my

2

13
SHORT
MYSTERY
NOVELS

ABOUT THE EDITORS

A full-time professional writer since 1969, BILL PRONZINI has published more than 30 novels, including a dozen in the "Nameless Detective" series; 275 short stories, articles, and essays in a wide variety of fields; and some 35 anthologies, including several in coeditorship with Martin H. Greenberg. *Hoodwink,* a "Nameless Detective" novel, won Pronzini the PWA (Private Eye Writers of America) Best Novel Award for 1981. His fiction has been translated into 17 languages and published in two dozen countries around the world. Pronzini was a charter member of PWA and served as its first president. He lives in San Francisco.

MARTIN H. GREENBERG, who has been called "the king of the anthologists," now has some 105 of them to his credit. Greenberg is professor of regional analysis and political science at the University of Wisconsin–Green Bay, where he also teaches a course in the history of science fiction. With Isaac Asimov and Charles G. Waugh, Greenberg is coeditor of *Baker's Dozen: 13 Short Fantasy Novels Presented by Isaac Asimov,* also published by Greenwich House.

BAKER'S
DOZEN

13
SHORT
MYSTERY
NOVELS

Edited by
Bill Pronzini
and
Martin H. Greenberg

GREENWICH HOUSE
Distributed by Crown Publishers, Inc.
New York

Grateful acknowledgment for permission to reprint material is hereby given to the following:

The Lawless Lady—Copyright 1929 by Leslie Charteris. Reprinted by permission of the author.
Introducing Susan Dare—from *The Cases of Susan Dare.* Copyright 1934, © renewed 1962 by Mignon G. Eberhart. Reprinted by permission of Brandt & Brandt Literary Agents, Inc.
Nightmare—by Cornell Woolrich. Copyright 1941 by the Frank A. Munsey Co. First published in *Argosy.* Reprinted by permission of the agents for the author's estate, the Scott Meredith Literary Agency, Inc., 845 Third Avenue, New York, NY 10022.
Death's Eye View—Copyright © renewed 1981 by John D. MacDonald Publishing, Inc. Reprinted by permission of John D. MacDonald Publishing, Inc.
The Murder Machine—Copyright 1950, © renewed 1978 by Judson Philips. Reprinted by permission of Brandt & Brandt Literary Agents, Inc.
Death Rides A Boxcar—Copyright 1944, © renewed 1972 by Erle Stanley Gardner. Reprinted by permission of Curtis Brown, Ltd.
The Bearded Lady—Copyright 1955, © renewed 1983 by Kenneth Millar. Reprinted by permission of Harold Ober Associates Incorporated.
Murder Set to Music—Copyright © 1957 by Fredric Brown. Reprinted by permission of International Creative Management.
The Zero Clue—from *Three Men Out* by Rex Stout. Copyright 1953 by Rex Stout. Copyright © renewed 1981 by Pola Stout, Barbara Selleck and Rebecca Bradbury. Reprinted by permission of Viking Penguin Inc.
Storm—from *The Empty Hours* Copyright © 1960, 1961, 1962 by Ed McBain. Reprinted by permission of John Farquharson Ltd.
Don't Look Now—from *Don't Look Now* by Daphne du Maurier. Copyright © 1970 by Daphne du Maurier. Reprinted by permission of Doubleday & Company, Inc.
Booktaker—Copyright © 1982, 1983 by Bill Pronzini. Reprinted by permission of the author.
The King in Yellow—from *The Simple Art of Murder* by Raymond Chandler. Copyright 1950 by Raymond Chandler, copyright © renewed 1978 by Helga Greene. Reprinted by permission of Houghton Mifflin Company.

This 1984 edition is published by Greenwich House, a division of Arlington House, Inc., distributed by Crown Publishers, Inc., One Park Avenue, New York, New York 10016, by arrangement with Bill Pronzini and Martin H. Greenberg.

Manufactured in the United States of America

Library of Congress Cataloging in Publication Data
Main entry under title:

Baker's dozen.

Contents: The lawless lady/Leslie Charteris—Introducing Susan Dare/
Mignon Eberhart—The king in yellow/Raymond Chandler—[etc.]
1. Detective and mystery stories, American.   2. Detective and mystery stories, English.
I. Pronzini, Bill.   II. Greenberg, Martin H. (Martin Harry)
PS648.D4B3   1984   813'.0872'08   84-6140
ISBN 0-517-444992

h g f e d c b a

CONTENTS

Introduction vii

Leslie Charteris
  The Lawless Lady 1

Mignon Eberhart
  Introducing Susan Dare 63

Cornell Woolrich
  Nightmare 89

John D. MacDonald
  Death's Eye View 147

Hugh Pentecost
  The Murder Machine 185

Erle Stanley Gardner
  Death Rides a Boxcar 233

Ross Macdonald
  The Bearded Lady 277

Fredric Brown
  Murder Set to Music 327

Rex Stout
  The Zero Clue 367

Ed McBain
  Storm 415

Daphne du Maurier
  Don't Look Now 469

Bill Pronzini
  Booktaker 513

Raymond Chandler
  The King in Yellow 549

INTRODUCTION

Baker's Dozen: 13 Short Mystery Novels brings together for the first time in book form thirteen top-quality mystery and detective novellas by some of the best writers in the field, both past and present.

These stories span more than fifty years of crime fiction writing in the United States and in England, and they feature a wide variety of heroes and heroines, villains, settings, story types, and stylistic approaches. Taken all together, they demonstrate how the mystery story has evolved in form, structure, and content over half a century and how authors have kept it fresh through thematic variation and ingenuity. The stories also reflect the times in which they were written so that they can be enjoyed from a historical perspective (both individually and in toto) as well as pure entertainment.

Several favorite sleuths populate these pages: Leslie Charteris's dashing rogue the Saint, in one of his most amusing early adventures, *The Lawless Lady*; Mignon Eberhart's writer detective Susan Dare, in her first recorded case, *Introducing Susan Dare*; Ross Macdonald's Lew Archer, hero of what has been praised by the *New York Times Book Review* as "the finest series of detective novels ever written by an American," in a powerful tale of thievery and murder, *The Bearded Lady*; Rex Stout's incomparable Nero Wolfe, who teams with Archie Goodwin to solve a mathematical crime-equation in *The Zero Clue*; Bill Pronzini's "Nameless Detective" in a book-shop mystery, *Booktaker,* about an "impossible" series of thefts. And Ed McBain's *Storm* features one member of his famed 87th Precinct Detective Squad, Cotton Hawes, who, while on vacation at a snowbound ski lodge, solves the brutal murders of two young women.

Nonseries stories also form an important part of this anthology. *The King in Yellow,* first published in the pulp magazine *Black Mask* in the 1930s and featuring a tough hotel detective named Steve Grayce, is Raymond Chandler at his hardboiled best. *Nightmare,* by the master of brooding suspense, Cornell Woolrich, is an eerie chiller whose title is apt indeed and which should definitely not be read while one is alone. Best-selling John D. Mac-Donald's *Death's Eye View* is a post-World War II mystery set in Florida (as are most of his superior novels and stories). Hugh Pentecost's *The Murder Machine* has a rural Pennsylvania setting, deals with murder by dynamiting in front of a hundred witnesses, and is ably solved by Lieutenant Pascal of New York City's Homicide Division. *Death Rides a Boxcar* is something of a departure for Erle Stanley Gardner, creator of Perry Mason, Bertha Cool, and Donald Lamb—a fast-paced tale that combines espionage and railroads with considerable success. Mayhem and jazz are the key components of Fredric Brown's *Murder Set to Music,* one of the most satisfying of this popular mystery and science fiction author's shorter works. Last but certainly not least, Daphne du Maurier, the author of *Rebecca* and the queen of the modern Gothic, offers a potent blend of suspense, magic, and the occult in modern-day Venice in *Don't Look Now.*

In short, we feel *Baker's Dozen* provides something for every mystery taste as well as a capsule course in mystery-making over the past fifty years. And we hope you derive as much pleasure from reading these thirteen novellas as we did from selecting them.

1984

BILL PRONZINI
MARTIN H. GREENBERG

LESLIE CHARTERIS
The Lawless Lady

1

FOR A law-breaker, in the midst of his law-breaking, to be attempting at the same time to carry on a feud with a chief inspector of police, might be called heroically quixotic. It might equally well be called pure blame-foolishness of the most suicidal variety—according to the way you look at these things. Simon Templar found it vastly entertaining.

Chief Inspector Claud Eustace Teal, of the Criminal Investigation Department, New Scotland Yard, that great detective (and he was nearly as great in mere bulk as he was in reputation) found it an interesting novelty. Teal was reputed to have the longest memory of any man at the Yard. It was said, perhaps with some exaggeration, that if the Records Office happened to be totally destroyed by fire, Teal could personally have rewritten the entire dossier of every criminal therein recorded, methods, habits, haunts, and notable idiosyncrasies completely included—and added thereto a rough but reliable sketch of every set of fingerprints therewith connected. Certainly, he had a long memory.

He distinctly remembered a mysterious Policeman, whom an enterprising journalist called the Policeman with Wings, who was strangely reincarnated some time after the originator and (normal) patentee of the idea had departed to heaven—or some other place beginning with the same letter—on top of a pile of dynamite, thereby depriving Teal of the pleasure of handing over to his commissioner fifty thousand pounds' worth of diamonds which had been lost for seven years. Mr. Teal suspected—not without reason—that Simon Templar's fertile brain had given birth to the dénouement of that gentle jest. And Mr. Teal's memory was long. Therefore the secret activities of the Saint came to be somewhat hampered by a number of massive gentlemen in bowler hats, who took to patrolling Brook Street in relays like members of a Scottish clan mounting guard over the spot where their chieftain is sure he had dropped a sixpence.

The day arrived when Simon Templar tired of this gloomy spectacle, and, having nothing else to do, armed himself with a stout stick and sallied forth for a walk, looking as furtive and conspiratorial as he knew how. He was as fit as a fiddle and shouting for exercise. He walked westward through London, and crossed the Thames by Putney Bridge. He left Kingston behind him. Continuing southwest, he took Esher and Cabham in his stride. He walked fast, enjoying himself. Not until he reached Ripley did he pause, and there he swung into a convenient hostel towards six o'clock, after twenty-three brisk miles had been spurned by his walking shoes.

The afternoon had been sunny and warm. Simon knocked back a couple of pints of beer as if he felt he had earned every drop of them, smoked a couple of cigarettes, and then started back to the road with a refreshed spring in his step. On his way out, in another bar, he saw a man with a very red face. The man had a bowler hat on the seat beside him, and he appeared to be melting steadily into a large spotted hand-kerchief.

Simon approached him like an old friend. "Are you ready to go on?" he asked. "I'm making for Guildford next. From there, I make for Winchester, where I shall have dinner, and I expect to sleep in South-ampton tonight. At six-thirty tomorrow morning I start for Liverpool, via Land's End. Near Manchester, I expect to murder a mulatto gasfit-ter with a false nose. After which, if you care to follow me to John o' Groats—" The rest of the conversation was conducted, on one side at least, in language which might have made a New York stevedore feel slightly shocked.

Simon passed on with a pained expression, and went on his way. A mile farther on, he slowed his pace to a stroll, and was satisfied that Red Face was no longer bringing up the rear. Shortly afterwards, a blue sports saloon swept past him with a rush and stopped a few yards away. As he reached it, a girl leaned out, and Simon greeted her with a smile. "Hullo, Pat, darling," he said. "Let's go and have a cocktail and some dinner."

He climbed in, and Patricia Holm let in the clutch.

"How's the market in bowler hats?" she asked.

"Weakening," murmured the Saint. "Weakening, old dear. The bulls weren't equal to the strain. Let's change the subject. Why are you so beautiful, Pat?"

She flung him a dazzling smile. "Probably," she said, "because I find I'm still in love with you—after a whole year. And you're still in love with me. The combination's enough to make anyone beautiful."

It was late when they got back to London. At the flat in Brook Street, Roger Conway and Dick Tremayne were drinking the Saint's beer. "There was some for you," said Roger, "only we drank it in case it went flat."

"Thoughtful of you," said the Saint.

He calmly annexed Mr. Conway's tankard, and sank into a chair. "Well, soaks," he remarked, "how was the English countryside looking this afternoon?"

"I took the North Road," said Roger. "My little Mary's lamb petered out at St. Albans, and Dicky picked me up just beyond. Twenty-one miles by the clock—in five hours forty-five minutes Fahrenheit. How's that?"

"Out," said the Saint. "I did twenty-three miles in five and a half hours dead. My sleuth was removed to hospital on an asbestos stretcher, and when they tried to revive him with brandy he burst into flames. We shall hear more of this."

Nevertheless, the following morning, Orace, bringing in his master's early tea, reported that a fresh detachment of bowler hats had arrived in Brook Street, and the Saint had to devote his ingenuity to thinking out other means of evading their vigilance.

In the next fortnight, the Saint sent £9,000 to charity, and Inspector Teal, who knew that to obtain that money the Saint must have "persuaded" someone to write him a check for £10,000, from which had been deducted the 10 percent commission which the Saint always claimed according to his rules, was annoyed. His squad, interrogated, were unable to make any suggestions as to the source of the gift. No, Simon Templar had done nothing suspicious. No, he had not been seen visiting or associating with any suspicious characters. No, he—"You're as much use as so many sick headaches," said Teal unkindly. "In fact, less use. You can stop watching that house. It's obviously a waste of your time—not," he added sweetly, "that the Department has missed you."

The climax came a few days later, when a cocaine smuggler whom Teal had been watching for months was at last caught with the goods as he stepped ashore at Dover. Teal, "acting on information received," snapped the bracelets on his wrists in the Customs House, and personally accompanied his prisoner on the train to London, sitting alone in a reserved compartment with his captive.

He did not know that Simon Templar was on the train until they were fifteen minutes out of Victoria Station, when the Saint calmly walked in and hailed him joyfully. "Can you read?" asked Teal.

"No," said the Saint.

Teal pointed to the red labels pasted on the windows. "R-E-S-E-R-V-E-D," he spelt out. "Do you know the word?"

"No," said the Saint. He sat down, after one curious glance at the man at Teal's side, and produced a gold cigarette-case. "I believe I owe you an apology for walking one of your men off his feet a while ago," he said. "Really, I think you asked for it, but I'm told you're sore. Can't we kiss and be friends?"

"No," said Teal.

"Have a cigarette?"

"I don't smoke cigarettes."

"A cigar, then?"

Teal turned warily. "I've had some of your jokes," he said. "Does this one explode, or is it the kind that blows soot all over your face when you light it?"

Simon handed over the weed. It was unmistakably excellent. Teal wavered, and bit off the end absent-mindedly. "Maybe I was unreasonable," he conceded, puffing. "But *you* asked for something before I ever did. And one day you'll get it. See this bright boy?" He aimed his cigar at the prisoner, and the Saint nodded. "I've been after him for the best part of a year. And he's had plenty of laughs off me before I got him. Now it's my turn. It'll be the same with you. I can wait. One day you'll go too far, you'll make a mistake, and—"

"I know that man," said the Saint. He looked across the compartment with cold eyes. "He is a blackmailer and a dealer in drugs. His name is Cyril Farrast, and he is thirty-two years old. He has one previous conviction."

Teal was surprised, but he concealed it by lowering his eyelids sleepily. He always looked most bored when he was most interested. "I know all that," he said. "But how do you know?"

"I've been looking for him," said the Saint simply, and the man stared. "Even now I still want him. Not for the dope business—I see you're going to take care of that—but for a girl in Yorkshire. There are thousands of stories like it, but this one happened to come to my notice. He'll recognize the name—but does he know who I am?"

"I'll introduce you," said Teal, and turned to his captive. "Cyril, this is Mr. Simon Templar. You've heard of him. He's known as the Saint."

The man shrank away in horror, and Simon grinned gently. "Oh, no," he drawled. "That's only Teal's nasty suspicious mind. . . . But if I *were* the Saint, I should want you, Cyril Farrast, because of Elsa Gordon, who committed suicide eleven days ago. I ought to kill you, but Teal has told me to be good. So, instead—"

Farrast was white to the lips. His mouth moved, but no sound came. Then—"It's a lie!" he screamed. "You can't touch me—"

Teal pushed him roughly back, and faced the Saint.

"Templar, if you think you're going to do anything funny—"

"I'm sure of it." Simon glanced at his watch. "That cigar, for instance, is due to function about now. No explosives. No soot. A much better joke than that." . . .

Teal was holding the cigar, staring at it. He felt very weak. His head seemed to have been aching for a long time. With a sudden convulsive effort he pitched the cigar through the window, and his hand began to reach round to his pocket. Then he sprawled limply sideways. A porter woke him at Victoria.

That night there were warrants out for the arrest of Simon Templar and all his friends. But the flat in Brook Street was shut up, and the janitor stated that the owners had gone away for a week—destination unknown. The press was not informed. Teal had his pride.

Three days later, a large coffin, labelled FRAGILE—HANDLE CARELESSLY—ANY OLD SIDE UP, was delivered at New Scotland Yard, addressed to Chief Inspector Teal. When examined, it was heard to tick loudly, and the explosives experts opened it at dead of night in some trepidation in the middle of Hyde Park. They found a large alarm clock—and Cyril Farrast. He was bound hand and foot, and gagged. And his bare back showed that he had been terribly flogged.

Also in the coffin was a slip of paper bearing the sign of the Saint. And in a box, carefully preserved in tissue paper and corrugated cardboard, was a cigar. When Teal arrived home that night he found Simon Templar patiently waiting on his doorstep. "I got your cigar," Teal said grimly.

"Smoke it," said the Saint. "It's a good one. If you fancy the brand, I'll mail you the rest of the box tomorrow."

"Come in," said Teal. He led the way, and the Saint followed. In the tiny sitting-room, Teal unwrapped the cigar, and the Saint lighted a cigarette. "Also," said Teal, "I've got a warrant for your arrest."

"And no case to use it on," said Simon. "You've got your man back."

"You flogged him."

"He's the only man who can bring that charge against me. You can't."

"If you steal something and send it back, that doesn't dispose of the charge of theft—if we care to prosecute."

"But you wouldn't," smiled the Saint, watching Teal light the cigar. "Frankly, now, between ourselves, would it be worth it? I notice the papers haven't said anything about the affair. That was wise of you. But if you charged me, you couldn't keep it out of the papers. And all England would be laughing over the story of how the great Claud Eustace Teal"—the detective winced—"was caught on the bend with the old, old doped cigar. Honestly—wouldn't it be better to call it a day?"

Teal frowned, looking straight at the smiling young man before him. From the hour of his first meeting with the Saint, Teal had recognized an indefinable superiority. It lay in nothing that the Saint did or said. It was simply there. Simon Templar was not common clay; and Teal, who was of the good red earth earthy, realized the fact without resentment. "Seriously, then, Templar," said Teal, "don't you see the hole you put me in? You took Farrast away and flogged him—that remains. And he saw you talking to me in the train. If he liked, he could say in court that we were secretly aiding and abetting you. The police are in the limelight just now, and a lot of the mud would stick."

"Farrast is dumb," answered Simon. "I promise you that. Because I told him that if he breathed a word of what had happened, I should find him and kill him. And he believes it. You see, I appreciated your difficulty."

Teal could think fast. He nodded. "You win again," he said. "I think the commissioner'll pass it—this once—since you've sent the man back. But another time—"

"I never repeat myself," said the Saint. "That's why you'll never catch me. But thanks, all the same."

He picked up his hat; but he turned back at the door. "By the way—has this affair, on top of the diamonds, put you in bad with the commissioner?"

"I won't deny it."

The Saint looked at the ceiling. "I'd like to put that right," he said. "Now, there's a receiver of stolen goods living in Notting Hill, named Albert Handers. Most of the big stuff passes through his hands, and I know you've been wanting him for a longish while."

Teal started. "How the deuce—"

"Never mind that. If you really want to smooth down the commissioner, you'll wait for Handers at Croydon Aërodrome tomorrow morning, when he proposes to fly to Amsterdam with the proceeds of the Asheton robbery. The diamonds will be sewn into the carrying handle of his valise. I wonder you've never thought of that, the times you've stopped him and searched him. . . . Night-night, sonny boy!" He was gone before the plump detective could stop him; and that night the Saint slept again in Brook Street.

But the information which the Saint had given came from Dicky Tremayne, another of the gang, and it signalled the beginning of the end of the coup to which Tremayne had devoted a year of patient preparation. This is the story of Dicky Tremayne.

2

DICKY TREMAYNE walked into the Saint's flat late one night, and found the Saint, in pajamas and dressing-gown, reading by the open window. Dicky Tremayne was able to walk in at any hour, because, like Roger Conway, he had his own key. Dicky Tremayne said: "Saint, I feel I'm going to fall in love."

The Saint slewed round, raising his eyes to heaven.

"What—not again?" he protested.

"Again," snapped Dicky. "It's an infernal nuisance, but there you are. A man must do something."

Simon put away his book and reached for a cigarette from the box that stood conveniently open on the table at his elbow. "Burn it," said Simon. "I always thought Archie Sheridan was bad enough. Till he went and got married, I used to spend my spare time wondering why he never got landed. But since you came out of your hermitage, and we let you go and live unchaperoned in Paris—"

"I know," snapped Dicky. "I can't help it. But it may be serious this time."

Match in hand, Simon regarded him. Norman Kent was the most darkly attractive of the Saints; Archie Sheridan had been the most delightfully irresponsible; Roger Conway was the most good-looking; but Dicky—Dicky Tremayne was dark and handsome in the clean keen-faced way which is the despairing envy of the Latin, and with it Dicky's elegance had a Continental polish and his eye a wicked Continental gleam. Dicky was what romantic maidens call a sheik—and yet he was unspoiled. Also he had a courage and a cheerfulness which never failed him. The Saint had a very real affection for Dicky. "Who is it this time, son?" he asked.

Tremayne walked to the window and stared out. "Her house in Park Lane was taken in the name of the Countess Anusia Marova," he said. "So was the yacht she's chartered for the season. But she was born in Boston, Mass., twenty-three years ago, and her parents called her Audrey Perowne. She's had a lot of names since then, but the Amsterdam police knew her best as 'Straight' Audrey. You know who I mean."

"And you—"

"You know what I've done. I spent all my time in Paris working in with Hilloran, who was her right-hand man in the States, because we were sure they'd get together sooner or later, and then we'd make one killing of the pair. And they *are* together again, and I'm in London as a fully accredited member of the gang. Everything's ready. And now I want to know why we ever bothered."

Simon shrugged. "Hilloran's name is bad enough, and she's made more money—"

"Why do they call her 'Straight' Audrey?"

"Because she's never touched or dealt in dope, which is considered eccentric in a woman crook. And because it's said to be unhealthy to get fresh with her. Apart from that, she's dabbled in pretty well everything—"

Dicky nodded helplessly. "I know, old man," he said. "I know it all. You're going to say that she and Hilloran, to us, were just a pair of crooks who'd made so much out of the game that we decided to make them contribute. We'd never met her. And it isn't as if she were a man—"

"And yet," said the Saint, "I remember a woman whom you wanted to kill. And I expect you'd have done it, if she hadn't died of her own accord."

"She was a—"

"Quite. But you'd've treated her exactly the same as you'd've treated a man engaged in the same traffic."

"There's nothing like that about Audrey Perowne."

"You're trying to argue that she's really hardly more of a crook than we are. Her crime record's pretty clean, and the man she's robbed could afford to lose."

"Isn't that so?"

Simon studied his cigarette-end. "Once upon a time," he observed, "there was a rich man named John L. Morganheim. He died at Palm

Beach—mysteriously. And Audrey Perowne was—er—keeping him company. You understand? It had to be hushed up, of course. His family couldn't have a scandal. Still—"

Tremayne went pale. "We don't know the whole of that story," he said.

"We don't," admitted the Saint. "We only know certain facts. And they mayn't be such thundering good facts, anyhow. But they're there —till we know something better." He got to his feet and laid a hand on Dicky's shoulder. "Let's have some straight talk, Dicky," he suggested. "You're beginning to feel you can't go through with the job. Am I right?"

Tremayne spread out his hands. "That's about the strength of it. We've got to be sure—"

"Let's be sure, then," agreed the Saint. "But meanwhile, what's the harm in carrying on? You can't object to the thrashing of Farrast. You can't feel cut up about the shopping of Handers. And you can't mind what sort of a rise we take out of Hilloran. What we do about the girl can be decided later—when we're sure. Till then, where's the point in chucking in your hand?"

Tremayne looked at him. "There's sense in that."

"Of course there's sense in it!" cried the Saint. "There's more in the gang than one girl. We want the rest. We want them like I want the mug of beer you're going to fetch me in a minute. Why shouldn't we have 'em?"

Dicky nodded slowly. "I knew you'd say that. But I felt you ought to know. . . ."

Simon clapped him on the back. "You're a great lad," he said. "And now, what about that beer?" Beer was brought and tasted with a fitting reverence. The discussion was closed.

With the Saint, momentous things could be brought up, argued, and dismissed like that. With Roger Conway, perhaps, the argument would have been pursued all night—but that was only because Roger and the Saint loved arguing. Dicky was reserved. Rarely did he throw off his reserve and talk long and seriously. The Saint understood, and respected his reticence. Dicky understood also. By passing on so light-heartedly to a cry for beer, the Saint did not lose one iota of the effect of sympathy; rather, he showed that his sympathy was complete.

Dicky could have asked for nothing more; and when he put down his tankard and helped himself to a cigarette, the discussion might never have raised its head between them. "To resume," he said, "we leave on the twenty-ninth."

Simon glanced at the calendar on the wall. "Three days," he murmured. "And the cargo of billionaires?"

"Complete." Dicky grinned. "Saint, you've got to hand it to that girl. Seven of 'em—with their wives. Of course, she's spent a year dry-nursing them. Sir Esdras Levy—George Y. Ulrig—Matthew Sankin—" He named four others whose names could be conjured with in the world of high finance. "It's a peach of an idea."

"I can't think of anything like it," said the Saint. "Seven bloated perambulating gold-mines with diamond studs, and their wives loaded up with enough jewelry to sink a battleship. She gets them off on the rolling wave—knowing they'll have all their sparklers ready to make a show at the ports they touch—on a motor yacht manned by her own crew—"

"Chief Steward, J. Hilloran—"

"And the first thing the world'll know of it will be when the cargo is found marooned on the Barbary coast, and the *Corsican Maid* has sailed off into the blue with the whichnots. . . . Oh, boy! As a philosophic student, I call that the elephant's tonsils."

Dicky nodded. "The day after tomorrow," he said, "we leave by special train to join the yacht at Marseilles. You've got to say that girl does her jobs in style."

"How do you go?"

"As her secretary. But—how do you go?"

"I haven't quite made up my mind yet. Roger's taking a holiday—I guess he deserves it. Norman and Pat are still cruising the Mediterranean. I'll handle this one from the outside alone. I leave the inside to you—and that's the most important part."

"I mayn't be able to see you again before we leave."

"Then you'll have to take a chance. But I think I shall also be somewhere on the ocean. If you have to communicate, signal in Morse out of a porthole, with an electric torch, either at midnight or four in the morning. I'll be on the look-out at those times. If . . ."

They talked for two hours before Tremayne rose to go. He did so at last. "It's the first real job I've had," he said. "I'd like to make it a good one. Wish me luck, Saint!"

Simon held out his hand. "Sure—you'll pull it off, Dicky. All the best, son. And about that girl—"

"Yes, about that girl," said Dicky shortly. Then he grinned ruefully. "Good-night, old man."

He went, with a crisp handshake and a frantic smile. He went as he had come, by way of the fire escape at the back of the building, for the

Saint's friends had caution thrust upon them in those days. The Saint watched him go in silence, and remembered that frantic smile after he had gone. Then he lighted another cigarette and smoked it thoughtfully, sitting on the table in the center of the room. Presently he went to bed. Dicky Tremayne did not go home to bed at once. He walked round to the side street where he had left his car, and drove to Park Lane.

The lights were still on in an upper window of the house outside which he stopped; and Tremayne entered without hesitation, despite the lateness of the hour, using his own key. The room in which he had seen the lights was on the first floor; it was used as a study and communicated with the Countess Anusia Marova's bedroom. Dicky knocked, and walked in. "Hullo, Audrey," he said.

"Make yourself at home," she said, without looking up. She was in a rich blue silk kimono and brocade slippers, writing at a desk. The reading lamp at her elbow struck gold from her hair.

There was a cut-glass decanter on the side table, glasses, a siphon, an inlaid cigarette-box. Dicky helped himself to a drink and a cigarette, and sat down where he could see her. The enthusiastic compilers of the gossip columns in the daily and weekly press had called her the most beautiful hostess of the season. That in itself would have meant little, seeing that fashionable hostesses are always described as "beautiful"— like fashionable brides, bridesmaids and debutantes. What, therefore, can it mean to be the most beautiful of such a galaxy?

But in this case something like the truth might well have been told. Audrey Perowne had grave grey eyes and an enchanting mouth. Her skin was soft and fine without the help of beauty parlours. Her color was her own. And she was tall, with the healthy grace of her kind; and you saw pearls when she smiled.

Dicky feasted his eyes. She wrote. She stopped writing. She read what she had written, placed the sheet in an envelope, and addressed it. Then she turned. "Well?"

"I just thought I'd drop in," said Dicky. "I saw the lights were on as I came past, so I knew you were up."

"Did you enjoy your golf?"

Golf was Dicky's alibi. From time to time he went out in the afternoon, saying that he was going to play a round at Sunningdale. Nearly always, he came back late, saying that he had stayed late playing cards at the club. Those were the times when he saw the Saint. Dicky said that he had enjoyed his golf.

"Give me a cigarette," she commanded. He obeyed. "And a

match. . . . Thanks. . . . What's the matter with you, Dicky? I shouldn't have had to ask for that."

He brought her an ashtray and returned to his seat. "I'm hanged if I know," he said. "Too many late nights, I should think. I feel tired."

"Hilloran's only just left," she said, with deceptive inconsequence. "Has he?"

She nodded. "I've taken back his key. In future, you'll be the only man who can stroll in here when and how he likes." Dicky shrugged, not knowing what to say. She added: "Would you like to live here?"

He was surprised. "Why? We leave in a couple of days. Even then, it hadn't occurred to me—"

"It's still occurring to Hilloran," she said, "even if we are leaving in a couple of days. But you live in a poky little flat in Bayswater, while there are a dozen rooms going to waste here. And it's never occurred to you to suggest moving in?"

"It never entered my head."

She smiled. "That's why I like you, Dicky," she said. "And it's why I let you keep your key. I'm glad you came tonight."

"Apart from your natural pleasure at seeing me again—why?"

The girl studied a slim ankle. "It's my turn to ask questions," she said. "And I ask you—why are you a crook, Dicky Tremayne?"

She looked up at him quickly as she spoke, and he met her eyes with an effort. The blow had fallen. He had seen it coming for months—the day when he would have to account for himself. And he had dreaded it, though he had his story perfectly prepared. Hilloran had tried to deliver the blow; but Hilloran, shrewd as he was, had been easy. The girl was not easy. She had never broached the subject before, and Dicky had begun to think that Hilloran's introduction had sufficiently disposed of questions. He had begun to think that the girl was satisfied, without making inquiries of her own. And that delusion was now rudely shattered.

He made a vague gesture. "I thought you knew," he said. "A little trouble in the Guards, followed by the O.B.E. You know. Order of the Boot—Everywhere. I could either accept the licking, or fight back. I chose to fight back. On the whole, it's paid me."

"What's your name?" she asked suddenly.

He raised his eyebrows. "Dicky Tremayne."

"I meant—your real name."

"Dicky is real enough."

"And the other?"

"Need we go into that?"

She was still looking at him. Tremayne felt that the grim way in which he was returning her stare was becoming as open to suspicion as shiftiness would have been. He glanced away, but she called him back peremptorily. "Look at me—I want to see you."

Brown eyes met grey steadily for an intolerable minute. Dicky felt his pulse throbbing faster, but the thin straight line of smoke that went up from his cigarette never wavered. Then, to his amazement, she smiled.

"Is this a joke?" he asked evenly.

She shook her head. "I'm sorry," she said. "I wanted to make sure if you were straight—straight as far as I'm concerned, I mean. You see, Dicky, I'm worried."

"You don't trust me?"

She returned his gaze. "I had my doubts. That's why I had to make sure—in my own way. I feel sure now. It's only a feeling, but I go by feelings. I feel that you wouldn't let me down—now. But I'm still worried."

"What about?"

"There's a squeaker in the camp," she said. "Somebody's selling us. Until this moment, I was prepared to believe it was you."

3

TREMAYNE SAT like an image, mechanically flicking the ash from his cigarette. Every word had gone through him like a knife, but never by a twitch of a muscle had he shown it. He said calmly enough: "I don't think anyone could blame you."

"Listen," she said. "You ask for it—from anyone like me. Hilloran's easy to fool. He's cleverer than most, but you could bamboozle him any day. I'm more inquisitive—and you're too secretive. You don't say anything about your respectable past. Perhaps that's natural. But you don't say anything about your disreputable past, either—and that's extraordinary. If it comes to the point, we've only got your word for it that you're a crook at all."

He shook his head. "Not good enough," he replied. "If I were a dick, sneaking into your gang in order to shop you—first, I'd have been smart enough to get Headquarters to fix me up with a convincing list of previous convictions, with the cooperation of the press, and, second, we'd have pulled in the lot of you weeks ago."

She had taken a chair beside him. With an utterly natural gesture, that nevertheless came strangely and unexpectedly from her, she laid a hand on his arm. "I know, Dicky," she said. "I told you I trusted you—now. Not for any logical reasons, but because my hunch says you're not that sort. But I'll let you know that if I hadn't decided I could trust you—I'd be afraid of you."

"Am I so frightening?"

"You were."

He stirred uncomfortably, frowning. "This is queer talk from you, Audrey," he said, rather brusquely. "Somehow, one doesn't expect any sign of weakness—or fear—from you. Let's be practical. What makes you so sure there's a squeaker?"

"Handers. You saw he was taken yesterday?" Dicky nodded. "It wasn't a fluke. I'll swear Teal would never have tumbled to that valise-handle trick. Besides, the papers said he was 'acting on information received.' You know what that means?"

"It sounds like a squeal, but—"

"The loss doesn't matter so much—ten thousand pounds and three weeks' work—when we're set to pull down twenty times that amount in a few days. But it makes me rather wonder what's going to happen to the big job."

Tremayne looked at her straightly. "If you don't think I'm the squeaker," he said, "who do you think it is?"

"There's only one other man, as far as I know, who was in a position to shop Handers."

"Namely?"

"Hilloran."

Dicky stared. The situation was grotesque. If it had been less grotesque, it would have been laughable; but it was too grotesque even for laughter. And Dicky didn't feel like laughing.

The second cut was overwhelming. First she had half accused him of being a traitor; and then, somehow, he had convinced her of a lie without speaking a word, and she had declared that she trusted him. And now, making him her confidant, she was turning the eyes of her suspicion upon the man who had been her chief lieutenant on the other side of the Atlantic. "Hilloran," objected Dicky lamely, "worked for you—"

"Certainly. And then I fired him—with some home truths in lieu of notice. I patched it up and took him back for this job because he's a darned useful man. But that doesn't say he's forgiven and forgotten."

"You think he's out to double-cross you and get his own back and salve his vanity?"

"It's not impossible."

"But—"

She interrupted with an impatient movement. "You don't get the point. I thought I'd made it plain. Apart from anything else, Hilloran seems to think I'd made a handsome ornament for his home. He's been out for that lay ever since I first met him. He was particularly pressing tonight, and I sent him away with several large fleas in each ear. I'll admit he was well oiled, and I had to show him a gun—"

Dicky's face darkened. "As bad as that?"

She laughed shortly. "You needn't be heroic about it, Dicky. The ordinary conventions aren't expected to apply in our world. Being outside the pale, we're reckoned to be frankly ruddy, and we usually are. However, I just happen to be funny that way—Heaven knows why. The point is that Hilloran's as sore and spiteful as a coyote on hot tiles, and if he didn't know it was worth a quarter of a million dollars to keep in with me—"

"He might try to sell you?"

"Even now," said the girl, "when the time comes, he mightn't be content with his quarter share."

Dicky's brain was seething with this new spate of ideas. On top of everything else, then, Hilloran was playing a game of his own. That game might lead him to laying information before the police on his own account, or, far more probably, to the conception of a scheme for turning the entire proceeds of the "big job" into his own pocket. It was a factor which Tremayne had never considered. He hadn't yet absorbed it properly. And he had to get the main lines of it hard and clear, get the map of the situation nailed out in his mind in a strong light, before—Zzzzzzzz . . . zzzzzzzz . . . "What's that?"

"The front door," said the girl, and pointed. "There's a buzzer in my bedroom. See who it is."

Dicky went to a window and peered out from behind the curtains. He came back soberly. "Hilloran's back again," he said. "Whatever he's come about, he must have seen my car standing outside. And it's nearly four o'clock in the morning." She met his eyes. "Shall we say it's—difficult."

She understood. It was obvious, anyway. "What would you like me to do?" asked Dicky.

The buzzer sounded again—a long, insistent summons. Then the smaller of the two telephones on the desk tinkled. The girl picked up the receiver. "Hullo. . . . Yes. He can come up." She put down the instrument and returned to her armchair. "Another cigarette, Dicky."

He passed her the box and struck a match. "What would you like me to do?" he repeated.

"Anything you like," she said coolly. "If I didn't think your gentlemanly instincts would be offended, I'd suggest that you took off your coat and tried to look abandoned, draping yourself artistically on the arm of this chair. In any case you can be as objectionable as Hilloran will be. If you can help him to lose his temper, he may show some of his hand."

Dicky came thoughtfully to his feet, his glass in his hand. Then the girl raised her voice, clearly and sweetly. "Dicky—darling—"

Hilloran stood in the doorway, a red-faced giant of a man, swaying perceptibly. His dinner jacket was crumpled, his tie askew, his hair tousled. It was plain that he had had more to drink since he left the house. "Audrey—"

"It is usual," said the girl coldly, "to knock."

Hilloran lurched forward. In his hand he held something which he flung down into her lap. "Look at that!"

The girl picked up the cards languidly. "I didn't know you were a proud father," she remarked. "Or have you been taking up art yourself?"

"Two of 'em!" blurted Hilloran thickly. "I found one pinned to my door when I got home. The other I found here—pinned to your front door—since I left! Don't you recognize it—the warning. It means that the Saint has been here tonight!"

The girl's face had changed color. She held the cards out to Dicky. Hilloran snatched them viciously away. "No, you don't!" he snarled. "I want to know what you're doing here at all, in this room, at this hour of the morning."

Audrey Perowne rose. "Hilloran," she said icily, "I'll thank you not to insult my friend in my own house."

The man leered at her. "You will, will you? You'd like to be left alone with him, when you know the Saint's sitting round waiting to smash us. If you don't value your own skin, I value mine. You're supposed to be the leader—"

"I am the leader."

"Are you? . . . Yes, you lead. You've led me on enough. Now you're leading him on. You little—"

Tremayne's fist smashed the word back into Hilloran's teeth. As the man crashed to the floor, Dicky whipped off his coat. Hilloran put a hand to his mouth, and the same came away wet and red. Then he shot out a shaky forefinger. "You—you skunk—I know you! You're here making love to Audrey, crawling in like a snake—and all the time you're planning to squeal on us. Ask him, Audrey!" The pointing finger stiffened, and the light of drunken hate in the man's eyes was bestial. *"Ask him what he knows about the Saint!"*

Dicky Tremayne stood perfectly still. He knew that the girl was looking at him. He knew that Hilloran could have no possible means of substantiating his accusation. He knew also how a seed sown in a bed of panic could grow, and realized that he was very near death. And he never moved. "Get up, Hilloran," he said quietly. "Get up and have the rest of your teeth knocked out."

Hilloran was scrambling to his feet. "Yes, I'll get up!" he rasped, and his hand was making for his pocket. "But I've my own way of dealing with rats—" And there was an automatic in his hand. His finger was trembling over the trigger. Dicky saw it distinctly.

Then, in a flash, the girl was between them. "If you want the police here," she said, "you'll shoot. But I shan't be here to be arrested with you."

Hilloran raved. "Out of the way, you—"

"Leave him to me," said Dicky. He put her aside, and the muzzle of the automatic touched his chest. He smiled into the flaming eyes. "May I smoke a cigarette?" he asked politely.

His right hand reached to his breast pocket in the most natural way in the world. Hilloran's scream of agony shattered the silence. Like lightning, Dicky's right hand had dropped and gripped Hilloran's right hand, at the same instant as Dicky's left hand fastened paralyzingly on Hilloran's right arm just above the elbow. The wrench that almost broke Hilloran's wrist was made almost in the same movement.

The gun thudded into the carpet at their feet, but Tremayne took no notice. Retaining and strengthening his grip, he turned Hilloran round and forced him irresistibly to his knees. Tremayne held him there with one hand. "We can talk more comfortably now," he remarked. He looked at the girl, and saw that she had picked up the fallen automatic. "Before we go any further, Audrey," he said, "I should like to know what you think of the suggestion—that I might be a friend of the Saint's. I needn't remind you that this object is jealous as well as drunk. I won't deny the charge, because that wouldn't cut any ice. I'd just like your opinion."

"Let him go, first."

"Certainly."

With a twist of his hand, Dicky released the man and sent him toppling over onto his face. "Hilloran, get up!"

"If you—"

"*Get up!*"

Hilloran stumbled to his feet. There was murder in his eyes, but he obeyed. No man of his calibre could have challenged that command. Dicky thought, "A crook—and she can wear power like a queen. . . ."

"I want to know, Hilloran," observed the girl frostily, "why you said what you said just now."

The man glared. "He can't account for himself, and he doesn't look or behave like one of us. We know there's a squeaker somewhere—someone who squealed on Handers—and he's the only one—"

"I see." The contempt in the girl's voice had the quality of concentrated acid. "What I see most is that because I prefer his company to yours, you're ready to trump up any wild charge against him that comes into your head—in the hope of putting him out of favour."

"And *I* see," sneered Hilloran, "that *I'm* the one who's out of favour—because he's taken my place. He's—"

"Either," said the girl, "you can walk out on your own flat feet, or you can be thrown out. Take your choice. And whichever way you go, don't come back here till you're sober and ready to apologize."

Hilloran's fists clenched. "You're supposed to be bossing this gang—"

"I am," said Audrey Perowne. "And if you don't like it, you can cut out as soon as you like."

Hilloran swallowed. "All right—"

"Yes?" prompted Audrey silkily.

"One day," said Hilloran, staring from under black brows, "you're going to be sorry for this. We know where we are. You don't want to fire me before the big job, because I'm useful. And I'll take everything lying down for the present time, because there's a heap of money in it for me. Yes, I'm drunk, but I'm not too drunk to be able to see that."

"That," said the girl sweetly, "is good news. Have you finished?"

Hilloran's mouth opened, and closed again deliberately. The knuckles showed whitely in his hands. He looked at the girl for a long time. Then, for a long time in exactly the same way, he looked at Tremayne, without speaking. At last. "Good-night," he said, and left the room without another word.

From the window, Tremayne watched him walk slowly up the street, his handkerchief to his mouth. Then Dicky turned and found Audrey Perowne beside him. There was something in her eyes which he could not interpret. He said: "You've proved that you trust me—"

"He's crazy," she said.

"He's mad," said Dicky. "Like a mad dog. We haven't heard the last of this evening. From the moment you step on board the yacht, you'll have to watch him night and day. You understand that, don't you?"

"And what about you?"

"A knowledge of ju-jitsu is invaluable."

"Even against a knife in the back?"

Dicky laughed. "Why worry?" he asked. "It doesn't help us."

The grey eyes were still holding his. "Before you go," she said, "I'd like your own answer—from your own mouth."

"To what question?"

"To what Hilloran said."

He was picking up his coat. He put it down and came towards her. A madness was upon him. He knew it, felt everything in him rebelling against it; yet he was swept before it out of reason, like a leaf before the wind. He held out his hand. "Audrey," he said, "I give you my word of honor that I'd be burnt alive sooner than let you down."

The words were spoken quite simply and calmly. The madness in him could only prompt them. He could still keep his face impassive and school the intensest meaning out of his voice. Her cool fingers touched his, and he put them to his lips with a smile that might have meant anything—or nothing. A few minutes later he was driving home with the first streaks of dawn in the sky, and his mouth felt as if it had been seared with a hot iron. He did not see the Saint again before they left for Marseilles.

4

THREE DAYS later, Dicky Tremayne, in white trousers, blue reefer and peaked cap, stood at the starboard rail of the *Corsican Maid* and stared moodily over the water. The sun shone high overhead, turning the water to a sea of quicksilver, and making of the Château d'If a fairy castle. The *Corsican Maid* lay in the open roadstead, two miles from Marseilles Harbour; for the Countess Anusia Marova, ever thoughtful for her guests, had decided that the docks, with their grime and noise and bustle, were no place for holiday-making millionaires and their wives to loiter, even for a few hours. But over the water, from the direction of the harbour, approached a fussy little tender. Dicky recognized it as the tender that had been engaged to bring the millionaires, with their wives and other baggage, to the countess's yacht, and watched it morosely.

That is to say that his eyes followed it intently; but his mind was in a dozen different places. The situation was rapidly becoming intolerable —far too rapidly. That, in fact, was the only reflection which was seriously concerned with the approach of the tender. For every yard of that approach seemed, in a way, to entangle him ten times more firmly in the web that he had woven for himself.

The last time he had seen the Saint, Dicky hadn't told him the half of it. One very cogent reason was that Dicky himself, at the time, hadn't even known the half well enough to call it Dear Sir or Madam. Now, he knew it much too well. He called it by its first name now—and others—and it sat back and grinned all over its ugly face at him. Curse it. . . .

When he said that he *might* fall in love with Audrey Perowne, he was underestimating the case by a mile. He *had* fallen in love with her, and there it was. He'd done his level best not to; and when it was done, he'd fought for all he was worth against admitting it even to himself. By this time, he was beginning to see that the struggle was hopeless.

And if you want to ask why the pink parrakeets he should put up a fight at all, the answer is that that's the sort of thing men of Dicky Tremayne's stamp do. If everything had been different—if the Saint had never been heard of—or, at least, if Tremayne had only known him through his morning newspaper—the problem would never have arisen. Say that the problem, having arisen, remains a simple one—and you're wrong. Wrong by the first principles of psychological arithmetic.

The Saint might have been a joke. The press, at first, had suggested that he must be a joke—that he couldn't, reasonably, be anything else. Later, with grim demonstrations thrust under their bleary eyes, the press admitted that it was no joke. In spite of which, the jest might have stood, had the men carrying it out been less under the Saint's spell.

There exists a loyalty among men of a certain type which defies instinct, and which on occasion can rise above the limitations of mere logic. Dicky Tremayne was of that breed. And he didn't find the problem simple at all. He figured it out in his own way.

"She's a crook. On the other hand, as far as that goes, so am I—

though not the way she thinks of it. She's robbing people who can afford to stand the racket. Their records, if you came to examine them closely, probably wouldn't show up any too clean. In fact, she's on much the same ground as we are ourselves. Except that she doesn't pass on ninety percent of the profits to charity. But that's only a private sentimentality of our own. It doesn't affect the main issue. Hilloran isn't the same proposition. He's a real bad *hombre*. I'd be glad to see him go down.

"The snag with the girl is the late John L. Morganheim. She probably murdered him. But then, there's not one of our crowd that hasn't got blood on his hands. What matters is why the blood was shed. We don't know anything about Morganheim, and action's going to be forced on me before I've time to find out. In a story, the girl's always innocent. Or, if she's guilty, she's always got a cast-iron reason to be. But I'm not going to be led away. I've seen enough to know that that kind of story is mostly based on vintage baloney, according to the recipe. I'm going to look at it coldly and sanely, till I find an answer or my brain busts. Because—

"Because, in fact, things being as they are, I've as good as sworn to the Saint that I'd bring home the bacon. Not in so many words, but that's what he assumes. And he's got every right to assume it. He gave me the chance to cry off if I wanted to—and I turned it down. I refused to quit. I dug this perishing pitfall, and it's up to me to fight my own way out—and no whining. . . ."

Thus Dicky Tremayne had balanced the ledger, over and over again, without satisfying himself. The days since the discomfiture of Hilloran had not made the account any simpler.

Hilloran had come round the next morning and apologized. Tremayne had been there—of course. Hilloran had shaken his hand heartily, boisterously disclaimed the least animosity, declared that it had been his own silly fault for getting canned, and taken Dicky and Audrey out to lunch. Dicky would have had every excuse for being deceived—but he wasn't. That he pretended to be was nobody's business.

But he watched Hilloran when he was not being watched himself; and from time to time he surprised in Hilloran's eyes a curiously abstracted intentness that confirmed his misgivings. It lasted only for a rare second here and there; and it was swallowed up again in a fresh flood of open-handed good humour so quickly that a less prejudiced observer might have put it down to imagination. But Dicky understood, and knew that there was going to be trouble with Hilloran.

Over the lunch, the intrusion of the Saint had been discussed, and a decision had been reached—by Audrey Perowne. "Whoever he is, and whatever he's done," she said, "I'm not going to be scared off by any comic-opera threats. We've spent six thousand pounds on ground bait, and we'd be a cheap lot of pikers to leave the pitch without a fight. Besides, sooner or later, this Saint's going to bite off more than he can chew, and this may very well be the time. We're going to be on the broad Mediterranean, with a picked crew, and not more than twenty percent of them can be double-crossing us. That gives us an advantage of four to one. Short of pulling out a ship of their own and making a pitched battle of it, I don't see what the Saint can do. I say we go on—with our eyes twice skinned." The argument was incontestable.

Tremayne, Hilloran and Audrey had left London quietly so as to arrive twelve hours before their guests were due. Dicky had spent another evening alone with the girl before the departure. "Do you believe in Hilloran's apology?" he had asked.

She had answered, at once: "I don't."

"Then why are you keeping him on?"

"Because I'm a woman. Sometimes, I think, you boys are liable to forget that. I've got the brain, but it takes a man to run a show like this, with a crew like mine to handle. You're the only other man I'd trust it to, but you—well, Dicky, honestly, you haven't the experience, have you?"

It had amazed him that she could discuss a crime so calmly. Lovely to look upon, exquisitely dressed, lounging at her ease in a deep chair, with a cigarette between white fingers that would have served the most fastidious sculptor for a model, she looked as if she should have been discussing, delightfully—anything but that. Of his own feelings he had said nothing. He kept them out of his face, out of his eyes, out of his voice and manner. His dispassionate calm rivalled her own. He dared hold no other pose. The reeling tumult of his thoughts could only be masked by the most stony stolidness. Some of the turmoil could inevitably have broken through any less sphinxlike disguise.

He was trying to get her in her right place—and, in the attempt, he was floundering deeper and deeper in the mire of mystification. There was about her none of the hard flashiness traditionally supposed to brand the woman criminal. For all her command, she remained completely feminine, gentle of voice, perfectly gracious. The part of the Countess Anusia Marova, created by herself, she played without effort; and, when she was alone, there was no travesty to take off. The charmingly broken English disappeared—that was all. But the same woman moved and spoke.

If he had not known, he would not have believed. But he knew—and it had rocked his creed to its foundations. There had only been one moment, that evening, when he had been in danger of stumbling. "If we bring this off," she had said, "you'll get your quarter share, of course. Two hundred and fifty thousand dollars. Fifty thousand pounds of your money. You need never do another job as long as you live. What will you do?"

"What will you do with yours?" he countered.

She hesitated, gazed dreamily into a shadowy corner as though she saw something there. Then: "Probably," she said lightly, "I'll buy a husband."

"I might buy a few wives," said Dicky, and the moment was past. Now he looked down into the blue Mediterranean and meditated that specimen of repartee with unspeakable contempt. But it had been the only thing that had come into his head, and he'd had to say something promptly. "Blast it all," thought Dicky, and straightened up with a sigh.

The tender had nosed up to the gangway, and Sir Esdras Levy, in the lead, was helping Lady Levy to the grating. Mr. George Y. Ulrig stood close behind. Dicky caught their eye. He smiled with his mouth, and saluted cheerily.

He ought to know them, for he himself had been the means of introducing them to the house in Park Lane. That had been his job, on the Continent, under Hilloran, for the past three months—to travel about the fashionable resorts, armed with plenty of money, an unimpeachable wardrobe and his natural charm of manner, and approach the Unapproachables when they were to be found in holiday moods with their armour laid aside.

It had been almost boringly simple. A man who would blow up high in the air if addressed by a perfect stranger in the lounge of the Savoy Hotel, London, may be addressed by the same stranger with perfect impunity in the lounge of the Heliopolis Hotel, Biarritz. After which, to a man of Dicky Tremayne's polished worldliness, the improvement of the shining hour came automatically. Jerking himself back to the realities of immediate importance, he went down to help to shepherd his own selected sheep to the slaughter.

Audrey Perowne stood at the head of the gangway, superbly gowned in a simple white skirt and colored jumper—superbly gowned because she wore them. She was welcoming her guests inimitably, with an intimate word for each, while Hilloran, in uniform, stood respectfully ready to conduct them to their cabins.

"Ah, Sir Esdras, ve 'ardly dare expec' you. I say, ' 'E vill not com' to my seely leetle boat.' But 'e is nize, and 'e com' to be oncomfortable to pleasse me. . . . And Lady Levy. My dear, each day you are more beautiful." Lady Levy, who was a fat fifty, glowed audibly. "And Mrs. Ulrig. Before I let you off my boat, you shall tell me 'ow eet iss you keep zo sleem." The scrawny and faded Mrs. George Y. Ulrig squirmed with pleasure. "George Y.," said the Countess, "I see you are vhat zey call a sheek. Ozairvize you could not 'ave marry 'er. And Mrs. Sankin . . ."

Dicky's task was comparatively childish. He had only to detach Sir Esdras Levy, Mr. George Y. Ulrig, and Matthew Sankin from their respective spouses, taking them confidentially by the arm, and murmur that there were cocktails set out in the saloon.

Luncheon, with Audrey Perowne for hostess, could not have been anything but a success. The afternoon passed quickly. It seemed no time before the bell rung by the obsequious Hilloran indicated that it was time to dress for dinner.

Tremayne went below with the rest to dress. It was done quickly; but the girl was already in the saloon when he arrived. Hilloran also was there, pretending to inspect the table. "When?" Hilloran was asking.

"Tomorrow night. I've told them we're due at Monaco about half-past six. We sha'n't be near the place, but that doesn't matter. We'll take them in their cabins when they go below to change."

"And afterwards?" questioned Dicky.

"We make straight across to Corsica during the night, and land them near Calvi the next morning. Then we make round the south of Sicily, and lose ourselves in the Greek Archipelago. We should arrive eventually at Constantinople—repainted, rechristened, and generally altered. There we separate. I'll give the immediate orders tomorrow afternoon. Come to my cabin about three."

Hilloran turned to Dicky. "By the way," he said, "this letter came with the tender. I'm afraid I forgot to give it to you before."

Dicky held the man's eyes for a moment, and then took the envelope. It was postmarked in London. With a glance at the flap, he slit it open. The letter was written in a round feminine hand.

DARLING:

This is just a line to wish you a jolly good time on your cruise.

You know I'll miss you terribly. Six weeks seems such a

long time for you to be away. Never mind. I'm going to drown my sorrows in barley-water.

I refuse to be lonely. Simple Simon, the man I told you about, says he'll console me. He wants me to go with a party he's taking to the Aegean Islands. I don't know yet if I shall accept, but it sounds awfully thrilling. He's got a big airplane, and wants us to fly all the way.

If I go, I shall have to leave on Saturday. Won't you be jealous?

Darling, I mustn't pull your leg any more. You know I'm always thinking of you, and I sha'n't be really happy till I get you back again.

Here come all my best wishes, then. Be good, and take care of yourself.

It's eleven o'clock, and I'm tired. I'm going to bed to dream of you. It'll be twelve by the time I'm there. My eyes are red from weeping for you.

You have all my love. I trust you.

PATRICIA.

Tremayne folded the letter, replaced it in its envelope, and put it in his pocket.

"Does she still love you?" mocked Audrey Perowne, and Dicky shrugged.

"So she says," he replied carelessly. "So she says."

5

MUCH LATER that night, in the privacy of his cabin, Dicky read the letter again. The meaning to him was perfectly obvious. The Saint had decided to work his end of the business by airplane. The reference to the Aegean Islands, Tremayne decided, had no bearing on the matter—the Saint could have had no notion that the *Corsican Maid's* flight would take her to that quarter. But Saturday—the next day—was mentioned, and Dicky took that to mean that the Saint would be on the lookout for signals from Saturday onwards. "Take care of yourself," was plain enough.

The references to "eleven o'clock" and "twelve" were ambiguous. "It'll be twelve by the time I'm there" might mean that, since the airplane would have to watch for signals from a considerable distance, to avoid being betrayed by the noise of the engines, it would be an hour from the time of the giving of the signal before the Saint could arrive on the scene. But why "eleven o'clock" and "twelve" instead of "twelve o'clock" and "one"—since they had previously arranged that signals were to be made either at midnight or four o'clock in the morning? Dicky pondered for an hour; and decided that either he was trying to read too much between the lines, or that a signal given an hour before the appointed time, at eleven o'clock instead of twelve, would not be missed.

"My eyes are red from weeping for you." He interpreted that to mean that he was to signal with a red light if there seemed to be any likelihood of their having cause to weep for him. He had a pocket flash-lamp fitted with color screens, and that code would be easy to adopt.

It was the last sentence that hit him fairly between the eyes. "I trust you." A shrewd blow—very shrewd. Just an outside reminder of what he'd been telling himself for the past three days. Simon couldn't possibly understand. He'd never met Audrey Perowne. And, naturally, he'd do his level best to keep Dicky on the lines.

Dicky crumpled the paper slowly into a ball, rolling it thoughtfully between his two palms. He picked up the envelope and rolled that into the ball also. Hilloran had steamed open that envelope and sealed it again before delivering the letter—Dicky was sure of that. He went to the porthole and pitched the ball far out into the dark waters.

He undressed and lay down in his bunk, but he could not compose his mind to sleep. The night was close and sultry. The air that came through the open porthole seemed to strike warm on his face, and to circulate that torrid atmosphere with the electric fan was pointless. He tried it, but it brought no relief. For an hour and a half he lay stifling; and then he rose, pulled on his slippers and a thin silk dressing-gown, and made his way to the deck.

He sprawled in a long cane chair and lighted a cigarette. Up there it was cooler. The ghost of a breeze whispered in the rigging and fanned his face. The soft hiss and wash of the sea cleft by the passage of their bows was very soothing. After a time, he dozed. He awoke with a curious sensation forcing itself through his drowsiness. It seemed as if the sea were rising, for the chair in which he lay was lurching and creaking under him. Yet the wind had not risen, and he could hear none of the thrash of curling waves which he should have been able to hear.

All this he appreciated hazily, roused but still half asleep. Then he opened one eye, and saw no rail before him, but only the steely glint of waters under the moon. Looking upwards and behind him he saw the foremast light riding serenely among the stars of a cloudless sky.

The convulsive leap he made actually spread-eagled him across the rail; and he heard his chair splash into the sea below as he tumbled over onto the deck.

Rolling on his shoulder, he glimpsed a sea-boot lashing at his head. He ducked wildly, grabbed, and kept his hold. All the strength he could muster went into the wrench that followed, and he heard the owner of the boot fall heavily with a strangled oath. An instant later he was on his feet—to find Hilloran's face two inches from his own. "Would you!" snapped Dicky.

He slipped the answering punch over his left shoulder, changed his feet, and crammed every ounce of his weight into a retaliatory jolt that smacked over Hilloran's heart and dropped the man as if his legs had been cut away from beneath him.

Dicky turned like a whirlwind as the man he had tripped up rose from the ground and leaped at him with flailing fists.

Scientific boxing, in that light, was hopeless. Dicky tried it, and stopped a right swing with the side of his head. Three inches lower, and it would probably have put an end to the fight. As it was, it sent him staggering back against the rail, momentarily dazed, and it was more by luck than judgment that his shoulder hunched in the way of the next blow. He hit back blindly, felt his knuckles make contact, and heard the man grunt with pain.

Then his sight cleared. He saw the seaman recover his balance and gather himself for a renewed onslaught. He saw Hilloran coming unsteadily off the deck, with the moonlight striking a silvery gleam from something in his right hand. And he understood the issue quite plainly.

They had tried to dump him overboard, chair and all, while he slept. A quiet and gentle method of disposing of a nuisance—and no fuss or mess. That having failed, however, the execution of the project had boiled down to a free fight for the same end. Dicky had a temporary advantage, but the odds were sticky. With the cold grim clarity of vision that comes to a man at such moments, Dicky Tremayne realized that the odds were very sticky indeed.

But not for a second could he consider raising his voice for help. Apart from the fact that the battle was more or less a duel of honor between Hilloran and himself—even if Hilloran didn't choose to fight his side single-handed—it remained to be assumed that, if Hilloran had one ally among the crew, he was just as likely to have half a dozen. The whole crew, finally, were just as likely to be on Hilloran's side as one.

The agreement had been that Audrey, Hilloran and Dicky were to divide equally three-quarters of the spoil, and the crew were to divide the last quarter. Knowing exactly the type of men of which the crew was composed, Tremayne could easily reckon the chance of their falling for the bait of a half share to divide instead of a quarter, when the difference would amount to a matter of about four thousand pounds per man.

And that, Tremayne realized, would be a pretty accurate guess at the position. He himself was to be eliminated as Audrey Perowne's one loyal supporter and a thorn in Hilloran's side. The quarter share thus saved would go to bribe the crew. As for Hilloran's own benefit, Audrey Perowne's quarter share . . .

Dicky saw the whole stark idea staring him in the face, and wondered dimly why he'd never thought of it before. Audrey Perowne's only use, for Hilloran, had been to get the millionaires on board the yacht and out to sea. After that, he could take his own peculiar revenge on her for the way she had treated him, revenge himself also on Tremayne for similar things, and make himself master of the situation and a half a million dollars instead of a quarter. A charming inspiration. . . . But Dicky didn't have to think it all out like that. He saw it in a flash, more by intuition than by logic, in the instant of rest that he had while he saw also the seaman returning to the attack and Hilloran rising rockily from the ground with a knife in his hand. And therefore he fought in silence.

The darkness was against him. Dicky Tremayne was a strong and clever boxer, quicker than most men, and he knew more than a little about ju-jitsu; but those are arts for which one needs the speed of vision that can only come with clear light. The light he had was meagre and deceptive—a light that was all on the side of sheer strength and bulk, and all against mere speed and skill.

He was pretty well cornered. His back was against the rail. Hilloran was on his left front, the huge seaman on his right. There was no room to pass between them, no room to escape past either of them along the rail. There was only one way to fight: their own way. The seaman was nearest, and Dicky braced himself. It had to be a matter of give and take, the only question being that of who was to take the most. As the seaman closed in, Tremayne judged his distance, dropped his chin, and drove with a long left.

The sailor's fist connected with Dicky's forehead, knocking back his head with a jar that wricked his neck. Dicky's left met something hard that seemed to snap under the impact. Teeth. But Dicky reeled, hazed

by the sickening power of the two tremendous blows he had taken; and
he could hardly see for the red and black clouds that swam before his
eyes.

But he saw Hilloran and dropped instinctively to one knee. He rose
again immediately under Hilloran's knife arm, taking the man about
the waist. Summoning all his strength, he heaved upwards, with some
mad idea of treating Hilloran to some of his own pleasant medicine—or
hurling the man over the rail into the glimmering black sea. And almost
at once he realized that he could not do it—Hilloran was too heavy,
and Dicky was already weakened. Nor was there time to struggle, for
in another moment Hilloran would lift his right arm again and drive
the knife into Dicky's back. But Tremayne, in this desperate effort, had
Hilloran off his feet for a second. He smashed him bodily against the
rail, hoping to slam the breath out of him for a momentary respite, and
broke away.

As he turned, the seaman's hands fastened on his throat, and Dicky
felt a sudden surge of joy. Against a man who knows his ju-jitsu, that
grip is more than futile: it is more than likely to prove fatal to the man
who employs it. Particularly was this fact proven then. For most of the
holds in ju-jitsu depend on getting a grip on a wrist or hand—which,
of course, are the hardest parts of the body to get a grip on, being the
smallest and most swift-moving. Dicky had been hampered all along by
being unable to trust himself to get his hold in that light, when the
faintest error of judgment would have been fatal. But now there could
be no mistake.

Dicky's hands went up on each side of his head, and closed on the
seaman's little fingers. He pulled and twisted at the same time, and the
man screamed as one finger at least was dislocated. But Dicky went on
and the man was forced sobbing to his knees. The surge of joy in
Dicky's heart rose to something like a shout of triumph—and died. Out
of the tail of his eye, he saw Hilloran coming in again.

Tremayne felt that he must be living a nightmare. There were two
of them, both far above his weight, and they were wearing him down,
gradually, relentlessly. As fast as he gained an advantage over one, the
other came to nullify it. As fast as he was able temporarily to disable
one, the other came back refreshed to renew the struggle. It was his own
stamina against their combined consecutive staminas—and either of
them individually was superior in brute strength to himself, even if one
left the knife out of the audit. Dicky knew the beginning of despair.

He threw the seaman from him, sideways, across Hilloran's very
knees, and leapt away. Hilloran stumbled, and Dicky's hands shot out

for the man's knife wrist, found its mark, twisted savagely. The knife tinkled into the scuppers.

If Dicky could have made a grip with both hands, he would have had the mastery, but he could only make it with one. His other hand, following the right, missed. A moment later he was forced to release his hold. He swung back only just in time to avoid the left cross that Hilloran lashed out at his jaw. Then both Hilloran and the sailor came at him simultaneously, almost shoulder to shoulder.

Dicky's strength was spent. He was going groggy at the knees, his arms felt like lead, his chest heaved terribly to every panting breath he took, his head swirled and throbbed dizzily. He was taking his licking. He could not counter the blows they both hurled at him at once. Somehow, he managed to duck under their arms, with some hazy notion of driving between them and breaking away into the open, but he could not do it. They had him cold.

He felt himself flung against the rail. The sailor's arms pinioned his own arms to his sides; Hilloran's hands were locked about his throat, strangling him to silence, crushing out life. His back was bent over the rail like a bow. His feet were off the ground.

The stars had gone out, and the moon had fallen from the sky. His chest was bound with ever-tightening iron bands. He seemed to be suspended in a vast void of utter blackness, and, though he could feel no wind, there was the roaring of a mighty wind in his ears.

And then, through the infinite distances of the dark gulf in which he hung, above even the great howling of that breathless wind, a voice spoke as a silver bell, saying: "What's this, Hilloran?"

6

DICKY SEEMED to awake from a hideous dream.

The fingers loosened from his throat, the iron cage that tortured his chest relaxed, the rushing wind in his ears died down to a murmur. He saw a star in the sky; and, as he saw it, a moon that had not been there before seemed to swim out of the infinite dark, back to its place in the heavens. And he breathed.

Also, he suddenly felt very sick. These things happened almost immediately. He knew that they must have been almost immediate, though they seemed to follow one another with the maddening slowness of the minute hand's pursuit of the hour hand round the face of a clock. He tried to whip them to a greater speed. He could not pause to savour the sensations of this return to life. His brain had never lost consciousness. Only his body was dead, and that had to be forced back to activity without a pause.

One idea stood out distinctly from the clearing fog that blurred his vision. Audrey Perowne was there, and she had caused an interruption that was saving him, but he was not safe yet. Neither was she.

She slept, he remembered, in a cabin whose porthole looked out onto the very stretch of deck where they had been fighting, and the noise must have roused her. But, in that light, she could have seen little but a struggling group of men, unless she had watched for a time before deciding to intervene—and that was unlikely. *And she must not be allowed to know the true reason for the disturbance.*

Tremayne now understood exactly how things were. If Hilloran was prepared to dispose of him, he was prepared to dispose of the girl as well—Dicky had no doubt of that. But that would require some determination. The habit of obedience would remain, and to break it would require a conscious effort. And that effort, at all costs, must not be stimulated by any provocation while Hilloran was able to feel that he had things mostly his own way.

All this Dick Tremayne understood, and acted upon it in an instant, before his senses had fully returned. His feet touched the deck; and he twisted and held the seaman in his arms as he himself had been held a moment earlier. Then he looked across and saw Audrey Perowne.

She stood by a bulkhead light, where they could see her clearly, and the light glinted on an automatic in her hand. She said again: "Hilloran—" And by the impatient way she said it, Dicky knew that she could not have been waiting long for her first question to be answered.

"It's all right," said Dicky swiftly. "One of the men's gone rather off his rocker, and he was trying to chuck himself overboard. Hilloran and I stopped him, and he fought. That's all."

The girl came closer, and neither Hilloran nor the seaman spoke. Now it was all a gamble. Would they take the lead he had offered them, and attest the lie? Or, rather, would Hilloran?—for the other man would take the cue from him.

It was a pure toss-up—with Audrey's automatic on Dicky's side. If Hilloran had a weapon—which he probably had—he would not dare to try and reach it when he was already covered, unless he had a supreme contempt for the girl's intelligence and straight shooting. And

Dicky had surmised that the man was not yet prepared for open defiance. . . .

But there was a perceptible pause before Hilloran said: "That's so, Audrey."

She turned to the sailor. "Why did you want to throw yourself overboard?"

Sullenly, the man said. "I don't know, miss."

She looked closely at him. "They seem to have been handling you pretty roughly."

"You should have seen the way he struggled," said Dicky. "I've never seen anyone so anxious to die. I'm afraid I did most of the damage. Here—"

He took the man's hand. "I'm going to put your finger back," he said. "It'll hurt. Are you ready?" He performed the operation with a sure touch; and then he actually managed a smile. "I should take him below and lock him up, Hilloran," he remarked. "He'll feel better in the morning. It must have been the heat. . . ."

Leaning against the rail, he watched Hilloran, without a word, take the man by the arm and lead him away. He felt curiously weak, now that the crisis was past and he hadn't got to fight any more. The blessing was that the girl couldn't see the bruises that must have been rising on his forehead and the side of his head. But something must have shown in his face that he didn't know was showing, or the way he leaned against the rail must have been rather limp, for suddenly he found her hand on his shoulder.

"It strikes me," she said softly, "that the man wasn't the only one who was roughly handled."

Dicky grinned. "I got some of the knocks, of course," he said.

"Did Hilloran?" she asked quietly.

He met her eyes, and knew then that she was not deceived. But he glanced quickly up and down the deck before he answered. "Hilloran took some knocks, too," he answered, "but it was a near thing."

"They tried to bump you off."

"That, I believe, was the general idea."

"I see." She was thoughtful. "Then—"

"I was trying to sleep on deck," said Dicky suddenly. "Hilloran was here when I arrived. We saw the man come along and try to climb over the rail—"

He broke up as Hilloran's shadow fell between them. "I've locked him up," said Hilloran, "but he seems quite sensible now."

"Good," said the girl casually. "I suppose you'd got the better of him by the time I came out. We'll discuss what's to be done with him in the morning. Dicky, you might take a turn round the deck with me before we go back to bed." She carried off the situation with such an utter naturalness that Hilloran was left with no answer. Her arm slipped through Dicky's, and they strolled away.

They went forward, rounded the deck-house, and continued aft, saying nothing; but when they came to the stern she stopped and leaned over the taffrail, gazing absorbedly down into the creaming wake.

Dicky stopped beside her. Where they stood, no one could approach within hearing distance without being seen. He took cigarettes and matches from his dressing-gown pocket. They smoked. He saw her face by the light of the match as he held it to her cigarette, and she seemed rather pale. But that might have been the light.

"Go on telling me about it," she ordered.

He shrugged. "You've heard most of it. I woke up when they were about to tip me over the side. There was some trouble. I did my best, but I'd have been done if you hadn't turned up when you did."

"Why did you lie to save them?"

He explained the instinctive reasoning which had guided him. "Not that I had time to figure it out as elaborately as that," he said, "but I'm still certain that it was a darned good guess."

"It's easily settled," she said. "We'll put Hilloran in irons—and you'll have to do the best you can in his place."

"You're an optimist," said Dicky sardonically. "Haven't I shown you every necessary reason why he should have the crew behind him to a man? They aren't the kind that started the story about honor among thieves."

She turned her head. "Are you suggesting that I should quit?"

He seemed to see his way clearly. "I am. We haven't an earthly— short of outbribing Hilloran, which 'ud mean sacrificing most of our own shares. We aren't strong enough to fight. And we needn't bank on Hilloran's coming back into the fold like a repentant sheep, because we'd lose our bets. He's got nothing to lose and everything to gain. We've served our purpose. He can handle the hold-up just as well without us, and earn another quarter of a million dollars for the shade of extra work. I don't say I wouldn't fight it out if I were alone. I would. But I'm not alone, and I suspect that Hilloran's got a nasty mind. If he's only thinking of taking your *money*—I'll be surprised."

She said coolly: "In that case, it doesn't look as if we'd gain anything by quitting."

"I could guarantee to get you away."

"How?"

"Don't ask me, Audrey. But I know how."

She appeared to contemplate the glowing end of her cigarette as though it were a crystal in which she could see the solution of all problems. Then she faced him. She said: "I don't quit."

"I suppose," said Dicky roughly, "you think that's clever. Let me tell you that it isn't. If you know that the decision's been framed against you right from the first gong, you don't lose caste by saving yourself the trouble of fighting."

"The decision on points may have been framed against you," she said, "but you can get round that one. You can win on a knockout."

"Possibly—if that were the whole of it. But you're forgetting something else, aren't you?"

"What's that?"

"The Saint."

He saw the exaggerated shrug of kimono'd shoulders. "I should worry about him. I'll stake anything he isn't among the passengers. I've had the ship searched from end to end, so he isn't here as a stowaway. And I haven't taken many chances with the crew. What is he going to do?"

"I don't know. But if the people he's beaten before now had known what the Saint was going to do—they wouldn't have been beaten. We aren't the first people who've been perfectly certain they were safe. We aren't the only clever crooks in the world."

Then she said again: "I've told you—I don't quit."

"All right—"

"This is the biggest game I've ever played!" she said, with a kind of savage enthusiasm. "It's more—it's one of the biggest games that ever *has* been played. I've spent months preparing the ground. I've sat up night after night planning everything out to the smallest detail, down to the last item of our getaways. It's a perfect machine. I've only got to press the button, and it'll run from tomorrow night to safety—as smoothly as any human machine ever ran. And you ask me to give that up!"

A kind of madness came over Dicky Tremayne. He turned, and his hands fell on her shoulders, and he forced her round with unnecessary violence. "All right!" he snapped. "You insist on keeping up this pose that you think's so brave and clever. You're damned pleased with yourself about it. Now listen to what I think. You're just a spoilt, silly fool—"

"Take your hands off me!"

"When I've finished. You're just a spoilt, silly little fool that I've a good mind to spank here and now, as I'd spank any other child—"

The moonlight gleamed on something blue-black and metallic between them. "Will you let me go?" she asked dangerously.

"No. Go ahead and shoot. I say you ought to be slapped, and, by the Lord . . . Audrey, Audrey, why are you crying?"

"Damn you," she said, "I'm not crying."

"I can see your eyes."

"Some smoke—"

"You dropped your cigarette minutes ago."

His fierce grip had slackened. She moved swiftly, and flung off his hands. "I don't want to get sentimental," she said shakily. "If I'm crying, it's my own business, and I've got my good reasons for it. You're quite right. I *am* spoilt. I *am* a fool. I want that quarter of a million dollars, and I'm going to have it—in spite of Hilloran—in spite of you, too, if you want to take Hilloran's side—"

"I'm not taking Hilloran's side, I'm—"

"Whose side are you taking, then? There's only two sides to this."

The moment had passed. He had chanced his arm on a show of strength—and failed. He wasn't used to bullying a girl. And through the dispersal of that shell-burst of madness he was aware again of the weakness of his position. A barefaced bluffer like the Saint might still have carried it off, but Dicky Tremayne couldn't. He dared not go too far. He was tied hand and foot. It had been on the tip of his tongue to throw up the game then—to tell the truth, present his ultimatum, and damn the consequences. Prudence—perhaps too great a prudence— had stopped him. In that, in a way, he was like Hilloran. Hilloran was in the habit of obedience; Tremayne was in the habit of loyalty; neither of them could break his habit on the spur of the moment. "I'm taking your side," said Dicky. And he wondered, at the same time, whether he oughtn't to have given way to the impulse of that moment's loss of temper.

"Then what's the point of all this?" she demanded.

"I'm taking your side," said Dicky, "better than you know. But we won't go into that any more—not just now, anyway. Let it pass. Since you're so clever—what's your idea for dealing with the situation?"

"Another cigarette."

He gave her one, lighted it, and turned to stare moodily over the sea. It was a hopeless dilemma. "I wonder," he thought bitterly, "why a man should cling so fanatically to his word of honor? It's sheer unnatural lunacy, that's what it is." He knew that was what it was. But he was on parole, and he would have no chance to take back his parole until the following night at the earliest.

"What do you think Hilloran'll do now?" she asked. "Will he try again tonight, or will he wait till tomorrow?"

The moment was very much past. It might never have been. Dicky tried to concentrate, but his brain seemed to have gone flabby. "I don't know," he said vaguely. "In his place, I'd probably try again tonight. Whether Hilloran has that type of mind is another matter. You know him better than I do."

"I don't think he has. He's had one chance tonight to make the stand against me, and he funked it. That's a setback, psychologically, that'll take him some time to get over. I'll bet he doesn't try again till tomorrow. He'll be glad to be able to do some thinking, and there's nothing to make him rush it."

"Will you have any better answer tomorrow than you have now?"

She smiled. "I shall have slept on it," she said carelessly. "That always helps. . . . Good-night, Dicky. I'm tired."

He stopped her. "Will you promise me one thing?"

"What is it?"

"Lock your door tonight. Don't open to anyone—on any excuse."

"Yes," she said. "I should do that, in any case. You'd better do the same."

He walked back with her to the cabin. Her hair stirred in the breeze, and the moon silvered it. She was beautiful. As they passed by a bulkhead light, he was observing the serenity of her proud lovely face. He found that he had not lost all his madness.

They reached the door. "Good-night, Dicky," she said again.

"Good-night," he said. And then he said, in a strange strained voice: "I love you, Audrey. Good-night, my dear." He was gone before she could answer.

7

DICKY DREAMED that he was sitting on Hilloran's chest, with his fingers round Hilloran's throat, banging Hilloran's head on the deck. Every time Hilloran's head hit the deck, it made a lot of noise. Dicky knew that this was absurd. He woke up lazily, and traced the noise to his cabin door. Opening one eye, he saw the morning sunlight streaming in through his porthole.

Yawning, he rolled out of the bunk, slipped his automatic from under the pillow, and went to open the door. It was a white-coated steward, bearing a cup of tea. Dicky thanked the man, took the cup, closed the door on him, locking it again.

He sat on the edge of the bunk, stirring the tea thoughtfully. He looked at it thoughtfully, smelt it thoughtfully, got up thoughtfully, and poured it thoughtfully out of the porthole. Then he lighted a cigarette. He went to his bath with the automatic in his dressing-gown pocket and his hand on the automatic. He finished off with a cold shower, and returned to his cabin to dress, with similar caution, but feeling better.

The night before, he had fallen asleep almost at once. Dicky Tremayne had an almost Saintly faculty for carrying into practice the ancient adage that the evil of the day is sufficient thereto; and, since he reckoned that he would need all his wits about him on the morrow, he had slept. But now the morrow had arrived, he was thoughtful.

Not that the proposition in front of him appeared any more hopeful in the clear light of day. Such things have a useful knack of losing many of their terrors overnight, in the ordinary way—but this particular specimen didn't follow the rules.

It was true that Dicky had slept peacefully, and, apart from the perils that might have lurked in the cup of tea which he had not drunk, no attempt had been made to follow up the previous night's effort. That fact might have been used to argue that Hilloran hadn't yet found his confidence. In a determined counter-attack, such trifles as locked doors would not for long have stemmed his march; but the counter-attack had not been made. Yet this argument gave Dicky little reassurance.

An estimated value of one million dollars' worth of jewelry was jay-walking over the Mediterranean in that yacht, and every single dollar of that value was an argument for Hilloran—and others. Audrey Perowne had described her scheme as a fool-proof machine. So it was—granted the trustworthiness of the various cogs and bearings. And that was the very snag upon which it was liable to take it into its head to seize.

The plot would have been excellent if its object had been monkey-nuts or hot dogs—things of no irresistible interest to anyone but an incorrigible collector. Jewels that were readily convertible into real live dollars were another matter. Even then, they might have been dealt with in comparative safety on dry land. But when they and their owners were more or less marooned in the open sea, far beyond the interference

of the policeman at the street corner, with a crew like that of the
Corsican Maid, each of those dollars became not only an argument but
also a very unstable charge of high explosive.

Thus mused Dicky Tremayne while he dressed, while he breakfasted
and while he strolled round the deck afterwards with Sir Esdras Levy
and Mr. Matthew Sankin. And the question that was uppermost in his
mind was how he could possibly stall off the impending explosion until
eleven or twelve o'clock that night.

He avoided Audrey Perowne. He saw her at breakfast, greeted her
curtly, and plunged immediately into a discussion with Mr. George Y.
Ulrig on the future of the American Negro—a point of abstract specula-
tion which interested Dicky Tremayne rather less than the future of the
Patagonian paluka. Walking round the deck, he had to pass and repass
the girl, who was holding court in a shady space under an awning. He
did not meet her eye, and was glad that she did not challenge him. If
she had, she could have made him feel intolerably foolish.

The madness of the night before was over, and he wondered what had
weakened him into betraying himself. He watched her out of the tail
of his eye each time he passed. She chattered volubly, joked, laughed
delightfully at each of her guests' clumsy sallies. It was amazing—her
impudent nerve, her unshakable self-possession. Who would have imagined, he asked himself, that before the next dawn she was proposing
that those same guests that she was then entertaining so charmingly
should see her cold and masterful behind a loaded gun?

And so to lunch. Afterwards—It was hot. The sun, a globe of eye-
aching fire, swung naked over the yard-arm in a burnished sky. It made
the tar bubble between the planks of the open deck, and turned the
scarcely rippling waters to a sheet of steel. With one consent, guests and
their wives, replete, sought long chairs and the shade. Conversation
suffocated—died.

At three o'clock, Dicky went grimly to the rendezvous. He saw
Hilloran entering as he arrived, and was glad that he had not to face
the girl alone.

They sat down on either side of the table, with one measured exchange of inscrutable glances. Hilloran was smoking a cigar. Dicky
lighted a cigarette.

"What have you done about that sailor?" asked Audrey.

"I let him out," said Hilloran. "He's quite all right now."

She took an armchair between them. "Then we'll get to business,"
she said. "I've got it all down to a time-table. We want as little fuss as
possible, and there's going to be no need for any shooting. While we're

at dinner, Hilloran, you'll go through all the cabins and clean them out. Do it thoroughly. No one will interrupt you. Then you'll go down to the galley and serve out—this."

She held up a tiny flask of a yellowish liquid. "Butyl," she said, "and it's strong. Don't overdo it. Two drops in each cup of coffee, with the last two good ones for Dicky and me. And there you are. It's too easy—and far less trouble than a gun holdup. By the time they come to, they'll be tied hand and foot. We drop anchor off the Corsican coast near Calvi at eleven, and put them ashore. That's all."

Dicky rose. "Very neat," he murmured. "You don't waste time."

"We haven't to do anything. It all rests with Hilloran, and his job's easy enough."

Hilloran took the flask and slipped it into his pocket.

"You can leave it to me," he said; and that reminder of the favourite expression of Dicky's friend, Roger Conway, would have made Dicky wince if his face hadn't been set so sternly.

"If that's everything," said Dicky, "I'll go. There's no point in anyone having a chance to notice that we're both absent together." It was a ridiculous excuse, but it was an excuse. She didn't try to stop him.

Hilloran watched the door close without making any move to follow. He was carefully framing a speech in his mind, but the opportunity to use it was taken from him.

"Do you trust Dicky?" asked the girl.

It was so exactly the point he had himself been hoping to lead up to that Hilloran could have gasped. As it was, some seconds passed before he could trust himself to answer. "It's funny you should say that now," he remarked. "Because I remember that when *I* suggested it, you gave me the air."

"I've changed my mind since last night. As I saw it—mind you, I couldn't see very well because it was so dark—but it seemed to me that the situation was quite different from the way you both described it. It seemed," said the girl bluntly, "as if Dicky were trying to throw *you* overboard, and the sailor was trying to stop him."

"That's the truth," said Hilloran blindly.

"Then why did you lie to save him?"

"Because I didn't think you'd believe me if I told the truth."

"Why did the sailor lie?"

"He'd take his tip from me. If I chose to say nothing, it wasn't worth his while to contradict me."

The girl's slender fingers drummed on the table.

"Why do you think Dicky should try to kill you?"

Hilloran had an inspiration. He couldn't stop to give thanks for the marvellous coincidence that had made the girl play straight into his hands. The thanksgiving could come later. The immediate thing was to leap for the heaven-sent opening. He took a sheet of paper from his pocket and leaned forward. "You remember me giving Dicky a letter yesterday evening before dinner?" he asked. "I opened it first and took a copy. Here it is. It looks innocent enough, but—"

"Did you test it for invisible ink?"

"I made every test I knew. Nothing showed up. But just read the letter. Almost every sentence in it might be a hint to anyone who knew how to take it."

The girl read, with a furrow deepening between her brows. When she looked up, she was frowning. "What's your idea?"

"What I told you before. I think Dicky Tremayne is one of the Saint's gang. An arrangement."

"That can't be right. I don't know much about the Saint, but I don't imagine he'd be the sort to send a man off on a job like this and leave his instructions to a letter delivered at the last minute. The least delay in the post, and he mightn't have received the letter at all."

"That's all very well, but—"

"Besides, whoever sent this letter, if it's what you think it is, must have guessed that it might be opened and read. Otherwise the instructions would have been written in plain language. Now, these people are clever. The hints may be good ones. They may just as probably be phoney. I wouldn't put it above them to use some kind of code that anyone might tumble to—and hide another code behind it. You think you've found the solution—in the hints, if you can interpret them—but I say that's too easy. It's probably a trap."

"Can you find any other code?"

"I'm not a code expert. But that doesn't say there isn't one."

Hilloran scowled. "I don't see that that makes any difference," he said. "I say that that letter's suspicious. If you agree with me, there's only one thing to be done."

"Certainly."

"He can go over the side, where he might have put me last night."

She shook her head. "I don't like killing, Hilloran. You know that. And it isn't necessary." She pointed to his pocket. "You have the stuff. Suppose there was only *one* coffee without it after dinner tonight?"

Hilloran's face lighted up with a brutal eagerness. He had a struggle to conceal his delight. It was too simple—too utterly, utterly simple. Verily, his enemies were delivered into his hands. . . . But he tried to make his acknowledgment of the idea restraining and calculating. "It'd be safer," he conceded. "I must say I'm relieved to find you're coming round to my way of thinking, Audrey."

She shrugged, with a crooked smile. "The more I know you," she said, "the more I realize that you're usually right."

Hilloran stood up. His face was like the thin crust of a volcano, under which fires and horrible forces boil and batter for release. "Audrey—"

"Not now, Hilloran—"

"I've got a first name," he said slowly. "It's John. Why don't you ever use it?"

"All right—John. But please . . . I want to rest this afternoon. When all the work's done, I'll—I'll talk to you."

He came closer. "You wouldn't try to double-cross John Hilloran, would you?"

"You know I wouldn't!"

"I want you!" he burst out incoherently. "I've wanted you for years. You've always put me off. When I found you were getting on too well with that twister Tremayne, I went mad. But he's not taking you in any more, is he?"

"No—"

"And there's no one else?"

"How could there be?"

"You little beauty!"

"Afterwards, Hilloran. I'm so tired. I want to rest. Go away now—"

He sprang at her and caught her in his arms, and his mouth found her lips. For a moment she stood passively in his embrace. Then she pushed him back, and dragged herself away. "I'll go now," he said unsteadily.

She stood like a statute, with her eyes riveted on the closing door, till the click of the latch snapping home seemed to snap also the taut cord that held her rigid and erect. Then she sank limply back into her chair. For a second she sat still. Then she fell forward across the table, and buried her face in her arms.

8

"VE VERE suppose'," said the Countess Anusia Marova, "to come to Monaco at nine o'clock. But ve are delay', and ze captayne tell me ve do nod zere arrive teel ten o'clock. So ve do nod af to urry past dinair to see ourselves come in ze port."

Dicky Tremayne heard the soft accents across the saloon, above the bull-voice drawl of Mr. George Y. Ulrig, who was holding him down with a discourse on the future of the Japanese colony in California. Dicky was rather less interested in this than he would have been in a discourse on the future of the Walloon colony in Cincinnati. A scrap of paper crumpled in the pocket of his dinner-jacket seemed to be burning his side.

The paper had come under his cabin door while he dressed. He had been at the mirror, fidgeting with his tie, and he had seen the scrap sliding on to the carpet. He had watched it, half-hypnotized, and it had been some time before he moved to pick it up. When he had read it, and jerked open the door, the alleyway outside was deserted. Only, at the end, he had seen Hilloran, in his uniform, pass across by the alley athwarthships without looking to right or left.

The paper had carried one line of writing, in block letters:

DON'T DRINK YOUR COFFEE

Nothing else. No signature, or even an initial. Not a word of explanation. Just that. But he knew that there was only one person on board who could have written it. He had hurried over the rest of his toilet in the hope of finding Audrey Perowne in the saloon before the other guests arrived, but she had been the last to appear. He had not been able to summon up the courage to knock on the door of her cabin. His desire to see her and speak to her again alone, on any pretext, was tempered by an equal desire to avoid giving her any chance to refer to his last words of the previous night.

"The Jap is a good citizen," George Y. Ulrig droned on, holding up his cocktail glass like a sceptre. "He has few vices, he's clean, and he doesn't make trouble. On the other hand, he's too clever to trust. He . . . Say, boy, what's eatin' you?"

"Nothing," denied Dicky hastily. "What makes you think the Jap's too clever to trust?"

"Now, the Chinaman's the honestest man in the world, whatever they say about him," resumed the drone. "I'll tell you a story to illustrate that. . . ."

He told his story at leisure, and Dicky forced himself to look interested. It wasn't easy. He was glad when they sat down to dinner. His partner was the less eagle-eyed Mrs. George Y. Ulrig, who was incapable of noticing the absent-minded way in which he listened to her detailed description of her last illness. But halfway through the meal he was recalled to attention by a challenge, and for some reason he was glad of it.

"Deeky," said the girl at the end of the table. Dicky looked up. "Ve are in ze middle of an argument," she said.

"Id iss this," interrupted Sir Esdras Levy. "Der Gountess asks, if for insdance you vos a friendt off mine, and I hat made a business teal mit odder friendts off mine, ant bromised to tell nobody nothing, ant I see you vill be ruined if you don't know off der teal, and I know der teal vill ruined be if you know off it—vot shoot I to?"

This lucid exposition was greeted with a suppressed titter which made Sir Esdras whiffle impatiently through his beard. He waved his hands excitedly. "I say," he proclaimed magisterially, "dot a a man's vort iss his pond. I am sorry for you, bud I must my vort keep."

"'Owever," chipped in Mr. Matthew Sankin, and, catching his wife's basilisk eye upon him, choked redly. "*However*," said Mr. Matthew Sankin, "I 'old by the British principle that a man oughter stick by his mates—friends—an' he ain't—'asn't—*hasn't* got no right to let 'em down. None of 'em. That's wot."

"Matthew, deah," said Mrs. Sankin silkily, "the Countess was esking Mr. Tremayne the question, ay believe. Kaindly give us a chance to heah his opinion."

"What about a show of hands?" suggested Dicky. "How many of you say that a man should stand by his word—whatever it costs him?" Six hands went up. Sankin and Ulrig were alone among the male dissenters. "Lost by one," said Dicky.

"No," said the Countess. "I do not vote. I make you ze chairman, Deeky, and you 'ave ze last vord. 'Ow do you say?"

"In this problem, there's no chance of a compromise? The man couldn't find a way to tell his friend so that it wouldn't spoil the deal for his other friends?"

"Ve hof no gompromises," said Sir Esdras sternly.

Dicky looked down the table and met the girl's eyes steadily. "Then," he remarked, "I should first see my partners and warn them that I was going to break my word, and then I should go and do it. But the first condition is essential."

"A gompromise," protested Sir Esdras. "Subbose you hof nod der dime or der obbortunity?"

"How great is this friend?"

"Der greatest friendt you hof," insisted the honorable man vehemently. "Id mags no tifference."

"Come orf it," urged Mr. Sankin. "A Britisher doesn't let 'is best pal dahn."

"Well," drawled George Y. Ulrig, "does an American?"

"You say I am nod Briddish?" fumed Sir Esdras Levy, whiffling. "You hof der imberdinence—"

"Deeky," said the girl sweetly, "you should make up your mind more queekly. Ozairvise ve shall 'ave a quarrel. Now, 'ow do you vote?" Dicky looked round the table. He wondered who had started that fatuous argument. He could have believed that the girl had done it deliberately, judging by the way she was thrusting the casting vote upon him so insistently. But, if that were so, it could only mean . . .

But it didn't matter. With zero hour only a few minutes away, a strange mood of recklessness was upon him. It had started as simple impatience—impatience with the theories of George. Y. Ulrig, impatience with the ailments of Mrs. Ulrig. And now it had grown suddenly to a hell-for-leather desperation.

Audrey Perowne had said it. "You should make up your mind more quickly." And Dicky knew that it was true. He realized that he had squandered all his hours of grace on fruitless shilly-shallying which had taken him nowhere. Now he answered in a kind of panic. "No," he said. "I'm against the motion. I'd let down any partners, and smash the most colossal deal under the sun, rather than hurt anyone I loved. Now you know—and I hope you're satisfied."

And he knew, as the last plates were removed, that he was fairly and squarely in the cart. He was certain then that Audrey Perowne had engineered the discussion, with intent to trap him into a statement. Well, she'd got what she wanted.

He was suspect. Hilloran and Audrey must have decided *that* after he'd left her cabin that afternoon. Then why the message before dinner? They'd decided to eliminate him along with the rest. That message must have been a weakness on her part. She must have been banking on his humanity—and she'd inaugurated the argument, and brought him into it, simply to satisfy herself on a stone-cold certainty. All right. . . .

That was just where she'd wrecked her own bet. A grim, vindictive resentment was freezing his heart. She chose to trade on the love he'd confessed—and thereby she lost it. He hated her now, with an increasing hatred. She'd almost taken him in. Almost she'd made him ready to sacrifice his honor and the respect of his friends to save her. And now she was laughing at him.

When he'd answered, she'd smiled. He'd seen it—too late—and even then the meaning of that smile hadn't dawned on him immediately. But he understood it all now. *Fool! Fool! Fool!* he cursed himself savagely and the knowledge that he'd so nearly been seduced from his self-respect by such a waster was like a worm in his heart.

"But she doesn't get away with it," he swore savagely to himself. "By God, she doesn't get away with it!"

And savagely that vindictive determination lashed down his first fury to an intensely simmering malevolence. Savagely he cursed the moment's panic that had made him betray himself—speaking from his heart without having fully reckoned all that might be behind the question. And then suddenly he was very cold and watchful. The steward was bringing in the tray of coffee.

As if from a great distance, Dicky Tremayne watched the cups being set before the guests. As each guest accepted his cup, Dicky shifted his eyes to the face above it. He hated nearly all of them. Of the women, Mrs. Ulrig was the only one he could tolerate—for all her preoccupation with the diseases which she imagined afflicted her. Of the men, there were only two whom he found human: Matthew Sankin, the henpecked Cockney who had, somehow, come to be cursed rather than blessed with more money than he knew how to spend, and George Y. Ulrig, the didactic millionaire from the Middle West. The others he would have been delighted to rob at any convenient opportunity—particularly Sir Esdras Levy, an ill-chosen advertisement for a noble race.

Dicky received his cup disinterestedly. His right hand was returning from his hip pocket. Of the two things which it brought with it, he had one under his napkin: the cigarette-case he produced, and offered. The girl caught his eye, but his face was expressionless. An eternity seemed to pass before the first cup was lifted. The others followed. Dicky counted them, stirring his own coffee mechanically. Three more to go . . . two more . . .

Matthew Sankin drank last. He alone dared to comment. "Funny taste in this cawfy," he said.

"It tastes good to me," said Audrey Perowne, having tasted.

And Dicky Tremayne, watching her, saw something in her eyes which he could not interpret. It seemed to be meant for him, but he hadn't the least idea what it was meant to be. A veiled mockery?

A challenge? A gleam of triumph? Or what? It was a curious look. Blind. . . .

Then he saw Lady Levy half rise from her chair, clutch at her head, and fall sprawling across the table.

"Fainted," said Matthew Sankin, on his feet. "It's a bit stuffy in here—I've just noticed. . . ."

Dicky sat still, and watched the man's eyes glaze open, and saw him fall before he could speak again. They fell one by one, while Dicky sat motionless, watching, with the sensation of being a spectator at a play. Dimly he appreciated the strangeness of the scene; dimly he heard the voices, and the smash of crockery swept from the table; but he himself was aloof, alone with his thoughts, and his right hand held his automatic pistol hidden under his napkin. He was aware that Ulrig was shaking him by the shoulder, babbling again and again: "Doped—that coffee was doped—some goldurned son of a coot!"—until the American in his turn crumpled to the floor. And then Dicky and the girl were alone, she standing at her end of the table and Dicky sitting at his end with the gun on his knee.

That queer blind look was still in her eyes. She said, in a hushed voice: "Dicky—"

"I should laugh now," said Dicky. "You needn't bother to try and keep a straight face any longer. And in a few minutes you'll have nothing to laugh about—so I should laugh now."

"I only took a sip," she said.

"I see the rest was spilt," said Dicky. "Have some of mine."

She was working round the table towards him, holding on the backs of the swivel chairs. He never moved. "Dicky, did you mean what you answered—just now?"

"I *did*. I suppose I might mean it still, if the conditions were fulfilled. You'll remember that I said—*anyone I loved*. That doesn't apply here. Last night, I said I loved you. I apologize for the lie. I don't love you. I never could. But I thought—" He paused, and then drove home the taunt with all the stony contempt that was in him: "I thought it would amuse me to make a fool of you."

He might have struck her across the face. But he was without remorse. He still sat and watched her, with the impassivity of a graven image, till she spoke again. "I sent you that note—"

"Because you thought you had a sufficient weapon in my love. Exactly. I understand that."

She seemed to be keeping her feet by an effort of will. Her eyelids were drooping, and he saw tears under them. "Who are you?" she asked.

"Dicky Tremayne is my real name," he said, "and I am one of the Saint's friends."

She nodded so that her chin touched her chest.

"And—I—suppose—you—doped—my coffee," she said, foolishly, childishly, in that small hushed voice that he had to strain to hear; and she slid down beside the chair she was holding and fell on her face without another word.

Dicky Tremayne looked down at her in a kind of numb perplexity, with the ice of a merciless vengefulness holding him chilled and unnaturally calm. He looked down at her, at her crumpled dress, at her bare white arms, at the tousled crop of golden hair tumbled disorderly over her head by the fall, and he was like a figure of stone.

But within him something stirred and grew and fought with the foundations of his calm. He fought back at it, hating it, but it brought him slowly up from his chair at last, till he stood erect, still looking down at her, with his napkin fallen to his feet and the gun naked in his right hand. "Audrey!" he cried suddenly.

His back was to the door. He heard the step behind him, but he could not move quicker than Hilloran's tongue. "Stand still!" rapped Hilloran.

Dicky moved only his eyes.

These he raised to the clock in front of him, and saw that it was twenty minutes past nine.

9

"DROP THAT gun," said Hilloran. Dicky dropped the gun.

"Kick it away." Dicky kicked it away.

"Now you can turn round." Dicky turned slowly.

Hilloran, with his own gun in one hand and Dicky's gun in the other, was leaning back against the bulkhead by the door with a sneer of triumph on his face. Outside the door waited a file of seamen. Hilloran motioned them in.

"Of course, I was expecting this," said Dicky.

"Mother's Bright Boy, you are," said Hilloran.

He turned to the seamen, pointing with his gun.

"Frisk him and tie him up."

"I'm not fighting," said Dicky. He submitted to the search imperturbably. The scrap of paper in his pocket was found and taken to Hilloran, who waived it aside after one glance at it.

"I guessed it was something like that," he said. "Dicky, you'll be glad to hear that I saw her slip it under your door. Lucky for me!"

"Very," agreed Dicky dispassionately. "She must have come as near fooling you as she was to fooling me. We ought to get on well after this."

"Fooling *you!*"

Dicky raised his eyebrows.

"How much did you hear outside that door?"

"Everything."

"Then you must have understood—unless you're a born fool."

"I understand that she double-crossed me, and warned you about the coffee."

"Why d'you think she did that? Because she thought she'd got me under her thumb. Because she thought I was so crazy about her that I was as soundly doped that way as I could have been doped by a gallon of 'knock-out.' And she was right—then."

The men were moving about with lengths of rope, binding wrists and ankles with methodical efficiency. Already pinioned himself, Dicky witnessed the guests being treated one by one in similar fashion, and remained outwardly unmoved. But his brain was working like lightning.

"When they're all safe," said Hilloran, with a jerk of one gun, "I'm going to ask you some questions—Mr. Dicky Tremayne! You'd better get ready to answer right now, because I sha'n't be kind to you if you give trouble."

Dicky stood in listless submission. He seemed to be in a kind of stupor. He had been like that ever since Hilloran had disarmed him. Except for the movements of his mouth, and the fact that he remained standing, there might have been no life in him. Everything about him pointed to a paralyzed and fatalistic resignation. "I sha'n't give any trouble," he said tonelessly. "Can't you understand that I've no further interest in anything—after what I've found out about her?"

Hilloran looked at him narrowly, but the words, and Dicky's slack pose, carried complete conviction. Tremayne might have been half-chloroformed. His apathetic, benumbed indifference was beyond dispute. It hung on him like a cloak of lead. "Have you any friends on board?" asked Hilloran.

"No," said Dicky flatly. "I'm quite alone."

"Is that the truth?"

For a moment Tremayne seemed stung to life.

"Don't be so damned dumb!" he snapped. "I say I'm telling you the truth. Whether you believe me or not, you're getting just as good results this way as you would by torture. You've no way of proving my statements—however you obtain them."

"Are you expecting any help from outside?"

"It was all in the letter you read."

"By airplane?"

"Seaplane."

"How many of your gang?"

"Possibly two. Possibly only one."

"At what time?"

"Between eleven and twelve, any night from tonight on. Or at four o'clock any morning. I should have called them by flashing—a red light."

"Any particular signal?"

"No. Just a regular intermittent flash," said Dicky inertly. "There's no catch in it."

Hilloran studied his face curiously. "I'd believe you—if the way you're surrendering wasn't the very opposite of everything that's ever been said about the Saint's gang."

Tremayne's mouth twitched. "For heaven's sake!" he burst out seethingly. "Haven't I told you, you poor blamed boob? I'm fed up with the Saint. I'm fed up with everything. I don't give another lonely damn for anything anyone does. I tell you, I was mad about that double-crossing little slut. And now I see what she's really worth, I don't care what happens to her or to me. You can do what you like. Get on with it!"

Hilloran looked round the saloon. By then, everyone had been securely bound except the girl, and the seamen were standing about uncertainly, waiting for further instructions. Hilloran jerked his head in the direction of the door. "Get out," he ordered. "There's two people here I want to interview—alone."

Nevertheless, when the last man had left the room, closing the door behind him, Hilloran did not immediately proceed with the interview. Instead, he pocketed one gun, and produced a large bag of soft leather. With this he went round the room, collecting necklaces, earrings, brooches, rings, studs, bracelets, wallets—till the bag bulged and weighed heavy. Then he added to it the contents of his pockets. More and more jewels slipped into the bag like a stream of glittering hailstones. When he had finished, he had some difficulty in tightening the cords that closed the mouth of the bag.

He balanced it appreciatively on the palm of his hand. "One million dollars," he said.

"You're welcome," said Dicky.

"Now I'll talk," said Hilloran.

He talked unemotionally, and Dicky listened without the least sign of feeling. At the end, he shrugged. "You might shoot me first," he suggested.

"I'll consider it."

No sentence of death could ever have been given or received more calmly. It was a revelation to Dicky, in its way, for he would have expected Hilloran to bluster and threaten luridly. Hilloran, after all, had a good deal to be vindictive about. But the man's restraint was inhuman.

Tremayne's stoicism matched it. Hilloran promised death as he might have promised a drink: Dicky accepted the promise as he might have accepted a drink. Yet he never doubted that it was meant. The very unreality of Hilloran's command of temper made his sincerity more real than any theatrical elaboration could have done. "I should like to ask a last favor," said Dicky calmly.

"A cigarette?"

"I shouldn't refuse that. But what I should appreciate most would be the chance to finish telling—her—what I was telling her when you came in."

Hilloran hesitated.

"If you agree," added Dicky callously, "I'd advise you to have her tied up first. Otherwise, she might try to untie me in the hope of saving her own skin. Seriously—we haven't been melodramatic about this tonight, so you might go on in the same way."

"You're plucky," said Hilloran.

Tremayne shrugged. "When you've no further interest in life, death loses its terror."

Hilloran went and picked up a length of rope that had been left over. He tied the girl's wrists behind her back; then he went to the door and called, and two men appeared. "Take those two to my cabin," he said. "You'll remain on guard outside the door." He turned back to Dicky. "I shall signal at eleven. At any time after that, you may expect me to call you out on deck."

"Thank you," said Dicky quietly. The first seaman had picked up Audrey Perowne, and Dicky followed him out of the saloon. The second brought up the rear. The girl was laid down on the bunk in Hilloran's cabin. Dicky kicked down the folding seat and made himself as comfortable as he could. The men withdrew, closing the door.

Dicky looked out of the porthole and waited placidly. It was getting dark. The cabin was in twilight; and, beyond the porthole, a faintly luminous blue-grey dusk was deepening over the sea. Sometimes he could hear the tramp of footsteps passing over the deck above. Apart from that, there was no sound but the murmuring undertone of slithering waters slipping past the hull, and the vibration, felt rather than heard, of the auxiliary engines. It was all strangely peaceful. And Dicky waited. After a long time, the girl sighed and moved. Then she lay still again. It was getting so dark that he could hardly see her face as anything but a pale blur in the shadow. But presently she said softly: "So it worked."

"What worked?"

"The coffee."

He said, "I had nothing to do with that."

"Almost neat butyl, it was," she said. "That was clever. I guessed my own coffee would be doped of course. I put the idea into Hilloran's head, because it's always helpful to know how you're going to be attacked. But I didn't think it'd be as strong as that. I thought it'd be safe to sip it."

"Won't you believe that I didn't do it, Audrey?"

"I don't care. It was somebody clever who thought of catching me out with my own idea."

He said: "I didn't do it, Audrey."

Then for a time there was silence.

Then she said: "My hands are tied."

"So are mine."

"He got you as well?"

"Easily. Audrey, how awake are you?"

"I'm quite awake now," she said. "Just very tired. And my head's splitting. But that doesn't matter. Have you got anything else to say?"

"Audrey, do you know who I am?"

"I know. You're one of the Saint's gang. You told me. But I knew it before."

"You knew it before?"

"I've known it for a long time. As soon as I noticed that you weren't quite an ordinary crook, I made inquiries—on my own, without anyone knowing. It took a long time, but I did it. Didn't you meet at a flat in Brook Street?"

Dicky paused. "Yes," he said slowly. "That's true. Then why did you keep it quiet?"

"That," she said, "is my very own business."

"All the time I was with you, you were in danger—yet you deliberately kept me with you."

"I chose to take the chance. That was because I loved you."

"You what?"

"I loved you," she said wearily. "Oh, I can say it quite safely now. And I will, for my own private satisfaction. You hear me, Dicky Tremayne? I loved you. I suppose you never thought I could have the feelings of an ordinary woman. But I did. I had it worse than an ordinary woman has it. I've always lived recklessly, and I loved recklessly. The risk was worth it—as long as you were with me. But I never thought you cared for me, till last night. . . ."

"Audrey, you tell me that!"

"Why not? It makes no difference now. We can say what we like—and there are no consequences. What exactly is going to happen to us?"

"My friends are coming in a seaplane. I told Hilloran, and he proposes to double-cross the crew. He's got all the jewels. He's going to give my signal. When the seaplane arrives, he's going to row out with me in a boat. My friends will be told that I'll be shot if they don't obey. Naturally, they'll obey—they'll put themselves in his hands, because they're that sort of fool. And Hilloran will board the seaplane and fly away—with you. He knows how to handle an airplane."

"Couldn't you have told the crew that?"

"What for? One devil's better than twenty."

"And what happens to you?"

"I go over this side with a lump of lead tied to each foot. Hilloran's got a grudge to settle—and he's going to settle it. He was so calm about it when he told me that I knew he meant every word. He's a curious type," said Dicky meditatively. "I wish I'd studied him more. Your ordinary crook would have been noisy and nasty about it, but there's nothing like that about Hilloran. You'd have thought it was the same thing to him as squashing a fly."

There was another silence, while the cabin grew darker still. Then she said: "What are you thinking, Dicky?"

"I'm thinking," he said, "how suddenly things can change. I loved you. Then, when I thought you were trading on my love, and laughing at me up your sleeve all the time, I hated you. And then, when you fell down in the saloon, and you lay so still, I knew nothing but that I loved you whatever you did, and that all the hell you could give me was nothing, because I had touched your hand and heard your blessed voice and seen you smile." She did not speak. "But I lied to Hilloran," he said. "I told him nothing more than that my love had turned to hate, and not that my hate had turned back to love again. He believed me. I asked to be left alone with you before the end, to hurl my dying contempt on you—and he consented. That again makes him a curious type—but I knew he'd do it. That's why we're here now."

"Why did you do that?"

"So that I could tell you the truth, and try to make you tell me the truth—and, perhaps, find some way out with you."

The darkness had become almost the darkness of night. She said, far away: "I couldn't make up my mind. I kept on putting myself off and putting myself off, and in order to do that I *had* to trade on your love. But I forced you into that argument at dinner to find out how great your love could be. That was a woman's vanity—and I've paid for it. And I told Hilloran to dope your coffee, and told you not to drink it, so that you'd be ready to surprise him and hold him up when he thought you were doped. I was going to double-cross him, and then leave the rest in your hands, because I couldn't make up my mind."

"It's a queer story, isn't it?" said Dicky Tremayne.

"But I've told you the truth now," she said. "And I tell you that if I can find the chance to throw myself out of the boat, or out of the seaplane, I'm going to take it. Because I love you." He was silent. "I killed Morganheim," she said, "because I had a sister—once." He was very quiet. "Dicky Tremayne," she said, "didn't you say you loved me—once?"

He was on his feet. She could see him.

"That was the truth."

"Is it—still—true?"

"It will always be true," he answered; and he was close beside her, on his knees beside the bunk. He was so close beside her that he could kiss her on the lips.

10

SIMON TEMPLAR sat at the controls of the tiny seaplane and stared thoughtfully across the water. The moon had not yet risen, and the parachute flares he had thrown out to land by had been swallowed up into extinction by the sea. But he could see, a cable's length away, the lights of the yacht riding sulkily on a slight swell; and the lamp in the stern of the boat that was stealing darkly across the intervening stretch of water was reflected a thousand times by a thousand ripples, making a smear of dancing luminance across the deep.

He was alone. And he was glad to be alone, for undoubtedly something funny was going to happen. He had himself, after much thought, written Patricia's letter to Dicky Tremayne, and he was satisfied that it had been explicit enough. "My eyes are red from weeping for you." It couldn't have been plainer. Red light—danger. A babe in arms couldn't have missed it.

And yet, when he had flown nearer, he had seen that the yacht was not moving; and his floats had hardly licked the first flurry of spray from the sea before the boat he was watching had put off from the ship's side. He could not know that Dicky had given away that red signal deliberately, hoping that it would keep him on his guard and that the inspiration of the moment might provide for the rest. All the same, the Saint was a good guesser, and he was certainly on his guard. He knew that something very fishy was coming towards him across that piece of fish-pond, and the only question was—what?

Thoughtfully the Saint fingered the butt of the Lewis gun that was mounted on the fuselage behind him. It had not been mounted there when he left San Remo that evening; for the sight of private seaplanes equipped with Lewis guns is admittedly unusual, and may legitimately cause comment. But it was there now. The Saint had locked it onto its special mounting as soon as his machine had come to rest. The tail of the seaplane was turned towards the yacht; and, twisting round in the roomy cockpit, the Saint could comfortably swivel the gun round and keep the sights on the approaching boat.

The boat, by that time, was only twenty yards away.

"Is that you, sonny boy?" called the Saint sharply.

The answering hail came clearly over the water.

"That's me, Saint."

In the dark, the cigarette between the Saint's lips glowed with the steady redness of intense concentration. Then he took his cigarette from his mouth and sighted carefully. "In that case," he said, "you can tell your pals to heave to, Dicky Tremayne. Because, if they come much nearer, they're going to get a lead shower-bath."

The sentence ended in a stuttering burst from the gun; and five tracer bullets hissed through the night like fireflies and cut the water in a straight line directly across the boat's course. The Saint heard a barked command, and the boat lost way; but a laugh followed at once, and another voice spoke.

"Is that the Saint?"

The Saint only hesitated an instant. "Present and correct," he said, "complete with halo. What do your friends call you, honey-bunch?"

"This is John Hilloran speaking."

"Good evening, John," said the Saint politely.

The boat was close enough for him to be able to make out the figure standing up in the stern, and he drew a very thoughtful bead upon it. A Lewis gun is not the easiest weapon in the world to handle with a microscopic accuracy, but his sights had been picked out with luminous paint, and the standing figure was silhouetted clearly against the reflection in the water of one of the lights along the yacht's deck.

"I'll tell you," said Hilloran, "that I've got your friend at the end of my gun—so don't shoot any more."

"Shoot, and be damned to him!" snapped in Dicky's voice. "I don't care. But Audrey Perowne's here as well, and I'd like her to get away."

"My future wife," said Hilloran, and again his throaty chuckle drifted through the gloom.

Simon Templar took a long pull at his cigarette, and tapped some ash fastidiously into the water. "Well—what's the idea, big boy?"

"I'm coming alongside. When I'm there, you're going to step quietly down into this boat. If you resist, or try any funny business, your friend will pass in his checks."

"Is—that—so?" drawled Simon.

"That's so. I want to meet you—Mr. Saint!"

"Well, well, *well!*" mocked the Saint alertly.

And there and then he had thrust upon him one of the most desperate decisions of a career that continued to exist only by the cool swift making of desperate decisions.

Dicky Tremayne was in that boat, and Dicky Tremayne had somehow or other been stung. That had been fairly obvious ever since the flashing of that red signal. Only the actual details of the stinging had been waiting to be disclosed. Now the Saint knew. And, although the Saint would willingly have stepped into a burning fiery furnace if he thought that by so doing he could help Dicky's getaway, he couldn't see how the principle applied at that moment. Once the Saint stepped down into that boat, there would be two of them in the *consommé* instead of one—and what would have been gained?

What, more important, would Hilloran have gained? Why should J. Hilloran be so anxious to increase his collection of Saints? The Saint thoughtfully rolled his cigarette-end between his finger and thumb, and dropped it into the water.

"Why," ruminated the Saint—"because the dear soul wants this blinkin' bus what I'm sitting in. He wants to take it and fly away into the wide world. Now, again—why? Well, there was supposed to be a million dollars' worth of jools in that there hooker. It's quite certain that their original owners haven't got them any longer—it's equally apparent that Audrey Perowne hasn't got them, or Dicky wouldn't have said that he wanted her to get away—and, clearly, Dicky hasn't got them. Therefore, Hilloran's got them. And the crew will want some of them. We don't imagine Hilloran proposes to load up the whole crew on this airyplane for their getaway: therefore, he only wants to load up himself and Audrey Perowne—leaving the ancient mariners behind to whistle for their share. Ha! Joke. . . ."

And there seemed to be just one solitary way of circumventing the opposition. Now, Hilloran wasn't expecting any fight at all. He'd had several drinks, for one thing, since the hold-up, and he was very sure of himself. He'd got everyone cold—Tremayne, Audrey, the crew, the Saint, and the jewels. He didn't see how anyone could get out of it.

He wasn't shaking with the anticipation of triumph, because he wasn't that sort of crook. He simply felt rather satisfied with his own ingenuity. Not that he was preening himself. He found it as natural to win that game as he would have found it natural to win a game of stud poker from a deaf, dumb, and blind imbecile child. That was all.

Of course, he didn't know the Saint except by reputation, and mere word-of-mouth reputations never cut much ice with Hilloran. He wasn't figuring on the Saint's uncanny intuition of the psychology of the crook, nor on the Saint's power of lightning logic and lightning decision. Nor had he reckoned on that quality of reckless audacity which lifted the Saint as far above the rut of ordinary adventurers as Walter Hagen is above the man who has taken up golf to amuse himself in his old age—a quality which infected and inspired also the men whom the Saint led.

There was one desperate solution to the problem, and Hilloran ought to have seen it. But he hadn't seen it—or, if he had, he'd called it too desperate to be seriously considered. Which was where he was wrong to all eternity.

He stood up in the stern of the boat, a broad dominant figure in black relief against the shimmering waters, and called out again: "I'm coming alongside now, Saint, if you're ready."

"I'm ready," said the Saint; and the butt of the Lewis gun was cuddled into his shoulder as steadily as if it had lain on a rock.

Hilloran gave an order, and the sweeps dipped again. Hilloran remained standing. If he knew what happened next, he had no time to coordinate his impressions. For the harsh stammer of the Lewis gun must have merged and mazed his brain with the sharp tearing agony that ripped through his chest, and the numbing darkness that blinded his eyes must have been confused with the numbing weakness that sapped all the strength from his body, and he could not have heard the choking of the breath of his throat, and the cold clutch of the waters that closed over him and dragged him down could have meant nothing to him at all. . . .

But Dicky Tremayne, staring stupidly at the widening ripples that marked the spot where Hilloran had been swallowed up by the sea, heard the Saint's hail. "Stand by for the mermaids!"

And at once there was a splash such as a seal makes in plunging from a high rock, and there followed the churning sounds of a strong swimmer racing through the water.

The two men, who were the boat's crew, seemed for a moment to sit in a trance; then, with a curse, one of them bent to his oars. The other followed suit.

Dicky knew that it was his turn. He came to his feet and hurled himself forward, throwing himself anyhow across the back of the man nearest to him. The man was flung sideways and over onto his knees, so that the boat lurched perilously. Then Dicky had scrambled up again, somehow, with bruised shins, and feet that seemed to weigh a ton, and launched himself at the back of the next man in the same way.

The first man whom he had knocked over struck at him, with an oath, but Dicky didn't care. His hands were tied behind his back, but he kicked out, swung his shoulders, butted with his head—fought like a madman. His only object was to keep the men from any effective rowing until the Saint could reach them.

And then, hardly a foot from Dicky's eyes, a hand came over the gunwale, and he lay still, panting. A moment later the Saint had hauled himself over the side, almost overturning the boat as he did so. "O.K., sonny boy!" said the Saint, in that inimitably cheerful way that was like new life to those who heard it on their side, and drove his fist into the face of the nearest man.

Then the other man felt the point of a knife prick his throat. "You heard your boss telling you to row over to the seaplane," remarked the

Saint gently, "and I'm very hot on carrying out the wishes of the dead. Put your back into it!"

He held the knife in place with one hand, with the other hand he reached for the second little knife which he carried strapped to his calf. "This way, Dicky boy, and we'll have you loose in no time." It was so. And then the boat was alongside the seaplane, and Dicky had freed the girl.

The Saint helped them up, and then went down to the stern of the boat and picked up the bag which lay fallen there. He tossed it into the cockpit, and followed it himself. From that point of vantage he leaned over to address the crew of the boat.

"You've heard all you need to know," he said. "I am the Saint. Remember me in your prayers. And when you've got the yacht to a port, and you're faced with the problem of accounting for all that's happened to your passengers—remember me again. Because tomorrow morning every port in the Mediterranean will be watching for you, and on every quay there'll be detectives waiting to take you away to the place where you belong. So remember the Saint!" And Simon Templar roused the engine of the seaplane and began to taxi over the water as the first shot spat out from the yacht's deck and went whining over the sea.

A week later, Chief Inspector Teal paid another visit to Brook Street. "I'm very much obliged to you, Mr. Templar," he said. "You'll be interested to hear that *Indomitable* picked up the *Corsican Maid* as she was trying to slip through the Straits last night. They didn't put up much of a scrap."

"You don't say!" murmured the Saint mockingly. "But have some beer."

Mr. Teal sank ponderously into the chair. "Fat men," he declined, "didn't ought to drink—if you won't be offended. But listen, sir—what happened to the girl who was the leader of the gang? And what happened to the jewels?"

"You'll hear today," said the Saint happily, "that the jewels have been received by a certain London hospital. The owners will be able to get them back from there, and I leave the reward they'll contribute to the hospital to their own consciences. But I don't think public opinion will let them be stingy. As for the money that was collected in cash, some twenty-five thousand dollars. I—er—well, that's difficult to trace, isn't it?"

Mr. Teal nodded sleepily. "And Audrey Perowne, *alias* the Countess Anusia Marova?"

"Were you wanting to arrest her?"

"There's a warrant—"

The Saint shook his head sadly. "What a waste of time, energy, paper, and ink! You ought to have told me that before. As it is, I'm afraid I—er—that is, she was packed off three days ago to a country where extradition doesn't work—I'm afraid I shouldn't know how to intercept her. Isn't that a shame?"

Teal grimaced. "However," said the Saint, "I understand that she's going to reform and marry and settle down, so you needn't worry about what she'll do next."

"How do you know that?" asked Teal suspiciously.

The Saint's smile was wholly angelic. He flung out his hand.

"A little Dicky bird," he said musically, "a little Dicky bird told me so this morning."

MIGNON EBERHART
Introducing Susan Dare

SUSAN DARE watched a thin stream of blue smoke ascend without haste from the long throat of a tiger lily. Michela, then, had escaped also. She was not, however, on the long veranda, for the clear, broadening light of the rising moon revealed it wide and empty, and nothing moved against the silvered lawn which sloped gently toward the pine woods.

Susan listened a moment for the tap of Michela's heels, did not hear it or any other intrusive sound, and then pushed aside the bowl of lilies on the low window seat, let the velvet curtains fall behind her, and seated herself in the little niche thus formed. It was restful and soothing to be thus shut away from the house with its subtly warring elements and to make herself part of the silent night beyond the open windows.

A pity, thought Susan, to leave. But after tonight she could not stay. After all, a guest, any guest, ought to have sense enough to leave when a situation develops in the family of her hostess. The thin trail of smoke from the lily caught Susan's glance again and she wished Michela wouldn't amuse herself by putting cigarette ends in flowers.

A faint drift of voices came from somewhere, and Susan shrank farther into herself and into the tranquil night. It had been an unpleasant dinner, and there would be still an hour or so before she could gracefully extract herself and escape again. Nice of Christabel to give her the guest house—the small green cottage across the terrace at the other side of the house, and through the hedge and up the winding green path. Christabel Frame was a perfect hostess, and Susan had had a week of utter rest and content.

But then Randy Frame, Christabel's young brother, had returned. And immediately Joe Bromfel and his wife Michela, guests also, had arrived, and with them something that had destroyed all content. The old house of the Frames, with its gracious pillars and long windows and generous dim spaces, was exactly the same—the lazy Southern air and the misty blue hills and the quiet pine woods and the boxed paths through the flowers—none of it had actually changed. But it was, all the same, a different place.

A voice beyond the green velvet curtains called impatiently: "Michela—Michela——"

It was Randy Frame. Susan did not move, and she was sure that the sweeping velvet curtains hid even her silver toes. He was probably at the door of the library, and she could see, without looking, his red hair and lithe young body and impatient, thin face. Impatient for Michela. Idiot, oh, idiot, thought Susan. Can't you see what you are doing to Christabel?

His feet made quick sounds upon the parquet floor of the hall and were gone, and Susan herself made a sharply impatient movement. Because the Frame men had been red-haired, gallant, quick-tempered, reckless, and (added Susan to the saga) abysmally stupid and selfish, Randy had accepted the mold without question. A few words from the dinner conversation floated back into Susan's memory. They'd been talking of fox hunting—a safe enough topic, one would have thought, in the Carolina hills. But talk had veered—through Michela, was it?— to a stableman who had been shot by one of the Frames and killed. It had happened a long time ago, had been all but forgotten, and had nothing at all to do with the present generation of Frames. But Christabel said hurriedly it had been an accident; dreadful. She had looked white. And Randy had laughed and said the Frames shot first and inquired afterwards and that there was always a revolver in the top buffet drawer.

"Here she is," said a voice. The curtains were pulled suddenly backward, and Randy, a little flushed, stood there. His face fell as he discovered Susan's fair, smooth hair and thin lace gown. "Oh," he said. "I thought you were Michela."

Others were trailing in from the hall, and a polite hour or so must be faced. Queer how suddenly and inexplicably things had become tight and strained and unpleasant!

Randy had turned away and vanished without more words, and Tryon Welles, strolling across the room with Christabel, was looking at Susan and smiling affably.

"Susan Dare," he said. "Watching the moonlight, quietly planning murder." He shook his head and turned to Christabel. "I simply don't believe you, Christabel. If this young woman writes anything, which I doubt, it's gentle little poems about roses and moonlight."

Christabel smiled faintly and sat down. Mars, his black face shining, was bringing in the coffee tray. In the doorway Joe Bromfel, dark and bulky and hot-looking in his dinner coat, lingered a moment to glance along the hall and then came into the room.

"If Susan writes poems," said Christabel lightly, "it is her secret. You are quite wrong, Tryon. She writes—" Christabel's silver voice hesitated. Her slender hands were searching, hovering rather blindly over the tray, the large amethyst on one white finger full of trembling purple lights. It was a barely perceptible second before she took a fragile old cup and began to pour from the tall silver coffeepot. "She writes murders," said Christabel steadily. "Lovely, grisly ones, with sensible solutions. Sugar, Tryon? I've forgotten."

"One. But isn't that for Miss Susan?"

Tryon Welles was still smiling. He, the latest arrival, was a neat gray man with tight eyes, pink cheeks, and an affable manner. The only obvious thing about him was a rather finical regard for color, for he wore gray tweed with exactly the right shades of green—green tie, green shirt, a cautious green stripe in gray socks. He had reached the house on the heels of his telephoned message from town, saying he had to talk business with Christabel, and he had not had time to dress before dinner.

"Coffee, Joe?" asked Christabel. She was very deft with the delicate china. Very deft and very graceful, and Susan could not imagine how she knew that Christabel's hands were shaking.

Joe Bromfel stirred, turned his heavy dark face toward the hall again, saw no one, and took coffee from Christabel's lovely hand. Christabel avoided looking directly into his face, as, Susan had noticed, she frequently did.

"A sensible solution," Tryon Welles was saying thoughtfully. "Do murders have sensible solutions?"

His question hung in the air. Christabel did not reply, and Joe Bromfel did not appear to hear it. Susan said:

"They must have. After all, people don't murder just—well, just to murder."

"Just for the fun of it, you mean?" said Tryon Welles, tasting his coffee. "No, I suppose not. Well, at any rate," he went on, "it's nice to know your interest in murder is not a practical one."

He probably thought he was making light and pleasant conversation, reflected Susan. Strange that he did not know that every time he said the word "murder" it fell like a heavy stone in that silent room. She was about to wrench the conversation to another channel when Michela and Randy entered from the hall; Randy was laughing and Michela smiling.

At the sound of Randy's laugh, Joe Bromfel twisted bulkily around to watch their approach, and, except for Randy's laugh, it was entirely silent in the long book-lined room. Susan watched too. Randy was holding Michela's hand, swinging it as if to suggest a kind of frank camaraderie. Probably, thought Susan, he's been kissing her out in the darkness of the garden. Holding her very tight.

Michela's eyelids were white and heavy over unexpectedly shallow dark eyes. Her straight black hair was parted in the middle and pulled severely backward to a knot on her rather fat white neck. Her mouth was deeply crimson. She had been born, Susan knew, in rural New England, christened Michela by a romantic mother, and had striven to live up to the name ever since. Or down, thought Susan tersely, and wished she could take young Randy by his large and outstanding ears and shake him.

Michela had turned toward a chair, and her bare back presented itself to Susan, and she saw the thin red line with an angle that a man's cuff, pressing into the creamy flesh, had made. It was unmistakable. Joe Bromfel had seen it, too. He couldn't have helped seeing it. Susan looked into her coffee cup and wished fervently that Joe Bromfel hadn't seen the imprint of Randy's cuff, and then wondered why she wished it so fervently.

"Coffee, Michela?" said Christabel, and something in her voice was more, all at once, than Susan could endure. She rose and said rather breathlessly:

"Christabel darling, do you mind—I have some writing to do—"

"Of course." Christabel hesitated. "But wait—I'll go along with you to the cottage."

"Don't let us keep you, Christabel," said Michela lazily.

Christabel turned to Tryon Welles and neatly forestalled a motion on his part to accompany her and Susan.

"I won't be long, Tryon," she said definitely. "When I come back— we'll talk."

A clear little picture etched itself on Susan's mind: the long, lovely room, the mellow little areas of light under lamps here and there, one falling directly upon the chair she had just left, the pools of shadows surrounding them; Michela's yellow satin, and Randy's red head and slim black shoulders; Joe, a heavy, silent figure, watching them broodingly; Tryon Welles, neat and gray and affable, and Christabel with her gleaming red head held high on her slender neck, walking lightly and gracefully amid soft mauve chiffons. Halfway across the room she paused to accept a cigarette from Tryon and to bend to the small flare of a lighter he held for her, and the amethyst on her finger caught the flickering light of it and shone.

Then Susan and Christabel had crossed the empty flagstone veranda and turned toward the terrace.

Their slippered feet made no sound upon the velvet grass. Above the lily pool the flower fragrances were sweet and heavy on the night air.

"Did you hear the bullfrog last night?" asked Christabel. "He seems to have taken up a permanent residence in the pool. I don't know what to do about him. Randy says he'll shoot him, but I don't want that. He *is* a nuisance of course, bellowing away half the night. But after all— even bullfrogs—have a right to live."

"Christabel," said Susan, trying not to be abrupt, "I must go soon. I have—work to do——"

Christabel stopped and turned to face her. They were at the gap in the laurel hedge where a path began and wound upward to the cottage.

"Don't make excuses, Susan honey," she said gently. "Is it the Bromfels?"

A sound checked Susan's reply—an unexpectedly eerie sound that was like a wail. It rose and swelled amid the moonlit hills, and Susan gasped and Christabel said quickly, though with a catch in her voice: "It's only the dogs howling at the moon."

"They are not," Susan said, "exactly cheerful. It emphasizes——" She checked herself abruptly on the verge of saying that it emphasized their isolation.

Christabel had turned in at the path. It was darker there, and her cigarette made a tiny red glow. "If Michela drops another cigarette into a flower I'll kill her," said Christabel quietly.

"*What*——"

"I said I'd kill her," said Christabel. "I won't, of course. But she—oh, you've seen how things are, Susan. You can't have failed to see. She took Joe—years ago. Now she's taking Randy."

Susan was thankful that she couldn't see Christabel's face. She said something about infatuation and Randy's youth.

"He is twenty-one," said Christabel. "He's no younger than I was when Joe—when Joe and I were to be married. That was why Michela was here—to be a guest at the wedding and all the parties." They walked on for a few quiet steps before Christabel added: "It was the day before the wedding that they left together."

Susan said: "Has Joe changed?"

"In looks, you mean," said Christabel, understanding. "I don't know. Perhaps. He must have changed inside. But I don't want to know that."

"Can't you send them away?"

"Randy would follow."

"Tryon Welles," suggested Susan desperately. "Maybe he could help. I don't know how, though. Talk to Randy, maybe."

Christabel shook her head.

"Randy wouldn't listen. Opposition makes him stubborn. Besides, he doesn't like Tryon. He's had to borrow too much money from him."

It wasn't like Christabel to be bitter. One of the dogs howled again and was joined by others. Susan shivered.

"You are cold," said Christabel. "Run along inside, and thanks for listening. And—I think you'd better go, honey. I meant to keep you for comfort. But—"

"No, no, I'll stay—I didn't know——"

"Don't be nervous about being alone. The dogs would know it if a stranger put a foot on the place. Good-night," said Christabel firmly, and was gone.

The guest cottage was snug and warm and tranquil, but Susan was obliged finally to read herself to sleep and derived only a small and fleeting satisfaction from the fact that it was over a rival author's book that she finally grew drowsy. She didn't sleep well even then, and was glad suddenly that she'd asked for the guest cottage and was alone and safe in that tiny retreat.

Morning was misty and chill.

It was perhaps nine-thirty when Susan opened the cottage door, saw that mist lay thick and white, and went back to get her rubbers. Tryon Welles, she thought momentarily, catching a glimpse of herself in the mirror, would have nothing at all that was florid and complimentary to say this morning. And indeed, in her brown knitted suit, with her fair hair tight and smooth and her spectacles on, she looked not unlike a chill and aloof little owl.

The path was wet, and the laurel leaves shining with moisture, and the hills were looming gray shapes. The house lay white and quiet, and she saw no one about.

It was just then that it came. A heavy concussion of sound, blanketed by mist.

Susan's first thought was that Randy had shot the bullfrog.

But the pool was just below her, and no one was there.

Besides, the sound came from the house. Her feet were heavy and slow in the drenched grass—the steps were slippery and the flagstones wet. Then she was inside.

The wide hall ran straight through the house, and away down at its end Susan saw Mars. He was running away from her, his black hands outflung, and she was vaguely conscious that he was shouting something. He vanished, and instinct drew Susan to the door at the left which led to the library.

She stopped, frozen, in the doorway.

Across the room, sagging bulkily over the arm of the green damask chair in which she'd sat the previous night, was a man. It was Joe Bromfel, and he'd been shot, and there was no doubt that he was dead.

A newspaper lay at his feet as if it had slipped there. The velvet curtains were pulled together across the window behind him.

Susan smoothed back her hair. She couldn't think at all, and she must have slipped down to the footstool near the door for she was there when Mars, his face drawn, and Randy, white as his pajamas, came running into the room. They were talking excitedly and were examining a revolver which Randy had picked up from the floor. Then Tryon Welles came from somewhere, stopped beside her, uttered an incredulous exclamation, and ran across the room too. Then Christabel came and stopped, too, on the threshold, and became under Susan's very eyes a different woman—a strange woman, shrunken and gray, who said in a dreadful voice:

"*Joe—Joe——*"

Only Susan heard or saw her. It was Michela, hurrying from the hall, who first voiced the question.

"I heard something—what was it? What——" She brushed past Christabel.

"Don't look, Michela!"

But Michela looked—steadily and long. Then her flat dark eyes went all around the room and she said: "Who shot him?"

For a moment there was utter shocked stillness.

Then Mars cleared his throat and spoke to Randy.

"I don' know who shot him, Mista Randy. But I saw him killed. An' I saw the han' that killed him——"

"*Hand!*" screamed Michela.

"Hush, Michela." Tryon Welles was speaking. "What do you mean, Mars?"

"They ain't nothin' to tell except that, Mista Tryon. I was just comin' to dust the library and was right there at the door when I heard the shot, and there was just a han' stickin' out of them velvet curtains. And I saw the han' and I saw the revolver and I—I do' know what I did then." Mars wiped his forehead. "I guess I ran for help, Mista Tryon."

There was another silence.

"Whose hand was it, Mars?" said Tryon Welles gently.

Mars blinked and looked very old.

"Mista Tryon, God's truth is, I do' know. I do' know."

Randy thrust himself forward.

"Was it a man's hand?"

"I reckon it was maybe," said the old Negro slowly, looking at the floor. "But I do' know for sure, Mista Randy. All I saw was—was the red ring on it."

"A red *ring?*" cried Michela. "What do you mean——"

Mars turned a bleak dark face toward Michela; a face that rejected her and all she had done to his house. "A red ring, Miz Bromfel," he said with a kind of dignity. "It sort of flashed. And it was red."

After a moment Randy uttered a curious laugh.

"But there's not a red ring in the house. None of us runs to rubies—" He stopped abruptly. "I say, Tryon, hadn't we better—well, carry him to the divan. It isn't decent to—just leave him—like that."

"I suppose so—" Tryon Welles moved toward the body. "Help me, Randy——"

The boy shivered, and Susan quite suddenly found her voice.

"Oh, but you can't do that. You can't——" She stopped. The two men were looking at her in astonishment. Michela, too, had turned toward her, although Christabel did not move. "But you can't do that," repeated Susan. "Not when it's—murder."

This time the word, falling into the long room, was weighted with its own significance. Tryon Welles's gray shoulders moved.

"She's perfectly right," he said. "I'd forgotten—if I ever knew. But that's the way of it. We'll have to send for people—doctor, sheriff, coroner, I suppose."

Afterward, Susan realized that but for Tryon Welles the confusion would have become mad. He took a quiet command of the situation, sending Randy, white and sick-looking, to dress, telephoning into town, seeing that the body was decently covered, and even telling Mars to bring them hot coffee. He was here, there, everywhere: upstairs, downstairs, seeing to them all, and finally outside to meet the sheriff . . . brisk, alert, efficient. In the interval Susan sat numbly beside

Christabel on the love seat in the hall, with Michela restlessly prowling up and down the hall before their eyes, listening to the telephone calls, drinking hot coffee, watching everything with her sullen, flat black eyes. Her red-and-white sports suit, with its scarlet bracelets and earrings, looked garish and out of place in that house of violent death.

And Christabel. Still a frozen image of a woman who drank coffee automatically, she sat erect and still and did not speak. The glowing amethyst on her finger caught the light and was the only living thing about her.

Gradually the sense of numb shock and confusion was leaving Susan. Fright was still there and horror and a queer aching pity, but she saw Randy come running down the wide stairway again, his red hair smooth now above a sweater, and she realized clearly that he was no longer white and sick and frightened; he was instead alert and defiantly ready for what might come. And it would be, thought Susan, in all probability, plenty.

And it was.

Questions—questions. The doctor, who was kind, the coroner, who was not; the sheriff, who was merely observant—all of them questioning without end. No time to think. No time to comprehend. Time only to reply as best one might.

But gradually out of it all certain salient facts began to emerge. They were few, however, and brief.

The revolver was Randy's, and it had been taken from the top buffet drawer—when no one knew or, at least, would tell. "Everybody knew it was there," said Randy sulkily. The fingerprints on it would probably prove to be Randy's and Mars's, since they picked it up.

No one knew anything of the murder, and no one had an alibi, except Liz (the Negro second girl) and Minnie (the cook), who were together in the kitchen.

Christabel had been writing letters in her own room: she'd heard the shot, but thought it was only Randy shooting a bullfrog in the pool. But then she'd heard Randy and Mars running down the front stairway, so she'd come down too. Just to be sure that that was what it was.

"What else did you think it could be?" asked the sheriff. But Christabel said stiffly that she didn't know.

Randy had been asleep when Mars had awakened him. He had not heard the sound of the shot at all. He and Mars had hurried down to the library. (Mars, it developed, had gone upstairs by means of the small back stairway off the kitchen.)

Tryon Welles had walked down the hill in front of the house to the mail box and was returning when he heard the shot. But it was muffled, and he did not know what had happened until he reached the library. He created a mild sensation at that point by taking off a ring, holding it so they could all see it, and demanding of Mars if that was the ring he had seen on the murderer's hand. However, the sensation was only momentary, for the large clear stone was as green as his neat green tie.

"No, suh, Mista Tryon," said Mars. "The ring on the han' I saw was red. I could see it plain, an' it was red."

"This," said Tryon Welles, "is a flawed emerald. I asked because I seem to be about the only person here wearing a ring. But I suppose that, in justice to us, all our belongings should be searched."

Upon which the sheriff's gaze slid to the purple pool on Christabel's white hand. He said, however, gently, that that was being done, and would Mrs. Michela Bromfel tell what she knew of the murder.

But Mrs. Michela Bromfel somewhat spiritedly knew nothing of it. She'd been walking in the pine woods, she said defiantly, glancing obliquely at Randy, who suddenly flushed all over his thin face. She'd heard the shot but hadn't realized it was a gunshot. However, she was curious and came back to the house.

"The window behind the body opens toward the pine woods," said the sheriff. "Did you see anyone, Mrs. Bromfel?"

"No one at all," said Michela definitely.

Well, then, had she heard the dogs barking? The sheriff seemed to know that the kennels were just back of the pine woods.

But Michela had not heard the dogs.

Someone stirred restively at that, and the sheriff coughed and said unnecessarily that there was no tramp about, then, and the questioning continued. Continued wearily on and on and on, and still no one knew how Joe Bromfel had met his death. And as the sheriff was at last dismissing them and talking to the coroner of an inquest, one of his men came to report on the search. No one was in the house who didn't belong there; they could tell nothing of footprints; the French windows back of the body had been ajar, and there was no red ring anywhere in the house.

"Not, that is, that we can find," said the man.

"All right," said the sheriff. "That'll be all now, folks. But I'd take it kindly if you was to stay around here today."

All her life Susan was to remember that still, long day with a kind of sharp reality. It was, after those first moments when she'd felt so ill and shocked, weirdly natural, as if, one event having occurred, another was bound to follow, and then upon that one's heels another, and all of them quite in the logical order of things. Even the incident of the afternoon, so trivial in itself but later so significant, was as natural, as unsurprising as anything could be. And that was her meeting with Jim Byrne.

It happened at the end of the afternoon, long and painful, which Susan spent with Christabel, knowing somehow that, under her frozen surface, Christabel was grateful for Susan's presence. But there were nameless things in the air between them which could be neither spoken of nor ignored, and Susan was relieved when Christabel at last took a sedative and, eventually, fell into a sleep that was no more still than Christabel waking had been.

There was no one to be seen when Susan tiptoed out of Christabel's room and down the stairway, although she heard voices from the closed door of the library.

Out the wide door at last and walking along the terrace above the lily pool, Susan took a long breath of the mist-laden air.

So this was murder. This was murder, and it happened to people one knew, and it did indescribable and horrible things to them. Frightened them first, perhaps. Fear of murder itself came first—simple, primitive fear of the unleashing of the beast. And then on its heels came more civilized fear, and that was fear of the law, and a scramble for safety.

She turned at the hedge and glanced backward. The house lay white and stately amid its gardens as it had lain for generations. But it was no longer tranquil—it was charged now with violence. With murder. And it remained dignified and stately and would cling, as Christabel would cling and had clung all those years, to its protective ritual.

Christabel: Had she killed him? Was that why she was so stricken and gray? Or was it because she knew that Randy had killed him? Or was it something else?

Susan did not see the man till she was almost upon him, and then she cried out involuntarily, though she as a rule was not at all nervous. He was sitting on the small porch of the cottage, hunched up with his hat over his eyes and his coat collar turned up, furiously scribbling on a pad of paper. He jumped up as he heard her breathless little cry and whirled to face her and took off his hat all in one motion.

"May I use your typewriter?" he said.

His eyes were extremely clear and blue and lively. His face was agreeably irregular in feature, with a mouth that laughed a great deal, a chin that took insolence from no man, and generous width of forehead. His hair was thinning but not yet showing gray and his hands were unexpectedly fine and beautiful. "Hard on the surface," thought Susan. "Terribly sensitive, really. Irish. What's he doing here?"

Aloud she said: "Yes."

"Good. Can't write fast enough and want to get this story off tonight. I've been waiting for you, you know. They told me you wrote things. My name's Byrne. James Byrne. I'm a reporter. Cover special stories. I'm taking a busman's holiday. I'm actually on a Chicago paper and down here for a vacation. I didn't expect a murder story to break."

Susan opened the door upon the small living room.

"The typewriter's there. Do you need paper? There's a stack beside it."

He fell upon the typewriter absorbedly, like a dog upon a bone. She watched him for a while, amazed at his speed and fluency and utter lack of hesitancy.

Presently she lighted the fire already laid in the tiny fireplace and sat there quietly, letting herself be soothed by the glow of the flames and the steady rhythm of the typewriter keys. And for the first time that day its experiences, noted and stored away in whatever place observations are stored, began to arouse and assort and arrange themselves and march in some sort of order through her conscious thoughts. But it was a dark and macabre procession, and it frightened Susan. She was relieved when Jim Byrne spoke.

"I say," he said suddenly, over the clicking keys, "I've got your name Louise Dare. Is that right?"

"Susan."

He looked at her. The clicking stopped.

"Susan. Susan Dare," he repeated thoughtfully. "I say, you can't be the Susan Dare that writes murder stories!"

"Yes," said Susan guardedly, "I can be that Susan Dare."

There was an expression of definite incredulity in his face. "But you——"

"If you say," observed Susan tensely, "that I don't look as if I wrote murder stories, you can't use my typewriter for your story."

"I suppose you are all tangled up in this mess," he said speculatively.

"Yes," said Susan, sober again. "And no," she added, looking at the fire.

"Don't commit yourself," said Jim Byrne dryly. "Don't say anything reckless."

"But I mean just that," said Susan. "I'm a guest here. A friend of Christabel Frame's. I didn't murder Joe Bromfel. And I don't care at all about the rest of the people here except that I wish I'd never seen them."

"But you do," said the reporter gently, "care a lot about Christabel Frame?"

"Yes," said Susan gravely.

"I've got all the dope, you know," said the reporter softly. "It wasn't hard to get. Everybody around here knows about the Frames. The thing I can't understand is why she shot Joe. It ought to have been Michela."

"*What——*" Susan's fingers were digging into the wicker arms of her chair, and her eyes strove frantically to plumb the clear blue eyes above the typewriter.

"I say, it ought to have been Michela. She's the girl who's making the trouble."

"But it wasn't—it couldn't—Christabel wouldn't——"

"Oh, yes, she could," said the reporter rather wearily. "All sorts of people could do the strangest things. Christabel could murder. But I can't see why she'd murder Joe and let Michela go scot-free."

"Michela," said Susan in a low voice, "would have a motive."

"Yes, she's got a motive. Get rid of a husband. But so had Randy Frame. Same one. And he's what the people around here call a Red Frame—impulsive, reckless, bred to a tradition of—violence."

"But Randy was asleep—upstairs——"

He interrupted her.

"Oh, yes, I know all that. And you were approaching the house from the terrace, and Tryon Welles had gone down after the mail, and Miss Christabel was writing letters upstairs, and Michela was walking in the pine woods. Not a damn alibi among you. The way the house and grounds are laid out, neither you nor Tryon Welles nor Michela would be visible to each other. And anyone could have escaped readily from the window and turned up innocently a moment later from the hall. I know all that. Who was behind the curtains?"

"A tramp—" attempted Susan in a small voice. "A burglar——"

"Burglar nothing," said Jim Byrne with scorn. "The dogs would have had hysterics. It was one of you. *Who?*"

"I don't know," said Susan. "*I don't know!*" Her voice was uneven, and she knew it and tried to steady it and clutched the chair arms tighter. Jim Byrne knew it, too, and was suddenly alarmed.

"Oh, look here, now," he cried. "Don't look like that. Don't cry. Don't——"

"I am not crying," said Susan. "But it wasn't Christabel."

"You mean," said the reporter kindly, "that you don't want it to be

Christabel. Well——" He glanced at his watch, said, "Golly," and flung his papers together and rose. "There's something I'll do. Not for you exactly—just for—oh, because. I'll let part of my story wait until tomorrow if you want the chance to try to prove your Christabel didn't murder him."

Susan was frowning perplexedly.

"You don't understand me," said the reporter cheerfully. "It's this. You write murder mysteries, and I've read one or two of them. They are not bad," he interpolated hastily, watching Susan. "Now, here's your chance to try a real murder mystery."

"*But I don't want*——" began Susan.

He checked her imperatively.

"You do want to," he said. "In fact, you've got to. You see—your Christabel is in a spot. You know that ring she wears——"

"When did you see it?"

"Oh, does it matter?" he cried impatiently. "Reporters see everything. The point is the ring."

"But it's an amethyst," said Susan defensively.

"Yes," he agreed grimly. "It's an amethyst. And Mars saw a red stone. He saw it, it has developed, on the right hand. And the hand holding the revolver. And Christabel wears her ring on her right hand."

"But," repeated Susan, "it *is* an amethyst."

"M-m," said the reporter. "It's an amethyst. And a little while ago I said to Mars: 'What's the name of that flowering vine over there?' And he said: 'That red flower, suh? That's wisteria.'"

He paused. Susan felt exactly as if something had clutched her heart and squeezed it.

"The flowers were purple, of course," said the reporter softly. "The color of a dark amethyst."

"But he would have recognized Christabel's ring," said Susan after a moment.

"Maybe," said the reporter. "And maybe he wishes he'd never said a word about the red ring. He was scared when he first mentioned it, probably; hadn't had a chance to think it over."

"But Mars—Mars would confess to murdering rather than——"

"No," said Jim Byrne soberly. "He wouldn't. That theory sounds all right. But it doesn't happen that way. People don't murder or confess to having murdered for somebody else. When it is a deliberate, planned murder and not a crazy drunken brawl, when anything can happen, there's a motive. And it's a strong and urgent and deeply personal and selfish motive and don't you forget it. I've got to hurry. Now then, shall I send in my story about the wisteria——"

"Don't," said Susan choking. "Oh, don't. Not yet."

He picked up his hat. "Thanks for the typewriter. Get your wits together and go to work. After all, you ought to know something of murders. I'll be seeing you."

The door closed, and the flames crackled. After a long time Susan moved to the writing table and drew a sheet of yellow manuscript paper toward her, and a pencil, and wrote: Characters; possible motives; clues; queries.

It was strange, she thought, not how different real life was to its written imitation, but how like. How terribly like!

She was still bent over the yellow paper when a peremptory knock at the door sent her pencil jabbing furiously on the paper and her heart into her throat. It proved to be, however, only Michela Bromfel, and she wanted help.

"It's my knees," said Michela irritably. "Christabel's asleep or something, and the three servants are all scared of their shadows." She paused to dig savagely at first one knee and then the other. "Have you got anything to put on my legs? I'm nearly going crazy. It's not mosquito bites. I don't know what it is. Look!"

She sat down, pulled back her white skirt and rolled down her thin stockings, disclosing just above each knee a scarlet blotchy rim around her fat white legs.

Susan looked and had to resist a wild desire to giggle. "It's n-nothing," she said, quivering. "That is, it's only jiggers—here, I'll get you something. Alcohol."

"Jiggers," said Michela blankly. "What's that?"

Susan went into the bathroom. "Little bugs," she called. Where was the alcohol? "They are thick in the pine woods. It'll be all right by morning." Here it was. She took the bottle in her hand and turned again through the bedroom into the tiny living room.

At the door she stopped abruptly. Michela was standing at the writing table. She looked up, saw Susan, and her flat dark eyes flickered.

"Oh," said Michela. "Writing a story?"

"No," said Susan. "It's not a story. Here's the alcohol."

Under Susan's straight look Michela had the grace to depart rather hastily, yanking up her stockings and twisting them hurriedly, and clutching at the bottle of alcohol. Her red bracelets clanked, and her scarlet fingernails looked as if they'd been dipped in blood. Of the few people who might have killed Joe Bromfel, Susan reflected coolly, she would prefer it to be Michela.

It was just then that a curious vagrant memory began to tease Susan. Rather it was not so much a memory as a memory *of* a memory—something that sometime she had known and now could not remember. It was tantalizing. It was maddeningly elusive. It floated teasingly on the very edge of her consciousness.

Deliberately, at last, Susan pushed it away and went back to work. Christabel and the amethyst. Christabel and the wisteria. Christabel.

It was dark and still drizzly when Susan took her way down toward the big house.

At the laurel hedge she met Tryon Welles.

"Oh, hello," he said. "Where've you been?"

"At the cottage," said Susan. "There was nothing I could do. How's Christabel?"

"Liz says she is still asleep—thank heaven for that. God, what a day! You oughtn't to be prowling around alone at this time of night. I'll walk to the house with you."

"Have the sheriff and other men gone?"

"For the time being. They'll be back, I suppose."

"Do they know any more about—who killed him?"

"I don't know. You can't tell much. I don't know of any evidence they have unearthed. They asked me to stay on." He took a quick puff or two of his cigarette and then said irritably: "It puts me in a bad place. It's a business deal where time matters. I'm a broker—I ought to be going back to New York tonight——" He broke off abruptly and said: "Oh, Randy—" as young Randy's pale, thin face above a shining mackintosh emerged from the dusk—"let's just escort Miss Susan to the steps."

"Is she afraid of the famous tramp?" asked Randy and laughed unpleasantly. He'd been drinking, thought Susan, with a flicker of anxiety. Sober, Randy was incalculable enough; drinking, he might be dangerous. Could she do anything with him? No, better leave it to Tryon Welles. "The tramp," Randy was repeating loudly. "Don't be afraid of a tramp. It wasn't any tramp killed Joe. And everybody knows it. You're safe enough, Susan, unless you've got some evidence. Have you got any evidence, Susan?"

He took her elbow and joggled it urgently.

"She's the quiet kind, Tryon, that sees everything and says nothing. Bet she's got evidence enough to hang us all. Evidence. That's what we need. Evidence."

"Randy, you're drunk," said Susan crisply. She shook off his clutch upon her arm and then, looking at his thin face, which was so white and tight-drawn in the dusk, was suddenly sorry for him. "Go on and take your walk," she said more kindly. "Things will be all right."

"Things will never be the same again," said Randy. "Never the same—do you know why, Susan?" He's very drunk, thought Susan; worse than I thought. "It's because Michela shot him. Yes, sir."

"Randy, shut up!"

"Don't bother me, Tryon, I know what I'm saying. And Michela," asserted Randy with simplicity, "makes me sick."

"Come on, Randy." This time Tryon Welles took Randy's arm. "I'll take care of him, Miss Susan."

The house was deserted and seemed cold. Christabel was still asleep, Michela nowhere to be seen, and Susan finally told Mars to send her dinner on a tray to the cottage and returned quietly like a small brown wraith through the moist twilight.

But she was an oddly frightened wraith.

She was alone on the silent terrace, she was alone on the dark path—strange that she felt as if someone else were there, too. Was the bare fact of murder like a presence hovering, beating dark wings, waiting to sweep downward again?

"Nonsense," said Susan aloud. "Nonsense——" and ran the rest of the way.

She was not, however, to be alone in the cottage, for Michela sat there, composedly awaiting her.

"Do you mind," said Michela, "if I spend the night here? There's two beds in there. You see—" she hesitated, her flat dark eyes were furtive —"I'm—afraid."

"Of what?" said Susan, after a moment. "Of whom?"

"I don't know who," said Michela, "or what."

After a long, singularly still moment Susan forced herself to say evenly:

"Stay if you are nervous. It's safe here." Was it? Susan continued hurriedly: "Mars will send up dinner."

Michela's thick white hand made an impatient movement.

"Call it nerves—although I've not a nerve in my body. But when Mars comes with dinner—just be sure it *is* Mars before you open the door, will you? Although as to that—*I* don't know. But I brought my revolver—loaded." She reached into her pocket, and Susan sat upright, abruptly. Susan, whose knowledge of revolvers had such a wide and peculiar range that any policeman, learning of it, would arrest her on suspicion alone, was nevertheless somewhat uneasy in their immediate vicinity.

"Afraid?" said Michela.

"Not at all," said Susan. "But I don't think a revolver will be necessary."

"I hope not, I'm sure," said Michela somberly and stared at the fire.

After that, as Susan later reflected, there was not much to be said. The only interruption during the whole queer evening was the arrival of Mars and dinner.

Later in the evening Michela spoke again, abruptly. "I didn't kill Joe," she said. And after another long silence she said unexpectedly: "Did Christabel ask you how to kill him and get by with it?"

"*No!*"

"Oh." Michela looked at her queerly. "I thought maybe she'd got you to plan it for her. You—knowing so much about murders and all."

"She didn't," said Susan forcefully. "And I don't plan murders for my friends, I assure you. I'm going to bed."

Michela, following her, put the revolver on the small table between the two beds.

If the night before had been heavy with apprehension, this night was an active nightmare. Susan tossed and turned and was uneasily conscious that Michela was awake and restless, too.

Susan must have slept at last, though, for she waked up with a start and sat upright, instantly aware of some movement in the room. Then she saw a figure dimly outlined against the window. It was Michela.

Susan joined her. "What are you doing?"

"Hush," whispered Michela. Her face was pressed against the glass. Susan looked, too, but could see only blackness.

"There's someone out there," whispered Michela. "And if he moves again I'm going to shoot."

Susan was suddenly aware that the ice-cold thing against her arm was the revolver.

"You are not," said Susan and wrenched the thing out of Michela's hand. Michela gasped and whirled, and Susan said grimly: "Go back to bed. Nobody's out there."

"How do you know?" said Michela, her voice sulky.

"I don't," said Susan, very much astonished at herself, but clutching the revolver firmly. "But I do know that you aren't going to start shooting. If there's any shooting to be done," said Susan with aplomb, "I'll do it myself. Go to bed."

But long after Michela was quiet Susan still sat bolt upright, clutching the revolver and listening.

Along toward dawn, out of the *mêlée* of confused, unhappy thoughts, the vagrant little recollection of a recollection came back to tantalize her. Something she'd known and now did not know. This time she returned as completely as she could over the track her thoughts had taken in the hope of capturing it by association. She'd been thinking of the murder and of the possible suspects; that if Michela had not murdered Joe, then there were left Randy and Christabel and Tryon Welles. And she didn't want it to be Christabel; it must not be Christabel. And that left Randy and Tryon Welles. Randy had a motive, but Tryon Welles had not. Tryon Welles wore a ring habitually, and Randy did not. But the ring was an emerald. And Christabel's ring was what Mars called red. Red—then what would he have called Michela's scarlet bracelet? Pink? But that was a bracelet. She wrenched herself back to dig at the troublesome phantom of a memory. It was something trivial —but something she could not project into her conscious memory. And it was something that somehow she needed. Needed now.

She awoke and was horrified to discover her cheek pillowed cosily upon the revolver. She thrust it away. And realized with a sinking of her heart that day had come and, with it, urgent problems. Christabel, first.

Michela was still silent and sulky. Crossing the terrace, Susan looked at the wisteria winding upward over its trellis. It was heavy with purple blossoms—purple like dark amethysts.

Christabel was in her own room, holding a breakfast tray on her lap and looking out the window with a blank, unseeing gaze. She was years older; shrunken somehow inside. She was pathetically willing to answer the few questions that Susan asked, but added nothing to Susan's small store of knowledge. She left her finally, feeling that Christabel wanted only solitude. But she went away reluctantly. It would not be long before Jim Byrne returned, and she had nothing to tell him—nothing, that is, except surmise.

Randy was not at breakfast, and it was a dark and uncomfortable meal. Dark because Tryon Welles said something about a headache and turned out the electric light, and uncomfortable because it could not be otherwise. Michela had changed to a thin suit—red again. The teasing ghost of a memory drifted over Susan's mind and away again before she could grasp it.

As the meal ended Susan was called to the telephone. It was Jim Byrne saying that he would be there in an hour.

On the terrace Tryon Welles overtook her again and said: "How's Christabel?"

"I don't know," said Susan slowly. "She looks—stunned."

"I wish I could make it easier for her," he said. "But—I'm caught, too. There's nothing I can do, really. I mean about the house, of course. Didn't she tell you?"

"No."

He looked at her, considered, and went on slowly.

"She wouldn't mind your knowing. You see—oh, it's tragically simple. But I can't help myself. It's like this: Randy borrowed money of me—kept on borrowing it, spent it like water. Without Christabel knowing it, he put up the house and grounds as collateral. She knows now, of course. Now I'm in a pinch in business and have got to take the house over legally in order to borrow enough money on it myself to keep things going for a few months. Do you see?"

Susan nodded. Was it this knowledge, then, that had so stricken Christabel?

"I hate it," said Tryon Welles. "But what can I do? And now Joe's— death—on top of it—" He paused, reached absently for a cigarette case, extracted a cigarette, and the small flame from his lighter flared suddenly clear and bright. "It's—hell," he said, puffing, "for her. But what can I do? I've got my own business to save."

"I see," said Susan slowly.

And quite suddenly, looking at the lighter, she did see. It was as simple, as miraculously simple as that. She said, her voice to her own ears marvelously unshaken and calm: "May I have a cigarette?"

He was embarrassed at not having offered it to her: he fumbled for his cigarette case and then held the flame of the lighter for her. Susan was very deliberate about getting her cigarette lighted. Finally she did so, said, "Thank you," and added, quite as if she had the whole thing planned: "Will you wake Randy, Mr. Welles, and send him to me? Now?"

"Why, of course," he said. "You'll be in the cottage?"

"Yes," said Susan and fled.

She was bent over the yellow paper when Jim Byrne arrived.

He was fresh and alert and, Susan could see, prepared to be kind. He expected her, then, to fail.

"Well," he said gently, "have you discovered the murderer?"

"Yes," said Susan Dare.

Jim Byrne sat down quite suddenly.

"I know who killed him," she said simply, "but I don't know why."

Jim Byrne reached into his pocket for a handkerchief and dabbed it lightly to his forehead. "Suppose," he suggested in a hushed way, "you tell all."

"Randy will be here in a moment," said Susan. "But it's all very simple. You see, the final clue was only the proof. I knew Christabel couldn't have killed him, for two reasons: one is, she's inherently incapable of killing anything; the other is—she loved him still. And I knew it wasn't Michela, because she is, actually, cowardly; and then, too, Michela had an alibi."

"Alibi?"

"She really *was* in the pine woods for a long time that morning. Waiting, I think, for Randy, who slept late. I know she was there, because she was simply chewed by jiggers, and they are only in the pine woods."

"Maybe she was there the day before."

Susan shook her head decidedly.

"No, I know jiggers. If it had been during the previous day they'd have stopped itching by the time she came to me. And it wasn't during the afternoon, for no one went in the pine woods then except the sheriff's men."

"That would leave, then, Randy and Tryon Welles."

"Yes," said Susan. Now that it had come to doing it, she felt ill and weak; would it be her evidence, her words, that would send a fellow creature over that long and ignominious road that ends so tragically?

Jim Byrne knew what she was thinking.

"Remember Christabel," he said quietly.

"Oh, I know," said Susan sadly. She locked her fingers together, and there were quick footsteps on the porch.

"You want me, Susan?" said Randy.

"Yes, Randy," said Susan. "I want you to tell me if you owed Joe Bromfel anything. Money—or—or anything."

"How did you know?" said Randy.

"Did you give him a note—anything?"

"Yes."

"What was your collateral?"

"The house—it's all mine——"

"When was it dated? Answer me, Randy."

He flung up his head.

"I suppose you've been talking to Tryon," he said defiantly. "Well, it was dated before Tryon got his note. I couldn't help it. I'd got some stocks on margin. I had to have——"

"So the house actually belonged to Joe Bromfel?" Susan was curiously cold. Christabel's house. Christabel's brother.

"Well, yes—if you want to put it like that."

Jim Byrne had risen quietly.

"And after Joe Bromfel, to Michela, if she knows of this and claims it?" pressed Susan.

"I don't know," said Randy. "I never thought of that."

Jim Byrne started to speak, but Susan silenced him.

"No, he really didn't think of it," she said wearily. "And I knew it wasn't Randy who killed him because he didn't, really, care enough for Michela to do that. It was—Tryon Welles who killed Joe Bromfel. He had to. For he had to silence Joe and then secure the note and, probably, destroy it, in order to have a clear title to the house, himself. Randy— did Joe have the note here with him?"

"Yes."

"It was not found upon his body?"

It was Jim Byrne who answered: "Nothing of the kind was found anywhere."

"Then," said Susan, "after the murder was discovered and before the sheriff arrived and the search began, only you and Tryon Welles were upstairs and had the opportunity to search Joe's room and find the note and destroy it. Was it you who did that, Randy?"

"*No—no!*" The color rose in his face.

"Then it must have been then that Tryon Welles found and destroyed it." She frowned. "Somehow, he must have known it was there. I don't know how—perhaps he had had words with Joe about it before he shot him and Joe inadvertently told him where it was. There was no time for him to search the body. But he knew——"

"Maybe," said Randy reluctantly, "I told him. You see—I knew Joe had it in his letter case. He—he told me. But I never thought of taking it."

"It was not on record?" asked Jim Byrne.

"No," said Randy, flushing. "I—asked him to keep it quiet."

"I wonder," said Susan, looking away from Randy's miserable young face, "just how Tryon Welles expected to silence you."

"Well," said Randy dully, after a moment, "it was not exactly to my credit. But you needn't rub it in. I never thought of this—I was thinking of—Michela. That she did it. I've had my lesson. And if he destroyed the note, how are you going to prove all this?"

"By your testimony," said Susan. "And besides—there's the ring."

"Ring," said Randy. Jim Byrne leaned forward intently.

"Yes," said Susan. "I'd forgotten. But I remembered that Joe had been reading the newspaper when he was killed. The curtains were pulled together back of him, so, in order to see the paper, he must have had the light turned on above his chair. It wasn't burning when I entered the library, or I should have noted it. So the murderer had pulled the cord of the lamp before he escaped. And ever since then he has been very careful to avoid any artificial light."

"What are you talking about?" cried Randy.

"Yet he had to keep on wearing the ring," said Susan. "Fortunately for him he didn't have it on the first night—I suppose the color at night would have been wrong with his green tie. But this morning he lit a cigarette and I saw."

"Saw what, in God's name," said Randy burstingly.

"That the stone isn't an emerald at all," replied Susan. "It's an Alexandrite. It changed color under the flare of the lighter."

"Alexandrite!" cried Randy impatiently. "What's that?"

"It's a stone that's a kind of red-purple under artificial light and green in daylight," said Jim Byrne shortly. "I had forgotten there was such a thing—I don't think I've ever happened to see one. They are rare—and costly. Costly," repeated Jim Byrne slowly. "This one has cost a life——"

Randy interrupted: "But if Michela knows about the note, why, Tryon may kill her——" He stopped abruptly, thought for a second or two, then got out a cigarette. "Let him," he said airily.

It had been Tryon Welles, then, prowling about during the night—if it had been anyone. He had been uncertain, perhaps, of the extent of Michela's knowledge—but certain of his ability to deal with her and with Randy, who was so heavily in his debt.

"Michela doesn't know now," said Susan slowly. "And when you tell her, Randy—she might settle for a cash consideration. And, Randy Frame, somehow you've got to recover this house for Christabel and do it honestly."

"But right now," said Jim Bryne cheerily, "for the sheriff. And my story."

At the doorway he paused to look at Susan. "May I come back later," he said, "and use your typewriter?"

"Yes," said Susan Dare.

CORNELL WOOLRICH
Nightmare

FIRST, ALL I could see was this beautiful face, this beautiful girl's face; like a white, slightly luminous mask, swimming detachedly against enfolding darkness. As if a little private spotlight of its own was trained on it from below. It was so beautiful and so false, and I seemed to know it so well, and my heart was wrung.

There was no danger yet, just this separate, shell-like face mask standing out. But there was danger somewhere around, I knew that already; and I knew that I couldn't escape it. I knew that everything I was about to do, I had to do, I couldn't avoid doing. And yet, oh, I didn't want to do it. I wanted to turn and flee, I wanted to get out of wherever this was.

I even turned and tried to, but I couldn't any more. There had been only one door when I slipped in just now. It had been simple enough. Now when I turned, the place was nothing but doors; an octagon of doors, set frame to frame with no free wall-space in between. I tried one, another, a third; they were the wrong ones, I couldn't get out.

And by doing this, I had unleashed the latent menace that was lurking there around me all the time; I had brought on all the sooner the very thing I had tried to escape from. Though I didn't know what it was yet.

The flickering white mask lost its cameolike placidity; slowly, before my horrified eyes, became malign, vindictive. It spoke, it snarled: "There he is right behind you, get him!" The eyes snapped like fuses, the teeth glistened in a grinning bite.

The light became more diffused, as if a stage-electrician were controlling the scene by a trick switch. It was a murky, bluish green now, the kind of light there would be under water. And in it danger, my doom, slowly reared its head, with typical under-water movements, too; sluggish and held back, with a terrible inevitability about them.

It was male, of course; menace is always male.

First it—he—was just a black huddle, an inchoate lumpy mass, say like solidified smoke, at the feet of this opalescent, revengeful mask. Then it slowly uncoiled, rose, lengthened and at the same time narrowed, until it loomed there before me upright. It was still anonymous, a hulk, an outline against the dark blue background, as though the light that had played up the mask until now, were coming from somewhere on the other side of it.

It came toward me, toward me, toward me, with cataleptic slowness. I wanted to get out, I wanted to turn and run, in the minute, the half-minute that was all there was left now. I couldn't move, I couldn't lift a foot, it was as though I was set into a concrete block. I just wavered back and forth, on a rigid base.

Why I wanted to get out, what It was going to do to me, wasn't clear, I didn't know. Only that there was soul-shriveling fear in it. And horror, more than the mind could contemplate.

The pace was beginning to accelerate now as it neared its climax, the way they always do.

He came on, using up the small remaining distance between us. His outline was still indistinct, clotted, like something daubed with mud, like a lumpy clay image. I could see the arms come up from the sides, and couldn't avoid their lobsterlike conjunction. I could feel the pressure of his hands upon my neck. He held it at the sides rather than in front, as if trying to break it rather than strangle me. The gouge of his thumbs, in particular was excruciating, digging into the straining cords right under the ears, pressing into the tender slack of flesh right beside and under the jawbone.

I went down in a sort of spiral, around and around, following my head and neck around as he sought to wrench them out of true with my spinal column. I had to keep it from snapping.

I clawed at the merciless hands, trying to pull them off. I pried one off at last, but it wrenched itself free of my restraint again, trailing a nail scratch on my forearm just across the knob of the wristbone. Fire was in the slight laceration, even in the midst of the total extinction threatening me. The hand clamped itself back where it had been, with the irresistibility of a suction-cup.

I beat at his arched body from underneath, then as my resistance weakened, only pushed at it, at last only grasped at it with the instinctive clutch of a drowning man. A button came off loose in my hand and I hung onto it with the senseless tenacity of the dying.

And then I was so long dying, my neck was so long breaking, he tired of the slower surer way. His voice sounded, he spoke to the macabre mask. I heard every word with Delphic clarity—like you do in those things. "Hand me that bore, that sharp-pointed bore lying over there, or this'll go on all night."

I raised mutely protesting hands, out and past him, and something was put into one of them. I could feel the short transverse handle. A thought flashed through my mind—and even one's thoughts are so distinct in those things—"She's put it into my hand instead of his!" I fixed my hand on it more securely, poised it high, and drove it into him from in back. The shock of its going in seemed to be transmitted to my own body, we were so inextricably intertwined. But, for all that, it seemed to go in effortlessly, like a skewer into butter. I could even feel myself withdraw it again, and it came out harder than it went in.

He went with it, or after it, and toppled back. After a moment, I drew near to him again, on hands and knees. And now that it was too late his face became visible at last, as if a wanly flickering light were playing over it, and he was suddenly no formless mud-blotted monster but a man just like I was. Harmless, helpless, inoffensive. The face looked reproachfully up at me, as if to say "Why did you have to do that?" I couldn't stand that, and I leaned over him, tentatively feeling for the position of his heart. Not for purposes of succor, but to make that face stop looking at me so accusingly. Then when I'd located it, I suddenly drove the metal implement in with ungovernable swiftness from straight overhead, and jumped back as I did so.

The mask, still present in the background, gave a horrid scream like something undone, foiled, and whisked away, like something drawn on wires.

I heard a door close and I quickly turned, to see which way she had gone, so that I might remember and find my own way out. But, as always in those things, I was too late. She was gone by the time I turned, and all the doors looked alike again.

I went to them and tried them one by one, and each one was the wrong one, wouldn't open, and now I couldn't get out of here, I was trapped, shut in with what was lying there on the floor, that still held fear and menace for me, greater even than when it had moved, attacked me. For the dread and horror that had been latent throughout, far from being expiated, was now more imminent than ever, seemed to gather itself to a head over me, about to burst and inundate me.

Its source, its focal point, was what lay there on the floor. I had to hide it, I had to shut it away. It was one of those compulsions, all the more inescapable for being illogical.

I threw open one of the many doors that had baffled me so repeatedly throughout. And behind it, in the sapphire pall that still shrouded the scene, I now saw a shallow closet. It was as though it hadn't been there until now, it was as though it had just formed itself for my purpose. I picked up what lay on the floor, and I could seem to do it easily, it had become light, as easy to shoulder as a rolled-up rug or mat; I propped it up behind the closet door; there was not depth enough behind it to do anything else.

Then I closed the door upon it, and pressed it here and there with the flats of my hands, up and down the frame that bordered the mirror, as if to make it hold tighter. But danger still seemed to exude through it, like a vapor. I knew that wasn't enough, I must do more than that, or it would surely open again.

Then I looked down, and below the knob there was a keyhead sticking out. It was shaped a little like a three-leaf clover, and the inner rim of each of the three scooped-out "leaves" was fretted with scroll-work and tracery. It was of some yellowish metal, either brass or iron gilded-over. A key such as is no longer made or used.

I turned it in the keyhole and I drew it slowly out. I was surprised at how long a stem it had, it seemed to keep coming forever. Then at last it ended, in two odd little teeth, each one doubled back on itself, like the single arm of a swastika.

After I had extricated it at last, I pocketed it, and then the knob started turning from the inside, the door started to open anyway. Very slowly but remorselessly, and in another minute I was going to see something unspeakably awful on the other side of it. Revelation, the thing the whole long mental film had been building to, was upon me.

And then I woke up.

I'd lost the pillow to the floor, and my head was halfway down after it, I was dangling partly over the side of the bed, and my face was studded with oozing sweatdrops. I righted it and propped myself up on one elbow and blew out my breath harrowedly. I mumbled, "Gee I'm glad that's over with!" and drew the back of my pajama sleeve across my forehead to dry it. I brushed the edge of my hand across my mouth, as if to remove a bad taste. I shook my head to clear the last clinging mists of the thing out of it. I looked at the clock, and it was time to get up anyway, but even if it hadn't been, who would have risked going back to sleep after such a thing? It might have re-formed and started in again, for all I knew.

I flung my legs out of the ravaged coverings, sat on the edge of the bed, picked up a sock and turned it inside-out preparatory to shuffling it on.

Dreams were funny things. Where'd they come from? Where'd they go?

The basinful of stinging cold water in the bathroom cleared away the last lingering vestiges of it, and from this point on everything was on a different plane, normal, rational and reassuringly familiar. The friendly bite of the comb. The winding of the little stem of my wrist-watch, the looping together of the two strap-ends around my—

They fell open and dangled down straight again, still unattached, and stayed that way. I had to rivet my free hand to the little dial to keep it from sliding off my wrist.

I stared at the thing for minutes on end.

I had to let my cuff slide back in place and cover it at last. I couldn't stand there staring at it forever. That didn't answer anything. What should it tell me? It was a scratch, that was all.

"Talk about your realistic dreams!" I thought. "I guess I must have done that to myself, with my other hand, in the throes of it. That was why the detail entered into the dream fabric."

It couldn't, naturally, be the other way around, because the other way around meant transference from the dream into the actuality of leaving a red scratch across my wristbone.

I went ahead. The familiar plane, the rational everyday plane. The blue tie today. Not that I changed them every day, I wasn't that much of a dude, but every second day I varied them. I threw up my collar, drew the tie-length through, folded it down again—

My hands stayed on it, holding it down flat on each side of my neck, as though afraid it would fly away, although it was a shirt-attached collar. Part of my mind was getting ready to get frightened, fly off the handle, and the rest of my mind wouldn't let it, held it steady just like I held the collar.

But I hadn't had those bruises, those brownish-purple discolorations, faintly, not vividly, visible at the side of my neck, as from the constriction of a powerful grip, the pressure of cruel fingers, last night when I undressed.

Well all right, but I hadn't yet had the dream last night when I undressed either. Why look for spooks in this? The same explanation that covered the wrist-scratch still held good for this too. I must have done it to myself, seized my own throat in trying to ward off the traumal attack passing through my mind just then.

I even stood there and tried to reconstruct the posture, to see if it were physically feasible. It was, but the result was almost grotesquely distorted. It resulted in crossing the arms over the chest and gripping the left side of the neck with the right hand, the right with the left. I didn't know; maybe troubled sleepers did get into those positions. I wasn't as convinced as I would have liked to be. One thing was certain, the marks had been made by two hands, not one; there were as many on one side as on the other, and the four fingers always go opposite to the thumb in a one-hand grip.

But more disturbing than their visibility, there was pain in them, soreness when I prodded them with my own fingertips, stiffness when I turned my neck acutely. It shouldn't have, but it seemed to weaken the theory of self-infliction. How was it I hadn't awakened myself, exerting that much pressure? To which the immediate and welcome corollary was: but if it had been exerted by someone else, I would have been apt to awaken even more quickly, wouldn't I?

I forced myself back to the everyday plane again. Buttoned the collar around the bruises, partly but not entirely concealing them, knotted the tie, shrugged on vest and coat. I was about ready to go now.

The last thing I did was what I always did last of all, one of those ineradicable little habits. I reached into my pocket to make sure I had enough change available for my meal and transportation, without having to stop and change a bill on the way. I brought out a palmful of it, and then I lost a good deal of it between my suddenly stiff, outspread fingers. Only one or two pieces stayed on, around the button. The large and central button. I let them roll, I didn't stoop to pick them up. I couldn't; my spine wouldn't have bent right then.

It was a strange button. Somehow I knew that even before I compared it. I knew I was going to check it with every article of clothing I owned, but I already knew it wasn't from one of my own things. Something about the shape, the color, told me; my fingers had never twisted it through a buttonhole, or they would have remembered it. That may sound far-fetched; but buttons can become personalized to nearly as great an extent as neckties.

And when I closed my hand over it—as I did now—it took up as much room inside my folded palm, it had the same feel, as it had had a little while ago *in that thing*.

It was the button from the dream.

I threw open the closet door so fast and frightenedly it swung all the way around flush with the wall, and rebounded off it, and started slowly back again with the recoil. There wasn't anything hanging up in there that I didn't hold it against, even where there was no button missing, even where its size and type utterly precluded its having been attached. Vests and jackets, a cardigan, a raincoat, a lumberjacket, a topcoat, bathing trunks, a bathrobe. Every stitch I owned.

It wasn't from anything of mine, it didn't belong anywhere.

This time I couldn't get back on the naturalistic plane, I was left dangling in midair. This time I couldn't say: "I did it to myself in the throes of that thing." It came from somewhere. It had four center holes, it even had a wisp or two of black tailor's thread still entwined in them. It was solid, not a phantom.

But rationality wouldn't give in, tried to rush into the breach, and I was on its side for all I was worth. "No, no. I picked this up on the street, and I don't remember doing it." That simply wasn't so; I'd never picked up a stray button in my life. "Or the last tailor I sent this suit out to left it in the pocket from someone else's clothing by mistake." But they always return dry-cleaning garments to you with the pocket-linings inside-out, I'd noticed that a dozen times.

That was the best rationalization could do, and it was none too good. "It just shows you what a thing like that will do to your nerves!" I took out a fresh handkerchief for the day, but I didn't just spade it into my pocket this time, I furtively touched my temples with it before I did—and it came away darkening with damp. "I better get out of here. I need a cup of coffee. I've got the jitters."

I shrugged into my coat fast, threw open my room door, poised it to close it after me. And the last gesture of all, before leaving each morning, came to me instinctively; feeling, to make sure I had my key and wouldn't be locked out when I returned that evening.

It came up across the pads of my fingers, but it was only visible at both ends, the middle part was bisected, obscured by something lying across it. My lips parted spasmodically, as when a sudden thrust is received, and refused to come together again.

It had a head—this topmost one—a little like a three-leaf clover and the inner rim of each of the three "leaves" was fretted with scrollwork and tracery. It had a stem disproportionately long for the size of its head, and it ended in two odd little teeth bent back on themselves, like the quarter part of a swastika. It was of some yellowish composition, either brass or iron gilded-over. A key such as is no longer made or used.

It lay lengthwise in the hollow of my hand, and I kept touching it repeatedly with the thumb of that same hand. That was the only part of me that moved for a long time, that foolish flexing thumb.

I didn't leave right then, for all my preparations. I went back into the room and closed the door after me on the inside, and staggered dazedly around for a moment or two. Once I dropped down limply on the edge of the bed, then turned around and noticed what it was, and got hastily up again, more frightened than ever. Another time, I remember, I thrust my face close to the mirror in the dresser, drew down my lower lid with one finger, stared intently at the white of my eyeball. Even as I did it, I didn't know what I meant by it myself, didn't know what it was to tell me. It didn't tell me anything.

And still another time, I looked out of the window, as if to see if the outside world was still there. It was. The houses across the way looked just like they'd looked last night. The lady on the third floor had her bedding airing over the windowsill, just like every morning. An iceman was gouging a partition across a cake of ice with one point of his tongs preparatory to picking it in two. A little boy was swinging his books on his way to school, killing as much time as he could by walking along spanning the curb, one foot up, one foot down.

There was nothing the matter out there. It was in here, with me.

I decided I'd better go to work, maybe that would exorcise me. I fled from the room almost as though it were haunted. It was too late to stop off at a breakfast counter now. I didn't want any, anyway. My stomach kept giving little quivers. In the end I didn't go to work, either. I couldn't, I wouldn't have been any good. I telephoned in that I was too ill to come, and it was no idle excuse, even though I was upright on my two legs.

I roamed around the rest of the day in the sunshine. Wherever the sunshine was the brightest, I sought and stayed in that place, and when it moved on I moved with it. I couldn't get it bright enough or strong enough. I avoided the shade, I edged away from it, even the slight shade of an awning or of a tree.

And yet the sunshine didn't warm me. Where others mopped their brows and moved out of it, I stayed—and remained cold inside. And the shade was winning the battle as the hours lengthened. It outlasted the sun. The sun weakened and died; the shade deepened and spread. Night was coming on, the time of dreams, the enemy.

I went to Cliff's house late. My mind had been made up to go there for hours past, but I went there late on purpose. The first time I got there they were still at the table, I could see them through the front window. I walked around the block repeatedly, until Lil had gotten up from the table and taken all the dishes with her, and Cliff had moved to another chair and was sitting there alone. I did all this so she wouldn't ask me to sit down at the table with them, I couldn't have stood it.

I rang the bell and she opened the door, dried her hands, and said heartily: "Hello, stranger. I was just saying to Cliff only tonight, it's about time you showed up around here."

I wanted to detach him from her, but first I had to sit through about ten minutes of her. She was my sister, but you don't tell women things like I wanted to tell him. I don't know why, but you don't. You tell them the things you have under control; the things that you're frightened of, you tell other men if you tell anyone.

Finally she said, "I'll just finish up the dishes, and then I'll be back."

The minute the doorway was empty I whispered urgently, "Get your hat and take a walk with me outside. I want to tell you something—alone."

On our way out he called in to the kitchen, "Vince and I are going out to stretch our legs, we'll be back in a couple of minutes."

She called back immediately and warningly: "Now Cliff, only beer—if that's what you're going for."

It put the idea in his head, if nothing else, but I said: "No, I want to be able to tell you this clearly, it's going to sound hazy enough as it is; let's stay out in the open."

We strolled slowly along the sidewalk; he was on his feet a lot and it was no treat to him, I suppose, but he was a good-natured sort of fellow, didn't complain. He was a detective. I probably would have gone to him about it anyway even if he hadn't been, but the fact that he was, of course, made it the inevitable thing to do.

He had to prompt me, because I didn't know where to begin. "So what's the grief, boy friend?"

"Cliff, last night I dreamed I killed a fellow. I don't know who he was or where it was supposed to be. His nail creased my wrist, his fingers bruised the sides of my neck, and a button came off him somewhere and got locked in my hand. And finally, after I'd done it, I locked the door of a closet I'd propped him up in, put the key away in my pocket. And when I woke up—well, look."

We had stopped under a street light. I turned to face him. I drew back my cuff to show him. "Can you see it?" He said he could. I dragged down my collar with both hands, first on one side, then on the other. "Can you see them? Can you see the faint purplish marks there? They're turning a little black now."

He said he could.

"And the button, the same shape and size and everything, was in my trouser pocket along with my change. It's on the dresser back in my own room now. If you want to come over, you can see it for yourself. And last of all, the key turned up on me, next to my own key, in the pocket where I always keep it. I've got it right here, I'll show it to you. I've been carrying it around with me all day."

It took me a little while to get it out, my hand was shaking so. It had shaken like that all day, every time I brought it near the thing to feel if it was still on me. And I had felt to see if it was still on me every five minutes on the minute. The lining caught around it and I had to free it, but finally I got it out.

He took it from me and examined it, curiously but noncommittally.

"That's just the way it looked in—when I saw it when I was asleep," I quavered. "The same shape, the same color, the same design. It even weighs the same, it even—"

He lowered his head a trifle, looked at me intently from under his brows, when he heard how my voice sounded. "You're all in pieces, aren't you?" he confirmed. He put his hand on my shoulder for a minute to steady it. "Don't take it that way, don't let it get you."

That didn't help. Sympathy wasn't what I wanted, I wanted explanation. "Cliff, you've got to help me. You don't know what I've been through all day; I've been turned inside-out."

He weighed the key up and down. "Where'd you get this from, Vince? I mean, where'd you *first* get it from, before you dreamed about it?"

I grabbed his one arm with both hands. "But don't you understand what I've just been telling you? I didn't *have* it before I dreamed about it. I never *saw* it before then. And then I wake up, and it turns *real!*"

"And that goes for the button too?"

I quirked my head.

"You're in bad shape over this, aren't you? Well what is it that's really got you going? It's not the key and button and scratch, is it? Are you afraid the dream really happened, is that it?"

By that I could see that he hadn't understood until now, hadn't really gotten me. Naturally it wasn't just the tokens carried over from the dream that had the life frightened out of me. It was the *implication* behind them. If it was just a key turned up in my pocket after I dreamed about it, why would I go to him? To hell with it. But if the key turned up real, then there was a mirrored closet door somewhere to go with it. And if there was a closet to match it, then there was a body crammed inside it. Also real. Real dead. A body that had scratched me and tried to wring my neck before I killed it.

I tried to tell him that. I was too weak to shake him, but I went through the motions. "Don't you understand? There's a room somewhere in this city right at this very minute, that this key belongs to! There's a man propped up dead behind it! And I don't know where; my God, I don't know where, nor who he is, nor how or why it happened—only that—that I must have been there, I must have done it—or why would it come to my mind like that in my sleep?"

"You're in a bad way." He gave a short whistle through his clenched teeth. "Do you need a drink, Lil or no Lil! Come on, we'll go someplace and get this thing out of your system." He clutched me peremptorily by the arm.

"But only coffee," I faltered. "Let's go where the lights are good and bright."

We went where there was so much gleam and so much dazzle even the flies walking around on the table cast long shadows.

"Now we'll go at this my way," he said, licking the beer foam off his upper lip. "Tell me the dream over again."

I told it.

"I can't get anything out of that." He shook his head baffled. "Did you know this girl, or face, or whatever it was?"

I pressed the point of one finger down hard on the table. "No, *now* I don't, but in the dream I did, and it made me broken-hearted to see her. Like she had double-crossed me or something."

"Well in the dream who was she, then?"

"I don't know; I knew her *then,* but now I don't."

"Jese!" he said, swallowing more beer fast. "I should have made this whiskey with tabasco sauce! Well was she some actress you've seen on the screen lately, maybe? Or some picture you've seen in a magazine? Or maybe even some passing face you glimpsed in a crowd? All those things could happen."

"I don't know, I don't know. I seemed to know her better than that; it hurt me to see her, to have her hate me. But I can't carry her over into—now."

"And the man, the fellow or whoever he was?"

"No, I couldn't seem to see his face through the whole thing. I only saw it at the very end, after it was already too late. And then when the door started to open again, after I'd locked him in, it seemed as though

I was going to find out something horrible—about him, I guess. But I woke up before there was time."

"And last of all, the place. You say nothing but doors all around you. Have you been in a place like that lately? Have you ever seen one? In a magazine illustration, in a story you read, in a movie?"

"No. No. No."

"Well then let's get away from the dream. Let's leave it alone." He flung his hand back and forth relievedly, as if clearing the air. "It was starting to get me myself. Now what'd you do last night—before this whole thing came up?"

"Nothing. Just what I do every night. I left work at the usual time, had my meal at the usual place—"

"Sure it wasn't a welsh rarebit?"

I answered his smile, but not light-heartedly. "A welsh rarebit is not responsible for that key. A locksmith is. Drop it on the table and hear it clash! Bite it between your teeth and chip them! *And I didn't have it when I went to bed last night.*"

He leaned toward me. "Now listen, Vince. There's a very simple explanation for that key. There has to be. And whatever it is, it didn't come to you in a dream. Either you were walking along, you noticed that key, picked it up because of its peculiar—"

I semaphored both hands before my face. "No, I tried to sell myself that this morning; it won't work. I have absolutely no recollection of ever having done that, at any time. I'd remember the key itself, even if I didn't remember the incident of finding it."

"Are you sitting there trying to say you've never in your life forgotten a single object, once you've seen it the first time?"

"No," I said unwillingly.

"You'd better not. Particularly a nondescript thing like a key—"

"This isn't a nondescript key, it's a unique key. And I *do* say I never saw it before, never picked it up; it's a strange key to me."

He spread his hands permissively. "All right, it don't have to be that explanation. There's a dozen-and-one other ways it could have gotten into your pocket without your knowledge. You might have hung the coat up under some shelf the key was lying on, and it dropped off and the open pocket caught it—"

"The pockets of my topcoat have flaps. What'd it do, make a U-turn to get in under them?"

"The flaps might have been left accidentally tucked-in, from the last time your hands were in your pockets. Or it may have fallen out of someone else's coat hung up next to yours in a cloakroom, and been lying there on the floor, and someone came along, thought it belonged in your coat, put it back in—"

"I shoved my hands in and out of those pockets a dozen times yesterday. And the day before. And the day before that. Where was it then? It wasn't in the pocket! But it was this morning. After I saw it clear as a photograph in my sleep during the night!"

"Suppose it was in the pocket and your hand missed it—yesterday and the day before and so on—until this morning? That would be physically possible, wouldn't it?"

I gave him a no on this; I had a right to. "It came up *over* my own key, it was the *top* one of the two, when I got them both out this morning. So if it was already in there last night, how could I have got my own key out—as I did when I came home—without bringing it up too? And last night I didn't bring it up."

He waived that point. Maybe because I had him, maybe not. "All right, have it your way, let's say that it *wasn't* in your pocket last night. That still doesn't prove that the dream itself was real."

"No?" I shrilled. "It gives it a damn good foundation-in-fact as far as I'm concerned!"

"Listen, Vince, there's no halfway business about these things. It's either one thing or the other. Either you dream a thing or you don't dream it, it really happens. You're twenty-six years old, you're not a kid. Don't worry, you'd know it and you'd remember it damn plainly afterwards if you ever came to grips with a guy and he had you by the throat, like in this dream, and you rammed something into his back. I don't take any stock in this stuff about people walking in their sleep and doing things without knowing it. They can walk a little ways off from their beds, maybe, but the minute anyone touches them or does something to stop them, they wake right up. They can't be manhandled and go right on sleeping through it—"

"I couldn't have walked in my sleep, anyway. It was drizzling when I went to bed last night; the streets were only starting to dry off when I first got up this morning. I don't own rubbers, and the soles of both my shoes were perfectly dry when I put them on."

"Don't try to get away from the main point at issue. Have you any recollection at all, no matter how faint, of being out of your room last night, of grappling with a guy, of ramming something into him?"

"No, all I have is a perfectly clear recollection of going to bed, *dreaming* I did all those things, and then waking up again."

He cut his hand short at me, to keep the button, key and bruises from showing up again, I guess. "Then that's all there is to it. Then it didn't happen." And he repeated stubbornly: "You either dream 'em or you *do* 'em. No two ways about it."

I ridged my forehead dissatisfiedly. "You haven't helped me a bit, not a dime's worth."

He was a little put out, maybe because he hadn't. "Naturally not, not if you expected me to arrest you for murdering a guy in a dream. The arrest would have to take place in a dream too, and the trial and all the rest of it. And I'm off-duty when I'm dreaming. What do you think I am, a witch doctor?"

"How much?" I asked the counterman disgruntledly.

"Seventeen cups of coffee—" he tabulated. It was two o'clock in the morning.

"I'm going to sleep in the living room at your place tonight," I said to him on the way over. "I'm not going back to that room of mine till broad daylight! Don't say anything to Lil about it, will you, Cliff?"

"I should say not," he agreed. "D'you think I want her to take you for bugs? You'll get over this, Vince."

"First I'll get to the bottom of it, then I'll get over it," I concurred sombrely.

I slept about an hour's worth, but that was the fault of the seventeen cups of coffee more than anything else. The hour that I did sleep had no images in it, was no different than any other night's sleep I'd had all my life. Until the night before; no better and no worse. He came in and he stood looking at me the next morning. I threw off the blanket they'd given me and sat up on the sofa.

"How'd it go?" he asked half-secretively. On account of her, I suppose.

I eyed him. "I didn't have any more dreams, if that's what you mean. But that has nothing to do with it. If I was convinced that was a dream, I would have gone home to my own room last night, even if I was going to have it over again twice as bad. But I'm not; I'm still not convinced, by a damn sight. Now are you going to help me or not?"

He rocked back and forth on his feet. "What d'you want me to do?"

How could I answer that coherently? I couldn't. "You're a detective. You've got the key. The button's over in my room. You must have often had less than that to work with. Find out where they came from! Find out what they're doing on me!"

He got tough. He had my best interests at heart maybe, but he thought the thing to do was bark at me. "Now listen, cut that stuff out, y'hear? I dowanna hear any more about that key! I've got it, and I'm keeping it, and you're not going to see it again! If you harp on this spooky stuff any more, I'll help you all right—in a way you won't appreciate. I'll haul you off to see a doctor."

The scratch on my wrist had formed a scab, it was already about to come off. I freed it with the edge of my nail, then I blew the little sliver of dried skin off. And I gave him a long look, more eloquent than words. He got it, but he wouldn't give in. Lil called in: "Come and get it, boys!"

I left their house—and I was on my own, just like before I'd gone there. Me and my shadows. I stopped in at a newspaper advertising bureau, and I composed an ad and told them I wanted it inserted in the real estate section. I told them to keep running it daily until further notice. It wasn't easy to word. It took me the better part of an hour, and about three dozen blank forms. This ad:

"WANTED: I am interested in inspecting, with a view toward leasing or buying, a house with an octagonal mirror-paneled room or alcove. Location, size and all other details of secondary importance, provided it has this one essential feature, desired for reasons of a sentimental nature. Communicate Box—, World-Express, giving exact details"

The first two days there was no reaction. That wasn't to be wondered at. It had only appeared on the first day, and any answer would still be in process of transmission through the mail on the second. On the third day there were two replies waiting when I stopped in at the advertising-bureau. One was from a Mrs. Tracy-Lytton, on deckled stationery. She had a house that she was anxious to dispose of for the winter season, with a view to going to Florida. It had a mirror lined powder-room on the second floor. It was not, she had to admit, eight-sided; it was only foursquare, but wouldn't that do? She was sure that once I had seen it—

The other was from a man by the name of Kern. He too had one that he thought would meet my requirements. It had an octagonal breakfast nook of glass bricks—

There wasn't anything on the fourth day. On the fifth there was a windfall of about half-a-dozen waiting for me when I stopped in. Before I'd set to work opening and reading them, I couldn't help being astonished that there should be this many prospective dwellings in the market with such a seldom-encountered feature as an eight-sided mirror-faced cubicle. By the time I'd waded through them I saw I needn't have worried; there weren't. Three of the six were from realty

agents offering their services, in case I couldn't find what I wanted
unassisted. Two more were from contractors, offering to install such a
feature to order for me, provided I couldn't find it ready-made. The last
one, the only one from an individual owner, and who was evidently
anxious to get a white elephant off his hands, likewise offered to have
one built in for me at his own expense, if I agreed to take a long-term
lease on the property.

They started tapering off after that. A desultory one or two more
drifted in by the end of the week. One of these for a moment seemed
to strike a spark when I read it, and my hopes flared up. It was from
a retired actress with a suburban villa which she did not occupy. She
was offering it furnished and mentioned that, although it had no eight-
sided built-in mirror arrangement, there was a small dressing room
fitted with a movable eight-paneled mirrored screen, which could be
adjusted so that it cut corners off and gave the room any number of
sides required.

I telephoned, arranged an appointment at her hotel, and she drove
me out in her car. I could see that my appearance and youth gave her
misgivings as to my financial ability to meet the terms involved, and she
only went through it because the appointment had been agreed upon.
The villa was a stucco affair, and at first sight of the screen, when we'd
gone in, my face got a little white and I thought I had something. It
was folded over to the width of one panel and leaning against the
dressing-room wall. "Here's how I used to arrange it when I was trying
on costumes," she said.

We rigged it up between us in octagon-shape, so that it made sort of
an inner-lining to the room, cutting off the four corners and providing
eight angles instead. I stood there in the middle of it, and she stood
beside me, waiting my decision. "No," I said finally, "no."

She couldn't understand. "But won't it do just as well? It's mirror,
and it's eight-sided."

There was no keyhole on any of the eight flaps to fit a key into, a key
such as I had found in my pocket that morning; that was the main
thing. I didn't explain. "I'll let you know," I said, and we went back
to the car and back to our starting-point.

That was the closest I'd come, and that wasn't very close. The ad
continued to run. But now it brought no further results, fell on barren
ground. The supply of mirrored compartments had been exhausted,
apparently. The advertising bureau phoned to find out if I wanted to
continue it. "No, kill it," I said disheartenedly.

Meanwhile, Cliff must have spotted it and recognized it. He was a very thorough paper-reader, when he came home at nights. Or perhaps he hadn't, he just wanted to see how I was getting along. Brace me up, "take me away from myself" as the phrase goes. At any rate he showed up good and early the next day, which was a Sunday. He was evidently off; I didn't ask him, but I hardly figured he'd wear a pullover and slacks like he had on, to Headquarters.

"Sit down," I invited.

"No," he said somewhat embarrassedly. "Matter of fact, Lil and I are going to take a ride out into the country for the day, and she packed a lunch for three. Cold beer, and, um—"

So that was it. "Listen, I'm all right," I said dryly. "I don't need any fresh-air jaunts, to exorcise the devils in me, if that's what the strategy is—"

He was going to be diplomatic—Lil's orders, I guess—and until you've seen a detective trying to be diplomatic, you haven't lived. Something about the new second-hand Chev (his actual phrase) that he'd just gotten in exchange for his old second-hand Chev. And just come down to the door a minute to say howdy to Lil, she was sitting in it. So I did, and he brought my coat out after me and locked up the room, so I went with him.

The thing was a hoodoo from the beginning. He wasn't much of a driver, but he wasn't the kind who would take back-seat orders on the road from anyone either; he knew it all. We never did reach where they'd originally intended going, he lost it on the way; we finally compromised on a fly-incubating meadow, after a thousand miles of detouring. Lil was a good sport about it. "It looks just like the other place, anyway," she consoled. We did more slapping at our ankles than eating, and the beer was warm, and the box of hard-boiled eggs had disappeared from the car at one of those ruts he'd hit. And then, to cap the climax, a menacing geyser of black clouds piled themselves up in the sky with effervescent suddenness, and we had to run for it. The storm was so instantaneous we couldn't even get back to the car before it broke, and the rest was a matter of sitting in sodden misery while he groped his way down one streaming, rain-misted country road and up another, surroundings completely invisible.

Lil's fortitude finally snapped short. The lightning was giving her a bad time of it—like most women, she abhorred it—and her new outfit was ruined. "Stop at the first place you come to and let's get in out of it!" she screamed at him. "I can't stand any more of this!" She hid her face against my chest.

"I can't even see through my windshield, much less offside past the road," he grunted. He was driving with his forehead pressed against the glass.

I scoured a peephole on my side of the car, peered out. A sort of rustic torii, one of those squared Japanese arches, sidled past in the watery welter. "There's a cut-off a little ways ahead, around the next turn," I said. "If you take that, it'll lead us to a house with a big wide porch; we can get in under there."

They both spoke at once. He said, "How did you know that?" She said, "Were you ever up around these parts before?"

I couldn't answer his question. I said "No" to hers, which was the truth.

Even after he'd followed the cut-off for quite some distance, there was no sign of a house.

"Are you getting us more tangled up than we were already, Vince?" he asked in mild reproach.

"No, don't stop, keep going," I insisted. "You'll come to it—two big stone lanterns, turn the car left between 'em—"

I shut up again, as jerkily as I'd commenced; the peculiar back-shoulder look he was giving me. I poked my fingers through my hair a couple of times. "Gee, I don't know how I knew that myself—" I mumbled half-audibly.

He became very quiet from then on, he didn't have much to say any more; I think he kept hoping I'd be wrong, there wouldn't be any—

Lil gave him a peremptory accolade on the shoulder without warning. "There they are, there they are! Turn, Cliff, like he told you!"

You could hardly make them out, even at that. Faint gray blurs against the obliterating pencil-strokes of rain. You certainly couldn't tell what they were.

He turned without a word and we glided between them. All I could see was his eyes, in the rear-sight mirror, on me. I'd never seen eyes with such black, accusing pupils before; like buckshot they were.

A minute passed, and then a house with a wide, sheltering veranda materialized through the mist, phantomlike, and came to a dead halt beside us. I heard his brakes go on.

I wasn't much aware of the business of making a dash for it through the intervening curtain of water that separated us from the porch roof, Lil squealing between us, my coat hooded over her head. Through it all I was conscious of the beer in my stomach; it had been warm when I drank it back at the meadow, but it had turned ice-cold now, as though it had been put into a refrigerator. I had a queasy feeling, and the rain had chilled me—but deep inside where it hadn't been able to wet me at all. And I knew those weren't raindrops on my forehead; they were sweat turned cold.

We stamped around on the porch for a minute, like soaked people do.

"I wish we could get in," Lil mourned.

"The key's under that window-box with the geraniums," I said.

Cliff traced a finger under it, and brought it out. He put it in the keyhole, his hand shaking a little, and turned it, and the door went in. He held his neck very stiff, to keep from looking around at me. That beer had turned to a block of ice now.

I went in last, like someone toiling through the coils of a bad dream.

It was twilight-dim around us at first, the rainstorm outside had gloomed up the afternoon so. I saw Lil's hands go out to a china switch-mount sitting on the inside of the door-frame, on the left. "Not that one, that's the one to the porch," I said. "The one that controls the hall is on the other side."

Cliff swept the door closed, revealing it; it had been hidden until now. This one was wood, not porcelain. He flicked it and a light went on a few yards before us, overhead. She tried out hers anyway, and the porch lit up; then blackened once more as she turned the switch off.

I saw them look at each other. Then she turned to me and said, "What is this a rib? How do you know so much about this place anyway, Vince?" Poor Lil, she was in another world.

Cliff said gruffly, "Just a lucky guess on his part." He wanted to keep her out of it, out of that darkling world he and I were in.

The light was showing us a paneled hall, and stairs going up, dark polished wood, with a carved handrail, mahogany or something. It wasn't a cheaply fitted-out place—whatever it was. And I could say that "whatever it was" as honestly as they could.

Cliff said, pointing his call up the stairs: "Good-afternoon! Anybody home?"

I said, "Don't do that," in a choked voice.

"He's cold," Lil said, "he's shaking."

She turned aside through a double doorway and lit up a living room. We both looked in there after her, without going in; we had other things on our minds, she just wanted warmth and comfort. There was an expensive parquet floor, but everything else was in a partial state of dismantlement. Not abandonment, just temporary dismantlement. Dustcovers making ghostly shapes of the chairs and sofa and a piano. An over-sized linen hornet's nest hanging from the ceiling, with indirect light peering from the top of it, was a crystal chandelier.

"Away for the summer," Lil said knowingly. "But funny they'd leave it unlocked like that, and with the electricity still connected. Your being a detective comes in handy, Cliff; we won't get in trouble walking in like this—" There was a black onyx fireplace, and after running her hands exploratively around it, she gave a little bleat of satisfaction, touched something. "Electric," and it glowed red. She started to rub her arms and shake out her skirt before it, to dry herself off, and forgot us for the time being.

I glanced at him, and then I backed away, out of the doorway. I turned and went up the staircase, silently but swiftly. I saw him make for the back of the hall, equally silent and swift. We were both furtive in our movements, somehow.

I found a bedroom, dismantled like downstairs. I left it by another door, and found myself in a two-entrance bath. I went out by the second entrance, and I was in another bedroom. Through a doorway, left open, I could see the hallway outside. Through another doorway, likewise unobstructed, I could see—myself.

Poised, quivering with apprehension, arrested in mid-search, white face staring out from above a collar not nearly so white. I shifted, came closer, dying a little, wavering as I advanced. Two of me. Three. Four, five, six, seven. I was across the threshold now. And the door, brought around from its position flat against the outside wall, pulled in after me, flashed the eighth image of myself on its mirror-backed surface.

I tottered there, and stumbled, and nearly went down—the nine of me.

Cliff's footfall sounded behind me, and the eighth reflection was swept away, leaving only seven. His hand gripped me by the shoulder, supporting me. I heard myself groan in infinite desolation, "This is the place; God above, this is the place, all right!"

"Yeh," he bit out in an undertone. He bit it off so short it was like a single letter, shorter than "No" even. Then he said, "Wipe off your forehead, you're all—" I don't know why, for lack of something better to say, I guess. I made a pass with my sleeve across it. We neither of us were really interested in that.

"Have you got it?" I said.

He knew what I meant. He fumbled. He had it on a ring with his other keys. I wished he hadn't kept it, I wished he'd thrown it away. Like an ostrich hides its head in the sand.

The other keys slithered away, and there it was. Fancy scroll-work . . . a key such as is no longer used or made. . . .

One was a door, the door we'd come in by. Four of the remaining seven were dummies, mirrors set into the naked wall-plaster. You could tell that because they had no keyholes. They were the ones that cut the corners of the quadrilateral. The real ones were the ones that paralleled the walls, one on each side.

He put it into one, and it went in, so smoothly, so easily, like a key goes into the keyhole for which it was made. Something went "Cluck" behind the wood, and he pulled open the mirror-door. A ripple coursed down the lining of my stomach. There was nothing in there, only empty wooden paneling.

That left two.

Lil's hail reached us. "What are you two up to, up there?" From that other world, so far away.

"Keep her downstairs a minute!" I breathed desperately. I don't know why; you don't want your agonies of soul witnessed by a woman.

He called down: "Hold it, Vince has taken off his pants to dry them."

She answered, "I'm hungry, I'm going to see if they left anything around to—" and her voice trailed off toward the kitchen at the back.

He was turning it in the second one. I thought the "Cluck" would never come, and when it did, I must have shuttered my eyes in mortal terror, his "Look!" caught me with them closed. I saw a black thing in the middle of it, and for a minute I thought—

It was a built-in safe, steel painted black but with the dial left its own color. It was jagged, had been cut or burned into.

"That's what he was crouched before, that—night, when he seemed just like a puddle on the floor," I heard myself say. "And he must have had a blow-torch down there on the floor in front of him—that's what made that bluish light. And made her face stand out in the reflection, like a mask—" A sob popped like a bubble in my throat. "And that one, that you haven't opened yet, is the one I propped him up in—"

He straightened and turned, and started over toward it, as though I had just then called his attention to it for the first time—which of course wasn't the case.

I turned to water, and there wasn't anything like courage in the whole world; I didn't know where other fellows got theirs. "No, don't," I pleaded, and caught ineffectively at his sleeve. "Not right away! Wait just a minute longer, give me a chance to—"

"Cut that out," he said remorselessly, and shook my hand off. He went ahead; he put the key in, deep it went, and turned it, and the panel backing the mirror grunted, and my heart groaned in company with it.

He opened it between us. I mean, I was standing on the opposite side from him. He looked in slantwise first, when it was still just open a crack, and then he widened it around my way for me to see. I couldn't until then.

That was his answer to my unspoken question, that widening of it like that for me to see. Nothing fell out on him, nothing was in there. *Not any more.*

He struck a match, and singed all up and down the perpendicular woodwork. There was light behind us, but it wasn't close enough. When the match stopped traveling, you could see the faint, blurred, old discoloration behind it. Old blood. Dark against the lighter wood. There wasn't very much of it; just about what would seep through a wound in a dead back, ooze through clothing, and be pressed out against the wood. He singed the floor, but there wasn't any down there, it hadn't been able to worm its way down that far. You could see where it had ended in two little tracks, one longer than the other, squashed out by the blotterlike clothed back before they had gotten very far.

The closet and I, we stared at one another.

The match went out, the old blood went out with it.

"Someone that was hurt was in here," he conceded grimly.

Someone that was dead, I amended with a silent shudder.

Lil dozed off right after the improvised snack she'd gotten up for us in the kitchen, tired out from the excitement of the storm and of getting lost. In that remote, secure world she still inhabited you did things like eat and take naps; not in the one I was in any more. But the two of us had to sit with her and go through the motions, while the knowledge we shared hung over us like a bloody axe, poised and waiting to crash.

I think if she hadn't started to nod, he would have hauled me outside into the dripping dusk with him then and there, if he'd had to, to get out of earshot. He couldn't wait to tackle me. All through the sketchy meal he'd sat there drumming the fingers of his left hand on the table-top, while he inattentively shoveled and spaded with his right. Like an engine all tuned-up and only waiting for the touch of the starter to go.

My own rigid wrist and elbow shoved stuff through my teeth, I don't know what it was. And then after it got in, it wouldn't go down anyway, stuck in my craw. "What's the matter, Vince, you're not very hungry," she said one time.

He answered for me. "No, he isn't!" He'd turned unfriendly.

We left her stretched out on the covered sofa-shape in the living room, the electric fireplace on, both our coats spread over her for a pieced blanket. As soon as her eyes were safely closed, he went out into the hall, beckoning me after him with an imperative hitch of his head without looking at me. I followed. "Close the doors," he whispered gutturally. "I don't want her to hear this."

I did, and then I followed him some more, back into the kitchen where we'd all three of us been until only a few minutes before. It was about the furthest you could get away from where she was. It was still warm and friendly from her having been in there. He changed all that with a look. At me. A look that belonged in a police-station basement.

He lit a cigarette, and it jiggled with wrath between his lips. He didn't offer me one. Policemen don't, with their suspects. He bounced the match down like he wanted to break it in three pieces. Then he shoved his hands deep in pockets, like he wanted to keep them down from flying at me.

"Let's hear about another dream," he said vitriolically.

I eyed the floor. "You think I lied, don't you—?"

That was as far as I got. He had a temper. He came up close against me, sort of pinning me back against the wall. Not physically—his hands were still in pockets—but by the scathing glare he sent into me. "You knew which cut-off to take that would get us here, from a *dream,* didn't you? You knew about those stone lanterns at the entrance from a *dream,* didn't you? You knew where the key to the front door was cached from a *dream,* didn't you? You knew which was the porch-switch and which the hall—from a *dream,* didn't you? You know what I'd do to you, if you weren't Lil's brother? I'd push your—lying face out through the back of your head!" And the way his hands hitched up, he had a hard time to keep from doing it then and there.

I twisted and turned as if I was on a spit, the way I was being tortured.

He wasn't through. He wasn't even half-through. "You came to me for help, didn't you! But you didn't have guts enough to come clean. To say, 'Cliff, I went out to such-and-such a place in the country last night and I killed a guy. Such-and-such a guy, for such-and-such a reason.' No, you had to cook up a dream! I can look up to and respect a guy, no matter how rotten a crime he's committed, that'll own up to it, make a clean breast of it. And I can even understand and make allowances for a guy that'll deny it flatly, lie about it—that's only human nature. But a guy that'll come to someone, trading on the fact that he's married to his sister and he knows he'll give him an ear, abusing his gullibility, making a fool out of him, like you did me—! I've got no use for him, he's low and lousy and no-good! He's lower than the lowest rat we ever brought in for knifing someone in an alley! 'Look, I found this key in my pocket when I got up this morning, how'd it get in there?' 'Look, I found this button—' Playing on my sympathies, huh? Getting me to think in terms of doctors and medical observation, huh?"

One hand came out of his pocket at last. He threw away his cigarette, not downward but on an even keel, he was so sore. He spit on the floor to one side of him. Maybe because he'd been talking so fast and furious, maybe just out of contempt. "Some dream that was, all right! Well the dream's over and baby's awake now." His left came out of the pocket and soldered itself to my shoulder and stiff-armed me there in front of him. "We're going to start in from scratch, right here in this place, you and me. I'm going to get the facts out of you, and whether they go any further than me or not, that's my business. But at least *I'm* going to have them!"

His right had knotted up, I could see him priming it. How could that get something out of me that I didn't have in me to give him?

"What were you doing out at this place the night it happened? What brought you here?"

I shook my head helplessly. "I never was here before—I never saw it until I came here today with you and Lil—"

He shot a short uppercut into my jaw. It was probably partly pulled, but it smacked my head back into the wallplaster. "Who was the guy you did it to? What was his name?"

"I'm in hell already, you blundering fool, without this," I moaned.

He sent another one up at me; I swerved my head, and this time it just grazed me. My recalcitrance—it must have seemed like that—only inflamed his anger. "Are you gonna answer me, Vince? Are you gonna answer me?"

"I can't. You're asking me things I can't." A sob of misery wrenched from me. "Ask God—or whoever it is watches over us in the night when we're unconscious."

It developed into a scuffle. He kept swinging at me; I sent one or two swings half-heartedly back at him—the instinctive reflex of anyone being struck at, no more.

"Who was the guy? Why'd you kill him? Why? Why? Why?"

Finally I wrenched myself free, retreated out of range. We stood there facing one another for an instant, puffing, glaring.

He closed in again. "You're not going to get away with this," he said. "I've handled close-mouthed guys before. I know how to. You're going to tell me, or I'm going to half-kill you with my own hands—where you killed somebody else!"

He meant it. I could see he meant it. The policeman's blood in him was up. All the stops were out now. He could put up with anything but what he took to be this senseless stubbornness, this irrational prevarication in the face of glaring, inescapable facts.

I felt the edge of the table the three of us had peacefully eaten at so short a time before grazing the fleshy part of my back. I shifted around behind it, got it between us. He swung up a ricketty chair, that didn't have much left to it but a cane seat and four legs, all the rungs were gone. It probably wouldn't have done much more than stun me. I don't think he wanted it to. He didn't want to break my head. He just wanted to get the truth out of it. And I—I wanted to get the truth into it.

He at least had someone he *thought* he could get the truth out of. I had no one to turn to. Only the inscrutable night that never repeats what it sees.

He poised the chair high overhead, and slung his lower jaw out of line with his upper.

I heard the door slap open. It was over beyond my shoulder. He could see it and I couldn't, without turning. I saw him sort of freeze and hold it, and looked over at it, not at me any more.

I looked too, and there was a man standing there eying the two of us, holding a drawn gun in his hand. Ready to use it.

He spoke first, after a second that had been stretched like an elastic band to cover a full minute, had snapped back in place. "What're you two men doing in here?" He moved one foot watchfully across the room threshold.

Cliff let the chair down the slow, easy way, with a neat little *tick* of its four legs. His stomach was still going in and out a little, I could see it through his shirt. "We came in out of the rain, that suit you?" he said with left-over truculence, that had been boiled up toward me originally and was only now simmering down.

"Identify yourselves—and hurry up about it!" The man's other foot came in the room. So did the gun. So did the cement ridges around his eyes.

Cliff took a wallet out of his rear trouser-pocket, shied it over at him so that it slithered along the floor, came up against his feet. "Help yourself," he said contemptuously. He turned and went over to the sink, poured himself a glass of water to help cool off, without waiting to hear the verdict.

He came back wiping his chin on his shirtsleeve, held out his hand peremptorily for the return of the credentials. The contents of the wallet had buried the gun muzzle-first in its holster, rubbed out the cement ridges around its owner's eyes. "Thanks, Dodge," the man said with noticeable respect. "Homicide Division, huh?"

Cliff remained unbending. "How about doing a little identifying yourself?"

"I'm a deputy attached to the sheriff's office." He silvered the mouth of his vest-pocket, looked a little embarrassed. "I'm detailed to keep an eye on this place, I was home having a little supper, and—uh—" He glanced out into the hall behind him questioningly. "How'd you get in? I thought I had it all locked up safe and sound—"

"The key was bedded in a flowerbox on the porch," Cliff said.

"It was!" He looked startled. "Must be a spare, then. I've had the original on me night and day for the past week. Funny, we never knew there was a second one ourselves—"

I swallowed at this point, but it didn't ease my windpipe any.

"I was driving by just to see if everything was okay," he went on, "and I saw a light peering out of the rear window here. Then when I got in, I heard the two of you—" I saw his glance rest on the ricketty chair a moment. He didn't ask the question: what had the two of us been scrapping about. Cliff wouldn't have answered it if he had, I could tell that by his expression. His attitude was, plainly it was none of this outsider's business; something just between the two of us.

"I thought maybe 'boes had broken in or something—" the deputy added lamely, seeing he wasn't getting any additional information.

Cliff said, "Why should this house be your particular concern?"

"There was a murder uncovered in it last week, you know."

Something inside me seemed to go down for the third time.

"There was," Cliff echoed tonelessly. There wasn't even a question mark after it. "I'd like to hear about it." He waited awhile, and then he added, "All about it."

He straddled the chair of our recent combat wrong-way-around, legs to the back. He took out his pack of smokes again. Then when he'd helped himself, he pitched it over at me, but without deigning to look at me. Like you throw something to a dog. No, not like that. You like the dog, as a rule.

I don't know how he managed to get the message across, it doesn't sound like anything when you tell it, but in that simple, unspoken act I got the meaning he wanted me to, perfectly. Whatever there is between us, I'm seeing that it says just between *us*—for the time being, anyway. So shut up and stay out of it. I'm not ready to give you away to anybody—yet.

It can't be analyzed, but that was the message he got across to me by cutting me in on his cigarettes in that grudging, unfriendly way.

"Give one to the man," he said in a stony-hard voice, again without looking at me.

"Much obliged, got my own." The deputy went over and rested one haunch on the edge of the table. That put me behind him, he couldn't see my face. Maybe that was just as well. He addressed himself entirely to Cliff, ignored me as though I were some nonentity. If there had been any room left for objectivity in my tormented, fear-wracked mind, I might have appreciated the irony of that: his turning his back on someone who might very well turn out to have been a principal in what he was about to relate.

He expanded, felt at home, you could see. This was shop-talk with a big-time city dick, on a footing of equality. He haloed his own head with comfortable smoke. "This house belonged to a wealthy couple named Fleming—"

Cliff's eyes flicked over at me, burned searchingly into my face for a second, whipped back to the deputy again before he had time to notice. How could I show him any reaction, guilty or otherwise? I'd never heard the name before, myself. It didn't mean anything to me.

"The husband frequently goes away on these long business trips. He was away at the time this happened. In fact we haven't been able to reach him to notify him yet. The wife was a pretty little thing—"

"Was?" I heard Cliff breathe.

The deputy went ahead; he was telling this his way.

"—Kind of flighty. In fact, some of the women around here say she wasn't above flirting behind his back, but no one was ever able to prove anything. There was a young fellow whose company she was seen in a good deal, but that don't have to mean anything. He was just as much a friend of the husband's as of hers, three of them used to go around together. His name was Dan Ayers—"

This time it was my mind soundlessly repeated, "Was?"

The deputy took time out, expectorated, scoured the linoleum with his sole. It wasn't his kitchen floor, after all. It was nobody's now. Some poor devil's named Fleming that thought he was coming back to happiness.

"Bob Evans, he leaves the milk around here, he was tooling his truck in through the cut-off that leads to this place, just about daybreak that Wednesday morning, and in the shadowy light he sees a bundle of rags lying there in the moss and brakes just offside. Luckily Bob's curious. Well sir, he stops, and it was little Mrs. Fleming, poor little Mrs. Fleming, all covered with dew and leaves and twigs—"

"Dead?" Cliff asked.

"Dying. She must have spent hours dragging herself flat along the ground toward the main road in the hope of attracting attention and getting help. She must have been too weak to cry out very loud, and even if she had, there wasn't anybody around to hear her. She must have groaned her life away unheard, there in those thickets and brambles. She'd gotten nearly as far as the foot of one of those stone entrance lanterns they have where you turn in. She was unconscious when Bob found her. He rushed her to the hospital, let the rest of his deliveries go hang. Both legs broken, skull fracture, internal injuries; they said right away she didn't have a chance, and they were right, she died early the next night."

Breathing was so hard; I'd never known breathing to be so hard before. It had always seemed a simple thing that anyone could do—and here I had to work at it so desperately.

The noise attracted the deputy. He turned his head, then back to Cliff with the comfortable superiority of the professional over the layman. "Kinda gets him, doesn't it? This stuff's new to him, guess."

Cliff wasn't having any of me. God, how he hated me right then! "What was it?" he went on tautly, without even giving me a look.

"Well that's it, we didn't know what it was at first. We knew that a car did it to her, but we didn't get the hang of it at first; had it all wrong. We even found the car itself, it was abandoned there under the trees, off the main road a little way down beyond the cut-off. There were hairs and blood on the tires and fenders—and it was Dan Ayers' car.

"Well, practically simultaneous to that find, Waggoner, that's my chief, had come up here to the house to look around, and he'd found the safe busted and looted. It's in an eight-sided mirrored room they got on the floor above, I'll take you up and show you afterwards—"

"Cut it out!" Cliff snarled unexpectedly. Not at the deputy.

I put the whiskey bottle back on the shelf where it had first caught my eye just now. This was like having your appendix taken out without ether.

"Why doesn't he go outside if this gets him?" the deputy said patronizingly.

"I want him in here with us; he should get used to this," Cliff said with vicious casualness.

"Well, that finding of the safe gave us a case, gave us the whole thing, entire and intact. Or so we thought. You know, those cases that you don't even have to build, that are there waiting for you—too good to be true? This was it: Ayers had caught on that Fleming left a good deal of money in the safe even when he was away on trips; had brought her back that night, and either fixed the door so that he could slip back inside again after pretending to leave, or else remained concealed in the house the whole time without her being aware of it. Sometime later she came out of her room unexpectedly, caught him in the act of forcing her husband's safe, and ran out of the house for her life—"

"Why didn't she use the telephone?" Cliff asked unmovedly.

"We thought of that. It wasn't a case of simply reporting an attempted robbery. She must have seen by the look on his face when she confronted him that he was going to kill her to shut her up. There wasn't any time to stop at a phone. She ran out into the open and down the cut-off toward the main road, to try to save her own life. She got clear of the house, but he tore after her in his car, caught up with her before she made the halfway mark to the stone lanterns. She tried to swerve offside into the brush, he turned the car after her, and killed her with it, just before she could get in past the trees that would have blocked him. We found traces galore there that reconstructed that angle of it to a T. And they were all offside, off the car path; it was no hit-and-run, it was no accident, it was a deliberate kill, with the car chassis for a weapon. He knocked her down, went over her, and then reversed and went over her a second time in backing out. He thought she was dead; she was next-door to it, but she was only dying."

I blotted the first tear before it got free of my lashes, but the second one dodged me, ran all the way down. Gee, life was lovely! All I kept saying over and over was: *I don't know how to drive, I don't know how to drive.*

Cliff took out his cigarettes again and prodded into the warped pack. He threw it at me, and looked at me and smiled. "Have another smoke, kid," he said. "I've only got one left, but you can have it." And I lit it and I smiled too, through all the wet junk in my eyes.

He rode the car a spell further down the main road away from there, and then he thought better of it, realized there must be traces all over it that would give him away even quicker than he could drive it, so he ran it off a second time, ditched it there out of sight where we found it, and lit out some less conspicuous way. I don't want to spent too much time on it. This is the case we *thought* we had, all Wednesday morning and up until about five that afternoon.

"We sent out a general alarm for Dan Ayers, broadcast his description, had the trains and roads and hauling-trucks out of here watched at the city end, we were all busy as a swarm of bees. And then at five that afternoon Mrs. Fleming regained consciousness for a short time— Waggoner had been waiting outside there the whole time to question her—and the first thing she whispered was, 'Is Dan all right? He didn't kill Dan, did he?' What she told us was enough to send us hotfooting back to the house. We pried open the various mirror-panels we'd overlooked the first time and found Ayers' dead body behind one of them. He'd been stabbed in the back with some kind of an awl or bit. He'd been dead since the night before. She died about eight that next evening. There went our case."

Cliff didn't ask it for quite awhile; maybe he hated to himself. Finally he did. "Did you get anything on the real killer?"

"Practically everything—but the guy himself. She was right in the alcove with the two of them when it happened. She got a pretty good look by torchlight, and she lasted long enough to give it to us. All the dope is over at my chief's office."

Cliff smacked his own knees, as if in reluctant decision. He got up. "Let's go over there," he said slowly. "Let's go over and give it the once over." He stopped and looked back at me from the doorway. "C'mon, Vince, you too. I'll leave a note for Lil."

He stood out there waiting, until I had to get up. My legs felt stiff. "C'mon, Vince," he repeated. "I know this is out of your line, but you better come anyway."

"Haven't you got any mercy at all?" I breathed muffledly, as I brushed past him with lowered head.

Cliff trod on my heel twice, going into the constabulary from the deputy's car, short as the distance was. He was bringing up behind me. It must have been accidental; but I think without it I might have faltered and come to a dead halt. I think he thought so, too.

Waggoner was a much younger-looking and trimmer man than I had expected. I'd never met a rural police official before. I'd thought they chewed straws and ran to galluses. Instead he was teething on a Dunhill pipe, and his trousers looked as though his wife ran a hot iron over them every day. The four of us went into his inner office, at the back of the front room, and the three of them chewed the rag about it—the case—in general terms for awhile. Then he said "Yes," to Cliff's question, opened a drawer in one of the filing cabinets and got out a folder; "we do have a pretty good general description of him, from her. Here's a transcription of my whole interview with her at the hospital. I had a stenographer take it down at her bedside." From the folder he removed in turn a quadruple-ply typescript on onion-skin, began finger-tracing its double-spaced lines.

"All that," I thought dismally. "Oh God, all that."

The room had gotten very quiet. "Our reconstruction of the car-assault on Mrs. Fleming was perfectly accurate, as was our motivation of the safe-looting and its interruption. The only thing is, there's a switch of characters involved; that's where we went wrong. Instead of Mrs. Fleming being killed by Ayers, Mrs. Fleming *and* Ayers were killed by this third person. She saw the awl plunged into Ayers' back, fled from the house for her life, was pursued down the cut-off by the murderer in Ayers' car and crushed to death. The murderer then went back, completed his interrupted ransacking of the safe, and concealed Ayers' body. He also relocked the house, to gain as much time as possible—" His voice became an unintelligible drone. "And so on, and so on." He turned a page, then his tracing finger stopped. "Here's what you want, Dodge. The killer was about twenty-five, and fairly skinny. His cheek-bones stood out, cast shadows in the torchlight as it wavered on his face—"

I cupped my hand lengthwise to my cheek, the one turned toward the three of them, and sat there as if holding my face pensively. I was over by the night-blacked window and they were more in the center of the room, under the conelight Waggoner had turned on over his desk.

His tracing finger dropped a paragraph lower, stopped again. "He had light-brown hair. She even remembered that it was parted low on the left side—take a woman to notice a thing like that even at such a moment—and an unusually long forelock that kept falling in front of his face."

My hand went up a little higher and brushed mine back. It only fell down again like it always did.

"His eyes were fixed and glassy, as though he was mentally un-balanced—"

I saw Cliff glance thoughtfully down at the floor, then up again.

"He had on a knitted sweater under his jacket, and she even took in that it had been darned or rewoven up at the neckline in a different color yarn—"

Lil had made me one the Christmas before, and then I'd burned a big hole in it with a cigarette-spark, and when I'd taken it back to her, she hadn't been able to get the same color again, it had left a big starlike patch that hit you in the eye— It was back at my room now. I looked out the window, and I didn't see anything.

His voice went on: "It took us hours to get all this out of her. We could only get it in snatches, a little at a time, she was so low. She went under without knowing Ayers had been killed along with her—"

I heard the onion-skin sheets crackle as he refolded them. No one said anything for awhile. Then Cliff asked, "They been buried yet?"

"Yeah, both. Temporarily, in her case; we haven't been able to contact the husband yet; I understand he's in South America—"

"Got pictures of them?"

"Yeah, we got death-photographs. Care to see them?"

I knew what was coming up. My blood turned to ice, and I tried to catch Cliff's eye, to warn him in silent desperation: Don't make me look, in front of them. I'll cave, I'll give myself away. I can't stand any more of it, I'm played out.

He said offhandedly, "Yeah, let's have a look."

Waggoner got them out of the same folder that had held the typescript. Blurredly, I could see the large, gray squares passing from hand to hand. I got that indirectly, by their reflections on the polished black window-square. I was staring with desperate intensity out into the night, head averted from them.

I missed seeing just how Cliff worked it, with my head turned away like that. I think he distracted their attention by becoming very animated and talkative all at once, while the pictures were still in his hands, so that Waggoner forgot to put them back where he'd taken them from. I lost track of them.

The next thing I knew the light had snapped out, they were filing out, and he was holding the inner office-door for me, empty-handed. "Coming, Vince?" We passed through the outside room to the street.

The deputy said, "I'll run you back there, it's on my own way home anyway." He got in under the wheel and Cliff got in next to him. I was just going to get in the back when Cliff's voice warded me off like a lazy whip. "Run back a minute and see if I left my cigarettes in Mr. Waggoner's office, Vince." Then he held Waggoner himself rooted to the spot there beside the car by a sudden burst of parting cordiality. "I want you to be sure and look me up anytime you're down our way—"

His voice dwindled behind me and I was in the darkened inner office again, alone. I knew what I'd been sent back for. He didn't have any cigarettes in here; he'd given me his last one back at the Fleming house. I found the still-warm cone, curbed its swaying, lit it. They were there on the table under my eyes, he'd left them out there for me purposely.

The woman's photograph was topmost. The cone threw a narrow pool of bright light. Her face seemed to come to life in it, held up in my hand. It lost its distortion, the stiff ugliness of death. Sight came into the vacant eyes. I seemed to hear her voice again. "There he is, right behind you!" And the man's came to life in my other hand. That look he'd given me when I'd bent over him, already wounded to death, on the floor. "What did you have to do that for?"

The conelight jerked high up into the ceiling, and then three pairs of feet were ranged around me, there where I was, flat on the floor. I could hear a blur of awed male voices overhead.

"Out like a light."

"What did it, you suppose, the pictures? Things like that get him, don't they? I noticed that already over at the house, before, when I was telling you about the case—"

"He's not well, he's under treatment by a doctor right now; he gets these dizzy spells now and then, that's all it is." The last was Cliff's. He squatted down by me on his haunches, raised my head, held a paper cup of water from the filter in the corner to my mouth.

His face and mine were only the cup's breadth away from one another.

"Yes," I sighed soundlessly.

"Shut up," he grunted without moving his lips.

I struggled up and he gave me an arm back to the car. It's a funny feeling, to lean on someone that's your natural enemy from now on; that has to be, through force of circumstances. "He'll be all right," he said, and he closed the rear car door on me. It sounded a little bit like a cell gate.

Waggoner was left behind, standing on the sidewalk in front of his office, in a welter of so-longs and much-obligeds.

We didn't say anything in the car. We couldn't; the deputy was at the wheel. We changed to Cliff's car at the Fleming house, picked Lil up and she was blazing sore. She laced it into him halfway back to the city. "I think you've got one hell of a nerve, Cliff Dodge, leaving me alone like that in a house where I had no business to be in the first place, and going off to talk shop with a couple of corny Keystone cops! Suppose you did leave a note saying where you were, that isn't the point! This was supposed to be your day off; I can't have one day in the year with you, without squad stuff, squad stuff, squad stuff! Don't you get enough of it all week long in the city—"

I think for once he was glad she kept his ears humming like that, kept him from thinking too steadily—about me. She only quit past the city limits, and then the cold, empty silence that descended could be ascribed to his sulking after the calling-down he'd gotten. Once, near the end, she said: "What's the matter, Vince, don't you feel well?" She'd caught me holding my head, in the rear-sight mirror.

"The outing was a little bit too strenuous for him," Cliff said bitterly.

That brought on a couple of postscripts. "No wonder, the way *you* drive! Next time, try *not* to get to the place we're going, and maybe you'll make it!"

I would have given all my hopes of heaven to be back in that blessed everyday world she was in—where you wrangled and you squabbled, but you didn't kill. I couldn't give that, because I didn't have any hopes of heaven left.

We stopped and he said, "I'll go up with Vince a minute."

I went up the stairs ahead of him. He closed the door after us. He spoke low and very undramatically, no fireworks. He said, "Lil's waiting downstairs, and I'm going to take her home—first, before I do anything. I love Lil. It's bad enough what this is going to do to her when she finds out; I'm going to see that she gets at least one good night's sleep before she does."

He went over to the door, got ready to leave. "Run out—that's about the best thing you can do. Meet your finish on the hoof, somewhere else, where your sister and I don't have to see it happen. If you're still here when I come back, I'm going to arrest you for the murder of Dan Ayers and Dorothy Fleming. I don't have to ask you if you killed those two people. You fainted dead on the floor when you saw their photographs in death." He gave the knob a twist, as though he was choking the life out of his own career. "Take my advice and don't be here when I get back. I'll turn in my information at my own precinct house and they can pass it on to Waggoner; then I'll hand over my own badge in the morning."

I was pressed up against the wall, as if I were trying to get out of the room where there was no door, arms making swimming-strokes. "I'm frightened," I said stifledly.

"Killers always are," he answered, "—afterwards. I'll be back in about half-an-hour." He closed the door and went out.

I didn't move for about half the time he'd given me, thrown scornfully into my face, so to speak. Then I put on the light over the washstand and turned the warm-water tap. I felt my jaw and it was a little bristly. I wasn't really interested in that. I opened the cabinet and took out my cream and blade and holder, from sheer reflex of habit. Then I saw I'd taken out too much, and I put back the cream and holder. The warm water kept running down. I was in such pain already I didn't even feel the outer gash when I made it. The water kept carrying the red away down the drain.

It would have been quicker at the throat, but I didn't have the guts. This was the old Roman way; slower but just as effective. I did it on the left one too, and then I threw the blade away. I wouldn't need it any more to shave with.

I was seeing black spots in front of my eyes when he tried to get in the door. I tried to keep very quiet, so he'd think I'd lammed and go away, but I couldn't stand up any more. He heard the thump when I went down on my knees, and I heard him threaten through the door, "Open it or I'll shoot the lock away!"

It didn't matter now any more, he could come in if he wanted to, he was too late. I floundered over to the door knee-high and turned the key. Then I climbed up it to my feet again. "You could have saved yourself the trip back," I said weakly.

All he said, grimly, was: "I didn't think of that way out," and then he ripped the ends off his shirt and tied them tight around the gashes, pulling with his teeth till the skin turned blue above them. Then he got me downstairs and into the car.

They didn't keep me at the hospital, just took stitches in the gashes, sent me home, and told me to stay in bed a day and take it easy. I hadn't even been able to do that effectively. These safety razor blades, no depth.

It was four when we got back to my room. He stood over me while I got undressed, then thumbed the bed for me to get in.

"What about the arrest?" I asked. "Postponed?" I asked it just as a simple question, without any sarcasm, rebuke or even interest. I didn't have any left in me to give.

"Canceled," he said. "I gave you your chance to run out, and you didn't take it. As a matter of fact, I sent Lil home alone, I've been downstairs watching the street-door the whole time. When a guy is willing to let the life ooze out of his veins, there must be something to his story. You don't die to back up lies. You've convinced me of your good faith, if not your innocence. I don't know what the explanation is, but I don't think you really know what you did that night, I think you're telling the truth to the best of your knowledge."

"I'm tired," I said, "I'm licked. I don't even want to talk about it any more."

"I think I better stick with you tonight." He took one of the pillows and furled it down inside a chair and hunched low in it.

"It's all right," I said spiritlessly. "I won't try it again. I still think it would have been the best way out—"

Our voices were low. We were both all in from the emotional stress we'd been through all night long. And in my case, there was the loss of blood. In another minute one or both of us would have dozed off. In another minute it would have eluded us forever. For no combination of time and place and mood and train of thought is ever the same twice. It's like a chemical formula. Vary it one iota and you don't get the same result.

This was the right minute now, our minute, mine and his. He yawned. He stretched out his legs to settle himself better, the chair had a low seat and he was long-legged. The shift brought them over a still-damp stain, from my attempt. There were traces of it in a straight line, from the washstand all the way over to the door. He eyed them. "You sure picked a messy way," he observed drowsily.

"Gas is what occurs to most people first, I imagine," I said, equally drowsily. "It did to me, but this house has no gas. So there was no other way but the blade—"

"Good thing it hasn't," he droned. "If more houses had no gas, there'd be fewer—"

"Yeah, but if the bulb in your room burns out unexpectedly, it can be damn awkward. That happened to the fellow in the next room one night, I remember, and he had to use a candle—" My eyes were closed already. Maybe his were too, for all I knew. My somnolent voice had one more phrase to unburden itself of before it, too, fell silent. "It was the same night I had the dream," I added inconsequentially.

"How do you know he had to use a candle? Were you in there at the time?"

His voice opened my eyes again, just as my last straggling remark had opened his. His head wasn't reared, he was still supine, but his face was turned toward me on the pillow.

"No, he rapped and stuck his head in my door a minute, and he was holding the candle. He wanted to know if my light had gone out, too; I guess he wanted to see if the current had failed through the whole house, or it was just the bulb in his room. You know how people are in rooming houses—"

"Why'd he have to do that? Couldn't he tell by the hall?" His voice wasn't as sleepy as before.

"They turn the lights out in the upper halls at eleven-thirty, here, and I guess the hall was dark already—"

His head had left the pillow now. "That's still no reason why he should bust in on you. I'd like to hear the rest of this."

"There isn't any rest, I've told you all there is to it."

"That's what you think! Watch what I get out of it. To begin with, who was he or had you ever seen him before?"

"Oh, sure," I smiled deprecatingly. "We weren't strangers. His name was Burg. He'd been living in the room for a week or ten days before that. We'd said howdy, passing each other on the stairs. We'd even stood and chatted down at the street door several times in the evening, when neither of us had anything to do."

"How is it you never mentioned this incident to me before, as many times as I've asked you to account for every single *minute* of that evening, before you fell asleep?"

"But this has nothing to do with *that,* with what—came up later. You've kept asking me if I was sure I didn't remember leaving the room at any time, and things like that. I didn't even step out into the hall, when he came to the door like that. I was in bed already, and I *didn't even get out of bed to let him in*—now what more d'you want?"

"Oh, you were in bed already."

"I'd been in bed some time past, reading the paper like I do every night. I'd just gotten through and put out my own light a couple minutes before, when I heard this light knock—"

He made an approving pass with his hands. "Tell it just like that. Step by step. Tell it like to a six-year-old kid." He'd left the chair long ago, was standing over me. I wondered why this trifling thing, this less-than-an-incident, should interest him so.

"I turned over, called out 'Who is it?' He answered in a low-pitched voice, 'Burg, from next-door.' "

Cliff wrinkled the skin under his eyes. "Low-pitched? Furtive—? Cagey—?"

I shrugged. "He didn't want to wake up everyone else on the whole floor I suppose."

"Maybe it was that. Go on."

"I can reach the door from my bed, you know. I stuck out my arm, flipped the key and opened the door. He was standing there in his suspenders, holding this lighted candle in front of him. So he asked if my room light was okay; we tried it, and it was."

"Then did he back right out again?"

"Well, not *instantly.* We put the light right out again, but he stayed on in the doorway a couple minutes."

"Why'd he have to stand in the doorway a couple minutes once he'd found out your light was okay?"

"Well—uh—winding up the intrusion, signing off, whatever you'd want to call it."

"In just what words?"

Gee, he was worse than a schoolteacher in the third grade. "You know how those things go. He said he was sorry he'd disturbed me, he wouldn't have if he'd realized I was in bed. He said, 'You're tired, aren't you? I can see you're tired.' "

"With the light out." It was a commentary, not a question.

"The candle was shining into my face. He said, 'Yes, you're tired. You're very tired.' And the funny part of it was, I hadn't been until then, but after he called it to my attention, I noticed he was right; I *was*."

"Kind of repetitious, wasn't he?" he drawled. "You've quoted him as saying it four times, already."

"He kept saying it over and over, I couldn't even keep track of how many times he said it, and his voice kept getting lower all the time." I smiled tolerantly. "I guess he's got kind of a one-track mind, used to mumbling to himself maybe."

"All right, keep going."

"There's no further to go. He closed the door and went away, and I dropped right off to sleep."

"Wait a minute, hold it right there. Are you sure that door closed after him? Did you *see* it close? Did you *hear* it? Or are you just tricking your senses into believing you did, because you figure that's what must have happened next anyway?"

Was he a hound at getting you mixed-up! "I wasn't so alert any more, I was sort of relaxed, like I say—" I said baffledly.

"Did it go like this?" He opened it slightly, eased it gently closed. The latch-tongue went *click* into the socket. "Did it go like this?" He opened it a second time, this time eased it back in place holding the knob fast so the latch-tongue couldn't connect. Even so, the edge of the door itself gave a little thump as it met the frame.

He waited, said: "I can see by the trouble you're having giving me a positive answer, that you didn't hear either of those sounds."

"But the door must've closed," I protested. "What was he going to do? Stay in here all night, keeping watch at my bedside? The candle seemed to go out, so he must've gone out and left me."

"The candle seemed to go out. How do you know it wasn't your eyes that dropped closed and shut it out?" I didn't say anything. "I want to ask you a few questions," he said. "What sort of an effect did his voice have on you, especially when he kept saying 'You're tired'?"

"Sort of peaceful. I liked it."

He nodded at that. "Another thing; where did he hold that candle, in respect to himself? Off to one side?"

"No, dead center in front of his own face, so that the flame was between his eyes, almost."

He nodded again. "Did you stare at the flame pretty steadily?"

"Yeah, I couldn't tear my eyes off it. You know how a flame in a dark room will get you—"

"And behind it—if he was holding it up like you say—you met his eyes."

"I guess—I guess I must have. He kept it on a straight line between my eyes and his the whole time."

Cliff worked his cheek around, like he was chewing a sour apple. "Eyes were fixed and glassy as though he were mentally unbalanced," I heard him mutter.

"What?"

"I was just remembering something in that deathbed statement Mrs. Fleming made to Waggoner. One more thing: when you chatted with him downstairs at the street door like you say you did once or twice, what were the topics, can you remember?"

"Oh, a little bit of everything, you know how those things go. At first general things like the weather and baseball and politics. Then later more personal things—you know how you get talking about yourself when you've got an interested listener."

"Getting the feel of your background." He must have meant that for himself, I couldn't make any sense out of it. "Did you ever catch yourself doing something you didn't want to do, while you were in his company?"

"No. Oh, wait, yes. One night he had a box of mentholated cough-drops in his pocket. He kept taking them out and offering them to me the whole time we were talking. Gosh, if there's one thing I hate it's mentholated coughdrops. I'd say no each time, and then I'd give in and take one anyway. Before I knew it, I'd finished the whole box."

He eyed me gloomily. "Testing your will-power to see if it was weak enough."

"You seem to make something out of this whole thing," I said helplessly. "What is it? Blamed if I can see!"

"Never mind. I don't want to frighten you right now. You get some sleep, kid. You're weak after what you tried to do just now." I saw him pick up his hat.

"Where you going?" I asked. "I thought you said you were staying here tonight?"

"I'm going back to the Fleming house—and to Waggoner's head-quarters too, while I'm at it."

"*Now?* You're going all the way back up there, at this hour of the morning?"

"And Vince," he added from the doorway, "don't give up yet. We'll find a way out somehow—don't take any more shortcuts."

It was high noon before I woke up, after all I'd been through, and even then he didn't show up for another two or three hours yet. I got dressed but I didn't dare leave my room, even for a cup of coffee; I was afraid if I did I'd miss him, and he'd think I'd changed my mind and lammed out after all.

Wild horses couldn't have dragged me away. Where was there to go, anyway? He was my only salvation—now.

He finally showed up around three, and found me worriedly coursing back and forth in my stocking-feet, holding one bandaged wrist with the opposite hand. Stiffening was setting in, and they hurt plenty.

But I was as fresh as a daisy compared to the shape he was in. He had big black crescents under his eyes from not getting to bed all night, and the first thing he did was sprawl back in the chair he'd originally intended occupying the night before, and kick off his shoes. Then he blew a big breath of relaxation that fanned halfway across the room.

"Were you up there all this time—until now?" I gasped.

"I've been back to town once, in-between—to pick up something I needed and get a leave of absence." He wasn't sanguine by any means, I could tell that just by looking at him. He didn't have that steely glint in his eye of your master detective on the home-stretch to a solution. But he looked less harassed than the night before. Maybe the activity of running around, in itself, was good for him.

He'd brought in with him a large flat slab wrapped in brown paper. He picked it up now, undid it, turning partly away from me, scissored his arms, and then turned back again. He was holding a large portrait-photograph in a leather frame against his chest for me to see. He didn't say anything, just watched me.

It took a minute for the identity to peer through the contradictory details, trifling as they were. The well-groomed hair, neatly tapered above the ears instead of shaggily unkempt; the clean-shaven upper lip instead of a sloppy walrus-tusk mustache—he helped this effect by holding one finger lengthwise under the picture's nose—; above all, an intangible aura of prosperity, radiating from the impeccable fit of the custom-tailored suit-collar, the careful negligence of the expensive necktie, the expression of the face itself, instead of the habitual unbuttoned, tieless, slightly soiled shirt-collar, the hangdog aura of middle-age running to seed.

I jolted. "That's Burg! The man that had the room next to me! Where'd you—?"

"I didn't have to ask you that, I already know it, from the landlord and one or two of the other roomers here I've shown it to." He reached under it with one hand and suddenly swung out a second panel, attached to the first. It was one of those double-easel arrangements that stand on dressers.

She stared back at me, and like a woman, she was different again. She'd been different on each of the three times. This was the third and last time I was to see her, though this crystallized, arrested glimpse of her preceded the other two in point of time. She had here neither the masklike scowl of hate at bay I had seen by torchlight, nor yet the rigid ghost-grin of death. She was smiling, calm, alive, lovely. I made a whimpering sound.

Somebody, I guess in Waggoner's office, had stuck a gummed tab uniting the two of them across the division of the folder. Uniting them symbolically in death and mystery. On it was inked: "B-20,263/Fleming-Ayers/7-21-40."

"He's also Dorothy Fleming's husband, Joel," Cliff said. "Waggoner gave me this, from their house."

He must have seen the wan light of hope beginning to flicker in my eyes. He snuffed it out, with a rueful gnaw at his under lip, a slight shake of his head. That was the kindest way, I guess; not to let it get fully kindled. Hope is so hard to kill, anyway. He closed the photo-folder and threw it aside. "No," he said, "no, there's no out in it for you. Look, Vince. D'you want to know now what we're up against, once and for all? You've got to sooner or later, and it isn't going to be easy for you to take."

"You've got bad news for me."

"Pretty bad. But at least it's better than this weird stuff that you've been shadow-boxing with ever since it happened. It's rational, down-to-earth, something that the mind can grasp. You killed a man that Wednesday night. You may as well get used to the idea. There's no dodging out of it, no possibility of mistake, no shrugging-off of responsibility. It isn't alone Mrs. Fleming's deathbed description, conclusive as that is—and she didn't make that up out of thin air, you know; *imagine* someone looking just like you. Fingerprints that Waggoner's staff took from that mirror door behind which Ayers' body was thrust check with yours. I compared them privately while I was up there, from a drinking-

glass I took out of this room and had dusted over at our own lab—"
I looked, and mine was gone.

"You and nobody but you found your way into the Fleming house
and punctured Dan Ayers' heart with an awl and secreted his body in
a closet."

He saw my face blanch. "Now steady a minute. You didn't kill
Dorothy Fleming. You would have, I guess, but she ran out of the
house and down the cut-off for her life. You can't drive, and she was
killed by somebody in a car. Somebody in Ayers' car, but not Ayers
himself obviously, since you had killed him upstairs a minute before
yourself. Now that proves, of course, that somebody *brought* you up
there—and was waiting outside for you at a safe distance, a distance
great enough to avoid implication, yet near enough to lend a hand when
something went wrong and one of the victims seemed on the point of
escaping."

That didn't help much. That halved my crime, but the half was still
as great as the whole. After being told you'd committed one murder,
where was the solace in being told you hadn't committed a dozen
others?

I folded over, seated, held my head. "But why didn't I *know* I was
doing it—?" I groaned anguishedly.

"We can take care of that later," he said. "I can't prove what I think
it was, right now, and what good is an explanation without proof? And
there's only one way to prove it: show it *could* have happened the first
time by getting it to happen all over again a second time—"

I thought he was going crazy—or I was. "You mean, go back and
commit the crime all over again—when they're both already buried?"

"No, I mean get the circumstances down on record, repeat the special
conditions that surrounded it the first time. Even then, it'll be purely
circumstantial and none too good, but it's about the best we can hope
for."

"But can't you tell me what—"

"I think it's safer if I don't, until afterwards. You'll get all tense,
keyed-up; you're liable to jeopardize the whole thing without meaning
to, make it miss fire. I want you to keep cool, everything'll depend on
that—"

I wondered what he was going to ask me.

"It's nearly four o'clock now," he said. "We haven't much time. A
telegram addressed to Mrs. Fleming was finally received from her
husband while I was up there; he's arriving back from South America
today. Waggoner took charge of it, showed it to me. He's ordered her

reburied in a private plot, will probably get there in time for the services—"

I trailed him downstairs to his car, got in beside him limply. "Where are we going?" I asked.

He didn't start the car right away, gave me a half-rueful, half-apologetic look. "Where is the place you would least rather go, of all places, right now?"

That wasn't hard. "That eight-sided mirrored alcove—where I did it."

"I was afraid of that. I'm sorry, kid, but that's the very place you're going to have to go back to, and stay in alone tonight—if you ever want to get out from under the shadows again. Whaddye say, shall we make the try?"

He still didn't start the car, gave me lots of time.

I only took four or five minutes, and I gave him the rest of it back. I slapped in my stomach, which made the sick feeling go up into my throat, and I said: "I'm ready."

I'd been sitting on the floor, outside it, to rest, when I heard him come in. There were other people with him. The silence of the house, tomblike until then, was abruptly shattered by their entrance into the lower hall, their voices, the sounds they made moving about. I couldn't tell how many of them there were. They went into the living room, and their voices became less distinct.

I stood up and got ready, but I stayed out a while longer, to be able to breathe better. I knew I had time yet, he wouldn't come up right away.

The voices were subdued, as befitted a solemn post-funeral occasion. Every once in a while, though, I could make out a snatch of something that was said. Once I heard someone ask: "Don't you want to come over to our place tonight, Joel? You don't mean you're going to stay here alone in this empty house after—after such a thing?"

I strained my ears for the answer—a lot depended on it—and I got it. "I'm closer to her here than anywhere else."

Presently they all came out into the hall again, on their way out, and I could hear goodnights being said. "Try not to think about it too much, Joel. Get some sleep."

The door closed. A car drove off outside, then a second one. No more voices after that. The tomblike silence almost returned. But not quite. A solitary tread down there, returning from the front door, told that someone had remained. It went into the living room and I heard the clink of a decanter against a glass. Then a frittering of piano notes struck at random, the way a person does who has found contentment, is eminently pleased with himself.

Then a light-switch ticked and the tread came out, started unhurriedly up the stairs. It was time to get in. I put one foot behind me, and followed it back. I drew concealment before me in the shape of a mirror-panel, all but the ultimate finger's breadth of gap, to be able to breathe and watch.

The oncoming tread had entered the bedroom adjacent to me, and a light went on in there. I heard a slatted blind spin down. Then the sound of a valise being shifted out into a more accessible position, and the click of the key used to open it. I could even glimpse the colored labels on the lid as it went up and over. South American hotels. I saw bodyless hands reach down, taking things out: striped pajamas and piles of folded linen, that had never seen South America. That had probably lain hidden on a shelf in some public checkroom in the city all this time.

My heart was going hard. The dried blood on the woodwork at my back, of someone I had killed, seemed to sear me where it touched. My flesh kept crawling away from it in ripples, though my body stood there motionless. It was the blood of someone *I* had killed, not that this man out there had killed. No matter what happened now, tonight, nothing could absolve me of that. There was no possibility of transfer of blame. Cliff had told me so, and it was true.

A light went up right outside where I was, and an ice-white needle of it splintered in at me, lengthwise, from top to bottom, but not broad enough to focus anything it fell on—from the outside.

I could see a strip of his back by it. He had come in and was squatting down by the damaged safe, mirror-covering swung out of the way. He swung its useless lid in and out a couple of times. I heard him give an almost soundless chuckle, as though the vandalism amused him. Then he took things out of his coat pockets and began putting them in. Oblong Manila envelopes such as are used to contain currency and securities, lumpy tissue-wrapped shapes that might have been jewelry. Then he gave the safe-flap an indifferent slap-to. As though whether it shut tight or not didn't matter; what it held was perfectly safe—for the present.

Then he stood, before turning to go out.

This was when, now. I took the gun Cliff had given me, his gun, out of my pocket, and raised it to what they call the wishbone of the chest and held it there, pointed before me. Then I moved one foot out before me, and that took the door away, in a soundless sweep.

I was standing there like that, when he turned finally. The mirror covering the safe-niche had been folded back until now, so he didn't see the reflection of my revelation.

The shock must have been almost galvanic. His throat made a sound like the creak of a rusty pulley. I thought he was going to fall down insensible for a minute. His body made a tortured corkscrew-twist all the way down to his feet, but he stayed up.

I had a lot to remember. Cliff had told me just what to say, and what not to say. I'd had to learn my lines by heart, and particularly the timing of them. That was even more important. He'd warned me I had a very limited time in which to say everything I was to say. I would be working against a deadline, that might fall at any minute, but he didn't tell me what it was. He'd warned me we both—this man I was confronting and I—would be walking a tightrope, without benefit of balancing-poles. Everything depended on which one of us made a false step first.

It was a lot to remember, staring at the man whom I had only known until now as Burg, a fellow rooming-house lodger, and who held the key to the mystery that had suddenly clouded my existence. And I had to remember each thing in the order they had been given me, in the proper sequence, or it was no good.

The first injunction was, Make him speak first. If it takes all night, wait until he speaks first. Some matter of recognition must have been involved, but I had no leisure for my own side-thoughts.

He spoke finally. Somebody had to, and I didn't. "How'd *you* get here?" It was the croak of a frog in mud.

"You showed me the way, didn't you?"

I could see the lump in his throat as he forced it down, to be able to articulate. "You're—You remembered coming here?"

"You didn't think I would, did you?"

His eyes rolled, as at the imminence of some catastrophe. "You—you couldn't have!"

The gun and I, we never moved. "Then how did I get back here again? You explain it."

His present situation pierced warningly at him through the muffling layers of his panic. I saw his eyes flick toward the entrance to the alcove. I shifted over a little, got it behind me, to seal him in. I felt with my foot and drew the door in behind me, not fast but leaving only a narrow gap. "How long have you been in here like—like this?"

"Since shortly after dark. I got in while you were away at the funeral services."

"Who'd you bring with you?"

"Just this." I righted the gun, which had begun to incline a little at the bore.

He couldn't resist asking it, he wouldn't have been human if he hadn't asked it, in his present predicament. "Just how much do you remember?"

I gave him a wise smile, that implied everything without saying so. It was Cliff's smile, not mine—but formed by my lips.

"You remember the drive up?" He said it low, but he'd wavered on the wire, that tightrope Cliff had mentioned. "You couldn't have! You had the look, the typical look—"

"What look?"

He shut up; he'd regained his equilibrium.

"I was holding a thumbtack pressed into the palm of each hand the whole way."

"Then why did you do everything I—you were directed to, so passively?"

"I wanted to see what it was leading up to. I thought maybe there might be some good in it for me later, if anyone went to all that trouble—"

"You purposely feigned—? I can't believe it! You didn't even draw back, exhibit a tremor, when I let you out of the car, put the knife in your hand, sent you on toward the house, told you how to get in and what to do! You mean you went ahead and consciously—?"

"Sure I went ahead and did it, because I figured you'd pay off heavy afterwards to keep me quiet. And if I'd tried to balk then, I probably would have gotten the knife myself, on the way back, for my trouble."

"What happened, what went wrong inside?"

"I accidentally dropped the knife in the dark somewhere in the lower hall and couldn't find it again. I went on up empty-handed, thinking I'd just frighten them out the back way and get a chance at the safe myself. But Ayers turned on me and got me down, he weighed more than I do, and he was going to kill *me*—to keep it from coming out that they were adulterous, and had been caught in the act of breaking into your safe in the bargain. Only by mistake, she put the awl that he cried out for into my hand instead of his. I plunged it into him in self-defense."

He nodded as though this cleared up something that had been bothering him. "Ah, that explains the change of weapon that had me mystified. Also how it was that she got out of the house like that and I had to go after her and—stop her myself. Luckily I was crouched behind the hood of Ayers' car, peering at the open door, when she came running out. She couldn't drive herself, so she didn't try to get in, ran screaming on foot down the cut-off. I jumped in without her seeing me, tore after her, and caught up with her. If I hadn't, the whole thing would have ended in a ghastly failure. I might have known you were under imperfect control—"

He'd fallen off long ago, gone hurtling down. But I still had a dead-line to work against, things to say, without knowing the why or where-fore. "Your control was perfect enough, don't let that worry you. You haven't lost your knack."

"But you just said—"

"And you fell for it. I didn't know what I was doing when you brought me up here, sent me in to do your dirty-work for you that night. Haven't you missed something from your late wife's bedroom since you've been back? There was a double photo-folder of you and her. The police took that. I happened to see both pictures in one of the papers. I recognized you as Burg. I'd also recognized my own description, by a darned sweater I wore that night, and had a vague recollection—like when you've been dreaming—of having been in such a house and taken part in such a scene. You've convicted yourself out of your own mouth to me, right now. I haven't come back here to be paid off for my participation or take a cut in any hush-money. Nothing you can give me from that safe can buy your life. You picked someone with weak will-power, maybe, but strong scruples. I was an honest man. You've made me commit murder. I can't clear myself in the eyes of the law— ever. You're going to pay for doing that to me. Now. *This* way."

"Wait, don't do that—that won't help *you* any. Alive, maybe I can do something for you. I'll give you money, I'll get you out of the country. No one needs to know."

"My conscience'll always know. I've got an honest man's conscience in a murderer's body, now. You should have let me alone. That was your mistake. Here you go, Fleming."

He was almost incoherent, drooling at the mouth. "Wait—one minute more! Just sixty seconds—" He took out a thin gold pocket watch, snapped up its burnished lid. He held it face toward me, open that way.

I saw what he was trying to do. Cliff had warned me to be careful. I dropped my eyes to his feet, kept them stubbornly lowered, brow furrowed with resistance, while I held the gun on him. Something kept trying to pull them up.

A flash from the burnished metal of the inside of the watchlid wavered erratically across my chest-front for an instant, like when kids tease you with sunlight thrown back from a mirror.

"Look up," he kept pleading, "look up. Just one minute more. See—the hands are at six-to. Look, just until they get to *here*."

Something was the matter with the trigger of the gun, it must have jammed. I kept trying to close the finger that was hooked around it, and it resisted. Or else maybe it was the finger that wouldn't obey my will.

I kept blinking more and more rapidly. The flash slithered across my shuttering eyes, slid off, came back again. They wanted so bad to look up into it; it prickled.

There was a slight snap, as though he had surreptitiously pulled out the stem-winder, to set the watch back. That did it. I glanced up uncontrollably. He was holding the watch up, brow-high—like he had the candle that night—as if to give me a good, unobstructed look at its dial. It was in about the position doctors carry those little attached head-mirrors with which they examine throats.

I met his eyes right behind it, and all of a sudden my own couldn't get away any more, as though they'd hit glue.

A sort of delicious torpor turned me into wax; I didn't have any ideas of my own any more. I was open to anyone else's. My voice-control lasted a moment longer than the rest of my functions. I heard it say, carrying a left-over message that no longer had any will-power behind it, "I'm going to shoot you."

"No," he said soothingly. "You're tired, you don't want to shoot anybody. You're tired. The gun's too heavy for you. Why do you want to hold that heavy thing?"

I heard a faraway thump as it hit the floor. As far away as though it had fallen right through to the basement. Gee, it felt good to be without it! I felt lazy all over. The light was going out, but very gradually, like it was tired too. The whole world was tired. Somebody was crooning, "You're tired, you're tired—you dirty bum, *now I've got you!*"

Mental Lapse—INDUCED BY HYPNOSIS

There was a white flash that seemed to explode inside my head, and hurt like anything. Something cold and wet pressed against my eyes when I tried to flicker them open. And when I had, instead of getting lighter as when you're slowly waking up, the world around me seemed to get darker and weigh against me crushingly, all over. The pain increased, traveled from my head to my lungs. Knives seemed to slash into them, and I couldn't breathe.

I could feel my eyeballs starting out of their sockets with strangulation, and my head seemed about to burst. The pressure of the surrounding darkness seemed to come against me in undulating waves. I realized that I was under water and was drowning. I could swim, but now I couldn't seem to. I tried to rise and something kept holding me down. I weaved there like a writhing seaweed, held fast to the bottom.

I doubled over, forced myself down against the surrounding resistance, groped blindly along my own legs. One seemed free and unencumbered, I could lift it from the mucky bottom. About the ankle of the other there was a triple constriction of tightly coiled rope, like a hideous hempen gaiter. It was tangled hopelessly about a heavy iron cross-bar. When I tried to raise this, one scimitarlike appendage came free, the other remained hopelessly hooked into the slime it had slashed into from above. It must have been some sort of a small but weighty anchor such as is used by launches and fishing craft.

I couldn't release it. I couldn't endure the bend of position against my inner suffocation. I spiraled upright again in death-fluid. My jaws kept going spasmodically, drinking in extinction.

A formless blur came down from somewhere, brushed lightly against me, shunted away again before I could grasp it, shot up out of reach. I couldn't see it so much as sense it as a disturbance in the water.

There were only fireworks inside my skull now, not conscious thoughts any more. The blurred manifestation shot down again, closer this time. It seemed to hang there, flounderingly, upside-down, beside me. I felt a hand close around my ankle. Then a knife grazed my calf, withdrew. I could feel a tugging at the rope, as if it were being sliced at.

Self-preservation was the only spark left in my darkening brain. I clutched at the hovering form in the death-grip of the drowning. I felt myself shooting up through water, together with it, inextricably entangled. I wouldn't let go. Couldn't. Something that felt like a small ridged rock crashed into my forehead. Even the spark of self-preservation went out.

When I came to I was lying out on a little pier or string-piece of some kind, and there were stars over me. I was in shorts and undershirt, wringing wet and shivering, and water kept flushing up out of my mouth. Somebody kept kneading my sides in and out, and somebody else kept flipping my arms up and down.

I coughed a lot, and one of them said: "There he is, he's all right now." He stood up and it was Cliff. He was in his underwear and all dripping too.

A minute later Waggoner stood up on the other side of me. He was equally sodden, but he'd left on everything but his coat and shoes. There hadn't been any time by then, I guess. He said, "Now get something around him and then the three of us better get back to the house fast and kill the first bottle we find."

There was light coming from somewhere behind us, through some fir trees that bordered the little lake. It played up the little pier. By it, I could see my own outer clothes neatly piled at the very lip of it. There was a paper on top of them, pressed down by one of my oxfords. Cliff picked it up and brought it over and read it to us.

> I'm wanted for the murder of those two people at the Fleming house, they're bound to get me sooner or later, and I have no chance. I see no other way but this.
>
> Vincent Hardy.

It was in my own handwriting; the light was strong enough for me to see that when he showed it to me.

He looked at Waggoner and said, "Do we need this?"

Waggoner pursed his lips thoughtfully and said, "I think we're better off without it. These coronery-inquest guys can be awfully dumb sometimes, it might sort of cloud their judgment."

Cliff took a match from his dry coat and struck it and held it to the note until there wasn't any to hold any more.

I was feeling better now, all but the shivering. I was sitting up. I looked back at the glow through the trees and said, "What's that?"

"Fleming's car," Cliff answered. "He tried to take a curve too fast getting away from here, when we showed up on his tail, and turned over and kindled."

I grimaced sickly. That was about all that could have stirred horror in me after the past ten days: a cremation alive.

"I shot him first," Cliff said quietly.

"One of us did," Waggoner corrected. "We all three fired after him. We'll never know which one hit him. We don't want to anyway. The machine telescoped and we couldn't get him out. And then I had to give Dodge a hand going down after you, he's no great shakes of a swimmer."

"We had to hit him," Cliff said. "It was the only way of breaking the hypnosis in time. You were drowning down there by your 'own' act, and there was no time to chase him and force him at gun-point to release his control, or whatever it is they do. We only found out about the anchor after we'd located you—"

A figure was coming back toward us from the glow, which was dwindling down now. It was the deputy. He said, "Nothing left now; I wet it down all I could to keep it from kindling the trees."

"Let's get back to the house," Cliff said. "The kid's all goose-pimples."

We went back and I got very soused on my third of the bottle. I couldn't even seem to do that properly. They let me sleep it off there, the four of us spent the night right there where we were. I found out later it was Fleming's own bed I'd occupied, but at the time I wouldn't have cared if it was the mirror-closet itself, with Ayers' body still in it.

In the morning Cliff came in and had a talk with me before the other two were up. I knew where I was going to have to go with him in a little while, but I didn't mind so much any more.

I said, "Did that help any, what I did last night? Did it do any good?"

"Sure," he said. "It was the works; it was what I wanted, had to have. What d'you suppose I was doing around here all day yesterday, before he got back? Why d'you suppose I warned you to make him stay right there in the alcove with you, not let the conversation drift outside? I had it all wired up, we listened in on the whole thing. The three of us were down in the basement, taking it all down. We've got the whole thing down on record now. I'd emptied that gun I gave you, and I figured he'd be too smart to do anything to you right here in his own house. Only, he got you out and into his car too quick, before we had a chance to stop him. We darned near lost you. We turned back after one false start toward the city, and a truckman told us he'd glimpsed a car in the distance tearing down the lake road. That gave us the answer.

"We wouldn't even have been able to hold the 'suicide' against him. You did all that yourself, you know, even to shackling your foot to that boat-anchor and dropping it over ahead of you. A person who is afraid of the jump into water but determined to go through with it might have taken such a precaution as that.

"I had a hunch it was hypnosis the minute you told me that candle incident. But how was I going to prove it? So much of that stuff is fake that most people don't want to believe in it. Now I've got two other police-officers, beside myself, who saw—or rather *heard*—the thing happen all over again. And that's going to carry weight that no coroner's jury will dare disregard.

"You were in a state of hypnosis when you committed this crime, that's the whole point. In other words, you were as unresponsible, as inanimate, as insensible, as the knife or club that a murderer wields to accomplish his deed. You were simply the weapon in the actual murderer's hands. Your own mind wasn't functioning, you had no mind. Two bodies were being directed by one mind. His." He stopped and looked at me. "Does that scare you?"

"Oh boy." I puffed out my cheeks.

"It would me too. I'd better begin at the beginning. Joel Fleming used to be a professional hypnotist in vaudeville years ago. I found enough scrapbooks, old theater-programs, and whatnot in trunks here in this house to testify to that. Stage-name 'Dr. Mephisto.' He undoubtedly possesses a gift of hypnotic control—over certain subjects. (With my wife Lil, for instance, I'm afraid he'd come a complete cropper—and even wind up helping her dry the dishes.)"

He was trying to cheer me up: I grinned appreciatively.

He went on, more seriously: "But there is such a thing, you know, it's not all bunk by any means. Only, certain types of people are more easily influenced than others. Well, he got out of vaudeville years ago while the getting out was still good, and he went into another line of business entirely, which doesn't need to concern us here, and he made good dough. Then, like they all do, he made the mistake of marrying someone years younger than him, a hat-check girl he met at a nightclub. It wasn't only that she married him simply for his money and to be able to quit handling people's sweat bands at four bits a throw; she was already the sweetie of a convict named Dan Ayers, who was doing time just then for embezzlement. You get the idea, don't you? Ayers got out, found a ready-made situation crying to be profited by—so he profited by it. He cultivated Fleming, got in solid with him; he didn't have to get in solid with Dorothy, he was already.

"All right. Fleming did make these trips to South America, all but the last time. It's obvious that he found out what was going on quite some time back, somewhere in between the last real trip he made and the fake one just now. It's equally obvious that he brooded and he planned revenge. They talk about a woman scorned. There's nothing more dangerous than a middle-aged husband who finds himself betrayed by a younger wife. It wasn't just a case of marital disloyalty involved, either; he found out they were planning to make off with all his available funds and securities the next time he was away, just strip him clean and goodbye. You notice he didn't entrust her with the combination of that safe here in the house.

"That's the basic situation. All that we've got to go on is just conjecture. The three principals are dead now and can't give evidence. I'm not trying to defend Fleming, but there is something to be said for his doing what he did. It turned him into a demon. He wanted Ayers dead, and he wanted Dorothy dead, too—now. But he picked a low, lousy way of effecting his purpose. He wasn't going to endanger himself, risk his own security. No, he started off for 'South America,' dropped from sight, holed-up in a rooming-house in the city under the name of Burg and picked an innocent kid, who had never done him any harm, who had just as much right as he had to life and the pursuit of happiness, to do his murdering for him.

"He tested you out, saw that you were a suitable subject, and—well, the rest we got over the dictaphone last night. To give him his due, he wasn't deliberately trying to have you apprehended for the crime either. He would have been just as satisfied if you were never caught yourself.

"But the point was, whatever clues came into the possession of the police pointing at the killer, would point at you, not him. He had provided himself with a buffer; he would always be one step removed from the crime. If they ever caught the man the clues pointed to, if they ever caught the actual killer, it would always be *you*, not him. It was a lot safer than just hiring a professional killer, in full possession of his faculties; it removed all danger of eventual betrayal and implication.

"True, he had to drive you up there, because you don't drive. Maybe he would have had to anyway; I don't know enough about hypnotism, I don't know if control can be effectively maintained over such a great distance. It was just as well he did, from his point of view. You lost the knife, only killed Ayers by a fluke in struggling with him, and Dorothy would have gotten away scotfree, if he hadn't been lurking outside to lend a hand himself. If she had lived to raise the alarm, you probably would have been nabbed then and there, before you could make a getaway in your dazed state; which would have brought the investigation back to the rooming-house too quickly to suit him, his presence there might have been revealed in spite of all his precautions. So he crushed her to death and whisked you back to immunity."

"How is it I remembered the whole murder-scene so vividly the next morning? Especially their *faces*—"

"His control wasn't one-hundred percent effective; I don't know if it ever is. The whole scene must have filtered dimly through to your conscious mind, remained in your memory the next morning after you woke up—just the way a dream does. And other particles, that remained imbedded in your subconscious at first, also came out later when they reproduced themselves in actuality: I mean your memory of the stone entrance lanterns, the cut-off, the spare doorkey, the hall light switch, etcetera. All that stuff is way over my head, I'm not qualified to pass expert judgment on it. I'd rather not even puzzle too hard about it; it scares me myself."

"Why did I seem to know her, when I didn't? Why was I so—sort of hurt, heartbroken, at the sight of her face?"

"Those were Fleming's thoughts, not yours, filtering through your mind. She was his wife, about to desert him, helping another man to rob him in his absence."

I was sitting down on the edge of the bed, lacing my shoes. That reminded me of something else. "It was drizzling in town that night when I went to bed—and the streets were only starting to dry off when I woke up the next morning. Yet the soles of my shoes were perfectly dry; how could they be, if I followed him even across the sidewalk to where he had a car waiting at the curb? And I doubt that he brought it up that close to the rooming-house entrance, for fear of being seen."

"I remember you mentioned that to me once before, and it's puzzled me too. The only possible explanation I can think of is this—and that's another thing we'll never know for sure, because that point didn't come up when he was giving himself away in the alcove last night: can you remember whether you got them off easily that night, when you were undressing in your own room, or as sometimes happens with nearly everyone, the laces got snarled, you couldn't undo the knot of one or both of them?"

I tried to remember. "I'm not sure—but I think a snag did form in the laces of one of them, so I pulled it off the way it was without really opening it properly."

"And in the morning?"

"They both seemed all right."

"That's what it was, then. You couldn't undo the knot in time while you were hurriedly getting dressed under his 'direction.' You followed him out and around to wherever the car was in your stocking feet, shoes probably shoved into the side-pockets of your coat. He got the knot out for you at his leisure in the car, before starting. It wasn't raining up here that night, and by the time you got back to town again the sidewalks were already starting to dry off, so your shoes stayed dry."

"But wouldn't my socks have gotten wet?"

"They probably did, but they'd dry off again quicker than shoes."

I was ready now. Waggoner and his deputy went over ahead without waiting for us. I guess he figured I'd rather just go alone with Cliff, and he wanted to make it as easy as he could for me. He said, "Bring the kid over whenever you're ready, Dodge."

Cliff and I started over by ourselves about half an hour later. I knew I'd have to go into a cell for awhile, but that didn't worry me any more; the shadows had lifted.

When we got out in front of the constabulary Cliff asked: "Are you scared, kid?"

I was a little, like when you're going in to have a tooth yanked or a broken arm reset. You know it's got to be done, and you'll feel a lot better after it's over. "Sort of," I admitted, forcing a smile.

"You'll be all right," he promised, giving me a heartening grip on the shoulder. "I'll be standing up right next to you the whole time. They probably won't even send it all the way through to prosecution."

We went in together.

JOHN D. MacDONALD
Death's Eye View

THE DAWN sky was silver grey, and he swam through the mist that drifted in patches over the warm water of the Atlantic. He had gotten the direction from the stars, but now they had faded. On the crest of the next swell he thrust himself upward, peering toward the coast, but he could see nothing. It was good that the water was so warm. Even so, he could sense the cramp that threatened his right calf. The girl was swimming ahead of him and to his right. He changed from slow crawl to sidestroke, both to rest his leg and to watch her more carefully. In the beginning her stroke had been crisp, but now he saw that she floundered a bit, her hands slapping limply into the water. It was in the lurid light of the burning cabin cruiser, an hour before, that he had helped her out of the sweater, the heavy tweed skirt that she had worn as protection against the night chill.

"Take a break," he called to her.

She rolled over onto her back and he moved up beside her to do the same. They lifted toward the sky, sank again, on the deep ground swell. She was breathing hard.

"Are we going the right way, Kelsy?" she asked. He knew that it had been a struggle for her to keep her voice calm.

"If we aren't, we'll make it to Casablanca, Dale. They can't drown us."

"My arms and legs have turned to concrete. I—I don't know how much longer I can go on."

"We were about six miles off shore. I think we've been going about an hour and a half. Two miles. With the current, I'd give us another mile. Halfway, Dale."

"God, if I hadn't come forward to help you with that light—"

"Don't think about it."

"We were supposed to be in the cabin, by the wheel, Kelsy. What was it?"

"Time bomb. No engine blows up that way. They can't kill us, baby."

She had a woman's buoyancy in the water. She floated high, back arched, the soaked nylon of her bra above the water. He had expected her to quit, long before this. He had wondered what he would do. Attempt to tow her. Support her in the water and hope to be sighted. He knew that he couldn't leave her to drown.

Her long hair, the precise shade of horse chestnuts he had collected as a kid, knocking them out of trees, cracking open the prickly green husk, was fanned out in the water. She was deeply tanned with the sun of Key West, the Miami interlude. She was a girl with an odd, almost Asiatic cast of features, but with eyes of Irish blue. Up until the very instant of the explosion, she had been his employer, and her faintly patronizing air had irritated him. Now it was no longer an employee-employer relationship. They were two people who wanted desperately one thing only—to survive.

"Do you think Steve was—"

"Mr. Markson never knew what hit him. Don't worry about that."

"I feel better now, Kelsy."

He tensed his right leg. The impending cramp was gone. "Okay. Look Dale. Try to ride a little lower in the water, and don't reach so far for your strokes. You'll last better. We've got all day."

She laughed, but he frowned as he heard the threat of hysteria. "Sure, Mr. McKewn, we've got all day."

Again they started. The pace settled into monotony. It was hypnotic. Stroke, stroke, breath. Stroke, stroke, breath. An eternity of effort. His arms quickly began to feel as though, around the wrists, he wore heavy lead bracelets. After a time you lost the feeling of being in water. It was as though you were suspended in grey space.

As he swam endlessly, he thought of the girl. He'd have to ask her why it had happened. She'd know. A peculiarly assorted pair, Mr. Steve Markson and Miss Dale Lamson. She'd done the hiring. Found him on the Miami docks, said that someone had told her about him. Would he take her cabin cruiser up to St. Augustine? Their man had quit. Kelsy McKewn didn't know yet why he'd agreed to do it. They were in a hurry. Weather reports good. Her cruiser, the *Mere Maid,* was a sturdy forty-footer, powered by a dependable high-speed diesel. A lot of boat. Weather reports good, the Atlantic flat in a warm May calm, so why mess with the inland waterway? Markson was a silent man . . . had been a silent man with a face like grey stone, a mouth like a coin slot.

The sound of strangled coughing brought him out of his reverie, his self-hypnosis. The girl was twenty feet away, slapping wildly at the water, her eyes wide with panic. He reached her as quickly as he could. She was beyond rational thought, and wrapped her arms around his neck, trying to climb up out of the water. He got the heel of his palm under her chin and broke the hold, slid around her and supported her, saying, "Easy, baby. Easy. I'll hold you up. Get your breath."

She coughed for a long time and then sighed. "Sorry, Kelsy. Got a mouthful and got panicky."

"Can you float for a while?"

"I don't know."

"Try it. Relax. There. That's the way." He watched her carefully. The fear had taken a lot out of her.

"Let me know when you're ready to go on, Dale."

"I can't go any farther," she said flatly.

"Giving up?"

"You can't challenge me that way, Kelsy. I just can't swim another stroke."

"I'm surprised you came this far."

She opened her eyes. "What do you mean by that?"

"I've seen your type in bad spots before."

"It won't work, Kelsy. I just can't lift my arms any more. So don't wear yourself out trying to needle me."

It had grown perceptibly lighter. He squinted toward the east, toward the rising sun that was beginning to cut the sea mist. He submarined to get enough impetus to surge waist high out of the water, timing the effort so that he would emerge at the high point of the swell. In the fraction of a second when he was at the highest, he saw the low dark line of coast against the horizon.

He moved back to her side. "So you can't swim any more, eh?"

"No."

"You quit in sight of land, eh?"

Her eyes opened wide. "You *can't* see land!"

"I just did. I'm not lying to give you courage, Dale. I saw land."

"My arms and legs, Kelsy. I—can't."

He took her upper arm between his hands and began kneading the muscles, much the way a second works on a fighter between rounds. He freshened the other arm, then prodded and dug at the long slim muscles of her calves and thighs, holding his breath when the effort sent him under water. Once she cried out at the force he was using.

"Now swim," he said grimly.

"Kelsy, I—"

"Swim, damn you! Roll over and swim."

She made one weary stroke and then another and another. "Good girl," he said.

"Please shut up," she gasped.

After a long time he let her rest, then drove her on again. The shoreline began to rise up out of the sea. At last he could see the tiny white flecks that were houses. They took the last rest within earshot of the distant mutter of surf on the packed beach. He could not orient himself. He knew that the cruiser had exploded a bit north of Fort Lauderdale, but he did not know how far north.

Then the waves began to curl and break with the friction drag of the bottom spilling them over, and they were being carried toward the beach.

After her solitary breakfast, as on every morning when the weather was not impossible, Mildred Coe walked down the rock stairs from her terrace to the wide expanse of beach. Of late she had the feeling that life was moving by her and she was caught in a black eddy, powerless to break free. She was a tall woman of thirty, with slightly gaunt cheeks, tiny weather wrinkles around her grey eyes, blonde hair bleached almost white by the sun. Her body was brown and trim and slim, and had changed in no measurement since she was twenty. She wore white tailored shorts and a sun bra. Her cigarettes and lighter were tucked in the waist band of the pocketless shorts and she walked with a free, swing stride on the packed sand where the tide had ebbed.

She knew that she was thinking of herself too often lately, and that such intensity of self-interest was morbid. Perhaps the small, efficient, almost bleak house was too lonely. It was on one of those oddly deserted sections of shore near Deerfield Beach where Route 1A1 curves briefly before returning to within sight of the sea.

She tried to measure the extent of the change in herself. At nineteen she had been Mildred Comer, a laughing girl, full of awkwardness and grace, a girl with too much money, and friends who had been made too easily, and popularity that she knew would never end. The world would always be right for Mildred Comer.

And then she had become Mrs. David Coe, bride, in 1941. A bad year for brides. A bad world for brides. One of Rommel's people had

smashed the skull of Lieutenant David Coe, and, in the same act had
forever broken the confidence of Mildred Coe, war widow.

Black grief had lasted for a year. And then she had an entanglement
which sickened her, because it was her first genuine taste of cheapness.
In flight she had moved from Miami to this place and had built this
house to suit her. It was not a gay house, and she had not been gay as
she planned it, superintended the construction.

Last year, out of restlessness, she had tried to pick up with old friends
once more. Old friends had lost their charm. Their worries seemed
petty, their lack of emotional security almost frightening. Loneliness
had done something to her, had made her think, had turned her into
an entirely new person, slow to smile, a woman with quiet eyes. She
quickly found that her married friends did not want her around. The
husbands seemed too anxious to delve beneath the lid of quietness and
find the hard vitality which they sensed was there.

And so she had retreated once more to the loneliness, knowing that
it was not enough, realizing for the first time that grief was no longer
poignant, was merely like an old dance card, a pressed flower, something to take out and look at sadly in idle moments. She knew that
David Coe would be ill at ease with the present Mildred Coe, that she
had outgrown the David she had married, that she now would most
probably find him to be unchallenging, a bit callow.

A few hundred yards up the beach gulls swooped and yelled in their
children's voices and minnows glinted silver in the early sun. She was
half tempted to go back and get her surf-casting rod and see if she could
get a strike from whatever was feeding on the school of minnows. But
the deep freeze was filled with the fileted slabs of striped bass from the
last good day of fishing. She stood shading her eyes, and then saw,
farther up the beach, the heads of two swimmers. She felt hard annoyance that they should come to use her beach.

As she stood watching, they came into shallow water. A man stood
up holding the wrist of a woman, and then fell forward like a tree going
down. The woman made feeble movements and the man floated motionless, face down, as a wave broke over him.

Mildred Coe sprinted down the beach line. She paused to kick off her
sandals, throw the cigarettes and lighter after them, then made a hard
running dive into the surf, came up swimming strongly, her head held
high, looking for the pair. The woman was crawling toward the beach.
She looked at Mildred out of a pretty face that was dead blank with
exhaustion. Mildred went by her, saw the man just as another wave
smothered him in white foam. She reached him, turned him over, got

a forearm across his throat and swam back to where she could stand in waist-deep water. The girl had reached the beach. She lay face down. Each breaking wave sent water swirling up as high as her waist. Mildred tugged the floating man along, noting absently that the girl wore underwear rather than a swimming suit.

Not until the man came aground did Mildred realize how big he was, and realize that he too wore underwear shorts. She got her hands under his arms and locked her fingers across his chest. She dug her heels into the wet sand and pulled back hard. She was able to make one big lurch at a time. His trailing feet channeled the sand. She got him up onto dry sand, dropped him, ran and got the girl's wrists, pulled her roughly up out of harm's way, then trotted back to the man. She rolled him over, put his head on his arm, put her fingers in his mouth and made certain that he hadn't swallowed his tongue. He was sun-blackened, and his hair was like a skull cap of copper wire. She knelt between his legs, came down firmly with the heels of her hands on his short ribs, holding it for the count, then snapping her hands off. His back was wide across the shoulders, tapering like a wedge to his waist. Even with the flaccidity of unconsciousness, his back looked hard and muscular. There was a three-cornered scar under his right shoulderblade.

Mildred maintained the rhythm of artificial respiration, waiting tensely for the first weak coughing that would announce the return of normal respiration.

The girl crawled up. Mildred glanced at her and saw that when she had dragged her up the beach, she unwittingly sandscuffed the skin from the side of her chin.

"Is he—dead?" the girl asked in a quiet voice.

"Ask me later," Mildred said breathlessly, acidly.

"What can I do?"

"Watch me so that—you can take over if—I should wear out."

The sun began to make its heat felt. Sweat began to run down Mildred's face, drip off onto the man.

"Swim far?" Mildred grunted.

"From six miles out. I couldn't have made it. He—made me do it."

"Good trick."

"I didn't even know he—was in trouble."

"He stood up and fell—probably from pure—exhaustion. Fainted."

"Our boat blew up."

"They have that habit."

The girl watched. Mildred's arms were aching. She estimated that she had been at it twenty minutes. She knew that soon the girl would have to take over, even though exhaustion had turned her grey under her tan. A rather pretty girl, that. Odd coloring. Like to paint her. Exotic setting. Drape that batique around her. Make a good model. Not a skin-and-bone clothes horse. Ripeness there. Damn the man! Is he going to die, after all this?

As though in answer to her unspoken question, the man's hand slowly tightened on the dry sand. He gave a strangled cough. She pressed down again and water gouted from his mouth, soaking immediately into the sand. She felt the lift of his first real intake of breath. She stopped the rhythm and watched him. He coughed wrenchingly and took another deep breath and another. Mildred moved sideways, sat down heavily, cradling her aching arms.

Muscles bunched in the man's back. He forced himself up onto hands and knees, lowered his head and vomited. He moved to one side, lay down and rolled over onto his back. The two women watched him.

"Kelsy," the girl said.

"Eh?"

"Kelsy, we made it! Six miles and we made it."

The man sat up. He pulled his knees up, locked his arms around his legs, his forehead on his knees. "Damn—I'm sick," he said.

"When you can walk, I have some brandy at the house," Mildred said.

He turned his head slowly and looked at her dully. Mildred felt an odd twinge as he looked into her eyes. His eyes were most odd. Brown, but not as soft as are most brown eyes.

"Who're you?" he asked.

"She hauled you out of the water, Kelsy. She's been giving you artificial respiration for hours!"

"Not hours," Mildred said. "Maybe a half hour." She got up and went over and cuffed into her sandals, picked up her cigarettes and lighter.

As Kelsy took the cigarette he looked up at her and said, "Thanks." He accented the word so that it included both the rescue and the cigarette.

"You're lucky I go for early walks on the beach," Mildred said.

The man smoked in silence. He flipped the cigarette out toward the water, then stood up with an obvious effort. Mildred came up beside him. "It's about a quarter of a mile. You can see it down there. Better lean on me."

Kelsy straightened his shoulders, flexed his arms, grinned. "I can make it." He glanced at the girl. "That's quite a beach costume, Dale."

She flushed under her tan. "With lace yet. Maybe I can borrow something from Mrs.—"

"Coe," Mildred said. "Mrs. Mildred Coe."

"I'm Dale Lamson and this is Kelsy McKewn, Mrs. Coe."

"I can lend you something to wear, Miss Lamson. A shame about your boat. Were you alone on it?"

The man said, "There was—"

"Just the two of us," the girl interrupted quickly. Mildred caught the odd, puzzled glance the man gave the girl.

The man asked where they had come ashore, and Mildred told him. They reached the foot of the rock steps that led thirty feet up the slanting cliff to the small cubical house atop the cliff. The man went up slowly. Mildred, behind him, saw how his long legs trembled as he took each step.

As they went into the small living room, Mildred said, "I have no phone. If you want me to drive into Boca Raton and phone for you—notify someone."

"That's very kind of you, but there's no hurry," the girl said. "No one was expecting us and, like a fool, I had no insurance on the cruiser. If we could just rest—"

"I'll show you to my room, Miss Lamson. Come along. Please wait, Mr. McKewn."

She took the girl down the short hallway. "The shower is in here. You'll want to get the salt out of your hair, I imagine. I'll get Mr. McKewn settled, then make your bed."

"We're causing you a great deal of trouble, Mrs. Coe."

Mildred looked at her for a few seconds. "As a matter of fact, I find I'm rather enjoying it. I was getting too set in my spinster habits, Miss Lamson."

McKewn was sitting on the couch, his eyes closed. Mildred went into the kitchen, poured two inches of brandy in a water glass, then shrugged and filled it to the half-way mark. She took it back to him, and had to speak quite loudly before he looked up at her. He took the glass and drained it, shuddered, handed it back. He followed her with silent docility back to the second bedroom. The bed was already made up. She mentioned the shower but he didn't seem to hear her. He tumbled across the bed and as she closed the door quietly she heard his first soft snore.

She made the bed as the shower roared. The girl came out in Mildred's flannel robe, drying her hair. Mildred indicated the brandy bottle and the clean glass. Miss Lamson poured a quarter tumbler, leaned against the bureau and sipped at it.

"I've laid out some things that ought to fit you," Mildred said.

"You're very kind."

"Sleep as long as you can."

An hour later Mildred looked in on the girl. She slept with her hands, palms together, under her cheek. Her mouth looked soft and childish. She looked very young.

Jubal Tabor sat behind the semi-circular desk in his tower office atop the Tabor Building in downtown Birmingham. The office measured precisely twenty by twenty. Set into each wall was a ten-foot bullseye window formed of one stationary sheet of polarized glass, a second disc of polarized glass which could be slowly revolved by a small electric motor concealed behind the paneling. The four control buttons for the windows were set into the edge of the desk. Jubal Tabor could adjust any window to any degree from complete opaqueness to crystal transparency.

The air conditioning equipment was nearly soundless. The private elevator, no larger than a phone booth, was rising slowly from the floor below where Tabor's two private secretaries worked at adjoining desks.

The tower office was furnished in warm, complimentary shades of brown. The desk top was clear. The inter-office communication equipment was built into the desk so that the speaker diaphragm was flush with the desk top. The only spots of color were the dark red French phone, the matching jackets of the hunters in the two wall prints.

With patience and care, a perfect replica of Jubal Tabor's face could be made. The only materials needed would be match sticks glued together for the delicate framework, grey paper glued over the framework, moistened so that it would draw tight, then allowed to dry. The naked skull was angular. The man was seventy years old. The face was seventy years old. The eyes had no age. The iris was the color of wet sand. The pupils were the shining black of the eyes of insects. He wore a brown tweed suit in a light-weight weave, a warm shade. His shirt was deep tan, almost matching his eyes. The tie was brown, so deep it was almost black.

He had the knack of stillness, of immobility like death.

The elevator came to a stop. Jubal Tabor looked at the light over the elevator door. The man was unarmed. If he were armed, the light would blink rapidly. He touched the button set into the arm of the chair and the elevator door slid back with a greased sound. The man came into the room, swinging heavy shoulders with over-confidence. He had a square, stupid face, animal shrewdness in his eyes. His loud and cheery greeting made Jubal Tabor wince. The man sat down.

"Those damn planes, Mr. Tabor. Always feel like I had a head full of cotton."

Jubal Tabor's voice was remote, dusty, frail. "Your report, Myron."

Myron made a circle of thumb and forefinger. "Silky. The guy brought the gimmick. He took it aboard the morning before they left. In a tool bag. Used a free inspection pitch. The pilot she hired, guy name of McKewn, fell for it. The guy reported back he stowed the gimmick in the bilge, taped it up where they wouldn't find it. He set it so the acid wouldn't eat through until maybe about four or five in the morning."

"What proof do you have that it worked?"

"I got a contact. A report come to the Coast Guard about a flash on the sky and something burning before dawn. As soon as I got that, I made my plane."

"And how about Mr. Cenelli?"

"Like a pie, Mr. Tabor. I think he was wise. He got a little nervous. It made it tougher. He wanted to stick around Collins Avenue—the bright lights. I finally got his drink loaded and used his car. Drove out through Coral Gables on Ninety-four and found the place I'd marked and put him and the car into the Tamiami Canal. If and when they find him, it'll be just another guy going too fast. He was a funny little guy. In love with his work, I guess. He kept patting that gimmick like it was a kitten when he showed it to me. Plastic explosive and napalm, he said. Made me nervous. I walked two miles from the place and got a truck ride back to town."

"Just the three of them were on the boat?"

"Uh-huh. That gal, that punk bodyguard of hers and the McKewn guy. They were running well out from the coast."

Jubal Tabor slid open a drawer of the desk. With dry, cool fingers he selected the three sealed stacks of bills. He put them on the desk where Myron could reach them. Myron picked them up. His face had gone pale. He riffled the edges of each stack, as though they were playing cards. He licked his lips, shoved the stacks into the inside pocket of his cream-colored jacket. They made an obvious bulge.

"Correct, Myron?" Jubal asked in his far-away voice.

Myron looked down at his hands. "As far as it goes."

"And what might that mean, Myron?"

The man was nervous. He kept wetting his lips. "I did a lot of thinking, Mr. Tabor. About Cenelli and—other things. I wrote it out pretty careful, and I got it in a safe place. With a—friend. Anything happens to me, Mr. Tabor, and it happens to you too. You get what I mean?"

"A very wise precaution, Myron."

"I was thinking that maybe you could keep on helping me out. I mean once this money is gone."

"I don't see why that wouldn't be fair, Myron."

The man's relief was evident. He gave Jubal a nervous smile. "And I thought you were going to be tough about it."

"I'm a reasonable man, Myron. I just wouldn't want you to get too greedy."

"I won't, Mr. Tabor. I sure won't."

"That's all, Myron."

"Sure," he said. "Sure."

He went into the elevator. The door slid shut. With a faint whine the elevator sank slowly down the shaft. After long minutes of thought, Jubal Tabor opened another drawer in his desk. He took out the long envelope on which was written, in Myron's cramped hand, "To Chief of Police, Birmingham." If Myron had not been a fool, he would have gone to a reputable lawyer with his document for safe-keeping. The thin-lipped blonde he had left it with had been loyal until the offer had reached half of what Jubal had been willing to pay. Then her eagerness to make a deal had been pathetic. Careful questioning had revealed that she had not opened the sealed envelope. She had agreed to tell Myron that it was still in safe-keeping. Myron was a fool. He had blundered in Key West. Only luck and Cenelli had made him successful at last.

Jubal Tabor opened the envelope and read the rambling, illiterate statement. He smiled thinly, tore it into neat strips and placed the strips in a large bronze ashtray. The smoke was whipped away by the air conditioning unit. He puddled the charred fragments with a letter opener.

He realized that he would never be able to get over a small, thin feeling of shame about Dale Lamson. A woman was not an entirely worthy opponent. Yet Dale, in her own way, had caused many troubles, and had been capable of causing many, many more.

The smog of industrial Birmingham screened out much of the afternoon sunshine. The old man sat motionless, thinking of the power, the warm heady sense of power that was so much better than any sun.

You did it the hard way. You started as an eight dollar a week clerk. You lived on five dollars and saved the three. Ten thousand dollars was the goal, and the money had to work for you. Ten thousand became fifty thousand. From nothing to ten was the hardest. From ten to fifty was easier. From fifty thousand to five hundred thousand was a bit easier. You learned that people were soft. You learned how to use emotional appeals. The showdowns came, one after another, and you were without mercy, because money knows no mercy. After you had the second million, you found out that you were a target. Money had made you too big. People wanted to knock you off the top of the hill. And so you hid behind the intricacies of interwebbed, interlocking corporations. You put a jungle growth between you and the world. No single guide, no matter how experienced, could track you back through that jungle. Firms of lawyers and accountants, working over a span of months, might unravel it all.

But there had to be a place where control could be exerted. Federal anti-trust legislation was rough on holding companies. But the reins had to be somewhere. Robat Enterprises, Incorporated. Tabor spelled backwards. A bit childish, but satisfying. Robat held shares of Swiss combines, reached deeply into the industrial heart of America, tapped gas fields, timber, oil, coal, steel, tin, rubber, plastics, electronics.

Never a straight controlling interest. That was both blatant and foolish. Always just the balance-of-power interest. The hidden hand. The light finger-touch on the scales. Robat incorporated as simply as possible, with just one thousand shares of voting stock.

The danger, the fear of the loss of power, had been with him for almost a year. Now, with the death of the girl, it was over. It was death and disappearance. Her will could not be probated for a long time. Delaying tactics would be helpful.

Fifty-five years of struggle for power, almost tipped over by a girl of twenty-three.

He could assess the exact limit of his own blame. He had tried to be too cautious, to hold personally too few shares of Robat. And the woman had blinded him, for a time.

In the beginning, his eldest son, Powell Tabor, had held three hundred shares. Nick, the younger son, held three hundred, and Jubal Tabor had held the remaining four hundred shares. Powell Tabor was amiable, ineffective. Nick was the hope of empire. Their mother died long ago.

When Jubal Tabor was forty-five, the woman had blinded him. She had come into his life like a flame racing through dry woods. A year later he had divorced her, having tired of her. Like a sentimental fool, he had settled one hundred shares of Robat on her. It had seemed safe.

Powell was amiable, and Nick was his right hand. The hundred shares
had been a sop to conscience, and an acknowledgment that money, as
such, was of no more use to Jubal Tabor—only the power was precious.
With Nick on his side, as Nick would always be, he controlled sixty
percent of Robat.

But Helen, after the divorce, married a great roaring man named
Lamson, and bore a daughter whom they named Dale. When the child
was ten, just old enough to have inherited Helen's heritage of hate for
Jubal Tabor, her parents died in an airline crash in Brazil, and she
inherited the hundred shares of Robat, to be held in trust for her until
she became of age.

Still there was no danger, no threatened loss of power. That same
year, when Jubal's only grandson was eleven, amiable Powell Tabor
was shot to death by the husband of a young actress in whom Powell
had taken more than a passing interest.

Three hundred shares held in trust for young Anthony Tabor, age
eleven. One hundred shares held in trust for young Dale, age ten.
Between them, forty percent. But Jubal and Nick held sixty percent,
and Nick was a carbon copy of Jubal. There was no danger. Nick was
Jubal's sole heir. Nick was empire. Immortality of a sort.

But Nick had fallen down and died one warm afternoon on the
corner of Third Avenue and Twentieth Street. He had never married.
He left everything he owned to his nephew, Anthony Tabor, son of
amiable Powell, with one exception. He split up his Robat stock. One
hundred and fifty-one shares to his father, Jubal. One hundred and
forty-nine to young Anthony. Anthony came of age six weeks later. A
young man owning four hundred and forty-nine shares of Robat. A
fortunate young man. Nick's cash position paid all the estate taxes. And
in its worst year, Robat had paid dividends in excess of ten thousand
dollars a share.

Jubal Tabor thus found himself in the very position in which he had
placed so many other people throughout the years. He owned four
hundred and fifty-one shares. Young Anthony owned four hundred and
forty-nine. And a girl named Dale Lamson owned the missing hundred
shares, would be able to vote them within a year.

Even so, there was no cause for worry. Jubal Tabor felt regret that
he had so completely ignored his grandson since the death of Powell.
He found, to his slight dismay, that young Anthony Tabor's primary
interest in life was ornithology. He put an end to that nonsense by
taking burly young Tony Tabor into the offices. Tony never had much
to say. He was intelligent. He learned to trace his way through the

corporate jungle with light-footed ease. He said yessir to his grandfather, and never gave away his thoughts.

When the girl, Dale Lamson, came of age, she directed that dividends no longer be sent to the bank which had acted as the executor for the estate of Helen Lamson, and asked that they be sent to a bank in Mexico City. Jubal Tabor made a request of an investigation agency. The report was completed in a month. Three pages of single-spaced typing. It was not what Jubal had hoped to read. Miss Lamson, in brief, appeared to be quite a do-gooder. Worked with the Friends Service Committee. Donated hospital facilities to isolated Indio villages. Actually went into the brush and gave shots. But two sides to her nature. Apparently gay, fun-loving, in fact, almost beautiful.

He filed the report and attempted to forget it. After all, the chances were exceedingly remote that Miss Dale Lamson and Anthony Tabor should ever meet. And if they did, it was most unlikely that they would join forces and, with the majority stock control, go against his wishes. Such a thing was unthinkable.

A year ago, when Dale was twenty-two and Tony was twenty-three, the fear started. That horrid fear of loss of power. Should that happen Jubal Tabor would become merely a dry-skinned old man with money. It was too late to start over, too late to fight.

Anthony went away for a week. Ostensibly, he was visiting a chemical plant in Gulfport, Texas.

He came back to the tower office. There seemed to be a new firmness about him, new force of decision. He was a thick-shouldered young man with dark curly hair, dark blue eyes.

He came to the point at once. "What do you think about beginning the liquidation of Robat holdings?"

"Should that concern me, Tony? It sounds like an exceptionally foolish idea."

Tony shrugged. "Most men your age have retired."

"What would you have me do? Sit in a park? Feed pigeons? Get a trained nurse?"

"What do you get out of it? You've got all the money you need. Liquidate, pay the capital gains and put the money into something you won't have to watch. Governments."

"It has taken me over fifty years to build this and—"

"And what have you got? You can play checkers with stock issues, push a few people around."

"Is that all it means to you?"

And Tony had smiled. "It means even less than that, grandfather.

I'm twenty-three. I'm a millionaire. Isn't that supposed to be the great American dream? I can't contribute anything by adding to what I've already got. I'll help with the liquidation. When it's over, I'm going to finance expeditions, go on them myself. I can make some contribution to human knowledge."

"Bird watching," Jubal said with thin-lipped contempt.

Tony smiled and shrugged. "Call it that if you want."

Jubal gingerly played his hole card. "Possibly you forget that I'm still in a position to make all Robat decisions, Tony."

Tony stood up. "Are you? I wonder. I'll draw up a tentative liquidation schedule."

"Wait, my boy. Look at my side of it for a moment." Jubal realized with disgust that he was going to plead. "This is my life, Tony. Without this, I'd die."

"I doubt that, grandfather."

"I need all this to keep me busy."

"You need it to make you feel like a big shot, grandfather. You like to push people around. You always have. Have you ever wondered if this power and influence business isn't just a little bit psychopathic?"

"Who has been influencing you, Tony? It's my dream to turn all of this over to you intact. You can be the—"

"Sorry, grandfather. Not interested. I'll have that liquidation schedule in a week. I think foreign interests should logically go first."

Three days later a small grey man put the report on Jubal's desk. Anthony Tabor had picked up a *turista* card and flown from San Antonio to Mexico City. He had taken a suite at the Del Prado. There he had been visited by Miss Dale Lamson. They had remained in Mr. Tabor's suite for nearly five hours. At the end of that time, they had gone to dinner at Jena, then returned to the hotel. Miss Lamson had left the hotel at one A.M., and Mr. Tabor had flown back to Texas on the early morning plane.

The next assigned task was more difficult. The agency man had a great deal of difficulty arranging an introduction to Miss Lamson, and considerably more difficulty in obtaining her confidence. He was unable to achieve any closeness to the young lady.

His written report was to the point.

Subject hates Jubal Tabor. Feels mother had a raw deal. Has guilt about money indirectly from Tabor, hence charity efforts. Well-versed, thru Anthony Tabor, on all Tabor operations. Feels old man's power and influence should be wiped out, for good of society or something. Fond of Anthony Tabor. Possibility of weakness there. Unable to ascertain. Cognizant of power of combined stock holdings. Believed to be constantly in touch with Anthony Tabor. No chance of buying her shares. From hint, believe her will leaves shares to hospital foundation. Unable to question closely without alerting subject. Subject plans new projects in Cuba starting this year.

Jubal Tabor was able to use delaying tactics. Liquidation was an easy word to use, but the corporations were formed like those carved Chinese spheres of ivory, one within the other, all as delicate as lace.

Anthony Tabor had become discomfortingly familiar with all Robat holdings and operations, and Jubal had to use all his skill, all his knowledge to prevent key holdings from being changed to the less satisfactory cash. It was a master game of chess, where Jubal reluctantly let one piece go in order to reinforce his position on another part of the board. The Belgian aircraft works went. A substantial holding in Canadian pulp mills went.

For a time Jubal believed that he could delay indefinitely, until Anthony lost patience and went his own way, leaving Robat intact. But as his moves grew more subtle, so did Anthony. The day, eight months after the declaration of battle, that Anthony forced through the relinquishing of Robat's hold on a promising natural gas field, Jubal knew that he must either admit eventual defeat, or take some step that would be outside the law. To harm his own flesh and blood was unthinkable. That left the girl. He had a file of pictures of her, pictures taken by the concealed cameras of the investigation agency. He had to admit that she was beautiful, as beautiful as Helen had been. Dale, climbing out of a taxi, long-legged, imperious. Dale, striding into a shop.

He called off any further investigation effort, severed all connections with the firm he had used on so many matters over so many years. One of the owners of the firm called on him, asked if he had been dissatisfied. Jubal stated mildly that he was in the process of liquidating his interests and retiring.

Myron was rather difficult to locate, to contact. He was on a plane of existence foreign to Jubal Tabor. Myron was a man hungry for money. His manners offended Jubal. But he understood almost at once.

"This girl, you want her rubbed out in such a way there's no body, so it goes as a disappearance."

Jubal had swallowed his distaste. "Precisely. If it is done the way I wish it to be done, you will receive thirty thousand dollars, plus all expenses. If you fail, you will get nothing."

Dale Lamson should have died in Key West. Myron had been a bit clumsy. She was saved by a fluke. And she was alerted. Her employee, Raymond Perez, had brought the *Mere Maid* from Havana to Key West, with Dale and a woman guest. The attempt had alerted Dale to the possibility of danger. The woman guest had been frightened away, as well as Perez. Perez consented to bring the *Mere Maid* to Miami before quitting. In Miami Dale hired Steve Markson, bodyguard of the Chicago school, found Kelsy McKewn to run the *Mere Maid*. Myron had followed them, contacted Cenelli, reported to Jubal, received permission, and planted the time bomb aboard the *Mere Maid*.

The shadows of dusk began to move slowly across Birmingham. Jubal Tabor sat at his desk, and thought of self-justification. The girl had come closer to blocking him than anyone ever had. So he was justified in using harsher methods than ever before.

He was an expert at covering up the moves he made in any game. Now his only connection with Dale's death was through Myron. And Myron's thin-lipped, greedy blonde. It was like a package that had been tied firmly, but with two lengths of string dangling from the knot. Once those two dangling bits had been clipped off, close to the knot, it would be over. Murder, and one might as well face the word, had slightly different characteristics than financial manipulation. You cannot hire B to kill A, and C to kill B, and D to kill C ad infinitum. Sooner or later you must step into line yourself and carefully remove the last one in the chain so that there is no possibility of either blackmail or detection. The girl knew nothing damaging. Were it to be staged in such a way that it appeared that the blonde, Beryl Kesh, had killed Myron. . . .

As the tower office steadily grew darker, Jubal set his mind to the problem, attempting to devise a plan that would not be beyond the abilities of his frail body.

Kelsy McKewn awoke abruptly, thinking on the moment of awakening that he was still in Al's apartment in Miami, then remembering, with the help of aching muscles, the flaring, full-throated grunt of the explosion that had hurled him and the girl off the bow of the cabin cruiser into the water. He glanced at his ruined wrist watch. It had stopped at five minutes to five. The small room was bright and cheerful. He sat up with an effort. Salt crust had stiffened the stubble on his chin and made a wiry sound under his fingers. He lay propped up on one elbow for a time, thinking idly of how many rooms he had awakened in over thirty years. Maybe it would be nice always to awaken in the same room. He had tried it, for a time, until restlessness became a disease, until he wanted to beat his head on the wall. There had been jobs, very good jobs, in fact. The pained expression on the face of management when he said he was moving along had become quite familiar. Owning the charter boat had been an attempt to find a compromise. But he had run into chronic engine trouble, poor fishing, haughty customers. And one day he had knocked a fat young banker from Gettysburg over the side, and that was the end of that. He had received fifty-three dollars for his equity in the *Howdy*.

The girl who had hired him had puzzled him. She seemed tense, nervous. The man with her, Markson, had been as demonstrative as a stone. There was a short in one of the running lights. He had told Markson to take the wheel. He had gone forward, onto the bow. The girl had come with him to hold the flash at the base of the light while he took a look at the wiring. Pure luck. In the water he had ripped off his sneakers, torn his shirt from his shoulders, eeled out of the jeans, then helped the girl. The *Mere Maid* had burned to the waterline with frightening speed. No life preserver had been hurled free. Some fragments of the cabin roof floated nearby, too small for support.

With a final bubbling hiss, the *Mere Maid* had gone under, leaving them alone on the slow dark breast of the sea.

There was a brand new T-shirt, khaki trousers, beach sandals, boxer shorts on the chair just inside the door. Kelsy showered, pulled on the clothes. The trousers were two inches too short but otherwise everything fitted. He wrinkled his nose. He could smell coffee. His stomach gave a convulsive hunger-lurch. He went out into the kitchen. The blonde woman was frowning down into the well of the deep freeze.

The sun was low in the west outside the kitchen windows. She gave him a quick smile. "Feel better?"

"Much. Thanks for the clothes."

"Don't mention it. I've got a problem here. How about steaks?"

"Don't say that word out loud. Is Dale up?"

"I heard her a few moments ago. She's in the process. Steaks it is, then."

"I've forgotten your name. I'm sorry."

"Mildred Coe, Mr. McKewn."

"Okay, Mildred. I'm Kelsy. What can I do to help?"

"Set the table. Everything we need is in that cupboard over there. Is your stomach too empty for cocktails?"

"Never."

In a few minutes, Dale Lamson came out. She looked fresh, rested. She wore a yellow two-piece sun dress, and her mahogany hair was tied with a bit of yellow yarn.

"Here is a girl," she said, "who can eat raw driftwood right off the beach."

"How do you feel, Dale?" Kelsy asked.

"Like somebody threaded my muscles with hot wire. Otherwise okay. Mrs. Coe, you are my friend for life."

"Thank you, Dale, and do call me Mildred. Would you like to use a phone now?"

"Not quite yet, thank you."

Kelsy concealed his frown by turning toward the table. Damn the girl, anyway. A man had died. The cabin cruiser hadn't blown itself up. A report ought to be made, and soon. He decided he'd give her until after dinner, and then start swinging a little weight around.

The Scotch old-fashioneds were crisp and good. As the steaks sputtered under the broiler, Kelsy sat on the couch and felt the glow spread through him. Dale came in and asked in a low tone, "Did you lose much?"

Her eyes were worried. "All my wordly possessions and my entire savings," he said.

Her eyes turned cool. "Just estimate the total valuation, please."

"Let me see. Say about forty bucks for clothes, and about thirty dollars in cash, and one wrist watch at about fifty, which I think is kaput. A hundred and twenty bucks ought to do it."

She smiled at him. "You fool. I thought it was going to be a holdup."

"That's the trouble with you moneyed types. Everybody is supposed to be out to gouge you."

"As soon as I get hold of a check book, I'll give you a check for a thousand dollars, Kelsy."

"You'll give me a check for two hundred and twenty. One hundred on our agreement, and one twenty for what I lost."

"Don't be so darned stuffy!" she flared.

"Come and get it, people," Mildred called.

The meal was oddly gay. They could have been a pair of welcome house guests. The steaks were wonderful, the salad special. Kelsy and Dale ate like wolves. Dale helped Mildred clear the table, then they came back to laze over the second cup of coffee while the dishwasher churned softly.

After a comfortable silence, Mildred said, "Don't you think you ought to let someone know you're all right?"

Kelsy saw Dale's knuckle whiten where she grasped the coffee cup. "There's plenty of time," she said casually.

"I believe the Coast Guard would like to know," Kelsy said firmly. "Probably somebody saw the flash and heard the noise. They'll be wondering."

"I'll phone later," Dale said, frowning down at the cup.

"You phone now or I'll phone now," Kelsy said, "that is, if Mildred is willing to drive us to Boca Raton."

"Any time," Mildred said.

Dale looked at Kelsy as he stood up. There was a pleading look in her eyes. "Would—could you take a short walk on the beach with me, Kelsy? Then we can go and make phone calls."

"If you'd like," he said, with no special show of interest.

They went down the rock steps to the beach. There was no moon. The phosphorescence in the waves gave the illusion of moonlight, and the sand glowed with the faint starlight. The night was warm, almost windless.

She walked along, her head down, her hands in the side pockets of the yellow skirt.

He waited until he grew impatient. "Well?" he said.

"Let's sit down up there, Kelsy." She led the way. She sat, her legs straight and ankles crossed, her arms braced against the sand. He squatted on his heels beside her.

"Do you have a family, Kelsy?"

"You mean is somebody worried if I don't show up? No."

"I have no family either. I'm quite alone."

"Look, a man was blown to bits out there and—"

"Please, Kelsy. Let me develop this my own way. I need help, badly. I'll tell you why in a moment. Would you be loyal to me, if I employed you?"

"When I think the stand you take is right, I'll be loyal. But you can't pay me enough to have me go along with anything that—"

"That's what I wanted you to say. For a person in my position, so few people can really be trusted. You know, of course, that the boat was blown up in an attempt to kill me."

"You sound remarkably calm about it, my friend."

"The first attempt was made in Key West. It failed. I've had a lot of time to think about why and sort of—adjust myself to the idea. The why is easy. I'll explain that to you. But first, understand my point of view. The first attempt failed. The second attempt failed. The third attempt might succeed, and isn't it better to have the person who did it think that the second attempt succeeded?"

"That's a point. Not much of a one, but a point."

"Helping me might be very dangerous. I'll pay all your expenses, pay you a thousand dollars for taking on the job, two hundred a week, and five thousand bonus when I don't need you any longer."

"You don't care how you throw it around, do you? What makes you think I can handle myself in a dangerous situation?"

"Oh, Kelsy! Remember me? I'm the girl who couldn't swim six miles, and did."

"Guns make me nervous. They make me want to hide under a bed. But you're still not making sense. Somebody tried to kill you. They missed, but they did kill Markson. There are laws against that, you know. So let's pin that murder on Mr. X and get out from under."

"It isn't that simple."

Kelsy eased himself down onto the sand. "I'm willing to be convinced."

He watched her profile as she talked. She looked out toward the sea. Never once did she turn and look at him. At first he became more and more incredulous at this talk of millions, of an old man's power threatened, and then incredulity began slowly to subside, as she added more and more facts, more and more details which would have been extremely hard to manufacture. In the end, he believed her utterly. Her voice stopped and there was only the soft wash of the sea.

"Holy kimono!" he said softly. "That old guy. That Jubal. What does he think? The laws don't fit him?"

"Maybe that's it, Kelsy. He was my mother's first husband. She hated him. The way I hate him now. But even as I hate him, I can still understand him. You see how hopeless it would be to attempt to make a big fuss. We don't know who put the bomb in the boat. If we did know, can you imagine trying to track it back to Jubal Tabor?"

"This holding company, this Robat, that's what you and that Anthony can take away from him, eh?"

"Not without a terrible fight, a fight that would drag through the courts until I'm a grey old lady. He thinks I'm dead. I know that. He thinks he has won. The only weapon we have to use against him is the fact that I am alive. And that has to be a weapon of surprise. Now do you see why I want none of this to get into the papers?"

"Yes, I can see, Dale."

"And—you'll help me?"

She turned toward him as she spoke. "Any way I can, Dale," he said.

She turned and half fell against his chest. He knew at once that it was the reaction from the fear of death. She had held it in until now. The new knowledge of having someone on her side had brought the release of tension. He lay back on the sand and held her closely through the storm of tears, through the sobs that seemed torn out of her. A girl who had been alone too much, who had been driven by money-guilt and by hate, and who now had felt the taste of death.

The interval between the sobs grew greater. She was sprawled with her cheek against his chest, the back of her hair barely touching his chin, his left arm around her.

"Messy," she muttered, struggling to sit up.

She propped herself on her elbows and looked at him. "Forgive the fuss," she said.

"No fuss, Dale."

"You're very patient, aren't you?"

He didn't answer. Her head was above his, blotting out a thousand stars. He put his right hand at the nape of her neck and brought her head down slowly, brought her lips down to his. Her kiss was warm—reluctant and then suddenly greedy with an emphasis that dizzied him. She spun quickly away to sit at a yard's distance and he could see her wipe her mouth with the back of her hand.

"That won't do at all," she said in a low voice.

"An improper employer-employee relationship, baby?"

"Oh, shut up!"

"Yes, ma'm!"

"It's just from being scared and being lonely, that's all."

She stood up. He linked his hands behind his head. She looked very tall against the sky. He said, "Any further instructions, ma'm?"

"You—you—" She kicked sand at him and ran fleetly down the beach.

Kelsy grinned up at the stars for a while, then slowly got to his feet and ambled after her. She was sitting up on the bottom rock step. She stood up as he walked up to her. She put her palms flat against his cheeks and kissed him soundly.

"That's just to show you that it doesn't mean a thing, Kelsy."

"I'm shore happy to know that, ma'm. I shorely am."

"Now stop being a fool. You have to make a phone call. To Anthony."

The girl had a thin, vital face, a mouth with expressiveness, mobility. Her pale silver-blonde hair was worn so long that in moments of confusion or emotional stress she could catch a strand of it between her teeth. It was a habit she was trying to break. Though she always looked scrubbed and shining, her clothes looked as though they had spent weeks wedged into a corner of the closet. She was always buttoned wrong, or had laces undone or zippers unfastened. She lost gloves and lighters, and never could find where she'd parked her car, and kept forgetting the names of her best friends whenever faced with an introduction. She had a passionate awareness that at first baffled and then obscurely frightened most men. Her name was Cassy Ling and she was a talented sculptor and she loved Anthony Tabor with all her heart. She refused to marry him, and didn't know why. She was child and woman and houri, and made his life alternately heaven and hell.

She sat on the deep window seat of Tony's apartment and watched him as he paced. She realized that she was nibbling on a strand of her hair, and she swung it away with a quick impatient movement of her head. She liked the strength in his face. The old man, Jubal, had strength, but of a different sort. She wanted to go up to him and make him hold still while, with her eyes shut, she traced the planes and angles of his face with thumbs and fingertips, retaining the memory so that she could reproduce that same expression in clay.

"Walk, walk, walk," she said.

He stopped and faced her. "I told you the old man knows something I don't. Today I took him the documents. He had agreed. I needed his signature. He looked like an owl full of mouse meat. He put them aside and said he'd think about it. I told him he'd already agreed. He said that maybe he'd change his mind. Dammit, he knows that Dale and I can force him, if we have to. What's the matter with that operator?"

He reached the phone in long strides, got hold of the long distance operator. "How about my call to Miss Dale Lamson in Miami?"

"We have been unable to reach your party."

"What does the hotel say?"

"She has checked out, sir. She checked out yesterday morning."

"Why didn't you tell me that before? How about St. Augustine?"

"Do you know which hotel in St. Augustine, sir?"

"Try them all, will you?"

"It will take some time, sir."

"I'll be right here." He hung up and turned toward Cassy. "She promised to phone me from Palm Beach today. So she's probably en route in that fool boat of hers."

"Then why worry?"

"I think she may have flown up to St. Augustine and had someone bring the boat up. It's just a hunch. I don't like the way Jubal acts. Maybe she sold out to him."

"From what you've told me about her, Tony, that doesn't sound very reasonable." She patted the window seat beside her. "Come here, now. Be good."

He sighed as he sat down. She wrapped thin eager arms around his neck, rubbed her lips slowly back and forth across his. "Hey," he said.

"Be good. Be my boy. Now tell me what you are really afraid of."

He let the silence grow. "That he's killed her, somehow—"

The phone rang. Tony ran to the phone.

A man's voice. "Hello, Tabor?"

"Who is this calling, please?"

"Never mind that. I've got a message for you. From Dale. She says it is very important. She says for you to act as though she is dead. Understand?"

"I—I don't know."

"She's okay. But she has to lie low. Pretend the old man has won. Stick around. Put an agency on it, without the old man knowing. See if you can find out who he hired to kill her. A time bomb was planted on the boat. Can you do that?"

Tony had regained control. "I can do that. I see—how do I contact her?"

"You don't. She'll contact you, Tabor. She wants five thousand in bills no larger than fifties. She's afraid checking accounts will be watched, just in case. Send them registered, general delivery, to Kelsy McKewn. M-c-K-e-w-n, at Lake Worth."

"How do I know this isn't a fancy scheme to—"

"You don't."

"Why doesn't she talk to me?"

"She doesn't want you getting a long distance call from a female. Or mail from her either. She's taking a chance that this call will stay private. She figured you might think this was a fake. So she told me to tell you that at Jena you two played the match game for drinks. You had three scotch Manhattans and lost every round."

"Okay, McKewn. That's good enough identification. I'll mail the money in the morning."

The man on the other end hung up with a muttered, "Thanks."

Tony walked slowly over to Cassy and sat down. He told her what had happened. She clasped her hands and said, "Oh boy! Intrigue!"

There was an enormous sadness in Tony. He expressed it at last. "To know that the old man is unscrupulous is one thing. To know that he would kill is something else. And I've got his damn blood in my veins."

Cassy finally comforted him in her own way, and her way was like the taste of honey, and the lick of blue flame.

They had to tell Mildred Coe. Even as Mildred listened, she sensed the conflict within herself. The years of seclusion had made her fearful of any outside influence that might upset her careful days. Yet she hungered for life, and this story they told her was like a cool wind blowing through a smoke-filled room.

Afterwards, in the dusk of the third day they stayed with her, she and Dale walked far up the beach, while Kelsy was still gone on his trip to Lake Worth. Mildred sensed that there was something fine and strong about Dale, but through some compulsion the girl didn't understand, she had fallen into the habit of playing the part of a girl with too much money, too much time, and too little direction.

"What are you going to do?" Mildred asked her.

"Kelsy and I, we decided we must rely on the experts Tony can hire. We must assume that the people Jubal hired were clever enough to cover their tracks. You see, there's just one flaw. Kelsy and I didn't die. We can give evidence, you know. And the most important bit is that Kelsy can identify the man who came aboard and planted the bomb. He posed as a man from a boat inspection service. We'd like to wait here a few more days and then go to Birmingham secretly and get in touch with Tony and find out if they've been able to unravel anything."

"And if they haven't?"

"I'm going to have to face Jubal Tabor and tell him what I know and use that knowledge as a club."

"Doesn't that frighten you?"

"A great deal. You see, I've never met him. Mother destroyed her pictures of him. He avoids all publicity. I don't know what he looks like, except from Tony's description. We shouldn't have stepped in here to take advantage of your kindness, Mildred."

"It's a good thing, in a way."

"Mildred, maybe Tony and I made a bad decision, to fight the old man. It's like fighting—shadows."

"You have to do what you believe. Or run away from yourself," Mildred said softly, her voice barely audible above the soft surge and crash of the waves.

"Have you been running? I shouldn't have said that. Forgive me."

"It's all right. Running? Probably. I don't really know."

"Shall we go back? Kelsy should be back by now. It's funny, Mildred. I've known him such a short time. But it seems as though I've known him for years."

Beryl Kesh made certain the door was locked. Then she took the money and laid it out on her bed, bill by bill, matching the edges neatly. Each bill had such a nice haughty look. A big-numbered look. When they were all laid out, the double bed was almost covered. She went over the pattern and turned the ones that were out of line so that all the men on the money were looking the same way. The hell with Myron and his mysterious envelopes. That dried-up old man had made a nice trade. And if she was any judge, there was a lot more where this money came from. Funny how furtive and nervous the old man had been, licking his lips and looking over his shoulder all the time. Wouldn't it be nice to get the old guy on the string? But hard to do. She pouted. He had seemed so intent on that damn envelope he hadn't looked at her, really looked at her.

These old guys. Sometimes they could really go for a young blonde. She turned her back on the money, pulled up the straps of her slip and looked at herself in the mirror, arching her back, turning slowly from side to side.

"Not too bad, kid," she said softly. "Not bad at all. Too good for that Myron, that's for sure."

Take off a few pounds here and there. Not much. Just a few. This money would parlay into some fine clothes. Knock the old guy's eyes out. Hell, he already had the envelope. This new desire of his to see her must be because he'd taken a better look at her than she'd realized.

Time to give Myron the brush. Little Beryl was going up in the world, just when she'd about figured it was too late. The old guy had tossed the money at her like it was so much scrap paper. You could tell about a guy from the way he handled money. Now Myron, give him a big bill and he always had to pop it between his fingers.

Of course, if she started spending any of this, Myron would wonder where the money had come from. And no use cutting loose from Myron until the old man was firmly on the hook, flopping around like a fish. She gathered the bills up quickly, like busting up a game of solitaire. She stacked them neatly, tapped the bundle on the bureau to align the edges. A nice bunch of portraits of Mr. Grant. Enough for a Cad, or a couple of blue-white carats, or a coat you'd want to walk barefoot on.

His voice had been so wispy over the phone. Cold-blooded old fish.

But life stirring in there somewhere. "Miss Kesh? My dear, this is your friend who—ah—made the purchase the other day."

"Hello, mister! I certainly remember *you*."

"You're alone, my dear?"

"Myron isn't here, if that's what you mean. Say, he hasn't asked me whether I still got that letter tucked away anyplace."

"You know what to say if he does ask you?"

"Sure, mister."

"I want to—ah—have another talk with you, Miss Kesh. In private, of course. It's rather difficult to arrange."

"How about like last time? Same park bench? Same time?"

"You're very kind, my dear."

"It's a date, mister. I'll give Myron some song and dance."

She hummed softly as she put the money back in the hiding place. It was a cinch Myron would never find it—she had carefully cut an oval piece of white cardboard to fit down into a hat box. The money went into the false bottom. That had been where she had hidden the letter he had considered so important that his voice had trembled when he asked her to keep it for him and mail to the cops if he ever suddenly disappeared.

She wondered what she would wear to the ten o'clock date. Something conservative. The grey tropical suit, with the aqua scarf and shoes. No hat, of course. And plenty of the scent. Those old guys, they probably had weak noses.

At twenty minutes of ten, ready to leave, she walked into the small living room of the flat where Myron lay on the couch, a magazine propped on his stomach, a radio comedian blaring at him from the small red-carved, Chinese table model.

"Where the hell are you going, Beryl?"

"Out."

He sat up and tossed the magazine on the floor. "What do you mean, out?"

"You think you own me or something? Out, I said."

"Maybe you're going out and maybe you're not. I'll decide that, kid."

She sighed. "Okay, okay. Bonny asked me to stop over and see the pictures she took at Virginia Beach. So you got to get dull about it."

"You look pretty fancy to go see Bonny, kid."

She went over to him, manufacturing a smile. "Honey, you got no need to be jealous of me. No need at all. Hey, watch the lipstick."

He grinned at her, picked up the magazine and lay back again. "Don't be late, kid."

She walked down the street, striking the sidewalk hard with her high heels. Let Myron wait and see. He'd find out a thing or two.

She was at the small park at five of ten. A couple was on the bench she wanted. The other benches were full too. So she strolled slowly up and down the curving walk. As soon as a bench was free, she took it. She saw the old man approaching. He walked like somebody crossing thin ice. It seemed to take him forever to get to the bench. He sat down at a careful distance and she slid over nearer him.

"Good evening, my dear," he said in that far-off voice.

"Hi, mister. Warm, isn't it?"

"I don't feel the heat much these days."

"You slim fellas are lucky, you know. Me, I carry too much weight. I'm reducing, though."

He lowered his voice. "My dear, I was very disappointed in that envelope."

"I hope you don't want your dough back. Because I spent it already."

His laugh was like the sound of wind in dry leaves. "Oh, nothing like that, my dear. In fact, I'd like to give you more."

"No kidding!"

"Yes, I'm afraid that what I want he carries on his person, and guards very carefully. I don't want you to take any risks, of course."

"How much is it worth?"

"Three times what I gave you before."

She whistled softly. "Man, you must really want that whatzit!"

"This time, my dear, I want to make absolutely certain that I get what I'm after. Here is the plan. Is he home now?"

"Sure. He's there."

"Here is half the money. Put it in your purse, quickly."

She slid the thick stack into her bag, and her breath came fast. He continued. "I want you to go back there and fix him a drink. Put this powder in it. He won't be able to taste it. It will knock him out. Give him the drink at about eleven thirty. I'll be there at twelve to search him, get what I want and give you the rest of the money. Then I rather think it would be wise for you to pack up and leave. He'll be very angry when he realizes what has happened."

"Mmmmm," she said. "How long will he be out?"

"Oh, until morning."

"That'll give me time to pack and clear out. Mister, you got a deal."

"Let me in quickly when I knock."

"I'll do that."

"Run along now, my dear."

Beryl Kesh walked back to the apartment. It was quarter of eleven when she let herself in. The radio still blared. Myron had fallen asleep, the magazine on his stomach. He snored hoarsely. She stared down at him with distaste, snapped the radio off. He gave a gargantuan groan, knuckled his eyes, yawned and sat up.

"Back, heh? How's Bonny?"

"Fine and dandy. Lousy pictures, though."

She walked into the kitchen, her mind racing. Trying to get the old guy on the string was a long shot. There was a better deal. Knock Myron out earlier than planned and grab the thing the old guy wanted. She'd probably recognize it when she saw it, she decided. If he was willing to pay that much for it, he'd pay more. Plenty more. And with Myron all through as a meal ticket, there would have to be plenty more.

Myron stared at her rigid back through the kitchen door. He frowned. There was something on her mind, if it could charitably be called that. Tiny warning bells rang in the back of his mind. Never trust that kind of a blonde.

He called to her. "Got that letter I give you in a safe place?"

"Sure, honey," she said, without turning.

"Let's see it, then."

"Okay. I'll get it in a minute. I got it hid good. Want a drink, honey?"

"A nightcap. Okay."

She moved out of sight. Myron had his shoes off. He drifted across the rug, as noiseless as a shadow. The counter extended behind the door. The door opened into the kitchen. He put his eye to the crack and saw her drop ice into the two glasses, splash in the liquor. She opened her purse, took out a small packet, dumped a white powder into one of the glasses. As she took the glasses over toward the sink, Myron hurried noiselessly back to the couch. He smiled up at her as she gave him his drink. He watched her carefully. Her smile was bland, but there was a pinched white look around her nostrils.

He pulled her down beside him. "Set that drink down, baby," he whispered into her hair. She put the drink on the floor and he put his down too. As he kissed her, he moved his stockinged foot with infinite caution. He pushed his drink over, hooked his foot around the base of her glass, pulled her drink over on his side.

He bent over and picked up his glass. "Salud, kid," he said.

"Skoal, baby," she said.

He took a long pull at his drink. She took two deep swallows. He finished his drink and set the glass aside. They sat and looked at each other. Suddenly her fingers opened. The glass bounded off her knee and fell to the floor. He laughed at her. She gasped deeply, gutturally and her glazed eyes went wide. Laughter died on his lips. As she doubled, he saw the pupils of her eyes roll up out of sight. Her fingers clawed at the couch upholstery. Her legs twisted, flexed. Suddenly she went utterly limp. She fell forward off the couch. Her head struck the rug and slid forward until she was flat on her face. He could see her cheek. It was blue as a summer sky.

Myron stood up. He balanced on the balls of his feet, knees and elbows flexed. He felt gingerly for her pulse. She was very thoroughly dead. He checked to see that the door was locked, the blinds shut.

It took him until two in the morning before he found the cache of money. When he found it he became fairly certain that the envelope was gone. He was intensely afraid, but at the same time grimly amused. Old Tabor had made his try. A very nice try, but an unsuccessful one. He sat down and stared at her body and tried to plan his next step.

Anthony Tabor, with a quiet young man named Rodgers sitting beside him, turned into the motor court on the outskirts of Birmingham at ten in the morning. Dale, in grey slacks and a white shirt, stood in the doorway of number nine. She smiled as he got out of the car and walked toward her, and he saw that she showed evidences of strain. A husky man with copper-colored hair came out of number eight with a tall tanned blonde woman and awaited introductions.

After they were all introduced, the five of them went into number nine. Kelsy McKewn stood and leaned against the frame of the bathroom door. Mr. Rodgers, briefcase on his knees, was in one of the two chairs, Mrs. Coe in the other. Anthony sat beside Dale on the bed.

Dale, smiling around, said, "Before we get started, let me explain that Mr. McKewn was the man I hired to pilot the *Mere Maid* up to St. Augustine. He managed to get me to dry land. Mrs. Coe took care of us. We told her the story and she drove us up here. It's only fair that she should be in on it all the way."

"Of course," Anthony murmured. "Mr. Rodgers represents the firm I employed to make the investigation you suggested, Dale. If you would proceed, Mr. Rodgers."

The quiet young man glanced around at them. "Let me say that this is an exceedingly delicate situation. Ever since I have been connected with the firm we have made it a policy never to withhold any information of criminal activities from the police. In this case we have violated our own policy. Now I believe that you, Miss Lamson, and you, Mr.

McKewn, can testify to the death of one Stephen Markson. This death has not been reported to the authorities."

"He's dead, all right," Kelsy said.

Mr. Rodgers continued, "Our first task was to find Mr. Jubal Tabor's contact with someone capable of carrying out such an assignment. One of our most—ah—attractive young men succeeded in winning the confidence of the receptionist at the Tabor offices. She was taken to Police Headquarters. There she identified one Paul Myron as having gone to see Mr. Tabor several times, using Mr. Tabor's private entrance. Paul Myron has a criminal record, and has been convicted twice for minor crimes, held often on suspicion of crimes more serious. However, there is no information to indicate that he has any knowledge of, or experience with, explosives."

Rodgers unbuckled his briefcase. "I have been able to borrow these photographs. I wonder if you could identify any one of them as being someone you saw in the vicinity of the boat, prior to leaving Miami."

Kelsy walked over and took the pictures. He leafed through them quickly, paused on the fourth, put it on top of the stack and returned the stack to Rodgers. "That one. He said he was from a free inspection service."

"Michael Cenelli," Rodgers said. "Excellent! We can prove that Myron and Cenelli know each other. Cenelli learned to handle dynamite on construction jobs years ago and went on from there. We'll try to have him picked up. Now to go on. Mr. Anthony Tabor already has my report in writing. He asked me to give it to you verbally. Three evenings ago we had, of course, operatives watching both Paul Myron and Mr. Jubal Tabor, in hopes of further proving the association. The woman living with Paul Myron met Mr. Jubal Tabor that night. They talked for fifteen minutes. Something was passed by Jubal Tabor to the woman. A third man was detailed to follow her. She returned to the apartment. Jubal Tabor returned to his home.

"Lights remained on in the apartment until three in the morning. Shortly after they went out, Mr. Paul Myron was observed carrying a heavy object out of the rear of the flat into the parking lot. He put it in the trunk of the car. He was followed. He drove by Oakhill Cemetery and out 18th Street across Village Creek. He drove into a patch of woods and we were unable to keep him under close observation. He then returned to the flat. At daybreak the woods were searched and the body of the woman, a Miss Kesh, was discovered in a shallow grave over which branches had been dragged. The police were brought in at once and it was determined that she had been poisoned. Laboratory methods disclosed that the body had been transported in the trunk compartment of Myron's car. In the meantime, as far as the police are concerned, Myron has disappeared.

"We have achieved—ah—a certain amount of cooperation. Mr. Jubal Tabor has been observed to have become quite nervous during the past two days. The authorities will not be patient with us much longer. We must produce Paul Myron. Myron, I might say, is exceedingly anxious to implicate Mr. Jubal Tabor, and accuses him of Miss Kesh's death. However, with the financial power of Mr. Tabor, and his un-doubted carefulness in most details, it is doubtful whether we have enough to cause him more than major annoyance. A contact in the district attorney's office confirms this. Mr. Myron's testimony is not enough, and for obvious reasons he pretends to know nothing about the explosion on the cabin cruiser."

Rodgers paused for breath. He was a very quiet, neat young man, evidently humorless.

Anthony said, "That's where we stand. We can inconvenience Jubal. But the rules of evidence are pretty flexible. If the authorities tried to force it to trial, Jubal's defense attorney would make hash of Myron's testimony, even if we could get Myron to say that Jubal hired him to kill Dale."

"Can the poison be traced to him?" Dale asked.

"If it could," Rodgers said, "it is equally evident that he would not have used it. Why do you assume Mr. Tabor gave the girl poison?"

"You said he gave her something, and then she died. I just jumped to the conclusion she was supposed to give it to Myron and something went wrong."

"Very sound," Rodgers murmured. "That's exactly what hap-pened."

"This is none of my business," Mildred Coe said. "But it would seem to me that your problem is to make Jubal Tabor convict himself by making an additional move."

They all looked at Mildred. She flushed.

"I've been alone a lot," she said. "Jubal Tabor sounds like a lonely man. Maybe it makes me feel as though I could anticipate how he might react. When you are alone you become too introspective. Reality becomes something that—can't be readily defined. The human animal is gregarious. There is something—twisted about a person who spends too much time alone. I don't want to be dramatic, but if we could use Dale in such a way that—"

* * *

For the hundredth time, Jubal Tabor told himself that the girl had merely been more intelligent than he had realized. When Myron had died, suddenly, alarmingly, the girl had managed to get rid of the body. Possibly some man she trusted had helped her. Even now she would be looking for him. Her chances of finding him were very slim. The public did not see Jubal Tabor. A few of his employees saw him—some in the office, the rest in the vast, ugly old house he had built for his first wife, the house in which the two dead sons had been born.

He sat alone in the paneled study of the old house. The lamp at his elbow left the high ceiling in darkness. If only the papers had reported the death of Paul Myron. Then he would know that at last he was safe. He sensed weakness in himself. There were too many emotions connected with this business of murder. It was almost a superstitious sort of fear, which was, of course, nonsense.

From a coldly practical point of view, a murder was no more emotional in context than the splitting of a stock issue, the refunding of bonds. It is a decision carried to the point of action.

The girl came in almost silently. He started as he saw her. He recognized her. That odd girl that Anthony seemed so fond of. What was her name? Cassy. Cassy Ling.

"How did you get in here?" he asked sharply.

"I wanted to see you. No one answered the door. I rang and rang. It was unlocked, so I came in."

"Nonsense," he said. "Pull the bell cord over there."

She went over and pulled the bell cord. They waited in silence.

"I can't understand this," Jubal said. "Why did you want to see me?"

"I'm frightened. Oh, not for myself. For Tony, Mr. Tabor. He wouldn't have wanted me to come here. I didn't tell him."

"Is he sick?"

"I think so. Something worse than sickness. He keeps seeing her. She keeps coming to him at night and trying to tell him something—"

Kelsy looked at Dale, in the dim light of the kitchen. Her face was whitened to the shade of chalk. Her water-soaked hair was flattened against her head and her clothes clung to her.

He put his hands on her shoulders. "If that Cassy does it right," he whispered, "you ought to give him a turn."

"This is no good," she said in a low voice. "It's a farce. He'll know at once that I'm alive, and trying, like a stupid child, to scare him."

"Baby, you look awful drowned to me," Kelsy said.

Anthony glanced at his watch and nodded to her. "Go ahead. The study is the second door off the hall, to the right."

Dale walked slowly, feeling like a fool. When they had gone over it, it had seemed like a good idea. To play on the old man's imagination, get him to say just one thing in front of witnesses which would strengthen the case against him. Rodgers, Anthony and Kelsy moved quietly behind her, to wait outside the study door.

At last she could see into the study. She saw Cassy Ling standing near the old man's chair, heard her low, vibrant, frightened voice.

"Utter nonsense, girl," the old man said in a frail voice.

Dale took a deep breath and moved slowly into the room. Water dripped from her clothes to the polished floor with tiny patting sounds, and then fell noiselessly to the rug.

In a strange, taut voice, the old man asked, "Who is that?" He pointed with a thin, dry finger.

Cassy turned and looked full at Dale. Then she said, "I must have made you nervous, Mr. Tabor. There's no one there."

The thin white hand sank slowly back to rest on the arm of the chair. Dale stood and looked at the old man's face. It was in shadow. She stood, waiting for the words that should come, would have to come. The long seconds went by.

Cassy said, "What made you think you saw someone?"

The old man giggled. It was a horrid, obscene sound in the dim room. Cassy moved back, one hand at her throat. The old man threw his head back and whinnied with laughter. They came in then, and turned on the overhead lights and stood in a semi-circle and looked at the old man's broken eyes and twisting mouth.

Between the laughter, the old man said, "*Amidst the mists and coldest frosts, with barest wrists and stoutest boasts—*"

The thin voice went on. Anthony said quietly, "They made me say that when I was little. I lisped. He must have learned it from me." He put his arm strongly around a trembling Cassy.

"*. . .he beats his fists against the posts and still . . .*"

"Horrible," Dale whispered, sensing the solid strength of Kelsy standing behind her.

"*. . . insists he sees the ghosts. Amidst the mists and . . .*"

Rodgers was talking quietly, firmly, over the phone.

In the sun-torrent of an August day, Kelsy McKewn planted his feet in the sand, swung the surf rod and sent the lead in a high whistling arc out beyond where the waves were breaking. He drew the line taut, set the drag and began reeling in. Almost at once the lure was hit violently. The fish headed diagonally out to sea, pulling out line against the drag. The rod bent and he fought the fish. It doubled back and he regained line, reeling fast, braced himself for its second run.

"Don't lose him now," she said, right behind him.

"If I do," he grunted, "you're going to see some boyish tears, gal."

Finally he got the fish onto the sand, hauled it up a way, got his hands under it and flipped it up further. It was as long as his leg and as big around as his thigh.

"A beauty!" she said.

He grinned at her, liking the slim clean strength of her. "Women clean fish," he said.

"And get help when they clean monster fish. Come on, now."

He got the hook out, looped a length of cord through the gill and mouth. He followed her up the rock stairs. Halfway up she stopped and turned. She frowned at him.

"Darling," she said, "a woman should never ask this. Why did it turn out to be me?"

"Would you like to be slapped in the kisser with a large fish?"

"Seriously now."

"I'll tell you. She was going to move around too fast. Me, I've decided I want to stay put."

"No more wanderlust?"

"Not while the fishing is like this, Mildred."

They went on up the steps and into the small house which no longer seemed as bleak.

HUGH PENTECOST
The Murder Machine

THE WOODS were peculiarly still. The gray dust from the limestone quarry had coated the leaves of the trees and shrubs, turning them into a photographic black and white instead of the lush green nature had intended. There was no life—no birds, no animals. The combination of the dust and the incessant noises from the quarry of secondary blasting, compressed-air drills, the high-powered shovels, the grinding of the jaw-crusher plant had driven them away.

When the clamor of work was at its height, the absence of life in the woods was not noticeable, but now, just past high noon of a hot July day, work had stopped as the men went to their midday meal, and the woods were silent. The only sound was the motor of the jeep that had started up the winding corduroy road toward the top of the quarry. The dark-haired man at the wheel of the jeep was aware of feeling that the countryside was abandoned, but there was no hint of death in the air.

Then, just as the jeep reached the outside point of the hairpin turn leading to the top, the ground under its wheels shuddered. The steep, white face of the quarry seemed to dissolve, like a wax dummy under heat. Then, with violent, almost unendurable sound, it burst outward. Thousands of cubic yards of white stone heaved out into space, while the earth thundered and rocked and the dust rose in an angry cloud.

The jeep, as if it had a living instinct for self-preservation, wrenched itself out of control of the dark-haired man and plunged off the road. It shot dizzily down a short embankment, turned over, then righted itself. The dark-haired man was thrown clear of it. He lay still, listening to the roar of the avalanche of white stone as it tumbled toward the floor of the quarry seemed to dissolve, like a wax dummy under the explosion, one thought remained clearly in focus in his mind: Somewhere in the heart of those thousands of tons of falling rock, ground to a meaningless pulp, was what had been seconds before, another human being.

The dark-haired man turned his face to one side and spat out the salty-tasting blood in his mouth. Two, three minutes more and he would have been in that white stone grave himself.

"Get moving, Pascal, you sucker," he said thickly to himself. He shook his head like a punch-drunk fighter and tried unsuccessfully to push himself up to a sitting position. This, he knew, was murder. . . .

Uncle Ben Michaels was responsible for Pascal's coming to the little Pennsylvania quarry town of Stone Ridge, a few days before. Uncle Ben was Pascal's last living relative, and when a vacation, annually delayed since before the war, finally became a reality, Pascal decided to spend it in Stone Ridge. Uncle Ben was getting along. There was no telling when they'd have a chance to spend a couple of weeks together again.

Uncle Ben had been a quarry worker in his youth, but for the last ten years he had held the post of County Sheriff, largely because of his relationship to Pascal. The voters seemed to think that the uncle of a police lieutenant in New York City's Homicide Division must also have special talents in the field of crime. Not that Uncle Ben had much crime to deal with. In ten years he had made a dozen arrests for disorderly conduct on paydays.

Pascal was not just any homicide man. A number of his successful cases had been written up in a national magazine, somewhat to his embarrassment. Uncle Ben was inordinately proud of him. He announced his coming for weeks. He booked him to make a speech at the local businessmen's club dinner. Pascal remarked to him, dryly, that he was sure it was just a coincidence that this exploitation happened to coincide with the fact that it was an election year.

Uncle Ben's leathery face wrinkled in a grin that was very like his nephew's. "I'd of done it any year, Dave," he said, "only I got to admit it won't do no special harm this year!"

But it was the businessmen's club dinner that resulted in Pascal's turning his holiday into something of a busman's outing, and led him to the bottom of a gully, bruised and bleeding, and squarely confronted by murder.

Pascal's speech at the dinner was off the cuff, and, by and large, humorous. The premature lines in his dark face had been placed there by good humor, which persistently rose above the grimness of his profession. But at the end of the speech he had made one or two quite serious remarks. He had said he felt it was a pity that so much of the modern scientific training of the police was directed toward solving the crime after the fact.

"It seems to be a national failing," he had said. "Our greatest surgeons cut out the cancer *after* it has developed; our statesmen have a genius for winning wars, but not much for avoiding them; our police, aided by modern science, can catch criminals after the crime, but they do very little toward preventing crime itself. We, as a people, have such great recuperative powers that we do very little to prevent disaster. We have always recovered and gone on to greater heights. But some day we may find we don't have as much bounce as we used to, and then it will be too late."

That evening of the speech was hot and humid, with the threat of a thunderstorm in the air, and when Pascal and Uncle Ben got back to the old man's cottage they sat on the front porch, each with a bottle of beer from the icebox. They'd only just gotten settled when a car pulled into the yard and stopped. The motor was switched off, the headlights turned down to dim, and a man got out and came up the path toward the porch.

"Looks like the new young doc," Uncle Ben said. "He was at the dinner, Dave. Don't know if you met him or not."

Pascal remembered Dr. Frank Lane. He was a slender, wiry young man in sports jacket and flannels. His brown hair was clipped short in a crew cut. He was not at all what Pascal would have expected the country doctor in a small town to be.

"Hello, Uncle Ben," Dr. Lane said. "Hope I'm not butting in on a private confab."

Everybody called the old man "Uncle Ben." He was rightly proud of the title.

"Just settin' here tryin' to breathe," Uncle Ben said. "Come on up. Dave'll get you a bottle of beer."

"No, thanks," Dr. Lane said. He sat down on the top step. "It's really Lieutenant Pascal I wanted to talk to. I was very much interested in your speech, Lieutenant—particularly the windup."

"I'm not sure I remember what I said," Pascal answered.

"About crime prevention," Dr. Lane said.

"Oh."

"You haven't visited Stone Ridge often, have you, Lieutenant?"

"This is the first time since I was a kid," Pascal said.

"Every small town has its personal complications," Dr. Lane said. "In a town dependent on one business, as this town is on the quarry, the complications usually center there."

Pascal sighed. Detectives, like doctors and lawyers, are always being asked for free advice. Well, this was Uncle Ben's town. The least he could do was listen.

"I'm new here myself," Dr. Lane said. "I came here on a special project, and when the old doctor died I agreed to fill in until someone took over the practice permanently. I'm really a research man. At the moment I'm working on N.G. headaches."

"N.G. headaches?" Pascal asked.

"Nitroglycerin. Men who handle explosives suffer from the most agonizing headaches," Lane said. "They make migraine seem like a Sunday-school picnic. They're caused by inhaling the fumes from nitroglycerin, or absorbing the oil through the pores. Unless the men build up an artificial tolerance they suffer the tortures of the damned."

"Interesting," Pascal said. "I'd never heard of it. What can the men do?"

"Old-timers used to smear nitro on their foreheads," Lane said, "under the sweatbands of their caps. But when they'd come to a week end, or any period when they weren't working, the headaches would return—in spades! I'm working on a capsule, to be taken internally, that will keep the tolerance even."

"I should think it was rather a limited occupational hazard," Pascal said.

Lane shook his head. "Did you know that, in this country, approximately a million pounds of dynamite are used every day? That takes a lot of handling. . . . But I didn't come here to talk to you about N.G. headaches, Lieutenant."

"You had another kind of headache in mind?" Pascal asked.

"Yes," Lane said gravely. "I think we are confronted with a situation at the quarry which is building toward violence that will cost a life—or lives. And not accidentally, Lieutenant."

Pascal frowned. "That would seem to be Uncle Ben's job."

"He hasn't been called in," Lane said. "And he won't be. Not till after the crime has been committed. That's why, when I heard your speech tonight, I wondered if you—"

"I have no authority here," Pascal said. "I couldn't do anything if I wanted to."

"You could observe," Lane said. "And you don't need authority to—to make a diagnosis. If someone got to the heart of this thing, murder might be prevented."

"Murder! Jumping Jehoshaphat!" Uncle Ben said. "What are you talking about, Doc?"

"Mind if I give the lieutenant a little background?" Lane asked.

"Shoot!" Uncle Ben said.

Lane drew a deep breath. "The quarry here had been owned for years by a family named Anderson," he said. "In this type of quarry, Lieutenant, they do two big blasts a year—spring and fall. That knocks out enough limestone to keep 'em going through the year. Of course, the blasts have to be perfect. If they don't come off right, if they leave a big toe at the base of the quarry and call for a lot of secondary drilling and blasting, the profits go out the window. The success of those blasts is the difference between profit and loss each year.

"Well, Tom Anderson inherited the quarry. I guess things had been pretty rough for young Tom. He'd had several offers to sell out to the Marshall Hewitt Company, a sort of limestone monopoly. He refused—something of family pride in it, I guess. But last year he was up against it. A fellow named Benson, a powder expert for a big company, came here to handle the blast. He persuaded Tom Anderson that by drilling in a different pattern and using a different quality of dynamite, he could get more stone at the same cost as in the past. Anderson needed that extra product and he let Benson sell him."

Lane shrugged. "The blast was a colossal dud. Anderson was faced with a highly expensive secondary blasting. He knew he couldn't swing it. His credit was exhausted at the banks. So he sold out to the Marshall Hewitt Company."

"It hit Tom Anderson hard," Uncle Ben said. "You see, Dave, this Marshall Hewitt started out here in Stone Ridge. He's about fifty-five. Used to work for Tom's father. Then he branched out on his own. Made a mint."

"One small-town boy makes good," Pascal said, "and one doesn't."

"That's it," Lane said. "Of course, Hewitt is many years older than Tom Anderson. Which is part of the rub. You see, Hewitt not only got Tom Anderson's quarry, but he also married Tom Anderson's girl."

"That's right," Uncle Ben said. "Everyone took it for granted Tom and Nora would get hitched, and then, right after Tom lost his business, Nora up and married the fella that took it from him. Fella old enough to be her father."

"From the sound of it maybe Anderson's well out of it," Pascal said. "The girl seems to have a nose for prosperity."

"Maybe—maybe not," Uncle Ben said.

"The point is, Lieutenant, there is a basis for ill-feeling," Dr. Lane said.

"I should think so."

"Things started to go wrong at the quarry," Lane said. "First some pieces of steel got in the jaw crusher and broke the jaws. That put the crusher plant out of business for weeks. Then the secondary blasting— which Hewitt was doing to clear up the mess Anderson had left—went wrong, and cost time and trouble. Powder trains were broken in the fuses; blasting caps had been soaked. Hose lines for the compression jackhammers were cut. The sump of the quarry pump was blocked and the quarry flooded. It was systematic sabotage."

"That all sounds like an inside job," Pascal said. "Surely Tom Anderson isn't working in the quarry?"

"No-o," Lane said, "but of course he knows every detail of its operation. The place isn't fenced in, you understand. Even with a couple of night watchmen on the job—"

"Go ahead," Pascal said.

"Well, the tension got heavy about three weeks ago," Lane said. "Hewitt's first blast is coming up in a day or two. The expert from the powder company arrived to supervise the drilling and make the plans. It was something of a shock to everyone locally when that expert turned out to be the same George Benson who'd ruined Tom Anderson with his bad advice last year. Anderson went a little crazy in the local pub. He accused Benson outright of having deliberately wrecked him, of being Hewitt's man, so to speak. He had to be restrained then from acting violently."

"Not an incomprehensible state of mind," Pascal said.

"Hewitt explains his hiring of Benson reasonably enough," Lane said. "He says just because Benson *did* make an error in judgment last year, he knows this particular quarry better than anyone else. He knows what not to do. Of course, he denies that he had any connections with Benson."

"Does he think Anderson is responsible for the sabotage?" Pascal asked.

"Hewitt isn't a man to publicize his opinions," Lane said. "I'm as close to him as anyone—he's very much interested in my experiments— but he doesn't tell me what he thinks. But I do know this: He's taken this situation as a kind of personal challenge. This quarry is only a tiny part of his holdings. He could abandon it, write the purchase price off as a loss, and forget it. But because this is his home town, and because someone is trying to stop him, he's concentrated all his interests here. He's been here steadily for the last three months and he intends to supervise the big blast personally."

"So?" Pascal said.

"Doesn't it seem to you," Lane asked, "that this may be exactly what the saboteur wants? That he's been working toward that end?"

"Why?"

"People get killed, Lieutenant, when blasts go wrong," Dr. Lane said.

The storm that had come in the early hours of the morning had cleared the air. It was bright and fresh when Pascal and Uncle Ben sat in the old man's kitchen drinking their second round of breakfast coffee.

"I feel," Pascal said, "like a wise old rat who sees a trap baited with cheese, knows it's a trap and that the cheese is bait, and still walks into it. Why did I tell Lane I'd look into this?"

"Can't help yourself," Uncle Ben said, methodically loading a pipe. "Old fire horse."

"Phooey!" Pascal said. He tossed a package of matches across the table to the old man. "Lane's an outsider, with maybe more imagination than's good for him. What's your opinion of the situation, Uncle Ben?"

The old man held a match to the bowl of his pipe till it was going evenly. Then he blew out the match. "Someone's gonna get hurt," he said.

"Who?"

"Maybe Hewitt. Maybe Benson. Maybe the fella who plans to do the hurting. People have been known to get caught in their own schemes."

"Frankenstein," Pascal said.

"Who?"

"Skip it," Pascal said, grinning.

"I was referring to Tom Anderson," the old man said.

"Tell me about him," Pascal said.

"Tom? Nice young fella," Uncle Ben said. "Raised in the quarry business. Knows it backwards."

"But he was had by this fellow Benson last year."

"Ever see a good boxer lose his head in the ring?" Uncle Ben asked. "Things are going fine. He uses his knowledge, he leads with his left, his footwork is okay. But the other fella is a little too good for him, starts wearing him down. Finally our boy is in a corner, absorbing a lot of punishment. He thinks, 'If I could just land one haymaker!' So he forgets his science, drops his guard, and starts throwing one from the outfield. Bang! The other fella lands one right on the button and our boy is down."

"But if he's a nice guy, does he start yelling 'Foul'?" Pascal asked.

"Maybe," Uncle Ben said, "if he convinces himself the other fella had a horseshoe inside his glove." The old man tamped the tobacco down in his pipe. "I've known Tom Anderson ever since he was born. I worked for his father and his grandfather. I could be a little prejudiced, Dave. You better figure it out for yourself. You'll be nearer right because you can keep your heart out of it."

"You think Anderson isn't responsible for the trouble?"

"I didn't say that, Dave. But if he is, I'd have a kind of sympathy for him."

"As the local representative of the law you can't afford to have sympathies," Pascal said.

The old man raised his pale eyes. "You learned how to turn off sympathy like a water faucet, Dave?"

"No," Pascal said, and heaved himself up out of his chair. He'd promised to meet Dr. Lane at the quarry at nine o'clock and it was time to go. . . .

Pascal drove Uncle Ben's jeep out to the quarry. When he was still a mile away he saw the ugly gray outlines of the crushing plant rising high against the morning sky. He turned the jeep off the main highway and drove into the quarry yard.

There was, in addition to the plant, the drab, gray, one-story office building, a parking lot where a couple of dozen dump trucks stood idle, and a dust-covered lunch wagon, with a little trickle of smoke coming from a tin chimney. Behind that, bleak in the shadow from the woods, rose the whitish-gray, clifflike walls of the quarry itself. As he parked the jeep, Pascal saw a big power shovel come waddling out of the quarry on its tractor treads.

There was a group of about a dozen men standing near the lunch wagon, and in the center of it was young Dr. Lane. Pascal paused to light a cigarette, and then wandered over in that direction. Dr. Lane saw him approaching and waved.

"Be with you in a second," he said. He was handing out small paper envelopes to the men. As each man received his envelope he climbed aboard a waiting truck. Finally they were all aboard, and the truck started toward the corduroy road that led to the top of the quarry.

"We're starting to load the holes today for the big blast," Dr. Lane said. "Those are the men who'll handle the dynamite, and I've been dishing out some of my magic headache pills. Some use the pills, some the old-fashioned method. Comparative test. Glad you were prompt, because I've got to go up top myself and check results."

"I really don't know what I'm doing here," Pascal said.

"You'll get a chance to look over some of the key figures in our little drama. Here comes the boss now."

Pascal turned, and saw a wine-red convertible, top down, pulling into the yard. A girl was driving. Her dark curly hair was cut short, and she was wearing a sports shirt and slacks, with a bright green handkerchief knotted around her neck. She had on dark sunglasses, which made it difficult to tell much about her face. Her mouth, Pascal thought, was almost defiantly scarlet, suggesting an unhappy person, but he couldn't really tell, with the eyes hidden behind the black lenses.

The man sitting beside her bent over for a second to brush her cheek with a good-by kiss before climbing out of the car. He was tall and angular. He had on work-worn corduroy trousers and a leather jacket. A fringe of iron-gray hair showed under the rim of a battered gray felt hat.

"I told Mr. Hewitt you were coming out here this morning," Lane said. "Had to if you were to see anything. He wouldn't have any unvouched-for strangers around at this point."

As Marshall Hewitt approached, Pascal saw that he had deep-set gray eyes with a glint of hardness in them. He turned once to wave to the girl who was driving away in the convertible.

"Is that Mrs. Hewitt?" Pascal asked Lane. "Tom Anderson's ex-girl-friend?"

"Right," Lane said.

Hewitt reached them. Pascal felt almost as if he were under the scrutiny of an X-ray machine.

"I take it you're Lieutenant Pascal," Hewitt said in a quiet voice.

"Glad to meet you," Pascal said, holding out his hand.

Hewitt didn't see it. "I'm surprised you'd pay any attention to old wives' tales, Lieutenant," he said.

Pascal grinned. "I'm a little surprised, myself," he said.

"I'll tell you something," Hewitt said. "No one fools around with high explosives. It's no respecter of persons, good or bad. As for anything going wrong with the blast—it can't. I'm double-checking every step of the process myself."

"It can't do any harm for Lieutenant Pascal to look over the setup," Dr. Lane said.

"Do you know anything about industrial explosives or this kind of quarry blasting, Lieutenant?" Hewitt asked.

"Not a thing," Pascal said blandly.

"I don't know how you can see anything if you don't understand what you're looking at," Hewitt said. "But come along. It will make Dr. Lane and my wife feel better."

"Your wife?"

Hewitt smiled grimly. "She's been listening to Lane's scare talk, too," he said. "Come on. Let's get started."

They rode to the top of the quarry in a small pickup truck. Hewitt drove, and he seemed preoccupied with his own problems. Lane, holding a small, black, doctor's bag on his knees, told Pascal a little something about procedure as they crawled up the winding, bumpy road.

"The quarry's about four hundred feet across and a hundred and sixty feet deep," he said. "The new holes have been drilled about twenty feet back from the face. They use a regular well-driller for the work, and the holes are sunk clear to the bottom. There are twenty of them. They'll be loaded with dynamite, capped, and packed. It'll take today and part of tomorrow to do the job. Then they blow all twenty holes at once, and if there are no mishaps, and the fragmentation is good, you've got enough limestone to keep the men busy for months."

"What could go wrong?" Pascal asked.

"Nothing!" It was Hewitt who answered, although he hadn't appeared to be listening. The conversation seemed to annoy him.

They reached the top, and Hewitt parked the truck. Pascal could see the men starting to carry boxes of dynamite from a shed marked "EXPLOSIVES."

"As long as you stay out of the way, Lieutenant, you're welcome," Hewitt said. "Lane, I want checks on the men every fifteen minutes. This ought to be a pretty good test of your pills. Good-by, Lieutenant."

"See you," Pascal said. Then, when Hewitt was out of earshot, he looked at the doctor with a faint smile. "To get back to my question, Lane, what *could* go wrong with this blast?"

"That's pretty hard to say," Lane said. "Let me tell you how it works. The drilling's all done, you understand. They'll load each of the holes with more than a ton of dynamite. Attached to the top sticks of the dynamite are blasting caps. They look like small firecrackers. Wires run from them to the tops of the holes. Then the holes are packed with wet sand, cuttings from the hole, anything to tamp the dynamite in solid, so it'll blow out and not up. When the holes are all loaded and packed, they test each blasting cap with a galvanometer. Then—"

"What's a galvanometer?" Pascal asked.

"Little gadget about the size of a small camera," Lane said. "It's a device for testing electric circuits. You hook the wires from the blasting cap onto the galvanometer, and it shows you whether the circuit is closed and ready for a blast, or whether it's open, due to faulty connections, or broken wires, or short circuits. You've got to make sure all your connections are right, because if one of the holes didn't blow you'd have a tricky and dangerous job to take care of later."

"I should think there'd be danger of setting off the blast with the galvanometer if it generates an electric current," Pascal said.

Lane shook his head. "They use a silver chloride cell in it," he said. "It produces only about a tenth enough juice to set off a blasting cap."

"So we've checked the holes," Pascal said.

"Then they run a connecting wire to all the holes," Lane said, "so they'll all go at once, you understand. They check that connecting wire with the galvanometer. If the circuit's properly closed, then they run a long lead wire back to the blasting machine, get everyone out of the way, and let her go."

"Hewitt will do the checking himself?" Pascal asked.

"Benson'll check, and Tiller, the quarry superintendent, and Hewitt."

"Then he's right," Pascal said. "Nothing *can* go wrong."

Lane took a pencil and a small black notebook from his pocket. "I'll feel better when it's over," he said. "Excuse me for a moment. I've got to check with my guinea pigs." He walked away toward the men who were handling the dynamite.

Pascal sat down on a rock. Hewitt was right, he told himself. It was absurd for him to be there, knowing as little as he did. Lane's explanation had been clear enough, and on the face of it, triple-checked by three experts, there didn't seem to be any room for a planned accident of any kind.

Just then Pascal saw one of the crew approaching the nearest hole to him with a stick of dynamite. Very casually the man held it over the hole and dropped it. Pascal's stomach did a flip-flop and his reflexes yanked him to his feet.

Someone behind Pascal chuckled. "Take it easy, Lieutenant. It takes a lot more than that to set off dynamite."

Pascal turned to confront a ruddy-faced, broad-shouldered man in a worn tweed jacket and slacks. He had a white, friendly smile. "My name's Benson," he said. "I'm the powder company expert. Doc Lane told me about you."

"Thanks for explaining," Pascal said. "Maybe I can swallow my heart now."

"They drop the sticks that way so they'll pack tighter," Benson said. "When they lower the last one with the blasting cap attached, that's something else. Kid-glove job."

Pascal studied him thoughtfully. This was the man whose advice had cost Tom Anderson his quarry. "Since you know why I'm here, Benson, maybe you'll give me your opinion of the sabotage that's been pulled here in the quarry."

Benson shrugged. "Not much doubt about the source," he said.

"Tom Anderson?"

"Who else?" Benson said. "He imagines he has a grievance."

"Imagines?" Pascal said.

Color mounted in Benson's cheeks. "I know the gossip, Lieutenant," he said. "That I deliberately gave Tom bad advice. That I was really working for Hewitt, and helped force Tom out of business so Hewitt could get the quarry."

"Is it true?" Pascal's voice was casual.

"Of course not. There are always unforeseeable risks," Benson said. "In this case there was something in the strata of the stone itself, way below the surface that kept the dynamite from blowing the stone out from the face of the quarry the way it should. It couldn't have been foreseen. It was bad luck for Anderson, and it could have been bad luck for me if Hewitt hadn't hired me to do this job. His show of confidence in me has probably saved me my career."

"But you're not using the same method you advised Anderson to use?"

"Of course not," Benson said. He was still flushed. "Why should we? It proved unsuccessful."

"Don't take offense," Pascal said. "I'm just trying to catch up on things. And I'm not concerned with technical errors. Dr. Lane has suggested something may go wrong with this blast, something deliberately planned by someone. Something that might result in the loss of life. That's what interests me."

"Anderson might like to see us all blown to kingdom come," Benson said. "But how? Every step of the process is being triple-checked. The galvanometer tests our circuits over and over again. What could anyone do?"

"You're the expert," Pascal said. "You should have the answer—if there is one."

"There isn't," Benson said. "This thing is foolproof. I promise you."

Pascal watched the loading of the holes for an hour or more and then he went back down to the floor of the quarry and to his parked jeep. Hewitt was right. You couldn't see much if you didn't understand what you were looking at. He decided his best bet was to hunt up Uncle Ben and arrange to meet young Tom Anderson. If it *was* Anderson who'd been sabotaging the work at the quarry, he could somehow be kept in check till any danger of the blast going wrong was past. If it wasn't Anderson, then there might really be a job for a detective.

He started the jeep back down the road toward town. He'd driven less than a mile when he saw that the road was blocked ahead of him. An ancient and battered black sedan was drawn squarely across the road. Pascal stopped the jeep and stood up on the seat. Then he saw the wine-red convertible stopped on the other side of the sedan. It had been heading for the quarry. The girl with the dark glasses was at the wheel, and a young man, tall and blond, was standing beside the car, leaning toward the girl and talking earnestly.

Pascal hopped out of the jeep and began sauntering toward them. Neither one of them saw him till he spoke. "Some kind of trouble?" he asked cheerfully.

The man spun around. "What do you want?" he demanded in a hoarse voice.

"My jeep is pretty handy," Pascal said, "but not handy enough to go through or over your road-block."

The young man hesitated. Then he said, "I'll move my car." He turned back to the girl, who was gripping the wheel, her head lowered. "Nora, you'll wait? We've *got* to have this out!"

Nora Hewitt murmured something Pascal couldn't hear, but it seemed to satisfy the young man. He got into the sedan and backed it off to one side of the road. Just as he was climbing out, the girl started the convertible.

"No!" the young man shouted. "Nora!"

Pascal waited by the side of the road. The young man started to get back into his car, and then he seemed to abandon the idea. He stood watching the convertible disappear, pain in his blue eyes.

"You're Tom Anderson, aren't you?" Pascal asked.

The blue eyes lifted. "I don't know you, do I?"

"No. Name is Pascal. I'm Ben Michaels' nephew."

"The cop!" Anderson said.

"Is that bad?" Pascal said, smiling.

Anderson's eyes narrowed. "What are you doing out at the quarry?" he asked.

"Looking into a potential murder."

"A *what*?"

"There seems to be an idea floating around," Pascal said, "that sometime before or during the big blast tomorrow you plan to polish off Marshall Hewitt, or George Benson, or both. Anything to it?"

Anderson let his breath out in a long sigh. "Tell me how, and I'll be glad to make your dream come true, Pascal. Naturally, I don't want to be caught!"

"That's what stops most people," Pascal said.

Tom Anderson took a pipe out of his pocket and began filling it from a plastic pouch. "So Hewitt's got the wind up," he said.

"No," Pascal said.

"Why else would be send for you?"

"He didn't."

Anderson squinted through the smoke from his pipe. "Old pros like you don't go investigating just for the fun of it."

"Dr. Lane asked me out," Pascal said. "Hewitt thinks he's crazy."

"But you don't?"

"Uncle Ben doesn't," Pascal said. "Uncle Ben knows the town and the people in it."

"So Uncle Ben's turned against me, too," Anderson said bitterly.

"Uncle Ben likes you," Pascal said. "He thinks if you're responsible for all that's happened at the quarry you've been pushed beyond endurance."

Anderson's teeth gritted down on his pipe stem. "I have," he said. "By heavens, I have!"

Pascal shrugged. "I might help."

"No one can help me," Anderson said. He reached for the door handle of his car. "Tell Uncle Ben I'm deeply touched that his belief in me permits him to think I might have a reason for being a criminal."

Pascal didn't reply, because at that moment the wine-red convertible went racing past in the direction of town.

When Pascal drove down the main street of Stone Ridge to Uncle Ben's cottage he saw the wine-red convertible parked in front of it. Nora Hewitt was twisted around in the seat, evidently watching for him to appear. She got out of the car as he came along the sidewalk toward her.

"I guess you know who I am, Lieutenant Pascal," she said. It was the first time he'd heard her voice. It was small and clear, and he got the impression she was trying very hard to keep it level and business-like.

"Yes, Mrs. Hewitt," he said.

"I've been waiting for you," she said.

"Will you come up on the porch?"

She didn't reply, but she walked beside him up the front steps and sat down in a wicker armchair.

"Frank told me that he's drawn you into this business," Nora said.

"Frank?"

"Dr. Lane. I saw you with him at the quarry earlier today."

"Dr. Lane is concerned about tomorrow's blast," Pascal said. "He thinks something may go wrong. Your husband and George Benson have just about persuaded me it's impossible."

"If anything does go wrong it will be too late, unless somebody does something now, Lieutenant."

"For example?"

Her fingers gripped the arms of the wicker chair. "He's got to be kept away from the quarry till the blast's over," she said.

"I don't quite see how that can be managed," Pascal said. "It's his business and he intends to check every step of it himself."

Nora raised her head and her lips parted in an expression of surprise. "I'm not talking about my husband!" she said. "It's Tom Anderson! If anything goes wrong he'll be blamed. If he's kept away, or if someone responsible, like yourself, is with him all the time, then he'll be in the clear."

This was a twist Pascal hadn't expected, not after the road-block, not after what he knew of the past. "You're concerned about Tom?"

"Yes." She leaned forward in the chair, and her voice was suddenly tense: "Don't you see? The whole thing has been built up so that it looks as if Tom were responsible for everything that has happened up till now. If there is more, people will conclude Tom's responsible for that, too."

"And you think he isn't responsible for anything that's happened so far?"

"I know he isn't," she said earnestly.

"Has he denied it to you?"

"No. He doesn't have to. Tom is bitter, Lieutenant. He has a right to be bitter. But he isn't a criminal."

"So your opinion is based on faith?"

"I've known Tom all my life," she said.

"And turned him down."

Her fingers were so tight on the arms of the chair that they had a dead-white look to them. "Yes. I turned him down," she said. "But I know him better than anyone else in the world knows him."

Pascal lit a cigarette, looked around for some place to throw the match, and then held it in his hand. "I confess to being a little bewildered, Mrs. Hewitt. You come here on behalf of Tom Anderson, a man you brutally rejected. Yet it's your husband who's presumably in danger."

"Marshall can take care of himself," Nora said. "He's not off guard.

But Tom is in terrible danger if something should happen. There'll be a circumstantial case against him he may not be able to beat. I just ask that he be forced to provide himself with an alibi."

"Then you think something is going to happen?" Pascal asked.

She shook her head from side to side. "I don't know what to think," she said. "Marshall says not. Frank thinks there's danger, but Marshall won't listen. Sometimes I think—" She stopped abruptly.

"You think what, Mrs. Hewitt?"

"I don't know," she said, with a kind of desperation. "Marshall is jealous of Tom. He knows how I—how Tom and I—"

"That you *were* in love?" Pascal asked, when she hesitated.

"Yes."

"Yet you married Hewitt. Doesn't that reassure him?"

She didn't answer. She just sat there in the chair, rigid, clinging to the arms.

"Were you going to suggest that your husband might try to frame Tom?"

"He hates Tom," she said, answering indirectly. "After all, the sabotage has been annoying, but it hasn't been serious. I mean, no one's been hurt. And Marshall just laughs when we talk about danger to him, as though he *knew* there wasn't any. How could he know, unless—?"

It was an intriguing idea. Pascal smoked his cigarette and thought about it. Uncle Ben and Dr. Lane had made it clear that financial loss at the quarry wouldn't even put a dent in Hewitt. Could the whole thing be an elaborate method for getting rid of a younger rival? But what next? The man certainly wouldn't commit suicide to get even.

"I can't put any sort of proper value on that theory, Mrs. Hewitt, without knowing more about your relationship with your husband. You did choose him as against Tom. Why?"

"Listen, Lieutenant. The only thing that's important is that Tom be kept from falling into some kind of trap."

"Was it for his money?" Pascal asked.

"No!" She stood up abruptly. "I see you won't help, Lieutenant. I'll have to go somewhere else, though heaven knows where!"

"I can't help unless I understand," Pascal said.

"It must be clear that I married Marshall because I loved him," she said in a flat, unconvincing tone. "I want him protected. But I—"

"—You also want Tom Anderson protected, because you used to love him, and because you have enough faith in him to ignore all the evidence, even though you refuse to talk to him without his setting up a road-block to stop you. I'm afraid I don't believe you're telling me everything, Mrs. Hewitt."

She hesitated, as if she were on the verge of blurting out some new information. Then, without saying anything, she turned and ran down the steps.

Pascal watched her go, brushing absently at the cigarette ashes that had dribbled down the front of his shirt. . . .

Time moved on, rather more rapidly than suited Pascal's taste.

"I should have stood in bed," he told Uncle Ben. "If I had decided to mind my own business, then I wouldn't be concerned. But having stuck my neck out, it would be nice if I had one good solid fact to go on."

"Nothing turned up?" Uncle Ben asked. They were at supper. Uncle Ben had broiled a couple of steaks that would have made a professional chef envious.

"Mrs. Hewitt turned up this morning," Pascal said.

"Nora?"

"A mixed-up cookie," Pascal said. "What about her, Uncle Ben?"

"I always liked Nora," the old man said. He reached for the coffeepot and refilled his cup. "Knew her father. He used to be engineer on the old steam engine at the quarry they used for pulling the stone cars into the crusher plant. A nice guy, Herb Mason. Widower. Brought up his two kids in a first-rate fashion. They were always neat and clean and polite."

"Two kids?"

"Nora and her brother," Uncle Ben said. "Larry, that's the brother, worked in the quarry, too, for a while. Ambitious young fellow. Went to night school over in Warrentown. Got into management end of the business. General sales manager, I think he is, for one of the biggest distributors of agricultural limestone in the country."

"He doesn't live here in Stone Ridge?"

"Nope. Hasn't for years. Used to drop back once in a while, but it's been two, three years since I've seen him."

"Not even for the wedding?" Pascal asked.

"Nora and Hewitt were married in Pittsburgh," Uncle Ben said. "Larry was there. He gave her away."

"And Nora's career before her marriage?" Pascal asked.

"Schoolteacher," Uncle Ben said. He chuckled. "They say the older boys used to try to stay in the seventh grade for two or three years! She was always a looker." Then the old man frowned. "But she was always

Tom Anderson's girl. Never went out with anyone else from the time they were in high school together."

"Then Hewitt snagged her out from under Tom's nose?"

Uncle Ben pushed away his plate. "Hewitt's a good man," he said. "A successful man. A plugger. If he'd married one of half a dozen eligible widows around the country, nearer his own age, everyone would have thought the lady'd done right well for herself. It's the difference in ages makes you feel kind of uncomfortable about him and Nora."

"Was Nora very much attached to her father?"

Uncle Ben snorted. "If you're going to start dishing out some of that new-fangled psychology stuff, or whatever it is, pardon me while I clean up the dishes!"

Pascal sighed. "Where does Tom Anderson spend his evenings?" he asked.

"Stone Ridge ain't Broadway and 42nd Street," Uncle Ben said. "There's one movie theater, one bar, and a couple of quick-lunch joints. Outside of that it's home, yours or someone else's."

One movie theater, one bar, and two lunchrooms failed to produce any sign of Tom Anderson. Inquiry brought out the fact that nobody had seen him around town since early that morning. Anderson's own house on the outskirts of town was dark, and there was no response to Pascal's knocking except the excited barking of a dog inside.

Shortly after midnight Pascal went to bed, feeling restlessly unhappy. So there were some personal complications, he told himself. But there wasn't any danger. The blast was foolproof. Hewitt and Benson said so.

Uncle Ben was an early riser, and Pascal joined him for breakfast about five-thirty.

"I've got the jitters," he told the old man. "They'll be pulling the blast after lunch today. If there's trouble brewing I haven't got a decent whiff of it."

"Maybe it's just jitters all around," Uncle Ben said.

"Could be," Pascal said. "But I'm going to find Tom Anderson and stick with him like a burr. If I can't do anything else I can see to it he stays out of trouble."

Shortly before seven Pascal was at Tom Anderson's house again, knocking on the door. The dog barked at him, still inside. That was all. Pascal walked around to the back and peered in the kitchen window. There was a coffee cup on the table, and in an ash tray the last eighth of an inch of a cigarette smoldered. Pascal knocked again. There was no answer. It looked as though he must have missed Anderson by only a minute or two. The black sedan was nowhere around.

Pascal went back to town and checked the eating places. No one had seen Tom. He drove out to the quarry. The dynamite crew was already at work loading the last of the holes. Pascal drove his jeep up to the top. Dr. Lane was there, checking on the action of his pills.

He saw Pascal after a minute or two and came over to speak to him. "Anything cooking, Lieutenant?"

"That's what I wanted to ask you," Pascal said. "Nothing wrong at the quarry this morning?"

"No. Did you expect there would be?"

Pascal shrugged. "Tom Anderson is a hard guy to locate," he said. "Could anything have been done to those holes that were loaded yesterday?"

"There's no sign of it," Dr. Lane said. "But here's Benson. You might ask him."

Benson joined them. He had something in a small leather case swung over his shoulder by a strap. "Still waiting around for a disaster, Lieutenant?"

"I'm getting a little sick of that question," Pascal said dryly. "I didn't dream this idea up, you know."

"I know," Benson said. "It's the Doc, here."

"Well, could anything have gone wrong in the night?"

"I'm about to recheck the loaded holes," Benson said. He tapped the leather case. "Galvanometer. Want to see for yourself?"

"Why not?"

They walked over to the first hole. Two wires lay on the top of the ground, one yellow, one red. Benson undid the leather flap of the galvanometer case, exposing the tester. There were two metal poles at the top and a glass face covering an indicator needle. Benson attached the two wires to the poles. Instantly the needle registered.

"All shipshape here," he said.

They repeated the process on all but the three holes on which the men were still working. As they checked the last one, Marshall Hewitt joined them.

"Good morning, Lieutenant," he said. He was more cheerful than he had been yesterday. "Sorry if I was a little sharp with you yesterday. Things on my mind. But I do appreciate your effort and your concern. I guess you can see, though, that this whole setup can be checked beyond a question of doubt."

"I begin to," Pascal said.

"These last three holes will be finished by noon. Then we'll attach the connecting wire. Then, after lunch, we'll make a final check on that, run off our lead wire to the detonator, and that will be that."

These men were busy and they went off to complete their job. Pascal sat down on the stone he'd occupied the day before. He felt a strange prickling of apprehension at the base of his neck. "I ought to be writing fiction," he thought to himself. "The great detective has a premonition of danger!"

He got up impatiently from the stone and went back to his jeep. He drove down the winding log road to the quarry yard. If he could just locate Tom Anderson things would feel better.

Then the wine-colored convertible drove into the yard. The girl with the black glasses made a tentative gesture of appeal to Pascal. He walked over and stood beside the car.

"Have you seen Tom?" Nora asked.

"No."

"One of the neighbors said they'd seen a stranger drive up in a jeep and stop at the house early this morning. I thought perhaps—"

"It was me," Pascal said. "Nobody home but the dog—and the burning remains of a cigarette which showed I was just too late."

"I thought you'd turned me down yesterday," Nora said. "Thanks for trying to find him."

"I am in my soap-opera mood this morning," Pascal said dryly. "Anderson smokes a pipe and he's kind to dogs. He must be innocent!"

"You've been up to the blasting site?" Nora asked.

"Just came down."

"Everything's all right? Nothing happened in the night?"

"Everything's perfect, they tell me."

Nora moistened her bright-red lips. "Maybe we're concerned for nothing," she said. "I hope so, *I hope so!*"

"Look," Pascal said. "Are you going into town?"

"I could," she said.

"If you could make a casual check on whether anyone has seen Anderson it would help," Pascal said.

"I'll go at once," she said.

He watched the convertible drive off and then he glanced at his wrist watch. Eleven-thirty. In half an hour the men would be coming down from the blasting site for the noon hour. After that, the blast. And after that, provided it went off according to schedule, he could go back to teaching Uncle Ben canasta.

Shortly after the sounding of the noon whistle the big dump truck came down from the top carrying the dynamite crew. It was followed by Hewitt, Benson, and Dr. Lane in the pickup. Pascal sat in his jeep, his hat tilted forward over his eyes. He didn't want to eat. He just wanted this to get over with so he could relax. Everyone had gone into the lunch wagon. Pascal felt drowsy. He didn't hear Dr. Lane's approach till the young man was almost at his elbow.

"There's a call for you in the office, Lieutenant," he said.

Pascal climbed out of the jeep. "Everything okay up top?" he asked the doctor.

"Seems perfect," Lane said. "The holes are loaded and tested, and they've attached the connecting wire. If there was anything afoot it looks as if it had been given up."

"Let's hope so," Pascal said.

"It's Uncle Ben on the phone," Dr. Lane said. "He sounded kind of urgent."

Pascal hurried over to the office shack. There was no one there. The telephone receiver lay on the desktop. Pascal picked it up.

"Nora asked me to call you," Uncle Ben said. "Didn't want anyone there to know what she was up to."

"Well?" Pascal said.

"No sign of the young man," Uncle Ben said. "Did a little checking myself. Neighbors say he left the house, driving his car, just a couple of minutes before you got there. You didn't pass him on the road, did you?"

"I didn't pass anyone," Pascal said.

"He was headed for the quarry, then," Uncle Ben said in an odd voice. "'Course that doesn't mean he stopped there."

"Of course," Pascal said.

"You drive to Warrentown that way," Uncle Ben said.

"Also Washington, D.C., or Bangor, Maine," Pascal said. "I'll keep my eyes open."

He went back to the jeep. Some of the dynamite crew had come out of the lunch wagon and were sitting around on the ground, smoking and laughing. At twenty minutes to one, Hewitt and Benson came out of the wagon. They were close enough by for Pascal to overhear their conversation. There was no attempt to guard it. Hewitt looked at his watch.

"Wish we could get started," he said. "The men still have twenty minutes. I'd like to get it over with."

"It won't take long to hook up the lead wire," Benson said.

Hewitt gave his hatbrim a tug. "I think I'll go on up," he said.

"Want me with you?" Benson asked.

"No. Have your smoke. Come on up with the crew. I just don't want to hang around here."

"See you in a few minutes, then," Benson said.

Hewitt got into the pickup truck and started up the road to the blasting site. Pascal watched him go. After a moment or so he shook his head. "Getting to be an old woman," he said. He started the jeep and drove over to where Benson was standing.

"Anybody else up there?" he asked the powder expert.

"No," Benson said. "Why?"

"Just wondered," Pascal said. "If something is being aimed at Hewitt it might be just as well if he wasn't left alone during this last stretch of time."

"Nothing can go wrong now," Benson said. "You can bank on that, Lieutenant."

"All the same," Pascal said, "I think I'll drive up there."

He turned the jeep and headed for the corduroy road. Pascal was aware of feeling that the countryside was abandoned, but there was no hint of death in the air.

Then, suddenly, the ground shuddered under the wheels of the jeep, and the face of the quarry burst outward, violently and thunderously. . . .

Pascal heard voices. Someone was scrambling down into the gully where he lay. He recognized the nearest voice as Dr. Lane's:

"Pascal! Pascal! Are you all right?"

"Now, that's a silly question," Pascal murmured.

"Thank heavens!" Lane said. "We weren't sure you hadn't reached the top. Here, let me have a look at you."

Dr. Lane knelt down beside him. His fingers explored Pascal's bones. There was something undignified about it, Pascal thought.

"I'm all right," he said. "Pretty badly shaken up, is all. I've tried moving everything. What about Hewitt? I had a glimpse of him standing by the nearest hole just before things happened."

"He was right on top of it when it blew," Lane said. "Not a chance for him. If the blast didn't kill him he's buried under thousands of tons of stone. Come on; lets get you on your feet. I can't dress those cuts and bruises here."

Pascal struggled up. Someone else was helping the doctor, and Pascal turned to look at him. It was Benson, his face the color of an old dustrag. The corner of Pascal's mouth turned down.

"Some foolproof!" he said.

Pascal must have passed out cold after that, because the next thing he knew he found himself lying on a cot in the office shack, with the anxious face of Uncle Ben bending over him.

"Hi," Pascal said.

"Jumping Jehoshaphat, it took you long enough to come around," Uncle Ben said. The immense relief in his eyes belied the sharpness of his voice.

Pascal reached out and touched his arm. "Thanks for worrying," he said. "Must have been shock and a touch of concussion from the blast. I seem to be all in one piece. How long have I been here?"

"You passed out after they found you," Uncle Ben said. "It's been about twenty minutes since they got you here. Doc Lane said you were okay. He'd gone back up top, just on a chance they might find Hewitt. He could have been blown away from the blast instead of going down under the rock. Outside chance. No one really thinks so."

Pascal swung his legs over the side of the cot and sat up. For a moment the office spun dizzily around him.

"I guess I'll do," he said, grinning at Uncle Ben. "Sorry about the jeep, though."

"Heck, the jeep's tougher than you are," Uncle Ben said. "They just drove her out of there."

Pascal inhaled on his cigarette. "So it happened in spite of us," he said.

"Yep," Uncle Ben said. His smile was acid. "They say it was a perfect blast. Best fragmentation of stone in years. They say there'll be almost no secondary blasting, except where they have to dig for Hewitt. Everything's perfect except the timing."

"How did it happen?" Pascal asked.

"Scientifically speaking, it didn't happen," Uncle Ben said grimly. "I talked to Benson. It wasn't hooked up to the blasting machine, so it couldn't have happened. It was an electrical circuit that had to be set off by the proper machinery. The proper machinery wasn't attached, and so it couldn't happen."

"Maybe someone attached the proper machinery during the lunch hour."

Uncle Ben shook his head. "No, sir. The lead wire and the blasting machine *were down here,* neatly packed in the truck, ready to be taken up by the crew. There wasn't any wire or machine up there. And if there was a second set of things, there wasn't time for anybody to remove 'em without trace."

"So it happened. So there is an answer," Pascal said. "An unaccountable, for the moment, accident."

"Nope," Uncle Ben said. "No room for accident. They can tell that by science. Somebody had to set it off on purpose—except that's impossible, too."

"Well, it wasn't gremlins," Pascal said.

"Who?"

"Skip it," Pascal said. He stood up, testing his legs. They were a little shaky but they worked. "Let's get moving."

He started for the door. Before he reached it, it was opened inward. Nora Hewitt stood there.

"They found him!" she whispered.

Uncle Ben went over and put his hand on her shoulder. "Then he didn't go down under the rock. That's a blessing, Nora."

She moved away from him as though his hand had burned her. "Not Marshall!" she said. "It's Tom they've found. He was up there—unconscious. He'd been struck on the head by a piece of flying stone and knocked unconscious."

Uncle Ben let his breath out in a long sigh. "So it was him, after all," he said.

"No! No! No!" Nora cried. "You've got to help him, you and the lieutenant, Uncle Ben! You've got to help him."

"Miracles are not in our line, Mrs. Hewitt," Pascal said. . . .

There was a well-equipped first-aid station in the shack next to the office. They had brought Tom Anderson there. He lay on a small operating table, with Lane bending over him as Pascal and Uncle Ben went in. Benson and Tiller, the quarry superintendent, were there. Nora Hewitt stood framed in the doorway.

Finally Lane straightened up. He saw Pascal. "You look pretty chipper," he said.

"I'm fine. What about Anderson?"

Lane walked toward a washbasin in the corner to scrub his hands. "He got smacked good by a piece of flying rock," he said. "I can't be certain without X-rays, but I don't think it's any worse than a mild concussion."

"He hasn't regained consciousness at all, enough to explain why he was there?"

"It'll take a lot of explaining," Tiller said angrily.

"How did he manage it?" Pascal asked, turning toward Tiller and Benson.

"He set off the blast when the boss was standing right over it," Tiller said.

"How?"

"He must have run a piece of lead wire off in the woods and had a detonator there."

"Did you find either a wire or a detonator?"

"No," Tiller said. "But the crew's still looking."

Pascal turned to Lane: "How far could he have run after he was hit in the head, Doctor?"

"Are you kidding?" Dr. Lane said. He came toward them, drying his hands on a towel. "He was knocked cold."

"The rock came from the blast," Pascal said. "It must have been only seconds after it went off. If he used a detonator he'd have to push down a sort of plunger to set it off, wouldn't he? That would leave only seconds before the blast went off. Right, Benson?"

"A fraction of one second," Benson said.

"All in all, if he moved ten feet from the detonator before he was struck it would have been a lot. So the wire and the detonator must be close to where you found him, if they are anywhere."

"Look, Lieutenant; you haven't got it all clear," Benson said. He wiped his sweating face with the sleeve of his shirt. "We found him about ten feet from the blasting line. He'd have been knocked cold by the concussion itself. He couldn't have moved one foot, let alone ten. Believe me, there's no lead wire and no detonator up there. That isn't how it was done."

"How, then?" Pascal's voice was hard.

"It sounds crazy," Benson said, "but there was no way."

"So it didn't happen," Uncle Ben said sourly. "In spite of that, I've got to send for the State Police. And I'm placing Tom Anderson under arrest on suspicion of murder." He turned toward the door and found himself facing Nora Hewitt. She looked like a bright flower that had wilted in the heat. "Dad blame it, Nora, it's my duty," he said.

Pascal was left with the doctor, Benson, and Tiller. Dr. Lane had moved back to the operating table and was feeling Tom Anderson's pulse.

"Stronger," he said. "He's coming along."

"I'm not good at guesing games," Pascal said. "You experts tell me this couldn't have been an accident. Then it had to be murder or suicide."

"Suicide!" Tiller exploded. "Are you crazy?"

"Probably," Pascal said, "but it's an angle to be considered. The point is, we need to know *how* it was done. Benson says there was no way, but of course he's wrong. Start thinking, Benson. Start thinking hard, because it did happen, so there was a way."

"The thing is clear as glass," Tiller said in his harsh voice. "Anderson's been making trouble around here for a year. We haven't been able to prove it, but we know it. He was there when the blast went off, so we know he's responsible. I don't need any more than that."

"A jury will," Pascal said. . . .

It was an hour before Tom Anderson regained consciousness, an unfruitful hour in which all reports were negative.

The dynamite crew discovered nothing at the site to explain the blast. Sergeant Gates, a tanned, gray-haired State Trooper, arrived and began questioning the crew. He didn't seem displeased to find Pascal there.

"Heard about you, Lieutenant. Glad you're here," he said, shaking hands warmly. "You had a close squeak."

"Too close," Pascal said. "If there's any way I can help—"

"Just act like you were in charge," Gates said. "A tricky homicide like this doesn't come my way every day."

Pascal listened to the questioning. It all added up to nothing. Anderson was on deck. Therefore he must be guilty.

About three o'clock Dr. Lane sent word from the first-aid station that Anderson had regained consciousness and was able to talk. Pascal, Gates, and Uncle Ben went there at once.

Anderson's blond head was swathed in a bandage and his face was painfully white. He looked defensively around at the circle of faces, but he didn't speak.

"Hello, Tom," Pascal said. "What happened up there?"

Anderson turned his head, and a spasm of pain twisted his mouth. "I know what's been going on here," he said. "Someone's been trying to frame me—all year. I hated Hewitt—hated his guts. But I'm not responsible for what's been going on at the quarry. That's the first thing you won't believe."

"Let's hear the second one," Pascal said.

"I didn't have anything to do with what happened up there this afternoon."

"You were just up there waiting for a streetcar," Pascal said.

"I was up there watching!" Anderson said. "I thought something might go wrong at the blast. I wanted to see what it was and who was responsible, because that person was the one trying to frame me.

"I got there this morning, just before the crew came to work. I climbed a tree about ten feet away from the line of holes. I sat there all morning, watching."

"Up a tree?"

"Yes," Anderson said. "And nothing happened. The work was all expertly done. I saw Benson check each hole and finally the connecting wire with his galvanometer. Hewitt and Tiller were with him, making sure. When everyone had gone down for lunch I got out of the tree and stretched my legs. Then I heard Hewitt's truck coming up, and got back up the tree again."

Anderson paused, and Dr. Lane handed him a glass of water. He drank a little and then went on:

"Hewitt parked the truck and walked over to the explosives shed. Benson had left the galvanometer hanging on a hook just inside the door. Hewitt took it and went over to the first hole where the ends of the connecting wires were. He hooked up one end to the galvanometer, and then he started to hook the other—and the world blew up in my face!"

Pascal was silent a moment. "Then the galvanometer set off the blast?"

"That's when it happened," Anderson said, "except the galvanometer couldn't do it. Not enough juice."

"What could go wrong with the silver chloride cell that sets up the juice in the galvanometer?"

"It could wear out," said Anderson dryly, "and then there'd be less juice."

"So it wasn't the galvanometer, and you were up a tree," Pascal said.

"I told you you wouldn't believe me," Anderson said bitterly.

Suddenly, in the distance, Pascal heard the machine-gun rattle of compressed air drills. They had started to dig in that monumental white rock pile for the body of Marshall Hewitt. . . .

"Despite a mass of fiction on the subject," Pascal said, "detectives rarely solve their cases through the use of black magic, Mrs. Hewitt." He was seated in the front seat of the wine-red convertible with Nora. The car was parked in the quarry yard. The drills chattered on. Almost everyone was at the huge rock pile, working or waiting his turn to work. "Most results are achieved by careful, methodical checking."

Nora shuddered, as if it were suddenly cold.

"I'm not sure what concerns you most, Mrs. Hewitt," Pascal went on quietly. "I'm not sure whether you are more interested in catching your husband's murderer—*if* he was murdered—or proving Tom Anderson's innocence."

" 'If he was murdered'?" Nora turned her pale face to him. "Is there any doubt of that, Lieutenant?"

"The build-up would certainly indicate it," Pascal said. "But there are some cloudy details. For instance, how could anyone have known Hewitt would go to the blasting site alone? If no one did, then the blast could have been meant for someone else, or simply sabotage again."

Nora was silent for a moment, and then she said steadily, "I knew."

"You knew he was going to make that check alone, while the men were still at lunch?"

"Yes."

"Would you mind explaining?"

"It was last night," she said. "Frank Lane and I are the only ones who seemed very much worried about today. Frank was at the house for a while, reporting on his headache tests. We both urged Marshall to take extra precautions today. Marshall laughed at us. But—later, when we were getting ready for bed, he came into my room. 'If you're really so worried,' he said to me, 'I promise to take special care. I'll make a private check of the whole blasting setup while the men are at lunch.' "

Pascal remembered the conversation he'd heard between Hewitt and Benson just before Hewitt had gone up to the site. Benson hadn't seemed to know that this was something planned in advance. Hewitt hadn't spoken of it as though it was something he'd meant to do all along. "Do you know if he told anyone else?" Pascal asked.

"No," Nora said. "He left in the morning before I was up. I—I never saw him again after he went to bed last night."

"But, of course, he may have told someone. He may have told several people," Pascal said.

"Yes."

"Except that no one has mentioned it," Pascal said. "If he'd told Tiller, or Benson, or Lane, you'd think they'd have mentioned it."

She turned to him quickly. "It's also obvious, isn't it, that he wouldn't have told Tom? That there wasn't any way Tom could know he'd be coming up to the blasting site alone?"

"Once information leaks, it can leak to the most unlikely places," Pascal said. "There are probably men working in the quarry who like Tom and think he got a raw deal. He could have heard. It's not impossible."

"You don't believe his story, do you?" Nora said.

Pascal sighed. "If it isn't true, it's the silliest invention I ever heard. If I had one wish in the world to ask my fairy godmother, it would be to beg protection from amateur detectives. They always get themselves in a mess. Your Mr. Anderson climbs a tree at the scene of the crime to discover, he says, who the criminal really was. It seems not to have occurred to him that the one sure way to clear himself, if there was to be trouble, was to stay away!"

"Tom thinks the whole world is against him!" Nora said.

"But he can't imagine the whole world is blind," Pascal said. "If he'd been sitting in the local hotel lobby when the blast went off he'd have had a dozen witnesses to prove his innocence, even if they were against him! But, no, he climbs a tree and gets himself caught red-handed in the one place he shouldn't be. You didn't, by any chance, turn him down because you suspected his mentality wasn't all it should be?"

Nora stared straight ahead of her. She didn't answer.

"Why did you marry Hewitt?" Pascal asked gently. "That's an answer I have to have, Nora."

"I told you," she said in a flat voice. "I loved him."

Pascal shrugged. "Have it your way, Nora. You could save me a lot of trouble, but if you refuse, I'll still find the answer." . . .

Uncle Ben and Sergeant Gates took Tom Anderson off to the local jail shortly after five o'clock.

"Holding him as a material witness," Uncle Ben told Pascal, "so long as he admits being there when it happened. Just in case he isn't guilty, there's no use having that 'suspicion of murder' charge against his record."

"You got any other likely candidates?" Pascal asked.

"No. But maybe it *was* an accident," Uncle Ben said hopefully.

"Maybe the moon is made of green cheese," Pascal said. "All the same—"

"You think you can prove this was murder, Dave?"

The two men were back at Uncle Ben's cottage, sitting on the front porch. Uncle Ben had a beef stew going on the stove.

"I want some answers, Uncle Ben," Pascal said. "When I have them they may not prove anything. But I'm not going to sleep too much until I do have them."

"Answers to such as what?" Uncle Ben asked, fiddling with his pipe.

Pascal ticked them off on his fingers: "One: What made the blast go off? Two: Did anyone besides Nora know that Hewitt intended to go up there alone? Three: Why did Nora turn down Tom Anderson and marry Hewitt?" Pascal cocked an eye at the old man. "Can you answer any of 'em?"

"Nope," Uncle Ben said. He put his pipe between his teeth and hunted for a match. Pascal tossed him a package. "Number one," the old man said, when his pipe was going, "is for the explosives experts to answer. Number three is for the lonely hearts department. Number two—well, that's for us, Dave."

"Who hated Hewitt besides Tom Anderson?"

"Nobody made it public," Uncle Ben said.

"Nora?"

"She's his wife."

"Does that exclude her?" Pascal asked.

"She was here in town when it happened, looking for Tom," Uncle Ben said. "She has an alibi."

"Maybe," Pascal said. "Nobody has an alibi till we know how it was worked. Maybe it was worked by remote control."

"Me, I got to believe in what I believe in," Uncle Ben said. "Nora wouldn't hurt a fly."

"What does that make Tom Anderson?" Pascal asked dryly. "She's just about wrecked him."

The old man took his pipe out of his mouth and stared at his nephew for a moment. Then he shook his head, slowly. "Tell you what, Dave. I'll be the detective for a while. I know everyone who works at the quarry. I know 'em well. They trust me. Maybe I can find out who knew Hewitt was going up there."

"Fine," Pascal said.

"You can wrassle with the explosives experts and the lonely hearts department. Okay?"

"Okay," Pascal said. "I'll want to make a couple of long-distance calls on your phone. That go on your expense account?"

"You solve this thing, Dave, and I'll pay it out of my own pocket. This ain't going to be a nice town to live in till this mess is cleared up." Uncle Ben raised his head and sniffed. "Stew's ready," he said.

Pascal put in his first call before he sat down to a savory bowl of beef and vegetables. It was to a friend of his in New York. The operator promised to call him.

After a couple of mouthfuls of stew he turned to Uncle Ben. "How do I locate Larry Mason, Nora's brother?"

"I don't know," Uncle Ben said. "I guess you ask her."

Pascal shook his head. "Might get the wind up," he said.

Uncle Ben thought a minute. "Ed Stevens is local correspondent for the *Warrentown Express.* He's probably got all the dope on the home-town boys that made good. But I don't see—"

"Before you start playing detective," Pascal said, "find out for me where Larry lives and the name of the limestone outfit he works for."

"Let a man eat his supper first, huh?" Uncle Ben said. But after a moment or two of silence he groaned, put down his fork, and went to the telephone. When he returned he had information, written on a slip of paper. Larry lived in and worked out of Pittsburgh. Pascal immediately got the toll operator on Larry Mason's trail.

"Supper's ruined," Uncle Ben complained a few minutes later. "Guess I better start playing detective. If you're waiting for calls you won't want the jeep."

"Help yourself," Pascal said. "And be a little devious, old-timer. You're not going to get a straight answer from someone." . . .

It was about a half-hour after Uncle Ben had left that Pascal got his first result. The operator informed him that she had Larry Mason for him in Pittsburgh.

Mason's voice sounded anxious. "Who is this?" he asked.

"My name is Pascal, nephew of Ben Michaels, the Stone Ridge sheriff."

"Oh?"

"Have you heard the news about your brother-in-law, Mr. Mason?"

"Marshall? What about him?"

"He was murdered this afternoon, Mr. Mason," Pascal said.

"*What!*"

"I'm assisting in the investigation," Pascal said. "I want you here, Mr. Mason."

"But what happened? Who did it?" Mason asked.

"A planned accident at the quarry," Pascal said. "You haven't heard from your sister?"

"No," Mason said.

"How soon can you get here, Mr. Mason?"

"Why—why, I can leave here fairly early in the morning. I'll have to go to my office first. Then—"

"Not nearly soon enough," Pascal said. "It takes about three hours to drive here from Pittsburgh. I'd like you here in three hours and a half."

"But that's impossible," Mason said.

"It would be a nuisance to have to get the Pittsburgh police to bring you here, Mason."

"What have the Pittsburgh police got to do with it?"

Pascal made it sound very casual: "I think you know what I mean, Mason."

There was a long silence at the other end. Then Pascal heard something that sounded like a heavy sigh. "I'll leave here within the next hour," Mason said. "Where will I find you?"

"I'm staying at Uncle Ben's in the village," Pascal said. "You'll find me there, or else I'll leave a message for you."

He hung up the receiver. Interesting conversation, he told himself. The threat about the Pittsburgh police had been a casual shot in the dark. He smiled faintly. "I wish *I* knew what I meant," he murmured.

He went back to the kitchen and reheated the coffee. Then he sat there smoking and waiting for his call from New York. It was almost an hour before it came.

"Doug? Dave Pascal, here," he said, when he was connected.

"Hi, you old so-and-so."

"You used to work for a chemical company, didn't you, Doug?"

"I still do, kid. You got an invention for sale cheap?"

"I want information," Pascal said. "You know what a galvanometer is?"

"The blaster's best friend," the voice said cheerfully.

"What could go wrong with one so that it would set off a blast, Doug?"

"Nothing. Nothing at all, Dave."

"Well, something did," Pascal said. "Killed a man."

"Impossible," was the answer.

"None the less, it happened," Pascal said. "I want the answer. This galvanometer worked fine one minute, and then, half an hour later, it shot off twenty to thirty tons of dynamite."

"Tomorrow morning I can talk to some of the boys who know."

"By midnight tonight at the latest," Pascal said.

"Listen, you jerk! I'm out with a beautiful blonde."

"Midnight, at the very latest," Pascal said. "Call me at Stone Ridge 64."

"The blonde will never forgive you, but okay. Midnight."

Pascal walked out onto the porch and sat down. A honeysuckle vine blotted out the light from a street lamp. It was dark and cool. Pascal leaned back in a wicker chair and drew on his cigarette. There had to be an answer about the "how." Doug would find that for him. There was an answer to Nora's marriage, and Mason might provide that.

Then he heard the jeep moving down the quiet village street. Uncle Ben was coming home, and he might have answers, too. Pascal glanced at his wrist watch. The old man had been gone just over two hours.

Pascal got up and walked to the top of the porch steps. He saw the jeep coming, with Uncle Ben at the wheel.

Then, just as the jeep was in the full spread of light from the street lamp, it exploded. It appeared to burst at every seam, and then it settled down on the road, a twisted heap of smoking junk.

Pascal froze on the top step of the porch. For a moment he could not believe what he had seen with his own eyes. Then his motor reflexes unlocked and he sprinted down the steps and across the street to the smoking wreckage. He plowed through the gathering crowd. Finally he stood by the jeep looking into the smoldering heap of metal.

Violence was Pascal's business. He had seen death in many forms, and had viewed it calmly and in a detached fashion. Mostly, the people he saw in death were strangers, or people with whom he'd had only the most casual contact. This was someone he had loved.

Pascal turned and staggered away to the curb. He was afraid he was going to faint.

A persistent cry rose from the crowd for someone to get a doctor. It was the hysterical reaction to something unbelievable.

Pascal leaned against the lamppost. Then adrenalin began to pump through his system, building slowly into a seething rage. As he turned back toward the crowd he heard the siren of Sergeant Gates's car wailing in a downward, mournful scale as the trooper jammed on his brakes and piled out into the throng around the wreck. People began to explain, all at once: "It just exploded!" "It blew up—all of a sudden!"

Pascal grabbed Gates's arm. "I want road-blocks set up so that not a single person in this town can leave!" Pascal said, not recognizing his own harsh voice. "I want everyone connected with the quarry brought here. I want Mrs. Hewitt, Lane, Benson, Tiller—everyone. I want them fast!"

Gates just stared at him as if he were a stranger. For the last time a wave of weakness swept over Pascal. He leaned his weight on the sergeant's shoulder. His voice cracked. "I'm sorry," he said. "I have no right to give orders. I—"

"I told you to act as if you were in charge," Gates said. "What happened?"

"I don't know," Pascal said. "I want Benson first. He's an explosives expert. He can tell us."

Dr. Lane arrived shortly after that. He looked in the jeep and turned away, almost as overcome as Pascal had been. He took a handkerchief out of his pocket and wiped his face. Then he saw Pascal.

"It *was* Uncle Ben?" he asked.

"Who else?" Pascal said grimly.

"I just—just hoped," Dr. Lane said.

Pascal left after Gates had deputized a couple of men to stand watch over the jeep. He went directly to the sheriff's office, which was about a block away, an adjunct to the jail. Gates was there, telephoning orders for the road-blocks.

"Benson's on his way," he said, when he hung up the receiver. "I called him first."

Pascal sat down in a chair beside the desk—Uncle Ben's desk. He felt a hard lump in his throat as he saw the pipe and can of tobacco, the scribbled notes in the old man's spidery handwriting. What was it Uncle Ben had said? That he, Pascal, could handle this best because he could keep his heart out of it!

He took a deep breath and proceeded to tell Gates what had happened earlier in the evening. "I was tracing the possible causes of the explosion at the quarry, and trying to get some facts about Nora Hewitt's marriage. Uncle Ben, because he knew people, was trying to find out who besides Nora might know that Hewitt planned to go to the blasting site alone." Pascal hesitated a moment. Then he said, "He must have found out! I sent him out to die."

"You shouldn't feel that way. It was his job," Gates said. "He never ducked a responsibility in his life."

"Thanks for talking sense," Pascal said. "Look here, Gates. You might as well release Tom Anderson. He wasn't responsible for this, and for my money that means he probably wasn't responsible for the other. He may be able to help us."

"How?"

"If he was telling the truth, and now I think he was, he can give us a lot more detail about the comings and goings at the blasting site."

"I'll get him," Gates said. He picked up a ring of keys from the desk and disappeared.

Pascal called the operator and gave instructions for his New York call, when it came, to be transferred to the sheriff's office. . . .

Anderson looked subdued when he was brought into the office. There was sympathy in his tone. "I can't tell you how sorry I am to hear what's happened, Lieutenant," he said. "Uncle Ben was a swell guy."

"He had his chips on you from the start," Pascal said. He leaned forward, "Listen, Tom; you can repay some of that faith he had in you by helping to catch his murderer."

"Anything I can do," Anderson said.

"Then answer me a question, Tom. It may not seem to you to have much bearing on this, but, believe me, it does. What happened between you and Nora? Why did she marry Hewitt?"

"I don't know," Anderson replied slowly. "That's the truth, Lieutenant. One day she wrote me a note saying it was all over between us and that she was going to marry Hewitt. I rushed over to see her, but she was gone. She'd timed it so that I'd be too late."

"Did you try to find out, when they came back here to live?"

"You saw what I had to do to get her to talk to me at all," Anderson said. "She's never explained."

"So that's that," Pascal said. "Now for your tree-climbing expedition."

"I was a fool," Anderson said.

"But you might save the day for us," Pascal said. "You're sure you saw no one around when Hewitt came up there alone?"

"I'm positive there wasn't anyone."

"All right," Pascal said. "Let's go back to the time when the men went down the hill for lunch. Benson had been testing the holes individually, and finally the connecting wire, with his galvanometer. Right?"

Anderson nodded.

"No hitch?"

"No hitch. Hewitt and Tiller were with him all the time. They were all satisfied."

"Then the crew came down for dinner?"

"Right. They all rode down in a dump truck. Hewitt, Benson, and Dr. Lane went down in the pickup."

"You said before that, when Hewitt came up alone, he went to the explosives shack and got the galvanometer off a hook where it was hanging inside the door. Was it common practice to leave the galvanometer there?"

"Sure. It's sort of a tool shed too."

"Who went into the shed before they came down?"

"Quite a few of them," Anderson said. "The men had jackets hanging there. They had tools they wanted to leave."

"But no one stayed behind?"

"No. I'm positive of that, Lieutenant. You see, I was on the lookout for anything out of the ordinary."

One of Gates's men stuck his head in the door. "Benson's here, ready to report, Sergeant."

"One minute," Pascal said. He turned to Anderson again: "You're free to go, Tom. I've asked Nora to come here. It isn't idle curiosity—

my question about why she ditched you. Maybe you can loosen her up. If you can't, tell her that her brother's due here presently, and that if she won't talk, I'm going to force it out of him."

"What's Larry got to do with it?"

"Everything—unless I'm way off base," Pascal said. "Now, get going, Tom." He turned to the deputy: "Send Benson in."

Benson was badly shaken. He stood there, looking at Pascal and moistening dry lips.

"What did it?" Pascal asked.

"I've only had a quick look at it," Benson said, "and it's a guess. But I'll bet I'm right. Someone poured some liquid nitroglycerin in the gas tank."

"But I saw the jeep coming down the street!" Pascal said. "No one had a chance."

"Look," Benson said; "it could have been done while he had the jeep parked somewhere. There's no telling exactly how long it would take for it to blow. The N.G. would have to work down into the motor, and it wouldn't blow till it contacted a spark. He might have driven five feet or a mile. I don't think anyone could say just how far. It's not a test anyone would make, you understand. But it wouldn't happen the instant the motor started. The stuff would have to work through."

"Where would anyone get liquid nitroglycerin?"

Benson lifted a hand to his throat. "You can't just buy it over the counter. I—I could get it through my company. But—"

"Did you?"

"No!"

"All right, Benson. Have they removed the—have they taken Uncle Ben away?" Pascal asked.

"Yes."

"Then I want you to go back to the jeep and start going through the wreckage with a fine-tooth comb. Uncle Ben may have found out something. He may have had something with him. Keep at it."

"Sure," Benson said.

The phone rang. Pascal picked it up, motioning at the same time for Benson to go out. It was the New York call.

"I've got a possible answer for you," Pascal's friend told him.

"I need it badly, Doug," Pascal said.

"If somebody monkeyed with that galvanometer it could set off a blast. But it would have to be deliberate, Dave."

"It was," Pascal said. "Keep talking."

"It's as simple as this, Dave. You take out the silver chloride cell and replace it with an ordinary, ten-cent flashlight battery. The flashlight battery would probably give off enough juice to blow your blasting caps. Mind you, nobody would be fool enough to do that, Dave. When a galvanometer goes sour they always send them back to the factory for adjustment or replacement. No one would fool with it unless—"

"Precisely," Pascal said. "Unless they wanted to set off a blast with it. Thanks a million, Doug." He put down the receiver. "A ten-cent holocaust!" he muttered. "How simple can it be, if you have the knowledge?"

Dr. Frank Lane came in the door then. He walked over to the desk. "As the coroner, I have to make a report," he said. "It's unpleasantly simple, Lieutenant. Uncle Ben was blown to pieces by an explosion that wrecked his car—probably nitroglycerin. I agree with Benson as to how it must have happened."

"You'll have to fill out forms, Doc," Sergeant Gates said. "And there'll be an inquest."

"I know," Lane said. He shook his head, an expression of disbelief in his eyes. "It's hard to take in. I saw Uncle Ben not an hour ago. Talked to him."

Pascal crushed out his cigarette in the ash tray on the desk. "What did he want of you, Doctor?"

"He was just checking on what happened this afternoon," Lane said. "Wanted to go over every detail of the day's doings at the quarry. There wasn't anything I could tell him that you didn't already know."

"Where did you see him?"

"He stopped at my house," Lane said. "I gathered he was making general inquiries from everyone who'd been on deck."

Pascal leaned back in his chair. "I think I know what set off the blast, Doctor. I think someone replaced the silver chloride cell in the galvanometer with a flashlight battery."

Lane's eyes widened. "Judas! That would blow things sky-high. But how was it managed? Of course, Anderson was up there alone. Anderson!"

"Anderson didn't blow up Uncle Ben's jeep," Pascal said. "He was shut up here in the hoosegow."

The deputy stuck his head in the door. "Mr. Mason and Mrs. Hewitt," he said.

Pascal's lips tightened. "I'll see you later, Doctor," he said. "Show them in, Deputy."

Larry Mason was a tall, thin young man with dark hair and rather small black eyes. Nora clung to his arm, protectively.

"I just got here, Lieutenant," Mason said. "I met my sister outside the building. I still haven't had a chance to find out what's happened. I hear Uncle Ben—"

"You can get a blow-by-blow account later," Pascal said in a hard voice. "Listen to me, Mason. I haven't time for evasions. What did Marshall Hewitt have on you?"

"Have on me? I don't know what you mean," Mason said.

"Your sister has chosen to give me a lot of doubletalk," Pascal said. "She says she married Hewitt because she loved him, but only an idiot would believe her. It's clear as crystal that she's in love with Tom Anderson, and always has been. So she smashed her life. Why? You're the only family she's got. I don't have to be a genius to guess that for some reason or other she sacrificed herself and her happiness on your account. Am I right?"

Mason swallowed hard. He looked helplessly at Nora and then back at Pascal. His voice was almost a whisper. "He—he could have had me sent up for twenty years," he said. "It was a matter of company funds. I—"

"That's all I wanted to know," Pascal interrupted. He turned to Gates: "Take this man somewhere and get a detailed account of every minute of his time for the last twenty-four hours. . . . No, wait, Mrs. Hewitt. I'm not through with you."

Gates took Mason into the next room. Nora sat down in the chair beside the desk and covered her face with her hands. There was no letup in the hardness of Pascal's voice.

"You know this doesn't make any sense," he said. "What possible reason could a man have for forcing a woman who doesn't love him into a marriage? Where's the satisfaction in that?"

Nora lowered her hands. "You didn't know Marshall," she said wearily. "He began paying me a great deal of attention a couple of years ago. Finally he asked me to marry him. I turned him down flat. I was in love with Tom."

"Go on."

"Marshall was a man who always got everything he wanted. He started with nothing and forged his way to a position of wealth and power. He couldn't stand rejection, Lieutenant. He hated me for it. But when he saw a way to force me into a marriage, he used it. It was out-and-out revenge on his part. Nothing else. He delighted in my misery. I—I could never give Tom the real explanation. He might really have killed Marshall if he'd known!"

There was a moment's silence; then Pascal went on. If he felt sympathy for her it wasn't revealed in his face or voice. "Mrs. Hewitt, did Uncle Ben come to see you tonight?"

She nodded.

"What time?"

"A little after eight."

"What did he want?"

"He asked the same questions you had earlier, Lieutenant. He—he thought I might have told someone that Marshall planned to go to the blasting site alone. I hadn't, as I told you."

"Did he ask for anything else?"

"No. That seemed to be all he was concerned with. He—he did urge me to be frank with you. Lieutenant, Larry's weak, but he's my brother. I—"

"He had a motive for wanting your husband dead," Pascal said. "But he couldn't have killed Uncle Ben. There wasn't time for him to get here. But what about you, Nora? You must have hated Marshall Hewitt."

She sat staring down at the floor. She didn't answer.

"You hated him," Pascal said. "He'd forced you into an unbearable situation. You knew he was going to the blasting site alone. You know a lot about the quarry and how things work. You were brought up here. Your father worked in the quarry. You could have tampered with the galvanometer when the men were at work."

"No," she said sharply. "I was here in town, Lieutenant. I have an alibi. You know that. Uncle Ben knew it! Besides, Tom was up at the blasting site. He can tell you I was never there."

"Can you imagine his telling me anything else?" Pascal said. "Maybe you and Tom have staged this whole act. He couldn't have killed Uncle Ben, but you could. You could have followed him when he left your house. You may have known he would catch up with you. Maybe you let something slip to him. When he stopped to talk to someone else, you could have poured that nitro into his gas tank."

"No, Lieutenant! No!" she cried.

He sat very still, studying her intently. "Motive, possible opportunity; they're there," he said. "The lovers in a murder pact, pretending to the outside world that they were not on speaking terms."

Just then Gates came back. He looked excited. "I think we've stumbled on something pretty hot, Lieutenant," he said. He glanced uncertainly at Nora.

"That's all for now, Mrs. Hewitt," Pascal said. "You and Tom better get together and straighten out your story. Don't leave. I'll want you again."

Without a word she went out. The moment the door closed behind her Gates began talking excitedly.

"The boys—two of the deputies—were helping Benson search the jeep," he said. "They came up with something you better see for yourself."

"Where are they?" Pascal said.

Gates went over to the side door and opened it. Into the room came the two deputies, with Benson walking, like a prisoner, between them. Benson's face was gray parchment. One of the deputies had something in his hand which he put down on the desk in front of Pascal. It was a small leather case, scratched and torn, but still in one piece. Inside it was a galvanometer. Written on the flap of the case in indelible ink were the words: "George Benson."

"This was under the seat," the deputy said. "Uncle Ben must have tucked it down beside him. When we found it Benson tried to make a break for it."

Pascal raised his eyes to Benson's face, slowly, "Well, Benson?" he said.

Benson went to pieces. His teeth chattered and tears ran down his face. "It's crazy," he said. "It's unbelievable. That thing should be buried in the rock pile with Hewitt's body if Anderson's telling the truth."

"Have they found Hewitt's body yet?" Pascal asked Gates.

The sergeant shook his head.

"Look, Benson; we know what happened," Pascal said. "Somebody put a flashlight battery in the galvanometer in place of the silver chloride cell. That's what set off the blast. Open that thing up."

Benson handled the galvanometer as though it was hot. It needed a small screw driver, which Pascal found in the desk, to get the back off. The five men peered down at it when it was open. No flashlight battery. The silver chloride cell had been smashed by the explosion of the jeep, but the remains of it were there.

"This is the galvanometer I used up there at the site this morning," Benson said. "It's mine. I don't deny that. I know the maker's number on it. It's the one I left in the explosives shed when we went to lunch. If Anderson's telling the truth, it's the one Hewitt had in his hands at the moment the blast went off. It should have been buried with him."

"Why did you try for a break when they found it?" Pascal asked.

"I lost my head," Benson said. "Seeing it there, I lost my head."

Pascal turned a pencil round and round in his fingers. "Did Uncle Ben come to see you tonight, Benson?"

"Yes."

"You didn't mention it before!"

"Well, why should I, Lieutenant? I'd just come from looking at—the jeep. You didn't ask me. I wasn't thinking about anything but what I'd just seen."

"What did Uncle Ben want with you?"

Benson closed his eyes as though it was an effort to remember. "He—he seemed to think the murderer must have known in advance that Hewitt planned to go up to the site alone during the noon hour. He asked me if I knew. I told him I didn't."

"What else did he ask you?"

"Nothing. He kept hammering at that one point." Benson's eyes widened. "You were close by, Lieutenant, when Hewitt sprang it on me. You must have heard me offer to go up with him."

Pascal didn't reply. His forehead was furrowed by a deep frown. "What time did Uncle Ben come to see you?"

"It was a little after nine. I know, because I'd just turned on a radio show I usually listen to on Thursday nights."

"It all checks," Pascal said, in an oddly tight voice.

"What checks?" Benson cried. "So help me, Lieutenant—"

"Shut up and listen to me," Pascal said. "This galvanometer clears things up a bit. I'd been wondering how someone had a chance to substitute the battery for the silver chloride cell without being seen. Nobody was alone long enough in the shed for that. And you used this for testing right up to the last minute. But it's clear enough now. Somebody substituted a different galvanometer, already prepared. Someone who knew Hewitt's plan. I think it was you, Benson. I think you brought this away with you. You probably hid it somewhere in your house."

"No!"

"I think Uncle Ben found it there when he visited you and sneaked it out with him when he left. I don't think you noticed it till after he was gone."

"No, I swear that isn't so, Lieutenant!" Benson protested. "I never saw this galvanometer after I left it in the shed before lunch, until we found it in the jeep."

"I think a little checking will prove you bought a second galvanometer. You knew we'd hang it on you when Uncle Ben delivered the galvanometer to us. You had to act quickly. You're about the only person in town who could normally be in possession of liquid nitroglycerin. Explosives are your business. I think you followed Uncle Ben. When he stopped at Dr. Lane's house you took that opportunity to pour the stuff into his gas tank. You expected the explosion would not only silence Uncle Ben, but also obliterate this galvanometer."

Benson's legs seemed to buckle under him. He sank down in the chair recently occupied by Nora Hewitt. "You've got it all wrong, Lieutenant," he said. "Nothing like that happened. I didn't have a second galvanometer. I didn't have any liquid nitro. I didn't even know Uncle Ben was going to Dr. Lane's."

Pascal turned to Sergeant Gates. "A little checking ought to wrap this up, Sergeant," he said.

"I'm satisfied now," Gates said.

Benson raised his face. "You've got to give me a break, Lieutenant. You can't prove any of this."

Pascal ignored him. "We're lucky to have cleaned this up so fast, Sergeant," he said. "The credit really belongs to Uncle Ben. It took sharp eyes for him to spot the galvanometer, wherever it was hidden."

And Pascal walked out of the office.

There was a crowd milling around outside. They turned silent as Pascal appeared. "It's all over," Pascal said. "We've got our man. It's Benson."

An angry murmur rose from the crowd. Then Dr. Lane stepped forward. "Benson!" he said. "It seems hard to believe. How did you get him?"

Pascal flipped away his cigarette. "I need a drink," he said. "And there are a few details you may be able to help me clear up, Doc. Come on back to the house with me."

They walked down the street together, and when they were out of earshot of the crowd Pascal gave Dr. Lane the outline of the case against Benson.

"But what was his motive?" Lane asked.

"I think he had big ideas, Doc," Pascal said. "He managed to get the quarry away from Anderson. I imagine Hewitt paid him well for that. How to get to the top in six easy lessons was his next problem. He may even have had his eye on the lovely Nora and Hewitt's money. With Hewitt dead and Anderson convicted of the murder he might have made it."

"Nora never even looked at him!" Lane said.

"You can't kill a man for hoping," Pascal said.

They walked up the front steps onto Uncle Ben's porch and into the house. Pascal locked the front door. "I don't want to be bothered with questions tonight," he said. He went through to the kitchen. The remains of supper were still there. Uncle Ben's unfinished plate of stew, their coffee cups. Pascal got a bottle of whiskey out of the pantry.

Pascal poured two drinks and set them down on the table. Both men drained their glasses. Pascal put his down on the table with a hard thud. He looked straight at Lane.

"Now, you murdering louse!" he said softly. "We're going to get to the bottom of this if I have to kill you!"

Lane stared at Pascal, his eyes widening. He had been about to put down his glass but he held it, suspended halfway to the table. "Good lord, Lieutenant, what's gone wrong with you?" he said.

Pascal's hand shot out and knocked Lane's glass spinning across the room, where it shattered against the old-fashioned coal range.

"I tell you what's wrong with me, young man," Pascal said in the same soft voice. "I loved Uncle Ben. By profession I'm a cop, but here I'm a private citizen with no obligations to anyone. I let Gates arrest Benson because I wanted to talk to you undisturbed for as long as it takes me to beat the truth out of you."

"Now, wait a minute!" Lane said, in a startled voice.

"I have a kind of special reputation," Pascal said. "I'm the man who always solves his case by detailed checking. Well, this is one case where I change techniques, my friend. I'm not going to bother to check. You're going to tell me the truth—provided you live through this."

Lane seemed caught and fascinated by Pascal's blazing eyes. "But your case against Benson—" he said.

"As full of holes as a Swiss cheese," Pascal said. "If Gates hadn't been so eager to make an arrest he'd have seen it. I wanted you to myself, Lane, so I helped him believe in it. Now you and I are going to clean this up."

"You've blown your top, Lieutenant," Lane said. "The shock of Uncle Ben's death—"

There was a crack like a pistol-shot as Pascal's open hand smacked against Lane's cheek. "We're not going to waste time with that kind of talk, Doctor."

Lane staggered back against the wall, and suddenly fear was in his eyes.

"You suckered me from the start," Pascal said. "Oh, it was smart, coming to me for help, pointing subtly all the time at Tom Anderson. I didn't pay any attention to you. I was focusing on Anderson. It was you who saw a future in Hewitt's widow, with both the men in her life dead."

"But Benson—"

"Benson's been in town just a couple of weeks," Pascal said. "Could he have been responsible for the sabotage at the quarry over the period of a year? No. It was you—the gent who had access to the quarry for your headache experiments, the gent who so graciously filled in for the local doctor when he died."

"That's guesswork!" Lane said.

"Backed by facts, sonny. You lied tonight. You lied your head off when you told me about Uncle Ben's visit to you."

"But he *did* visit me!"

"Sure, he did; only, you weren't there. That's when he found that galvanometer and came hot-footing home with it."

"That's guesswork, too."

"Is it?" Pascal said. "I asked you what Uncle Ben wanted. You said he was just checking on what happened this afternoon. You said he wanted to go over the details of the day's doings at the quarry. That proved to me, Lane, that he never talked to you about what was on his mind. *Because Uncle Ben was after quite a different piece of information.* He wanted to know who might have known that Hewitt planned to go to the blasting site alone. You didn't know that, so you gave me the wrong answer. That's because he never questioned you."

Lane opened his mouth to speak, and then closed it.

"You had to say Uncle Ben had called on you because his jeep was parked in front of your house. People knew that jeep and who owned it. If you'd denied the call you'd have been trapped. Because they'd have seen your car, too!"

"Then someone did—?" Lane said.

"No, Doctor, but it had to be that way. I think you were out—came home and saw Uncle Ben's jeep in front of your house. Being guilty, you acted like a guilty man. You snaked up to one of the windows and looked in. Uncle Ben had found that galvanometer. You knew your goose was cooked if he got back to me with it. It cost him him life that he didn't leave at once. He probably stayed because he thought he might find other evidence. I imagine your car was parked behind the jeep.

"You, Doctor—*you* had liquid nitro in that little black bag of yours. You were using it in your headache experiments. Some of the men were taking your pills; some of them were smearing liquid nitro in their hatbands, the old-fashioned way. You were making comparative tests.

So you got the nitro out of your bag and poured it into Uncle Ben's gas tank. It wasn't too risky. It was dark. If anyone happened along you could have pretended to be doing something to your own car. Then you went in and saw Uncle Ben!"

Again Lane opened his mouth, and again no sound came.

"It was perfect for you, because you could let him go. And, naturally, he wanted to go, since he had that galvanometer tucked away in his pocket. So he went—and he died!"

"You're—you're still guessing!"

"Am I? Well, I could still check, if I had a mind to, Doctor. I could prove *you* bought a galvanometer; I could probably prove the purchase of flashlight batteries; I can certainly prove the possession of liquid nitro. But I'm not going to bother, Doctor. Any more than I'm going to bother to do the necessary checking to prove it was you who murdered Hewitt. You knew, of course, he planned to go up there alone. You were the solicitous friend, who'd worried about him all along! You probably suggested that trip alone!

"When you went up to the site this morning for the final loading and checking, you had that second galvanometer, loaded with a battery, in your bag. At noon, when everybody was starting down, you probably left the bag in the shed. At the last minute you probably pretended to remember it and went back for it, alone. Hewitt and Benson waited in the pickup. It only took seconds to switch galvanometers. The stage was set. The murder machine was ready."

"Guesswork," Lane mumbled. "The same facts would fit Benson."

"He wasn't here for the sabotage," Pascal said. "And one more thing, sonny boy, Uncle Ben visited Nora Hewitt about eight. He saw Benson a little after nine. *After that,* by your own admission, he was at your house. Do you think, if he'd found that galvanometer at Benson's, he'd have bothered to stop and see you? He would not! He'd have come hot-footing for me, just as fast as that jeep could go!"

Pascal drew a deep breath. "You're it, Lane. Nora Hewitt is wealthy now. If things had gone as you planned, Hewitt would be dead and Tom Anderson would have paid the penalty for murder. Then you, the always sympathetic friend, would have had the field to yourself. In time you'd have had a good chance of getting what you wanted. You could afford to be patient—there was a big fortune at stake."

Lane moistened his lips. "You've built up an interesting case, Lieutenant, but—"

"I want to know," Pascal said softly, "where you bought the galvanometer. I want to know where you bought the flashlight batteries. I want to know where you got the liquid nitro. In short, Doctor, I want a full confession."

Lane started to laugh, and the laugh was smashed to an abrupt end by Pascal's fist. Lane sagged toward the floor.

"I've got all night. I've got all week. I've got all my life," Pascal said. "I could take that time to check and prove my case. But I'll get much more pleasure doing it this way." He yanked Lane to his feet. "Well, Doctor?"

For an instant, resistance flared once more in Lane's eyes, and then slowly faded. Perhaps it was the fear of further punishment. Perhaps he realized this was a dead-end street, whether he resisted or gave in. He lifted the back of his hand to wipe the blood away from his mouth. "What's the use?" he said thickly. "You could check. I—I'll make a statement for you."

Pascal loosened his hold on the doctor's coat. He let his breath out in a long sigh. "I wish you had put it off a while, Lane," he said. "I wish you'd made it just a little harder!"

ERLE STANLEY GARDNER
Death Rides a Boxcar

WHEN THE leg gave its first warning twinge, I stood still for a while and let the rest of the crowd stream on past, up the sloping passenger exit of the big Los Angeles terminal, up to the place where friends and relatives, wives and sweethearts waited in a roped-off space.

It was going to be a job, remembering to favor that leg, but anything was better than hanging around the insipid routine of the hospital.

"Gabby" Hilman was coming in by bus. He was to meet me at the Palm Court Hotel around ten o'clock. Until then I was just killing time. I could have started a little celebration over my release from the hospital, but I didn't want to do it without Gabby. He'd been my buddy, and I wanted to start even with him.

There was no such thing as getting a cab to yourself these days. They piled them in two, three, and four at a time. A starter grabbed the light bag I was carrying. "Where to?" he asked.

"Palm Court Hotel."

"Get in."

He held the door open, and that was when I saw class waiting in the cab.

She moved over as I got in. For a moment her eyes rested on mine— large dark eyes that were built to register expression.

I was careful about getting into the cab. "Sorry if I'm a little awkward," I apologized. "I'm nursing a knee back to life."

She smiled, but she didn't say anything.

The cab starter said abruptly, "Where to, sir?" and a man answered, "The corner of Sixth and Figueroa Street."

The cab starter said, "Hop in."

A woman came through the door first, an elderly, white-haired

235

woman with a beaming cheerful face and kindly gray eyes that blinked at me through silver-rimmed spectacles. The man with her looked to be somewhere around 70, so I pulled down the jump seat and moved over. It was rather a slow process because I didn't want to throw the leg out, and I thought the girl on my left watched me with just a little more interest than she'd shown before.

The elderly woman moved over to the middle of the seat, the man got in on the right side. The cab door slammed, and we were off.

It was a short run to Sixth and Figueroa. The man and the woman got off. The girl said to me, "If you're going much farther, you'd better come back to a more comfortable seat."

"Thanks," I told her, and moved back.

Her eyes were solicitous as she watched the way I moved my leg. "Hurt?" she asked.

"It's just a habit," I told her. "It will take some time to get accustomed to throwing the leg around."

She didn't say anything more for a while, and not knowing just how far she was going I decided I'd have to work fast. I took a notebook from my pocket, pulled out a pencil, and said, "I'm an investigator gathering statistics for a Gallup poll. These are questions we have to ask in the line of duty. Have you purchased war bonds?—Not the amount; just yes or no."

She looked at me with a peculiar, half-quizzical expression, and said shortly, "Yes,"

"Question Number Two," I went blithely on. "Do you feel sympathetic toward the personnel in the armed forces?"

"Of course."

"Question Number Three. Recognizing the fact that members of the armed forces whom you may encounter are frequently far from home, inclined to be lonely, and with no personal contacts, do you feel it is not only all right, but commendable, to let them make your acquaintance and perhaps, under favorable circumstances, act as your escort for an evening?"

I looked up at her expectantly, holding the pencil poised over the page.

There was just a twinkle in the dark eyes. "You're asking this question impersonally, of course?"

"Oh, certainly."

"Only as an investigator?"

"That's right."

"Collecting statistics?"

"Correct."

"Therefore, I presume you ask these questions of every woman you encounter who is over eighteen and under thirty?"

She had me there. I saw a bit of triumph in her eyes. "That's not exactly correct," I said.

"Why not?"

"Over *sixteen* and under eighty," I told her, without smiling. "My employers want the field thoroughly covered."

She laughed, and just then the cab made a little lurch as it swung in to the curb over on the left side of the street. "I'm sorry, soldier. Here's where I get off."

"Question Number Four," I said, hurrying the pencil down the page. "Correct name, address, and telephone number."

She just laughed. The cab driver came around and opened the door for her.

"Good night," she said.

I closed the notebook and slipped it back in my pocket. Gabby could probably have done better. He's a whiz at pulling a line out of thin air and getting by with it.

She flashed me a smile. I raised my hat.

In a few minutes we pulled up in front of the Palm Court. I paid the driver and started easing my weight out of the cab.

My hand, resting on the seat cushion, felt something. I looked at it. It was a woman's black leather purse. Returning that purse might give me a chance to begin all over again—starting where I had left off.

I should have said to the cab driver, "That woman left her purse," but there's no use insulting Fortune when she gives a fellow a second chance. I simply slid the purse under my coat and held it there with my elbow.

"Leg bothering you?" the cab driver asked.

"A little stiff, that's all."

The first thing I saw when I opened the purse in my hotel room was a long thin strip of paper about 12 inches long, an inch and a half wide, and covered with a string of figures written with a soft pencil. First was the figure 6, with four straight lines just below it; then the figure 23, four lines, and a tally; then 10 and three lines below that—and so on down the entire strip of paper. On the other side a message had been written in the same soft pencil: "Puzzle No. 2 a little after midnight."

That meant nothing to me, so I placed the strip of paper on the bed and turned so the light would shine into the purse.

There was a wad of greenbacks in there that would have stuffed a sofa cushion.

I felt my heart start pounding as I pulled them out and dumped them on the bed. They were in twenties, fifties, and hundreds, with a small sprinkling of tens and fives.

I started counting. It added up to $7523 in currency, with a coin purse containing $1.68 in small change.

Then a disquieting thought struck me. The girl who had been in the taxi cab had paid her fare when she got to the sidewalk. I distinctly remembered seeing her hand the cab driver the fare. And I was almost certain she was holding an open purse in her hand as she did so—come to think of it, I was certain. This, then, must be the purse that belonged to the white-haired woman.

I started digging down into the lower regions of the purse.

I found a small leather key container which held four keys, then I took out a lipstick, a compact, four cleansing tissues, a small address book of red leather with a loop in front which held a little pencil, and an opened envelope which evidently contained a letter. The envelope was addressed to Muriel Comley, Redderstone Apartments, Los Angeles.

Then I reached for the telephone book.

The voice that answered the telephone sounded very much like that of the girl in the taxicab.

"Is this Muriel Comley?"

An interval—just long enough to be noticeable. Then the smoothly modulated voice said, "Who is this speaking, please?"

"Before I answer," I said, "I'd like to ask you a question. Did you lose something tonight—within the last hour?"

I felt her voice freeze. "I'm sorry, if you can't give me your name, I . . . oh, you mean you've found the purse? oh!" That last exclamation was filled with sudden dismay. "Will you hold the phone a moment?"

After a while I began to think it was just some sort of runaround. Then she was back.

"Yes. I lost my purse. Do you have it?"

Her voice sounded different from what it had been before—as though her throat had gone dry. I could imagine how she'd feel when she realized she'd lost a wad of dough like that. "I have it," I said, "and it's all safe."

She asked, "Is this, by any chance, the man who is collecting information for the Gallup poll on how women feel toward service men?"

"None other."

"I'm so relieved. If you'll just send—"

"I'll deliver it in exactly twelve minutes and thirty seconds," I interpolated, and hung up before she could argue the point.

I found the name Muriel Comley on the list of names to the right of the apartment-house entrance. She was in Apartment 218.

I pressed the bell, and almost immediately the buzzer announced that the door was being unlatched.

I pushed through the door and into the lobby. It wasn't the sort of apartment house in which one would have expected to find a tenant who carried a small fortune in cash in her purse.

I went up to the second floor, found 218, and pressed my finger against the door button.

The girl opened the door, smiling at me with her lips. Her eyes were wide and dark. When she turned so they caught the light, I saw she was afraid. There was terror in those eyes.

Her lips kept smiling. "Won't you come in? I'm sorry I can't offer you a drink, but the apartment seems to be fresh out of drinkables . . . So you found my purse? It certainly was stupid of me."

I kept the purse under my coat, holding it against my body with my left arm. I said, "I really couldn't believe it was yours."

"Why?"

"I thought you opened a purse when you paid off the cab driver."

She laughed. "Just a coin purse. I happened to have it in my pocket. Do sit down."

I stretched my left leg out in front of me.

"Is it bothering you?" she asked solicitously.

"No. Just habit . . . Of course, there are certain little formalities. You can describe the purse?"

"Of course. It's black leather with a silver border. The metal at the top has polished silver roses."

"And the contents?"

Her face went blank.

I kept waiting.

"You opened it?"

"Certainly. I had to get your name and address."

She said, "Surely, Mr.—I don't believe I have your name."

"Burr—Jayson Burr."

"Oh, yes. Mr. Burr. Surely you don't doubt that it's my purse," and she was laughing at me now, actually making me feel uncomfortable.

"I'm afraid you're going to have to describe the contents."

"Well, let me see. There was my lipstick, my compact, and—yes, I left my keys in there."

"Have any trouble getting into the apartment?" I asked casually, and watched her.

She said, without batting an eyelash "I always keep a duplicate key in my pocket. I've lost my purse before. I'm a bit absent-minded."

"All right. So far we've got lipstick, compact, and keys. What else?"

"Isn't that enough?"

"I'm afraid that's too general an inventory. It would describe the contents of any woman's purse."

"Well, let's see," she said archly, as though playing some very interesting game. "Since I'm accused of stealing my own purse—or *am* I accused of stealing it?"

"No accusation," I smiled, "no stealing. Simply for my own protection."

"That's right; you *are* entitled to some protection. Well, let's see. There was my address book in there, and some cleansing tissues, and—and a coin purse."

"Can you tell me how much money?"

"I'm sorry, I simply can't. I always carry an extra coin purse in my pocket. Sort of mad money, you know, and then carry the balance in—oh, I suppose there's ten or twelve dollars probably, altogether, but I can't be certain at all."

"And was there anything else?" I asked.

She frowned. "Really, Mr. Burr, I can't remember *all* the little details. Surely I've identified the purse well enough . . . You have it with you?"

I looked her squarely in the eyes and lied like a trooper. "I decided I'd better leave it in the hotel until you'd identified it."

"Why, what a strange way to—" she broke off and looked puzzled, a frown furrowing her forehead.

"I'm sorry," I said, "but, you see, you failed to describe the most important thing that was in the purse."

She was silent for a matter of seconds, then, abruptly, she got to her feet. "Mr. Burr, I've tried to be patient. I've tried to make allowances. But don't you think that, in the first place, you should have returned the purse to the cab driver? In the second place, you should have carried your investigation of the contents of the purse only far enough to have ascertained my name and address. In the third place, I *have* described the purse to you—in the greatest detail."

"The exterior."

"The exterior!" she repeated with icy dignity. "And that should be enough in dealing with a *gentleman.*"

I just grinned at her.

She said angrily, "You know I *could* have you arrested for taking that purse."

"Why don't you? Then I'll tell the judge to turn it over to you just as soon as you've described the contents."

"That wouldn't help *you* any."

"I don't know much law, but I think you'd have to convince a jury that it was *your* purse before you could convict me of stealing it, wouldn't you?"

Suddenly she was sarcastic. "Very well, if *that's* the way you feel about it I would prefer to lose the purse than put up with your insolence."

She swept toward the door and held it open.

That wasn't the way I had planned the interview to go at all. "Look here," I said. "All I want is a reasonable assurance that—"

"Thank you, Mr. Burr," she interrupted. "All I want is my purse. You admit that you came over here without it. Therefore, no matter *what* I may say, you can't deliver my purse to me here and now. Under the circumstances I see no use in prolonging the discussion. I will say this, that if you don't have that purse in my hands before tomorrow morning I'll have you arrested."

"You can have your purse just as soon as you—"

"I don't care to discuss it any more."

She was watching me as I stood holding my left arm against my side. She must have realized that the purse was under my coat, but she said nothing.

I walked out of the door and said, "Good night," without looking back. I heard the vicious slam of the door.

I was halfway to the elevator before I was aware she was following me.

The elevator was waiting there at the second floor. I pulled the door open and stepped to one side for her to get in.

She walked in ahead of me, chin up, eyes cold. I got in, closed the door, and pushed the button for the ground floor.

Neither one of us said anything.

The cage rattled to a stop. I opened the door, waited for her to get out. She was careful not to touch me as she walked past.

A man was sitting at the horseshoe desk behind a sign reading Manager. He was a narrow-shouldered chap with thick-lensed spectacles which gave his face a look of studious abstraction. He blinked owlishly in my general direction, and then lowered his eyes to a day-book in which he was making some entries.

The girl cleared her throat loudly, then said, "Pardon me."

The man at the desk looked up.

When she was sure his eye was on her, she grabbed for my left arm, which was holding the purse firmly against my body on the inside of my coat.

I was ready for her, and lowered my shoulder.

Her body struck against the shoulder and glanced off. Her hands clawed at my coat.

The clerk at the desk said, in mildly bewildered reproof, "Come, come, we can't have—"

The girl hung on to me. "Will you please call the police! This man has stolen my purse!"

The clerk blinked.

I smiled at him and said, "I've found *a* purse. She *says* it's hers, but she can't identify it."

She said to the clerk indignantly, "I've described it in detail. Please do as I say. Call the police!"

The clerk looked at me, then looked at her rather dubiously. "You're with Mrs. Comley?" he asked. "Aren't you the lady who just moved in?"

That question did it. She was licked the minute he asked her that question.

The clerk seemed surprised by her sudden surrender. "Oh, all *right*," she stormed. "Take the purse if you think it will do you any good." She flounced toward the elevator.

I raised my hat. "Good evening," I said, and walked out.

I was dozing in the hotel lobby and didn't see Gabby when he came in. The first I knew, I woke up with a start, and there he was looking down with that good-natured grin of his.

"Hi, soldier," he said.

I came up out of the chair, forgetting everything the doc had told me about the leg. Gabby thumped me on the shoulder and I made a quick pass at his chin. Then we shook hands.

We went up to the room. Gabby splashed around in the bathtub and I told him all about the purse.

"Where you got this purse now?" Gabby asked.

"I did it up in a bundle and told the hotel clerk that the package contained important military documents, to put it in a safe, and to be darn sure no one else got it."

Gabby, pulling clean clothes out of his bag, thought things over while he got dressed. "This jane is class?" he asked.

"With a capital C."

"Why wouldn't she tell you what was in the bag?"

"She didn't know. She isn't Muriel Comley."

"Then what was she doing in Muriel Comley's apartment?"

"I don't know. Seemed like she was visiting, from what the clerk said."

"Seems like we'd ought to do something about this," Gabby said, and winked.

"That's the way I felt."

"Maybe Muriel's good-looking," Gabby suggested.

"Could be."

"What," Gabby asked, "are we waiting for?"

"You."

Gabby grinned, struggled into his coat, and said, "Let's go."

At the apartment-house entrance I rang the bell of 218 and we stood there waiting, tingling with that feeling of excitement which comes from doing something interesting and not being quite certain what is going to happen next. After a few seconds I pressed the button again. When there was still no answer I said to Gabby, "Perhaps she's been expecting this and decided nothing doing."

"Perhaps she's gone to bed."

I said, "Oh, well then, we wouldn't want to get her up. Oh, no! We'll go right on back to the hotel."

Gabby laughed.

I moved over to the front door, pressed my face against the glass, looked inside, holding my hands up at the side of my face to shut out the reflection of the street lights. There was no one at the desk. The lobby looked deserted.

"Anything doing?" Gabby asked.

"No. Evidently the clerk's gone to bed and this outer door is kept locked at night."

I pressed a couple of other buttons. On my second try the buzzer on the door whirred, and Gabby, pushing against the door, stumbled in as the door opened. We walked up the one flight of stairs.

Just as I raised my hand to knock on the door of 218, Gabby caught my wrist. Then I saw that the door lacked about a sixteenth of an inch of being closed. The apartment was dark behind it and from where I was standing, the door looked to be securely closed. Standing over at Gabby's angle, you could see it wasn't.

We stood there for a second or two in silence, looking at the door. Then Gabby pushed the door open.

I went in. We found the light switch, snapped on the lights, and Gabby heeled the door shut behind us.

The apartment was just as I had last seen it. Nothing seemed to have been touched or moved.

Gabby tried a door which led to a kitchenette. While Gabby was prowling around in there, I opened the other door.

"Gabby!" I yelled.

Gabby's heels pounded the floor, and his fingers dug into my shoulder as we stood looking at what lay there on the bed.

The body was sprawled in that peculiarly awkward position which is the sign of death. By the weird, unreal light cast by a violet globe in the bed lamp I could see his features. I had the feeling I'd seen him before, and recently, too. Then I remembered. "It's the clerk at the desk downstairs," I said.

Gabby gave a low whistle, moved around the end of the bed, paused, looking down at the floor.

"Don't touch it," I warned as I saw him bend over. I moved around and joined him, looking down at the thing on the floor lying near the side of the bed.

It was a club some two feet long, square at one end, round at the other, and covered with sinister stains which showed black in the violet light. There were three rings cut in the billet, up near the round end, and, between these rings were crosses; first a cross like a sign of addition, then a conventional cross with the horizontal arm two-thirds of the way up the perpendicular, then another cross of addition.

We searched the rest of the place. No one was there.

"I think," I said, "someone's putting in too many chips for us to sit in the game."

"Looks like it to me," Gabby admitted.

We left the door slightly ajar, just as we had found it. We couldn't be bothered with the elevator, but went tiptoeing down the corridor at a constantly accelerating rate. I wanted to get out of the place.

Suddenly down at the far end of the corridor a dog barked twice. Those two short barks made me jump half out of my clothes and sent a chill up my spine. Gabby moved right along. I doubt if he even heard them . . .

We didn't say any more all the way to the hotel. We went up to our room. Gabby sat down in the big chair by the window and lit a cigarette. I pulled up my bag and started scooping up the stuff on the bed and cramming it in. When I had my clean clothes packed, I spread out my soiled shirt so I could wrap clothes in it for the laundry. A slip of paper fluttered to the floor.

"What's that?" Gabby asked.

I picked it up. "That's the piece of paper that was in the purse. I put stuff from the purse out on the bed, and I'd also dumped my bag—"

"Let's see it."

I handed it over.

Gabby frowned. " 'Puzzle No. 2 a little after midnight.' That mean anything, Jay?"

"Not to me."

Gabby's eyes were cold and hard. "Never heard of a switch list—or a puzzle switch?"

"No." I knew then, just from the way Gabby was looking at me, that we were in for something.

"You see, Jay, there's just a chance this is a trap we're being invited to walk into."

"Sort of will-you-walk-into-my-parlor-asked-the-spider-of-the-fly?" I inquired inanely.

"Exactly."

"So what do we do?"

Gabby's lips were a thin line. "We walk in. Come on, Jay. We're going to the freight yards. I have to see a man down there anyway, and this is as good a time as any."

We got across the yards in a series of jerks and dashes to a big wooden building. Gabby led me up a flight of stairs, down a long corridor lined with offices, and pushed open a door.

A man who had been writing down figures on the page of a book glanced up. An expression of annoyance gave way to astonishment. Then the swivel chair went swirling back on its casters as he jumped to his feet.

"You old son of a gun!" the man exclaimed.

Gabby gave that slow grin of his and said, "Fred, this is Jay Burr," and to me, jerking his head toward the man in the green eyeshade, "Fred Sanmore."

Just then a train came rumbling through and it sounded as though the building was within a half mile or so of a heavy bombardment.

Everything shook and trembled. The roar of sound filled the room so there was no chance to talk. We simply sat there and waited.

When the train had passed, Sanmore went back of the desk, took off his eyeshade, and said to Gabby, "You old so and so, you want something."

"How did you know?" Gabby asked.

"Because I know you. You're here on furlough. This is your first night in town. You've been here for a couple of hours. By this time you'd be buying drinks for a blonde, a brunette, and a redhead—if you didn't want something. What is it?"

Gabby pulled the strip of paper out of his pocket. "List of cars going past the puzzle switch?" he asked.

"Probably coming on a switch from over the hump."

"What," I asked, "is a hump?"

Sanmore started to answer me, then turned to Gabby instead. "Why do you want to know, Gabby?"

"Just checking up."

Sanmore sighed and turned back to me. "Sorry, Burr. A hump is the high point on a two-way incline. You push cars up to the hump, then cut 'em loose, and gravity takes 'em down across the yards. It saves a lot of wear and tear, a lot of steam, releases a lot of rolling stock, and handles a cut a lot faster than you can any other way."

"And a cut?" I asked.

He grinned. "Any number of freight cars taken from a train and switched around yards. Even if it's a whole train. The minute a switch engine gets hold of it, it's a cut."

Gabby said, "Any idea whose figures these are?"

Sanmore shook his head. "We might be able to find out."

"You're certain that's what this list is?" I asked.

"Positive."

"Would it be too much to ask just what makes you certain?"

He said, "Well, in the first place, notice the numbers. There aren't any of them higher than ninety-seven. We have ninety-seven numbers on our terminal card index. Whenever a train comes in, a switch list is made up, and numbers are put on the cars for different destinations.

"For instance, here's Number One, and underneath it are three lines. That means there are three cars in a row for T N O Manifest. Then here's two lines under Number Eleven. That means two cars in a row for Indio. Then there are two lines under the figure four, which means two successive cars for the El Paso Manifest.

"Now then, loosen up and tell me what brings you two goofs in here at this hour of the night to ask questions about railroading."

Gabby said awkwardly, "Just got curious, that was all. Jay thought it might be a code."

Sanmore kept looking at Gabby.

Gabby reached for the strip of paper.

Sanmore started to hand it to him, then idly turned it over.

Gabby grabbed for it.

Sanmore jerked his hand back and read the message on the back: " 'Puzzle No. 2 a little after midnight.' " I saw his eyebrows get level.

Gabby didn't say anything.

Sanmore slid down off the corner of the desk. "Come on, you birds."

He led the way down the stairs, out through a door, and up along the tracks bearing off to the left.

"This is a bit tricky," Sanmore said, as the tracks began to converge. "Watch your step along here." Abruptly he reached out, grabbed our arms. "Hold it!"

I couldn't see what had stopped us, when all at once a great bulk loomed out of the night. It was so close and seemed so ominously massive I wanted to jump back, but Sanmore's grip held me. And I realized then that another big shape was moving along just behind me.

"Putting cars over the hump," Sanmore explained.

As the car passed I could hear the sound of its wheels rumbling over the steel rails. But its approach had been as quiet as though I had been in the jungle and some huge elephant had come padding softly up behind me.

"All right," Sanmore said, and we went forward again.

"This is dangerous," Sanmore said. "You get one of those big boxcars rolling along by gravity and it's like a fifty-ton steel ball moving slowly down an incline. You can't stop 'em; you can't turn 'em. They don't have any whistle or any bell. They don't make very much noise against the background of noise from the yards, particularly when they're coming toward you. Okay; here we are, boys. Here's one of the puzzle switches."

A man sat at a complicated switch mechanism, a slip of narrow paper in his hands similar to the one I had found in Muriel Comley's purse. A seemingly endless stream of cars was rolling down the tracks that fed into the intricate mechanism of the switch—a remorselessly steady procession which called for carefully co-ordinated thought and action.

Sanmore said, "He's too busy to talk now. Let's go find the hump foreman."

We started moving up the tracks. I paused as I saw a line of men seated by a stretch of track. In front of them was a string of holes and in many of these holes there were billets of hickory, substantial clubs some two feet or more in length, identical, as nearly as I could tell, with the club we had seen on the floor by the murdered man.

Sanmore answered my unspoken question. "These are the men who ride the cars down," he said. "The hump is back up here. We put the cars over the hump. The pinmen uncouple the cars in units according to the numbers on them. Then one of these boys—notice that chap on the end now."

Two cars came rumbling down the track. A man swung lazily up out of a chair, picked up one of the hickory clubs, stood for a moment by the track gauging the speed of the oncoming cars, then swung casually up the iron ladder, climbed to the brake wheel, inserted his billet to give leverage on the wheel, tightened it enough to get the feel of the brakes, and then clung to the car, peering out into the darkness.

The car moved onward, seeming neither to gather speed nor to slow down as it moved. The man at the puzzle switch flipped a little lever. The car rattled across switch frogs, turned to the left, and melted away into the darkness.

A stocky competent man, who looked hard and seemed to have a deep scorn for anything that wasn't as hard and as tough as he was, came walking down the track.

Sanmore said, "Cuttering, couple of friends of mine looking the ground over . . . Whose figures are these?"

The man took one look at the long list of figures on the slip of paper; he looked at Sanmore, then he looked at Gabby, and finally at me.

"They're *my* figures," he said in a voice that had an edge of truculence. "What about it?"

Silently Sanmore turned over the slip and showed Cuttering the writing on the back.

"Not my writing," Cuttering said.

"Know whose it is?"

"No."

"Any idea what this message means?"

"No. Look here; there's a half a dozen of these old lists lying along the tracks. We throw 'em away after a cut has gone over the hump and through the switches. Anyone who wanted to write a message to someone and wanted a piece of paper to write it on could pick up one of these slips."

There was an uneasy silence for half a minute.

"What's so important about this?" Cuttering asked sharply.

"It may be evidence."

"Of what?"

I met the steady hostility of his eyes. "I don't know."

I reached for the strip of paper. "You'll have to make a copy of it," I said. "This one is evidence."

Wordlessly, while we watched, Cuttering copied off the string of numbers with the lines underneath them. Then, just before he reached the end, he frowned and said, "Wait a minute. We put this through yesterday night about eleven fifteen."

Sanmore didn't waste any more time. His voice was packed with the authority of a man giving an order. "Get me everything you have on that, Bob." Then he turned to Gabby. "We'll check those cars through the Jumbo Book, Gabby, if you think it's that important."

Gabby said simply, "I think it's that important. We're at the Palm Court. You can phone us there."

Gabby said to the cab driver, "Go a little slow in the next block, will you? I want to take a look on the side street."

The driver obligingly slowed. "This the place you want?" he called back.

"Next street," Gabby said, swinging around to look at the Redderstone Apartments.

Then Gabby and I exchanged puzzled looks. The apartments were dark. The street in front showed no activity. There was no unusual congestion of vehicles parked at the curb.

"Okay?" the driver asked as he crawled past the next side street.

"Okay," I said.

We went on to the Palm Court, paid off the cab driver, stood for a moment on the sidewalk. Neither of us wanted to go in.

"What do you make of it?" Gabby asked in a low voice.

I said, "We've got to tip off the police."

"We'll be in bad if we do it now."

"We've got to do it, Gabby."

"You don't think the police have been notified, cleaned up the place, and gone?"

I didn't even bother to answer.

"Okay," Gabby said. "Let's go."

We went into the lobby, nodded to the clerk on duty, and I walked over to the telephone booth. Gabby stood by the door until I motioned him away so I could close the door tightly.

I dialed Police Headquarters and said, "This is the Redderstone Apartments. Did you get a call about some trouble up here—about an hour and a half ago?"

"Just a minute," the voice said at the other end of the line.

"I'll check with the broadcasting department . . . What was it about?"

I said, "You'll find it all right—if it's there."

"Okay. Just a minute."

I held onto the line while the receiver made little singing noises in my ear. Then the voice said, "No, we haven't anything from the Redderstone Apartments. Why? What's the trouble?"

"Apartment two-eighteen," I said, "has a murdered man. You should have known about it an hour ago," and hung up.

Gabby was waiting for me in the lobby. His brows raised in a question.

"They know nothing about it."

"You reported it?"

I nodded.

Gabby and I went over to the desk to get the key.

The clerk took a memo out of the box, along with the key. "Some young woman's been trying to get to you. She waited here nearly half an hour."

"A good-looking brunette with large dark eyes," I asked, "about twenty-two or twenty-three, good figure?"

"Easy on the eyes," he said somewhat wistfully, "but she isn't a brunette. She's a redhead, blue eyes, dark red hair—guess you'd call it auburn. A quick-stepping little number."

"She didn't leave any name?"

"No name."

"Want to wait?" I asked Gabby.

He said, for the clerk's benefit, "Time was when I'd have waited all night on a hundred-to-one chance a girl like that would come back, but now I want shut-eye."

"Same here," I told him.

We went up in the elevator and hadn't much more than unlocked the door of the room when the telephone rang.

I picked up the receiver, and the voice of the clerk, who was evidently taking over the switchboard on the night shift, said, "She's here again. Wants to come up."

"Send her up," I told him, hung up the phone, and said to Gabby, "A redheaded gal is about to cross our paths."

Gabby walked over to the mirror, hitched his tie into position, ran a comb through his wavy hair. "Let's not fire until we see the whites of her eyes. Perhaps she has a friend."

Knuckles tapped with gentle impatience against the panel of the door.

I opened it.

The girl was something to take pictures of and then pin the pictures up on the wall.

"Won't you come in?" I asked.

She walked in as easily and naturally as though this was where she lived. She took off her gloves, smiled affably up at me, and said, "Which one of you is Mr. Burr?"

I nodded. "I have the—"

"Honor," Gabby finished.

We all laughed then and the tension let down. She said casually, "I'm Muriel Comley."

"*You* are!"

The blue eyes widened in surprise. "Why, yes. Why not?"

I said, "You aren't the Muriel Comley I saw earlier."

She looked puzzled for a minute, and then said, "Oh, you must have seen Lorraine."

"Who's Lorraine?"

"Lorraine Dawson."

"Tell me a little more about Lorraine."

"Lorraine was looking for an apartment on a fifty-fifty basis. I had this place on a lease. It was too big for me, and too much rent. Lorraine came in with me about a week ago."

I said, "You might tell me how it happens Lorraine got hold of your purse."

"She didn't get hold of it. I merely left it in the taxi. I got out. Lorraine stayed in."

"And how did you know where to come for your purse?"

"The taxi driver said you had it."

I raised my eyebrows.

"You see," she said, "I called up the cab company. The purse hadn't been turned in. They got hold of the cab driver. He said he remembered you had picked something up from the seat of the cab when you got out. He thought it might have been the purse."

"I didn't know you had been in that cab."

She sighed. "Lorraine and I went to the depot," she explained "I got out and went to meet a train. Lorraine was coming on home, and wasn't going to wait. I waited down there at the depot for the train to come in. The person I expected to meet wasn't on it. Then suddenly I realized I didn't have my purse. I thought back, and remembered that I must have left it in the cab. That was when I called the cab company. Now do I have to explain to you anything more about my private affairs in order to get what belongs to me? After all, Mr. Burr, your own actions are subject to considerable question."

Gabby said, "He's just trying to be sure, that's all."

She turned to him, and her eyes softened into a smile.

I said, "I'm not interested in your private affairs. But, under the circumstances, since you're the second person this evening who has claimed to be Muriel Comley, I'd like some proof."

"Very well," she said, dropped her hand to the pocket of her light coat, and pulled out a transparent envelope which contained a driver's license.

The driver's license was made out to Muriel Comley. The description fit her to a T.

"The purse," she said, "is of black leather with a smooth glossy finish. The mountings are silver with narrow borders stamped around the edges of the metal, silver curlicues embossed against a dull-finished background. The handles are of braided leather. Is that enough?"

"The contents?"

"You looked inside?"

"Naturally."

She met my eyes. "The purse," she said, "contained something over seven thousand five hundred dollars in cash, in addition to having my lipstick, keys, a small coin purse with about a dollar and a half in change, an embroidered handkerchief, some cleansing tissues, an address book, and a compact."

Gabby sighed. "I guess," he said to me, "she gets the purse."

I hesitated.

"Well!" she demanded.

"All right," I said.

At length, after I had signed my name on a receipt, being the receiving end of suspicious scrutiny from the clerk, the package was returned to me.

Back in the apartment I unwrapped the purse, handed it to her, and said, "Please count the money."

She opened the purse, took out the money, spread the bills on the floor, and counted them carefully. Then she said, "Thank you, Mr. Burr," snapped the purse shut, and started for the door.

Gabby opened it for her. Her eyes caressed his. "Thank you very much, Mr. Hilman," she said, and was gone.

I stood looking after her. "I don't like it," I said.

"For the love of Mike, Jay! Snap out of it! She owns the purse. You've got her address. You—"

"And there's a murdered man in her apartment."

"Well, what of it? You can see she doesn't know anything about it."

"Don't be too certain," I said.

I was just getting into bed, and Gabby, in his pajamas, was sitting on the edge of the chair smoking a last-minute cigarette, when knuckles tapped on the door.

Gabby looked at me in surprise.

Suddenly I remembered. "She's back after that slip of paper, I bet."

"My gosh!" Gabby said. "You got a robe, Jay?"

"Gosh, no," I told him. "You're decent. Go to the door."

"What do you mean I'm decent?" Gabby demanded, looking down at his pajamas.

The light tapping on the door was resumed. "Stick your head out if you're so damned modest," I said. "After all, she's been married. She must know what pajamas are. Tell her you're going to get dressed and take her down to a cocktail bar."

"*That's* an idea!" Gabby barefooted across to the door, opened it a scant three inches, cleared his throat, and said, in the very dulcet tone he reserved for particularly good-looking women, "I'm sorry—you see, I was just getting into bed. I—"

The door pushed open as though a steam roller had been on the other end of it. Gabby jumped up in the air, grabbed his left big toe, and started hopping around in agonized circles.

A tall competent-looking man in a gray suit, a gray hat to match, with a face that was lean and bronzed, pushed his way into the room and slammed the door shut behind him.

Gabby managed to sidetrack the pain of his skinned toe long enough to get belligerent. "Say," he demanded, "who the hell do you think *you* are? Get out of here, and—"

"Now then," the man announced, "what kind of a damn racket are you two guys pulling?"

"And just who are you?" I asked.

"Inspector Fanston. Headquarters. What's the idea?"

"The idea of what?"

"Who was the jane who was just up in the room?"

I said "I'm not going to lie to you, Inspector. Her mother and I are estranged and she came to get me to go home. But I told her nothing doing. I shouldn't have married a woman who was forty-five years older than I was, in the first place, and I should never have had a daughter who was only five years younger. It makes for a terrific strain on family life. Or don't you think so?"

"Do you," he asked, "think this is a gag?"

"Why not? We're over twenty-one. And if a woman can't pay us a five-minute visit in a hotel bedroom without some house dick—"

"Forget it. I'm not a house dick. I'm from Headquarters. I want to know who the woman was, and when you get done making wisecracks I want to know what the hell the idea was ringing up Headquarters and telling them a murder had been committed at the Redderstone Apartments."

Neither Gabby nor I said anything for a minute.

The Inspector grinned, settled down on the edge of the bed, and said "That makes it different, doesn't it, wise guy?"

"That makes it very much different," I told him. "How—how did you—?"

"Easy," he said. "When the desk sergeant told you he was consulting with the broadcasting system he was tracing the call. The hotel clerk remembered you going in to telephone, and there's been a cute little number dropping in . . . What the hell's the idea? What are you two guys trying to do?"

I cleared my throat. "About the purse," I said.

"Let's talk about the murder first, if you don't mind."

I said, "I—er—thought—"

"Did you?" he interrupted. "Well, try thinking it out straight this time. I suppose you boys are on the loose for a little night life, and it's okay by me just so you don't start pulling practical jokes about murders."

"Practical jokes!" I exclaimed. "A man had the back of his head caved in."

"What man?"

"The man in 218 at the Redderstone Apartments."

He said, "Get up and get your clothes on," and nodded to Gabby, "You, too."

We went to the Redderstone Apartments and up to the second floor. An officer in uniform was on guard in the living room of 218. The bedroom was just as we had left it, except now the bed was a spotless expanse of smooth counterpane.

I had been bracing myself for the shock of being called on to identify the body—perhaps being accused of having had something to do with the crime, and wondering just how I could establish an alibi. But the sight of that smooth bed was too much for me. I stood there for a good two or three seconds.

"Any old time," Fanston said.

Gabby and I both started talking at once. Then Gabby quit and let me tell the story. I knew there was only one thing to do. I told it right from the beginning, with the uniformed cop looking at me skeptically and Fanston's eyes drilling tunnels right into my brain.

"You *sure* this was the apartment?"

"Absolutely."

Inspector Fanston didn't give up. "All right, let's concede that he looked dead—that you thought he was dead. Those things don't just happen, you know."

"It happened this time."

"Wait a minute until you see what I'm getting at. Suppose it was all planned. A purse is planted where you'll be certain to find it. There's enough money in it so you'll really start doing something about it. It's a foregone conclusion that you're coming to this apartment—not once, but twice. And the second time you come back you find the outer door open. A man is lying sprawled on the bed. There's a violet-colored bulb in the lamp over the bed. That would make anyone look dead as a doornail.

"My best guess is that it's either some new racket or a frame-up to get you two guys on a spot because you two guys just happen to be you two guys. If it's a racket, you look old enough to take care of yourselves. If either one of you has any particular military information, or is here on some secret mission—well, I think that now would be a good time to take the police into your confidence."

He looked at Gabby. "Right, soldier?"

Gabby just looked innocent. Then he took a leather case from his pocket and handed it to the Inspector. "Keep it to yourself," he said.

The Inspector turned his back. I saw slight motion in his shoulders as he opened the leather case. Then he was motionless and silent for a few seconds.

I heard the snap of a catch, and the Inspector turned, poker-faced. He handed the leather case back to Gabby.

"Then you don't think there really was anybody?" I asked.

Fanston said, "Hell, no. Now, go home. If you start buzzing these janes in the morning, be careful—that's all."

Gabby snorted. "They're so dumb they think they've fooled us. Do you want to go back to the hotel now, Jay?"

"No. Let's find out some more about that stick—and what's happening at Puzzle Number Two shortly after midnight."

We found Fred Sanmore still on duty, tired to the point of utter weariness, but still shoving traffic through the yards.

"Look, Fred," Gabby said, "those brake sticks the men use—does it make any difference which is which?"

"What do you mean?"

"Can any man pick up any stick?"

Sanmore laughed. "Gosh, no. That's a sure way to pick a fight. Each man has his own stick. When a shift comes on duty, they'll bundle up all of the sticks and heave them out as far as they can throw them. The man whose stick goes the farthest puts it in the last hole. He's the last one out."

"How do they tell them apart?"

"Oh, various markings."

Gabby said, with what seemed to me just a little too much innocence, "I don't suppose you happen to know who owns the stick that has three rings out near the end with a series of crosses between the rings?"

"No, but I can find out for you."

"If you could do it quietly," Gabby said, "so your inquiries didn't attract too much attention, that might help."

"Come on," Sanmore said.

We started up toward the place where the men were sitting in front of the line of pegs. There weren't so many of them now. The cut that was going over the hump was getting down to the last ten or fifteen cars.

Sanmore left us and talked with two or three of the switchmen in a low voice, then was back to say, "As nearly as I can tell, it's a man named Carl Greester. He went off duty at midnight, but he's still around somewhere. He has a friend visiting him in the yards."

"What do you mean, a friend?"

Sanmore grinned. "I mean a *friend*," and holding up his hands in front of him he made an hourglass outline of a woman's figure. "She came down with a pass from headquarters. And she had another woman with her. Greester is having a confab with them."

"You don't know where Greester lives, do you?" I asked.

"Gosh, no. But I can find out."

"Look, Fred," Gabby said suddenly. "Could Jay and I ride one of these cars down to its destination, just to see what it's like?"

"Absolutely against the rules," Sanmore told him brusquely. "If I saw you do it, I'd have to jerk you off the car and have you put out of the yards." And then he deliberately walked away.

A big freight car came lumbering down the incline. One of the switchmen, moving with lazy coordination, picked up his stick and swung aboard the front of the car.

Gabby and I, acting just as though we had received formal permission from the foreman, walked over to the back ladder.

"You first," Gabby said.

I favored the leg as much as possible, taking it easy up to the top of the car.

"Hang on," Gabby said, as his head came up over the edge of the boxcar. I looked ahead and saw we were right on the puzzle switch, and braced myself, expecting that I would be thrown from one side to the other as the trucks went over the frogs; but the big loaded car moved along in majestic dignity. There was only a little jar as the wheels underneath us made noise. Then we were gliding out from the well-lighted area into the half darkness, then out to where it was completely dark.

We clicked over a couple of other switches, then veered sharply to the right and were coasting along when I heard a scream coming from almost directly beneath the car.

Gabby was where he could look down on the side. Then he was climbing down the ladder. "Come on, Jay!"

I looked back and caught a glimpse of two girls. A man was with them. Evidently he'd put his arms around them and jerked them back out of the way of the car.

I forgot all about the leg as I came down the iron ladder, but Gabby was running alongside and eased me to the ground on that last jump.

My knee gave me a little twinge just as we passed a couple of boxcars on a track on the left. I dropped back and said, "Go ahead, Gabby. I'll catch up."

Gabby turned to look at me, and then I saw him stiffen. At what I saw on his face I forgot about the leg and whirled.

Three men, armed with brake sticks, were right on top of us. A year ago I'd have been frightened into giving ground and making useless motions, but I'd learned a lot since then. The man who was nearest me raised his club. I shot my left straight to the Adam's apple. I saw Gabby pivot sideways to let a blow slide harmlessly past him, grab the man's wrist, give the arm a swift wrench, then heave. The air became filled with arms and legs as the man went flying through the darkness, to crash against the side of a boxcar, then drop limply to the ground.

The man I had hit was on the ground. He made a wild swing at my shins with the brake stick. Automatically, and without thinking, I tried to jump back out of the way. The injured knee gave way without warning. Then the brake stick cracked against my shin and I went down on my knees. Suddenly I lost balance and fell forward. As I fell I spread apart the first and second fingers of my right hand and jabbed the fingers toward his eyes. If he wanted to play dirty I could teach him something about that. I'd specialized in it.

I heard a faint swish. Something—perhaps the sixth sense which wild things have and which we develop under the spur of life-and-death conflict—warned me. I jerked my head to one side, but not soon enough and not far enough . . .

The next thing I remembered, I was in a warm musty darkness with a sore head and an aching sensation at my wrists. I tried to move my arms, and realized my hands were tied behind my back.

From the stuffy thick blackness I heard Gabby's voice. "How's it coming, Jay?"

"What," I asked, "happened?"

"The guy from behind," Gabby explained. "The one who was with the two girls. He caught you on the head just as you went down. I smeared his nose all over his face with a straight right, and then the guy behind me hit me just over the kidneys with everything he had."

"What about the girls?"

Gabby said, "The redhead ran away. I think she's gone for help. The other one just stood there watching. The damn spy."

My head was feeling a little better, although it still ached. I said, "If you ask me, it was the redhead who was the decoy. They wouldn't have let her run away if she hadn't been. Where are we?"

"Inside a boxcar."

"What," I asked, "is it all about?"

Once more Gabby was silent, but this time it was the tight-lipped silence of a man who is carefully guarding a secret.

I tried to roll over so I could take some of the pressure off my wrists. My shoulder hurt and it was hard to keep my balance.

Gabby heard me move. "Take it easy, Jay. I'm getting this knot worked loose, I think."

After a minute or two Gabby said triumphantly, "I've got it, Jay. Just another minute and we'll be loose, and then we'll be out of here."

I heard his feet on the planks, heard him starting toward me—

With an ominous rumble the door slid back along its tracks. The beam of a flashlight stabbed into the darkness.

Gabby flung himself flat on the floor, keeping his ankles crossed, his hands behind his back.

There was a peculiar scuffling sound from the outer darkness, then the sobbing breathing of a woman.

I got my head around to where I could see a little more of what was happening.

Lorraine Dawson was literally lifted and thrown into the car by three men.

The beam of the flashlight swung around and then suddenly stopped. "Do you," demanded a voice, "see what I see?"

I looked along the beam of the flashlight. It was centered on the pieces of rope that Gabby had untied from his wrists and ankles.

The three men were bunched there in the doorway, the beam of the flashlight holding Gabby as a target like a helpless airplane caught in a vortex of searchlights.

Gabby made one swift leap and hit the group feet first.

I heard the thud of his heels striking against flesh. The flashlight was jerked up, looped the loop, hit the side of the boxcar, hesitated a moment at the edge of the door, then fell to the tracks. The sounds of bodies threshing around in a struggle, the thud of blows filled the night. All of a sudden there was a lull, then shouts and curses as our assailants piled out of the boxcar. Good old Gabby had given them the slip and was leading them away.

Almost immediately the rumbling noise from the trucks indicated that the car had been banged into rapid motion. The door was still open. I could feel the fresh night air coming in through the opening to eddy around the interior of the boxcar.

"You all right?" I asked the girl.

"Yes . . . Who are you?"

"Believe it or not, I'm Jayson Burr, who wanted to return the purse you lost. That was when you were masquerading as Muriel Comley. Remember?"

I heard the quick intake of her breath. "How did you get here?" she demanded.

"It's a long story. Would you mind telling me just what your name really is?"

"I'm Lorraine," she said.

"And who's Muriel?"

"Believe it or not, I don't know. About all I do know is that she had an attractive apartment and wanted a roommate to share expenses. I moved in."

I swung around and managed to get into a sitting position. "Would you," I asked, "mind telling me something of what this is all about?"

"I don't know."

"Then perhaps you can tell me why you don't know."

She said, "I only moved in with Muriel a few days ago. She seemed nice, and just recently secured a divorce. Tonight Muriel was to meet someone who was due to come in on a train. I don't even know whether it was a man or a woman. We were in town. I wanted to take a cab to the apartment, so I dropped Muriel at the depot. They said the cab had to take on a full load before it started back. You know the rest. I never realized Muriel had left her purse until she telephoned me at the apartment; then, just after she'd hung up, you telephoned."

The cars were rattling and banging over switches, lurching crazily.

"And then you said *you* were Muriel?"

"Yes, of course. I didn't know who you were, but you had Muriel's purse, and I wanted to get it back for her. I thought it was easier to pretend to be Muriel than to do a lot of explaining, and then have you insist on waiting for Muriel to come back to claim the purse."

"And when I got up there," I said, "you were frightened."

"I'll tell the world I was frightened."

"Can you tell me what happened?"

She said, "There was a man in the apartment all the time, hiding in the bedroom. I didn't know it until after you'd telephoned."

The freight car gave a series of short quick jerks and bangs, slowed almost to a stop, then slammed in another string of cars, and after a moment the whole string began to roll.

"Sounds as though we're making up a train," I said. "Look here, do you suppose you could lie over on your side and I'd get over as close to you as I could? We'd lie back to back, and you could work on the knots on my wrists with your fingers, and I'd try to untie your wrists."

"We could try," she said.

We rolled and hitched along the floor until we were lying back to back. Somehow I couldn't get my fingers working. The cords around my wrists made my fumbling fingers seem all thumbs. But she was more successful. I felt the knot slip, heard her say, "I'm getting it, all right— ouch! I'll bet I lost a fingernail there—hold still, it's coming loose."

A few moments later my wrists were free. I sat up and untied her.

Abruptly, with that jerking lurch so characteristic of car switching, the engineer applied the brakes. Lorraine was thrown up against me, and I kept from falling only by grabbing at the side of the car. The partially opened door slammed back until it came up with a bang against the end of the iron track, leaving the square doorway wide-open. The whole string of cars abruptly slowed.

Suddenly our view was cut off. The doorway seemed to be pushed up against a solid wall of darkness.

"What is it?" Lorraine asked. "A warehouse?"

At that moment the train slammed to a dead stop.

I saw then that our car had been stopped directly opposite another string of boxcars.

"Can you jump across to the ladder on that car opposite?" I asked quickly.

She didn't even bother to answer, simply leaned out of the car, caught the iron ladder on the car opposite, and stepped across. I had to wait a second for her to climb up, so as to leave me a handhold, and in that second the engine gave a snort and a jerk. The car started forward.

"Quick!" Lorraine shouted.

I just missed her leg as I grabbed an iron rung of the ladder and leaned out. It seemed that the car was literally jerked out from under me.

"You all right?" she asked.

"Yes, I took the shock on my other leg." I started down the ladder. "Watch your step," I warned. "The—" I broke off, as I saw the flash of a red light, heard a little toot from the engine whistle, and saw the whole string of cars ahead slide to an abrupt stop. I saw the gleam of a flashlight, then another. Then a beam came slithering along the string of cars.

"Quick!" I said. "Get up to the top and lie down. They're searching for us."

I heard the slight scrape of her feet on the iron rungs as she scampered up the ladder, and I followed, making the best time I could. We flattened out, I on one side of the walk on top of the car, she on the other.

There were voices after that. Shadows danced along the side of a concrete warehouse just above us. I listened, trying to determine if these men were friends, sent by Gabby to rescue us, or if they were our captors returning. Then, within ten yards of me, a man's voice said, "This is the end of the cut. They must have swung off while it was moving. They're not in the car. You can see the ropes there on the floor. Why in hell can't Jim tie 'em so they stay tied!"

Another voice: "You can't hold things up any longer without making everybody suspicious. Give them the high-ball. We'll have to catch 'em as they leave the yards. We'll spread out. They can't get away."

Once more shadows danced. The switch engine gave two muted toots of the whistle and started the string of cars into rattling motion.

"Now what?" Lorraine asked.

"Now," I said, "we get out of here just as fast as we can. Come on, let's go."

"Where?"

"Back to the Redderstone Apartments. Unless I'm mistaken, we'll find a police inspector by the name of Fanston somewhere in the building, and we can get action out of him a whole lot quicker than we can explain to some strange cop. Tell me one thing. You said there was a man in your apartment?"

"Yes. He heard me talking on the telephone. I don't know whether you noticed it or not, but I gave an exclamation and then asked you to hold the line a minute."

"I noticed it," I said. "What happened?"

"A man stepped out of the bedroom. The first thing I knew I felt the cold circle of a gun muzzle sticking in the back of my neck. Then the man took me away from the telephone for a minute or two, and demanded to know who was talking. I told him it was just someone who wanted to return Muriel's purse."

"What did he do?" I asked.

"Marched me back to the telephone with instructions to get you up there at any cost and to insist that I was Muriel."

"And when I came up," I asked, "where was he?"

"In the bedroom. He had the door open a crack. He wasn't where he could see—only listen. That's why I took a chance and slipped out after you. All I wanted at the time was to get out. Later on, downstairs, when I saw the clerk on duty, I got the idea of trying to make you give up the purse. I was sure you had it under your coat."

"You knew that Muriel came to the hotel and got it back?"

"Yes, of course. She told me you gave it to her."

"Did she tell you what was in it?"

"No. What was in it?"

"Would you," I asked abruptly, "be shocked to learn Muriel is an enemy agent?"

"Good heavens! She can't be. Why, she's just a young married woman who found out she made a mistake and—"

"And what does she live on?"

"I don't know. She said she was looking for a job. I supposed she had some money—alimony, perhaps."

I didn't say anything for a few seconds, letting Lorraine get herself adjusted to the idea I'd given her. Then I said, "Just when did you meet Muriel?"

"A little over a week ago. She had an ad in the—"

"No, no. I mean tonight, after I left."

She said, "I pretended to go back up to the second floor to the apartment. That was just to fool you and the clerk. Actually, I just took the elevator all the way up to the top floor, waited for five or ten minutes, then went back down and walked out."

"The clerk was at the desk then?"

"No. No one was in the lobby."

"Where did you go?"

"There's a little tearoom down the block where Muriel usually drops in before she comes to the apartment to go to bed. I went there and waited, frightened stiff."

"How long did you wait?"

"It seemed like ages."

"But you don't know exactly how long it was?"

"No. It was quite a while."

"And she finally came in?"

"Oh, yes."

"That was before she had been to see us?"

"No, afterward. She had her purse."

"And you told her about what had happened in the apartment?"

"Yes."

"What did she do?"

"She seemed quite disturbed. She said she'd notify the police, but it would have to wait until tomorrow, because she had an important appointment to keep."

"And how did you happen to come down here to the switchyard?"

"I didn't want to go back to the apartment alone. Muriel said she had arranged for a pass and that I could come with her. She didn't seem particularly anxious to have me, though."

"Then you and Muriel came down here without first going back to the apartment?"

"That's right."

"Hadn't it occurred to you to call the police as soon as you got out of the apartment?"

"Of course."

"Why didn't you do it?"

"Because—well, Muriel's rather secretive about her affairs and somehow I had an idea she wouldn't like it. You see, she's had a divorce and—well, you know how those things are. I thought perhaps it might be something that was connected with the divorce, or an attempt on the part of her ex-husband to get evidence so he could get out of paying alimony, or something of that sort."

"Did Muriel tell you who she was meeting?"

"Yes, a man named Greester, but he never showed up."

"And what did he want?"

"Apparently it was something about her husband. Greester wasn't there, and Muriel didn't tell much. We started to walk down the tracks, and then the next thing I knew that car was almost on us. I think I screamed. I remember a man's arm around me, pulling me off the tracks; then I saw you and this other man jump off the car and start toward us. Then three men started toward you—there was that awful fight. I tried to help and—well, they grabbed me and tied me up."

"And Muriel?"

"Muriel got away."

"Anyone try to stop her?"

"I think one of the men did. He made a grab for her, but she jerked herself loose."

"It may have been an act?" I asked.

"It might have been an act," she said wearily.

I said, "All right, sister. Now I'm going to tell you something. Muriel is an enemy agent, and in case you want to know what was in that purse it was a great big wad of currency totaling seven thousand five hundred dollars. And *that's* why I was so cagey about delivering it."

Lorraine sat perfectly still on top of the boxcar, looking at me, her eyes wide and startled. After a while she said, "I can't believe it."

I didn't argue about it. I peered over the side of the car that was against the warehouse. "I think," I said, "we can manage to squeeze through here. We'll walk back down the length of the train, keeping behind these cars; and we'd better start. I'm going first."

It was dark as a pocket in the narrow space between the cars and the warehouse. There was just room to squeeze along, and I knew that if the train jerked into motion we'd be caught and rolled along between the moving cars and the warehouse until we dropped down under the wheels; but it was our only way out.

Halfway down the string of cars I crawled under and looked back at the track. I could see little spots of light that stabbed the darkness, then they were snuffed out, only to glow again. They were still hunting for us.

"See anything?" Lorraine asked as I crawled back to the dark side of the cars.

"No," I said. There was no use scaring the kid to death.

We worked our way down to the end of the cars. There was a stretch of open track, curved rails running up to an iron bumper. Back of that was a concrete wall.

We were trapped.

I felt my way along the wall, hoping I might find a door. That was when Lorraine saw the flashlights.

"Look," she whispered. "*Lights!* I think they're coming this way."

I simply pulled her in behind the protection of that steel and concrete bumper.

We huddled there for what seemed five or ten minutes. The lights were coming closer. We could see shadows on the concrete wall.

The lights were swinging around now in wider arcs, making bright splotches on the concrete wall, intensifying the shadows. Then, when they must have been within twenty yards of us, they quit.

I got to my hands and knees, held my head low down, and peeked out. The track was a vague, distinct ribbon vanishing into a wall of darkness. I looked for several seconds and couldn't see anything. I decided to chance it.

We turned off the tracks when we came to the end of the warehouse, walked across the yards, and found a gate that was locked from the inside. We unlocked it and went out without seeing a soul.

"You have a key?" I asked Lorraine when we reached the Redderstone Apartments.

She opened her purse, fumbled around for a moment, and handed me a key.

I hesitated before putting it in the lock. "Someone on your floor have a dog?" I asked.

"Yes. I don't know which apartment it is. A cute little woolly dog."

"I heard him barking."

"Yes, he barks once in a while."

"Which end of the corridor from your apartment? Toward the front of the house or the back?"

"The back."

I fitted the key to the lock, held the door open, and Lorraine and I went in. The dimly lit foyer was silent as a tomb.

Halfway to the elevator I paused. "Look, Lorraine, you wait here. If you hear any commotion upstairs, get out just as fast as you can. Go to the nearest telephone and call Police Headquarters. If you *don't* hear anything, wait for me to come back and pick you up."

The door was locked with a night latch. I carefully inserted the key that Lorraine had given me and silently slipped back the latch. Then I eased the door open, ready to leap forward and go into action if necessary.

Gabby was sitting in the overstuffed chair, his feet propped up on a straight-backed chair, smoking a cigarette. He was all alone in the room.

"How," I asked, "did *you* get here?"

He turned and grinned. I saw, then, that his left eye was all puffed up. His lip had been cut, and when he grinned it opened up the cut and a few drops of blood started trickling down his chin.

I closed the door behind me. "How'd you make out?"

"Okay," Gabby said. "Did the Military find you?"

"No one found me. I rode a train out of the yards. What about the Military?"

Gabby said, "I sewed that place up. Nobody gets in or out, and they're going through it with a fine-tooth comb."

"Where," I asked, "did you get all that authority?"

"I didn't, I haven't, I ain't," Gabby said. "But in case I forgot to tell you I'm sort of working under a colonel here, and we're checking up on certain things that happened to freight shipments. At first we didn't think it could have happened in the freight yards, because the records were all straight, but now we're changing our minds mighty fast. I came here to start tracing this stuff from the time it hit the terminal yards until it was delivered."

"Yes," I said, "you neglected to tell me."

Gabby grinned again. "I was afraid I had. Where's the girl spy?"

"That's what I wanted to ask you."

"Cripes!" Gabby said, frowning. "I thought you'd be able to keep *her* lined up."

"You mean you didn't see her?"

"No. What happened to her?"

"Just that she took to her heels is all I know.

Gabby straightened up. "Say, who do you think I'm talking about?"

"Muriel."

"Muriel, nothing!" Gabby snorted. "Muriel's little roommate, Lorraine Dawson, is the one I mean."

"You're all wrong, but we won't argue that now. Where *is* Muriel?"

"In case it's any of your business," Gabby said angrily, "She's in the bedroom changing her clothes."

I started for the bedroom door.

Gabby said, "Don't."

"Why not?"

"She's a decent kid."

I said, "She may be a decent kid, but she's an enemy agent," and flung the door open.

Gabby came out of the chair and toward me fast, but something he saw in my face made him turn toward the bedroom.

It was empty.

"You see?"

Gabby walked across the room to the bedroom window and looked out to the iron platform of the fire escape.

After a minute I said, "Look, Gabby, we're going to get her back. She can't get away with it. I think Lorraine can help us."

Gabby turned. "Where is Lorraine?"

"Down by the elevator. I left her there while I came up to see that the coast was clear."

Gabby said, "Go get her. We can't wait."

Lorraine wasn't there.

I walked over to the door and looked out on the street. She wasn't there. I came back and climbed the stairs. No sign of her on the stairs.

I went back to the apartment.

Gabby looked up. "Where is she?"

"I don't know." I said, "Suppose you and I quit making damned fools of ourselves. There was a dead man in that bedroom. I don't know what the big idea was with the police claiming it was a plant. You call the law in on a murder case and right away they start telling you it's all a pipe dream."

"I know," Gabby said.

"All right; it was a body. You can't pick up a body and carry it downstairs under your arm. You can't change the mattress and the sheet and the blankets and the spread and the pillows on a bed in the middle of the night. The way I see it, there's only one answer."

"The adjoining apartment?"

I nodded.

Gabby said, "How's your leg?"

"Okay."

Gabby said, "Remember, I've got my automatic, so in case the party gets rough let's not break any legs over it."

"We won't," I said.

Gabby said, "If you'd come down to earth and be reasonable—I could tell you what happened—just so you won't crack the wrong girl over the head."

"I won't crack the wrong girl."

"Look, Jay, when Muriel came to her apartment this evening she found a man's suit hanging in the closet. It looked as though the suit had just come back from the cleaners. She noticed a bulge in one pocket which turned out to be the seventy-five hundred."

"So little Muriel figures finders keepers."

"Muriel happens to be a gal who can look out for herself. The whole thing struck her as fishy, so she decided to sit tight until she discovered what was going on—or at least part of it. It seems there was quite a splash in the papers when her divorce came up and she's allergic to publicity. She had sense enough to realize that either by design or accident she had become involved in something, and she couldn't be sure her husband didn't have a hand in it. Unless it became absolutely necessary she didn't want the cops in on it."

"I still don't see why she carried all that around with her."

"She wanted to get it to a place of safekeeping, but a guy started to tail her when she left the apartment. She was almost sure she had lost him, but just as she was stepping out of the taxi she thought she saw him again. Apparently without Lorraine seeing her, she slipped her purse back on the seat and then got out. As soon as she was certain she had lost the tail she telephoned the cab company to see if the driver had found her purse."

"How come she didn't tell any of this to Lorraine?"

"I didn't ask her, but my guess is that she thought it would be best all around if she didn't."

"And the switch list with the message?"

"Don't be so damn sarcastic. A railroad friend of hers gave her that, earlier in the afternoon, and arranged for a pass. In case you want to know all about her private life, her husband made a property settlement prior to the divorce. Then he ran out on her and quit paying. This man tipped her off that a chap was working on the night shift at the hump who owed her husband a wad of dough, and told her that she could go down there tonight and he'd take her to this man. She wanted to get the rest of the money her husband had promised her on the property settlement and then forgot to pay."

"Who was this friend," I asked, "and will he corroborate her statement?"

Gabby said stiffly, "I haven't had a chance to get her entire story."

I started for the window and got out onto the steel platform of the fire escape. The window which opened on the farther edge of the platform was closed. I slid my knife blade under it and found it wasn't locked.

"Step to one side as soon as you raise it," Gabby whispered.

I got the window up, and was too mad to care about anything. I slipped under Gabby's arm and went in headfirst. Gabby was behind me with the gun, and he could take care of anything that happened.

Nothing happened.

We were in an apartment very similar to the one we'd just left, only arranged in reverse order. The window opened into the bedroom. I could see the bed. It was clean and white, and apparently hadn't been slept in. For all I could see, there was no one in the apartment, and then somehow I had an uneasy feeling that the place was occupied. You could feel the presence of human beings.

We moved on a few steps from the window.

"The light switch will be over by the door," I whispered.

"Think we dare to risk the lights?" Gabby asked.

"Gosh, yes. This place gives me the willies."

"Stick 'em up!"

The beam of a flashlight sprang out of nothing and hit my eyes with such a bright glare that it hurt. I saw Gabby's wrist snap around so that his gun was pointed toward the flashlight. Then Inspector Fanston's voice yelled, "Hold it, soldier! This is the law."

Gabby said, "Put out that damn flashlight. What are you doing here?"

"What are *you* doing here?" the Inspector asked.

"There's no one here?" Gabby asked.

Fanston said, "Switch on the lights, Smitty."

The light switch clicked the room into illumination.

"Where's the girl?" I asked.

"What girl?" the Inspector asked.

"The one who came through the window a few minutes before we did."

"No one came through that window."

"For how long?"

"Ever since we came over here with you. I doped it out that if you saw a body it must have been moved. It looked as though it must have moved out the window to the fire escape, then across to here. I made a stall to get you boys out of the way, then Smitty and I went to work."

"And you've been waiting here all that time," I demanded, "simply on a hunch that the body might have been—"

"Take it easy," the Inspector interrupted. "Show him what we found, Smitty."

The cop opened the closet door.

I looked inside and saw a bundle of bedclothes wadded up into a ball. There were red splotches on the bedclothes—blood that wasn't old enough even yet to get that rusty-brown tint. It looked red and fresh.

"I'll be damned," Gabby said.

"That's the only way they could have come in," Fanston said. "It's perfectly logical. What's more, there are bloodstains on the iron ribs of the fire-escape platform."

"And why," I asked, "are you guarding the bloody bedclothes and letting the other apartment take care of itself?"

Fanston looked at Smitty, and the look was a question.

"Why not?" Smitty said.

Fanston decided to tell us. "Because when we looked through that other apartment, we found something. I'll show you."

He led the way back through the window out to the fire escape and then to the girl's apartment. Over in a corner of the bedroom was a fine sprinkle of plaster dust on the floor near the baseboard.

Gabby was the one who got it first. He moved a mirror back out of the way. Behind it was a neat little hole in the plaster and the diaphragm of a dictograph.

That point established, we returned to the other apartment.

"The receiving end of the installation is in here," Fanston continued; "also, the bloody bedclothes are in here. You can figure what that means. Having put up that dictograph, with the receiving end in this apartment, they're naturally due to come back to watch it—if you fellows haven't messed things up so that you've scared away the quarry we're after."

Suddenly I remembered something. Without waiting to explain my hunch, I hurried out of the room.

I walked down the long corridor, looking at numbers on the doors. I found the apartment I wanted down at the far end of the corridor. The place was dark and silent. The hallway had that peculiar clammy feel which clings to crowded apartment houses along toward morning. A dog yapped once, then quit.

I gently turned the doorknob. When I felt that the latch was free I pushed tentatively against the door.

The door was jerked open from the inside. Before I could let loose, I was thrown off balance and came stumbling on into the room.

A man's voice said, "All right—you asked for this."

It was dark in the room, with just the faint hint of distant lights seeping through the windows.

They had fed me enough carrots and vitamins to improve my night vision and taught me enough about rough-and-tumble fighting in the dark, so that what came next didn't bother me at all. It was just like going through a training routine.

I knew a blackjack was swinging for my head somewhere in the darkness. I sidestepped, felt a swish of air as something whizzed past where my head had been, saw a dark object in front of me, and, somewhat off balance, figured out where his bread basket would be, and hit him where he was thickest.

I felt surprised muscles collapsing beneath the force of my blow, heard a *whoosh* as the breath went out of him.

Someone cursed behind me. A flame split the darkness wide-open. I could feel the hot breath of burning gunpowder against my cheek. I never did hear the bullet crash. My ears were numbed by the sound, but I whirled and struck out with my left.

It was then the knee gave way. I went down in a heap. But they'd taught me all about that in the Army, too. I caught the man's knees as I went down. He struck at my head in the dark with the gun barrel and missed by a couple of inches. I grabbed for his wrists and didn't connect. He kicked me in the shin and broke loose.

There was a quarter second of silence. I realized then he had enough light to show him where I was. He was going to shoot.

I flung myself into a quick roll, kicking as I came over. My heel grazed against his knee. A dog was barking frenziedly.

I heard running steps in the corridor. The beam of a flashlight danced around the opening of the door. There were scrambling steps, someone barking an order, a back door opening, and a pell-mell of stampeding feet running down a staircase.

The two officers went storming past me, following the beam of the flashlight. I saw Gabby's long arms raise the window, saw him slide matter-of-factly out to the edge of the sill, and heard him say, "All right, boys. That'll be enough. Stick up your hands."

The windowpane above him split into fragments of glass as two bullets crashed through.

I saw Gabby's arm swing the automatic.

"You all right, Jay?" he asked.

I rolled over on my hands and knees and started getting up. The knee felt weak, the way a thumb feels when you've bent it all the way back and all the strength is gone out of it; but I could hobble along all right.

"Okay," I said.

I went into the bedroom. Before I found the light switch, I could see two long rolls of something stretched out on the bed. Then I found the switch and clicked on illumination.

They were tied up in sheets, their lips taped shut. Two pair of eyes looked up at me—large expressive dark eyes and big blue eyes.

I reached over and tried pulling off the tape from their lips. I held the side of Lorraine's cheek, got a good hold on the tape, and gave it a quick jerk.

"Hurt?" I asked.

She looked up at me. "Not much."

I went around the bed to Muriel, worked a corner loose, and then gave her the same treatment.

"You *would* have to do it the hard way!" she flared.

I started untying sheets.

From the outer room I heard Inspector Fanston saying in an odd voice, "Good Lord! How did you do it, shooting in the dark? Knocking the legs out from under them."

Gabby didn't even bother to answer the question. He said, "Listen, Inspector, this is purely civilian, see? We don't figure in it at all. We're just witnesses who happened to be in an apartment in the building. Here's a number. Call this number and make a report. They'll tell you what to do. As far as you know, it's a gang of housebreakers that had headquarters here. You even keep the railroad angle out of it. Get me?"

I waited, expecting to hear Fanston ask Gabby who the hell he thought he was. But, instead, Fanston's voice sounded meek and subdued. I knew then the shield in the leather case Gabby was carrying in his pocket was big stuff.

The Inspector said, "I get you. Smitty, go out in the hallway and get those people back where they belong. Tell them there may be more shooting. And don't let anyone talk with the prisoners."

I heard the whir of a telephone and Inspector Fanston's voice saying "Police Headquarters," then Muriel Comley saying, "Leave that sheet where it is. All I've got on is underwear." Her eyes went past me to the doorway and softened. "Oh, hello, Gabby!"

Gabby said, "We can stay right here until things quiet down, and then you can go and—"

"Not in *this* room," Lorraine said.

"What's the matter with it?" Gabby asked.

I looked at Lorraine's eyes, got up and walked across to the closet door, opened it a few inches, and then hastily pushed it shut.

Gabby took one look at my face and knew the answer.

"Oh, Fanston," he said, "the body you're looking for is in here."

Over a breakfast of ham, eggs, and coffee, Gabby told us as much as he ever told us.

"For a long time," he said, "we'd been running into a peculiar type of trouble. Machinery would be tested and double-tested. It would be put aboard freight cars, shipped to various army camps, and tested when it got there. Everything would be all right, but after a while, usually under the stress of combat, the machinery would suddenly go haywire. Part of it we found was due to the old familiar sabotage of putting a little acid on critical metal parts, and then carefully covering up the slight discoloration.

"But the other part of it had us completely baffled. A machine would get into combat and suddenly fail. Later on, we'd post-mortem, and find sugar had been introduced into the gasoline. You know what *that* does to an internal combustion motor.

"After a while we found out that all the machinery with which we had this trouble had come through the yards in this city, but that in itself didn't seem to mean anything, because the machinery was tested on arrival at destination and everything was seemingly all right. But we still kept coming back to the peculiar coincidence that our troubles came only with stuff that went through these freight yards.

"I'd had some railroad experience, and I was sent up here to check the whole situation. In the meantime, Carl Greester was working on the hump, and he stumbled onto what was going on. The enemy agents had duplicate tags slightly larger than the regular numbered tags which went on the cars as they came through the switch. By putting on those phony numbers they'd have the cars they wanted switched down to a siding where they had sufficient opportunity to do their work. And it didn't take them long.

"After the cars had been entered and sabotaged they'd be resealed, the phony numbers taken off, a couple of dummy cars added, and a switch engine sent down to pick up the cut and redistribute it.

"When Greester found out what was happening, he didn't go to the F.B.I. He went to the men who were mixed up in it. They bought his silence for seven thousand five hundred dollars. But Greester was afraid to take a bribe in the ordinary manner, and they weren't foolish enough to just park seven thousand five hundred somewhere and go away and leave it for him to pick up. Greester kept insisting that the money be given to him under such circumstances that if there was a double-cross, the F.B.I. couldn't claim he had accepted a bribe.

"Finally they agreed that Greester would send a suit out to be cleaned. When the suit came back, it was to be given to the clerk to hang up in Greester's apartment. The bribe money would be in the inside pocket. In that way, if anyone suspected what was happening, Greester could have a perfect alibi. He'd sent his suit to the cleaners. The cleaner had returned the suit to the clerk while Greester was at the yards.

"But when the go-between picked up the suit at the cleaners, planted the seventy-five hundred bucks in the pocket, and handed the suit to the desk, he either got mixed up on the numbers, or the clerk did. No names were mentioned, merely apartment numbers. The suit went to two-eighteen instead of two-eighty-one.

"Greester came home, looked for the suit and the bribe money. No suit, no money. He asked the clerk if anything had been left for him at the desk. The clerk said no. The gang knew the suit had been delivered. They thought the clerk had got the dough.

"They got the thing straightened out, finally. The clerk was a little nincompoop who was always getting figures mixed up. They decided he must have delivered the suit to the wrong apartment. One of the men got into Muriel's apartment with a passkey and found the suit; but the money was gone. He was in there when Lorraine came in, and he had an idea the money might have found its way into Muriel's purse. That's why he was so interested in the telephone conversation."

"And the clerk?" I asked.

"The clerk kept thinking over Greester's questions, finally remembered about the suit, and wondered if he hadn't put it in two-eighteen instead of two-eighty-one. He went up to two-eighteen, let himself in with a passkey, and found a man boring holes in the wall and installing a dictograph. We know what happened to the clerk."

"Why the dictograph?" I asked.

"Don't you see? They didn't know whether Muriel was a government agent and they were leading with their chins, or whether it was just a mixup. Naturally, killing the clerk hadn't entered into their plans. They had to get rid of the body."

"They knew we'd discovered that body?" I asked.

"Sure they did. They were on the other end of the dictograph when we stumbled on it before they'd had a chance to remove it. They evidently waited a while to see if we were going to report it. When they found out we didn't, they tried to whisk it away."

"But Greester must have thrown in with them," I said. "His apartment was two-eighty-one—"

"He didn't throw in with them," Gabby said. "Greester tried to play smart. It was unfortunate that he did."

"You mean—?"

"The police discovered his body about daylight this morning, when one of the gang confessed."

"But," Muriel said, "Carl Greester seemed so nice. He told me that a man who owed my husband some money was working down at the switchyard on a night shift, that if I'd come down and see him I could arrange to get the balance of the money that was due under the property settlement with my husband. He wrote out where I was to meet him shortly after midnight. I . . . Oh, I guess I see now."

Gabby said, "He found out about this man and tipped you off just as a favor, but all the time he was playing with this personal dynamite. He thought he was being smart. He was signing his own death warrant."

"So they took over Greester's apartment?" I asked.

"Sure. It was bad enough finding Greester's suit in the girl's apartment. But when the girls came down to the switchyard to join Greester around midnight, they became suspicious. They made an excuse to grab Muriel, jerk her out of the way of a freight car, and frisk her purse while they were doing it. As soon as they found out that the purse contained seventy-five hundred dollars, the girls were on the spot. Then you and I put in our two-bits worth."

"What's become of the money?" I asked.

"The money," Gabby said, "is in the hands of Uncle Sam. Three men were placed under arrest for tampering with the seals of freight cars. One of them started talking. He's talked enough so Fanston can pin the murder of the clerk and Carl Greester on the two other men. And the third, who turned state's evidence, will get life as an accessory after the fact."

"How about the man who owed my husband money?" Muriel asked. "Is he one of them?"

Gabby shook his head. "I think you're okay on that. His name is Gulliver. He works under Bob Cuttering. Cuttering's a grouch-face who is pretty much overworked, but he's a good egg just the same."

I said, "I don't see why this man in the bedroom didn't stick me up for Muriel's purse—"

"Because you *said* you didn't have it with you. Lorraine could tell, from the way you were holding your left arm against your body, that you did have it. The man in the bedroom could only hear what you'd said. He couldn't see. That's why Lorraine was able to get out of the apartment—talking as though she were slamming the door indignantly on her visitor, but actually slamming herself on the other side of it."

Lorraine said, "I was never so frightened in my life. While I was waiting down there, a man poked the muzzle of a gun into my back and marched me down the corridor."

"The dog was a sort of watchman?" I asked.

Gabby nodded. "When they moved into Greester's apartment they took the dog with 'em. The dog had been trained on one of those inaudible dog whistles. Whenever he heard it he'd bark and try to get out. Whenever anyone entered the place who might make trouble, a guy posted outside would blow the whistle, and the dog would bark. The dog had also been taught to give warning when anyone came near the apartment."

"Well," I said, "I guess that winds up the case."

"Of course," Gabby said, "the colonel insists that he's going to hold us responsible to see nothing happens to these girls—my buddy and me. I told the colonel it might be a little embarrassing. But you know the colonel; he just barked into the telephone, 'Keep those two girls lined up. I don't want them going out with anyone except you and Jay!' "

"You mean we can't have any dates," Muriel demanded, "unless—"

"Exactly," Gabby said sternly. "Those are orders direct from the colonel."

Muriel lowered her lashes. "Well," she conceded, "if it's for my country."

I looked at Lorraine.

She said, "He's got the idea now, Gabby, so you can take your foot away. It's *my* toe you're on."

"What are you two talking about?" Muriel demanded.

"Our patriotic duty to our government," Lorraine said self-righteously.

ROSS MACDONALD
The Bearded Lady

THE UNLATCHED door swung inward when I knocked. I walked into the studio, which was high and dim as a hayloft. The big north window in the opposite wall was hung with monkscloth draperies that shut out the morning light. I found the switch beside the door and snapped it on. Several fluorescent tubes suspended from the naked rafters flickered and burnt blue-white.

A strange woman faced me under the cruel light. She was only a charcoal sketch on an easel, but she gave me a chill. Her nude body, posed casually on a chair, was slim and round and pleasant to look at. Her face wasn't pleasant at all. Bushy black eyebrows almost hid her eyes. A walrus moustache bracketed her mouth, and a thick beard fanned down over her torso.

The door creaked behind me. The girl who appeared in the doorway wore a starched white uniform. Her face had a little starch in it, too, though not enough to spoil her good looks entirely. Her black hair was drawn back severely from her forehead.

"May I ask what you're doing here?"

"You may ask. I'm looking for Mr. Western."

"Really? Have you tried looking behind the pictures?"

"Does he spend much time there?"

"No, and another thing he doesn't do—he doesn't receive visitors in his studio when he isn't here himself."

"Sorry. The door was open. I walked in."

"You can reverse the process."

"Just a minute. Hugh isn't sick?"

She glanced down at her white uniform and shook her head.

"Are you a friend of his?" I said.

279

"I try to be." She smiled slightly. "It isn't always easy, with a sib. I'm his sister."

"Not the one he was always talking about?"

"I'm the only one he has."

I reached back into my mental grab bag of war souvenirs. "Mary. The name was Mary."

"It still is Mary. Are *you* a friend of Hugh's?"

"I guess I qualify. I used to be."

"When?" The question was brusque. I got the impression she didn't approve of Hugh's friends, or some of them.

"In the Philippines. He was attached to my group as a combat artist. The name is Archer, by the way. Lew Archer."

"Oh. Of course."

Her disapproval didn't extend to me, at least not yet. She gave me her hand. It was cool and firm, and went with her steady gaze. I said:

"Hugh gave me the wrong impression of you. I thought you were still a kid in school."

"That was four years ago, remember. People grow up in four years. Anyway, some of them do."

She was a very serious girl for her age. I changed the subject.

"I saw the announcement of his show in the L.A. papers. I'm driving through to San Francisco, and I thought I'd look him up."

"I know he'll be glad to see you. I'll go and wake him. He keeps the most dreadful hours. Sit down, won't you, Mr. Archer?"

I had been standing with my back to the bearded nude, more or less consciously shielding her from it. When I moved aside and she saw it, she didn't turn a hair.

"What next?" was all she said.

But I couldn't help wondering what had happened to Hugh Western's sense of humor. I looked around the room for something that might explain the ugly sketch.

It was a typical working artist's studio. The tables and benches were cluttered with things that are used to make pictures: palettes and daubed sheets of glass, sketch pads, scratchboards, bleeding tubes of paint. Pictures in half a dozen mediums and half a dozen stages of completion hung or leaned against the burlap-covered walls. Some of them looked wild and queer to me, but none so wild and queer as the sketch on the easel.

There was one puzzling thing in the room, besides the pictures. The wooden doorframe was scarred with a row of deep round indentations, four of them. They were new, and about on a level with my eyes. They looked as if an incredible fist had struck the wood a superhuman blow.

"He isn't in his room," the girl said from the doorway. Her voice was very carefully controlled.

"Maybe he got up early."

"His bed hasn't been slept in. He's been out all night."

"I wouldn't worry. He's an adult after all."

"Yes, but he doesn't always act like one." Some feeling buzzed under her calm tone. I couldn't tell if it was fear or anger. "He's twelve years older than I am, and still a boy at heart. A middle-aging boy."

"I know what you mean. I was his unofficial keeper for a while. I guess he's a genius, or pretty close to it, but he needs somebody to tell him to come in out of the rain."

"Thank you for informing me. I didn't know."

"Now don't get mad at me."

"I'm sorry. I suppose I'm a little upset."

"Has he been giving you a bad time?"

"Not really. Not lately, that is. He's come down to earth since he got engaged to Alice. But he still makes the weirdest friends. He can tell a fake Van Gogh with his eyes shut, literally, but he's got no discrimination about people at all."

"You wouldn't be talking about me? Or am I having ideas of reference?"

"No." She smiled again. I liked her smile. "I guess I acted terribly suspicious when I walked in on you. Some pretty dubious characters come to see him."

"Anyone in particular?" I said it lightly. Just above her head I could see the giant fist-mark on the doorframe.

Before she could answer, a siren bayed in the distance. She cocked her head. "Ten to one it's for me."

"Police?"

"Ambulance. The police sirens have a different tone. I'm an X-ray technician at the hospital, so I've learned to listen for the ambulance. And I'm on call this morning."

I followed her into the hall. "Hugh's show opens tonight. He's bound to come back for that."

She turned at the opposite door, her face brightening. "You know, he may have spent the night working in the gallery. He's awfully fussy about how his pictures are hung."

"Why don't I phone the gallery?"

"There's never anybody in the office till nine." She looked at her unfeminine steel wristwatch. "It's twenty to."

"When did you last see him?"

"At dinner last night. We ate early. He went back to the gallery after dinner. He said he was only going to work a couple of hours."

"And you stayed here?"

"Until about eight, when I was called to the hospital. I didn't get home until quite late, and I thought he was in bed." She looked at me uncertainly, with a little wrinkle of doubt between her straight eyebrows. "Could you be cross-questioning me?"

"Sorry. It's my occupational disease."

"What do you do in real life?"

"Isn't this real?"

"I mean now you're out of the army. Are you a lawyer?"

"A private detective."

"Oh. I see." The wrinkle between her eyebrows deepened. I wondered what she'd been reading.

"But I'm on vacation." I hoped.

A phone burred behind her apartment door. She went to answer it, and came back wearing a coat. "It *was* for me. Somebody fell out of a loquat tree and broke a leg. You'll have to excuse me, Mr. Archer."

"Wait a second. If you'll tell me where the art gallery is, I'll see if Hugh's there now."

"Of course, you don't know San Marcos."

She led me to the French windows at the rear end of the hall. They opened on a blacktop parking space which was overshadowed on the far side by a large stucco building, the shape of a flattened cube. Outside the windows was a balcony from which a concrete staircase slanted down to the parking lot. She stepped outside and pointed to the stucco cube:

"That's the gallery. It's no problem to find, is it? You can take a shortcut down the alley to the front."

A tall young man in a black leotard was polishing a red convertible in the parking lot. He struck a pose, in the fifth position, and waved his hand:

"Bonjour, Marie."

"Bonjour, my phony Frenchman." There was an edge of contempt on her good humor. "Have you seen Hugh this morning?"

"Not I. Is the prodigal missing again?"

"I wouldn't say missing—"

"I was wondering where your car was. It's not in the garage." His voice was much too musical.

"Who's he?" I asked her in an undertone.

"Hilary Todd. He runs the art shop downstairs. If the car's gone, Hugh can't be at the gallery. I'll have to take a taxi to the hospital."

"I'll drive you."

"I wouldn't think of it. There's a cabstand across the street." She added over her shoulder: "Call me at the hospital if you see Hugh."

I went down the stairs to the parking lot. Hilary Todd was still polishing the hood of his convertible, though it shone like a mirror. His shoulders were broad and packed with shifting muscle. Some of the ballet boys were strong and could be dangerous. Not that he was a boy, exactly. He had a little round bald spot that gleamed like a silver dollar among his hair.

"Bonjour," I said to his back.

"Yes?"

My French appeared to offend his ears. He turned and straightened. I saw how tall he was, tall enough to make me feel squat, though I was over six feet. He had compensated for the bald spot by growing side-burns. In combination with his liquid eyes, they gave him a Latin look. Pig Latin.

"Do you know Hugh Western pretty well?"

"If it's any concern of yours."

"It is."

"Now why would that be?"

"I asked the question, sonny. Answer it."

He blushed and lowered his eyes, as if I had been reading his evil thoughts. He stuttered a little. "I—I—well, I've lived below him for a couple of years. I've sold a few of his pictures. Why?"

"I thought you might know where he is, even if his sister doesn't."

"How should I know where he is? Are you a policeman?"

"Not exactly."

"Not at all, you mean?" He regained his poise. "Then you have no right to take this overbearing attitude. I know absolutely nothing about Hugh. And I'm very busy."

He turned abruptly and continued his polishing job, his fine useless muscles writhing under the leotard.

I walked down the narrow alley which led to the street. Through the cypress hedge on the left, I caught a glimpse of umbrella tables growing like giant multi-colored mushrooms in a restaurant patio. On the other side was the wall of the gallery, its white blankness broken by a single iron-barred window above the level of my head.

The front of the gallery was Greek-masked by a high-pillared porch. A broad flight of concrete steps rose to it from the street. A girl was standing at the head of the steps, half leaning on one of the pillars.

She turned towards me, and the slanting sunlight aureoled her bare head. She had a startling kind of beauty: yellow hair, light hazel eyes, brown skin. She filled her tailored suit like sand in a sack.

"Good morning."

She pretended not to hear me. Her right foot was tapping the pavement impatiently. I crossed the porch to the high bronze door and pushed. It didn't give.

"There's nobody here yet," she said. "The gallery doesn't open until ten."

"Then what are you doing here?"

"I happen to work here."

"Why don't you open up?"

"I have no key. In any case," she added primly, "we don't allow visitors before ten."

"I'm not a tourist, at least at the moment. I came to see Mr. Western."

"Hugh?" She looked at me directly for the first time. "Hugh's not here. He lives around the corner on Rubio Street."

"I just came from there."

"Well, he isn't here." She gave the words a curious emphasis. "There's nobody here but me. And I won't be here much longer if Dr. Silliman doesn't come."

"Silliman?"

"Dr. Silliman is our curator." She made it sound as if she owned the gallery. After a while she said in a softer voice: "Why are you looking for Hugh? Do you have some business with him?"

"Western's an old friend of mine."

"Really?"

She lost interest in the conversation. We stood together in silence for several minutes. She was tapping her foot again. I watched the Saturday-morning crowd on the street: women in slacks, women in shorts and dirndls, a few men in ten-gallon hats, a few in berets. A large minority of the people had Spanish or Indian faces. Nearly half the cars in the road carried out-of-state licenses. San Marcos was a unique blend of western border town, ocean resort, and artists' colony.

A small man in a purple corduroy jacket detached himself from the crowd and bounded up the steps. His movements were quick as a monkey's. His lined face had a simian look, too. A brush of frizzled gray hair added about three inches to his height.

"I'm sorry if I kept you waiting, Alice."

She made a *nada* gesture. "It's perfectly all right. This gentleman is a friend of Hugh's."

He turned to me. His smile went on and off. "Good morning, sir. What was the name?"

I told him. He shook my hand. His fingers were like thin steel hooks.

"Western ought to be here at any minute. Have you tried his flat?"

"Yes. His sister thought he might have spent the night in the gallery."

"Oh, but that's impossible. You mean he didn't come home last night?"

"Apparently not."

"You didn't tell me that," the blond girl said.

"I didn't know you were interested."

"Alice has every right to be interested." Silliman's eyes glowed with a gossip's second-hand pleasure. "She and Hugh are going to be married. Next month, isn't it, Alice? Do you know Miss Turner, by the way, Mr. Archer?"

"Hello, Mr. Archer." Her voice was shallow and hostile. I gathered that Silliman had embarrassed her.

"I'm sure he'll be along shortly," he said reassuringly. "We still have some work to do on the program for the private showing tonight. Will you come in and wait?"

I said I would.

He took a heavy key ring out of his jacket pocket and unlocked the bronze door, relocking it behind us. Alice Turner touched a switch which lit up the high-ceilinged lobby and the Greek statues standing like frozen sentinels along the walls. There were several nymphs and Venuses in marble, but I was more interested in Alice. She had everything the Venuses had, and the added advantage of being alive. She also had Hugh Western, it seemed, and that surprised me. He was a little old for her, and a little used. She didn't look like one of those girls who'd have to settle for an aging bachelor. But then Hugh Western had talent.

She removed a bundle of letters from the mail box and took them into the office which opened off the lobby. Silliman turned to me with a monkey grin.

"She's quite a girl, is she not? Trust Hugh to draw a circle around the prettiest girl in town. And she comes from a very good family, an excellent family. Her father, the Admiral, is one of our trustees, you know, and Alice has inherited his interest in the arts. Of course she has a more personal interest now. Had you known of their engagement?"

"I haven't seen Hugh for years, not since the war."

"Then I should have held my tongue and let him tell you himself."

As we were talking, he led me through the central gallery, which ran the length of the building like the nave of a church. To the left and right, in what would have been the aisles, the walls of smaller exhibition rooms rose halfway to the ceiling. Above them was a mezzanine reached by an open iron staircase.

He started up it, still talking: "If you haven't seen Hugh since the war, you'll be interested in the work he's been doing lately."

I was interested, though not for artistic reasons. The wall of the mezzanine was hung with twenty-odd paintings: landscapes, portraits, groups of semi-abstract figures, and more abstract still lifes. I recognized some of the scenes he had sketched in the Philippine jungle, transposed into the permanence of oil. In the central position there was a portrait of a bearded man whom I'd hardly have known without the label, "Self-Portrait."

Hugh had changed. He had put on weight and lost his youth entirely. There were vertical lines in the forehead, gray flecks in the hair and beard. The light eyes seemed to be smiling sardonically. But when I looked at them from another angle, they were bleak and somber. It was a face a man might see in his bathroom mirror on a cold gray hangover morning.

I turned to the curator hovering at my elbow. "When did he raise the beard?"

"A couple of years ago, I believe, shortly after he joined us as resident painter."

"Is he obsessed with beards?"

"I don't quite know what you mean."

"Neither do I. But I came across a funny thing in his studio this morning. A sketch of a woman, a nude, with a heavy black beard. Does that make sense to you?"

The old man smiled. "I've long since given up trying to make sense of Hugh. He has his own esthetic logic, I suppose. But I'd have to see this sketch before I could form an opinion. He may have simply been doodling."

"I doubt it. It was big, and carefully done." I brought out the question that had been nagging at the back of my mind. "Is there something the matter with him, emotionally? He hasn't gone off the deep end?"

His answer was sharp. "Certainly not. He's simply wrapped up in his work, and he lives by impulse. He's never on time for appointments." He looked at his watch. "He promised last night to meet me here this morning at nine, and it's almost nine-thirty."

"When did you see him last night?"

"I left the key of the gallery with him when I went home for dinner. He wanted to rehang some of these paintings. About eight or a little after he walked over to my house to return the key. We have only the one key, since we can't afford a watchman."

"Did he say where he was going after that?"

"He had an appointment, he didn't say with whom. It seemed to be urgent, since he wouldn't stop for a drink. Well." He glanced at his watch again. "I suppose I'd better be getting down to work, Western or no Western."

Alice was waiting for us at the foot of the stairs. Both of her hands gripped the wrought-iron bannister. Her voice was no more than a whisper, but it seemed to fill the great room with leaden echoes:

"Dr. Silliman, the Chardin's gone."

He stopped so suddenly I nearly ran into him. "That's impossible."

"I know. But it's gone, frame and all."

He bounded down the remaining steps and disappeared into one of the smaller rooms under the mezzanine. Alice followed him more slowly. I caught up with her:

"There's a picture missing?"

"Father's best picture, one of the best Chardins in the country. He loaned it to the gallery for a month."

"Is it worth a lot of money?"

"Yes, it's very valuable. But it means a lot more to Father than the money—" She turned in the doorway and gave me a closed look, as if she'd realized she was telling her family secrets to a stranger.

Silliman was standing with his back to us, staring at a blank space on the opposite wall. He looked badly shaken when he turned around.

"I *told* the board that we should install a burglar alarm—the insurance people recommended it. But Admiral Turner was the only one who supported me. Now of course they'll be blaming me." His nervous eyes roved around and paused on Alice. "And what is your father going to say?"

"He'll be sick." She looked sick herself.

They were getting nowhere, and I cut in: "When did you see it last?"

Silliman answered me. "Yesterday afternoon, about five-thirty. I showed it to a visitor just before we closed. We check the visitors very closely from the office, since we have no guards."

"Who was the visitor?"

"A lady—an elderly lady from Pasadena. She's above suspicion, of course. I escorted her out myself, and she was the last one in, I know for a fact."

"Aren't you forgetting Hugh?"

"By George, I was. He was here until eight last night. But you surely don't suggest that Western took it? He's our resident painter, he's devoted to the gallery."

"He might have been careless. If he was working on the mezzanine and left the door unlocked—"

"He always kept it locked," Alice said coldly. "Hugh isn't careless about the things that matter."

"Is there another entrance?"

"No," Silliman said. "The building was planned for security. There's only one window in my office, and it's heavily barred. We do have an air-conditioning system, but the inlets are much too small for anyone to get through."

"Let's have a look at the window."

The old man was too upset to question my authority. He led me through a storeroom stacked with old gilt-framed pictures whose painters deserved to be hung, if the pictures didn't. The single casement in the office was shut and bolted behind a Venetian blind. I pulled the cord and peered out through the dusty glass. The vertical bars outside the window were no more than three inches apart. None of them looked as if it had been tampered with. Across the alley, I could see a few tourists obliviously eating breakfast behind the restaurant hedge.

Silliman was leaning on the desk, one hand on the cradle phone. Indecision was twisting his face out of shape. "I do hate to call the police in a matter like this. I suppose I must, though, mustn't I?"

Alice covered his hand with hers, the line of her back a taut curve across the desk. "Hadn't you better talk to Father first? He was here with Hugh last night—I should have remembered before. It's barely possible he took the Chardin home with him."

"Really? You really think so?" Silliman let go of the telephone and clasped his hands hopefully under his chin.

"It wouldn't be like Father to do that without letting you know. But the month is nearly up, isn't it?"

"Three more days." His hand returned to the phone. "Is the Admiral at home?"

"He'll be down at the club by now. Do you have your car?"

"Not this morning."

I made one of my famous quick decisions, the kind you wake up in the middle of the night reconsidering five years later. San Francisco could wait. My curiosity was touched, and something deeper than curiosity. Something of the responsibility I'd felt for Hugh in the Philippines, when I was the practical one and he was the evergreen adolescent who thought the jungle was as safe as a scene by Le Douanier Rousseau. Though we were nearly the same age, I'd felt like his elder brother. I still did.

"My car's around the corner," I said. "I'll be glad to drive you."

The San Marcos Beach Club was a long low building painted an unobtrusive green and standing well back from the road. Everything about it was unobtrusive, including the private policeman who stood inside the plate-glass doors and watched us come up the walk.

"Looking for the Admiral, Miss Turner? I think he's up on the north deck."

We crossed a tiled lanai shaded with potted palms, and climbed a flight of stairs to a sun deck lined with cabanas. I could see the mountains that walled the city off from the desert in the northeast, and the sea below with its waves glinting like blue fish scales. The swimming pool on the lee side of the deck was still and clear.

Admiral Turner was taking the sun in a canvas chair. He stood up when he saw us, a big old man in shorts and a sleeveless shirt. Sun and wind had reddened his face and crinkled the flesh around his eyes. Age had slackened his body, but there was nothing aged or infirm about his voice. It still held the brazen echo of command.

"What's this, Alice? I thought you were at work."

"We came to ask you a question, Admiral." Silliman hesitated, coughing behind his hand. He looked at Alice.

"Speak out, man. Why is everybody looking so green around the gills?"

Silliman forced the words out: "Did you take the Chardin home with you last night?"

"I did not. Is it gone?"

"It's missing from the gallery," Alice said. She held herself uncertainly, as though the old man frightened her a little. "We thought you might have taken it."

"Me take it? That's absurd! Absolutely absurd and preposterous!" The short white hair bristled on his head. "When was it taken?"

"We don't know. It was gone when we opened the gallery. We discovered it just now."

"God damn it, what goes on?" He glared at her and then he glared at me, from eyes like round blue gun muzzles. "And who the hell are you?"

He was only a retired admiral, and I'd been out of uniform for years, but he gave me a qualm. Alice put in:

"A friend of Hugh's, Father. Mr. Archer."

He didn't offer his hand. I looked away. A woman in a white bathing suit was poised on the ten-foot board at the end of the pool. She took three quick steps and a bounce. Her body hung jack-knifed in the air, straightened and dropped, cut the water with hardly a splash.

"Where is Hugh?" the Admiral said petulantly. "If this is some of his carelessness, I'll ream the bastard."

"Father!"

"Don't father me. Where is he, Allie? You ought to know if anyone does."

"But I don't." She added in a small voice: "He's been gone all night."

"He has?" The old man sat down suddenly, as if his legs were too weak to bear the weight of his feelings. "He didn't say anything to me about going away."

The woman in the white bathing suit came up the steps behind him. "Who's gone away?" she said.

The Admiral craned his wattled neck to look at her. She was worth the effort from anyone, though she wouldn't see thirty again. Her dripping body was tanned and disciplined, full in the right places and narrow in others. I didn't remember her face, but her shape seemed familiar. Silliman introduced her as Admiral Turner's wife. When she pulled off her rubber cap, her red hair flared like a minor conflagration.

"You won't believe what they've been telling me, Sarah. My Chardin's been stolen."

"Which one?"

"I've only the one. The 'Apple on a Table.' "

She turned on Silliman like a pouncing cat. "Is it insured?"

"For twenty-five thousand dollars. But I'm afraid it's irreplaceable."

"And who's gone away?"

"Hugh has," Alice said. "Of course it's nothing to do with the picture."

"You're sure?" She turned to her husband with an intensity that made her almost ungainly. "Hugh was at the gallery when you dropped in there last night. You told me so yourself. And hasn't he been trying to buy the Chardin?"

"I don't believe it," Alice said flatly. "He didn't have the money."

"I know that perfectly well. He was acting as agent for someone. Wasn't he, Johnston?"

"Yes," the old man admitted. "He wouldn't tell me who his principal was, which is one of the reasons I wouldn't listen to the offer. Still, it's foolish to jump to conclusions about Hugh. I was with him when he left the gallery, and I know for a fact he didn't have the Chardin. It was the last thing I looked at."

"What time did he leave you?"

"Some time around eight—I don't remember exactly." He seemed to be growing older and smaller under her questioning. "He walked with me as far as my car."

"There was nothing to prevent him from walking right back."

"I don't know what you're trying to prove," Alice said.

The older woman smiled poisonously. "I'm simply trying to bring out the facts, so we'll know what to do. I notice that no one has suggested calling in the police." She looked at each of the others in turn. "Well? Do we call them? Or do we assume as a working hypothesis that dear Hugh took the picture?"

Nobody answered her for a while. The Admiral finally broke the ugly silence. "We can't bring in the authorities if Hugh's involved. He's virtually a member of the family."

Alice put a grateful hand on his shoulder, but Silliman said uneasily, "We'll have to take some steps. If we don't make an effort to recover it, we may not be able to collect the insurance."

"I realize that," the Admiral said. "We'll have to take that chance."

Sarah Turner smiled with tight-lipped complacency. She'd won her point, though I still wasn't sure what her point was. During the family argument I'd moved a few feet away, leaning on the railing at the head of the stairs and pretending not to listen.

She moved towards me now, her narrow eyes appraising me as if maleness was a commodity she prized.

"And who are you?" she said, her sharp smile widening.

I identified myself. I didn't smile back. But she came up very close to me. I could smell the chlorine on her, and under it the not so very subtle odor of sex.

"You look uncomfortable," she said. "Why don't you come swimming with me?"

"My hydrophobia won't let me. Sorry."

"What a pity. I hate to do things alone."

Silliman nudged me gently. He said in an undertone: "I really must be getting back to the gallery. I can call a cab if you prefer."

"No, I'll drive you." I wanted a chance to talk to him in private.

There were quick footsteps in the patio below. I looked down and saw the naked crown of Hilary Todd's head. At almost the same instant he glanced up at us. He turned abruptly and started to walk away, then changed his mind when Silliman called down.

"Hello there. Are you looking for the Turners?"

"As a matter of fact, I am."

From the corner of my eye, I noticed Sarah Turner's reaction to the sound of his voice. She stiffened, and her hand went up to her flaming hair.

"They're up here," Silliman said.

Todd climbed the stairs with obvious reluctance. We passed him going down. In a pastel shirt and a matching tie under a bright tweed jacket he looked very elegant, and very self-conscious and tense. Sarah Turner met him at the head of the stairs. I wanted to linger a bit, for eavesdropping purposes, but Silliman hustled me out.

"Mrs. Turner seems very much aware of Todd," I said to him in the car. "Do they have things in common?"

He answered tartly: "I've never considered the question. They're no more than casual acquaintances, so far as I know."

"What about Hugh? Is he just a casual acquaintance of hers, too?"

He studied me for a minute as the convertible picked up speed. "You notice things, don't you?"

"Noticing things is my business."

"Just what is your business? You're not an artist?"

"Hardly. I'm a private detective."

"A detective?" He jumped in the seat, as if I had offered to bite him. "You're not a friend of Western's then? Are you from the insurance company?"

"Not me. I'm a friend of Hugh's, and that's my only interest in this case. I more or less stumbled into it."

"I see." But he sounded a little dubious.

"Getting back to Mrs. Turner—she didn't make that scene with her husband for fun. She must have had some reason. Love or hate."

Silliman held his tongue for a minute, but he couldn't resist a chance to gossip. "I expect that it's a mixture of love and hate. She's been interested in Hugh ever since the Admiral brought her here. She's not a San Marcos girl, you know." He seemed to take comfort from that. "She was a Wave officer in Washington during the war. The Admiral noticed her—Sarah knows how to make herself conspicuous—and added her to his personal staff. When he retired he married her and came here to live in his family home. Alice's mother has been dead for many years. Well, Sarah hadn't been here two months before she was making eyes at Hugh." He pressed his lips together in spinsterly disapproval. "The rest is local history."

"They had an affair?"

"A rather one-sided affair, so far as I could judge. She was quite insane about him. I don't believe he responded, except in the physical sense. Your friend is quite a demon with the ladies." There was a whisper of envy in Silliman's disapproval.

"But I understood he was going to marry Alice."

"Oh, he is, he is. At least he certainly was until this dreadful business came up. His—ah—involvement with Sarah occurred before he knew Alice. She was away at art school until a few months ago."

"Does Alice know about his affair with her stepmother?"

"I daresay she does. I hear the two women don't get along at all well, though there may be other reasons for that. Alice refuses to live in the same house; she's moved into the gardener's cottage behind the Turner house. I think her trouble with Sarah is one reason why she came to work for me. Of course, there's the money consideration, too. The family isn't well off."

"I thought they were rolling in it," I said, "from the way he brushed off the matter of the insurance. Twenty-five thousand dollars, did you say?"

"Yes. He's quite fond of Hugh."

"If he's not well heeled, how does he happen to have such a valuable painting?"

"It was a gift, when he married his first wife. Her father was in the French Embassy in Washington, and he gave them the Chardin as a wedding present. You can understand the Admiral's attachment to it."

"Better than I can his decision not to call in the police. How do you feel about that, doctor?"

He didn't answer for a while. We were nearing the center of the city and I had to watch the traffic. I couldn't keep track of what went on in his face.

"After all it *is* his picture," he said carefully. "And his prospective son-in-law."

"You don't think Hugh's responsible, though?"

"I don't know what to think. I'm thoroughly rattled. And I won't know what to think until I have a chance to talk to Western." He gave me a sharp look. "Are you going to make a search for him?"

"Somebody has to. I seem to be elected."

When I let him out in front of the gallery, I asked him where Mary Western worked.

"The City Hospital." He told me how to find it. "But you will be discreet, Mr. Archer? You won't do or say anything rash? I'm in a very delicate position."

"I'll be very suave and bland." But I slammed the door hard in his face.

There were several patients in the X-ray waiting room, in various stages of dilapidation and disrepair. The plump blonde at the reception desk told me that Miss Western was in the darkroom. Would I wait? I sat down and admired the way her sunburned shoulders glowed through her nylon uniform. In a few minutes Mary came into the room, starched and controlled and efficient-looking. She blinked in the strong light from the window. I got a quick impression that there was a lost child hidden behind her facade.

"Have you seen Hugh?"

"No. Come out for a minute." I took her elbow and drew her into the corridor.

"What is it?" Her voice was quiet, but it had risen in pitch. "Has something happened to him?"

"Not to *him.* Admiral Turner's picture's been stolen from the gallery. The Chardin."

"But how does Hugh come into this?"

"Somebody seems to think he took it."

"Somebody?"

"Mrs. Turner, to be specific."

"*Sarah!* She'd say anything to get back at him for ditching her."

I filed that one away. "Maybe so. The fact is, the Admiral seems to suspect him, too. So much so that he's keeping the police out of it."

"Admiral Turner is a senile fool. If Hugh were here to defend himself—"

"But that's the point. He isn't."

"I've got to find him." She turned towards the door.

"It may not be so easy."

She looked back in quick anger, her round chin prominent. "You suspect him, too."

"I do not. But a crime's been committed, remember. Crimes often come in pairs."

She turned, her eyes large and very dark. "You do think something has happened to my brother."

"I don't think anything. But if I were certain that he's all right, I'd be on my way to San Francisco now."

"You believe it's as bad as that," she said in a whisper. "I've got to go to the police."

"It's up to you. You'll want to keep them out of it, though, if there's the slightest chance—" I left the sentence unfinished.

She finished it: "That Hugh is a thief? There isn't. But I'll tell you what we'll do. He may be up at his shack in the mountains. He's gone off there before without telling anyone. Will you drive up with me?" She laid a light hand on my arm. "I can go myself if you have to get away."

"I'm sticking around," I said. "Can you get time off?"

"I'm taking it. All they can do is fire me, and there aren't enough good technicians to go around. Anyway, I put in three hours' overtime last night. Be with you in two minutes."

And she was.

I put the top of the convertible down. As we drove out of the city the wind blew away her smooth glaze of efficiency, colored her cheeks and loosened her sleek hair.

"You should do this oftener," I said.

"Do what?"

"Get out in the country and relax."

"I'm not exactly relaxed, with my brother accused of theft, and missing into the bargain."

"Anyway, you're not working. Has it ever occurred to you that perhaps you work too hard?"

"Has it ever occurred to you that somebody has to work or nothing will get done? You and Hugh are more alike than I thought."

"In some ways that's a compliment. You make it sound like an insult."

"I didn't mean it that way, exactly. But Hugh and I are so different. I admit he works hard at his painting, but he's never tried to make a steady living. Since I left school, I've had to look after the bread and butter for both of us. His salary as resident painter keeps him in artist's supplies, and that's about all."

"I thought he was doing well. His show's had a big advance buildup in the L.A. papers."

"Critics don't buy pictures," she said bluntly. "He's having the show

to try to sell some paintings, so he can afford to get married. Hugh has
suddenly realized that money is one of the essentials." She added with
some bitterness, "The realization came a little late."

"He's been doing some outside work, though, hasn't he? Isn't he a
part-time agent or something?"

"For Hendryx, yes." She made the name sound like a dirty word.
"I'd just as soon he didn't take any of that man's money."

"Who's Hendryx?"

"A man."

"I gathered that. What's the matter with his money?"

"I really don't know. I have no idea where it comes from. But he has
it."

"You don't like him?"

"No. I don't like him, and I don't like the men who work for him.
They look like a gang of thugs to me. But Hugh wouldn't notice that.
He's horribly dense where people are concerned. I don't mean that
Hugh's done anything wrong," she added quickly. "He's bought a few
paintings for Hendryx on commission."

"I see." I didn't like what I saw, but I named it. "The Admiral said
something about Hugh trying to buy the Chardin for an unnamed
purchaser. Would that be Hendryx?"

"It could be," she said.

"Tell me more about Hendryx."

"I don't know any more. I only met him once. That was enough. I
know that he's an evil old man, and he has a bodyguard who carries
him upstairs."

"Carries him upstairs?"

"Yes. He's crippled. As a matter of fact, he offered me a job."

"Carrying him upstairs?"

"He didn't specify my duties. He didn't get that far." Her voice was
so chilly it quick-froze the conversation. "Now could we drop the
subject, Mr. Archer?"

The road had begun to rise towards the mountains. Yellow and black
Slide Area signs sprang up along the shoulders. By holding the gas
pedal nearly to the floor, I kept our speed around fifty.

"You've had quite a busy morning," Mary said after a while, "meeting the Turners and all."

"Social mobility is my stock in trade."

"Did you meet Alice, too?"

I said I had.

"And what did you think of her?"

"I shouldn't say it to another girl, but she's a lovely one."

"Vanity isn't one of my vices," Mary said. "She's beautiful. And she's really devoted to Hugh."

"I gathered that."

"I don't think Alice has ever been in love before. And painting means almost as much to her as it does to him."

"He's a lucky man." I remembered the disillusioned eyes of the self-portrait, and hoped that his luck was holding.

The road twisted and climbed through red clay cutbanks and fields of dry chaparral.

"How long does this go on?" I asked.

"It's about another two miles."

We zigzagged up the mountainside for ten or twelve minutes more. Finally the road began to level out. I was watching its edge so closely that I didn't see the cabin until we were almost on top of it. It was a one-story frame building standing in a little hollow at the edge of the high mesa. Attached to one side was an open tarpaulin shelter from which the rear end of a gray coupe protruded. I looked at Mary.

She nodded. "It's our car." Her voice was bright with relief.

I stopped the convertible in the lane in front of the cabin. As soon as the engine died, the silence began. A single hawk high over our heads swung round and round on his invisible wire. Apart from that, the entire world seemed empty. As we walked down the ill-kept gravel drive, I was startled by the sound of my own footsteps.

The door was unlocked. The cabin had only one room. It was a bachelor hodgepodge, untouched by the human hand for months at a time. Cooking utensils, paint-stained dungarees and painter's tools and bedding were scattered on the floor and furniture. There was an open bottle of whiskey, half empty, on the kitchen table in the center of the room. It would have been just another mountain shack if it hadn't been for the watercolors on the wall, like brilliant little windows, and the one big window which opened on the sky.

Mary had crossed to the window and was looking out. I moved up to her shoulder. Blue space fell away in front of us all the way down to the sea, and beyond to the curved horizon. San Marcos and its suburbs were spread out like an air map between the sea and the mountains.

"I wonder where he can be," she said. "Perhaps he's gone for a hike. After all, he doesn't know we're looking for him."

I looked down the mountainside, which fell almost sheer from the window.

"No," I said. "He doesn't."

The red clay slope was sown with boulders. Nothing grew there except a few dust-colored mountain bushes. And a foot, wearing a man's shoe, which projected from a cleft between two rocks.

I went out without a word. A path led round the cabin to the edge of the slope. Hugh Western was there, attached to the solitary foot. He was lying, or hanging head down with his face in the clay, about twenty feet below the edge. One of his legs was doubled under him. The other was caught between the boulders. I climbed around the rocks and bent to look at his head.

The right temple was smashed. The face was smashed; I raised the rigid body to look at it. He had been dead for hours, but the sharp strong odor of whiskey still hung around him.

A tiny gravel avalanche rattled past me. Mary was at the top of the slope.

"Don't come down here."

She paid no attention to the warning. I stayed where I was, crouched over the body, trying to hide the ruined head from her. She leaned over the boulder and looked down, her eyes bright black in her drained face. I moved to one side. She took her brother's head in her hands.

"If you pass out," I said, "I don't know whether I can carry you up."

"I won't pass out."

She lifted the body by the shoulders to look at the face. It was a little unsettling to see how strong she was. Her fingers moved gently over the wounded temple. "This is what killed him. It looks like a blow from a fist."

I kneeled down beside her and saw the row of rounded indentations in the skull.

"He must have fallen," she said, "and struck his head on the rocks. Nobody could have hit him that hard."

"I'm afraid somebody did, though." Somebody whose fist was hard enough to leave its mark in wood.

Two long hours later I parked my car in front of the art shop on Rubio Street. Its windows were jammed with Impressionist and Post-Impressionist reproductions, and one very bad original oil of surf as stiff and static as whipped cream. The sign above the windows was lettered in flowing script: *Chez Hilary.* The cardboard sign on the door was simpler and to the point; it said: *Closed.*

The stairs and hallway seemed dark, but it was good to get out of the sun. The sun reminded me of what I had found at high noon on the mesa. It wasn't the middle of the afternoon yet, but my nerves felt stretched and scratchy, as though it was late at night. My eyes were aching.

Mary unlocked the door of her apartment, stepped aside to let me pass. She paused at the door of her room to tell me there was whiskey on the sideboard. I offered to make her a drink. No, thanks, she never drank. The door shut behind her. I mixed a whiskey and water and tried to relax in an easy chair. I couldn't relax. My mind kept playing back the questions and the answers, and the questions that had no answers.

We had called the sheriff from the nearest firewarden's post, and led him and his deputies back up the mountain to the body. Photographs were taken, the cabin and its surroundings searched, many questions asked. Mary didn't mention the lost Chardin. Neither did I.

Some of the questions were answered after the county coroner arrived. Hugh Western had been dead since some time between eight and ten o'clock the previous night; the coroner couldn't place the time more definitely before analyzing the stomach contents. The blow on the temple had killed him. The injuries to his face, which had failed to bleed, had probably been inflicted after death. Which meant that he was dead when his body fell or was thrown down the mountainside.

His clothes had been soaked with whiskey to make it look like a drunken accident. But the murderer had gone too far in covering, and outwitted himself. The whiskey bottle in the cabin showed no fingerprints, not even Western's. And there were no fingerprints on the steering wheel of his coupe. Bottle and wheel had been wiped clean.

I stood up when Mary came back into the room. She had brushed her black hair gleaming, and changed to a dress of soft black jersey which fitted her like skin. A thought raced through my mind like a nasty little rodent. I wondered what she would look like with a beard.

"Can I have another look at the studio? I'm interested in that sketch."

She looked at me for a moment, frowning a little dazedly. "Sketch?"

"The one of the lady with the beard."

She crossed the hall ahead of me, walking slowly and carefully as if the floor were unsafe and a rapid movement might plunge her into black chaos. The door of the studio was still unlocked. She held it open for me and pressed the light switch.

When the fluorescent lights blinked on, I saw that the bearded nude was gone. There was nothing left of her but the four torn corners of the drawing paper thumbtacked to the empty easel. I turned to Mary.

"Did you take it down?"

"No. I haven't been in the studio since this morning."

"Somebody's stolen it then. Is there anything else missing?"

"I can't be sure, it's such a mess in here." She moved around the room looking at the pictures on the walls and pausing finally by a table in the corner. "There was a bronze cast on this table. It isn't here now."

"What sort of a cast?"

"The cast of a fist. Hugh made it from the fist of that man—that dreadful man I told you about."

"What dreadful man?"

"I think his name is Devlin. He's Hendryx' bodyguard. Hugh's always been interested in hands, and the man has enormous hands."

Her eyes unfocused suddenly. I guessed she was thinking of the same thing I was: the marks on the side of Hugh's head, which might have been made by a giant fist.

"Look." I pointed to the scars on the doorframe. "Could the cast of Devlin's fist have made these marks?"

She felt the indentations with trembling fingers. "I think so—I don't know." She turned to me with a dark question in her eyes.

"If that's what they are," I said, "it probably means that he was killed in this studio. You should tell the police about it. And I think it's time they knew about the Chardin."

She gave me a look of passive resistance. Then she gave in. "Yes, I'll have to tell them. They'll find out soon enough, anyway. But I'm surer now than ever that Hugh didn't take it."

"What does the picture look like? If we could find it, we might find the killer attached to it."

"You think so? Well, it's a picture of a little boy looking at an apple. Wait a minute: Hilary has a copy. It was painted by one of the students at the college, and it isn't very expert. It'll give you an idea, though, if you want to go down to his shop and look at it."

"The shop is closed."

"He may be there anyway. He has a little apartment at the back."

I started for the hall, but turned before I got there. "Just who is Hilary Todd?"

"I don't know where he's from originally. He was stationed here during the war, and simply stayed on. His parents had money at one time, and he studied painting and ballet in Paris, or so he claims."

"Art seems to be the main industry in San Marcos."

"You've just been meeting the wrong people."

I went down the outside stairs to the parking lot, wondering what that implied about her brother. Todd's convertible stood near the mouth of the alley. I knocked on the back door of the art shop. There was no answer, but behind the Venetian-blinded door I heard a murmur of voices, a growling and a twittering. Todd had a woman with him. I knocked again.

After more delay the door was partly opened. Todd looked out through the crack. He was wiping his mouth with a red-stained handkerchief. The stains were too bright to be blood. Above the handkerchief his eyes were very bright and narrow, like slivers of polished agate.

"Good afternoon."

I moved forward as though I fully expected to be let in. He opened the door reluctantly under the nudging pressure of my shoulder, and backed into a narrow passage between two wallboard partitions.

"What can I do for you, Mr.—? I don't believe I know your name."

Before I could answer, a woman's voice said clearly, "It's Mr. Archer, isn't it?"

Sarah Turner appeared in the doorway behind him, carrying a highball glass and looking freshly groomed. Her red hair was unruffled, her red mouth gleaming as if she had just finished painting it.

"Good afternoon, Mrs. Turner."

"Good afternoon, Mr. Archer." She leaned in the doorway, almost too much at ease. "Do you know Hilary, Mr. Archer? You should. Everybody should. Hilary's simply loaded and dripping with charm, aren't you, dear?" Her mouth curled in a thin smile.

Todd looked at her with hatred, then turned to me without changing his look. "Did you wish to speak to me?"

"I did. You have a copy of Admiral Turner's Chardin."

"A copy, yes."

"Can I have a look at it?"

"What on earth for?"

"I want to be able to identify the original. It's probably connected with the murder."

I watched them both as I said the word. Neither showed surprise.

"We heard about it on the radio," the woman said. "It must have been dreadful for you."

"Dreadful," Todd echoed her, injecting synthetic sympathy into his dark eyes.

"Worse for Western," I said, "and for whoever did it. Do you still think he stole the picture, Mrs. Turner?"

Todd glanced at her sharply. She was embarrassed, as I'd intended her to be. She dunked her embarrassment in her highball glass, swallowing deeply from it and leaving a red half-moon on its rim.

"I never thought he stole it," her wet mouth lied. "I merely suggested the possibility."

"I see. Didn't you say something about Western trying to buy the picture from your husband? That he was acting as agent for somebody else?"

"I wasn't the one who said that. I didn't know it."

"The Admiral said it then. It would be interesting to know who the other man was. He wanted the Chardin, and it looks to me as if Hugh Western died because somebody wanted the Chardin."

Todd had been listening hard and saying nothing. "I don't see any necessary connection," he said now. "But if you'll come in and sit down I'll show you my copy."

"You wouldn't know who it was that Western was acting for?"

He spread his palms outward in a Continental gesture. "How would I know?"

"You're in the picture business."

"I *was* in the picture business." He turned abruptly and left the room.

Sarah Turner had crossed to a portable bar in the corner. She was splintering ice with a silver-handled ice pick. "May I make you one, Mr. Archer?"

"No, thanks." I sat down in a cubistic chair designed for people with square corners, and watched her take half of her new highball in a single gulp. "What did Todd mean when he said he *was* in the picture business? Doesn't he run this place?"

"He's having to give it up. The *boutique's* gone broke, and he's going around testing shoulders to weep on."

"Yours?" A queer kind of hostile intimacy had risen between us, and I tried to make the most of it.

"Where did you get that notion?"

"I thought he was a friend of yours."

"Did you?" Her laugh was too loud to be pleasant. "You ask a great many questions, Mr. Archer."

"They seem to be indicated. The cops in a town like this are pretty backward about stepping on people's toes."

"You're not."

"No. I'm just passing through. I can follow my hunches."

"What do you hope to gain?"

"Nothing for myself. I'd like to see justice done."

She sat down facing me, her knees almost touching mine. They were pretty knees, and uncovered. I felt crowded. Her voice, full of facile emotion, crowded me more:

"Were you terribly fond of Hugh?"

"I liked him." My answer was automatic. I was thinking of something else: the way she sat in her chair with her knees together, her body sloping backward, sure of its firm lines. I'd seen the same pose in charcoal that morning.

"I liked him, too," she was saying. "Very much. And I've been thinking—I've remembered something. Something that Hilary mentioned a couple of weeks ago, about Walter Hendryx wanting to buy the Chardin. It seems Hugh and Walter Hendryx were talking shop—"

She broke off suddenly. She had looked up and seen Todd leaning through the doorway, his face alive with anger. His shoulders moved slightly in her direction. She recoiled, clutching her glass. If I hadn't been there, I guessed he would have hit her. As it was, he said in a monotone:

"How cozy. Haven't you had quite a bit to drink, Sarah darling?"

She was afraid of him, but unwilling to admit it. "I have to do something to make present company bearable."

"You should be thoroughly anesthetized by now."

"If you say so, darling."

She hurled her half-empty glass at the wall beside the door. It shattered, denting the wallboard and splashing a photograph of Nijinsky as the Faun. Some of the liquid splattered on Todd's blue suede shoes.

"Very nice," he said. "I love your girlish antics, Sarah. I also love the way you run at the mouth." He turned to me: "This is the copy, Mr. Archer. Don't mind her, she's just a weensy bit drunky."

He held it up for me to see, an oil painting about a yard square showing a small boy in a blue waistcoat sitting at a table. In the center of the linen tablecloth there was a blue dish containing a red apple. The boy was looking at the apple as if he intended to eat it. The copyist had included the signature and date: Chardin, 1744.

"It's not very satisfactory," Todd said, "if you've ever seen the original. But of course you haven't?"

"No."

"That's too bad. You probably never will now, and it's really perfect. It's the finest Chardin west of Chicago."

"I haven't given up hope of seeing it."

"You might as well, old boy. It'll be well on its way by now, to Europe, or South America. Picture thieves move fast, before the news of the theft catches up with them and spoils the market. They'll sell the Chardin to a private buyer in Paris or Buenos Aires, and that'll be the end of it."

"Why 'they'?"

"Oh, they operate in gangs. One man can't handle the theft and the disposal of a picture by himself. Division of labor is necessary, and specialization."

"You sound like a specialist yourself."

"I am, in a way." He smiled obliquely. "Not in the way you mean. I was in museum work before the war."

He stooped and propped the picture against the wall. I glanced at Sarah Turner. She was hunched forward in her chair, still and silent, her hands spread over her face.

"And now," he said to me, "I suppose you'd better go. I've done what I can for you. And I'll give you a tip if you like. Picture thieves don't do murder, they're simply not the type. So I'm afraid your precious hypothesis is based on bad information."

"Thanks very much," I said. "I certainly appreciate that. Also your hospitality."

"Don't mention it."

He raised an ironic brow, and turned to the door. I followed him out through the deserted shop. Most of the stock seemed to be in the window. Its atmosphere was sad and broken-down, the atmosphere of an empty-hearted, unprosperous, second-hand Bohemia. Todd didn't look around like a proprietor. He had already abandoned the place in his mind, it seemed.

He unlocked the front door. The last thing he said before he shut it behind me was:

"I wouldn't go bothering Walter Hendryx about that story of Sarah's. She's not a very trustworthy reporter, and Hendryx isn't as tolerant of intruders as I am."

So it was true.

I left my car where it was and crossed to a taxi stand on the opposite corner. There was a yellow cab at the stand, with a brown-faced driver reading a comic book behind the wheel. The comic book had dead women on the cover. The driver detached his hot eyes from its interior, leaned wearily over the back of the seat and opened the door for me. "Where to?"

"A man called Walter Hendryx—know where he lives?"

"Off of Foothill Drive. I been up there before. It's a two-fifty run, outside the city limits." His Jersey accent didn't quite go with his Sicilian features.

"Newark?"

"Trenton." He showed bad teeth in a good smile. "You want to make something out of it?"

"Nope. Let's go."

He spoke to me over his shoulder when we were out of the heavy downtown traffic. "You got your passport?"

"What kind of a place are you taking me to?"

"They don't like visitors. You got to have a visa to get in, and a writ of habeas corpus to get out. The old man's scared of burglars or something."

"Why?"

"He's got about ten million reasons, the way I hear it. Ten million bucks." He smacked his lips.

"Where did he get it?"

"You tell me. I'll drop everything and take off for the same place."

"You and me both."

"I heard he's a big contractor in L.A.," the driver said. "I drove a reporter up here a couple of months ago, from one of the L.A. papers. He was after an interview with the old guy, something about a tax case."

"What about a tax case?"

"I wouldn't know. It's way over my head, friend, all that tax business. I have enough trouble with my own forms."

"What happened to the reporter?"

"I drove him right back down. The old man wouldn't see him. He likes his privacy."

"I'm beginning to get the idea."

"You a reporter, too, by any chance?"

"No."

He was too polite to ask me any more questions.

We left the city limits. The mountains rose ahead, violet and unshadowed in the sun's lengthening rays. Foothill Drive wound through a canyon, across a high-level bridge, up the side of a hill from which the sea was visible like a low blue cloud on the horizon. We turned off the road through an open gate on which a sign was posted: *Trespassers Will Be Prosecuted.*

A second gate closed the road at the top of the hill. It was a double gate of wrought iron hung between a stone gatepost and a stone gatehouse. A heavy wire fence stretched out from it on both sides, following the contours of the hills as far as I could see. Hendryx' estate was about the size of a small European country.

The driver honked his horn. A thick-waisted man in a Panama hat came out of the stone cottage. He squeezed through a narrow postern and waddled up to the cab. "Well?"

"I came to see Mr. Hendryx about a picture."

He opened the cab door and looked me over, from eyes that were heavily shuttered with old scar tissue. "You ain't the one that was here this morning."

I had my first good idea of the day. "You mean the tall fellow with the sideburns?"

"Yeah."

"I just came from him."

He rubbed his heavy chin with his knuckles, making a rasping noise. The knuckles were jammed.

"I guess it's all right," he said finally. "Give me your name and I'll phone it down to the house. You can drive down."

He opened the gate and let us through into a shallow valley. Below, in a maze of shrubbery, a long, low house was flanked by tennis courts and stables. Sunk in the terraced lawn behind the house was an oval pool like a wide green eye staring at the sky. A short man in bathing trunks was sitting in a Thinker pose on the diving board at one end.

He and the pool dropped out of sight as the cab slid down the eucalyptus-lined road. It stopped under a portico at the side of the house. A uniformed maid was waiting at the door.

"This is further than that reporter got," the driver said in an undertone. "Maybe you got connections?"

"The best people in town."

"Mr. Archer?" the maid said. "Mr. Hendryx is having his bath. I'll show you the way."

I told the driver to wait, and followed her through the house. I saw when I stepped outside that the man on the diving board wasn't short at all. He only seemed to be short because he was so wide. Muscle bulged out his neck, clustered on his shoulders and chest, encased his arms and legs. He looked like a graduate of Muscle Beach, a subman trying hard to be a superman.

There was another man floating in the water, the blotched brown swell of his stomach breaking the surface like the shellback of a Galapagos tortoise. Thinker stood up, accompanied by his parasitic muscles, and called to him:

"Mr. Hendryx!"

The man in the water rolled over lazily and paddled to the side of the pool. Even his head was tortoise-like, seamed and bald and impervious-looking. He stood up in the waist-deep water and raised his thin

brown arms. The other man bent over him. He drew him out of the
water and steadied him on his feet, rubbing him with a towel.

"Thank you, Devlin."

"Yessir."

Leaning far forward with his arms dangling like those of a withered,
hairless ape, Hendryx shuffled towards me. The joints of his knees and
ankles were knobbed and stiffened by what looked like arthritis. He
peered up at me from his permanent crouch:

"You want to see me?" The voice that came out of his crippled body
was surprisingly rich and deep. He wasn't as old as he looked. "What
is it?"

"A painting was stolen last night from the San Marcos gallery:
Chardin's 'Apple on a Table'. I've heard that you were interested in it."

"You've been misinformed. Good afternoon." His face closed like a
fist.

"You haven't heard the rest of it."

Disregarding me, he called to the maid who was waiting at a distance:
"Show this man out."

Devlin came up beside me, strutting like a wrestler, his great curved
hands conspicuous.

"The rest of it," I said, "is that Hugh Western was murdered at the
same time. I think you knew him?"

"I knew him, yes. His death is unfortunate. Regrettable. But so far
as I know, it has nothing to do with the Chardin and nothing to do with
me. Will you go now, or do I have to have you removed?"

He raised his cold eyes to mine. I stared him down, but there wasn't
much satisfaction in that.

"You take murder pretty lightly, Hendryx."

"Mr. Hendryx to you," Devlin said in my ear. "Come on now, bud.
You heard what Mr. Hendryx said."

"I don't take orders from him."

"I do," he said with a lopsided grin like a heat-split in a melon. "I
take orders from him." His light small eyes shifted to Hendryx. "You
want for me to throw him out?"

Hendryx nodded, backing away. His eyes were heating up, as if the
prospect of violence excited him. Devlin's hand took my wrist. His
fingers closed around it and overlapped.

"What is this, Devlin?" I said. "I thought Hugh Western was a pal
of yours."

"Sure thing."

"I'm trying to find out who killed him. Aren't you interested? Or did you slap him down yourself?"

"The hell." Devlin blinked stupidly, trying to hold two questions in his mind at the same time.

Hendryx said from a safe distance: "Don't talk. Just give him a going-over and toss him out."

Devlin looked at Hendryx. His grip was like a thick handcuff on my wrist. I jerked his arm up and ducked under it, breaking the hold, and chopped at his nape. The bulging back of his neck was hard as a redwood bole.

He wheeled, and reached for me again. The muscles in his arm moved like drugged serpents. He was slow. My right fist found his chin and snapped it back on his neck. He recovered, and swung at me. I stepped inside of the roundhouse and hammered his ridged stomach, twice, four times. It was like knocking my fists against the side of a corrugated iron building. His great arms closed on me. I slipped down and away.

When he came after me, I shifted my attack to his head, jabbing with the left until he was off balance on his heels. Then I pivoted and threw a long right hook which changed to an uppercut. An electric shock surged up my arm. Devlin lay down on the green tiles, chilled like a side of beef.

I looked across him at Hendryx. There was no fear in his eyes, only calculation. He backed into a canvas chair and sat down clumsily.

"You're fairly tough, it seems. Perhaps you used to be a fighter? I've owned a few fighters in my time. You might have a future at it, if you were younger."

"It's a sucker's game. So is larceny."

"Larceny-farceny," he said surprisingly. "What did you say you do?"

"I'm a private detective."

"Private, eh?" His mouth curved in a lipless tortoise grin. "You interest me, Mr. Archer. I could find a use for you—a place in my organization."

"What kind of an organization?"

"I'm a builder, a mass-producer of houses. Like most successful entrepreneurs, I make enemies: cranks and bleeding hearts and psychopathic veterans who think the world owes them something. Devlin here isn't quite the man I thought he was. But you—"

"Forget it. I'm pretty choosy about the people I work for."

"An idealist, eh? A clean-cut young American idealist." The smile was still on his mouth; it was saturnine. "Well, Mr. Idealist, you're wasting your time. I know nothing about this picture or anything connected with it. You're also wasting *my* time."

"It seems to be expendable. I think you're lying, incidentally."

Hendryx didn't answer me directly. He called to the maid: "Telephone the gate. Tell Shaw we're having a little trouble with a guest. Then you can come back and look after this." He jerked a thumb at Muscle-Boy, who was showing signs of life.

I said to the maid: "Don't bother telephoning. I wouldn't stick around here if I was paid to."

She shrugged and looked at Hendryx. He nodded. I followed her out.

"You didn't stay long," the cab driver said.

"No. Do you know where Admiral Turner lives?"

"Curiously enough, I do. I should charge extra for the directory service."

I didn't encourage him to continue the conversation. "Take me there."

He let me out in a street of big old houses set far back from the sidewalk behind sandstone walls and high eugenia hedges. I paid him off and climbed the sloping walk to the Turner house. It was a weathered frame building, gabled and turreted in the style of the nineties. A gray-haired housekeeper who had survived from the same period answered my knock.

"The Admiral's in the garden," she said. "Will you come out?"

The garden was massed with many-colored begonias, and surrounded by a vine-covered wall. The Admiral, in stained and faded suntans, was chopping weeds in a flowerbed with furious concentration. When he saw me he leaned on his hoe and wiped his wet forehead with the back of his hand.

"You should come in out of the sun," the housekeeper said in a nagging way. "A man of your age—"

"Nonsense! Go away, Mrs. Harris." She went. "What can I do for you, Mr.—?"

"Archer. I guess you've heard that we found Hugh Western's body."

"Sarah came home and told me half an hour ago. It's a foul thing, and completely mystifying. He was to have married—"

His voice broke off. He glanced towards the stone cottage, at the rear of the garden. Alice Turner was there at an open window. She wasn't looking in our direction. She had a tiny paintbrush in her hand, and she was working at an easel.

"It's not as mystifying as it was. I'm starting to put the pieces together, Admiral."

He turned back to me quickly. His eyes became hard and empty again, like gun muzzles.

"Just who are you? What's your interest in this case?"

"I'm a friend of Hugh Western's, from Los Angeles. I stopped off here to see him, and found him dead. I hardly think my interest is out of place."

"No, of course not," he grumbled. "On the other hand, I don't believe in amateur detectives running around like chickens with their heads cut off, fouling up the authorities."

"I'm not exactly an amateur. I used to be a cop. And any fouling up there's been has been done by other people."

"Are you accusing me?"

"If the shoe fits."

He met my eyes for a time, trying to master me and the situation. But he was old and bewildered. Slowly the aggressive ego faded from his gaze. He became almost querulous.

"You'll excuse me. I don't know what it's all about. I've been rather upset by everything that's happened."

"What about your daughter?" Alice was still at the window, working at her picture and paying no attention to our voices. "Doesn't she know that Hugh is dead?"

"Yes. She knows. You mustn't misunderstand what Alice is doing. There are many ways of enduring grief, and we have a custom in the Turner family of working it out of our system. Hard work is the cure for a great many evils." He changed the subject, and his tone, abruptly. "And what is your idea of what's happened?"

"It's no more than a suspicion, a pretty foggy one. I'm not sure who stole your picture, but I think I know where it is."

"Well?"

"There's a man named Walter Hendryx who lives in the foothills outside the city. You know him?"

"Slightly."

"He probably has the Chardin. I'm morally certain he has it, as a matter of fact, though I don't know how he got it."

The Admiral tried to smile, and made a dismal failure of it. "You're not suggesting that Hendryx took it? He's not exactly mobile, you know."

"Hilary Todd is very mobile," I said. "Todd visited Hendryx this morning. I'd be willing to bet even money he had the Chardin with him."

"You didn't see it, however?"

"I don't have to. I've seen Todd."

A woman's voice said from the shadow of the back porch: "The man is right, Johnston."

Sarah Turner came down the path towards us, her high heels spiking the flagstones angrily.

"Hilary did it!" she cried. "He stole the picture and murdered Hugh. I saw him last night at midnight. He had red mountain clay on his clothes."

"It's strange you didn't mention it before," the Admiral said dryly.

I looked into her face. Her eyes were bloodshot, and the eyelids were swollen with weeping. Her mouth was swollen, too. When she opened it to reply, I could see that the lower lip was split.

"I just remembered."

I wondered if the blow that split her lip had reminded her.

"And where did you see Hilary Todd last night at midnight?"

"Where?"

In the instant of silence that followed, I heard footsteps behind me. Alice had come out of her cottage. She walked like a sleepwalker dreaming a bad dream, and stopped beside her father without a word to any of us.

Sarah's face had been twisting in search of an answer, and found it. "I met him at the Presidio. I dropped in there for a cup of coffee after the show."

"You are a liar, Sarah," the Admiral said. "The Presidio closes at ten o'clock."

"It wasn't the Presidio," she said rapidly. "It was the bar across the street, the Club Fourteen. I had dinner at the Presidio, and I confused them—"

The Admiral brushed past her without waiting to hear more, and started for the house. Alice went with him. The old man walked unsteadily, leaning on her arm.

"Did you really see Hilary last night?" I asked her.

She stood there for a minute, looking at me. Her face was disorganized, raddled with passion. "Yes, I saw him. I had a date with him at ten o'clock. I waited in his flat for over two hours. He didn't show up until after midnight. I couldn't tell *him* that." She jerked one shoulder contemptuously toward the house.

"And he had red clay on his clothes?"

"Yes. It took me a while to connect it with Hugh."

"Are you going to tell the police?"

She smiled a secret and unpleasant smile. "How can I? I've got a marriage to go on with, such as it is."

"You told me."

"I like you." Without moving, she gave the impression of leaning towards me. "I'm fed up with all the little stinkers that populate this town."

I kept it cool and clean, and ver nasty: "Were you fed up with Hugh Western, Mrs. Turner?"

"What do you mean?"

"I heard that he dropped you hard a couple of months ago. Somebody dropped *him* hard last night in his studio."

"I haven't been near his studio for weeks."

"Never did any posing for him?"

Her face seemed to grow smaller and sharper. She laid one narrow taloned hand on my arm. "Can I trust you, Mr. Archer?"

"Not if you murdered Hugh."

"I didn't; I swear I didn't. Hilary did."

"But you were there last night."

"No."

"I think you were. There was a charcoal sketch on the easel, and you posed for it, didn't you?"

Her nerves were badly strained, but she tried to be coquettish. "How would you know?"

"The way you carry your body. It reminds me of the picture."

"Do you approve?"

"Listen, Mrs. Turner. You don't seem to realize that that sketch is evidence, and destroying it is a crime."

"I didn't destroy it."

"Then where did you put it?"

"I haven't said I took it."

"But you did."

"Yes, I did," she admitted finally. "But it isn't evidence in this case. I posed for it six months ago, and Hugh had it in his studio. When I heard he was dead this afternoon, I went to get it, just to be sure it wouldn't turn up in the papers. He had it on the easel for some reason, and had ruined it with a beard. I don't know why."

"The beard would make sense if your story was changed a little. If you quarreled while Hugh was sketching you last night, and you hit him over the head with a metal fist. You might have drawn the beard yourself, to cover up."

"Don't be ridiculous. If I had anything to cover up I would have destroyed the sketch. Anyway, I can't draw."

"Hilary can."

"Go to hell," she said between her teeth. "You're just a little stinker like the rest of them."

She walked emphatically to the house. I followed her into the long, dim hallway. Halfway up the stairs to the second floor she turned and flung down to me: "I hadn't destroyed it, but I'm going to now."

There was nothing I could do about that, and I started out. When I passed the door of the living room, the Admiral called out, "Is that you, Archer? Come here a minute, eh?"

He was sitting with Alice on a semicircular leather lounge, set into a huge bay window at the front of the room. He got up and moved toward me ponderously, his head down like a charging bull's. His face was a jaundiced yellow, bloodless under the tan.

"You're entirely wrong about the Chardin," he said. "Hilary Todd had nothing to do with stealing it. In fact, it wasn't stolen. I removed it from the gallery myself."

"You denied that this morning."

"I do as I please with my own possessions. I'm accountable to no one, certainly not to you."

"Dr. Silliman might like to know," I said with irony.

"I'll tell him in my own good time."

"Will you tell him why you took it?"

"Certainly. Now, if you've made yourself sufficiently obnoxious, I'll ask you to leave my house."

"Father." Alice came up to him and laid a hand on his arm. "Mr. Archer has only been trying to help."

"And getting nowhere," I said. "I made the mistake of assuming that some of Hugh's friends were honest."

"That's enough!" he roared. "Get out!"

Alice caught up with me on the veranda. "Don't go away mad. Father can be terribly childish, but he means well."

"I don't get it. He lied this morning, or else he's lying now."

"He isn't lying," she said earnestly. "He was simply playing a trick on Dr. Silliman and the trustees. It's what happened to Hugh afterwards that made it seem important."

"Did you know that he took the picture himself?"

"He told me just now, before you came into the house. I made him tell you."

"You'd better let Silliman in on the joke," I said unpleasantly. "He's probably going crazy."

"He is," she said. "I saw him at the gallery this afternoon, and he was tearing his hair. Do you have your car?"

"I came up here in a taxi."

"I'll drive you down."

"Are you sure you feel up to it?"

"It's better when I'm doing something," she said.

An old black sedan was standing in the drive beside the house. We got in, and she backed it into the street and turned downhill toward the center of town.

Watching her face, I said, "Of course you realize I don't believe his story."

"Father's, you mean?" She didn't seem surprised. "I don't know what to believe, myself."

"When did he say he took the Chardin?"

"Last night. Hugh was working on the mezzanine. Father slipped away and took the picture out to the car."

"Didn't Hugh keep the door locked?"

"Apparently not. Father said not."

"But what possible reason could he have for stealing his own picture?"

"To prove a point. Father's been arguing for a long time that it would be easy to steal a picture from the gallery. He's been trying to get the board of trustees to install a burglar alarm. He's really hipped on the subject. He wouldn't lend his Chardin to the gallery until they agreed to insure it."

"For twenty-five thousand dollars," I said, half to myself. Twenty-five thousand dollars was motive enough for a man to steal his own picture. And if Hugh Western witnessed the theft, there was motive for murder. "Your father's made a pretty good story out of it. But where's the picture now?"

"He didn't tell me. It's probably in the house somewhere."

"I doubt it. It's more likely somewhere in Walter Hendryx' house."

She let out a little gasp. "What makes you say that? Do you know Walter Hendryx?"

"I've met him. Do you?"

"He's a horrible man," she said. "I can't imagine why you think he has it."

"It's purely a hunch."

"Where would he get it? Father wouldn't dream of selling it to him."

"Hilary Todd would."

"Hilary? You think Hilary stole it?"

"I'm going to ask him. Let me off at his shop, will you? I'll see you at the gallery later."

The *Closed* sign was still hanging inside the plate glass, and the front door was locked. I went around to the back of the shop by the alley. The door under the stairs was standing partly open. I went in without knocking.

The living room was empty. The smell of alcohol rose from the stain on the wall where Sarah had smashed the glass. I crossed the passage to the door on the other side. It, too, was partly open. I pushed it wider and went in.

Hilary Todd was sprawled face down on the bed, with an open suitcase crushed under the weight of his body. The silver handle of his ice pick stood up between his shoulder blades in the center of a wet, dark stain. The silver glinted coldly in a ray of light which came through the half-closed Venetian blinds.

I felt for his pulse and couldn't find it. His head was twisted sideways, and his empty dark eyes stared unblinking at the wall. A slight breeze from the open window at the foot of the bed ruffled the hair along the side of his head.

I burrowed under the heavy body and went through the pockets. In the inside breast pocket of the coat I found what I was looking for: a plain white business envelope, unsealed, containing $15,000 in large bills.

I was standing over the bed with the money in my hand when I heard someone in the hallway. A moment later Mary appeared at the door.

"I saw you come in," she said. "I thought—" Then she saw the body.

"Someone killed Hilary."

"*Killed Hilary?*" She looked at the body on the bed and then at me. I realized that I was holding the money in plain view.

"What are you doing with that?"

I folded the bills and tucked them into my inside pocket. "I'm going to try an experiment. Be a good girl and call the police for me."

"Where did you get that money?"

"From someone it didn't belong to. Don't tell the sheriff about it. Just say that I'll be back in half an hour."

"They'll want to know where you went."

"And if you don't know, you won't be able to tell them. Now do as I say."

She looked into my face, wondering if she could trust me. Her voice was uncertain: "If you're sure you're doing the right thing."

"Nobody ever is."

I went out to my car and drove to Foothill Drive. The sun had dipped low over the sea, and the air was turning colder. By the time I reached the iron gates that cut off Walter Hendryx from ordinary mortals, the valley beyond them was in shadow.

The burly man came out of the gatehouse as if I had pressed a button, and up to the side of the car. "What do you want?" He recognized me then, and pushed his face up to the window. "Beat it, chum. I got orders to keep you away from here."

I restrained an impulse to push the face away, and tried diplomacy. "I came here to do your boss a favor."

"That's not the way he feels. Now blow."

"Look here." I brought the wad of bills out of my pocket, and passed them back and forth under his nose. "There's big money involved."

His eyes followed the moving bills as if they hypnotized him. "I don't take bribes," he said in a hoarse and passionate whisper.

"I'm not offering you one. But you should phone down to Hendryx, before you do anything rash, and tell him there's money in it."

"Money for him?" There was a wistful note in his voice. "How much?"

"Fifteen thousand, tell him."

"Some bonus." He whistled. "What kind of a house is he building for you, bud, that you should give him an extra fifteen grand?"

I didn't answer. His question gave me too much to think about. He went back into the gatehouse.

Two minutes later he came out and opened the gates. "Mr. Hendryx will see you. But don't try any funny stuff or you won't come out on your own power."

The maid was waiting at the door. She took me into a big rectangular room with French windows on one side, opening on to the terrace. The rest of the walls were lined with books from floor to ceiling—the kind of books that are bought by the set and never read. In front of the fireplace, at the far end, Hendryx was sitting half submerged in an overstuffed armchair, with a blanket over his knees.

He looked up when I entered the room and the firelight danced on his scalp and lit his face with an angry glow. "What's this? Come here and sit down."

The maid left silently. I walked the length of the room and sat down in an armchair facing him. "I always bring bad news, Mr. Hendryx. Murder and such things. This time it's Hilary Todd."

The turtle face didn't change, but his head made a movement of withdrawal into the shawl collar of his robe. "I'm exceedingly sorry to hear it. But my gatekeeper mentioned the matter of money. That interests me more."

"Good." I produced the bills and spread them fanwise on my knee. "Do you recognize this?"

"Should I?"

"For a man that's interested in money, you're acting very coy."

"I'm interested in its source."

"I had an idea that you were the source of this particular money. I have some other ideas. For instance, that Hilary Todd stole the Chardin and sold it to you. One thing I have no idea about is why you would buy a stolen picture and pay for it in cash."

His false teeth glistened coldly in the firelight. Like the man at the gate, he kept his eyes on the money. "The picture wasn't stolen. I bought it legally from its rightful owner."

"I might believe you if you hadn't denied any knowledge of it this afternoon. I think you knew it was stolen."

His voice took on a cutting edge: "It was not." He slipped his blue-veined hand inside his robe and brought out a folded sheet of paper, which he handed me.

It was a bill of sale for the picture, informal but legal, written in longhand on the stationery of the San Marcos Beach Club, signed by Admiral Johnston Turner, and dated that day.

"Now may I ask you where you got hold of that money?"

"I'll be frank with you, Mr. Hendryx. I took it from the body of Hilary Todd, when he had no further use for it."

"That's a criminal act, I believe."

My brain was racing, trying to organize a mass of contradictory facts. "I have a notion that you're not going to talk to anyone about it."

He shrugged his shoulders. "You seem to be full of notions."

"I have another. Whether or not you're grateful to me for bringing you this money, I think you should be."

"Have you any reason for saying that?" He had withdrawn his eyes from the money on my knee and was looking into my face.

"You're in the building business, Mr. Hendryx?"

"Yes." His voice was flat.

"I don't know exactly how you got this money. My guess is that you gouged it out of home-buyers, by demanding a cash side-payment in addition to the appraised value of the houses you've been selling to veterans."

"That's a pretty comprehensive piece of guesswork, isn't it?"

"I don't expect you to admit it. On the other hand, you probably wouldn't want this money traced to you. The fact that you haven't banked it is an indication of that. That's why Todd could count on you to keep this picture deal quiet. And that's why you should be grateful to me."

The turtle eyes stared into mine and admitted nothing. "If I were grateful, what form do you suggest my gratitude should take?"

"I want the picture. I've sort of set my heart on it."

"Keep the money instead."

"This money is no good to me. Dirty money never is."

He threw the blanket off and levered himself out of the chair. "You're somewhat more honest than I'd supposed. You're offering, then, to buy the picture back from me with that money."

"Exactly."

"And if I don't agree?"

"The money goes to the Intelligence Unit of the Internal Revenue Bureau."

There was silence for a while, broken by the fire hissing and sputtering in an irritable undertone.

"Very well," he said at length. "Give me the money."

"Give me the picture."

He waded across the heavy rug, moving his feet a few inches at a time, and pressed a corner of one of the bookcases. It swung open like a door. Behind it was the face of a large wall safe. I waited uncomfortably while he twirled the double dials.

A minute later he shuffled back to me with the picture in his hands. The boy in the blue waistcoat was there in the frame, watching the apple, which looked good enough to eat after more than two hundred years.

Hendryx' withered face had settled into a kind of malevolent resignation. "You realize that this is no better than blackmail."

"On the contrary, I'm saving you from the consequences of your own poor judgment. You shouldn't do business with thieves and murderers."

"You still insist the picture was stolen?"

"I think it was. You probably know it was. Will you answer one question?"

"Perhaps."

"When Hilary Todd approached you about buying this picture, did he claim to represent Admiral Turner?"

"Of course. You have the bill of sale in your hand. It's signed by the Admiral."

"I see that, but I don't know his signature."

"I do. Now, if you have no further questions, may I have my money?"

He held out his brown hand with the palm upward. I gave him the sheaf of bills.

"And the bill of sale, if you please."

"It wasn't part of the bargain."

"It has to be."

"I suppose you're right." I handed it to him.

"Please don't come back a third time," he said as he rang for the maid. "I find your visits tiring and annoying."

"I won't come back," I said. I didn't need to.

I parked in the alley beside the art gallery and got out of the car with the Chardin under my arm. There was talk and laughter and the tinny din of cutlery in the restaurant patio beyond the hedge. On the other side of the alley a light was shining behind the barred window of Silliman's office. I reached up between the bars and tapped on the window. I couldn't see beyond the closed Venetian blinds.

Someone opened the casement. It was Alice, her blond head aureoled against the light. "Who is it?" she said in a frightened whisper.

"Archer." I had a sudden, rather theatrical impulse. I held up the Chardin and passed it to her edgewise between the bars. She took it from my hands and let out a little yelp of surprise.

"It was where I thought it would be," I said.

Silliman appeared at her shoulder, squeaking, "What is it? What is it?"

My brain was doing a double take on the action I'd just performed. I had returned the Chardin to the gallery without using the door. It could have been stolen the same way, by Hilary Todd or anyone else who had access to the building. No human being could pass through the bars, but a picture could.

Silliman's head came out of the window like a gray mop being shaken. "Where on earth did you find it?"

I had no story ready, so I said nothing.

A gentle hand touched my arm and stayed, like a bird alighting. I started, but it was only Mary.

"I've been watching for you," she said. "The sheriff's in Hilary's shop, and he's raving mad. He said he's going to put you in jail, as a material witness."

"You didn't tell him about the money?" I said in an undertone.

"No. Did you really get the picture?"

"Come inside and see."

As we turned the corner of the building, a car left the curb in front of it, and started up the street with a roar. It was Admiral Turner's black sedan.

"It looks like Alice driving," Mary said.

"She's gone to tell her father, probably."

I made a sudden decision, and headed back to my car.

"Where are you going?"

"I want to see the Admiral's reaction to the news."

She followed me to the car. "Take me."

"You'd better stay here. I can't tell what might happen."

I tried to shut the door, but she held on to it. "You're always running off and leaving me to make your explanations."

"All right; get in. I don't have time to argue."

I drove straight up the alley and across the parking lot to Rubio Street. There was a uniformed policeman standing at the back door of Hilary's shop, but he didn't try to stop us.

"What did the police have to say about Hilary?" I asked her.

"Not much. The ice pick had been wiped clean of fingerprints, and they had no idea who did it."

I went through a yellow light and left a chorus of indignant honkings at the intersection behind me.

"You said you didn't know what would happen when you got there. Do you think the Admiral—" She left the sentence unfinished.

"I don't know. I have a feeling I soon will, though." There were a great many things I could have said. I concentrated on my driving.

"Is this the street?" I asked her finally.

"Yes."

My tires shrieked on the corner, and again in front of the house. She was out of the car before I was.

"Stay back," I told her. "This may be dangerous."

She let me go up the walk ahead of her. The black sedan was in the drive with the headlights burning and the left front door hanging open.

The front door of the house was closed but there was a light behind it. I went in without knocking.

Sarah came out of the living room. All day her face had been going to pieces, and now it was old and slack and ugly. Her bright hair was ragged at the edges, and her voice was ragged. "What do you think you're doing?"

"I want to see the Admiral. Where is he?"

"How should I know? I can't keep track of any of my men." She took a step toward me, staggered, and almost fell.

Mary took hold of her and eased her into a chair. Her head leaned limply against the wall, and her mouth hung open. The lipstick on her mouth was like a rim of cracked dry blood.

"They must be here."

The single shot that we heard then was an exclamation point at the end of my sentence. It came from somewhere back of the house, muffled by walls and distance.

I went through into the garden. There were lights in the gardener's cottage, and a man's shadow moved across the window. I ran up the path to the cottage's open door, and froze there.

Admiral Turner was facing me with a gun in his hand. It was a heavy-caliber automatic, the kind the Navy issued. From its round, questioning mouth a wisp of blue smoke trailed. Alice lay face down on the carpeted floor between us.

I looked into the mouth of the gun, into Turner's granite face. "You killed her."

But Alice was the one who answered. "Go away." The words came out in a rush of sobbing that racked her prostrate body.

"This is a private matter, Archer." The gun stirred slightly in the Admiral's hand. I could feel its pressure across the width of the room. "Do as she says."

"I heard a shot. Murder is a public matter."

"There has been no murder, as you can see."

"You don't remember well."

"I have nothing to do with that," he said. "I was cleaning my gun, and forgot that it was loaded."

"So Alice lay down and cried? You'll have to do better than that, Admiral."

"Her nerves are shaken. But I assure you that mine are not." He took three slow steps towards me, and paused by the girl on the floor. The gun was very steady in his hand. "Now go, or I'll have to use this."

The pressure of the gun was increasing. I put my hands on the doorframe and held myself still. "You seem to be sure it's loaded now," I said.

Between my words I heard the faint, harsh whispering of shifting gravel on the garden path behind me. I spoke up loudly, to drown out the sound.

"You had nothing to do with the murder, you say. Then why did Todd come to the beach club this morning? Why did you change your story about the Chardin?"

He looked down at his daughter as if she could answer the questions. She made no sound, but her shoulders were shaking with inner sobbing.

As I watched the two of them, father and daughter, the pattern of the day came into focus. At its center was the muzzle of the Admiral's gun, the round blue mouth of death.

I said, very carefully, to gain time, "I can guess what Todd said to you this morning. Do you want me to dub in the dialogue?"

He glanced up sharply, and the gun glanced up. There were no more sounds in the garden. If Mary was as quick as I thought, she'd be at a telephone.

"He told you he'd stolen your picture and had a buyer for it. But Hendryx was cautious. Todd needed proof that he had a right to sell it. You gave him the proof. And when Todd completed the transaction, you let him keep the money."

"Nonsense! Bloody nonsense." But he was a poor actor, and a worse liar.

"I've seen the bill of sale, Admiral. The only question left is why you gave it to Todd."

His lips moved as if he was going to speak. No words came out.

"And I'll answer that one, too. Todd knew who killed Hugh Western. So did you. You had to keep him quiet, even if it meant conniving at the theft of your own picture."

"I connived at nothing." His voice was losing its strength. His gun was as potent as ever.

"Alice did," I said. "She helped him to steal it this morning. She passed it out the window to him when Silliman and I were on the mezzanine. Which is one of the things he told you at the beach club, isn't it?"

"Todd has been feeding you lies. Unless you give me your word that you won't repeat those lies, not to anyone, I'm going to have to shoot you."

His hand contracted, squeezing off the automatic's safety. The tiny noise it made seemed very significant in the silence.

"Todd will soon be feeding worms," I said. "He's dead, Admiral."

"Dead?" His voice had sunk to an old man's quaver, rustling in his throat.

"Stabbed with an ice pick in his apartment."

"When?"

"This afternoon. Do you still see any point in trying to shoot me?"

"You're lying."

"No. There's been a second murder."

He looked down at the girl at his feet. His eyes were bewildered. There was danger in his pain and confusion. I was the source of his pain, and he might strike out blindly at me. I watched the gun in his hand, waiting for a chance to move on it. My arms were rigid, braced against the doorframe.

Mary Western ducked under my left arm and stepped into the room in front of me. She had no weapon, except her courage.

"He's telling the truth," she said. "Hilary Todd was stabbed to death today."

"Put down the gun," I said. "There's nothing left to save. You thought you were protecting an unfortunate girl. She's turned out to be a double murderess."

He was watching the girl on the floor. "If this is true, Allie, I wash my hands of you."

No sound came from her. Her face was hidden by her yellow sheaf of hair. The old man groaned. The gun sagged in his hand. I moved, pushing Mary to one side, and took it away from him. He didn't resist me, but my forehead was suddenly streaming with sweat.

"You were probably next on her list," I said.

"No."

The muffled word came from his daughter. She began to get up, rising laboriously from her hands and knees like a hurt fighter. She flung her hair back. Her face had hardly changed. It was as lovely as ever, on the surface, but empty of meaning, like a doll's plastic face.

"I was next on my list," she said dully. "I tried to shoot myself when I realized you knew about me. Father stopped me."

"I didn't know about you until now."

"You did. You must have. When you were talking to Father in the garden, you meant me to hear it all—everything you said about Hilary."

"Did I?"

The Admiral said with a kind of awe: "You killed him, Allie. Why did you want his blood on your hands? Why?" His own hand reached for her, gropingly, and paused in midair. He looked at her as if he had fathered a strange, evil thing.

She bowed her head in silence. I answered for her: "She'd stolen the Chardin for him and met his conditions. But then she saw that he couldn't get away, or if he did he'd be brought back, and questioned. She couldn't be sure he'd keep quiet about Hugh. This afternoon she made sure. The second murder comes easier."

"No!" She shook her blond head violently. "I didn't murder Hugh. I hit him with something, I didn't intend to kill him. He struck me first, he *struck* me, and then I hit him back."

"With a deadly weapon, a metal fist. You hit at him twice with it. The first blow missed and left its mark on the doorframe. The second blow didn't miss."

"But I didn't mean to kill him. Hilary knew I didn't mean to kill him."

"How would he know? Was he there?"

"He was downstairs in his flat. When he heard Hugh fall, he came up. Hugh was still alive. He died in Hilary's car, when we were starting for the hospital. Hilary said he'd help me to cover up. He took that horrible fist and threw it into the sea.

"I hardly knew what I was doing by that time. Hilary did it all. He put the body in Hugh's car and drove it up the mountain. I followed in his car and brought him back. On the way back he told me why he was helping me. He needed money. He knew we had no money, but he had a chance to sell the Chardin. I took it for him this morning. I had to. Everything I did, I did because I had to."

She looked from me to her father. He averted his face from her.

"You didn't have to smash Hugh's skull," I said. "Why did you do that?"

Her doll's eyes rolled in her head, came back to me, glinting with a cold and deathly coquetry. "If I tell you, will you do one thing for me? One favor? Give me father's gun for just a second?"

"And let you kill us all?"

"Only myself," she said. "Just leave one shell in it."

"Don't give it to her," the Admiral said. "She's done enough to disgrace us."

"I have no intention of giving it to her. And I don't have to be told why she killed Hugh. While she was waiting in his studio last night, she found a sketch of his. It was an old sketch, but she didn't know that. She'd never seen it before, for obvious reasons."

"What kind of a sketch?"

"A portrait of a nude woman. She tacked it up on the easel and decorated it with a beard. When Hugh came home he saw what she'd done. He didn't like to have his pictures spoiled, and he probably slapped her face."

"He hit me with his fist," Alice said. "I killed him in self-defense."

"That may be the way you've rationalized it. Actually, you killed him out of jealousy."

She laughed. It was a cruel sound, like vital tissue being ruptured. "Jealousy of *her?*"

"The same jealousy that made you ruin the sketch."

Her eyes widened, but they were blind, looking into herself. "Jealousy? I don't know. I felt so lonely, all alone in the world. I had nobody to love me, since my mother died."

"It isn't true, Alice. You had me." The Admiral's tentative hand came out and paused again in the air, as though there were an invisible wall between them.

"I never had you. I hardly saw you. Then Sarah took you. I had no one, no one until Hugh. I thought at last that I had some one to love me, that I could count on—"

Her voice broke off. The Admiral looked everywhere but at his daughter. The room was like a cubicle in hell where lost souls suffered under the silent treatment. The silence was finally broken by the sound of a distant siren. It rose and expanded until its lamentation filled the night.

Alice was crying, with her face uncovered. Mary Western came forward and put her arm around her. "Don't cry." Her voice was warm. Her face had a grave beauty.

"You hate me, too."

"No. I'm sorry for you, Alice. Sorrier than I am for Hugh."

The Admiral touched my arm. "Who was the woman in the sketch?" he said in a trembling voice.

I looked into his tired old face and decided that he had suffered enough. "I don't know."

But I could see the knowledge in his eyes.

FREDRIC BROWN
Murder Set to Music

IT STARTED on a Tuesday evening in early October. It had been a fine evening, up to then. I'd made a good sale and when the phone rang I guessed that it was Danny and was glad he'd called so I'd have a chance to tell him about it.

Danny Bushman and I run a used car lot together. My name is Ralph Oliver. Danny and I have been close friends since we started high school together. He played trumpet and I played sax and we played together in the high school band and orchestra, and in our junior and senior years we made our spending money playing at parties and dances.

After graduation we were apart for a year. Danny got a few thousand bucks from his father's life insurance—his mother had died before he entered high school—and he threw it into starting a small but hot dance band, which he called *The Bushmen,* from his own name which, in case you've forgotten already, was Bushman. He wanted me to go with him on it, but I had other ideas. I enrolled as a student at the Wisconsin Conservatory of Music. Both of my parents had died by then too (funny how many parallels there have been in Danny's life and mine, in big things as well as little ones) but I figured I could work my way through by playing evenings. I found that I could, but I also found within a year that longhair, although not for the birds was not for me either, and I quit. And in just the same length of time Danny found out that he was a better trumpet player than a band leader and *The Bushmen,* as Danny put it, went back to the bushes.

For the next ten years we blew for our bread and butter, and managed most of the time to stick together. If not in the same band, at least in bands in the same city.

Something happened then that might have broken up our friendship, but only showed how strong it was. We both fell in love with the same girl, Doris Dennis, who was a singer with Tommy Drum's orchestra, with which both Danny and I were playing at the time. She liked both of us but Danny was the one she fell for. They were married, and still we were friends. All three of us, in fact.

A few months later, Tommy Drum got behind the eight ball and had to break up the orchestra. Almost any musician who's really good, and Tommy Drum was, tries his hand as an orchestra leader once; few of them are businessmen enough to make a go of it.

Danny and I, with Doris kibitzing, had a conference to decide what band might be able to take both of us on, and ended up deciding, with Doris abetting, that we were getting a little old for the game. Most dance musicians quit and get into something else by the time they're thirty, and that's how old we were. And we both happened to be solvent enough for it to be a good time for us to make the break. We'd all been working steadily for quite a while and I had a fairish sum salted. Danny had somewhat less, mostly because he had a weakness for the ponies, but Doris had some savings and wanted to advance Danny enough to make his share match mine, if we could find a good place to put it.

We kicked it around, and the only thing we both knew and liked besides music was cars. So we ended up with a used car lot. Back in the small city Danny and I had come from.

That was almost a year ago, and we were beginning to do all right. At least we were out of the red and into the black, and we made money when we had a good day. A good day is one when we make two good sales of relatively late model cars; one sale gets us off the nut and a second one is gravy.

It was a quarter of nine when Danny phoned and I was just getting ready to shut up shop. We keep open from nine to nine, with Danny opening the lot in the morning and quitting at dinner time and with me starting after lunch and working till closing, which puts two of us on the lot during the afternoon and one each mornings and evenings. Danny said, "Hi, Ralph. How goes it?"

"Crazy," I told him. "I sold the fifty-three Buick."

"Attaboy. Full price?"

"Full price, except that for cash I promised him four new tires. It's still a good deal."

"I'm flipping," he said. "But I got some good news too. Guess who's in town?"

"I'll bite. Who? Eisenhower?"

"Better than that. Tommy Drum. He's got a cool combo, and they're opening tonight at the Casanova Club. Need I say more?"

"Did you make reservations?"

"For three. Only you'll have to pick me up and take me there. Doris is at a hen party and she took my heap, so I'm afoot. But I phoned her and she'll join us as soon as her party breaks up, probably around eleven. Can you come right here, or will you have to go home first?"

"I'll come right there. I can wash up and shave there and bum a clean shirt. The rest of my clothes will do."

"Hit it, man. My pad is panting."

We don't ordinarily talk that way, but it came natural to go back to the jive when we were going to see Tommy again and dig his combo. It could be good if he had the right support. Tommy Drum, despite his name, plays a very cool piano.

It took me ten or fifteen minutes to put the lot to sleep and to climb aboard the old Merc I use for my own transportation—although when I'm on the lot it's there too, in case anybody wants to buy it—and another fifteen or twenty to Danny's "pad." He and Doris have a small apartment on the north side. Neat but not gaudy. It's in a small building, only four apartments, two on each floor, and the Bushmans' is the downstairs one on the left.

I tried the knob first, thinking Danny would probably have left it unlocked so I could walk right in, and was surprised when the door wouldn't open. I knocked, and then again and louder.

There was only silence on the other side. Could Danny have dozed off? Hardly, and besides he was a light sleeper; even my first light knock would have wakened him. It didn't make sense, that silence. Expecting me any minute, he wouldn't have gone out anywhere.

It had been minutes now, and I began to get worried. Anywhere in that small apartment he must have heard me. But I tried again and still harder, and called out his name.

This got me an open door on the other side of the hall, and a man with rumpled gray hair looking at me through the doorway. I'd been introduced to him once—but didn't remember his name—as a neighbor of the Bushmans. He said, "Oh—it's you," so he recognized me too, and then, "Is something wrong?"

I said, "I know Danny's home—he must be. But—"

He stared at me. "You know," he said, "I thought I heard a kind of thud across there a little while ago. If you think— These locks are awfully flimsy. I think together we could—"

But already I'd thrown my weight against the door, and he was right about the lock; it broke and the door flew open on my first lunge.

Danny, fully dressed except for his suit coat, lay stretched, spread-eagled, on the living room rug with his feet toward the door. I ran to him and bent over him, fumbling to open his shirt at the collar to give him air and farther down to reach in and feel for a heartbeat. The neighbor had come as far as the doorway and I yelled over my shoulder to him to phone for an ambulance. I said a police ambulance because I thought it would get us faster service whatever this was, whatever had happened. And I thought I knew because his otherwise spotless white shirt was dirty just where it would have been dirtied by someone giving him a few kicks after knocking him out. It looked like a going-over.

His heart was okay. I ran to the bathroom and wet a washrag with cold water. I had his head in my lap and was using it on his forehead when the neighbor came back. He said, "They're coming. Is he—all right?"

"He's alive. I think he's been beaten up." Danny was moaning a little now, beginning to come around.

"Is there anything I can—?"

I said, "There's brandy in the cabinet over the kitchen sink. Bring some."

He brought the bottle, a pint about half full. He took the cap off and handed it to me. Danny's eyes were open now, but a bit glazed. His lips opened, though, when I held the mouth of the bottle against them, and he gulped and shuddered when I raised the bottle enough to give him a good sized slug.

Then he tried weakly to sit up but I held him back lightly by a shoulder. I said, "Take it easy, kid. There's an ambulance coming and you'd better lie still. You might have something broken."

Two uniformed cops were coming in the doorway. From a radio car, we learned later, that had happened to be cruising only a few blocks away when they'd got the message.

I beat them to the punch by asking if an ambulance was coming.

"Yeah," one of them said. "What's up?"

"A beating, I think," I told him. Danny tried to say something but I shushed him. "Wait for some strength, Danny. Let us tell our stories first; they're simpler."

But we all three had time to tell our stories before the ambulance came and Danny's was as simple to tell as ours. Or simpler. A few minutes after talking to me on the phone he'd been going to the door to unlock it so I could let myself in when I came, and there was a knock

on the door before he reached it. Danny's first reaction had been that
he'd misjudged the time and that I was here already and he'd thrown
the door wide open. A big man with a handkerchief tied over his face
and a hat pulled down over his eyes stepped through the doorway and
had swung a right at Danny's jaw that Danny had barely seen coming
and didn't have time even to try to duck. And that was the last thing
he remembered until he came to, with his head in my lap.

Did he know the guy? No, and he wouldn't be able to identify him
if he saw him again. A big guy, maybe six feet and at least a couple of
hundred pounds, and that was all the description he could give. Danny
thought he wore a brown suit but he wasn't even sure of that. There'd
probably been quite literally only a second between the time he'd
opened the door and the time he'd gone down and out.

And no, he didn't have any enemies that he knew of and didn't have
the faintest idea what it was all about. Either the guy was crazy or it
was a case of mistaken identity and he thought he was beating up
somebody else.

Danny kept saying he was okay and trying to sit up, but I told him
for all we knew he could have some broken ribs and we didn't want one
puncturing a lung. When the ambulance came, they were gentle about
getting him on the stretcher.

I rode with him to the emergency hospital, but we didn't talk much
on the ride. Danny said that from the hospital I'd better get to the
Casanova Club fast to be sure of being there in time to meet Doris; she'd
be worried if she got there first and didn't find either of us. I said okay,
but it was still only half past nine; there was lots of time and I'd wait
until they'd at least have given him a quick once over. So that, if there
wasn't anything serious—and we were both beginning to think there
wasn't—I could reassure Doris and not frighten her.

It didn't take long, once we got there. I was in the waiting room only
twenty minutes when a doctor came in and gave me the news: nothing
broken, nothing seriously wrong.

Danny was going to have a sore jaw and some sore ribs, a few bruises
other places, but nothing worse. As far as the hospital was concerned
he could be released right away, if he felt up to going home, although
the doctor advised him to lie quietly and rest another half hour or so
before leaving.

"You say as far as the hospital is concerned," I said. "What else?"

"The police," he said. "They are sending a detective around to talk
to him."

They let me in to talk to Danny again. They'd stripped him for the examination and he was getting his clothes back on, a bit painfully. He said, "Listen, Ralph, I'm stuck here till some dick comes to grill me, but maybe I can still get to the Casanova before Doris does. And if so, don't say anything—"

"Nuts," I said. "You can't keep this from Doris. It may or may not make the papers, but you're going to be a lot sorer tomorrow morning when you wake up than you are right now. You'll probably need help to get dressed. And your jaw will probably be too sore to chew toast for breakfast. You'll have to tell her *something* and it might as well be the truth. Why not?"

He saw that, and gave in, provided I'd play it down instead of up if I had to be the one to tell her.

I caught a cab from the hospital back to his place to get the Merc, and it was ten o'clock by the time I got it. The Casanova's well west of town, about an hour's drive, but I drove fast and made it well before eleven. I thought ruefully about how much cab fare was going to cost Danny, but there wasn't any out on that.

The joint was jumping. It was a good thing Danny had phoned and reserved a table. Even so, it was a lousy table for our purpose; the room was L-shaped and this one was around the corner and out of sight of the bandstand. No doubt we'd be able to get ourselves a better one later, though; the people who had come mostly for dinner would be starting to leave now.

So I took the table without argument and ordered myself a highball. It might be amusing to listen to the combo before I saw it, to see if I could guess who Tommy Drum had with him. Tommy's piano I'd have known anywhere. The sax was not quite up to it, and I couldn't place it; it could have been any one of a hundred tenor saxes. Smooth tone and no goofing, but weak on improvisation; Tommy's piano could lead him just so far out but no farther. But it was adequate and it was something the squares could dig. The skins were much better but I didn't place the drummer until he took a solo and started to go to town—but in a civilized way—on the Chinese cymbal. It was Frank Ritchie; I'd never played with him but I knew him and had heard him often, always with combos. He was a combo man and didn't like band work. He was right in his element with Tommy; it could have been a great combo with a better sax.

Well, I'd identified the drummer and I'd given up on the sax so I left my half-finished drink on the table and strolled out to where I could see the bandstand. I knew the sax after all, although not well. It was Mick O'Neill, a guy Danny and I had played with two or three times for short periods. Danny had never liked him, had almost had a fight with him once, but I got along okay with him. Mick had got his start in New Orleans and he was strictly a Dixieland man; he was good at that but way over his head in the kind of stuff Tommy Drum was playing tonight. I wondered why Tommy had picked him.

A hand touched my sleeve and a voice said, "Hi, Oliver. Sit down." I looked down and saw it was Max Stivers. Bookmaker and racketeer, I'd heard. I'd met him around a few places.

He said, "This is Gino Itule," and nodded to his companion. "Gino, Ralph Oliver." And I reached across and shook hands with a man built like a beer barrel.

"Sit down," Stivers repeated. "Saw the lousy table they gave you. You can't see from there."

I slid into the vacant seat beside him. "Thanks," I said. "Until somebody I'm expecting shows up." I looked around for a waiter. "I'll have my drink brought over."

"Forget it," Stivers said. "I'll get you a fresh one." He reached a hand in the air and snapped his fingers and suddenly we had not one but three waiters coming toward us. I ordered a rye and soda from one of them and grinned at Stivers. "Real service you get."

"I should. I own a piece of the joint. Say, you're an ex-musician, aren't you? What do you think of the combo that's starting tonight?"

"Came to catch them; they're old friends of mine. So my opinion would be prejudiced."

When the waiter brought my drink it occurred to me that now, while I was sitting with the owner of a piece of the joint, would be a good time to start pushing for a better table, but Stivers stopped me and waved the waiter away. He said, "Take this table. Gino and I are leaving in a minute. And it's bigger; your friends in the band will probably want to join you when they take a break."

That solved that and I thanked him. Racketeers may not be nice people but they're nice people to know, when they're on your side.

They left a minute later and a minute after that Tommy Drum looked my way and I caught his eye and waved. He didn't wave back or even nod, but his music went into a tricky little phrase that had once been a joke between us. And a few minutes later he ended the number and came over to my table.

I said it was swell to see him again.

"Crazy," he said, grinning ear to ear. "How goes the filling station?"

"Used car lot. It goes, somewhat. How goes the combo?"

"You heard it," he said. He shook his head sadly. "My kingdom for a saxophone. You don't want a job again, do you, Ralph?"

"Off it for good, Tommy. I'm a car salesman now, and a business-man. Maybe there isn't much dough in it yet, but we're building it up; we'll get there."

"Just evenings, just while we're booked here—a month. You can put in some time on the lot days."

I shook my head. "Sorry, Tommy, but it's out. But what gives? How come you hired Mick? You know he's a Dixie boy."

"Do I, do I? It's a long sad story, Ralph. Wingy Tyler's blowing for me—one of the best in the business, short of the real top boys I couldn't afford. Man, can that cat blow. And this morning, two hours or so before plane time for our booking here, he goofs on me. Know what he does, like?"

"What does he do, like?"

"Ruptures his appendix, that's all. Well, the operation went fine; we couldn't wait but I had the doc send me a telegram. But Wingy's out for the month we're booked here. So there I am in Pittsburg, two hours to plane time, and I run into Mick just when I think I'm going to have to cancel. He says he's going west anyway so he'll come along for the ride and fill in till I get somebody. It's fine with Mick the minute I replace him—you won't be undercutting him. Nohow, Jackson."

He lighted a cigarette for me that I'd just stuck in my mouth. "Think it over, anyway. Talk to Danny about it; *he'll* tell you not to let an old man down. Where is he?"

"Coming later. So's Doris."

"Crazy. Why don't you people stay home, though? Found both you and Danny in the fun book, and kept calling first one number then the other till I finally got Danny at half past eight."

"You should have called the lot; we were both there all afternoon."

"I looked for it, but I looked under filling stations." He glanced at his watch and got up quickly. "Back to the mountain," he said. "This is supposed to be in the middle of a set, so that's why I told the other boys to stay up there. We'll all be over later. Hasta banana."

I looked at my watch too, wondering about Doris. It was almost half past eleven. Well, half an hour isn't late for a woman.

Danny came in a few minutes later. There was a stocky middle aged man with him and if the man wasn't a cop then he was disguised as one; he wore a shiny blue serge suit, carried a soft black felt hat that the check girl hadn't been able to take away from him, and wore the first pair of high shoes I'd seen in a long time. He had a round face and sad eyes.

Danny introduced him as Lieutenant Andrews.

Danny grinned at me. "I persuaded him to third-degree me while driving me out here. Look at the cab fare I saved."

"He didn't have to talk me into it," Andrews said. "I wanted to talk to you, and to Drum. He's the one playing piano there, isn't he?"

I nodded, but I asked, "Why to him? He couldn't have had anything to do with what happened to Danny."

He gave me a level look. "Then you know all about what happened to your partner?"

"Of course not. But I see what you mean." I happened to look toward the entrance and I said, "Here comes Doris. Listen, Lieutenant, how's about you and me strolling over to the bar for a few minutes. You want to question me anyway, and that'll give Danny a chance to tell his wife what happened without—well, it would worry her more if there's a cop with him when he has to tell it."

He nodded and we stood up. That's when Doris caught sight of us and I waved to her and pointed to Danny still seated, and Andrews and I started toward the bar. But halfway there he took me by the arm and started steering at right angles. "Let's go out on the terrace instead. I don't drink on duty and besides the bar's pretty crowded."

It was all right by me, and we went out into the cool darkness and sat down on a concrete railing. We could hear the music from here and I heard Mick O'Neill start what might have been a far out wail and then suddenly butter a large ear of corn; I winced.

"All right," Andrews said. "Tell it your way, what happened."

I told it my way and he listened without interrupting.

When I'd finished, he asked, "How sure are you it was a quarter to nine when Mr. Bushman phoned you?"

"Within a minute or two. I'd just looked at my watch, wondering how soon I could start turning out lights and closing up."

"I guess it checks," he said. "Mr. Bushman happened to notice the time when he got a call from Mr. Drum, half past eight. He didn't notice any times after that, but the first thing he did was to call the club here for a reservation and—"

"Why didn't he ask Tommy to take care of it? Simpler."

"Says he didn't think of it until they'd hung up. Anyway, then he phoned his wife at the party she was attending, a baby shower, and then called you. That would make it a quarter of nine by the time he called you, as near as matters."

"As nears as matters, but what does it matter?"

"Just trying to reconstruct things. Maybe the exact timing doesn't matter. Neighbor across the hall was watching television when he heard that thud. Thinks it was about the middle of the second half, after the midway commercial break, of a half hour dramatic show he was watching. That would put it between, say, ten minutes of nine and five of nine. Could you have driven from the lot to the Bushmans' place in five or ten minutes?"

"Ten minutes maybe, if I went pretty fast. But I didn't. I closed up the lot first and that took till almost nine. Then, since I didn't speed, it must have taken me at least fifteen minutes more to get out there. But why? You don't think *I* slugged Danny?"

"No, I don't," he said mildly. "Just not overlooking the possibility. After all, you're about six feet tall and two hundred pounds, like he described the man who hit him. And you're wearing a brownish suit and I'll bet you've got a handkerchief."

I had to laugh. I said, "Put on the cuffs, Lieutenant. You've got me cold. But tell me why I did it?"

"His wife, maybe. You were both in love with her once and maybe you both still are. Mr. Bushman told me that—I mean the fact that you both *were* in love with her—when he was telling me how close friends the two of you were. But what if you never gave up?"

I said, "I did give up, but even if I hadn't, what would beating up Danny do me toward taking his wife away from him? That's nutty, Lieutenant."

He sighed. "I guess it is. Does your friend have any enemies that you know of?"

"None that I know of and a buck gets you twenty he hasn't any that I don't know of. A few guys who don't like him too well, maybe, back in the old days—all musicians aren't one big happy family, sometimes we get in one another's hair—but nobody who'd still be carrying a grudge."

"Uh-huh. Does he gamble?"

"Nope. Used to a little, just small horse bets, when we were playing, but he's a reformed character now. We both are."

"Yeah? What are you reformed from?"

"Knocking out my friends and kicking them in the ribs," I told him.

He sighed again. "Well, thanks. Guess I had that coming. Shall we go back?"

When we got inside I saw that the combo had apparently finished the set because all three of them were at the table with Danny and Doris. I wondered for a second if Danny had had time to tell Doris what had happened, then realized he must have had because the combo had played two numbers after Andrews and I had gone out on the terrace.

I stopped Andrews just inside. I said, "Listen, Lieutenant, this is a family reunion, people who haven't seen one another for over a year. If you go asking questions at the table, you'll be a spectre at the feast. How about making that corner of the terrace your office and talking one at a time to whoever you want to talk to, like you did with me?"

"Son, I'm tired," he said. And seeing him so closely in the bright light I saw now that his face did look tired, and older than I'd thought at first. "And it's way past my quitting time. Yes, I'll want to talk to everybody there, but I think it can safely wait till tomorrow."

"Good," I said. "That's best all around."

"Yeah. I don't think there's any more danger. The goon who beat your friend up had him down and out; he could've hurt him worse if he wanted to, so why would he come back for more? But I got one more question for you and the fact that I forgot to ask it out there shows my brain is through working for the night."

"Shoot," I said.

"Could your friend by any chance be playing around on the side with a woman who might have a jealous husband or lover?"

"No," I said. "That's one vice Danny hasn't got. And believe me, we're close enough that I'd know it if he was doing any philandering. I'd guess it before Doris would."

"You sound sure. All right, I'll buy it. Thanks, Son, and goodnight."

I went back to the table, said hi to Doris and shook hands with Frank Ritchie and Mick. Danny gave me a raised eyebrow and I knew he was wondering what had happened to the cop, so I leaned over and told him.

And that was an end to serious discussion for a while. For the next half hour it was musicians' talk and old home week and a ball. Then the combo had to climb the mountain for another set, and as soon as Tommy started tickling the keys, Doris looked at Danny, "Mind if I dance one with Ralph?"

Danny grinned at her. "You don't really want to dance with him, Honey. You just want a chance to pump him to find out if I told all. Go ahead."

When we were out on the floor dancing, Doris said, "Danny was right, Ralph. I do want to pump you."

"Sorry I'm such a lousy dancer."

"Don't be foolish. You know you're a wonderful dancer or you wouldn't say that. But about Danny—he's not playing this down, is he? I mean, about how badly he got hurt."

"Only some bruises, Doris. That's the McCoy because I got it straight from the doc, not roundabout. But he may be pretty sore in the morning and maybe he shouldn't open the lot. Tell you what, I'll phone around breakfast time and if he doesn't feel up to it, I'll get to the lot at nine. And if he doesn't feel up to coming in later, it won't hurt me to work the whole twelve hours for once."

"That's sweet of you, Ralph. Do you have any idea who might have done it to him or why?"

"Not a glimmer. Like Danny said when we were talking to the squad car cops, it could have been mistaken identity. Which, in that case, would mean the guy was a professional goon sent to beat up someone he didn't know and knocked on the wrong door or got the wrong building. Either that or the guy was a nut."

"But if he's *that,* what if he comes back again?"

I reassured her on that by repeating the lieutenant's reasoning, that the man had had Danny down and out and if he'd wanted to hurt him any worse, he could have done so there and then, without taking the added risk of making a second trip.

Then to change the subject I asked her if the dress she was wearing was a new one. It was a strapless black velvet that set off her page boy blonde hair beautifully, and I was sure I'd never seen her wear it before.

She leaned back against my arm and laughed up at me. "It's borrowed, Ralph. You don't think I wore an evening gown to a baby shower, do you? After the shower I explained to Winnie what my phone call had been about, and she loaned me this." She added a little wistfully, "It *is* gorgeous."

That was all there was to say and we danced just one number.

We'd scarcely got back to the table when Mick O'Neill came over from the bandstand. He put a hand on my shoulder. "How about sitting in for a number, Ralph boy? Use my sax. I just wiped the mouthpiece and put in a new reed for you."

He slid into a chair. I hesitated and he grinned at me. "G'wan, man, I don't care if you show me up. Ride it high and funky."

Doris put her hand on my arm and said, "Go ahead, Ralph," so I nodded and climbed the mountain. Tommy said, "Hi, man. You name it." "You name it," I said, "and start it. But let me wet this reed first." I wetted the reed and blew a few soft arpeggios, and then nodded.

"All right, *Body,*" Tommy said. "I'll take an eight-bar intro and you come in." He swung into a smooth introduction to *Body and Soul,* and we were off.

I took my first chorus reasonably straight, and then started out, not far out but getting farther. Tommy, grinning, gave me a modulation into a new key and a swinging beat, and I found myself and blew. Way out and knowing I'd get back. Tommy looked around at me. "Dig that crazy tenor man," he said. And it sounded good and felt better than it sounded.

Then, when I laid off for thirty-two to give Frank a solo on the skins I looked toward our table and Danny was sitting there alone, and looking beyond I saw Mick dancing with Doris. I hoped Danny wasn't working up a peeve over that. Not that he minds other men dancing with Doris, but it might be different with Mick if Danny still had a grudge against him. But it was probably all right, I told myself, Danny wouldn't hold a grudge that long; it had been three years ago he'd almost had that fight with Mick. I couldn't remember now what it had been about, and like as not Danny wouldn't remember either.

At the end of the number, Tommy tried to talk me into finishing the set; I told him no, but that I'd be out again within a few days and next time I came I'd bring my own sax and I'd sit in a full set, maybe more.

So I went back to the table and sent Mick, who'd just returned Doris to Danny, back to the combo. Danny said, "Nice going, Ralph," and Doris said "Cool," and I tried to blush modestly.

Danny leaned toward me. He said, "Mick was telling me about Tommy wanting you to join the combo. Why don't you, Ralph? Just while they're playing here, I mean. We could work it out."

"No, Danny," I said. "Remember our promise; we're through blowing for money. Jamming or sitting in, sure. But once one or both of us starts taking jobs on the side, the lot goes downhill. We talked that out and made it definite."

"But this is different. Tommy's a friend of ours and he *needs* a sax. We can't let a friend down. If we trade shifts on the lot so I work evenings—"

I said, "If Tommy was really in a jam, it might be different. But Mick agreed to stick with him till he gets somebody else. And how many in a crowd like this one know the difference? One in thirty, maybe; Tommy isn't going to lose his booking."

Danny shrugged. "If that's the way you feel about it, okay." Which surprised me a little; I'd expected him to give me more of an argument and if he had, who knows? Maybe I'd have let myself be talked into it.

You've got to have principles in business, but that doesn't mean you can't weaken a little *once* in a while.

Doris said, "Ralph's right, Danny. You're going to make a go of that business, but only if you both stick to it tight and don't go goofing off."

And that ended any chance of my being talked into playing with Tommy; I'd look like a fool now if I changed my mind.

We had another round of drinks and Danny danced a couple of numbers with Doris and I danced one, and when I brought her back Danny was stifling a yawn.

"Chillun," he said, "I better go, I'm the one that gets up early, and it's pushing midnight and an hour's drive from home."

I told him he was going to be sore in the morning and should let me open up for a change, but he insisted that he'd be all right. But he went along with the idea when I said I'd arranged with Doris to phone at breakfast time to make sure he felt up to working.

He told Doris she could stay and come in with me if she wanted to, but she vetoed that. He asked me to explain things to the boys so they wouldn't have to go over to the bandstand and to say good night for them. "If this was a one-night stand," he said, "I'd buck up and stick around. But they'll be here a month; we'll be out often."

"Okay," I told them, "scram before they finish this number then, because it's maybe the last one, and you'll get tied up if you're not gone. Take care of yourself, Danny. 'Night, Doris."

It *was* the combo's last number, it turned out, so it was lucky they'd made their getaway. The Casanova is an early club in an early town. Most people come for dinner and don't stay too long afterwards, so the entertainment is off and on between six and midnight. The club stays open another two hours, until the legal closing time, for those who want to stick around that long, but they have to entertain themselves.

The combo now adjourned to the table I had all to myself and after I'd explained and excused Danny and Doris for leaving early, we entertained ourselves, talking, until they closed.

Meanwhile, I sold another car, although not on a very profitable basis. Tommy brought up that they were thinking about renting a car for the month they'd be here, since they'd flown in and didn't have any local transportation. He said one car would do for the three of them, even if they fought over it once in a while. I told them what renting a car for a month would cost them—plenty—and pointed out they'd do better to buy a cheap but usable car and resell it when they took off. I told them we had a '49 Ford on the lot priced at four-fifty and said if they chipped in and bought it for that we'd buy it back at the end of the month for four hundred if they hadn't banged it up any, or for whatever price was fair if they'd damaged it any. They said that sounded swell to them and that they'd be down tomorrow afternoon to look it over and would probably drive it away. We wouldn't make anything on a deal like that, but I knew Danny would back me up on it.

"Where are you boys staying?" I asked. "I'll run you home."

I was mildly surprised to learn that they were staying at a motel—Tommy had to look at his key to tell me the name of it—when they didn't have a car. But they'd intended to rent one tomorrow, so it made sense. They'd seen this one on the way in from the airport in a taxi and because it had a sizeable swimming pool and both Tommy and Mick, especially Mick, liked to swim, they'd had the taxi drop them off there. They'd taken two rooms, Tommy and Frank sharing one and Mick taking the other.

At the motel they tried to talk me into coming in for a nightcap, but I knew that would lead to another hour or two of yak and refused to get out of the car. It was already half past two and I had to get up early to call Danny at breakfast time. But I gave Tommy the telephone number of the office on the lot and told him to call early in the afternoon. If Danny and I were both there I'd probably be able to drop out and pick them up for a look at the car I had in mind for them.

It was three when I got home and I set the alarm for eight and went right to bed.

When the alarm went off I staggered to the telephone, trying to wake myself up as little as possible, and dialed Danny's number. If he was okay, there was no reason why I shouldn't grab a couple more hours of sleep.

But he wasn't okay. It was Doris who answered the phone and she said, "He's pretty stiff and sore, Ralph. He says to tell you he *can* get down there, but he'll appreciate it if you'll swap shifts today and let him have a few more hours."

"Sure," I told her. "Tell him to come in whenever he feels like it, or not at all. It won't hurt me to do the whole thing one day. Sometime I'll take a day off and get revenge."

"Thanks, Ralph. But he thinks he'll be able to come in by afternoon. Maybe sooner."

"He won't need to let me know," I said. "I'll look for him when and if I see him."

So that ended any chance of my going back to sleep. I took a cold shower to wake up and then shaved and dressed. I remembered my promise to Tommy to bring my own sax when I came out next, and

decided that I might decide to do so that evening if Danny came to
relieve me, so I put my sax case in the car. I stopped for breakfast en
route and got to the lot a little, but not much, after nine o'clock.

It was a dull morning. Not a nibble, unless you could count as such
a pair of teen-agers wanting to sell a jalopy. In our business you don't
buy jalopies. You *have* jalopies, ones that you've had to take in as trades
to sell somewhat better cars, and you're very lucky if you get out of the
jalopy whatever trade-in you had to allow on it. So I had to turn the
boys down.

A little before noon another jalopy drove onto the lot, and Lieutenant
Andrews got out of it. He didn't look as tired as he had last night but
he didn't look exactly cheerful either.

I said, "Sorry, but we can't buy it. Or do you want to trade it in on
a better one?"

"Might do that, but not today. Mr. Bushman around?"

I told him Danny was still at home, but might be in later.

"He isn't home. I just came from there. His Missus said he'd left
about eleven o'clock. Well, I wanted to talk to her anyway, and I had
a chance to do that. Where do you suppose Mr. Bushman might have
gone?"

I shrugged. "Some errands, maybe. We're trading shifts today so he
isn't due here till one o'clock. Anything new on the matter?"

"Not on our end. Thought maybe after a night's sleep, your friend
might be able to remember and tell us something he might have missed
before." He took off his hat and wiped his forehead with his handkerchief. "Nobody else has been beat up yet."

For a second I didn't get it and said "Huh?" but I realized what he
meant before he went on to explain, "If that was mistaken identity or
wrong address, somebody's going to find out he made a mistake."

I said, "Or maybe the right victim won't report it—if he knows he
had it coming."

"Could be. You haven't thought of anything to add, have you? Or
learned anything new out at that club after I left?"

I told him no to both questions. But then I added, "You said you
wanted to talk to the boys in the combo. I drove them home last night
so I can tell you where they're holing in—the Cypress Lodge, a motel
out on Centralia."

"Thanks. Don't think I'll look them up today, though, if ever.
There's no way they could be involved in this that I can see; they were
playing at the club when it happened."

"That's right," I said. "And even if they weren't playing at that moment, there wouldn't be time between sets for anyone at the club to get into town and back again. It's at least three quarters of an hour each way."

"I know." He got back into his car and started the engine but instead of driving off he leaned his elbows on top of the door and looked at me.

He said, "I'll level with you, Son. Unless something new develops, there's nothing more we can do on this case. Especially where the victim can't identify his attacker even if he sees him. If it was mistaken identity and if another beating is reported, then we'll have a lead. If it wasn't—"

He hesitated and I prompted him. "If it wasn't, then what?"

"Then we're still not going to get anywhere unless your friend decides to level with us. If a man gets beat up on purpose, he knows why it happened all right. If, for reasons of his own, he won't tell us that, then we can't help him."

"You've got a point there," I admitted. "Shall I tell Danny you'll be back?"

"No, because I won't. I've got something else to do this afternoon, but it's paper work and I'll be at headquarters. You have a talk with your friend and tell him what I told you, and tell him to drop by and see me, or else telephone, if he wants to add anything."

"Right, Lieutenant," I said.

Danny showed up a few minutes before one, but I didn't get a chance to talk to him right away because I was talking to a prospect at the time. By the time I was free Danny was busy.

Then there was a lull and I was able to tell him about the lieutenant's call and what he had said.

"Guess he's right," Danny said. "I mean, about there being nothing more they can do about it. And about the fact that if the guy corrects his mistake and beats up the right guy, or already has, it may never get reported to us."

"Uh-huh. How do you feel? Sure you're up to working the rest of the day?"

"Sure. Wouldn't want to climb into the ring with anyone, but nothing hurts any worse when I'm on my feet than when I'm sitting down, so what's to lose working? Any business this morning?"

I told him there hadn't been, but that reminded me to tell him about the deal I'd made—subject to their trying out the car, of course—with the boys in the combo.

Danny approved. "Not much profit if we have to buy it back for only fifty less," he said, "but maybe they won't turn it back. If their next booking turns out to be within driving distance they'll probably decide to keep it. You better run and get yourself some lunch so you'll be free when they call up."

I went to the restaurant across the street and had myself some lunch and when I came back Danny said that Tommy Drum had already called. They were ready.

I hesitated whether to take the Ford—and make one of them drive me back in it if they bought it—or to pick them up in my own car and bring them to the lot. It made sense either way, but I decided on my own car and used it. If we got them on the lot, maybe—if they were solvent enough—they'd fall for one of the better cars instead of the one I'd told them about. By showing them the Ford first I might goof us out of a bigger sale. And a sale it would be, if, as Danny had suggested might happen, they should decide to keep the car and drive to their next booking.

The boys had told me their room numbers but I didn't know where the rooms were located so I parked in front of the motel and walked back. I came to the number that would be Mick's single first and knocked on the door but there wasn't any answer. So I went down the line a few more doors and knocked again. Tommy's voice called out for me to come in.

Tommy Drum was sitting in a chair reading *Downbeat* and Frank Ritchie was sprawled across the bed busily doing nothing. Tommy said, "Hi, Ralph. Did you bring the Ford?"

"No. Thought I'd take you in to the lot. You might want to look at some others too, before you make up your minds. Where's the Mick?"

"In his room, I guess."

"Isn't," I told him. "I passed his door first and knocked."

Tommy shrugged. "Probably went for a walk like the fresh air fiend he is. Doesn't matter. The three of us talked it over last night after you dropped us off and figured it's a better idea for just Frank and I to buy the car. Mick won't be here the full month if I can get a replacement for him, so he'll just chip in on the running expenses and we'll let it go at that."

"Sounds sensible," I said. "Well, shall we take off?"

"Drink first," Tommy said. "I refuse to look at cars on an empty stomach. Want yours straight, Ralph? Or plain?"

He went to the dresser and poured a shot into each of three glasses, handed them around. I said I didn't want mine either straight or plain and took my glass into the bathroom; I poured about half of it out because he'd made it too big a slug for me to want that early in the day when I'd have to go back to selling cars, and I diluted the rest of it with a couple inches of water.

We sat around with our drinks and Frank said, "Let's kill a little time with these. Maybe Mick just went around the block or something. And even if he isn't shopping on the car, he'd probably want to go into town with us."

"I didn't knock loudly," I said. "Maybe he's still asleep."

Tommy shook his head. "He's up long since. We got up around ten and he was swimming in the pool then. Told us which way to walk to find a restaurant for breakfast within a block. He was out of the pool when we came back but he wouldn't have gone back to sleep. Mick doesn't take naps."

We batted the breeze about nothing until we'd killed our drinks and then tried Mick O'Neill's door again with the same result I'd got twenty minutes before, and we piled into the Merc and went down to the lot.

They looked at several other cars but finally settled for the '49 Ford; I'd guessed right the first time on how high they'd want to go under the circumstances. They made out checks and I made out the papers and they had a car. They offered to drive one or both of us to the nearest bar for a drink to celebrate the deal, and I told Danny to go, since I'd already had a drink with them back at the motel.

Alone on the lot, I found myself drowning in prospects looking at cars, but as soon as the boys brought Danny back the rush dropped off and there was not much doing.

At five, Danny said, "Why don't you run along, Ralph? I can take it from here."

"Sure you're up to working all evening?"

"Sure I'm sure. I'll probably be ready to sleep by the time I'm through though, so I'll give the Casanova a miss tonight. You going?"

I said, "Think I'll have dinner there. At six, when they start serving. Then maybe sit in with the boys for a few numbers. I've got my sax in the car."

"Have a ball. See you tomorrow."

"Maybe sooner. If I don't spend more than an hour or two at the club, I'll drop by the lot on my way home and see how things are going."

But on the way out to the Casanova I decided I didn't want to eat there after all; I just wasn't hungry enough to do justice to a five-buck dinner. So I stopped at a less expensive restaurant en route and saved myself three and a half bucks by having a lighter meal. It was a quarter after six when I got to the club.

Tommy Drum and Frank Ritchie were playing when I walked in with my sax case; Mick O'Neill wasn't on the stand, or in sight. I started over to them and someone touched my arm and said, "Hi, Oliver. Sit down and have a drink with us." It was Max Stivers, the bookie-racketeer who had bought me a drink last night. The beer barrel shaped Gino Itule was with him again.

I said, "I'd better see the boys first. Hasn't Mick O'Neill shown up yet?"

I had to explain to Stivers that Mick O'Neill was the sax man with the combo and he said no, there hadn't been a sax on the stand yet tonight.

Tommy saw me coming and brought the number to an end just as I got there.

"Where's Mick?" I asked him.

"Don't know. He hasn't shown up. Thank God you got here. I just phoned the lot and Danny said you were on your way and had your sax with you."

I started getting the sax out of the case and putting it together. I asked, "Didn't you stop by at the motel to get him?"

"Sure, and waited around as long as we could without being late ourselves. Then I shoved a note under his door telling him to take a taxi, and we scrammed. Thought maybe we'd find him already out here, but he wasn't."

"You sure he couldn't have been asleep in his room, Tommy?"

"We knocked loud enough to wake the dead, and Mick's a light sleeper. Must have gone somewhere and lost track of the time. He ought to show up any minute."

"It's not like Mick to be late," I said. "Maybe something happened to him."

"I'm a little worried too, Ralph. But let's run off two numbers and call this a set, and if he isn't here by then—well, we can phone the motel and ask the guy who runs it to use his pass key and look in Mick's room. And—anything else we can do?"

"Phone the police maybe and see if there's an accident report or something. But okay, we'll give him till half past before we try either of those. Want to give *Stardust* a spin?"

We gave *Stardust* a spin, and then *Don't Stop*. But we did stop, despite applause that wanted us to keep on.

"Come on," Tommy said, "we'll use the phone in the manager's office."

The door of the manager's office was ajar but the room was empty.

We were hesitating in the doorway when Max Stivers' voice spoke behind us. "Something wrong, boys?"

"We were looking for the manager," I told him.

"Green? He's around somewhere. Shall I have one of the waiters look for him? Or anything else I can do?"

I explained briefly and Stivers said, "Sure, take over his office, use the phone all you want. When you've found out the score, join me at my table, all three of you."

Tommy called the motel first and explained to and then argued with the proprietor. He swore and put down the phone. "Guy won't check the room. Says if Mick's there and won't answer the door it's his business. Says if we call the cops he'll give them the pass key, but he won't use it himself. Guess we'll have to do it that way."

"Let me," I suggested. I was remembering that Lieutenant Andrews had said he had a lot of paper work at headquarters; he might be working late.

He was. I told him what the situation was, listened to what he had to say. I thanked him and hung up.

"He'll take care of both ends of it," I told Tommy and Frank. "He's right at headquarters so he'll check on accident reports. And he'll have the radio operator instruct the nearest radio car to look in the room. He'll call back as soon as he gets anything."

Tommy sighed. "I can use a drink. I'm getting scared now, Ralph. If it was some guys I'd just figure it didn't mean anything, but not Mick. He'd at least have phoned us."

I took the boys to Stivers' table. There was a third man there whom I didn't know, but Tommy and Frank knew him and introduced him as Harvey Green, the manager. I told about the call we'd made, and Stivers took over again. He clapped Green on the shoulder and said, "You wait in your office for that call, Harv, so the boys can relax and have a drink." And a snap of his fingers brought a waiter running and got us our round of drinks in a lot less time than we could have got them ourselves.

Stivers tried to keep it from being a wake but none of us felt much like talking and he didn't succeed. Mostly we just sat and nursed our drinks until Green came back and said I was wanted on the phone.

I got there fast. Andrews' voice said. "Bad news, Oliver. Your friend Mick is dead."

My mouth felt suddenly dry. "Dead, how?" I asked.

"Murdered. Beaten up like your partner was, but the beating didn't stop there this time. Hit over the head several times after he was down and out. Probably with a blackjack."

"In his room at the motel?"

"Yeah. I think you boys better come down here, all three of you. The Casanova will have to get by without music, one evening. If anybody out there objects tell 'em it's a police order."

"All right. You mean headquarters or the motel?"

"Make it headquarters. I'm going around to the motel now, but I'll be back here by the time you can make it in from there. Or not much after."

He hung up on me before I could ask any more questions. Back at the table I gave it to them straight, without sitting down again. Tommy Drum looked stunned. He opened his mouth, probably to call me a liar or to ask if I was kidding him, then realized I wouldn't possibly be either lying or kidding about something like that, and closed his mouth again.

Frank Ritchie just stood up and said, "All right, what are we waiting for?"

We took my car, going in, because it was faster. I don't know why we felt there was any hurry, but we did. We didn't talk much, except about one thing. Tommy and Frank had known about Danny's being beaten up last night; it had been mentioned at the table, but played down as something that must have been a mistake. Now they wanted details and I told them the little I knew that they didn't.

I drove to the police station and we all trouped in. A sergeant at the desk had been alerted to our coming; he showed us into a kind of waiting room and told us Lieutenant Andrews would be back soon. The chairs were hard and uncomfortable, but we sat on them. And waited.

Frank said, "I don't get it. It must have been the same guy who beat up Danny, but who could possibly have a down on both Danny and Mick?"

Neither of us answered him. And that was all the conversation there was until, after half an hour or so, Danny came in. He looked white and shaken, more worried than I'd ever seen him before.

He told us that Andrews had stopped by the lot on his way to the motel and had asked him a few questions and then had asked him to come to the station when he closed the lot at nine. He'd stuck around for a while and then decided to close early and head for headquarters to get it over with.

"Did you phone Doris?" I asked him. And he nodded.

Another half an hour and Andrews came in. He put the finger on Tommy first and took him through a door to a smaller office marked *Private.* After a while—I didn't time it—Tommy came back and said the lieutenant wanted Frank next, so Frank went in.

"Are you free to go, or does he want you to stick around?" I asked Tommy.

"Free to go, but where? Nowhere I want to go alone. Maybe when he's through with Frank, he and I can go somewhere where we can have a drink and wait for you guys."

Danny looked at his watch. "May be pretty late when we get through. Here's a thought. Doris is home alone and probably worried stiff. Why don't you go round to my place and keep her company? We can all head there one at a time as the police get through with us here. And there's liquor."

Tommy said it sounded like a good idea but that he'd wait till Frank was through and the two of them could go around together. But he suggested that meanwhile Danny phone Doris and make sure she liked the idea. Danny nodded and went out into the hallway to use a pay phone. He came back and nodded. "She says it's a swell idea."

We gave Tommy the address of the Bushmans' apartment and I tried to give them the key to my Mercury, since their car was still out at the Casanova, but he insisted they'd rather take a cab than try to follow directions in a strange town by night, so I didn't insist.

And then Frank Ritchie rejoined us and said Andrews wanted to talk to me next. A minute later the lieutenant was looking at me across his desk. The chair I sat on was even harder and more uncomfortable than the ones in the outer office.

He said wearily, "Let's start with your running through the day for me. Where you were and when."

I started with my alarm going off at eight o'clock and went through it for him.

He nodded when I'd finished. He said, "At least you fellows tell stories that fit together, as far as times concerned. Not that any of you has an alibi this time."

"What time was Mick O'Neill killed, Lieutenant?" I asked him.

"Give or take an hour, around one o'clock. That makes it between twelve and two. It would have been right around two when you knocked on his door. And he could have answered, and asked you in."

"He could have," I said, "but he didn't. But how about Tommy and Frank? Don't they alibi each other? Unless you think they *both* killed Mick."

The lieutenant sighed. "I don't think anything. But no, they don't alibi each other. About half past one, Mr. Drum left Ritchie in their room at the motel and went out to make that phone call to the lot that brought you out there to pick them up. He didn't make it from the motel office because he was out of cigarettes anyway so he walked to a store two blocks off and phoned from there. So he could have dropped in on Mr. O'Neill either going or coming. Or Mr. Ritchie could have done it while Mr. Drum was gone."

He got out a crumpled pack of cigarettes, put one in his mouth and lighted it. He said, "And your partner—he hasn't got an alibi either. He left home at eleven and didn't get to the lot until one. Did you ask him what he was doing then?"

"No," I said. "It wasn't any of my business."

"I thought you might have got curious anyway. Well, he says he was just driving around thinking. Does that make sense to you?"

"Why not? He sure had something to think about, after what happened to him last night."

"Yeah. Well, he says when he left home at eleven he intended to drive right to the lot and then he got to thinking that there wasn't any point in showing before one, anyway. Says around half past twelve, just before he did come to the lot, he stopped in at a diner and had a sandwich. We can check that, but it doesn't give him an alibi even if it checks because if Mr. O'Neill was killed at twelve, whoever killed him could still have made that diner by half past, or sooner."

I said, "If you think—Listen, it doesn't make sense. Danny is inches shorter than Mick, and fifty or sixty pounds lighter, and Mick was an athlete to boot. You say Mick was knocked unconscious *before* he was killed with a blackjack or whatever?"

"That's right. And I'll admit I can't see your friend Mr. Bushman doing that, especially picking a fight when he himself had sore ribs and a sore jaw to start with."

"And especially when it could not have been because he thought Mick had beaten him up first, last night. Mick was over twenty miles away when that happened, and playing sax in front of a hundred people."

"Yeah. So more likely the same guy attacked both of them. Who might that have been?"

"I don't know," I said. "I couldn't even guess."

"Nor any reason at all why anyone might have had it in for either one of them, let alone both of them?"

"No," I said. "I wish I could help you, Lieutenant, but it makes nuts." I thought a minute and added, "Maybe quite literally. Last night Danny thought, and I thought with him, that his beating was probably a case of mistaken identity. It's hard to figure it that way now. But our second thought last night—that whoever did it was off his rocker—looks better now than it did then. Nobody could possibly have a sane motive for attacking both Danny and Mick."

"Even a crazy killer would have a motive. One that made sense to him. Could someone have had a grudge against both of them, from way back?"

I said, "It would have to be from way back. There's been no contact direct or indirect between Danny and Mick for longer than the year he and I have been in business here. Probably a year before that would have been the last time they saw one another. That would have been when we were playing with Nick Frazer's band."

"For how long?"

"Danny and I were with Mick for about three months. Mick got taken on two weeks before we left. No connection between his joining and our leaving; we got a better offer, that's all."

"And before that?"

"I'd have to think back to remember times and places but I'd say about three or four times before that Danny and Mick played in the same band, maybe up to two or three months at a time. Always a big band."

"Why always a big band?"

"Any competent musician can read notes and play the arrangements a big band uses. Smaller groups—even small bands, let alone combos—improvise, and when it comes to improvisation, there are different types of musicians. Mick was a Dixieland man, the righteous stuff. Neither Danny nor I swing that way. Did Tommy explain how he happened to have Mick with the combo?"

"Yeah. How did you get along with Mick?"

"Okay. We weren't close friends, but we got along."

"And Danny?"

"They didn't get along very well. But they weren't enemies and neither had anything specific against the other. Just—well, call it a personality clash. Danny can answer that better than I can, and give you reasons, but don't take it seriously because it was nothing serious, believe me."

"I believe you. Mr. Drum tells me he offered you Mick's job last night and you turned it down."

"That's right. Not because Mick would have minded; he wanted me to take it. But when Danny and I bought the lot we decided between us, no more playing. Not professionally, I mean; we sit in on jam sessions once in a while. Or just play together, with Doris on piano."

"She was a singer, wasn't she?"

"Yes. But she plays enough piano to give us a background."

"Going to play saxophone with the combo now?"

I said, "I haven't thought about it."

"Think about it a minute. Won't this make it different?"

"Maybe it will. I doubt if Tommy could get another sax man in town here, even as good as Mick was. He'd probably have to cancel his booking and he's too good a friend for us to want that to happen to. And under those circumstances I'm sure it'll be okay with Danny. In fact, it would have been all right with him if I'd said yes last night, when there wasn't any emergency involved."

"Uh-huh. Well, just one more question, Mr. Oliver. Can you tell me anything at all that even might possibly be helpful, something I might not have asked the right questions to bring out?"

"Not a thing," I said.

"Okay, that's all for now. You're not planning to leave town, I take it. I'll be able to find you on the lot or out at the Casanova."

"Right," I said. "Shall I send Danny in?"

In the outer office I asked Danny if he thought I should wait for him, but he said it would be silly because we each had a car parked outside and couldn't go together anyway.

I found Doris plenty worried and Tommy and Frank both trying to reassure her by telling her Danny couldn't possibly be in any further danger.

"But why," she wanted to know, "was Mick killed? If we don't know that, how can we know there won't be any second attack on Danny?"

Because, I pointed out again and patiently, the man who'd attacked Danny had had him completely at his mercy; if he'd wanted to kill Danny or even injured him any worse than he had, he could have done so then, in perfect safety.

"That's right, Doris," Tommy said. "You know how I dope it? I don't think that cat intended to kill Mick at all, just to beat him up like he beat Danny. Only Danny went down and out from that first sneak punch—and I'm guessing Mick didn't. Mick was big and tough himself and I'm guessing he put up more of a fight. And got the handkerchief down off the guy's face so he knew who was attacking him, see? So when he did kayo Mick, he went ahead and finished the job so Mick couldn't put the finger on him. Makes sense?"

"Makes sense," I said. "Believe me, if I'm next on his list, I'm going to go down for the count without making a grab for any handkerchief. I'd rather be a live coward than a dead hero."

"Me too," Tommy said. "And because we don't know *why* he put the slug on Danny and Mick, we can't be sure we're not on his list too. Say, Ralph, Frank and I were talking this over on the way here and— Wait, one thing first. You're going to play with us now, aren't you? You're not going to let us down and make us lose that booking, are you?"

Frank said, "It would put us in an awful jam, Ralphie boy. On account that cop ordered us not to leave town, and we'd be strictly on the nut having to stay and not working."

I said, "I want to talk it over with Danny. If he thinks I should—"

"Swell," Tommy said. "Then it's in the bag because I know what Danny'll say. How's about a drink to that? We're ready for another and Ralph hasn't even had one yet. What kind of a hostess are you, Doris?"

Doris laughed and went out into the kitchen to make a round of drinks and Tommy said, "Attaboy, Ralph. Knew you wouldn't let us down. Now here's what we were talking about on the way over here. What kind of a pad you got?"

"Bachelor apartment. Two rooms and a kitchenette I never use."

"Sleep three?"

"If somebody sleeps on the couch, yes."

"Then why don't we check out of the motel and triple up? Big as that guy is, he isn't going to tangle with three of us at once and if we stick together as much as possible it'll be that much tougher for him to dope a way to get at any one of us alone."

Doris came in with a tray of drinks just as I was saying that it sounded like a good idea to me.

We told her what we'd decided and she said it sounded sensible to her.

"And we'll all save money," Frank said. "We chip in on Ralph's rent, natch, but it probably won't come to as much as the motel. What do you pay, Ralph?"

We were still trying to figure out what one third of eighty dollars was when Danny came in. We briefed him while Doris went out to make him a drink. He approved down the line and said that if I *didn't* help the boys out by playing with them, he'd disown me.

And we worked out a schedule for handling the lot. Danny would work the regular shift I'd been working, one o'clock in the afternoon till nine at night. I'd take the shift he'd had, but shorten it at both ends by not opening the lot until ten in the morning—we never did much business the first hour anyway—and working until three or four o'clock, depending on whether we were busy or not. That would give me two or three hours to clean up, rest a little, and go out to the club with Tommy and Frank in time for the combo to start swinging at six. Because I'd be putting in fewer hours than he on the lot, I talked Danny into agreeing to take two thirds of our profits for the next month, instead of half. I pointed out that with what Tommy would be paying me I'd still be coming out way ahead on the deal. Doris backed me up on that, and Danny gave in and said okay.

Tommy decided he'd better call the club and tell them the combo had a new sax lined up, and that they could count on us tomorrow evening. While he was making the call, I asked Danny if the lieutenant, in talking to him, had come up with anything new.

Danny shook his head. "He isn't through with me, though; just called it off because it was getting so late. He's going to come here tomorrow morning to talk some more. Wants to talk to Doris too, or he'd probably have asked me to come back there."

We broke it up just short of midnight. I drove the boys to the motel and waited till they'd packed their stuff, then took them home with me. We made our sleeping arrangements, had a nightcap, and turned in.

That was the end of the second day.

Nothing startling happened for the next week. The investigation brought out some things about Mick that we hadn't known, including the fact that he'd really been stashing his dough during the dozen-odd years he'd been playing. He was more solvent than all the rest of us put together, with bank accounts and stocks and bonds adding up to nearly twenty thousand dollars. We'd talked about chipping in for a funeral for him, but when we learned that, we quit talking about it. Or, for that matter, about having the funeral here. It turned out that both his parents were still living, in Cincinnati. His body was flown there for the funeral, as soon as the police released it. Since Mick had been working with them at the time he died, Tommy and Frank thought they ought to go to the funeral, but since the Casanova manager didn't look kindly on the idea of a second comboless evening, they compromised on letting Frank Ritchie represent both of them; I was able to find them a local skin man who was free and who was good enough to hold down Frank's end of the combo for the one evening he'd have to be gone if he flew both ways. Tommy Drum's piano held the combo together and was irreplaceable so he had to stay. We all sent flowers, of course. Frank came back looking a bit stunned and said he was surprised that a Dixie man could have so many friends. He said cats had come to the funeral from as far away as New Orleans and San Francisco.

Toward the end of the week Danny came out twice and brought Doris, after closing the lot. The second time he brought his trumpet and sat in with us for a few numbers. And we talked Doris into singing a couple of numbers, and the customers really got their money's worth that night.

That was a Wednesday night, and the next night was a Thursday and the night after that a Friday; it was around half past seven and we'd finished our second set and were sitting at one of the tables. With Max Stivers and his friend Gino; Stivers had invited us over again. Had offered to buy us drinks too, but we'd turned them down except that Tommy Drum had taken a coke. When you're playing till midnight you can't start drinking too early and unless there was special occasion for it, we laid off taking our first drink of the evening until ten or eleven o'clock, when a lift would be welcome to carry us the rest of the way. But we'd sat down with them and were batting the breeze with them. With Stivers, anyway, Gino never said much.

Then there was a hand lightly on my shoulder and I looked up and saw Lieutenant Andrews was standing beside me. He said, "Mind if I sit down?"

The chair next to mine was empty and I said, "Sure, Lieutenant." And then corrected myself. "That is, this is Mr. Stivers' table, so I really shouldn't invite you." I started to introduce them, but Stivers smiled. "We know one another, Ralph. Sit down, Andrews. Drink?"

The lieutenant shook his head. "Didn't know you knew these boys, Mr. Stivers."

"Sure I know them. I hang out here. And like music."

"Do any business with them?"

Max Stivers quit smiling. "Is that any business of yours, Andrews? You're not in your territory here. This is outside city limits, way outside."

"Yeah," the lieutenant said. "Forget I asked."

Stivers smiled again. "But since you did ask, the answer is no. None of these boys are horse players."

"Is their friend, Mr. Danny Bushman, a horse player?"

The smile stayed on Stivers' lips but went out of his eyes. He said shortly, "I've met him. I don't know him well enough to know that. Andrews, is this an interrogation?"

The lieutenant sighed and took a pipe and tobacco pouch from his pocket. "No, it isn't. But I was just wondering. And I'm wondering, too, if Mr. O'Neill was a horse player."

Tommy Drum cut in. "I can answer that, Lieutenant. Mick was down on gambling, all kinds. He wouldn't even match pennies with you."

The lieutenant got his pipe going and didn't ask any more questions, and gradually things got less tense than they'd seemed to be for a few minutes. The conversation got on Dave Brubeck and from Brubeck it got, somehow, to Bix Beiderbecke. Musicians' talk.

I'd just glanced at my watch—Tommy never wears one and he'd put me in charge of keeping time on our breaks—and decided we had a few minutes left before we had to start playing again, when there was another hand on my shoulder and I looked up again. It was a man I knew only very slightly and only by his last name, Hart. He owned a sporting goods store a couple of blocks from the lot and I'd bought a set of golf clubs from him, and once he'd been on the lot and looked at cars, but hadn't bought one.

I said, "Hi," and he said, "Hi, Oliver. Don't bother introducing me around; I've got to get back to my table. Just want to ask you one question."

"Shoot," I said.

"Drove past your lot on my way here but didn't have time to stop or I'd have made myself late. But what's the price on that Cad you've got there?"

"Cad?" I said blankly. "There isn't any Cad on the lot. You must've mistaken some other car for one."

"No, this was a Cad all right. I pulled in to the curb and had a close look at it. But I saw your partner was busy with another customer and I'd have made myself late here if I'd waited to ask him. It's a yellow hardtop, late model, couldn't be over a year old. Looked practically brand new."

I shook my head. "It wasn't there this afternoon, when I left at three o'clock. Danny must have taken it in."

He shrugged and said, "Okay, I'll drop by tomorrow sometime. It's sure a sweet car."

He started to turn away but Lieutenant Andrews' voice said, "Just a minute, Sir." And I realized that everyone at the table had been listening to the conversation.

Hart turned back and said, "Yes?" politely to the lieutenant. Since they were going to talk anyway, I said, "Lieutenant Andrews, Mr. Hart."

"Glad to know you, Mr. Hart. Just want to ask this. Could that Cadillac have been a customer's car?"

"Not the way it was parked, lined up with the others. A customer wouldn't drive in and park his car that way. It was between an Olds Rocket 88 convertible and a Buick Special. All three of them look like almost new cars." He turned back to me. "When I drop by tomorrow I want to look at that Rocket too."

"Thanks, Mr. Hart," the lieutenant said.

And then he was looking at me hard, across the table. "Mr. Oliver, was there a late model Buick Special on the lot this afternoon?"

I said, "A Buick Roadmaster. He just got the model wrong."

"Was there on Olds convertible?"

I shook my head.

"All right, let's say he made a mistake on the Buick. Would your partner be likely to have bought *two* almost new, expensive cars in one afternoon without consulting you?"

I said, "It would be unusual, but he's got the authority to. If he got them at a good enough price—"

"Is there enough cash in your checking account for him to have bought them?"

I said, "They could have been trades. Trade-downs. Sometimes a man has an expensive car but goes broke and needs dough. He'll trade it for an older model and a cash difference. Or they could have been left on consignment."

"How does that work?"

"Well, we don't do this often but sometimes we don't want to buy a car outright for what a customer wants for it but if he wants us to we leave it on the lot and try to sell it for him if we can get enough to give him his price and leave a profit for us. We used to do that oftener when we were first starting and didn't have enough cars to make a good showing on the lot."

The lieutenant said, "Uh-huh," and stood up slowly. "Well, I thought I was through for the day but I think I'll want to talk to Mr. Bushman. And if any of you have in mind to telephone him and warn him I'm coming, it won't do any good. If I find those two or three cars gone off the lot, he's going to have to do a lot more explaining than if they're still there."

He looked around the table to take in all of us, and stiffened suddenly. He snapped at Max Stivers. "Where's your goon?"

"You mean Gino?" Stivers asked blandly. "I don't know. I guess I didn't notice him leave."

"You sent him to—" He broke off and swung around to grab me by the shoulder. "Take me to a telephone."

I hurried with him to the manager's office. The door was closed. He jerked it open without knocking and bolted in; the office was vacant. He hurried to the desk and then swore and held up a broken phone cord. "What other phones—? Never mind, if he yanked this cord, he took care of the others. Son, have you got a fast car and can you handle it?"

"Yes," I said. We were already running out. I saw Tommy and Frank starting after us, but we didn't wait.

I led him to the Merc and Tommy and Frank caught up with us and started to pile in the back seat. Andrews stopped them. "You fellows got another car?"

"Yeah," Tommy said, "but not as fast—"

"Never mind that. Take your car and find the nearest public phone you can use. Don't waste time calling your friend—call the police. Tell them to get cops on that lot *fast*. Tell 'em they may have to stop a murder."

They were running for the car I'd sold them while I got the Merc percolating and gunned it. I asked, "Do you really think—?"

"Don't talk, Son. Concentrate on driving and I'll do the talking. Your night vision's good?"

"Yes."

"Mine's a little under standard. I'll drive as fast as I have to by day, but at night I don't dare go over forty or so, even on a clear road. You go as fast as you think is safe. Don't worry about tickets. If a cop car gets on our tail, that's fine. I'll ask him to go ahead of us and use his siren. And his radio, if he's got one."

Out of the corner of my eye I could see that he'd taken a gun out of a shoulder holster. It was a flat automatic. He worked the slide to jack a bullet from the clip into the firing chamber and then put the gun back in the holster.

"Watch it, Son," he said, as I passed a car with a rather risky margin of safety against a truck coming the other way. "I've got guts, but I don't want them strewn along the highway. And we aren't going to help your partner any getting ourselves killed. Did you notice Gino leave, how long it was before we missed him?"

"Right after Hart came up and started asking me about the Cad, I think."

"Then he's got a pretty fair start on us. You argued with Mr. Hart a while, and then you and I did some yakking. Even allowing him a couple of minutes to pull out telephone cords, he's got at least five minutes start and maybe ten. 'Course we don't know what kind of a car he's got or how well he can handle it. You're doing fine on this one, but don't try it any faster."

I had to slow down a little as we flashed through a block with lighted stores. The lieutenant said, "That's where your friends will be able to phone from. I'd say it's about a dead toss-up whether or not we get there before they get their call through and get results from it."

I said, "You called Gino a goon. Do you think he killed Mick and beat up Danny? But Danny described his attacker as six feet tall and Gino's built like—"

"Don't talk, Son. Yeah, Gino's built short and broad, but he's got power. Used to fight pro, and used to wrestle. Yeah, he's a goon, for Stivers. People who are beaten up by goons sometimes give wrong descriptions, on purpose. We'll worry about that later. It's funny, I knew Stivers was in on a lot of things, but I never thought he had a part in a hot car racket. And I never thought of your used car lot being used to unload them. It's a natural. Now don't run off the road when I ask you this, but are you sure you weren't onto what was going on?"

I said, "I'm still not onto what's going on. Especially how *Mick* figures in on it."

"I'm beginning to get a hunch on that. Well, Son, we're getting close." He took the pistol out of its holster again and this time kept it in his hand. "You don't by any chance have a gun on you or in the car, do you?"

I told him I hadn't. "Then I want you to stay out of whatever happens," he said. "You just pull up and park in front of—"

We were a block and a half away then, and we heard the shots. Two of them. And we were half a block away when a dark green coupe pulled out of the lot and turned away from us.

It didn't have speed as yet and at the speed we were going I could easily have caught it and boxed it to the curb, but a light turned red in my face and another car pulled out in front of me from an intervening intersection and I had to slam on brakes and barely avoided a smashup. The screeching stop killed my engine and before I could start it again there was another screeching—of sirens. A car with two men in it slowed down alongside ours, and the lieutenant yelled to them to get the green coupe—and to be careful because there was an armed killer in it. The car took off, siren going and red light flashing, and another like it came from behind us and joined the chase.

"They'll get Gino," the lieutenant said. "He hasn't a chance. We stay here."

I had the engine going again now, and I drove onto the lot.

It was two o'clock in the morning when a doctor came into the hospital waiting room and told us Danny was dead. He said, "Lieutenant Andrews asked me to tell you that he'll appreciate if you'll all wait here a few minutes. He's on the telephone now, but he wants to talk to you."

Doris was crying softly. She had hold of my hand and was squeezing my fingers spasmodically, so hard that it almost hurt.

Danny had recovered consciousness for a while, and Doris and I had each had a few minutes with him. I don't know what he told her, but he'd asked me to take care of Doris if he died—and I think he knew that he was going to. And he'd made a full statement to the police and had lived to sign it. Anyway, he'd lived longer than Gino. The green coupe, doing better than eighty, had gone off the road and into a tree when a police bullet had found a back tire. And Pat Stivers was under arrest. The lieutenant had come into the waiting room and told us both of those things before Danny had recovered consciousness.

And now the lieutenant came in again. As he looked from one of us to another—Tommy and Frank were there too, of course—he looked more tired than I'd ever seen him look before.

He spoke to Doris. "Do you want the details tonight, Mrs. Bushman? Or would you rather wait?"

Doris got her sobbing under control and told him she'd rather hear it now.

He said, "Your husband got to playing the horses again; he's been playing heavily for six months now. And he got deeper into debt trying to get out, and Stivers let him do it, gave him credit. As of last week he owed Stivers three and a half thousand dollars. And Stivers decided it was time to close the trap.

"He sent his goon, Gino Itule, to see Mr. Bushman. What happened there wasn't just what your husband told us. Gino wasn't masked and he didn't swing the second he came through the door. He told your husband to see Stivers the next day, and either to bring cash for what he owed or be ready to listen to a proposition about using the used car lot as an outlet for stolen cars until the commissions Stivers would pay him for selling them would cover that debt. Your husband said no to that, and that's when Gino knocked him out and gave him a few kicks to help him think it over.

"When your husband left at eleven the next day he went to see Stivers—and he'd been convinced. But he said you, Mr. Oliver, wouldn't go for it and he couldn't risk having the hot cars on the lot even when you were off shift because you often dropped in even when you were not working, to see how things were going. Stivers had an answer for that. Gino was still around, and with a broken leg you wouldn't be dropping in for a while."

The lieutenant was looking at me now. He said, "Naturally your partner, because he was your friend too, wouldn't agree to that. But he had another answer. He said that if Mr. O'Neill was hurt, maybe a broken arm, badly enough so he wouldn't be able to play saxophone for a month then he was certain you'd not let Mr. Drum down, but would agree to join him.

"So he sent Gino to beat up Mr. O'Neill and what happened there was like we figured. Mr. O'Neill resisted and was strong enough to get the mask down off Gino's face. It hadn't been intended as a murder—till then.

"That scared Mr. Bushman, but it was too late for him to back out. He himself had suggested the beating up and that made him an accessory to murder now. Anyway, he could count on you being away from the lot—and far enough away that you couldn't drop in accidentally—all evening every evening. The stolen cars, three or four at a time, were garaged nearby and every evening after you were on your way to the Casanova, Gino would help drive them onto the lot. And off the lot again at closing time. Your partner had sold three of those cars the first week. Four or five more and his commissions on them would have put him in the clear—or so he thought; I doubt if Stivers would have let him off the hook that easily. But that doesn't matter now.

"The blow-up tonight was when, by sheer accident, someone told you about cars being on the lot that you knew didn't belong there—and told you when I was listening and when Stivers and Gino were there too. Stivers acted quick; he saw right at the start of that conversation what it was going to lead to and whispered quick orders to Gino. But Gino wasn't quite fast enough to make a clean getaway. If he had, we might have guessed down the line, but we would not have had positive proof."

"I—I think I understand everything now, Lieutenant," Doris said. "Is that all?"

"Not quite. There's something else I think you should understand. Mr. Oliver's part in this. If he hadn't done what he did, Mr. Bushman wouldn't be dead, might not even have got into serious trouble."

I said. "You're crazy, Andrews. What did I do?"

"Nothing, Son. Nothing at all. That's the whole trouble. You *must* have known your partner was gambling again and getting in over his head. Why, when you assured me he wasn't tangled with some other woman you admitted you and he were so much together you'd know something like that even if his wife didn't suspect it. And he wouldn't have been as secretive about horse playing as he would about that, especially from you. And you mean to tell me he could go that far in debt and worry about it without your even suspecting?"

I said, "I knew he was worrying about something, but—"

"And you knew, or guessed, what. When you found him beaten up that night, you knew he was in over his head, and what did you do about it? Try to talk him into leveling with you so you could help him straighten out whatever it was? Or pretend to believe what he told you, so he'd get himself in deeper?"

I said, "I *did* believe it. And why do you think I wanted Danny in trouble. He was my best friend."

"Until he got married, he was. But you were both in love with the same woman, and I think you still want her. And I think that six months or a year from now, except for what I'm saying, you'd be getting her. Son, you figured it that way. Your Danny was weak, you'd probably saved him from getting into serious trouble more than once since you went to school together. And you knew that if you pretended to keep on being his friend sooner or later his weakness would get him in trouble again and that all you'd have to do was what you did this time—nothing. Am I right?"

"You're *not*. This is slander, Lieutenant. I could—"

"You could sue me, Son, but you won't, because I'm right. You could have stopped things from happening as they did easily, when he first started gambling again. Even after he was beaten up, if you'd talked him into leveling with you. The only trouble he was in up to then was owing money."

Sometime long ago Doris' hand had dropped mine.

The lieutenant said, "And tonight, Son, was the real clincher. You saw Gino leave the table—right after we'd learned that there was a strange Cadillac on your lot. You had more information then than I did; you guessed the truth quicker. So what did you do? You kept me busy and distracted as long as you could, explaining how strange cars could have been taken in as trade-downs or could have been taken onto the lot on consignment. You kept me distracted just long enough to let your partner get killed. And there's no charge I can bring against you."

Doris stood up suddenly. "Thank you, Lieutenant. Thank you very much. Tommy, Frank, will you take me home please?"

They followed, and at the doorway Tommy Drum turned. He said, "There isn't any more combo; I'll cancel the booking. The Casanova manager will send you a check."

The door closed behind them. Definitely.

"Happy, Son?" the lieutenant asked.

"Damn you," I said. "Don't call me Son!"

"You'd rather I use all four words of the phrase, Son?"

REX STOUT
The Zero Clue

1

IT BEGAN with a combination of circumstances, but what doesn't? To mention just one, if there hadn't been a couple of checks to deposit that morning I might not have been in that neighborhood at all.

But I was, and, approving of the bright sun and the sharp clear air as I turned east off Lexington Avenue into Thirty-seventh Street, I walked some forty paces to the number and found it was a five-story yellow brick, clean and neat, with greenery in tubs flanking the entrance. I went in. The lobby, not much bigger than my bedroom, had a fancy rug, a fireplace without a fire, more greenery, and a watchdog in uniform who challenged me with a suspicious look.

As I opened my mouth to meet his challenge, circumstances combined. A big guy in a dark blue topcoat and homburg, entering from the street, breezed past me, heading for the elevator, and as he did so the elevator door opened and a girl emerged. Four of us in that undersized lobby made a crowd, and we had to maneuver. Meanwhile I was speaking to the watchdog.

"My name's Goodwin, and I'm calling on Leo Heller."

Gazing at me, his expression changing, he blurted at me, "Ain't you Archie Goodwin works for Nero Wolfe?"

The girl, making for the exit, stopped a step short of it and turned, and the big guy, inside the elevator, blocked the door from closing and stuck his head out, while the watchdog was going on, "I've saw your picture in the paper, and look, I want Nero Wolfe's autograph."

It would have been more to the point if he had wanted mine, but I'm no hog. The man in the elevator, which was self-service, was letting the door close, but the girl was standing by, and I hated to disappoint her by denying I was me, as of course I would have had to do if I had been there on an operation that needed cover.

I'll have to let her stand there a minute while I explain that I was actually not on an operation at all. Chiefly, I was satisfying my curiosity. At five in the afternoon the day before, in Nero Wolfe's office, there had been a phone call. After taking it I had gone to the kitchen—where Fritz was boning a pig's head for what he calls *fromage de cochon*—to get a glass of water, and told Fritz I was going upstairs to do a little yapping.

"He is so happy up there," Fritz protested, but there was a gleam in his eye. He knows darned well that if I quit yapping the day would come when there would be no money in the bank to meet the payroll, including him.

I went up three flights, on past the bedroom floors to the roof, where ten thousand square feet of glass in aluminum frames make a home for ten thousand orchid plants. The riot of color on the benches of the three rooms doesn't take my breath any more, but it is unquestionably a show, and as I went through that day I kept my eyes straight ahead to preserve my mood for yapping intact. However, it was wasted. In the intermediate room Wolfe stood massively, with an Odontoglossum seedling in his hand, glaring at it, a mountain of cold fury, with Theodore Horstmann, the orchid nurse, standing nearby with his lips tightened to a thin line.

As I approached, Wolfe transferred the glare to me and barked savagely, "Thrips!"

I did some fast mood shifting. There's a time to yap and a time not to yap. But I went on.

"What do you want?" he rasped.

"I realize," I said politely but firmly, "that this is ill timed, but I told Mr. Heller I would speak to you. He phoned—"

"Speak to me later! If at all!"

"I'm to call him back. It's Leo Heller, the probability wizard. He says that calculations have led him to suspect that a client of his may have committed a serious crime, but it's only a suspicion and he doesn't want to tell the police until it has been investigated, and he wants us to investigate. I asked for details, but he wouldn't give them on the phone. I thought I might as well run over there now—it's over on East Thirty-seventh Street—and find out if it looks like a job. He wouldn't—"

"No!"

"My eardrums are not insured. No what?"

"Get out!" He shook the thrips-infested seedling at me. "I don't want it! That man couldn't hire me for any conceivable job on any imaginable terms! Get out!"

I turned, prompt but dignified, and went. If he had thrown the seedling at me I would of course have dodged, and the fairly heavy pot would have sailed on by and crashed into a cluster of Calanthes in full bloom, and God only knew what Wolfe would have done then.

On my way back down to the office I was wearing a grin. Even without the thrips, Wolfe's reaction to my message would have been substantially the same, which was why I had been prepared to yap. The thrips had merely keyed it up. Leo Heller had been tagged by fame, with articles about him in magazines and Sunday newspapers. While making a living as a professor of mathematics at Underhill College, he had begun, for amusement, to apply the laws of probability, through highly complicated mathematical formulas, to various current events, ranging from ball games and horse races to farm crops and elections. Checking back on his records after a couple of years, he had been startled and pleased to find that the answers he had got from his formulas had been 86.3 percent correct, and he had written a piece about it for a magazine. Naturally requests had started coming from all kinds of people for all kinds of calculations, and he had granted some of them to be obliging, but when he had tried telling a woman in Yonkers where to look for thirty-one thousand dollars in currency she had lost, and she had followed instructions and found it and had insisted on giving him two grand, he side-stepped to a fresh slant on the laws of probability as applied to human problems and resigned his professorship.

That had been three years ago, and now he was sitting pretty. It was said that his annual take was in six figures, that he returned all his mail unanswered, accepting only clients who called in person, and that there was nothing on earth he wouldn't try to dope a formula for, provided he was furnished with enough factors to make it feasible. It had been suggested that he should be hauled in for fortunetelling, but the cops and the DA's office let it lay, as well they might, since he had a college degree and there were at least a thousand fortunetellers operating in New York who had never made it through high school.

It wasn't known whether Heller was keeping his percentage up to 86.3, but I happened to know it wasn't goose eggs. Some months earlier a president of a big corporation had hired Wolfe to find out which member of his staff was giving trade secrets to a competitor. I had been busy on another case at the time, and Wolfe had put Orrie Cather on the collection of details. Orrie had made a long job of it, and the first we knew we were told by the corporation president that he had got impatient and gone to Leo Heller with the problem, and Heller had cooked up a formula and come out with an answer, the name of one of the junior vice-presidents, and the junior VP had confessed! Our client freely admitted that most of the facts he had given Heller for the ingredients of his formula had been supplied by us, gathered by Orrie Cather, and he offered no objection to paying our bill, but Wolfe was so sore he actually told me to send no bill—an instruction I disregarded, knowing how he would regret it after he had cooled off. However, as I was aware through occasional mutterings from him, he still had it in for Leo Heller, and taking on any kind of job for him would have been absolutely off the program that day or any other day, even if there had been no thrips within a mile of Thirty-fifth Street.

Back downstairs in the office, I phoned Heller and told him nothing doing. "He's extremely sensitive," I explained, "and this is an insult. As you know, he's the greatest detective that ever lived, and—do you know that?"

"I'm willing to postulate it," Heller conceded in a thin voice that tended to squeak. "Why an insult?"

"Because you want to hire Nero Wolfe—meaning me, really—to collect facts on which you can base a decision whether your suspicion about your client is justified. You might as well try to hire Stan Musial as bat boy. Mr. Wolfe doesn't sell the raw material for answers; he sells answers."

"I'm quite willing to pay him for an answer, any amount short of exorbitance, and in cash. I'm gravely concerned about this client, this situation, and my data is insufficient. I shall be delighted if with the data I get an answer from Mr. Wolfe, and—"

"And," I put in, "if his answer is that your client has committed a serious crime, as you suspect, he decides whether and when to call a cop, not you. Yes?"

"Certainly." Heller was eager to oblige. "I do not intend or desire to shield a criminal—on the contrary."

"Okay. Then it's like this. It wouldn't do any good for me to take it up with Mr. Wolfe again today because his feelings have been hurt. But tomorrow morning I have to go to our bank on Lexington Avenue not far from your place, to deposit a couple of checks, and I could drop in to see you and get the sketch. I suspect that I make this offer mostly because I'm curious to see what you look like and talk like, but I haven't enough data to apply the laws of probability to it. Frankly, I doubt if Mr. Wolfe will take this on, but we can always use money, and I'll try to sell him. Shall I come?"

"What time?"

"Say a quarter past ten."

"Come ahead. My business day begins at eleven. Take the elevator to the fifth floor. An arrow points right, to the waiting room, but go left to the door at the end of the hall, and push the button, and I'll let you in. If you're on time we'll have more than half an hour."

"I'm always on time."

That morning I was a little early. It was nine minutes past ten when I entered the lobby on Thirty-seventh Street and gave the watchdog my name.

2

I TOLD the watchdog I would try to get Nero Wolfe's autograph for him, and wrote his name in my notebook: Nils Lamm. Meanwhile the girl stood there facing us, frowning at us. She was twenty-three or -four, up to my chin, and without the deep frown her face would probably have deserved attention. Since she showed no trace of embarrassment, staring fixedly at a stranger, I saw no reason why I should, but something had to be said, so I asked her, "Do you want one?"

She cocked her head. "One what?"

"Autograph. Either Mr. Wolfe's or mine, take your pick."

"Oh. You are Archie Goodwin, aren't you? I've seen your picture too."

"Then I'm it."

"I—" She hesitated, then made up her mind. "I want to ask you something."

"Shoot."

Someone trotted in from the street, a brisk female in mink, executive type, between twenty and sixty, and the girl and I moved aside to clear the lane to the elevator. The newcomer told Nils Lamm she was seeing Leo Heller and refused to give her name, but when Lamm insisted she coughed it up: Agatha Abbey, she said, and he let her take the elevator. The girl told me she had been working all night and was tired, and we went to a bench by the fireplace. Close up, I would still have said twenty-three or -four, but someone or something had certainly been harassing her. Naturally there was a question in my mind about the night work.

She answered it. "My name's Susan Maturo, and I'm a registered nurse."

"Thanks. You know mine, and I'm a registered detective."

She nodded. "That's why I want to ask you something. If I hired Nero Wolfe to investigate a—a matter, how much would it cost?"

I raised my shoulders half an inch and let them down. "It all depends. The kind of matter, the amount of time taken, the wear and tear on his brain, the state of your finances. . . ."

I paused, letting it hang, to return a rude stare that was being aimed at us by another arrival, a thin tall bony specimen in a brown suit that badly needed pressing, with a bulging briefcase under his arm. When my gaze met his he called it off and turned and strode to the elevator, without any exchange with Nils Lamm.

I resumed to Susan Maturo. "Have you got a matter, or are you just researching?"

"Oh, I've got a matter." She set her teeth on her lip—nice teeth, and not a bad lip—and kept them that way a while, regarding me. Then she went on, "It hit me hard, and it's been getting worse in me instead of better. I began to be afraid I was going batty, and I decided to come to this Leo Heller and see what he could do, so I came this morning, but I was sitting up there in his waiting room—two people were already there, a man and a woman—and it went all through me that I was just being bitter and vindictive, and I don't think I'm really like that—I'm pretty sure I never have been—"

Apparently she needed some cooperation, so I assured her, "You don't look vindictive."

She touched my sleeve with her fingertips to thank me. "So I got up and left, and then as I was leaving the elevator I heard that man saying your name and who you are, and it popped into my head to ask you. I asked how much it would cost to have Nero Wolfe investigate, but that was premature, because what I really want is to tell him about it and get his advice about investigating."

She was dead serious and she was all worked up, so I arranged my face and voice to fit. "It's like this," I told her, "for that kind of approach to Mr. Wolfe, with no big fee in prospect, some expert preparation is required, and I'm the only expert in the field." I glanced at my wrist and saw 10:19. "I've got a date, but I can spare five minutes if you want to brief me on the essentials, and then I'll tell you how it strikes me. What was it that hit you?"

She looked at me, shot a glance at Nils Lamm, who couldn't have moved out of earshot in that lobby if he had wanted to, and came back to me. Her jaw quivered, and she clamped it tight and held it for a moment, then released it and spoke. "When I start to talk about it, it sticks in my throat and chokes me, and five minutes wouldn't be enough, and anyway I need someone old and wise like Nero Wolfe. Won't you let me see him?"

I promised to try. I told her that it would be hard to find any man in the metropolitan area more willing to help an attractive girl in distress than I was, but it would be a waste of time and effort for me to take her in to Wolfe cold, and though I was neither old nor wise she would have to give me at least a full outline before I could furnish either an opinion or help. She agreed that that was reasonable and gave me her address and phone number, and we arranged to communicate later in the day. I went and opened the door for her, and she departed.

On the way up in the elevator my watch said 10:28, so I wasn't on time after all, but we would still have half an hour before Heller's business day began. On the fifth floor a plaque on the wall facing the elevator was lettered LEO HELLER, WAITING ROOM, with an arrow pointing right, and at that end of the narrow hall a door bore the invitation, WALK IN. I turned left, toward the other end, where I pushed a button beside a door, noticing as I did so that the door was ajar a scanty inch. When my ring brought no response, and a second one, more prolonged, didn't either, I shoved the door open, crossed the sill, and called Heller's name. No reply. There was no one in sight.

Thinking that he had probably stepped into the waiting room and would soon return, I glanced around to see what the lair of a probability wizard looked like, and was impressed by some outstanding features. The door, of metal, was a good three inches thick, either for security or for soundproofing, or maybe both. If there were any windows they were behind the heavy draperies; the artificial light came indirectly from channels in the walls just beneath the ceiling. The air was conditioned. There were locks on all the units of a vast assembly of filing cabinets that took up all the rear wall. The floor, with no rugs, was tiled with some velvety material on which a footfall was barely audible.

The thick door was for soundproofing. I had closed it, nearly, on entering, and the silence was complete. Not a sound of the city could be heard, though the clang and clatter of Lexington Avenue was nearby one way and Third Avenue the other.

I crossed for a look at the desk, but there was nothing remarkable about it except that it was twice the usual size. Among other items it held a rack of books with titles that were not tempting, an abacus of ivory or a good imitation, and a stack of legal-size working pads. Stray sheets of paper were scattered, and a single pad had on its top sheet some scribbled formulas that looked like doodles by Einstein. Also a jar of sharpened lead pencils had been overturned, and some of them were in a sort of a pattern near the edge of the desk.

I had been in there ten minutes, and no Heller; and when, at eleven o'clock by schedule, Wolfe came down to the office from his morning session with the orchids, it was desirable that I should be present. So I went, leaving the door ajar as I had found it, walked down the hall to the door of the waiting room at the other end, and entered.

This room was neither air-conditioned nor soundproofed. Someone had opened a window a couple of inches, and the din was jangling in. Five people were here and there on chairs; three of them I had seen before: the big guy in the dark blue topcoat and homburg, the brisk female in mink who called herself Agatha Abbey, and the tall thin specimen with a briefcase. Neither of the other two was Leo Heller. One was a swarthy little article, slick and sly, with his hair pasted to his scalp, and the other was a big blob of an overfed matron with a spare chin.

I addressed the gathering. "Has Mr. Heller been in here?"

A couple of them shook their heads, and the swarthy article said hoarsely, "Not visible till eleven o'clock, and you take your turn."

I thanked him, left, and went back to the other room. Still no Heller. I didn't bother to call his name again, since even if it had flushed him I would have had to leave immediately. So I departed. Down in the lobby I again told Nils Lamm I'd see what I could do about an autograph. Outside, deciding there wasn't time to walk it, I flagged a taxi. Home again, I hadn't been in the office more than twenty seconds when the sound came of Wolfe's elevator descending.

That was a funny thing. I'm strong on hunches, and I've had some beauts during the years I've been with Wolfe, but that day there wasn't the slightest glimmer of something impending. You might think that was an ideal spot for a hunch, but no, not a sign of a tickle. I was absolutely blithe as I asked Wolfe how the anti-thrips campaign was doing, and later, after lunch, as I dialed the number Susan Maturo had given me, though I admit I was a little dampened when I got no answer, since I had the idea of finding out someday how she would look with the frown gone.

But still later, shortly after six o'clock, I went to answer the doorbell and through the one-way glass panel saw Inspector Cramer of Manhattan Homicide there on the stoop. There was an instant reaction in the lower third of my spine, but I claim no credit for a hunch, since after all a homicide inspector does not go around ringing doorbells to sell tickets to the Policemen's Annual Ball.

I let him in and took him to the office, where Wolfe was drinking beer and scowling at three United States senators on television.

3

CRAMER, BULKY and burly, with a big red face and sharp and skeptical gray eyes, sat in the red leather chair near the end of Wolfe's desk. He had declined an offer of beer, the TV had been turned off, and the lights had been turned on.

Cramer spoke. "I dropped in on my way down, and I haven't got long." He was gruff, which was normal. "I'd appreciate some quick information. What are you doing for Leo Heller?"

"Nothing." Wolfe was brusque, which was also normal.

"You're not working for him?"

"No."

"Then why did Goodwin go to see him this morning?"

"He didn't."

"Hold it," I put in. "I went on my own, just exploring. Mr. Wolfe didn't know I was going, and this is the first he's heard of it."

There were two simultaneous looks of exasperation—Cramer's at Wolfe, and Wolfe's at me. Cramer backed his up with words. "For God's sake. This is the rawest one you ever tried to pull! Been rehearsing it all afternoon?"

Wolfe let me go temporarily, to cope with Cramer. "Pfui. Suppose we have. Justify your marching into my house to demand an accounting of Mr. Goodwin's movements. What if he did call on Mr. Heller? Has Mr. Heller been found dead?"

"Yes."

"Indeed." Wolfe's brows went up a little. "Violence?"

"Murdered. Shot through the heart."

"On his premises?"

"Yeah. I'd like to hear from Goodwin."

Wolfe's eyes darted to me. "Did you kill Mr. Heller, Archie?"

"No, sir."

"Then oblige Mr. Cramer, please. He's in a hurry."

I obliged. First telling about the phone call the day before, and

Wolfe's refusal to take on anything for Heller, and my calling Heller back, I then reported on my morning visit at Thirty-seventh Street, supplying all details, except that I soft-pedaled Susan Maturo's state of harassment, putting it merely that she asked me to arrange for her to see Wolfe and didn't tell me what about. When I had finished, Cramer had a few questions. Among them:

"So you didn't see Heller at all?"

"Nope."

He grunted. "I know only too well how nosy you are, Goodwin. There were three doors in the walls of that room besides the one you entered by. You didn't open any of them?"

"Nope."

"One of them is the door to the closet in which Heller's body was found by a caller, a friend, at three o'clock this afternoon. The medical examiner says that the sausage and griddle cakes he ate for breakfast at nine-thirty hadn't been in him more than an hour when he died, so it's practically certain that the body was in the closet while you were there in the room. As nosy as you are, you're telling me that you didn't open the door and see the body?"

"Yep. I apologize. Next time I'll open every damn door in sight."

"A gun had been fired. You didn't smell it?"

"No. Air-conditioned."

"You didn't look through the desk drawers?"

"No. I apologize again."

"We did." Cramer took something from his breast pocket. "In one drawer we found this envelope, sealed. On it was written in pencil, in Heller's hand, 'Mr. Nero Wolfe.' In it were five one-hundred-dollar bills."

"I'm sorry I missed that," I said with feeling.

Wolfe stirred. "I assume that has been examined for fingerprints."

"Certainly."

"May I see it, please?"

Wolfe extended a hand. Cramer hesitated a moment, then tossed it across the desk, and Wolfe picked it up. He took out the bills, crisp new ones, counted them, and looked inside.

"This was sealed," he observed dryly, "with my name on it, and you opened it."

"We sure did." Cramer came forward in his chair with a hand stretched. "Let me have it."

It was a demand, not a request, and Wolfe reacted impulsively. If he had taken a second to think he would have realized that if he claimed it he would have to earn it, or at least pretend to, but Cramer's tone of voice was the kind of provocation he would not take. He returned the bills to the envelope and put it in his pocket.

"It's mine," he stated.

"It's evidence," Cramer growled, "and I want it."

Wolfe shook his head. "Evidence of what? As an officer of the law, you should be acquainted with it." He tapped his pocket with a fingertip. "My property. Connect it, or connect me, with a crime."

Cramer was controlling himself, which wasn't easy under the circumstances. "I might have known," he said bitterly. "You want to be connected with a crime? Okay. I don't know how many times I've sat in this chair and listened to you making assumptions. I'm not saying you never make good on them, I just say you're strong on assumptions. Now I've got some of my own to offer, but first here are a few facts. In that building on Thirty-seventh Street, Heller lived on the fourth floor and worked on the fifth, the top floor. At five minutes to ten this morning, on good evidence, he left his living quarters to go up to his office. Goodwin says he entered that office at ten-twenty-eight, so if the body was in the closet when Goodwin was there—and it almost certainly was—Heller was killed between nine-fifty-five and ten-twenty-eight. We can't find anyone who heard the shot, and the way that room is proofed we probably never will. We've tested it."

Cramer squeezed his eyes shut and opened them again, a trick of his. "Very well. From the doorman we've got a list of everyone who entered the place during that period, and most of them have been collected, and we're getting the others. There were six of them. The nurse, Susan Maturo, left before Goodwin went up, and the other five left later, at intervals, when they got tired waiting for Heller to show up—according to them. As it stands now, and I don't see what could change it, one of them killed Heller. Any one of them, on leaving the elevator at the fifth floor, could have gone to Heller's office and shot him, and then to the waiting room."

Wolfe muttered, "Putting the body in the closet?"

"Of course, to postpone its discovery. If someone happened to see the murderer leaving the office, he had to be able to say he had gone in to look for Heller and Heller wasn't there, and he couldn't if the body was there in sight. There are marks on the floor where the body—and Heller was a featherweight—was dragged to the closet. In leaving, he left the door ajar, to make it more plausible, if someone saw him, that he had found it that way. Also—"

"Fallacy."

"I'll tell him you said so the first chance I get. Also, of course, he couldn't leave the building. Knowing that Heller started to see callers at eleven o'clock, those people had all come early so as not to have a long wait. Including the murderer. He had to go to the waiting room and wait with the others. One of them did leave, the nurse, and she made a point of telling Goodwin why she was going, and it's up to her to make it stick under questioning."

"You were going to connect me with a crime."

"Right." Cramer was positive. "First one more fact. The gun was in the closet with the body, under it on the floor. It's an old Gustein flug, a nasty little short-nose, and there's not a chance in a thousand of tracing it, though we're trying. Now here are my assumptions. The murderer went armed to kill, pushed the button at the door of Heller's office, and was admitted. Since Heller went to his desk and sat, he couldn't—"

"Established?"

"Yes. He couldn't have been in fear of a mortal attack. But after some conversation, which couldn't have been more than a few minutes on account of the timetable as verified, he was not only in fear, he felt that death was upon him, and in that super-soundproofed room he was helpless. The gun had been drawn and was aimed at him. He knew it was all up. He talked, trying to stall, not because he had any hope of living, but because he wanted to leave a message to be read after he was dead. Shaking with nervousness, with a trembling hand, perhaps a pleading one, he upset the jar of pencils on his desk, and then he nervously fumbled with them, moving them around on the desk in front of him, all the while talking. Then the gun went off, and he wasn't nervous any more. The murderer circled the desk, made sure his victim was dead, and dragged the body to the closet. It didn't occur to him that the scattered pencils had been arranged to convey a message—if it had, one sweep of a hand would have taken care of it. It was desperately urgent for him to get out of there and into the waiting room."

Cramer stood up. "If you'll let me have eight pencils I'll show you how they were."

Wolfe opened his desk drawer, but I got there first with a handful taken from my tray. Cramer moved around to Wolfe's side, and Wolfe, making a face, moved his chair to make room.

"I'm in Heller's place at his desk," Cramer said, "and I'm putting them as he did from where he sat." After getting the eight pencils arranged to his satisfaction, he stepped aside. "There it is, take a look."

Wolfe inspected it from his side, and I from mine. It was like this from Wolfe's side:

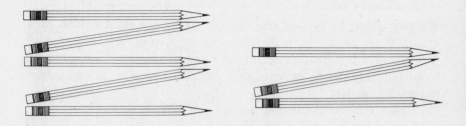

"You say," Wolfe inquired, "that was a message?"

"Yes," Cramer asserted. "It has to be."

"By mandate? Yours?"

"Blah. You know damn well there's not one chance in a million those pencils took that pattern by accident, Goodwin, you saw them. Were they like that?"

"Approximately," I conceded. "I didn't know there was a corpse in the closet at the time, so I wasn't as interested in it as you were. But since you ask me, the pencil points were not all in the same direction, and an eraser from one of them was there in the middle." I put a fingertip on the spot. "Right there."

"Fix it as you saw it."

I went around and joined them at Wolfe's side of the desk and did as requested, removing an eraser from one of the pencils and placing it as I had indicated. Then it was like this:

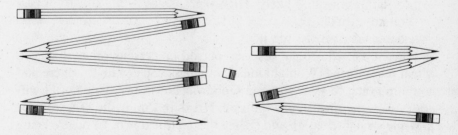

"Of course," I said, "you had the photographer shoot it. I don't say that's exact, but they were pointing in different directions, and the eraser was there."

"Didn't you realize it was a message?"

"Nuts. Someday you'll set a trap that'll catch me, and I'll snarl. Sure,

I thought it was Heller's way of telling me he had gone to the bathroom and would be back in eight minutes. Eight pencils, see? Pretty clever. Isn't that how you read it?"

"It is not." Cramer was emphatic. "I think Heller turned it sideways to make it less likely that his attacker would see what it was. Move around here, please. Both of you. Look at it from here."

Wolfe and I joined him at the left end of the desk and looked as requested. One glance was enough. You can see what we saw by turning the page a quarter-turn counter-clockwise.

Cramer spoke. "Could you ask for a plainer NW?"

"I could," I objected. "Why the extra pencil on the left of the W?"

"He put it there deliberately, for camouflage, to make it less obvious, or it rolled there accidentally, I don't care which. It is unmistakably NW." He focused on Wolfe. "I promised to connect you with a crime."

Wolfe, back in his chair, interlaced his fingers. "You're not serious."

"The hell I'm not." Cramer returned to the red leather chair and sat. "That's why I came here, and came alone. You deny you sent Goodwin there, but I don't believe you. He admits he was in Heller's office ten minutes, because he has to, since the doorman saw him go up and five people saw him enter the waiting room. In a drawer of Heller's desk is an envelope addressed to you, containing five hundred dollars in cash. But the clincher is that message. Heller, seated at his desk, sure that he is going to be killed in a matter of seconds, uses those seconds to leave a message. Can there be any question what the message was about? Not for me. It was about the person or persons responsible for his death. I am assuming that its purpose was to identify that person or persons. Do you reject that assumption?"

"No. I think it quite likely. Highly probable."

"You admit it?"

"I don't admit it, I state it."

"Then I ask you to suggest any person or persons other than you whom the initials NW might identify. Unless you can do that here and now I'm going to take you and Goodwin downtown as material witnesses. I've got men in cars outside. If I didn't do it the DA would."

Wolfe straightened up and sighed deep, clear down. "You are being uncommonly obnoxious, Mr. Cramer." He got to his feet. "Excuse me a moment." Detouring around Cramer's feet, he crossed to the other side of the room, to the bookshelves back of the big globe, reached up to a high one, took a book down, and opened it. He was too far away for me to see what it was. He turned first to the back of the book, where the index would be if it had one, and then to a page near the middle of it. He went on to another page, and another, while Cramer, containing his emotions under pressure, got a cigar from a pocket, stuck it in his mouth and sank his teeth in it. He never lit one.

Finally Wolfe returned to his desk, opened a drawer and put the book in it, and closed and locked the drawer. Cramer was speaking. "I'm not being fantastic. You didn't kill him; you weren't there. I'm not even assuming Goodwin killed him, though he could have. I'm saying that Heller left a message that would give a lead to the killer, and the message says NW, and that stands for Nero Wolfe, and therefore you know something, and I want to know what. I want a yes or no to this. Do you or do you not know something that indicates, or may indicate, who murdered Leo Heller?"

Wolfe, settled in his chair again, nodded. "Yes."

"Ah. You do. What?"

"The message he left."

"The message only says NW. Go on from there."

"I need more information. I need to know—are the pencils still there on his desk as you found them?"

"Yes. They haven't been disturbed."

"You have a man there, of course. Get him on the phone and let me talk to him. You will hear us."

Cramer hesitated, not liking it, then decided he might as well string along, came to my desk, dialed a number, got his man, and told him Wolfe would speak to him. Wolfe took it with his phone while Cramer stayed at mine.

Wolfe was courteous but crisp. "I understand those pencils are there on the desk as they were found, that all but one of them have erasers in their ends, and that an eraser is there on the desk, between the two groups of pencils. Is that correct?"

"Right." The dick sounded bored. I was getting it from the phone on the table over by the globe.

"Take the eraser and insert it in the end of the pencil that hasn't one in it. I want to know if the eraser was loose enough to slip out accidentally."

"Inspector, are you on? You said not to disturb—"

"Go ahead," Cramer growled. "I'm right here."

"Yes, sir. Hold it, please."

There was a long wait, and then he was back on. "The eraser couldn't have slipped out accidentaly. Part of it is still clamped in the end of the pencil. It had to be pulled out, torn apart, and the torn surfaces are bright and fresh. I can pull one out of another pencil and tell you how much force it takes."

"No, thank you, that's all I need. But to make certain, and for the record, I suggest that you send the pencil and eraser to the laboratory to check that the torn surfaces fit."

"Do I do that, Inspector?"

"Yeah, you might as well. Mark them properly."

"Yes, sir."

Cramer returned to the red leather chair, and I went to mine. He tilted the cigar upward from the corner of his mouth and demanded, "So what?"

"You know quite well what," Wolfe declared. "The eraser was yanked out and placed purposely, and was a part of the message. No doubt as a dot after the N to show it was an initial? And he was interrupted permanently before he could put one after the W?"

"Sarcasm don't change it any. It's still NW."

"No. It isn't. It never was."

"For me and the district attorney it is. I guess we'd better get on down to his office."

Wolfe upturned a palm. "There you are. You're not hare-brained, but you are pigheaded. I warn you, sir, that if you proceed on the assumption that Mr. Heller's message says NW, you are doomed; the best you can expect is to be tagged a jackass."

"I suppose you know what it does say."

"Yes."

"You do?"

"Yes."

"I'm waiting."

"You'll continue to wait. If I thought I could earn this money"— Wolfe tapped his pocket—"by deciphering that message for you, that would be simple, but in your present state of mind you would only think I was contriving a humbug."

"Try me."

"No, sir." Wolfe half closed his eyes. "An alternative. You can go on as you have started and see where it lands you, understanding that Mr. Goodwin and I will persistently deny any knowledge of the affair or those concerned in it except what has been given you, and I'll pursue my own course; or you can bring the murderer here and let me at him—with you present."

"I'll be glad to. Name him."

"When I find him. I need all six of them, to learn which one Heller's message identifies. Since I can translate the message and you can't, you need me more than I need you, but you can save me much time and trouble and expense."

Cramer's level gaze had no trace whatever of affection or sympathy. "If you can translate that message and refuse to disclose it, you're withholding evidence."

"Nonsense. A conjecture is not evidence. Heaven knows your conjecture that it says NW isn't. Nor is mine, but it should lead to some if I do the leading." Wolfe flung a hand impatiently, and his voice rose. "Confound it, am I suggesting a gambol for my refreshment? Do you think I welcome an invasion of my premises by platoons of policemen herding a drove of scared and suspected citizens?"

"No. I know damn well you don't." Cramer took the cigar from his mouth and regarded it as if trying to decide exactly what it was. That accomplished, he glanced at Wolfe and then looked at me, by no means as a bosom friend.

"I'll use the phone," he said, and got up and came to my desk.

4

WITH THREE of the six scared citizens, it was a good thing that Wolfe didn't have to start from scratch. They had been absolutely determined not to tell why they had gone to see Leo Heller, and, as we learned from the transcripts of interviews and copies of statements they had signed, the cops had had a time dragging it out of them.

By the time the first one was brought to us in the office, a little after eight o'clock, Wolfe had sort of resigned himself to personal misery and was bravely facing it. Not only had he had to devour his dinner in one-fourth the usual time; also he had been compelled to break one of his strictest rules and read documents while eating—and all that in the company of Inspector Cramer, who had accepted an invitation to have a bite. Of course Cramer returned to the office with us and called in, from the assemblage in the front room, a police stenographer, who settled himself in a chair at the end of my desk. Sergeant Purley Stebbins, who once in a spasm of generosity admitted that he couldn't prove I was a hoodlum, after bringing the citizen in and seating him facing Wolfe and Cramer, took a chair against the wall.

The citizen, whose name as furnished by the documents was John R.

Winslow, was the big guy in a dark blue topcoat and homburg who had stuck his head out of the elevator for a look at Archie Goodwin. He now looked unhappy and badly wilted, and was one of the three who had tried to refuse to tell what he had gone to Heller for; and considering what it was I couldn't blame him much.

He started in complaining. "I think—I think this is unconstitutional. The police have forced me to tell about my private affairs, and maybe that couldn't be helped, but Nero Wolfe is a private detective, and I don't have to submit to questioning by him."

"I'm here," Cramer said. "I can repeat Wolfe's questions if you insist, but it will take more time."

"Suppose," Wolfe suggested, "we start and see how it goes. I've read your statement, Mr. Winslow, and I—"

"You had no right to! They had no right to let you! They promised me it would be confidential unless it had to be used as evidence!"

"Please, Mr. Winslow, don't bounce up like that. A hysterical woman is bad enough, but a hysterical man is insufferable. I assure you I am as discreet as any policeman. According to your statement, today was your third visit to Mr. Heller's office. You were trying to supply him with enough information for him to devise a formula for determining how much longer your aunt will live. You expect to inherit a considerable fortune from her, and you wanted to make plans intelligently based on reasonable expectations. So you say, but reports are being received which indicate that you are deeply in debt and are hard pressed. Do you deny that?"

"No." Winslow's jaw worked. "I don't deny it."

"Are your debts, or any part of them, connected with any violation of the law? Any criminal act?"

"No!"

"Granted that Mr. Heller could furnish a valid calculation on your aunt's life, how would that help you any?"

Winslow looked at Cramer and met only a stony stare. He went back to Wolfe. "I was negotiating to borrow a very large sum against my—expectations. There was to be a certain percentage added for each month that passed before repayment was made, and I had to know what my chances were. It was a question of probabilities, and I went to an expert."

"What data had you given Heller as a basis for his calculations?"

"My God, I couldn't—all kinds of things."

"For instance?" Wolfe insisted.

Winslow looked at the police stenographer and me, but we couldn't help. He returned to Wolfe. "Hundreds of things. My aunt's age, her habits—eating, sleeping, everything I could—her health as far as I knew about it, the ages of her parents and grandparents when they died, her weight and build—I gave him photographs—her activities and interests, her temperament, her attitude to doctors, her politics—"

"Politics?"

"Yes. Heller said her pleasure or pain at the election of Eisenhower was a longevity factor."

Wolfe grunted. "The claptrap of the charlatan. Did he also consider as a longevity factor the possibility that you might intervene by dispatching your aunt?"

That struck Winslow as funny. He did not guffaw, but he tittered, and it did not suit his build. Wolfe insisted, "Did he?"

"I really don't know, really." Winslow tittered again.

"From whom did your aunt inherit her fortune?"

"Her husband. My Uncle Norton."

"When did he die?"

"Six years ago. In nineteen forty-seven."

"How? Of what?"

"He was shot accidentally while hunting. Hunting deer."

"Were you present?"

"Not present, no. I was more than a mile away at the time."

"Did you get a legacy from him?"

"No." Some emotion was mobilizing Winslow's blood and turning his face pink. "He sneered at me. He left me six cents in his will. He didn't like me."

Wolfe turned to speak to Cramer, but the inspector forestalled him. "Two men are already on it. The shooting accident was up in Maine."

"I would like to say how I feel about this," Winslow told them. "I mean the questions that have been asked me about my uncle's death. I regard them as a compliment. They assume that I might have been capable of shooting my uncle, and that is a very high compliment, and you say there are two men on it, so it is being investigated, and that is a compliment too. My aunt would be amused at the idea of my having killed Uncle Norton, and she would be amused at the idea that I might try to kill her. I wouldn't mind a bit having her know about that, but if she finds out what I went to Leo Heller for—God help me." He gestured in appeal. "I was promised, absolutely promised."

"We disclose people's private affairs," Cramer rumbled, "only when it is unavoidable."

Wolfe was pouring beer. When the foam was at the rim he put the bottle down and resumed. "I have promised nothing, Mr. Winslow, but I have no time for tattle. Here's a suggestion. You're in this pickle only because of your association with Mr. Heller, and the question is, was there anything in that association to justify this badgering? Suppose you tell us. Start at the beginning, and recall as well as you can every word that passed between you. Go right through it. I'll interrupt as little as possible."

"You've already seen it," Cramer objected. "The transcript, the statement—what the hell, have you got a lead or haven't you?"

Wolfe nodded. "We have a night for it," he said, not happily. "Mr. Winslow doesn't know what the lead is, and it's Greek to you." He went to Winslow. "Go ahead, sir. Everything that you said to Mr. Heller, and everything he said to you."

It took more than an hour, including interruptions. The interruptions came from various city employees who were scattered around the house —the front room, the dining room, and three upstairs bedrooms— working on other scared citizens, and from the telephone. Two of the phone calls were from homicide dicks who were trying to locate a citizen who had got mislaid—one named Henrietta Tillotson, Mrs. Albert Tillotson, the overfed matron whom I had seen in Heller's waiting room with the others. There were also calls from the police commissioner and the DA's office and other interested parties.

When Purley Stebbins got up to escort Winslow from the room, Wolfe's lead was still apparently Greek to Cramer, as it was to me. As the door closed behind them Cramer spoke emphatically. "I think it's a goddam farce. I think that message was NW, meaning you, and you're stalling for some kind of a play."

"And if so?" Wolfe was testy. "Why are you tolerating this? Because if the message did mean me I'm the crux, and your only alternative is to cart me downtown, and that would merely make me mum, and you know it." He drank beer and put the glass down. "However, maybe we can expedite it without too great a risk. Tell your men who are now interviewing these people to be alert for something connected with the figure six. They must give no hint of it, they must themselves not mention it, but if the figure six appears in any segment of the interview they should concentrate on that segment until it is exhausted. They all know, I presume, of Heller's suspicion that one of his clients had committed a serious crime?"

"They know that Goodwin says so. What's this about six?"

Wolfe shook his head. "That will have to do. Even that may be foolhardy, since they're your men, not mine."

"Winslow's uncle died six years ago and left him six cents."

"I'm quite aware of it. You say that is being investigated. Do you want Mr. Goodwin to pass this word?"

Cramer said no thanks, he would, and left the room.

By the time he returned, citizen number two had been brought in by Stebbins, introduced to Wolfe, and seated where Winslow had been. She was Susan Maturo. She looked fully as harassed as she had that morning, but I wouldn't say much more so. There was now, of course, a new aspect to the matter: did she look harassed or guilty? She was undeniably attractive, but so had Maude Vail been, and she had poisoned two husbands. There was the consideration that if Heller had been killed by the client whom he suspected of having committed a crime, it must have been a client he had seen previously at least once, or how could he have got grounds for a suspicion; and, according to Susan Maturo, she had never called on Heller before and had never seen him. But actually that eliminated neither her nor Agatha Abbey, who also claimed that that morning had been her first visit. It was known that Heller had sometimes made engagements by telephone to meet prospective clients elsewhere, and Miss Maturo and Miss Abbey might well have been among that number.

Opening up on her, Wolfe was not too belligerent, probably because she had accepted an offer of beer and, after drinking some, had licked her lips. It pleases him when people share his joys.

"You are aware, Miss Maturo," he told her, "that you are in a class by yourself. The evidence indicates that Mr. Heller was killed by one of the six people who entered that building this morning to call on him, and you are the only one of the six who departed before eleven o'clock, Mr. Heller's appointment hour. Your explanation of your departure as given in your statement is close to incoherent. Can't you improve on it?"

She looked at me. I did not throw her a kiss, but neither did I glower. "I've reported what you told me," I assured her, "exactly as you said it."

She nodded at me vaguely and turned to Wolfe. "Do I have to go through it again?"

"You will probably," Wolfe advised her, "have to go through it again a dozen times. Why did you leave?"

She gulped, started to speak, found no sound was coming out, and had to start over again. "You know about the explosion and fire at the Montrose Hospital a month ago?"

"Certainly. I read newspapers."

"You know that three hundred and two people died there that night. I was there working, in Ward G on the sixth floor. In addition to those who died, many were injured, but I went all through it and I didn't get a scratch or any burn. My dearest friend was killed, burned to death trying to save the patients, and another dear friend is crippled for life, and a young doctor I was engaged to marry—he was killed in the explosion, and others I knew. I don't know how I came out of it without a mark, because I'm sure I tried to help. I'm positively sure of that, but I did, and that's one trouble, I guess, because I couldn't be glad about it—how could I?"

She seemed to expect an answer, so Wolfe muttered, "No. Not to be expected."

"I am not," she said, "the kind of person who hates people."

She stopped, so Wolfe said, "No?"

"No, I'm not. I never have been. But I began to hate the man—or if it was a woman, I don't care which—that put the bomb there and did it. I can't say I went out of my mind because I don't think I did, but that's how I felt. After two weeks I tried to go back to work at another hospital, but I couldn't. I read all there was in the newspapers, hoping they would catch him, and I couldn't think of anything else, and I dreamed about it every night, and I went to the police and wanted to help, but of course they had already questioned me and I had told everything I knew. The days went by, and it looked as if they never would catch him, and I wanted to do something, and I had read about that Leo Heller, and I decided to go to him and get him to do it."

Wolfe made a noise and her head jerked up. "I said I hated him!"

Wolfe nodded. "So you did. Go on."

"And I went, that's all. I had some money saved, and I could borrow some, to pay him. But while I was sitting there in the waiting room, with that man and woman there, I suddenly thought I must be crazy, I must have got so bitter and vindictive I didn't realize what I was doing, and I wanted to think about it, and I got up and went. Going down in the elevator I felt as if a crisis had passed—that's a feeling a nurse often has about other people—and then as I left the elevator I heard the names Archie Goodwin and Nero Wolfe, and the idea came to me, why not get them to find him? So I spoke to Mr. Goodwin, and there I was again, but I couldn't make myself tell him about it, so I just told him I wanted to see Nero Wolfe to ask his advice, and he said he would try to arrange it, and he would phone me or I could phone him."

She fluttered a hand. "That's how it was."

Wolfe regarded her. "It's not incoherent, but neither is it sapient. Do you consider yourself an intelligent woman?"

"Why—yes. Enough to get along. I'm a good nurse, and a good nurse has to be intelligent."

"Yet you thought that quack could expose the man who planted the bomb in the hospital by his hocus-pocus?"

"I thought he did it scientifically. I knew he had a great reputation, just as you have."

"Good heavens." Wolfe opened his eyes wide at her. "It is indeed a bubble, as Jacques said. What were you going to ask my advice about?"

"Whether you thought there was any chance—whether you thought the police were going to find him."

Wolfe's eyes were back to normal, half shut again. "This performance I'm engaged in, Miss Maturo—this inquisition of a person involved by circumstance in a murder—is a hubbub in a jungle, at least in its preliminary stage. Blind, I grope, and proceed by feel. You say you never saw Mr. Heller, but you can't prove it. I am free to assume that you had seen him, not at his office, and talked with him; that you were convinced, no matter how, that he had planted the bomb in the hospital and caused the holocaust; and that, moved by an obsessive rancor, you went to his place and killed him. One ad—"

She was gawking. "Why on earth would I think he had planted the bomb?"

"I have no idea. As I said, I'm groping. One advantage of that assumption would be that you have confessed to a hatred so overpowering that surely it might have impelled you to kill if and when you identified its object. It is Mr. Cramer, not I, who is deploying the hosts of justice in this enterprise, but no doubt two or three men are calling on your friends and acquaintances to learn if you have ever hinted a suspicion of Leo Heller in connection with the hospital disaster. Also they are probably asking whether you had any grudge against the hospital that might have provoked you to plant the bomb yourself."

"My God!" A muscle at the side of her neck was twitching. "Me? Is that what it's like?"

"It is indeed. That wouldn't be incongruous. Your proclaimed abhorrence of the perpetrator could be simply the screeching of your remorse."

"Well, it isn't." Suddenly she was out of her chair, and a bound took her to Wolfe's desk, and her palms did a tattoo on the desk as she leaned forward at him. "Don't you dare say a thing like that! The six people

I cared for most in the world—they all died that night! How would you feel?" More tattoo. "How would anybody feel?"

I was up and at her elbow, but no bodily discipline was required. She straightened and for a moment stood trembling all over, then got her control back and went to her chair and sat. "I'm sorry," she said in a tight little voice.

"You should be," Wolfe said grimly. A woman cutting loose is always too much for him. "Pounding the top of my desk settles nothing. What were the names of the six people you cared for most in the world, who died?"

She told him, and he wanted to know more about them. I was beginning to suspect that actually he had no more of a lead than I did, that he had given Cramer a runaround to jostle him loose from the NW he had fixed on, and that, having impulsively impounded the five hundred bucks, he had decided to spend the night trying to earn it. The line he now took with Susan Maturo bore me out. It was merely the old grab-bag game—keep her talking, about anything and anybody, in the hope that she would spill something that would faintly resemble a straw. I had known Wolfe, when the pickings had been extremely slim, to play that game for hours on end.

He was still at it with Susan Maturo when an individual entered with a message for Cramer which he delivered in a whisper. Cramer got up and started for the door, then thought better of it and turned.

"You might as well be in on this," he told Wolfe. "They've got Mrs. Tillotson, and she's here."

That was a break for Susan Maturo, since Wolfe might have kept her going another hour or so, though I suppose all it got her was an escort to some lieutenant or sergeant in another room, who started at her all over again. As she arose to go she favored me with a glance. It looked as if she intended it for a smile to show there were no hard feelings, but if so it was the poorest excuse for a smile I had ever seen. If it hadn't been unprofessional I would have gone and given her a pat on the shoulder.

The newcomer who was ushered in was not Mrs. Tillotson but an officer of the law, not in uniform. He was one of the newer acquisitions on Homicide, and I had never seen him before, but I admired his manly stride as he approached and his snappy stance when he halted and faced Cramer, waiting to be spoken to.

"Who did you leave over there?" Cramer asked him.

"Murphy, sir. Timothy Murphy."

"Okay. You tell it. Hold it." Cramer turned to Wolfe. "This man's name is Roca. He was on post at Heller's place. It was him you asked about the pencils and the eraser. Go on, Roca."

"Yes, sir. The doorman in the lobby phoned up that there was a woman down there that wanted to come up, and I told him to let her come. I thought that was compatible."

"You did."

"Yes, sir."

"Then go ahead."

"She came up in the elevator. She wouldn't tell me her name. She asked me questions about how much longer would I be there and did I expect anybody else to come, and so on. We bantered back and forth, my objective being to find out who she was, and then she came right out with it. She took a roll of bills from her bag. She offered me three hundred dollars, and then four hundred, and finally five hundred, if I would unlock the cabinets in Heller's office and let her be in there alone for an hour. That put me in a quandary."

"It did."

"Yes, sir."

"How did you get out?"

"If I had had keys to the cabinets I would have accepted her offer. I would have unlocked them and left her in there. When she was ready to go I would have arrested her and taken her to be searched, and we would have known what she had taken from the cabinet. That would have broken the case. But I had no keys to the cabinets."

"Uh-huh. If you had had keys and had unlocked the cabinets and left her in there, and she had taken something from a cabinet and burned it up, you would have collected the ashes and sent them to the laboratory for examination by modern scientific methods."

Roca swallowed. "I admit I didn't think about burning. But if I had had keys I would have thought harder."

"I bet you would. Did you take her money for evidence?"

"No, sir. I thought that might be instigation. I took her into custody. I phoned in. When a relief came, I brought her here to you. I am staying here to face her."

"You've faced her enough for tonight. Plenty. We'll have a talk later. Go and tell Burger to bring her in."

ALTHOUGH MY stay in Heller's waiting room that morning had been brief, I have long been trained to see what I look at and to remember what I see, and I would hardly have recognized Mrs. Albert Tillotson. She had lost five pounds and gained twice that many wrinkles, and the contrast between her lipstick and her drained-out skin made her look more like a woman-hater's pin-up than an overfed matron.

"I wish to speak with you privately," she told Inspector Cramer.

She was one of those. Her husband was president of something, and therefore it was absurd to suppose that she was not to expect privileges. It took Cramer a good five minutes to get it into her head that she was just one of the girls, and it was such a shock that she had to take time out to decide how to react to it.

She decided on a barefaced lie. She demanded to know if the man who had brought her there was a member of the police force, and Cramer replied that he was.

"Well," she declared, "he shouldn't be. You may know that late this afternoon a police officer called at my residence to see me. He told me that Leo Heller had been killed, murdered, and wanted to know for what purpose I had gone to his office this morning. Naturally I didn't want to be involved in an ugly thing like that, so I told him I hadn't gone to see Leo Heller, but he convinced me that that wouldn't do, so I said I had gone to see him, but on an intimate personal matter that I wouldn't tell—Is that man putting down what I'm saying?"

"Yes. That's his job."

"I wouldn't want it. Nor yours either. The officer insisted that I must tell why I had gone to see that Heller, and I refused, and he insisted, and I refused. When he said he would have to take me to the district attorney's office, under arrest if necessary, and I saw that he meant it, I told him. I told him that my husband and I have been having some difficulty with our son, especially his schooling, and I went to Heller to ask what college would be best for him. I answered the officer's questions, within reason, and finally he left. Perhaps you knew all this."

Cramer nodded. "Yes."

"Well, after the officer had gone I began to worry, and I went to see a friend and ask her advice. The trouble was that I had given Heller many details about my son, some of them very intimate and confidential, and since he had been murdered the police would probably go through all his papers, and those details were private and I wanted to keep them private. I knew that Heller had made all his notes in a personal shorthand that no one else could read—anyhow he had said so, but I couldn't be sure, and it was very important. After I had discussed it with my friend a long time, for hours, I decided to go to Heller's place and ask whoever was in charge to let me have any papers relating to my family affairs, since they were not connected with the murder."

"I see," Cramer assured her.

"And that's what I did. And the officer there pretended to listen to me, he pretended to be agreeing with me, and then suddenly he arrested me for trying to bribe an officer; and when I indignantly denied it, as of course I did, and started to leave, he detained me by force, and he actually was going to put handcuffs on me! So I came with him, and here I am, and I hope you realize I have a complaint to make and I am making it!"

Cramer was eying her. "Did you try to bribe him?"

"No, I didn't!"

"You didn't offer him money?"

"No!"

Purley Stebbins permitted a low sound, half growl and half snort, to escape him. Cramer, ignoring that impertinence from a subordinate, took a deep breath and let it out again.

"Shall I take it?" Wolfe inquired.

"No, thank you," Cramer said acidly. He was keeping his eyes at Mrs. Tillotson. "You're making a mistake, madam," he told her. "All these lies don't do you any good. They just make it harder for you. Try telling the truth for a change."

She drew herself up, but it wasn't very impressive because she was pretty well fagged after her hard day. "You're calling me a liar," she accused Cramer, "and in front of witnesses." She pointed a finger at the police stenographer. "You get that down just the way he said it!"

"He will," Cramer assured her. "Look, Mrs. Tillotson. You admit you lied about going to see Heller until you saw it wouldn't work, when you realized that the doorman would swear that you were there not only this morning but also previously. Now about your trying to bribe an officer. That's a felony. If we charge you with it, and you go to trial, I can't say who the jury will believe, you or the officer, but I know who I believe. I believe him, and you're lying about it."

"Get him in here," she challenged. "I want to face him."

"He wants to face you too, but that wouldn't help any. I'm satisfied that you're lying, and also that you're lying about what you wanted to get from Heller's files. He made his notes in a private code that it will take a squad of experts to decipher, and you knew that, and I do not believe that you took the risk of going there and trying to bribe an officer just to get his notes about you and your family. I believe there is something in his files that can easily be recognized as pertaining to you or your family, and that's what you were after. In the morning we'll have men going through the contents of the files, item by item, and if anything like that is there they'll spot it. Meanwhile I'm holding you for further questioning about your attempt to bribe an officer. If you want to telephone a lawyer, you may—one phone call, with an officer present."

Cramer's head swiveled. "Stebbins, take her in to Lieutenant Rowcliff, and tell Rowcliff how it stands."

Purley arose. Mrs. Tillotson was shrinking, looking less overfed every second, right in front of our eyes. "Will you wait a minute?" she demanded.

"Two minutes, madam. But don't try cooking up any more lies. You're no good at it."

"That man misunderstood me. I wasn't trying to bribe him."

"I said you may phone a lawyer—"

"I don't want a lawyer." She was sure about that. "If they go through those files they'll find what I was after, so I might as well tell you. It's some letters in envelopes addressed to me. They're not signed, they're anonymous, and I wanted that Heller to find out who sent them."

"Are they about your son?"

"No. They're about me. They threaten me with something, and I was sure it was leading up to blackmail."

"How many letters?"

"Six."

"What do they threaten you with?"

"They—they don't exactly threaten. They're quotations from things. One of them says, 'He that cannot pay, let him pray.' Another one says, 'He that dies pays all debts.' Another one says, 'So comes a reckoning when the banquet's o'er.' The others are longer, but that's what they're like."

"What made you think they were leading up to blackmail?"

"Wouldn't you? 'He that cannot pay, let him pray.' "

"And you wanted Heller to identify the sender. How many times had you seen him?"

"Twice."

"Of course you had given him all the information you could. We'll

get the letters in the morning, but you can tell us now what you told
Heller. As far as possible, everything that was said by both of you."

I permitted myself to grin, not discreetly, and glanced at Wolfe to
see if he was properly appreciative of Cramer's adopting his approach,
but he was just sitting there looking patient.

It was hard to tell, for me at least, how much Mrs. Tillotson was
giving and how much she was covering. If there was something in her
past that someone might have felt she should pay for or give a reckoning
of, either she didn't know what it was, or she had kept it from Heller,
or she had told him but certainly didn't intend to let us in on it. It went
on and on, with her concentrating hard on remembering her conversations with Heller and all the data she had given him for factors of his
formulas, and with Cramer playing her back and forth until she was
so tied up in contradictions that it would have taken a dozen mathematical wizards to make head or tail of it.

Wolfe finally intervened. He glanced up at the wall clock, shifted in
his chair to get his seventh of a ton bearing on another spot, and
announced, "It's after midnight. Thank heaven you have an army to
start sorting this out and checking it. If your Lieutenant Rowcliff is still
here, let him have her, and let's have some cheese. I'm hungry."

Cramer, as ready for a recess as anybody, had no objection. Purley
Stebbins removed Mrs. Tillotson. The stenographer went on a private
errand. I went to the kitchen to give Fritz a hand, knowing that he was
running himself ragged furnishing trays of sandwiches to flocks of
Homicide personnel distributed all over the premises. When I returned
to the office with a supply of provender, Cramer was riding Wolfe,
pouring it on, and Wolfe was leaning back in his chair with his eyes
shut. I passed around plates of Fritz's *il pesto* and crackers, with beer
for Wolfe and the stenographer, coffee for Cramer and Stebbins, and
milk for me.

In four minutes Cramer inquired, "What is this stuff?"

Wolfe told him. "*Il pesto.*"

"What's in it?"

"Canestrato cheese, anchovies, pig liver, black walnuts, chives, sweet
basil, garlic, and olive oil."

"Good God."

In another four minutes Cramer addressed me in the tone of one
doing a gracious favor. "I'll take some more of that, Goodwin."

But while I was gathering the empty plates he started in on Wolfe
again. Wolfe didn't bother to counter. He waited until Cramer halted

for breath and then growled, "It's nearly one o'clock, and we have three more."

Cramer sent Purley for another scared citizen. This time it was the thin tall bony specimen who, entering the lobby on Thirty-seventh Street that morning, had stopped to aim a rude stare at Susan Maturo and me seated on the bench by the fireplace. Having read his statement, I now knew that his name was Jack Ennis, that he was an expert diemaker, at present unemployed, that he was unmarried, that he lived in Queens, and that he was a born inventor who had not yet cashed in. His brown suit had not been pressed.

When Cramer told him that questions from Wolfe were to be considered a part of the official inquiry into Leo Heller's death, Ennis cocked his head to appraise Wolfe, as if deciding whether or not such a procedure deserved his okay.

"You're a self-made man," he told Wolfe. "I've read about you. How old are you?"

Wolfe returned his gaze. "Some other time, Mr. Ennis. Tonight you're the target, not me. You're thirty-eight, aren't you?"

Ennis smiled. He had a wide mouth with thin colorless lips, and his smile wasn't especially attractive. "Excuse me if you thought I was being fresh, asking how old you are, but I don't really give a damn. I know you're right at the top of your racket, and I wondered how long it took you to get started up. I'm going to the top too, before I'm through, but it's taking me a hell of a time to get a start, and I wondered about you. How old were you when you first got your name in the paper?"

"Two days. A notice of my birth. I understand that your call on Leo Heller was connected with your determination to get a start as an inventor?"

"That's right." Ennis smiled again. "Look. This is all a lot of crap. The cops have been at me now for seven hours, and where are they? What's the sense in going on with it? Why in the name of God would I want to kill that guy?"

"That's what I'd like to know."

"Well, search me. I've got patents on six inventions, and none of them is on the market. One of them is not perfect—I know damn well it's not—but it needs only one more trick to make it an absolute whiz. I can't find the trick. I've read about this Heller, and it seemed to me that if I gave him all the dope, all the stuff he needed for one of his formulas, there was a good chance he would come up with the answer. So I went to him. I spent three long sessions with him. He finally thought he had enough to try to work up a formula, and he was taking a crack at it, and I had a date to see him this morning and find out how it was going."

Ennis stopped for emphasis. "So I'm hoping. After all the sweating I've done and the dough I've spent, maybe I'm going to get it at last. So I go. I go upstairs to his office and shoot him dead, and then I go to the waiting room and sit down and wait." He smiled. "Listen. If you want to say there are smarter men than me, I won't argue. Maybe you're smarter yourself. But I'm not a lunatic, am I?"

Wolfe's lips were pursed. "I won't commit myself on that, Mr. Ennis. But you have by no means demonstrated that it is fatuous to suppose you might have killed Heller. What if he devised a formula from the data you supplied, discovered the trick that would transform your faulty contraption into a whiz, as you expressed it, and refused to divulge it except on intolerable terms? That would be a magnificent motive for murder."

"It sure would," Ennis agreed without reservation. "I would have killed him with pleasure." He leaned forward and was suddenly intense and in dead earnest. "Look. I'm headed for the top. I've got what I need in here"—he tapped his forehead—"and nothing and nobody is going to stop me. If Heller had done what you said, I might have killed him, I don't deny it; but he didn't." He jerked to Cramer. "And I'm glad of a chance to tell you what I've told those bozos that have been grilling me. I want to go through Heller's papers to see if I can find the formula he worked up for me. Maybe I can't recognize it, and if I do I doubt if I can figure it out, but I want to look for it, and not next year either."

"We're doing the looking," Cramer said dryly. "If we find anything that can be identified as relating to you, you'll see it, and eventually you may get it."

"I don't want it eventually, I want it now. Do you know how long I've been working on that thing? Four years! It's mine, you understand that, it's mine!" He was getting upset.

"Calm down, bud," Cramer advised him. "We're right with you in seeing to it that you get what's yours."

"Meanwhile," Wolfe said, "there's a point or two. When you entered that building this morning, why did you stop and gape at Mr. Goodwin and Miss Maturo?"

Ennis's chin went up. "Who says I did?"

"I do, on information. Archie. Did he?"

"Yes," I stated. "Rudely."

"Well," Ennis told Wolfe, "he's bigger than I am. Maybe I did, at that."

"Why? Any special reason?"

"It depends on what you call special. I thought I recognized her, a girl I knew once, and then saw I was wrong. She was much too young."

"Very well. I would like to explore my suggestion, which you reject, that Heller was trying to chouse you out of your invention as perfected by his calculations. I want you to describe the invention as you described it to him, particularly the flaw which you had tried so persistently to rectify."

I won't attempt to report what followed, and I couldn't anyhow, since I understood less than a tenth of it. I did gather that the invention was a gadget intended to supersede all existing X-ray machines, but beyond that I got lost in a wilderness of cathodes and atomicity and coulombs, and if you ask me, Wolfe and Cramer were no better off. If talking like a character out of space-science fiction proves you're an inventor, that bird was certainly one. He stood up to make motions to illustrate, and grabbed a pad and pencil from Wolfe's desk to explain with drawings, and after a while it began to look as if it would be impossible to stop him. They finally managed it, with Sergeant Stebbins lending a hand by marching over and taking his elbow. On his way out he turned at the door to call back, "I want that formula, and don't you forget it!"

6

THE FEMALE of an executive type was still in mink, or rather she had it with her, but she was not so brisk. As I said before, that morning I would have classified her as between twenty and sixty, but the day's experiences had worn her down closer to reality, and I would now have put her at forty-seven. However, she was game. With all she had gone through, at that late hour she still let us know, as she deposited the mink on a chair, sat on another, crossed her legs, got out a cigarette and let me light it, and thanked me for an ashtray, that she was cool and composed and in command.

My typing her as an executive had been justified by the transcripts. Her name really was Agatha Abbey, and she was executive editor of a magazine, *Mode,* which I did not read regularly. After Cramer had explained the nature of the session, including Wolfe's status, Wolfe took aim and went for the center of the target.

"Miss Abbey. I presume you'd like to get to bed—I know I would— so we won't waste time flouncing around. Three things about you." He held up a finger. "First. You claim that you never saw Leo Heller. It is corroborated that you had not visited his place before today, but whether you had seen him elsewhere will be thoroughly investigated by men armed with pictures of him. They will ask people at your place of business, at your residence, and at other likely spots. If it is found that you had in fact met him and conferred with him, you won't like it."

He raised two fingers. "Second. You refused to tell why you went to see Heller. That does not brand you as a miscreant, since most people have private matters which they innocently and jealously guard, but you clung to your refusal beyond reason, even after it was explained that that information had to be given by all of the six persons who called on Heller this morning, and you were assured that it would be revealed to no one unless it proved to be an item of evidence in a murder case. You finally did give the information, but only when you perceived that if you didn't there would be a painstaking investigation into your affairs and movements."

He raised three fingers. "Third. When the information was wormed out of you, it was almost certainly flummery. You said that you wanted to engage Heller to find out who had stolen a ring from a drawer of your desk some three months ago. That was childish nonsense. I grant that even though the ring was insured you may have been intent on disclosing the culprit, and the police had failed you; but if you have enough sense to get and hold a well-paid job in a highly competitive field, as you have, surely you would have known that it was stupid to suppose Heller could help you. Even if he were not a humbug, if he were honestly applying the laws of probability to complex problems with some success, singling out a sneak thief from among a hundred possibilities was plainly an operation utterly unsuited to his technique, and even to his pretensions."

Wolfe moved his head an inch to the left and back again. "No, Miss Abbey, it won't do. I want to know whether you saw Leo Heller before today, and in any case what you wanted of him."

The tip of her tongue had appeared four times, to flick across her lips. She spoke in a controlled, thin, steely voice. "You make it sound overwhelming, Mr. Wolfe."

"Not I. It *is* overwhelming."

Her sharp dark eyes went to Cramer. "You're an inspector, in charge of this business?"

"That's right."

"Do the police share Mr. Wolfe's—skepticism?"

"You can take what he said as coming from me."

"Then no matter what I tell you about why I went to see Heller, you'll investigate it? You'll check it?"

"Not necessarily. If it fits all right, and if we can't connect it with the murder, and if it's a private confidential matter, we'll let it go at that. If we do check any, we'll be careful. There are enough innocent citizens sore at us already."

Her eyes darted back to Wolfe. "What about you, Mr. Wolfe? Will you have to check?"

"I sincerely hope not. Let Mr. Cramer's assurance include me."

Her eyes went around. "What about these men?"

"They are trained confidential assistants. They hold their tongues or they lose their jobs."

The tip of her tongue came out and went in. "I'm not satisfied, but what can I do? If my only choice is between this and the whole New York detective force pawing at me, the Lord knows I take this. I phoned Leo Heller ten days ago, and he came to my office and spent two hours there. It was a business matter, not a personal one. I'm going to tell you exactly what it was, because I'm no good at ad libbing a phony. I was a damn fool to say that about the stolen ring."

She was hating it, but she went on. "You said I have sense enough to get and hold a well-paid job in a highly competitive field, but if you only knew. It's not a field, it's a corral of wild beasts. There are six female tigers trying to get their claws on my job right now, and if they all died tonight there would be six others tomorrow. If it came out what I went to Leo Heller for, that would be the finish of me."

The tip of her tongue flashed out and in. "So that's what this means to me. A magazine like *Mode* has two main functions, reporting and predicting. American women want to know what is being made and worn in Paris and New York, but even more they want to know what is going to be made and worn next season. *Mode's* reporting has been good enough—I've been all right on that—but for the past year our predictions have been utterly rotten. We've got the contacts, but something has gone haywire, and our biggest rival has made monkeys of us. Another year like that, even another season, and good-by."

Wolfe grunted. "To the magazine?"

"No, to me. So I decided to try Leo Heller. We had carried a piece about him, and I had met him. The idea was to give him everything we had—and we had plenty—about styles and colors and trends for the past ten years, and have him figure the probabilities six months ahead. He thought it was feasible, and I don't think he was a faker. He had to come to the office to go through our stuff, and of course I had to camouflage it, what he was there for, but that wasn't hard. Do you want to know what I told them he was doing?"

"I think not," Wolfe muttered.

"So he came. I phoned him the next day, and he said it would take him at least a week to determine whether he had enough information to make up a probability formula. Yesterday I phoned again, and he said he had something to discuss and asked me to call at his place this morning. I went. You know the rest of it."

She stopped. Wolfe and Cramer exchanged glances. "I would like," Wolfe said, "to have the name of the six female tigers who are after your job."

She turned white. I have never seen the color leave a face faster or more completely. "Damn you," she said in bitter fury. "So you're a rat like everybody else!"

Wolfe showed her a palm. "Please, madam. Mr. Cramer will speak for himself, but I have no desire to betray you to your enemies. I merely want—"

He saved his breath, because his audience was leaving. She got up, retrieved her mink from the other chair, draped it over her arm, turned, and headed for the door. Stebbins looked at Wolfe, Wolfe shook his head, and Stebbins trailed after her.

As he left the room at her heels, Cramer called to him, "Bring Busch!" Then he turned on Wolfe to protest. "What the hell, you had her open. Why give her a breath?"

Wolfe made a face. "The wretch. The miserable wretch. Her misogyny was already in her bones; now her misandry is too. She was dumb with rage, and it would have been futile to keep at her. But you're keeping her?"

"You're right we are. For what?" He was out of his chair, glaring down at Wolfe. "Tell me for what! Except for dragging that out of that woman, there's not one single . . ."

He was off again. I miss no opportunity of resenting Inspector Cramer—I enjoy it, and it's good for my appetite—but I must admit that on that occasion he seemed to me to have a point. I still had seen or heard no indication whatever that Wolfe's statement that he had a lead was anything but a stall, and it was half-past two in the morning, and five of them had been processed, with only one to go. So as Cramer yapped at my employer I did not cheer him on or offer him an orchid, but I had a private feeling that some of the sentiments he expressed were not positively preposterous. He was still at it when the door opened to admit Stebbins with the sixth customer.

The sergeant, after conducting this one to the seat the others had occupied, facing Wolfe and Cramer, did not go to the chair against the wall, which he had favored throughout the evening. Instead, he lowered his bulk onto one at Cramer's left, only two arms' lengths from the subject. That was interesting because it meant that he was voting for Karl Busch as his pick of the lot, and while Stebbins had often been wrong I had known him, more than once, to be right.

Karl Busch was the slick, sly, swarthy little article with his hair pasted to his scalp. In the specifications on his transcript I had noted the key NVMS, meaning No Visible Means of Support, but that was just a nod to routine. The details of the report on him left no real doubt as to the sources he tapped for jack. He was a Broadway smoothie, third grade. He was not in the theater or sports or the flicks or any of the tough rackets, but he knew everyone who was, and as the engraved lettuce swirled around the midtown corners and got trapped in the nets of the collectors, legitimate and otherwise, he had a hundred little dodges for fastening onto a specimen for himself.

To him Cramer's tone was noticeably different. "This is Nero Wolfe," he rasped. "Answer his questions. You hear, Busch?"

Busch said he did. Wolfe, who was frowning, studying him, spoke. "Nothing is to be gained, Mr. Busch, by my starting the usual rigmarole with you. I've read your statement, and I doubt if it would be worthwhile to try to pester you into a contradiction. But you had three conversations with Leo Heller, and in your statement they are not reported, merely summarized. I want the details of those conversations, as completely as your memory will furnish. Start with the first one, two months ago. Exactly what was said?"

Busch slowly shook his head. "Impossible, mister."

"Word by word, no. Do your best."

"Huh-uh."

"You won't try?"

"It's this way. If I took you to the pier and ast you to try to jump across to Brooklyn, what would you do? You'd say it was impossible and why get your feet wet. That's me."

"I told you," Cramer snapped, "to answer his questions."

Busch extended a dramatic hand in appeal. "What do you want me to do, make it up?"

"I want you to do what you were told, to the best of your ability."

"Okay. This will be good. I said to him, 'Mr. Heller, my name's Busch, and I'm a broker.' He said broker of what, and I said of anything people want broken, just for a gag, but he had no sense of humor and I saw he didn't, so I dropped that and explained. I told him there was a great demand among all kinds of people to know what horse was going to win a race the day before the race was run or even an hour before, and I had read about his line of work and was thinking that he could help to meet that demand. He said that he had thought several times about using his method on horse races, but he didn't care himself to use the method for personal bets because he wasn't a betting man, and for him to make up one of his formulas for just one race would take an awful lot of research and it would cost so much it wouldn't be worth it for any one person unless that person made a high-bracket plunge."

"You're paraphrasing it," Wolfe objected. "I'd prefer the words that were used."

"This is the best of my ability, mister."

"Very well. Go on."

"I said I wasn't a high-bracket boy myself, but anyway that wasn't here or there or under the rug, because what I had in mind was a wholesale setup. I had figgers to show him. Say he did ten races a week. I could round up at least twenty customers right off the bat. He didn't need to be any God Almighty always right; all he had to do was crack a percentage of forty or better, and it would start a fire you couldn't put out if you ran a river down it. We could have a million customers if we wanted 'em, but we wouldn't want 'em. We would hand-pick a hundred and no more, and each one would ante one C per week, which if I can add at all would make ten grand every sennight. That would—"

"What?" Wolfe exploded. "Ten grand every what?"

"Sennight."

"Meaning a week?"

"Sure."

"Where the deuce did you pick up that fine old word?"

"That's not old. Some big wit started it around last summer."

"Incredible. Go on."

"Where was— Oh, yeah. That would make half a million little ones per year, and Heller and me would split it. Out of my half I would expense the operating, and out of his half he would expense the dope. He would have to walk on his nose to cut under a hundred grand all clear, and I wouldn't do so bad. We didn't sign no papers, but he could smell it, and after two more talks he agreed to do a dry run on three races. The first one he worked on, his answer was the favorite, a horse named White Water, and it won, but what the hell, it was just exercise for that rabbit. The next one, there were two sweethearts in a field of nine, and it was heads or tails between those two, and Heller had the winner all right, a horse named Short Order, but on a fifty-fifty call you don't exactly panic. But get this next one."

Busch gestured dramatically for emphasis. "Now get it. This animal was forty to one, but it might as well have been four hundred. It was a musclebound sore-jointed hyena named Zero. That alone, a horse named Zero, was enough to put the curse of six saints on it, but also it was the kind of looking horse which if you looked at it would make you think promptly of canned dog food. When Heller came up with that horse, I thought oh-oh, he's a loon after all, and watch me run. Well, you ast me to tell you the words we used, me and Heller. If I told you some I used when that Zero horse won that race, you would lock me up. Not only was Heller batting a thousand, but he had kicked through with the most— What are you doing, taking a nap?"

We all looked at Wolfe. He was leaning back with his eyes shut tight, and was motionless except for his lips, which were pushing out and in, and out and in, and again out and in. Cramer and Stebbins and I knew what that meant: something had hit his hook, and he had yanked and had a fish on. A tingle ran up my spine. Stebbins arose and took a step to stand at Busch's elbow. Cramer tried to look cynical but couldn't make it; he was as excited as I was. The proof of it was that he didn't open his trap; he just sat with his eyes on Wolfe, along with the rest of us, looking at the lip movements as if they were something really special.

"What the hell!" Busch protested. "Is he having a fit?"

Wolfe's eyes opened, and he came forward in his chair. "No, I'm not," he snapped, "but I've been having one all evening. Mr. Cramer. Will you please have Mr. Busch removed? Temporarily."

Cramer, with no hesitation, nodded at Purley, and Purley touched Busch's shoulder, and they went. The door closed behind them, but it wasn't more than five seconds before it opened again and Purley was back with us. He wanted as quick a look at the fish as his boss and me.

"Have you ever," Wolfe was asking Cramer, "called me, pointblank, a dolt and a dotard?"

"Those aren't my words, but I've certainly called you."

"You may do so now. Your opinion of me at its lowest was far above my present opinion of myself." He looked up at the clock, which said five past three. "We now need a proper setting. How many of your staff are in my house?"

"Fourteen or fifteen."

"We want them all in here, for the effect of their presence. Half of them should bring chairs. Also, of course, the six persons we have interviewed. This shouldn't take too long—possibly an hour, though I doubt it. I certainly won't prolong it."

Cramer was looking contrary. "You've already prolonged it plenty. You mean you're prepared to name him?"

"I am not. I haven't the slightest notion who it is. But I am prepared to make an attack that will expose him—or her—and if it doesn't, I'll have no opinion of myself at all." Wolfe flattened his palms on his desk, for him a violent gesture. "Confound it, don't you know me well enough to realize when I'm ready to strike?"

"I know you too damn well." Cramer looked at his sergeant, drew in a deep breath, and let it out. "Oh, nuts. Okay, Purley. Collect the audience."

7

THE OFFICE is a good-sized room, but there wasn't much unoccupied space left when that gathering was fully assembled. There were twenty-seven of us all told. The biggest assortment of Homicide employees I had ever gazed upon extended from wall to wall in the rear of the six subjects, with four of them filling the couch. Cramer was planted in the red leather chair, with Stebbins on his left, and the stenographer was hanging on at the end of my desk.

The six citizens were in a row up front, and none of them looked merry. Agatha Abbey was the only person present who rated two chairs, one for herself and one for her mink, but no one was bothering to resent it in spite of the crowding. Their minds were on other matters.

Wolfe's eyes went from right to left and back again, taking them in. He spoke. "I'll have to make this somewhat elaborate, so that all of you will clearly understand the situation. I could not at the moment hazard even a venturesome guess as to which of you killed Leo Heller, but I now know how to find out, and I propose to do so."

The only reaction visible or audible was John R. Winslow clearing his throat.

Wolfe interlaced his fingers in front of his middle mound. "We have from the first had a hint that has not been imparted to you. Yesterday— Tuesday, that is—Heller telephoned here to say that he suspected that one of his clients had committed a serious crime and to hire me to investigate. I declined, for reasons we needn't go into, but Mr. Goodwin, who is subordinate only when it suits his temperament and convenience, took it upon himself to call on Heller this morning to discuss the matter."

He shot me a glance, and I met it. Merely an incivility. He went on to them, "He entered Heller's office but found it unoccupied. Tarrying there for some minutes, and meanwhile exercising his highly trained talent for observation, he noticed, among other details, that some pencils and an eraser from an overturned jar were arranged on the desk in a sort of pattern. Later that same detail was of course noted by the police, after Heller's body had been found and they had been summoned; and it was a feature of that detail which led Mr. Cramer to come to see me. He assumed that Heller, seated at his desk and threatened with a gun, knowing or thinking he was about to die, had made the pencil pattern to leave a message, and that the purpose of the message was to give a clue to the identity of the murderer. On that point I agreed with Mr. Cramer. Will you all approach, please, and look at this arrangement on my desk? These pencils and the eraser are placed approximately the same as those on Heller's desk, with you, not me, on Heller's side of the desk. From your side you are seeing them as Heller intended them to be seen."

The six did as requested, and they had company. Not only did most of the homicide subordinates leave their chairs and come forward for a view, but Cramer himself got up and took a glance—maybe just curiosity, but I wouldn't put it past him to suspect Wolfe of a shenanigan. However, the pencils and eraser were properly placed, as I ascertained by arising and stretching to peer over shoulders.

When they were all seated again Wolfe resumed. "Mr. Cramer had a notion about the message which I rejected and will not bother to expound. My own notion of it, conceived almost immediately, came not as a *coup d'éclat,* but merely a stirring of memory. It reminded me vaguely of something I had seen somewhere; and the vagueness disappeared when I reflected that Heller had been a mathematician, academically qualified and trained. The memory was old, and I checked it by going to my shelves for a book I had read some ten years ago. Its title is *Mathematics for the Million,* by Hogben. After verifying my recollection, I locked the book in a drawer because I thought it would be a pity for Mr. Cramer to waste time leafing through it."

"Let's get on," Cramer growled.

Wolfe did so. "As told in Mr. Hogben's book, more than two thousand years ago what he calls a matchstick number script was being used in India. Three horizontal lines stood for three, two horizontal lines stood for two, and so on. That was indeed primitive, but it had greater possibilities than the clumsy devices of the Hebrews and Greeks and Romans. Around the time of the birth of Christ some brilliant Hindu improved upon it by connecting the horizontal lines with diagonals, making the units unmistakable." He pointed to the arrangement on his desk. "These five pencils on your left form a three exactly as the Hindus formed a three, and the three pencils on your right form a two. These Hindu symbols are one of the great landmarks in the history of number language. You will note, by the way, that our own forms of the figure three and of the figure two are taken directly from these Hindu symbols."

A couple of them got up to look, and Wolfe politely waited until they were seated again. "So, since Heller had been a mathematician, and since those were famous patterns in the history of mathematics, I assumed that the message was a three and a two. But evidence indicated that the eraser was also a part of the message and must be included. That was simple. It is the custom of an academic mathematician, if he wants to scribble 'four times six,' or 'seven times nine,' to use for the 'times' not an X, as we laymen do, but a dot. It is so well-known a custom that Mr. Hogben uses it in his book without thinking it necessary to explain it, and therefore I confidently assumed that the eraser was meant for a dot, and that the message was three times two, or six."

Wolfe compressed his lips and shook his head. "That was an impetuous imbecility. During the whole seven hours that I sat here poking at you people, I was trying to find some connection with the figure six that would either set one of you clearly apart, or relate you to the commission of some crime, or both. Preferably both, of course, but either would serve. In the interviews the figure six did turn up with persistent monotony, but with no promising application, and I could only ascribe it to the mischief of coincidence.

"So at three o'clock in the morning I was precisely where I had been when I started. Without a fortuitous nudge, I can't say how long it would have taken me to become aware of my egregious blunder; but I got the nudge, and I can at least say that I responded promptly and effectively. The nudge came from Mr. Busch when he mentioned the name of a horse, Zero."

He upturned a palm. "Of course. Zero! I had been a witless ass. The use of the dot as a symbol for 'times' is a strictly modern device. Since the rest of the message, the figures three and two, were in Hindu number script, surely the dot was too—provided that the Hindus had made any use of the dot. And what made my blunder so unforgivable was that the Hindus had indeed used a dot; they had used it, as is explained in Hogben's book, for the most brilliant and imaginative invention in the whole history of the language of numbers. For when you have once decided how to write three and how to write two, how are you going to distinguish among thirty-two and three hundred and two and three thousand and two and thirty thousand and two? That was the crucial problem in number language, and the Greeks and Romans, for all their intellectual eminence, never succeeded in solving it. Some Hindu genius did, twenty centuries ago. He saw that the secret was position. Today we use our zero exactly as he did, to show position, but instead of a zero he used a dot. That's what the dot was in the early Hindu number language; it was used like our zero. So Heller's message was not three times two, or six; it was three zero two, or three hundred and two."

Susan Maturo started, jerking her head up, and made a noise. Wolfe rested his eyes on her. "Yes, Miss Maturo. Three hundred and two people died in the explosion and fire at the Montrose Hospital a month ago. You mentioned that figure when you were talking with me, but even if you hadn't, it is so imbedded in the consciousness of everyone who reads newspapers or listens to radio, it wouldn't have escaped me. The moment I realized that Heller's message was the figure three hundred and two, I would certainly have connected it with that disaster, whether you had mentioned it or not."

"But it's—" She was staring. "You mean it is connected?"

"I'm proceeding on that obvious assumption. I am assuming that through the information one of you six people furnished Leo Heller as factors for a formula, he formed a suspicion that one of you had commited a serious crime, and that his message, the figure three hundred and two, indicates that the crime was planting in the Montrose Hospital that bomb that caused the deaths of three hundred and two people—or at least involvement in that crime."

It seemed as if I could see or feel muscles tightening all over the room. Most of those dicks, maybe all of them, had of course been working on the Montrose thing. Cramer pulled his feet back and his hands were fists. Purley Stebbins took his gun from his holster and rested it on his knee and leaned forward, the better to have his eyes on all six of them.

"So," Wolfe continued, "Heller's message identified not the person who was about to kill him, not the criminal, but the crime. That was superbly ingenious, and, considering the situation he was in, he deserves our deepest admiration. He has mine, and I retract any derogation of him. It would seem natural to concentrate on Miss Maturo, since she was certainly connected with that disaster, but first let's clarify the matter. I'm going to ask the rest of you if you have at any time visited the Montrose Hospital, or been connected with it in any way, or had dealings with any of its personnel. Take the question just as I have stated it." His eyes went to the end of the row, at the left. "Mrs. Tillotson? Answer, please. Have you?"

"No." It was barely audible.

"Louder, please."

"No!"

His eyes moved. "Mr. Ennis?"

"I have not. Never."

"We'll skip you, Miss Maturo. Mr. Busch?"

"I've never been in a hospital."

"That answers only a third of the question. Answer all of it."

"The answer is no, mister."

"Miss Abbey?"

"I went there once about two years ago, to visit a patient, a friend. That was all." The tip of her tongue came out and went in. "Except for that one visit I have never been connected with it in any way or dealt with any of its personnel."

"That is explicit. Mr. Winslow?"

"No to the whole question. An unqualified no."

"Well." Wolfe did not look frustrated. "That would seem to isolate Miss Maturo, but it is not conclusive." His head turned. "Mr. Cramer. If the person who not only killed Leo Heller but also bombed that hospital is among these six, I'm sure you won't want to take the slightest risk of losing him. I have a suggestion."

"I'm listening," Cramer growled.

"Take them in as material witnesses, and hold them without bail if possible. Starting immediately, collect as many as you can of the former staff of that hospital. There were scores who survived, and other scores who were not on duty at the time. Get all of them if possible, spare no effort, and have them look at these people and say if they have ever seen any of them. Meanwhile, of course, you will be working on Miss Maturo, but you have heard the denials of the other five, and if you get reliable evidence that one of them has lied I'm sure you will need no further suggestion from me. Indeed, if one of them has lied and leaves this room in custody with that lie undeclared, that alone will be half the battle. I'm sorry—"

"Wait a minute."

All eyes went to one spot. It was Jack Ennis, the inventor. His thin colorless lips were twisted, with one end up, but not in an attempt to smile. The look in his eyes showed that he had no idea of smiling.

"I didn't tell an exact lie," he said.

Wolfe's eyes were slits. "Then an inexact lie, Mr. Ennis?"

"I mean I didn't visit that hospital as a hospital. And I didn't have dealings with them, I was just trying to. I wanted them to give my X-ray machine a trial. One of them was willing to, but the other two talked him down."

"When was this?"

"I was there three times, twice in December and once in January."

"I thought your X-ray machine had a flaw."

"It wasn't perfect, but it would work, and it would have been better than anything they had. I was sure I was going to get it in, because he was for it—his name is Halsey—and I saw him first, and he wanted to try it. But the other two talked him out of it, and one of them was very—he—" He petered out.

Wolfe prodded him. "Very what, Mr. Ennis?"

"He didn't understand me! He hated me!"

"There are people like that. There are all kinds of people. Have you ever invented a bomb?"

"A bomb?" Ennis's lips worked, and this time I thought he actually was trying to smile. "Why would I invent a bomb?"

"I don't know. Inventors invent many things. If you have never tried your hand at a bomb, of course you have never had occasion to get hold of the necessary materials—for instance, explosives. It's only fair to tell you what I now regard as a reasonable hypothesis: that you placed the bomb in the hospital in revenge for an injury, real or fancied; that included in the data you gave Leo Heller was an item or items which led him to suspect you of that crime; that something he said led you, in turn, to suspect that he suspected; that when you went to his place this morning you went armed, prepared for action if your suspicion was verified; that when you entered the building you recognized Mr. Goodwin as my assistant; that you went up to Heller's office and asked him if Mr. Goodwin was there for an appointment with him, and his answer heightened or confirmed your suspicion, and you produced the gun; that—"

"Hold it," Cramer snapped. "I'll take it from here. Purley, get him out and—"

Purley was a little slow. He was up, but Ennis was up faster and off in a flying dive for Wolfe. I dived too, and got an arm and jerked. He tore loose, but by then a whole squad was there, swarming into him, and since I wasn't needed I backed off. As I did so someone dived at me, and Susan Maturo was up against me, gripping my lapels.

"Tell me!" she demanded. "Tell me! Was it him?"

I told her promptly and positively, to keep her from ripping my lapels off. "Yes," I said, in one word.

Two months later a jury of eight men and four women agreed with me.

ED McBAIN
Storm

1

THE GIRL with Cotton Hawes had cold feet.

He didn't know what to do about her feet because he'd already tried everything he could think of, and they were still cold. He had to admit that driving in subzero temperatures with a storm some fifteen minutes behind him wasn't exactly conducive to warm pedal extremities. But he had turned the car heater up full, supplied the girl with a blanket, taken off his overcoat and wrapped that around her—and she still had cold feet.

The girl's name was Blanche Colby, a very nice euphonic name which she had adopted the moment she entered show business. That had been a long time ago. Blanche's real name was Bertha Cooley, but a press agent those many years back told her that Bertha Cooley sounded like a mentholated Pullman, and not a dancer. Blanche Colby had class, he told her, and if there was one thing Bertha Cooley wanted, it was class. She had taken the new name and gone into the chorus of a hit musical twenty-two years ago, when she was only fifteen. She was not thirty-seven, but all those years of prancing the boards had left her with a youthful body, lithe and long-legged. She was still, with a slight assist from Clairol, a soft honey-blonde. Her green eyes were intelligent and alert. Her feet, unfortunately, *ahhhh,* her feet.

"How are they now?" he asked her.

"Freezing," she said.

"We're almost there," Hawes told her. "You'll like this place. One of the guys on the squad—Hal Willis—comes up here almost every weekend he's off. He says the skiing is great."

"I know a dancer who broke her leg in Switzerland," Blanche said. "Skiing?"

417

"Sure, skiing."

"You've never skied before?"

"Never."

"Well . . ." Hawes shrugged. "Well, I don't think you'll break any legs."

"That's reassuring," Blanche said. She glanced through the window on her side of the car. "I think that storm is catching up to us."

"Just a few flurries."

"I wonder how serious it'll be. I have a rehearsal Monday night."

"Four to six inches, they said. That's not very much."

"Will the roads be open?"

"Sure. Don't worry."

"I know a dancer who got snowed in for six days in Vermont," Blanche said. "It wouldn't have been so bad, but she was with a Method actor."

"Well, I'm a cop," Hawes said.

"Yeah," Blanche answered noncommittally.

They were silent for several moments. The light snow flurries drifted across the road, turning it into a dreamlike, white, flowing stream. The headlights illuminated the shifting macadam. Sitting behind the wheel, Hawes had the peculiar feeling that the road was melting. He was glad to see the sign for Rawson Mountain Inn. He stopped the car, picking out the sign from the tangle of other signs announcing accommodations in the area. He set the car in motion again, turning left over an old wooden bridge, the timbers creaking as the convertible passed over them. A new sign, blatant red and white, shouted the features of the area—a sixteen-hundred-foot mountain, two chair lifts, a T-Bar, a rope tow, and, definitely not needed with a storm on the way, a snow-making machine.

The inn lay nestled in the foothills at the base of the mountain. The trees around the inn were bare, standing in gaunt silhouette against the snow-threatening sky. Snow-nuzzled lights beckoned warmly. He helped Blanche out of the car, put on his overcoat, and walked with her over old packed snow to the entrance. They stamped their feet in the doorway and entered the huge room. A fire was going at one end of the room. Someone was playing the piano. A handful of tired weekday skiers were sprawled around the fireplace, wearing very fashionable after-ski boots and sweaters, drinking from bottles onto which they'd hand-lettered their names. Blanche went directly to the fire, found a place on one of the couches, and stretched her long legs to the blaze. Hawes found the desk, tapped a bell on it, and waited. No one appeared.

He tapped the bell again. A skier passing the desk said, "He's in the office. Over there on your left."

Hawes nodded, found the door marked OFFICE, and knocked on it. A voice inside called, "Yes, come in," and Hawes twisted the knob and entered.

The office was larger than he'd expected, a good fifteen feet separating the entrance door from the desk at the opposite end of the room. A man in his late twenties sat behind the desk. He had dark hair and dark brows pulled low over deep brown eyes. He was wearing a white shirt open at the throat, a bold reindeer-imprinted sweater over it. He was also wearing a plaster cast on his right leg. The leg was stretched out stiffly in front of him, the foot resting on a low ottoman. A pair of crutches leaned against the desk, within easy reach of his hands. Hawes was suddenly glad he'd left Blanche by the fire.

"You're not a new skier, I hope," the man said.

"No, I'm not."

"Good. Some of them get scared by the cast and crutches."

"Was it a skiing accident?" Hawes asked.

The man nodded. "Spiral break of the tibia and fibula. Someone forgot to fill in a sitzmark. I was going pretty fast, and when I hit the hole . . ." He shrugged. "I won't be able to walk without the crutches for at least another month."

"That's too bad," Hawes said. He paused, and then figured he might as well get down to business. "I have a reservation," he said. "Adjoining rooms with bath."

"Yes, sir. What was the name on that?"

"Cotton Hawes and Blanche Colby."

The man opened a drawer in his desk and consulted a typewritten sheet. "Yes, sir," he said. "Two rooms in the annex."

"The annex?" Hawes said. "Where's that?"

"Oh, just a hundred yards or so from the main building, sir."

"Oh. Well, I guess that'll be . . ."

"And that's *one* bath, you understand."

"What do you mean?"

"They're adjoining rooms, but the bathroom is in 104. 105 doesn't have a bath."

"Oh. Well, I'd like two rooms that *do* have baths," Hawes said, smiling.

"I'm sorry, sir. 104 and 105 are the only available rooms in the house."

"The fellow I spoke to on the phone . . ."

"Yes, sir, that's me. Elmer Wollender."

"How do you do?" Hawes said. "You told me both rooms had baths."

"No, sir. You said you wanted adjoining rooms with bath, and I said I could give you adjoining rooms with bath. And that's what I've given you. Bath. Singular."

"Are you a lawyer, Mr. Wollender?" Hawes asked, no longer smiling.

"No, sir. Out of season, I'm a locksmith."

"What are you in season?"

"Why, a hotel-keeper, sir," Wollender said.

"Don't test the theory," Hawes answered. "Let me have my deposit back, Mr. Wollender. We'll find another place to stay."

"Well, sir, to begin with, we can't make any cash refunds, but we'll be happy to keep your deposit here against another time when you may wish . . ."

"Look, Mr. Wollender," Hawes said menacingly, "I don't know what kind of a . . ."

"And of course, sir, there *are* lots of places to stay here in town, but none of them, sir, *none* of them have any private baths at all. Now if you don't mind walking down the hall . . ."

"All I know is . . ."

". . . and sharing the john with a hundred other skiers, why then . . ."

"You told me on the phone . . ."

"I'm sure you can find other accommodations. The *lady,* however, might enjoy a little privacy." Wollender waited while Hawes considered.

"If I give her 104 . . ." Hawes started and then paused. "Is that the room with the bath?"

"Yes, sir, 104."

"If I give her that room, where's the bath for 105?"

"Down at the end of the hall, sir. And we *are* right at the base of the mountain, sir, and the skiing *has* been excellent, and we're expecting at least twelve inches of fresh powder."

"The radio said four to six."

"That's in the city, sir. We normally get a lot more snow."

"Like what I got on the phone?" Hawes asked. "Where do I sign?"

2

COTTON HAWES was a detective, and as a member of the 87th Squad he had flopped down in a great many desirable and undesirable rooms throughout the city and its suburbs. Once, while posing as a dock walloper, he had taken a furnished room overlooking the River Harb, and had been surprised during the night by what sounded like a band of midgets marching at the foot of his bed. The midgets turned out to be giants, or at least giants of the species *Rattus muridae*—or as they say in English, rats. He had turned on the light and picked up a broom, but those brazen rat bastards had reared back on their hind legs like boxers and bared their teeth, and he was certain the pack of them would leap for his throat. He had checked out immediately.

There were no rats in rooms 104 and 105 of the annex to Rawson Mountain Inn. Nor was there very much of anything else, either. Whoever had designed the accommodations was undoubtedly steeped in Spartan philosophy. The walls were white and bare, save for a single skiing poster over each bed. There was a single bed in each room, and a wooden dresser painted white. A portable cardboard clothes closet nestled in the corner of each room. The room Hawes hoped to occupy, the one without the bath, was excruciatingly hot, the vents sending in great waves of heated air. The room with the bath, Blanche's room, was unbearably cold. The single window was rimmed with frost, the floor was cold, the bed was cold, the heating ducts and vents were either clogged or blocked, but certainly inoperative.

"And *I'm* the one with the cold feet," Blanche said.

"I'd let you have the heated room," Hawes said gallantly, "but this is the one with the bath."

"Well, we'll manage," Blanche said. "Shall we go down for the bags?"

"I'll get them," Hawes answered. "Stay in my room for now, will you? There's no sense freezing in here."

"I may get to like your room," Blanche said archly, and then turned and walked past him through the connecting door.

He went down the long flight of steps to the front porch, and then beyond to where the car was parked. The rooms were over the ski shop, which was closed for the night now, silent and dark. He took the two valises out of the trunk, and then pulled his skis from the rack on top of the car. He was not a particularly distrustful man, but a pair of Head skis had been stolen from him the season before, and he'd been a cop long enough to know that lightning sometimes *did* strike twice in the same place. In his right hand, and under his right arm, he carried the two bags. In his left hand, and under his left arm, he carried his skis and his boots. He struggled through the deepening snow and onto the front porch. He was about to put down the bags in order to open the door when he heard the heavy thud of ski boots on the steps inside. Someone was coming down those steps in a hell of a hurry.

The door opened suddenly, and a tall thin man wearing black ski pants and a black-hooded parka came onto the porch, almost colliding with Hawes. His face was narrow, handsome in a fine-honed way, the sharply hooked nose giving it the edged striking appearance of an ax. Even in the pale light filtering from the hallway, Hawes saw that the man was deeply tanned, and automatically assumed he was an instructor. The guess was corroborated by the Rawson Mountain insignia on the man's right sleeve, an interlocking R and M in bright red letters. Incongruously, the man was carrying a pair of white figure skates in his left hand.

"Oh, I'm sorry," he said. His face broke into a grin. He had spoken with an accent, German or Swedish, Hawes couldn't tell which.

"That's all right," Hawes said.

"May I help you?"

"No, I think I can manage. If you'd just hold the door open for me . . ."

"It will be my pleasure," the man said, and he almost clicked his heels together.

"Has the skiing been good?" Hawes asked as he struggled through the narrow doorway.

"Fairly good," the man answered. "It will be better tomorrow."

"Well, thanks," Hawes said.

"My pleasure."

"See you on the mountain," Hawes said cheerfully and continued up the steps. There was something slightly ridiculous about the entire situation, the adjoining rooms with only one bath, the pristine cells the rooms had turned out to be, the heat in one, the cold in the other, the fact that they were over the ski shop, the fact that it had begun snowing very heavily, even the hurried ski instructor with his polite Teutonic manners and his guttural voice and his figure skates, there was something faintly reminiscent of farce about the whole setup. He began chuckling as he climbed the steps. When he came into his room, Blanche was stretched out on his bed. He put down the bags.

"What's so funny?" she asked.

"I've decided this is a comic-opera hotel," Hawes said. "I'll bet the mountain out there is only a backdrop. We'll go out there tomorrow morning and discover it's painted on canvas."

"This room is nice and warm," Blanche said.

"Yes, it is," Hawes answered. He slid his skis under the bed, and she watched him silently.

"Are you expecting burglars?"

"You never can tell." He took off his jacket and pulled his holstered service revolver from his back hip pocket.

"You going to wear that on the slopes tomorrow?" Blanche asked.

"No. You can't get a gun into those zippered pockets."

"I think I'll stay in *this* room tonight," Blanche said suddenly.

"Whatever you like," Hawes said. "I'll take the icebox next door."

"Well, actually," she said, "that wasn't exactly what I had in mind."

"Huh?"

"Don't detectives kiss people?"

"Huh?"

"We've been out twice together in the city, and we've just driven three hours alone together in a car, and you've never once tried to kiss me."

"Well, I . . ."

"I wish you would," Blanche said thoughtfully. "Unless, of course, there's a department regulation against it."

"None that I can think of," Hawes said.

Blanche, her hands behind her head, her legs stretched luxuriously, suddenly took a deep breath and said, "I think I'm going to like this place."

3

THERE WERE sounds in the night.

Huddled together in the single bed, the first sound of which they were aware was the noise of the oil burner. At regularly spaced intervals, the thermostat would click, and there would be a thirty-second pause, and then a 707 jet aircraft would take off from the basement of the old wooden building. Hawes had never heard a noisier oil burner in his life. The aluminum ducts and vents provided a symphony all their own, too, expanding, contracting, banging, clanking, sighing, exhaling, whooshing. Down the hall, the toilet would be flushed every now and again, the noise sounding with cataract sharpness on the still mountain air.

There was another noise. A rasping sound, the narrow shrill squeak of metal upon metal. He got out of bed and went to the window. A light was burning in the ski shop below, casting a yellow rectangle onto the snow. Sighing, he went back to bed and tried to sleep.

Down the corridor, there was the constant thud of ski boots as guests returned to their rooms, the slamming of doors, the occasional high giggle of a girl skier intoxicated by the mountain air.

Voices.

". . . will mean a slower track for the slalom . . ."

"Sure, but everyone'll have the same handicap . . ."

Fading.

More voices.

". . . don't even think they'll open the upper trails."

"They have to, don't they?"

"Not Dead Man's Fall. They won't even be able to get up there with all this snow. Seventeen inches already, and no end in sight."

The 707 taking off again from the basement. The vents beginning their orchestral suite, the ducts supplying counterpoint. And more voices, raised in anger.

". . . because he thinks he's God almighty!"

"I tell you you're imagining things."

"I'm warning you! Stay away from him!"

A young girl's laughter.

"I'm warning you. If I see him . . ."

Fading.

At two o'clock in the morning, the Cats started up the mountain. They sounded like Rommel's mechanized cavalry. Hawes was certain they would knock down the outside walls and come lumbering into the room. Blanche began giggling.

"This is the noisiest hotel I've ever slept in," she said.

"How are your feet?"

"Nice and warm. You're a very warm man."

"You're a very warm girl."

"Do you mind my sleeping in long johns?"

"I thought they were leotards."

"Leotard is singular," Blanche said.

"Singular or plural, those are the sexiest long johns I've ever seen."

"It's only the girl in them," Blanche said modestly. "Why don't you kiss me again?"

"I will. In a minute."

"What are you listening for?"

"I thought I heard an unscheduled flight a moment ago."

"What?"

"Didn't you hear it? A funny buzzing sound?"

"There are so many noises . . ."

"Shhhh."

They were silent for several moments. They could hear the Cats grinding their way up the mountain. Someone down the hall flushed the toilet. More boots in the corridor outside.

"Hey!" Blanche said.

"What?"

"You asleep?"

"No," Hawes answered.

"That buzzing sound you heard?"

"Yes?"

"It was my blood," she told him, and she kissed him on the mouth.

4

IT WAS still snowing on Saturday morning. The promised storm had turned into a full-fledged blizzard. They dressed in the warm comfort of the room, Blanche putting on thermal underwear, and then two sweaters and stretch pants, the extra clothing padding out her slender figure. Hawes, standing six feet two inches tall in his double-stockinged feet, black pants and black sweater, presented a one-hundred-and-ninety pound V-shaped silhouette to the window and the gray day outside.

"Do you think I'll get back in time for Monday night's rehearsal?" Blanche asked.

"I don't know. I'm supposed to be back at the squad by six tomorrow night. I wonder if the roads are open."

They learned during breakfast that a state of emergency had been declared in the city and in most of the towns lining the upstate route. Blanche seemed blithely indifferent to the concept of being snowbound. "If there's that much snow," she said, "they'll cancel the rehearsal, anyway."

"They won't cancel the police department," Hawes said.

"The hell with it," Blanche said happily. "We're here now, and there's marvelous snow, and if the skiing is good it'll be a wonderful weekend."

"Even if the skiing is *lousy,*" Hawes said, "it'll be a wonderful week-end."

They rented boots and skis for her in the ski rental shop, and then took to the mountain. Both chair lifts were in operation, but as one of the midnight voices had prophesied, the upper trails were not yet opened. A strong wind had arisen, and it blew the snow in driving white sheets across the slopes. Hawes took Blanche to the rope tow first, had her practice climbing for a while, teaching her to edge and to herring-bone, and then illustrated the use of the tow—left hand clamped around the rope, right hand and arm behind the back and gripping the rope. The beginner's slope was a gentle one, but Blanche seemed immediately capable of more difficult skiing. She was a trained dancer, and she automatically thought of the skis as part of a difficult stage costume, encumbering movement, but simply something to overcome. With re-markable coordination, she learned how to snowplow on the beginner's slope. By midmorning, she had graduated to the T-Bar, and was begin-ning to learn the rudiments of the stem christie. Hawes patiently stayed with her all morning, restricting his own skiing to the elementary slopes. He was becoming more and more grateful for the snow-clogged roads. With the roads impassable, the number of weekend skiers was limited; he and Blanche were enjoying weekday skiing on a Saturday, and the fresh snow made everything a delight.

After lunch, she suggested that he leave her alone to practice for a while. Hawes, who was itching to get at the chair lift and the real trails, nonetheless protested that he was perfectly content to ski with her on the baby slopes. But Blanche insisted, and he finally left her on the slope serviced by the T-Bar, and went to the longest of the chair lifts, Lift A.

He grinned unconsciously as he approached the lift. Eight or ten skiers were waiting to use the chairs, as compared to the long lines one usually encountered on weekends. As he approached the loading area, he caught a blur of black movement from the corner of his eye, turned and saw his German or Swedish ski instructor from the night before *wedeln* down the mountain, and then turning, parallel in a snow-spray-ing stop near the lift. He did not seem to recognize Hawes, but Hawes was not at all surprised. Every skier on the line was wearing a hooded parka, the hoods covering their heads and tied securely beneath their chins. In addition, all the skiers were wearing goggles, most with tinted yellow lenses in defense against the grayness of the day, some with darker lenses in spite of the grayness. The result, in any case, was almost total anonymity. Male and female, they all looked very much alike. They could have been a band of Martians waiting to be taken to a leader. Instead, they were waiting for chairs. They did not have to wait very long.

The chairs on their cable kept rounding the bend, came past the grinding machinery. Hawes moved into position, watched the girl ahead of him sit abruptly as the chair came up under her behind. He noticed that the chair gave a decided lurch as it cleared the platform, and he braced himself for the expected force, glanced back over his shoulder as another chair rounded the turn. Ski poles clutched in his left hand, his right hand behind him to grip the edge of the chair as it approached, he waited. The chair was faster and had a stronger lurch than he'd anticipated. For a moment, he thought it would knock him down. He gripped the edge of the seat with his mittened right hand, felt himself sliding off the seat, and automatically grabbed for the upright supporting rod with his left hand, dropping his poles.

"Dropped your poles!" one of the loaders shouted behind him.

"We'll send them up!" the other loader called.

He turned slightly in the chair and looked back. He could see one of the loaders scrambling to pick up his poles. There were two empty chairs behind him, and then a skier got into the third chair, and the loader handed him the poles Hawes had dropped. Behind that chair, two other skiers shared a chair. The wind and the snow made it difficult to see. Hawes turned his head abruptly, but the wind was even stronger coming down the mountain. The chair ahead of him was perhaps thirty feet away, but he could barely make out the shadowy figure of the person sitting in it. All he saw was a dim silhouette obscured by blinding snow and keening wind. He could feel snow seeping under the edges of his hood. He took off his mittens and tightened the string. Quickly, before the biting cold numbed his fingers, he put the mittens on again.

The lift was a new one, and it pulled the chairs silently up the mountain. On his right, Hawes could see the skiers descending, a damn fool snowplowing out of control down a steep embankment pocked with moguls, an excellent skier navigating turns in parallel precision. The wind keened around and under his hood, the only sound on the mountain. The ride was a pleasant one, except for the wind and the cold. In some spots, the chair was suspended some thirty feet above the snow below. In other places, the chair came as close as six feet to the ground. He was beginning to anticipate the descent. He saw the unloading station ahead, saw the sign advising him to keep the tips of his skis up, and prepared to disembark. The skier ahead of him met with difficulty as he tried to get off his chair. The snow had been falling too heavily to clear, and there was no natural downgrade at the top of the lift; the chair followed its occupant, rather than rising overhead at the unloading point. The girl ahead of Hawes was almost knocked off her feet by her own chair. She managed to free herself as the chair gave a sharp lurch around the bend to begin its trip down the mountain again. Hawes concentrated on getting off the chair. Surprisingly, he did so with a minimum of effort and without poles, and then waited while the two empty chairs passed by. The third following chair approached the station. A man clambered off the chair, handed Hawes his poles with a "These yours?" and skied to the crest of the slope. Hawes stood just outside the station booth, hanging his poles over his wrists. He was certain that the fourth chair behind his had contained *two* skiers at the bottom of the lift, and yet it seemed to be approaching now with only a single person in it. Hawes squinted through the snow, puzzled. Something seemed odd about the person in the fourth chair, something was jutting into the air at a curious angle—a ski? a leg? a . . . ?

The chair approached rapidly.

The skier made no move to disembark.

Hawes opened his eyes wide behind his yellow-tinted goggles as the chair swept past the station.

Through the driving snow, he had seen a skier slumped back into the passing chair, gloved hands dangling limply. And sticking out of the skier's chest at a malicious angle over the heart, buffeted by the wind and snow so that it trembled as if it were alive, thrust deep through the parka and the clothing beneath it like an oversized, slender aluminum sword, was a ski pole.

5

THE CHAIR gave its sharp lurch as it rounded the bend.

The skier slid from the seat as the chair made its abrupt turn. Skis touched snow, the body fell forward, there was a terrible snapping sound over the keening of the wind, and Hawes knew instantly that a leg had been broken as bone yielded to the unresisting laminated wood and the viselike binding. The skier fell face downward, the ski pole bending as the body struck the snow, one leg twisted at an impossible angle, the boot still held firmly in its binding.

For a moment, there was only confusion compounded.

The wind and the snow filled the air, the body lay motionless, face down in the snow as the chair whipped around the turn and started its descent. An empty chair swept past, another, a third, and then a chair came into view with a man poised to disembark, and Hawes shouted to the booth attendant, "Stop the lift!"

"What?"

"Stop the goddamn lift!"

"What? What?"

Hawes moved toward the body lying in the snow just as the man on the chair decided to get off. They collided in a tangle of poles and skis, the relentless chair pushing them along like a bulldozer, sending them sprawling onto the body in the snow, before it snapped around for its downward passage. The booth attendant finally got the message. He ran into the small wooden shack and threw the control switch. The lift stopped. There was a deeper silence on the mountain.

"You okay?" he called.

"I'm fine," Hawes said. He got to his feet and quickly unsnapped his bindings. The man who'd knocked him down was apologizing profusely, but Hawes wasn't listening. There was a bright red stain spreading into the snow where the impaled skier had fallen. He turned the body over and saw the ashen face and sightless eyes, saw the blood-soaked parka where the pole had been pushed through the soft and curving breast into the heart.

The dead skier was a young girl, no more than nineteen years old.

On the right sleeve of her black parka was the insignia of a Rawson Mountain ski instructor, the interlocking R and M in red as bright as the blood which seeped into the thirsty snow.

"What is it?" the booth attendant shouted. "Shall I get the ski patrol? Is it an accident?"

"It's no accident," Hawes said, but his voice was so low that no one heard him.

As BEFITTED this farcical hotel in this comic-opera town, the police were a band of Keystone cops led by an inept sheriff who worked on the premise that a thing worth doing was a thing worth doing badly. Hawes stood by helplessly as he watched these cracker-barrel cops violate each and every rule of investigation, watched as they mishandled evidence, watched as they made it hopelessly impossible to gain any information at all from whatever slender clues were available.

The sheriff was a gangling oaf named Theodore Watt who, instead of putting Lift A out of commission instantly while his men tried to locate the victim's chair, instead rode that very lift to the top of the mountain, followed by at least three dozen skiers, hotel officials, reporters, and local cretins who undoubtedly smeared any latent prints lingering on *any* of the chairs, and made the task of reconstructing the crime almost impossible. One girl, wearing bright lavender stretch pants and a white parka, climbed off the chair near the booth and was promptly informed there was blood all over the seat of her pants. The girl craned her neck to examine her shapely behind, touched the smear of blood, decided it was sticky and obscene, and almost fainted dead away. The chair, meantime, was happily whisking its way down the mountain again to the loading station where, presumably, another skier would again sit into a puddle of the dead girl's blood.

The dead girl's name, as it turned out, was Helga Nilson. She was nineteen years old and had learned to ski before she'd learned to walk, as the old Swedish saying goes. She had come to America when she was fifteen, had taught in the ski school at Stowe, Vermont, for two years before moving down to Mt. Snow in that same fair state, and then abandoning Vermont and moving to Rawson Mountain, further south. She had joined the Rawson ski school at the beginning of the season, and seemed to be well-liked by all the instructors and especially by many beginning skiers who, after one lesson with her, repeatedly asked for "Helga, the little Swedish girl."

The little Swedish girl had had a ski pole driven into her heart with such force that it had almost exited through her back. The pole, bent out of shape when Helga fell from the chair, was the first piece of real evidence the Keystone cops mishandled. Hawes saw one of the deputies kneel down beside the dead girl, grasp the pole with both hands, and attempt to pull it out of her body.

"Hey, what are you doing?" he shouted, and he shoved the man away from the body.

The man glanced up at him with a baleful upstate eye. "And just who in hell're *you?*" he asked.

"My name's Cotton Hawes," Hawes said. "I'm a detective. From the city." He unzipped the left hip pocket of his ski pants, pulled out his wallet, and flashed the tin. The deputy seemed singularly unimpressed.

"You're a little bit aways from your jurisdiction, ain't you?" he said.

"Who taught you how to handle evidence?" Hawes asked heatedly.

Sheriff Watt sauntered over to where the pair were arguing. He grinned amiably and said, "What seems to be the trouble here, hmmm?" He sang out the "hmmm," his voice rising pleasantly and cheerfully. A nineteen-year-old girl lay dead at his feet, but Sheriff Watt thought he was an old alumnus at Dartmouth's Winter Carnival.

"Feller here's a city detective," the deputy said.

"That's good," Watt said. "Pleased to have you with us."

"Thanks," Hawes said. "Your man here was just smearing any latent prints there may be on that weapon."

"What weapon?"

"The ski pole," Hawes said. "What weapon do you think I . . . ?"

"Oh, won't be no fingerprints on that, anyway," Watt said.

"How do you know?"

"No damn fool's gonna grab a piece of metal with his bare hands, is he? Not when the temperature's ten below zero, now is he?"

"He might have," Hawes said. "And while we're at it, don't you think it'd be a good idea to stop that lift? You've already had one person smearing up whatever stuff you could have found in the . . ."

"I got to get my men up here before I order the lift stopped," Watt said.

"Then restrict it to the use of your men."

"I've already done that," Watt said briefly. He turned back to his deputy. "Want to let me see that pole, Fred?"

"Sheriff, you let him touch that pole again, and . . ."

"And *what?*"

". . . and you may ruin . . ."

"Mister, you just let me handle this my own which-way, hmmm? We been in this business a long time now, and we know all about skiing accidents."

"This wasn't an accident," Hawes said angrily. "Somebody shoved a ski pole into that girl's chest, and that's not . . ."

"I know it wasn't an accident," Watt said. "That was just a manner of speaking. Let me have the pole, Fred."

"Sheriff . . ."

"Mister, you better just shut up, hmmm? Else I'll have one of my men escort you down the mountain, and you can warm your feet by the fire."

Hawes shut up. Impotently, he watched while the deputy named Fred seized the ski pole in both hands and yanked it from Helga's chest. A spurt of blood followed the retreating pole, welled up into the open wound, overflowed it, was sopped up by the sodden sweater. Fred handed the bent pole to the sheriff. Watt turned it over and over in his big hands.

"Looks like the basket's been taken off this thing," he said.

The basket, Hawes saw, had indeed been removed from the bottom of the aluminum pole. The basket on a ski pole is a circular metal ring perhaps five inches in diameter, crossed by a pair of leather thongs. A smaller ring stamped into the thongs fits over the end of the pointed pole and is usually fastened by a cotter pin or a tight rubber washer. When the basket is in place on the end of a pole, it prevents the pole from sinking into the snow, thereby enabling the skier to use it in executing turns or maintaining balance. The basket had been removed from this particular pole and, in addition, someone had sharpened the normally sharp point so that it was as thin as a rapier. Hawes noticed this at once. It took the sheriff a little while longer to see that he was holding a razor-sharp weapon in his hands, and not a normally pointed pole.

"Somebody been working on the end of this thing," he said, the dawn gradually breaking.

A doctor had come up the lift and was kneeling beside the dead girl. To no one's particular surprise, he pronounced her dead. One of the sheriff's bumbling associates began marking the position of the body, tracing its outline on the snow with a blue powder he poured liberally from a can.

Hawes couldn't imagine what possible use this imitation of investigatory technique would serve. They were marking the position of the body, true, but this didn't happen to be the scene of the crime. The girl had been murdered on a chair somewhere between the base of the mountain and the top of the lift. So far, no one had made any attempt to locate and examine the chair. Instead, they were sprinkling blue powder onto the snow, and passing their big paws all over the murder weapon.

"May I make a suggestion?" he asked.

"Sure," Watt said.

"That girl got on the lift with someone else. I know because I dropped my poles down there, and when I turned for a look, there were two people in that chair. But when she reached the station here, she was alone."

"Yeah?" Watt said.

"Yeah. I suggest you talk to the loader down below. The girl was a ski instructor, and they may have recognized her. Maybe they know who got on the chair with her."

"Provided anyone did."

"Someone did," Hawes said.

"How do you know?"

"Because . . . ." Hawes took a deep breath. "I just told you. I *saw* two people in that chair."

"How far behind you?"

"Four chairs behind."

"And you could see four chairs behind you in this storm, hmmm?"

"Yes. Not clearly, but I could see."

"I'll just bet you could," Watt said.

"Look," Hawes insisted, "someone was in that chair with her. And he undoubtedly jumped from the chair right after he killed her. I suggest you start combing the ground under the lift before this snow covers any tracks that might be there."

"Yes, we'll do that," Watt said. "When we get around to it."

"You'd better get around to it soon," Hawes said. "You've got a blizzard here, and a strong wind piling up drifts. If . . ."

"Mister, I hadn't *better* do anything. You're the one who'd just better butt his nose out of what we're trying to do here."

"What is it you're trying to do?" Hawes asked. "Compound a felony? Do you think your murderer's going to sit around and wait for you to catch up to him? He's probably halfway out of the state by now."

"Ain't nobody going noplace, mister," Watt said. "Not with the condition of the roads. So don't you worry about that. I hate to see anybody worrying."

"Tell that to the dead girl," Hawes said, and he watched as the ski patrol loaded her into a basket and began taking her on her last trip down the mountain.

DEATH IS a cliché, a tired old saw.

He had been a cop for a good long time now, starting as a rookie who saw death only from the sidelines, who kept a timetable while the detectives and the photographers and the assistant M.E. and the laboratory boys swarmed around the victim like flies around a prime cut of rotten meat. Death to him, at that time, had been motion-picture death. Standing apart from death, being as it were a uniformed secretary who took the names of witnesses and jotted in a black book the arrivals and departures of those actually concerned with the investigation, he had watched the proceedings dispassionately. The person lying lifeless on the sidewalk, the person lying on blood-soaked sheets, the person hanging from a light fixture, the person eviscerated by the onrushing front grille of an automobile, these were all a trifle unreal to Hawes, representations of death, but not death itself, not that grisly son of a bitch.

When he became a detective, they really introduced him to death.

The introduction was informal, almost casual. He was working with the 30th Squad at the time, a very nice respectable squad in a nice respectable precinct where death by violence hardly ever came. The introduction was made in a rooming house. The patrolman who had answered the initial squeal was waiting for the detectives when they arrived. The detective with Hawes asked, "Where's the stiff?" and the patrolman answered, "He's in there," and the other detective turned to Hawes and said, "Come on, let's take a look."

That was the introduction.

They had gone into the bedroom where the man was lying at the foot of the dresser. The man was fifty-three years old. He lay in his undershorts on the floor in the sticky coagulation of his own blood. He was a small man with a pinched chest. His hair was black and thinning, and bald patches showed his flaking scalp. He had probably never been handsome, even when he was a youth. Some men do not improve with age, and time and alcohol had squeezed everything out of this man, and drained him dry until all he possessed was sagging flesh and, of course, life. The flesh was still there. The life had been taken from him. He lay at the foot of the dresser in his undershorts, ludicrously piled into a heap of inert flesh, so relaxed, so impossibly relaxed. Someone had worked him over with a hatchet. The hatchet was still in the room, blood-flecked, entangled with thin black hair. The killer had viciously attacked him around the head and the throat and the chest. He had stopped bleeding by the time they arrived, but the wounds were still there to see, open and raw.

Hawes vomited.

He went into the bathroom and vomited. That was his introduction to death.

He had seen a lot of death since, had come close to being dead himself. The closest, perhaps, was the time he'd been stabbed while investigating a burglary. The woman who'd been burglarized was still pretty hysterical when he got there. He asked his questions and tried to comfort her, and then started downstairs to get a patrolman. The woman, terrified, began screaming when he left. He could hear her screams as he went down the stair well. The superintendent of the building caught him on the second floor landing. He was carrying a bread knife, and he thought that Hawes was the burglar returned, and he stabbed repeatedly at his head, ripping a wound over his left temple before Hawes finally subdued him. They let the super go; the poor guy had actually thought Hawes was the thief. And then they'd shaved Hawes' red hair to get to the wound, which time of course healed as it does all wounds, leaving however a reminder of death, of the closeness of death. The red hair had grown in white. He still carried the streak over his temple. Sometimes, particularly when it rained, death sent little signals of pain to accompany the new hair.

He had seen a lot of death, especially since he'd joined the 87th, and a lot of dying. He no longer vomited. The vomiting had happened to a very young Cotton Hawes, a very young and innocent cop who suddenly awoke to the knowledge that he was in a dirty business where the facts of life were the facts of violence, where he dealt daily with the sordid and grotesque. He no longer vomited. But he still got angry.

He had felt anger on the mountain when the young girl fell out of the chair and struck the snow, the ski pole bending as she dropped into that ludicrously ridiculous posture of the dead, that totally relaxed and utterly frightening posture. He had felt anger by juxtaposition, the reconstruction of a vibrant and life-bursting athlete against the very real image of the same girl, no longer a girl, only a worthless heap of flesh and bones, only a body now, a corpse, "Where's the stiff?"

He had felt anger when Theodore Watt and his witless assistants muddied the residue of sudden death, allowing the killer a precious edge, presenting him with the opportunity for escape—escape from the law and from the outrage of humanity. He felt anger now as he walked back to the building which housed the ski shop and the rooms overhead.

The anger seemed out of place on the silent mountain. The snow still fell, still and gentle. The wind had died, and now the flakes drifted aimlessly from overhead, large and wet and white, and there was a stillness and a peace to Rawson Mountain and the countryside beyond, a lazy white quiet which denied the presence of death.

He kicked the packed snow from his boots and went up the steps.

He was starting down the corridor toward his room when he noticed the door was slightly ajar. He hesitated. Perhaps Blanche had come back to the room, perhaps . . .

But there was silence in the corridor, a silence as large as noise. He stooped and untied the laces on his boots. Gently, he slipped them from his feet. Walking as softly as he could—he was a big man and the floor boards in the old building creaked beneath his weight—he approached the room. He did not like the idea of being in his stockinged feet. He had had to kick men too often, and he knew the value of shoes. He hesitated just outside the door. There was no sound in the room. The door was open no more than three inches. He put his hand against the wood. Somewhere in the basement, the oil burner clicked and then *whooooomed* into action. He shoved open the door.

Elmer Wollender, his crutches under his arms, whirled to face him. His head had been bent in an attitude of . . . prayer, was it? No. Not prayer. He had been listening, that was it, listening *to* something, or *for* something.

"Oh, hello, Mr. Hawes," he said. He was wearing a red ski parka over his white shirt. He leaned on his crutches and grinned a boyish, disarming grin.

"Hello, Mr. Wollender," Hawes said. "Would you mind telling me, Mr. Wollender, just what the hell you're doing in my room?"

Wollender seemed surprised. His eyebrows arched. He tilted his head to one side, almost in admiration, almost as if he too would have behaved in much the same way had he come back to *his* room and found a stranger in it. But the admiration was also tinged with surprise. This was obviously a mistake. Head cocked to one side, eyebrows arched, the boyish smile on his mouth, Wollender leaned on his crutches and prepared to explain. Hawes waited.

"You said the heat wasn't working, didn't you?" Wollender said. "I was just checking it."

"The heat's working fine in this room," Hawes said. "It's the room next door."

"Oh." Wollender nodded. "Oh, is that it?"

"That's it, yes."

"No wonder. I stuck my hand up there to check the vent, and it seemed fine to me."

"Yes, it would be fine," Hawes said, "since there was never anything wrong with it. I told you at the desk this morning that the heat wasn't working in 104. This is 105. Are you new here, Mr. Wollender?"

"I guess I misunderstood you."

"Yes, I guess so. Misunderstanding isn't a wise practice, Mr. Wollender, especially with your local cops crawling all over the mountain."

"What are you talking about?"

"I'm talking about the girl. When those imitation cops begin asking questions, I suggest . . ."

"What girl?"

Hawes looked at Wollender for a long time. The question on Wollender's face and in his eyes looked genuine enough, but could there possibly be someone on the mountain who still had not heard of the murder? Was it possible that Wollender, who ran the inn, the center of all activity and gossip, did not know Helga Nilson was dead?

"The girl," Hawes said. "Helga Nilson."

"What about her?"

Hawes knew enough about baseball to realize you didn't throw your fast ball until you'd tried a few curves. "Do you know her?" he asked.

"Of course, I know her. I know all the ski instructors. She rooms right here, down the hall."

"Who else rooms here?"

"Why?"

"I want to know."

"Just her and Maria," Wollender said. "Maria Fiers. She's an instructor, too. And, oh yes, the new man. Larry Davidson."

"Is he an instructor?" Hawes asked. "About this tall?"

"Yes."

"Hooked nose? German accent."

"No, no. You're thinking of Helmut Kurtz. And that's an Austrian accent." Wollender paused. "Why? Why do you want to . . . ?"

"Anything between him and Helga?"

"Why, no. Not that I know of. They teach together, but . . ."

"What about Davidson?"

"Larry Davidson?"

"Yes."

"Do you mean, is he dating Helga, or . . ."

"Yes, that's right."

"Larry's married," Wollender said, "I would hardly think . . ."

"What about you?"

"I don't understand."

"You and Helga. Anything?"

"Helga's a good friend of mine," Wollender said.

"Was," Hawes corrected.

"Huh?"

"She's dead. She was killed on the mountain this afternoon."

There was the fast ball, and it took Wollender smack between the eyes. "Dea—" he started, and then his jaw fell slack, and his eyes went blank. He staggered back a pace, colliding with the white dresser. The crutches dropped from his hands. He struggled to maintain his balance, the leg with the cast stiff and unwieldy; he seemed about to fall. Hawes grabbed at his elbow and pulled him erect. He stooped down for Wollender's crutches and handed them to him. Wollender was still dazed. He groped for the crutches, fumbled, dropped them again. Hawes picked them up a second time, and forced them under Wollender's arms. Wollender leaned back against the dresser. He kept staring at the wall opposite, where a poster advertising the pleasures of Kitzbühel was hanging.

"She . . . she took too many chances," he said. "She always went too fast. I told her . . ."

"This wasn't a skiing accident," Hawes said. "She was murdered."

"No." Wollender shook his head. "No."

"Yes."

"No. Everyone liked Helga. No one would . . ." He kept shaking his head. His eyes stayed riveted to the Kitzbühel poster.

"There are going to be cops here, Mr. Wollender," Hawes said. "You seem like a nice kid. When they start asking questions, you'd better have a more plausible story than the one you invented about being in my room. They're not going to fool around. They're looking for a killer."

"Why . . . why do you *think* I came here?" Wollender asked.

"I don't know. Maybe you were looking for some pocket money. Skiers often leave their wallets and their valu—"

"I'm not a thief, Mr. Hawes," Wollender said with dignity. "I only came here to give you some heat."

"That makes it even," Hawes answered. "The cops'll be coming here to give *you* some."

HE FOUND the two loaders in the lodge cafeteria. The lifts had been closed at four-thirty, the area management having reached the conclusion that most skiing accidents took place in the waning hours of the afternoon, when poor visibility and physical exhaustion combined to create gentle havoc. They were both burly, grizzled men wearing Mackinaws, their thick hands curled around coffee mugs. They had been loading skiers onto chairs ever since the area was opened, and they worked well together as a team. Even their dialogue seemed concocted in one mind, though it issued from two mouths.

"My name's Jake," the first loader said. "This here is Obey, short for Obadiah."

"Only I ain't so short," Obadiah said.

"He's short on brains," Jake said and grinned. Obadiah returned the grin. "You're a cop, huh?"

"Yes," Hawes said. He had shown them his buzzer the moment he approached them. He had also told an outright lie, saying he was helping with the investigation of the case, having been sent up from the city because there was the possibility a known and wanted criminal had perpetrated the crime, confusing his own doubletalk as he wove a fantastic monologue which Jake and Obadiah seemed to accept.

"And you want to know who we loaded on them chairs, right? Same as Teddy wanted to know."

"Teddy?"

"Teddy Watt. The sheriff."

"Oh. Yes." Hawes said. "That's right."

"Whyn't you just ask *him?*" Obadiah said.

"Well, I have," Hawes lied. "But sometimes a fresh angle will come up if witnesses can be questioned directly, do you see?"

"Well, we ain't exactly witnesses," Jake said. "We didn't see her get killed, you know."

"Yes, but you did load her on the chair, didn't you?"

"That's right. We did, all right."

"And someone was in the chair with her, is that right?"

"That's right," Jake said.

"Who?" Hawes asked.

"Seems like everybody wants to know *who,*" Jake said.

"Ain't it the damnedest thing?" Obadiah said.

"Do you remember?" Hawes asked.

"We remember it was snowing, that's for sure."

"Couldn't hardly see the chairs, it was snowing that hard."

"Pretty tough to reckernize one skier from another with all that wind and snow, wouldn't you say, Obey?"

"Next to impossible," Obadiah answered.

"But you did recognize Helga," Hawes suggested.

"Oh, sure. But she said hello to us, you see. She said, 'Hello, Jake. Hello, Obey.' And also, she took the chair closest to the loading platform, the inside chair. The guy took the other chair."

"Guy?" Hawes asked. "It was a man then? The person who took the chair next to her was a man?"

"Well, can't say for sure," Jake said. "Was a time when men's ski clothes was different from the ladies', but that don't hold true no more."

"Not by a long shot," Obadiah said.

"Nowadays, you find yourself following some pretty girl in purple pants, she turns out to be a man. It ain't so easy to tell them apart no more."

"Then you don't know whether the person who sat next to her was a man or a woman, is that right?" Hawes asked.

"That's right."

"Coulda been either."

"Did this person say anything?"

"Not a word."

"What was he wearing?"

"Well, we ain't established it was a *he,*" Jake reminded him.

"Yes, I know. I meant the . . . the person who took the chair. It'll be easier if we give him a gender."

"Give him a *what?*"

"A gen—if we assume for the moment that the person was a man."

"Oh." Jake thought this over. "Okay, if you say so. Seems like pretty sloppy deduction to me, though."

"Well, I'm not actually making a deduction. I'm simply trying to facilitate . . ."

"Sure, I understand," Jake said. "But it's sure pretty sloppy."

Hawes sighed. "Well . . . what *was* he wearing?"

"Black," Jake said.

"Black ski pants, black parka," Obadiah said.

"Any hat?" Hawes asked.

"Nope. Hood on the parka was pulled clear up over the head. Sun glasses over the eyes."

"Gloves or mittens?" Hawes asked.

"Gloves. Black gloves."

"Did you notice whether or not there was an insignia on the man's parka?"

"What kind of insignia?"

"An R-M interlocked," Hawes said.

"Like the instructors wear?" Jake asked.

"Exactly."

"They wear it on their *right* sleeves," Obadiah said. "We told you this person took the outside chair. We couldn'ta seen the right sleeve, even if there *was* anything on it."

Hawes suddenly had a wild idea. He hesitated before he asked, and then thought *What the hell, try it.*

"This person," he said, "was he . . . was he carrying crutches?"

"Carrying *what?*" Jake asked incredulously.

"Crutches. Was his leg in a cast?"

"Now how in hell . . . of *course* not," Jake said. "He was wearing skis, and he was carrying ski poles. Crutches and a cast! My God! It's hard enough getting on that damn lift as it is. Can you just picture . . ."

"Never mind," Hawes said. "Forget it. Did this person say anything to Helga?"

"Not a word."

"Did she say anything to him?"

"Nothing we could hear. The wind was blowing pretty fierce."

"But you heard her when she said hello to you."

"That's right."

"Then if she'd said anything to this person, you might have heard that, too."

"That's right. We didn't hear nothing."

"You said he was carrying poles. Did you notice anything unusual about the poles?"

"Seemed like ordinary poles to me," Jake said.

"Did both poles have baskets?"

Jake shrugged. "I didn't notice. Did you notice, Obey?"

"Both seemed to have baskets," Obadiah said. "Who'd notice a thing like that?"

"Well, you might have," Hawes said. "If there'd been anything unusual, you might have noticed."

"I didn't notice nothing unusual," Obadiah said. "Except I thought to myself this feller must be pretty cold."

"Why?"

"Well, the hood pulled up over his head, and the scarf wrapped almost clear around his face."

"What scarf? You didn't mention that before."

"Sure. He was wearing a red scarf. Covered his mouth and his nose, reached right up to the sunglasses."

"Hmmm," Hawes said, and the table went still.

"You're the fellow dropped his poles on the way up, ain't you?" Jake asked.

"Yes."

"Thought I remembered you."

"If you remember *me,* how come you can't remember the person who took that chair alongside Helga's?"

"You saying I *should,* mister?"

"I'm only asking."

"Well, like maybe if I seen a guy wearing black pants and a black hood, and sunglasses, and a scarf wrapped clear around his face, why maybe then I would recognize him. But, the way I figure it, he ain't likely to be wearing the same clothes right now, is he?"

"I don't suppose so," Hawes said, sighing.

"Yeah, neither do I," Jake answered. "And I ain't even a cop."

9

DUSK WAS settling upon the mountain.

It spread into the sky and stained the snow a purple-red. The storm was beginning to taper off, the clouds vanishing before the final triumphant breakthrough of the setting sun. There was an unimaginable hush to the mountain, and the town, and the valley beyond, a hush broken only by the sound of gently jingling skid-chains on hard-packed snow.

He had found Blanche and taken her to the fireplace in the inn, settling her there with a brace of double Scotches and a half-dozen copies of a skiing magazine. Now, with the mountain and the town still, the lifts inoperative, the distant snow brushed with dying color, he started climbing the mountain. He worked through the deep snow directly under the lift, the chairs hanging motionless over his head. He was wearing ski pants and after-ski boots designed for lounging beside a fire. He had forsaken his light parka for two sweaters. Before he'd left the room, he had unholstered the .38 and slipped it into the elastic-reinforced waistband of his trousers. He could feel it digging into his abdomen now as he climbed.

The climb was not an easy one.

The snow under the lift had not been packed, and he struggled against it as he climbed, encountering drifts which were impassable, working his way in a zigzagging manner across the lift line, sometimes being forced to leave the high snow for the Cat-packed trail to the right of the lift. The light was waning. He did not know how much longer it would last. He had taken a flashlight from the glove compartment of his car, but he began to wonder whether its glow would illuminate very much once the sun had set. He began to wonder, too, exactly what he hoped to find. He was almost certain that any tracks the killer had left would already have been covered by the drifting snow. Again, he cursed Theodore Watt and his inefficient slobs. Someone should have made this climb immediately after they discovered the dead girl, while there was still a possibility of finding a trail.

He continued climbing. After a day of skiing, he was physically and mentally exhausted, his muscles protesting, his eyes burning. He thumbed on the flashlight as darkness claimed the mountain, and pushed his way through knee-deep snow. He stumbled and got to his feet again. The snow had tapered almost completely, but the wind had returned with early evening, a high keening wind that rushed through the trees on either side of the lift line, pushing the clouds from the sky. There was a thin sliver of moon and a scattering of stars. The clouds raced past them like silent dark horsemen, and everywhere on the mountain was the piercing shriek of the wind, a thin scream that penetrated to the marrow.

He fell again.

Loose snow caught under the neck of his sweater, slid down his back. He shivered and tried to brush it away, got to his feet, and doggedly began climbing again. His after-ski boots had not been designed for deep snow. The tops ended just above his ankles, offering no protection whatever. He realized abruptly that the boots were already packed with snow, that his feet were literally encased in snow. He was beginning to regret this whole foolhardy mission, when he saw it.

He had come perhaps a third of the way up the lift line, the mountain in absolute darkness now, still except for the maiden scream of the wind. The flashlight played a small circle of light on the snow ahead of him as he stumbled upward, the climb more difficult now, the clouds rushing by overhead, skirting the thin moon. The light touched something which glinted momentarily, passed on as he continued climbing, stopped. He swung the flashlight back. Whatever had glinted was no longer there. Swearing, he swung the flashlight in a slow steady arc. The glint again. He swung the light back.

The basket was half-covered by the snow. Only one edge of its metallic ring showed in the beam of his light. It had probably been covered completely earlier in the day, but the strong fresh wind had exposed it to view again, and he stopped quickly to pick it up, almost as if he were afraid it would vanish. He was still bending, studying the basket in the light of the flash, when the man jumped onto his back.

The attack came suddenly and swiftly. He had heard nothing but the wind. He had been so occupied with his find, so intent on studying the basket which, he was certain, had come from the end of the ski-pole weapon, that when he felt the sudden weight on his back he did not connect it immediately with an attack. He was simply surprised, and his first thought was that one of the pines had dropped a heavy load of snow from its laden branches, and then he realized this was no heavy load of snow, but by that time he was flat on his belly.

He rolled over instantly. He held the ski pole basket in his left hand, refusing to let go of it. In his right hand, he held the flashlight, and he swung that instantly at the man's head, felt it hitting the man's forearm instead. Something solid struck Hawes' shoulder; a wrench? a hammer? and he realized at once that the man was armed, and suddenly the situation became serious. He threw away the flashlight and groped for the .38 in his waistband.

The clouds cleared the moon. The figure kneeling over him, straddling him, was wearing a black parka, the hood pulled up over his head. A red scarf was wrapped over his chin and his mouth and his nose. He was holding a hammer in his right hand, and he raised the hammer over his head just as the moon disappeared again. Hawes' fingers closed on the butt of the .38. The hammer descended.

It descended in darkness, striking Hawes on his cheek, ripping the flesh, glancing downward and catching his shoulder. Hawes swore violently, drew the .38 in a ridiculously clumsy draw, brought it into firing position, and felt again the driving blow of the other man's weapon, the hammer lashing out of the darkness, slamming with brute force against his wrist, almost cracking the bone. His fingers opened involuntarily. The gun dropped into the snow. He bellowed in pain and tried to kick out at his attacker, but the man moved away quickly, gained his feet, and braced himself in the deep snow for the final assault. The moon appeared again. A thin silvery light put the man in silhouette against the sky, the black hooded head, the face masked by the scarf. The hammer went up over his head.

Hawes kicked out at his groin.

The blow did nothing to stop the man's attack. It glanced off his thigh, missing target as the hammer came down, but throwing him off balance slightly so that the hammer struck without real force. Hawes threw a fist at him, and the man grunted and again the hammer came out of the new darkness. The man fought desperately and silently, frightening Hawes with the fury of his animal strength. They rolled over in the snow, and Hawes grasped at the hood, tried to pull it from the man's head, found it was securely tied in place, and reached for the scarf. The scarf began to unravel. The man lashed out with the hammer, felt the scarf coming free, pulled back to avoid exposing his face, and suddenly staggered as Hawes' fist struck home. He fell into the snow, and all at once, he panicked. Instead of attacking again, he pulled the scarf around his face and began to half run, half stumble through the deep snow. Hawes leaped at him, missing, his hands grabbing air. The man scrambled over the snow, heading for the pines lining the lift. By the time Hawes was on his feet again, the man had gone into the trees. Hawes went after him. It was dark under the trees. The world went black and silent under the pines.

He hesitated for a moment. He could see nothing, could hear nothing. He fully expected the hammer to come lashing out of the darkness.

Instead, there came the voice.

"Hold it right there."

The voice startled him, but he reacted intuitively, whirling, his fist pulling back reflexively, and then firing into the darkness. He felt it connecting with solid flesh, heard someone swearing in the dark, and then—surprisingly, shockingly—Hawes heard the sound of a pistol shot. It rang on the mountain air, reverberated under the pines. Hawes opened his eyes wide. A pistol? But the man had only a hammer. Why hadn't . . . ?

"Next time, I go for your heart," the voice said.

Hawes stared into the darkness. He could no longer locate the voice. He did not know where to jump, and the man was holding a pistol.

"You finished?" the man asked.

The beam of a flashlight suddenly stabbed through the darkness. Hawes blinked his eyes against it, tried to shield his face.

"Well, well," the man said. "You never can tell, can you? Stick out your hands."

"What?" Hawes said.

"Stick out your goddamn hands."

Hesitantly, he held out his hands. He was the most surprised human being in the world when he felt the handcuffs being snapped onto his wrists.

10

THE OFFICE from which Theodore Watt, sheriff of the town of Rawson, operated was on the main street alongside an Italian restaurant whose neon sign advertised LASAGNA * SPAGHETTI * RAVIOLI. Now that the snow had stopped, the plows had come through and banked snow on either side of the road so that the door of the office was partially hidden by a natural fortress of white. Inside the office, Theodore Watt was partially hidden by the fortress of his desk, the top of which was covered with Wanted circulars, FBI flyers, carbon copies of police reports, a pair of manacles, a cardboard container of coffee, a half-dozen chewed pencil stubs, and a framed picture of his wife and three children. Theodore Watt was not in a very friendly mood. He sat behind his desk-fortress, a frown on his face. Cotton Hawes stood before the desk, still wearing the handcuffs which had been clamped onto his wrists on the mountain. The deputy who'd made the collar, the self-same Fred who had earlier pulled the ski pole from Helga Nilson's chest, stood alongside Hawes, wearing the sheriff's frown, and also wearing a mouse under his left eye, where Hawes had hit him.

"I could lock you up, you know," Watt said, frowning. "You hit one of my deputies."

"You ought to lock *him* up," Hawes said angrily. "If he hadn't come along, I might have had our man."

"You might have, huh?"

"Yes."

"You had no right being on that damn mountain," Watt said. "What were you doing up there?"

"Looking."

"For what?"

"Anything. He gave you the basket I found. Apparently it was important enough for the killer to have wanted it, too. He fought hard enough for it. Look at my cheek."

"Well now, that's a shame," Watt said drily.

"There may be fingerprints on that basket," Hawes said. "I suggest . . ."

"I doubt it. Weren't none on the ski pole, and none on the chair, neither. We talked to the two loaders, and they told us the one riding up with Helga Nilson was wearing gloves. I doubt if there's any fingerprints on that basket at all."

"Well . . ." Hawes said, and he shrugged.

"What it amounts to, hmmmm," Watt said, "is that you figured we wasn't handling this case to your satisfaction, ain't that it? So you figured you'd give us local hicks a little big-time help, hmmmm? Ain't that about it?"

"I thought I could possibly assist in some . . ."

"Then you shoulda come to me," Watt said, "and *asked* if you could help. This way, you only fouled up what we was trying to do."

"I don't understand."

"I've got six men on that mountain," Watt said, "waiting for whoever killed that girl to come back and cover his mistakes. This basket here was one of the mistakes. But did our killer find it? No. Our helpful big-city detective found it. You're a lot of help, mister, you sure are. With all that ruckus on the mountain, that damn killer won't go anywhere near it for a month!"

"I almost had him," Hawes said. "I was going after him when your man stopped me."

"Stopped you, hell! *You're* the one who was stopping *him* from doing his job. Maybe I *ought* to lock you up. There's a thing known as impeding the progress of an investigation. But, of course, you know all about that, don't you? Being a big-city detective. Hmmm?"

"I'm sorry if I . . ."

"And of course we're just a bunch of local hicks who don't know nothing at all about police work. Why, we wouldn't even know enough to have a autopsy performed on that little girl, now would we? Or to have tests made of the blood on that chair, now would we? We wouldn't have no crime lab in the next biggest town to Rawson, would we?"

"The way you were handling the investigation . . ." Hawes started.

". . . was none of your damn business," Watt concluded. "Maybe we like to make our own mistakes, Hawes! But naturally, you city cops never make mistakes. That's why there ain't no crime at all where you come from."

"Look," Hawes said, "you were mishandling evidence. I don't give a damn what you . . ."

"As it turns out, it don't matter because there wasn't no fingerprints on that pole, anyway. And we had to get our men up the mountain, so we had to use the lift. There was a hell of a lot of confusion there today, mister. But I don't suppose big-city cops ever get confused, hmmmm?" Watt looked at him sourly. "Take the cuffs off him, Fred," he said.

Fred looked surprised, but he unlocked the handcuffs. "He hit me right in the eye," he said to Watt.

"Well, you still got the other eye," Watt said drily. "Go to bed, Hawes. We had enough of you for one night."

"What did the autopsy report say?" Hawes asked.

Watt looked at him in something close to astonishment. "You still sticking your nose in this?"

"I'd still like to help, yes."

"Maybe we don't need your help."

"Maybe you can use it. No one here knows . . ."

"There we go with the damn big-city attitu—"

"I was going to say," Hawes said, overriding Watt's voice, "that no one in the area knows I'm a cop. That could be helpful to you."

Watt was silent. "Maybe," he said at last.

"*May* I hear the autopsy report?"

Watt was silent again. Then he nodded. He picked up a sheet of paper from his desk and said. "Death caused by fatal stab wound of the heart, penetration of the auricles and pulmonary artery. That's where all the blood came from, Hawes. Wounds of the ventricles don't usually bleed that much. Coroner figures the girl died in maybe two or three minutes, there was that much loss of blood."

"Anything else?"

"Broke her ankle when she fell out of that chair. Oblique fracture of the lateral malleolus. Examiner also found traces of human skin under the girl's fingernails. Seems like she clawed out at whoever stabbed her, and took a goodly part of him away with her."

"What did the skin tell you?"

"Not a hell of a lot. Our killer is white and adult."

"That's all?"

"That's all. At least, that's all from the skin, except the possibility of using it later for comparison tests—if we ever get anybody to compare it with. We found traces of blood on her fingers and nails, too, not her own."

"How do you know?"

"Blood on the chair, the girl's blood, was in the AB grouping. Blood we found on her hands was in the O grouping, most likely the killer's."

"Then she scratched him enough to cause bleeding."

"She took a big chunk of skin from him, Hawes."

"From the face?"

"Now how in hell would I know?"

"I thought maybe . . ."

"Couldn't tell from the skin sample whether it came from the neck or the face or wherever. She coulda scratched him anyplace."

"Anything else?"

"We found a trail of the girl's blood in the snow under the lift. Plenty of it, believe me, she bled like a stuck pig. The trail started about four minutes from the top. Took her two or three minutes to die. So, assuming the killer jumped from the chair right soon's he stabbed her, then the girl . . ."

". . . was still alive when he jumped."

"That's right."

"Find any tracks in the snow?"

"Nothing. Too many drifts. We don't know whether he jumped with his skis on or not. Have to have been a pretty good skier to attempt that, we figure."

"Well, anyway, he's got a scratch," Hawes said. "That's *something* to look for."

"You gonna start looking tonight?" Watt asked sarcastically.

11

BLANCHE COLBY was waiting for him when he got back to the room. She was sitting up in his bed propped against the pillows, wearing a shapeless flannel nightgown which covered her from her throat to her ankles. She was holding an apple in her hand, and she bit into it angrily as he entered the room, and then went back to reading the open book in her lap.

"Hi," he said.

She did not answer him, nor did she even look up at him. She continued destroying the apple, continued her pretense of reading.

"Good book?"

"*Excellent* book," she answered.

"Miss me?"

"Drop dead," Blanche said.

"I'm sorry. I . . ."

"Don't be. I enjoyed myself immensely in your absence."

"I got arrested, you see."

"You got *what?*"

"Arrested. Pinched. Pulled in. Collared. Apprehen—"

"I understood you the first time. Who arrested you?"

"The cops," Hawes said, and he shrugged.

"Serves you right." She put down the book. "Wasn't it you who told me a girl was killed on this mountain today? Murdered? And you run off and leave me when a killer . . ."

"I told you where I was going. I told you . . ."

"You said you'd be back in an hour!"

"Yes, but I didn't know I was going to be arrested."

"What happened to your cheek?"

"I got hit with a hammer."

"Good," Blanche said, and she nodded emphatically.

"Aren't you going to kiss my wound?" Hawes asked.

"*You* can kiss my . . ."

"Ah-ah," he cautioned.

"I sat by that damn fireplace until eleven o'clock. Then I came up here and . . . what time is it, anyway?"

"After midnight."

Blanche nodded again. "I would have packed up and gone home, believe me, if the roads were open."

"Yes, but they're closed."

"Yes, damn it!"

"Aren't you glad I'm back?"

Blanche shrugged. "I couldn't care less. I was just about to go to sleep."

"In here?"

"In the other room, naturally."

"Honey, honey . . ."

"Yes, honey-honey?" she mimicked. "*What,* honey-honey baby?"

Hawes grinned. "That's a very lovely nightgown. My grandmother used to wear a nightgown like that."

"I thought you'd like it," Blanche said sourly. "I put it on especially for you."

"I always liked the touch of flannel," he said.

"Get your big hands . . ." she started, and moved away from him swiftly. Folding her arms across the front of her gown, she sat in the center of the bed and stared at the opposite wall. Hawes studied her for a moment, took off his sweaters, and then began unbuttoning his shirt.

"If you're going to undress," Blanche said evenly, "you could at least have the modesty to go into the . . ."

"Shhh!" Hawes said sharply. His hands had stopped on the buttons of his shirt. He cocked his head to one side now and listened. Blanche, watching him, frowned.

"What . . . ?"

"Shhh!" he said again, and again he listened attentively. The room was silent. Into the silence came the sound.

"Do you hear it?" he asked.

"Do I hear what?"

"Listen."

They listened together. The sound was unmistakable, faint and faraway, but unmistakable.

"It's the same buzzing I heard last night," Hawes said. "I'll be right back."

"Where are you going?"

"Downstairs. To the ski shop," he answered, and swiftly left the room. As he went down the corridor toward the steps, a door at the opposite end of the hall opened. A young girl wearing a quilted robe over her pajamas, her hair done in curlers, came into the hallway carrying a towel and a tooth brush. She smiled at Hawes and then walked past him. He heard the bathroom door locking behind her as he went down the steps.

The lights were on in the ski shop. The buzzing sound came from somewhere in the shop, intermittent, hanging on the silent night air, ceasing abruptly, beginning again. He walked silently over the snow, stopping just outside the door to the shop. He put his ear to the wood and listened, but the only sound he heard was the buzzing. He debated kicking in the door. Instead, he knocked gently.

"Yes?" a voice from inside called.

"Could you open up, please?" Hawes said.

He waited. He could hear the heavy sound of ski boots approaching the locked door. The door opened a crack. A sun-tanned face appeared in the opening. He recognized the face at once—Helmut Kurtz, the ski instructor who had helped him the night before, the man he'd seen today on the mountain just before he'd got on the chair lift.

"Oh, hello there," Hawes said.

"Yes? What is it?" Kurtz asked.

"Mind if I come in?"

"I'm sorry, no one is allowed in the shop. The shop is closed."

"Yes, but *you're* in it, aren't you?"

"I'm an instructor," Kurtz said. "We are permitted . . ."

"I just saw a light," Hawes said, "and I felt like talking to someone."

"Well . . ."

"What are you doing, anyway?" Hawes asked casually, and casually
he wedged one shoulder against the door and gently eased it open,
casually pushing it into the room, casually squeezing his way into the
opening, casually shouldering his way past Kurtz, and then squinting
past the naked hanging light bulb to the work bench at the far end of
the room, trying to locate the source of the buzzing sound which filled
the shop.

"You are really not allowed . . ." Kurtz started, but Hawes was
already halfway across the room, moving toward the other small area
of light where a green-shaded bulb hung over the work bench. The
buzzing sound was louder, the sound of an old machine, the sound
of . . .

He located it almost at once. A grinding wheel was set up on one end
of the bench. The wheel was still spinning. He looked at it, nodded and
then flicked the switch to turn it off. Turning to Kurtz, he smiled and
said, "Were you sharpening something?"

"Yes, those skates," Kurtz said. He pointed to a pair of white figure
skates on the bench.

"Yours?" Hawes asked.

Kurtz smiled. "No. Those are women's skates."

"Whose?"

"Well, I don't think that is any of your business, do you?" Kurtz
asked politely.

"I suppose not," Hawes answered gently, still smiling. "Were you in
here sharpening something last night, too, Mr. Kurtz?"

"I beg your pardon?"

"I said, were you . . ."

"No, I was not." Kurtz walked up to the bench and studied Hawes
slowly and deliberately. "Who *are* you?" he asked.

"My name's Cotton Hawes."

"How do you do? Mr. Hawes, I'm sorry to have to be so abrupt, but
you are really not allowed . . ."

"Yes, I know. Only instructors are allowed in here, isn't that right,
Mr. Kurtz?"

"After closing, yes. We sometimes come in to make minor repairs on
our skis or . . ."

"Or sharpen up some things, huh, Mr. Kurtz?"

"Yes. Like the skates."

"Yes," Hawes repeated. "Like the skates. But you weren't in here last night, were you, Mr. Kurtz?"

"No, I was not."

"Because, you see, I heard what could have been the sound of a file or a rasp or something, and then the sound of this grinding wheel. So you're sure you weren't in here sharpening something? Like skates? Or . . ." Hawes shrugged. "A ski pole?"

"A ski pole? Why would anyone . . . ?" Kurtz fell suddenly silent. He studied Hawes again. "What are you?" he asked. "A policeman?"

"Why? Don't you like policemen?"

"I had nothing to do with Helga's death," Kurtz said immediately.

"No one said you did."

"You implied it."

"I implied nothing, Mr. Kurtz."

"You asked if I were sharpening a ski pole last night. The implication is . . ."

"But you weren't."

"No, I was *not!*" Kurtz said angrily.

"What *were* you sharpening last night?"

"Nothing. I was nowhere near this shop last night."

"Ahh, but you were, Mr. Kurtz. I met you outside, remember? You were coming down the steps. Very fast. Don't you remember?"

"That was earlier in the evening."

"But I didn't say anything about time, Mr. Kurtz. I didn't ask you *when* you were in this shop."

"I was *not* in this shop! Not at any time!"

"But you just said 'That was earlier in the evening.' Earlier than what, Mr. Kurtz?"

Kurtz was silent for a moment. Then he said, "Earlier than . . . than whoever was here."

"You saw someone here?"

"I . . . I saw a light burning."

"When? What time?"

"I don't remember. I went to the bar after I met you . . . and I had a few drinks, and then I went for a walk. That was when I saw the light."

"Where do you room, Mr. Kurtz?"

"In the main building."

"Did you see Helga at any time last night?"

"No."

"Not at any time?"

"No."

"Then what were you doing upstairs?"

"I came to get Maria's skates. Those." He pointed to the figure skates on the bench.

"Maria who?"

"Maria Fiers."

"Is she a small girl with dark hair?"

"Yes. Do you know her?"

"I think I just saw her in the hallway," Hawes said. "So you came to get her skates, and then you went for a drink, and then you went for a walk. What time was that?"

"It must have been after midnight."

"And a light was burning in the ski shop?"

"Yes."

"But you didn't see who was in here?"

"No, I did not."

"How well did you know Helga?"

"Very well. We taught together."

"How well is very well?"

"We were good friends."

"How good, Mr. Kurtz?"

"I *told* you!"

"Were you sleeping with her?"

"How dare you . . ."

"Okay, okay." Hawes pointed to the skates. "These are Maria's, you said?"

"Yes. She's an instructor here, too. But she skates well, almost as well as she skis."

"Are you good friends with her, too, Mr. Kurtz?"

"I am good friends with *everyone!*" Kurtz said angrily. "I am normally a friendly person." He paused. *"Are* you a policeman?"

"Yes. I am."

"I don't like policemen," Kurtz said, his voice low. "I didn't like them in Vienna, where they wore swastikas on their arms, and I don't like them here, either. I had nothing to do with Helga's death."

"Do you have a key to this shop, Mr. Kurtz?"

"Yes. We *all* do. We make our own minor repairs. During the day, there are too many people here. At night, we can . . ."

"What do you mean by *all?* The instructors?"

"Yes."

"I see. Then any of the instructors could have . . ."

The scream was a sentient thing which invaded the room suddenly and startlingly. It came from somewhere upstairs, ripping down through the ancient floor boards and the ancient ceiling timbers. It struck the room with its blunt force, and both men looked up toward the ceiling, speechless, waiting. The scream came again. Hawes got to his feet and ran for the door. *"Blanche,"* he whispered, and slammed the door behind him.

She was standing in the corridor outside the hall bathroom, not really standing, but leaning limply against the wall, her supporting dancer's legs robbed of stance, robbed of control. She wore the long flannel nightgown with a robe over it, and she leaned against the wall with her eyes shut tight, her blond hair disarrayed, the scream unvoiced now, but frozen in the set of her face and the trembling openness of her mouth. Hawes came stamping up the steps and turned abruptly right, and stopped stock still when he saw her, an interruption of movement for only a fraction of a second, the turn, the stop, and then a forward motion again which carried him to her in four headlong strides.

"What is it?" he said.

She could not answer. She clung to the wall with the flat palms of her hands, her eyes still squeezed shut tightly, the scream frozen in her throat and blocking articulation. She shook her head.

"Blanche, what is it?"

She shook her head again, and then pulled one hand from the wall, as if afraid that by doing so she would lose her grip and tumble to the floor. The hand rose limply. It did not point, it only indicated, and that in the vaguest manner, as if it too were dazed.

"The bathroom?" he asked.

She nodded. He turned from her. The bathroom door was partly open. He opened it the rest of the way, rushing into the room, and then stopping instantly, as if he had run into a stone wall.

Maria Fiers was inside her clothing and outside of it. The killer had caught her either dressing or undressing, had caught her in what she supposed was privacy, so that one leg was in the trousers of her pajamas and the other lay twisted beneath her body, naked. Her pajama top had ridden up over one delicately curved breast, perhaps as she fell, perhaps as she struggled. Even her hair seemed in a state of uncertain transition, some of it held firmly in place by curlers, the rest hanging in haphazard abandon, the loose curlers scattered on the bathroom floor. The hook latch on the inside of the door had been ripped from the jamb when the door was forced. The water in the sink was still running. The girl lay still and dead in her invaded privacy, partially clothed, partially disrobed, surprise and terror wedded in the death mask of her face. A towel was twisted about her throat. It had been twisted there with tremendous force, biting into the skin with such power that it remained twisted there now, the flesh torn and overlapping it in places, the coarse cloth almost embedded into her neck and throat. Her tongue protruded from her mouth. She was bleeding from her nose where her face had struck the bathroom tile in falling.

He backed out of the room.

He found a pay telephone in the main building, and from there he called Theodore Watt.

12

BLANCHE SAT on the edge of the bed in room 105, shivering inside her gown, her robe, and a blanket which had been thrown over her shoulders. Theodore Watt leaned disjointedly against the dresser, puffed on his cigar, and said, "Now you want to tell me exactly what happened, Miss Colby?"

Blanche sat shivering and hunched, her face pale. She searched for her voice, seemed unable to find it, shook her head, nodded, cleared her throat, and seemed surprised that she could speak. "I . . . I was alone. Cotton had gone down to see what . . . what the noise was."

"What noise, Hawes?" Watt asked.

"A grinding wheel," he answered. "Downstairs in the ski shop. I heard it last night, too."

"Did you find who was running the wheel?"

"Tonight, it was a guy named Helmut Kurtz. He's an instructor here, too. Claims he was nowhere near the shop last night. But he did see a light burning after midnight."

"Where's he now?"

"I don't know. Sheriff, he was with me when the girl was killed. He couldn't possibly have . . ."

Watt ignored him and walked to the door. He opened it, and leaned into the corridor. "Fred," he said, "find me Helmut Kurtz, an instructor here."

"I got that other guy from down the hall," Fred answered.

"I'll be right with him. Tell him to wait."

"What other guy?" Hawes asked.

"Instructor in 102. Larry Davidson." Watt shook his head. "Place is crawling with goddamn instructors, excuse me, miss. Wonder there's any room for guests." He shook his head again. "You said you were alone, Miss Colby."

"Yes. And I . . . I thought I heard something down the hall . . . like . . . I didn't know what. A loud sudden noise."

"Probably the bathroom door being kicked in," Watt said. "Go on."

"And then I . . . I heard a girl's voice saying, 'Get out of here! Do you hear me? Get out of here!' And . . . and then it was quiet, and I heard someone running down the hall and down the steps, so I . . . I thought I ought to . . . to look."

"Yes, go on."

"I went down the . . . the hallway and looked down the steps, but I didn't see anyone. And then, when I . . . when I was starting back for the room, I . . . I heard the water running in the bathroom. The . . . the door was open, so I . . . Oh Jesus, do I *have* to?"

"You found the girl, is that right?"

"Yes," Blanche said, her voice very low.

"And then you screamed."

"Yes."

"And then Hawes came upstairs, is that right?"

"Yes," Hawes said. "And I called you from the main building."

"Um-huh," Watt said. He went to the door and opened it. "Want to come in here, Mr. Davidson?" he asked.

Larry Davidson came into the room hesitantly. He was a tall man, and he stooped as he came through the doorway, giving an impression of even greater height, as if he had to stoop to avoid the top of the door frame. He was wearing dark trousers and a plaid woolen sports shirt. His hair was clipped close to his scalp. His blue eyes were alert, if not wary.

"Guess you know what this is all about, huh, Mr. Davidson?" Watt asked.

"Yes, I think so," Davidson answered.

"You don't mind answering a few questions, do you?"

"No. I'll . . . I'll answer anything you . . ."

"Fine. Were you in your room all night, Mr. Davidson?"

"Not all night, no. I was up at the main building part of the time."

"Doing what?"

"Well, I . . ."

"Yes, Mr. Davidson, what were you doing?"

"I . . . I was fencing. Look, I didn't have anything to do with this."

"You were *what,* Mr. Davidson?"

"Fencing. We've got some foils and masks up there, and I . . . I was just fooling around. Look, I *know* Helga was stabbed, but . . ."

"What time did you get back here, Mr. Davidson?"

"About . . . about ten-thirty, eleven."

"And you've been in your room since then?"

"Yes."

"What did you do when you got back here?"

"I wrote a letter to my wife, and then I went to sleep."

"What time did you go to sleep?"

"About midnight."

"Did you hear any loud noise in the hall?"

"No."

"Did you hear any voices?"

"No."

"Did you hear Miss Colby when she screamed?"

"No."

"Why not?"

"I guess I was asleep."

"You sleep in your clothes, Mr. Davidson?"

"What? Oh. Oh, no. Your fellow . . . your deputy said I could put on some clothes."

"What *were* you sleeping in?"

"My pajamas. Listen, I barely knew those girls. I only joined the school here two weeks ago. I mean, I knew them to talk to, but that's all. And the fencing is just a coincidence. I mean, we always fool around with the foils. I mean, ever since I came here, somebody's been up there fooling around with . . ."

"How many times did you scream, Miss Colby?" Watt asked.

"I don't remember," Blanche said.

"She screamed twice," Hawes said.

"Where were you when you heard the screams, Hawes?"

"Downstairs. In the ski shop."

"But you were in your room, right down the hall, Mr. Davidson, and you didn't hear anything, hmmm? Maybe you were too busy . . ."

And suddenly Davidson began crying. His face twisted into a grimace, and the tears began flowing, and he said, "I didn't have anything to do with this, I swear. Please, I didn't have anything to do with it. Please, I'm married, my wife's in the city expecting a baby, I *need* this job, I didn't even *look* at those girls, I swear to God, what do you want me to do? Please, please."

The room was silent except for his sobbing.

"I swear to God," he said softly. "I swear to God. I'm a heavy sleeper. I'm very tired at night. I swear. Please. I didn't do it. I only knew them to say hello. I didn't hear anything. Please. Believe me. Please. I *have* to keep this job. It's the only thing I know, skiing. I can't get involved in this. Please."

He lowered his head, trying to hide the tears that streamed down his face, his shoulders heaving, the deep sobs starting deep inside him and reverberating through his entire body.

"Please," he said.

For the first time since the whole thing had started, Watt turned to Hawes and asked his advice.

"What do you think?" he said.

"I'm a heavy sleeper, too," Hawes said. "You could blow up the building, and I wouldn't hear it."

13

ON SUNDAY morning, the church bells rang out over the valley.

They started in the town of Rawson, and they rang sharp and clear on the mountain air, drifting over the snow and down the valley. He went to the window and pulled up the shade, and listened to the sound of the bells, and remembered his own youth and the Reverend Jeremiah Hawes who had been his father, and the sound of Sunday church bells, and the rolling, sonorous voice of his father delivering the sermon. There had always been logic in his father's sermons. Hawes had not come away from his childhood background with any abiding religious fervor—but he had come away with a great respect for logic. "To be believed," his father had told him, "it must be reasonable. And to be reasonable, it must be logical. You could do worse than remembering that, Cotton."

There did not seem to be much logic in the killing of Helga Nilson and Maria Fiers, unless there was logic in wanton brutality. He tried to piece together the facts as he looked out over the peaceful valley and listened to the steady tolling of the bells. Behind him, Blanche was curled in sleep, gently breathing, her arms wrapped around the pillow. He did not want to wake her yet, not after what she'd been through last night. So far as he was concerned, the weekend was over; he could not ski with pleasure anymore, not this weekend. He wanted nothing more than to get away from Rawson Mountain, no, that wasn't quite true. He wanted to find the killer. That was what he wanted more than anything else. Not because he was being paid for the job, not because he wanted to prove to Theodore Watt that maybe big-city detectives *did* have a little something on the ball—but only because the double murders filled him with a sense of outrage. He could still remember the animal strength of the man who'd attacked him on the mountain, and the thought of that power directed against two helpless young girls angered Hawes beyond all reason.

Why? he asked himself.

Where is the logic?

There was none. No logic in the choice of the victims, and no logic in the choice of the scene. Why would anyone have chosen to kill Helga in broad daylight, on a chair suspended anywhere from six to thirty feet above the ground, using a ski pole as a weapon? A ski pole sharpened to a deadly point, Hawes reminded himself, don't forget that. This thing didn't just happen, this was no spur-of-the-moment impulse, this was planned and premeditated, a pure and simple Murder One. Somebody had been in that ski shop the night before the first murder, using a file and then a grinding wheel, sharpening that damn pole, making certain its end could penetrate a heavy ski parka, *and* a ski sweater, *and* a heart.

Then there must have been logic to the choice of locale, Hawes thought. Whoever killed Helga had at least planned far enough ahead to have prepared a weapon the night before. And admitting the existence of a plan, then logic could be presupposed, and it could further be assumed that killing her on the chair lift was a *part* of the plan—perhaps a very necessary part of it.

Yes, that's logic, he thought—*except that it's illogical.*

Behind him, Blanche stirred. He turned to look at her briefly, remembering the horror on her face last night, contrasting it now with her features relaxed in sleep. She had told the story to Watt three times, had told him again and again how she'd found the dead girl.

Maria Fiers, twenty-one years old, brunette, a native of Montpelier, Vermont. She had begun skiing when she was six years old, had won the woman's slalom four times running, had been an instructor since she was seventeen. She skated, too, and had been on her high school swimming team, an all-around athlete, a nice girl with a gentle manner and a pleasant smile—dead.

Why?

She lived in the room next door to Helga's, had known Helga for close to a year. She had been nowhere near the chair lift on the day Helga was killed. In fact, she had been teaching a beginner's class near the T-Bar, a good distance from the chair lift. She could not have seen Helga's murder, nor Helga's murderer.

But someone had killed her nonetheless.

And if there were a plan, and if there were supposed logic to the plan, and if killing Helga on a chair halfway up the mountain was part of that logic, then the death of Maria Fiers was also a part of it.

But how?

The hell with it, Hawes thought. I can't think straight any more. I want to crack this so badly that I can't think straight, and that makes me worse than useless. So the thing to do is to get out of here, wake Blanche and tell her to dress and pack, and then pay my bill and get out, back to the city, back to the 87th where death comes more frequently perhaps, and just as brutally—but not as a surprise. I'll leave this to Theodore Watt, the sheriff who wants to make his own mistakes. I'll leave it to him and his nimble-fingered deputies, and maybe they'll bust it wide open, or maybe they won't, but it's too much for me, I can't think straight any more.

He went to the bed and woke Blanche, and then he walked over to the main building, anxious to pay his bill and get on his way. Someone was at the piano, practicing scales. Hawes walked past the piano and the fireplace and around the corner to Wollender's office. He knocked on the door, and waited. There was a slight hesitation on the other side of the door, and then Wollender said, "Yes, come in," and Hawes turned the knob.

Everything looked exactly the way it had looked when Hawes checked in on Friday night, an eternity ago. Wollender was sitting behind his desk, a man in his late twenties with dark hair and dark brows pulled low over deep brown eyes. He was wearing a white shirt open at the throat, a bold reindeer-imprinted sweater over it. The plaster cast was still on his right leg, the leg stretched out stiffly in front of him, the foot resting on a low ottoman. Everything looked exactly the same.

"I want to pay my bill," Hawes said. "We're checking out."

He stood just inside the door, some fifteen feet from the desk. Wollender's crutches leaned against the wall near the door. There was a smile on Wollender's face as he said, "Certainly," and then opened the bottom drawer of the desk and took out his register and carefully made out a bill. Hawes walked to the desk, added the bill, and then wrote a check. As he waved it in the air to dry the ink, he said, "What *were* you doing in my room yesterday, Mr. Wollender?"

"Checking the heat," Wollender said.

Hawes nodded. "Here's your check. Will you mark this bill 'Paid,' please?"

"Be happy to," Wollender said. He stamped the bill and handed it back to Hawes. For a moment, Hawes had the oddest feeling that something was wrong. The knowledge pushed itself into his mind in the form of an absurd caption: WHAT'S WRONG WITH THIS PICTURE? He looked at Wollender, at his hair, and his eyes, and his white shirt, and his reindeer sweater, and his extended leg, and the cast on it, and the ottoman. Something was different. This was not the room, not the picture as it had been on Friday night. WHAT'S WRONG WITH THIS PICTURE? he thought, and he did not know.

He took the bill. "Thanks," he said. "Have you heard any news about the roads?"

"They're open all the way to the Thruway. You shouldn't have any trouble."

"Thanks," Hawes said. He hesitated, staring at Wollender. "My room's right over the ski shop, you know," he said.

"Yes, I know that."

"Do you have a key to the shop, Mr. Wollender?"

Wollender shook his head. "No. The shop is privately owned. It doesn't belong to the hotel. I believe the proprietor allows the ski instructors to . . ."

"But then, you're a locksmith, aren't you?"

"What?"

"Isn't that what you told me when I checked in? You said you were a locksmith out of season, didn't you?"

"Oh. Oh, yes. Yes, I did." Wollender shifted uneasily in the chair, trying to make his leg comfortable. Hawes looked at the leg again, and then he thought, Damn it, what's wrong?

"Maybe you went to my room to listen, Mr. Wollender. Is that possible?"

"Listen to what?"

"To the sounds coming from the ski shop below," Hawes said.

"Are the sounds that interesting?"

"In the middle of the night, they are. You can hear all sorts of things in the middle of the night. I'm just beginning to remember all the things I heard."

"Oh? What did you hear?"

"I heard the oil burner clicking, and the toilet flushing, and the Cats going up the mountain, and someone arguing down the hall, and somebody filing and grinding in the ski shop." He was speaking to Wollender, but not really speaking to him. He was, instead, remembering those midnight voices raised in anger, and remembering that it was only later he had heard the noises in the shop, and gone to the window, and seen the light burning below. And then a curious thing happened. Instead of calling him "Mr. Wollender," he suddenly called him "Elmer."

"Elmer," he said, "something's just occurred to me."

Elmer. And with the word, something new came into the room. With the word, he was suddenly transported back to the interrogation room at the 87th, where common thieves and criminals were called by their first names, Charlie, and Harry, and Martin, and Joe, and where this familiarity somehow put them on the defensive, somehow rattled them and made them know their questioners weren't playing games.

"Elmer," he said, leaning over the desk, "it's just occurred to me that since Maria couldn't have *seen* anything on the mountain, maybe she was killed because she *heard* something. And maybe what she heard was the same arguing I heard. Only *her* room is right next door to Helga's. And maybe she knew *who* was arguing." He hesitated. "That's pretty logical, don't you think, Elmer?"

"I suppose so, Wollender said pleasantly. "But if you know who killed Maria, why don't you go to . . ."

"I don't know, Elmer. Do *you* know?"

"I'm sorry. I don't."

"Yeah, neither do I, Elmer. All I have is a feeling."

"And what's the feeling?" Wollender asked.

"That you came to my room to listen, Elmer. To find out how much *I* had heard the night before Helga was murdered. And maybe you decided I heard too damn much, and maybe that's why I was attacked on the mountain yesterday."

"Please, Mr. Hawes," Wollender said, and a faint superior smile touched his mouth, and his hand opened limply to indicate the leg in the cast.

"Sure, sure," Hawes said. "How could I have been attacked by a man with his leg in a cast, a man who can't get around without crutches? Sure, Elmer. Don't think that hasn't been bugg—" He stopped dead. "Your crutches," he said.

"What?"

"Your crutches! Where the hell are they?"

For just an instant, the color went out of Wollender's face. Then, quite calmly, he said, "Right over there. Behind you."

Hawes turned and looked at the crutches, leaning against the wall near the door.

"Fifteen feet from your desk," he said. "I thought you couldn't walk without them."

"I . . . I used the furniture to . . . to get to the desk. I . . ."

"You're lying, Elmer," Hawes said, and he reached across the desk and pulled Wollender out of the chair.

"My leg!" Wollender shouted.

"Your leg, my ass! How long have you been walking on it, Elmer? Was that why you killed her on the mountain? So that . . ."

"I didn't kill anybody!"

". . . so that you'd have a perfect alibi? A man with his leg in a cast couldn't possibly ride a lift or jump from it, could he? Unless he'd been in and out of that cast for God knows how long!"

"My leg is broken! I can't walk!"

"Can you *kill*, Elmer?"

"I didn't kill her!"

"Did Maria hear you arguing, Elmer?"

"No. No . . ."

"Then why'd you go after her?"

"I didn't!" He tried to pull away from Hawes. "You're crazy. You're hurting my leg! Let go of . . ."

"*I'm* crazy? You son of a bitch, *I'm* crazy? You stuck a ski pole in one girl and twisted a towel around . . ."

"I didn't, I didn't!"

"We found the basket from your pole!" Hawes shouted.

"What basket? I don't know what . . ."

"Your fingerprints are all over it!" he lied.

"You're crazy," Wollender said. "How could I get on the lift? I can't walk. I broke the leg in two places. One of the bones came right through the skin. I couldn't get on a lift if I wanted . . ."

"The skin," Hawes said.

"What?"

"The skin!" There was a wild look in his eyes now. He pulled Wollender closer to him and yelled, "Where'd she scratch you?"

"What?"

He seized the front of Wollender's shirt with both hands, and then ripped it open. "Where's the cut, Elmer? On your chest? On your neck?"

Wollender struggled to get away from him, but Hawes had his head captured in both huge hands now. He twisted Wollender's face viciously, forced his head forward, pulled back the shirt collar.

"Let go of me!" Wollender screamed.

"What's this, Elmer?" His fingers grasped the adhesive bandage on the back of Wollender's neck. Angrily, he tore it loose. A healing cut, two inches long and smeared with iodine, ran diagonally from a spot just below Wollender's hairline.

"I did that myself," Wollender said. "I bumped into . . ."

"Helga did it," Hawes said. "When you stabbed her! The sheriff's got the skin, Elmer. It was under her fingernails."

"No," Wollender said. He shook his head.

The room was suddenly very still. Both men were exhausted. Hawes kept clinging to the front of Wollender's shirt, breathing hard, waiting. Wollender kept shaking his head.

"You want to tell me?"

Wollender shook his head.

"How long have you been walking?"

Wollender shook his head again.

"Why'd you keep your leg in the cast?"

Again, Wollender shook his head.

"You killed two young girls!" Hawes bellowed. He was surprised to find himself trembling. His hand tightened on the shirt front, the knuckles showing white through his skin. Perhaps Wollender felt the sudden tension, perhaps Wollender knew that in the next instant Hawes would throttle him.

"All right," he said. His voice was very low. "All right."

"Why'd you keep wearing the cast?"

"So . . . so . . . so she wouldn't know. So she would think I . . . I was . . . was unable to walk. And that way, I could . . . could watch her. Without her knowing."

"Watch who?"

"Helga. She . . . She was my girl, you see. I . . . I loved her, you see."

"Yeah, you loved her enough to kill her," Hawes said.

"That's *not* why I . . ." He shook his head. "It was because of Kurtz. She kept denying it, but I knew about them. And I warned her. You have to believe that I warned her. And I . . . I kept the cast on my leg to . . . to fool her."

"When did it come off?" Hawes asked.

"Last week. The . . . the doctor took it off right in this room. He did a bivalve, with an electric saw, cut it right down the side. And

. . . and when he was gone, I . . . I figured I could put the two halves together again, and . . . and . . . hold it in place with . . . with tape. That way, I could watch her. Without her knowing I could get around."

"And what did you see?"

"You *know* what I saw!"

"Tell me."

"Friday night, she . . . I . . . I saw Kurtz leaving the annex. I knew he'd been with her."

"He was there to pick up Maria's skates," Hawes said. "To sharpen them."

"No!" Wollender shouted, and for a moment there was force in his voice, a vocal explosion, fury and power, and Hawes remembered again the brute strength of Wollender's attack on the mountain. Wollender's voice died again. "No," he said softly, "you're mistaken. He was with Helga. I know. Do you think I'd have killed her if . . ." His voice caught. His eyes suddenly misted. He turned his head, not looking at Hawes, staring across the room, the tears solidifying his eyes. "When I went up to her room, I warned her," he said, his voice low. "I told her I had seen him, seen him with my own eyes, and she . . . she said I was imagining things. And she laughed." His face went suddenly tight. "She laughed, you see. She . . . she shouldn't have laughed." His eyes filled with tears, had a curiously opaque look. "She shouldn't have laughed," he said again. "It wasn't funny. I loved her. It wasn't funny."

"No," Hawes said wearily. "It wasn't funny at all."

14

THE STORM was over.

The storm which had started suddenly and filled the air with fury was gone. The wind had died after scattering the clouds from the sky. They drove in the warm comfort of the convertible, the sky a clear blue ahead of them, the snow banked on either side of the road.

The storm was over.

There were only the remains of its fury now, the hard-packed snow beneath the automobile, and the snow lining the roads, and the snow hanging in the branches of the trees. But now it was over and done, and now there was only the damage to count, and the repairs to be made.

He sat silently behind the wheel of the car, a big redheaded man who drove effortlessly. His anger was gone, too, like the anger of the storm. There was only a vast sadness inside him.

"Cotton?" Blanche said.

"Mmmm?" He did not take his eyes from the road. He watched the winding white ribbon and listened to the crunch of snow beneath his heavy-duty tires, and over that the sound of her voice.

"Cotton," she said, "I'm very glad to be with you."

"I am, too."

"In spite of everything," she said, "I'm very very glad."

He did a curious thing then. He suddenly took his right hand from the wheel and put it on her thigh, and squeezed her gently. He thought he did it because Blanche was a very attractive girl with whom he had just shared a moment of communication.

But perhaps he touched her because death had suddenly shouldered its way into that automobile, and he had remembered again the two young girls who had been Wollender's victims.

Perhaps he touched her thigh, soft and warm, only as a reaffirmation of life.

DAPHNE DU MAURIER
Don't Look Now

"DON'T LOOK now," John said to his wife, "but there are a couple of old girls two tables away who are trying to hypnotize me."

Laura, quick on cue, made an elaborate pretence of yawning, then tilted her head as though searching the skies for a nonexistent aircraft.

"Right behind you," he added. "That's why you can't turn round at once—it would be much too obvious."

Laura played the oldest trick in the world and dropped her napkin, then bent to scrabble for it under her feet, sending a shooting glance over her left shoulder as she straightened once again. She sucked in her cheeks, the first tell-tale sign of suppressed hysteria, and lowered her head.

"They're not old girls at all," she said. "They're male twins in drag."

Her voice broke ominously, the prelude to uncontrolled laughter, and John quickly poured some more chianti into her glass.

"Pretend to choke," he said, "then they won't notice. You know what it is, they're criminals doing the sights of Europe, changing sex at each stop. Twin sisters here on Torcello. Twin brothers tomorrow in Venice, or even tonight, parading arm-in-arm across the Piazza San Marco. Just a matter of switching clothes and wigs."

"Jewel thieves or murderers?" asked Laura.

"Oh, murderers, definitely. But why, I ask myself, have they picked on me?"

The waiter made a diversion by bringing coffee and bearing away the fruit, which gave Laura time to banish hysteria and regain control.

"I can't think," she said, "why we didn't notice them when we arrived. They stand out to high heaven. One couldn't fail."

"That gang of Americans masked them," said John, "and the bearded man with a monocle who looked like a spy. It wasn't until they all went just now that I saw the twins. Oh God, the one with the shock of white hair has got her eye on me again."

Laura took the powder compact from her bag and held it in front of her face, the mirror acting as a reflector.

"I think it's me they're looking at, not you," she said. "Thank heaven I left my pearls with the manager at the hotel." She paused, dabbing the sides of her nose with powder. "The thing is," she said after a moment, "we've got them wrong. They're neither murderers nor thieves. They're a couple of pathetic old retired schoolmistresses on holiday, who've saved up all their lives to visit Venice. They come from some place with a name like Walabanga in Australia. And they're called Tilly and Tiny."

Her voice, for the first time since they had come away, took on the old bubbling quality he loved, and the worried frown between her brows had vanished. At last, he thought, at last she's beginning to get over it. If I can keep this going, if we can pick up the familiar routine of jokes shared on holiday and at home, the ridiculous fantasies about people at other tables, or staying in the hotel, or wandering in art galleries and churches, then everything will fall into place, life will become as it was before, the wound will heal, she will forget.

"You know," said Laura, "that really was a very good lunch. I did enjoy it."

Thank God, he thought, thank God. . . . Then he leant forward, speaking low in a conspirator's whisper. "One of them is going to the loo," he said. "Do you suppose he, or she, is going to change her wig?"

"Don't say anything," Laura murmured. "I'll follow her and find out. She may have a suitcase tucked away there, and she's going to switch clothes."

She began to hum under her breath, the signal, to her husband, of content. The ghost was temporarily laid, and all because of the familiar holiday game, abandoned too long, and now, through mere chance, blissfully recaptured.

"Is she on her way?" asked Laura.

"About to pass our table now," he told her.

Seen on her own, the woman was not so remarkable. Tall, angular, aquiline features, with the close-cropped hair which was fashionably called Eton crop, he seemed to remember, in his mother's day, and about her person the stamp of that particular generation. She would be in her middle sixties, he supposed, the masculine shirt with collar and tie, sports jacket, grey tweed skirt coming to mid-calf. Grey stockings and laced black shoes. He had seen the type on golf-courses and at dog-shows—invariably showing not sporting breeds but pugs—and if you came across them at a party in somebody's house they were quicker on the draw with a cigarette-lighter than he was himself, a mere male, with pocket-matches. The general belief that they kept house with a more feminine, fluffy companion was not always true. Frequently they boasted, and adored, a golfing husband. No, the striking point about this particular individual was that there were two of them. Identical twins cast in the same mould. The only difference was that the other one had whiter hair.

"Supposing," murmured Laura, "when I find myself in the toilette beside her she starts to strip?"

"Depends on what is revealed," John answered. "If she's hermaphrodite, make a bolt for it. She might have a hypodermic syringe concealed and want to knock you out before you reach the door."

Laura sucked in her cheeks once more and began to shake. Then, squaring her shoulders, she rose to her feet. "I simply must not laugh," she said, "and whatever you do, don't look at me when I come back, especially if we come out together." She picked up her bag and strolled self-consciously away from the table in pursuit of her prey.

John poured the dregs of the chianti into his glass and lit a cigarette. The sun blazed down upon the little garden of the restaurant. The Americans had left, and the monocled man, and the family party at the far end. All was peace. The identical twin was sitting back in her chair with her eyes closed. Thank heaven, he thought, for this moment at any rate, when relaxation was possible, and Laura had been launched upon her foolish, harmless game. The holiday could yet turn into the cure she needed, blotting out, if only temporarily, the numb despair that had seized her since the child died.

"She'll get over it," the doctor said. "They all get over it, in time. And you have the boy."

"I know," John had said, "but the girl meant everything. She always did, right from the start, I don't know why. I suppose it was the difference in age. A boy of school age, and a tough one at that, is someone in his own right. Not a baby of five. Laura literally adored her. Johnnie and I were nowhere."

"Give her time," repeated the doctor, "give her time. And anyway, you're both young still. There'll be others. Another daughter."

So easy to talk. . . . How replace the life of a loved lost child with a dream? He knew Laura too well. Another child, another girl, would have her own qualities, a separate identity, she might even induce hostility because of this very fact. A usurper in the cradle, in the cot, that had been Christine's. A chubby, flaxen replica of Johnnie, not the little waxen dark-haired sprite that had gone.

He looked up, over his glass of wine, and the woman was staring at him again. It was not the casual, idle glance of someone at a nearby table, waiting for her companion to return, but something deeper, more intent, the prominent, light blue eyes oddly penetrating, giving him a sudden feeling of discomfort. Damn the woman! All right, bloody stare, if you must. Two can play at that game. He blew a cloud of cigarette smoke into the air and smiled at her, he hoped offensively. She did not register. The blue eyes continued to hold his, so that finally he was obliged to look away himself, extinguish his cigarette, glance over his shoulder for the waiter and call for the bill. Settling for this, and fumbling with the change, with a few casual remarks about the excellence of the meal, brought composure, but a prickly feeling on his scalp remained, and an odd sensation of unease. Then it went, as abruptly as it had started, and stealing a furtive glance at the other table he saw that her eyes were closed again, and she was sleeping, or dozing, as she had done before. The waiter disappeared. All was still.

Laura, he thought, glancing at his watch, is being a hell of a time. Ten minutes at least. Something to tease her about, anyway. He began to plan the form the joke would take. How the old dolly had stripped to her smalls, suggesting that Laura should do likewise. And then the manager had burst in upon them both, exclaiming in horror, the reputation of the restaurant damaged, the hint that unpleasant consequences might follow unless . . . The whole exercise turning out to be a plant, an exercise in blackmail. He and Laura and the twins taken in a police launch back to Venice for questioning. Quarter of an hour . . . Oh, come on, come on . . .

There was a crunch of feet on the gravel. Laura's twin walked slowly past, alone. She crossed over to her table and stood there a moment, her tall, angular figure interposing itself between John and her sister. She was saying something, but he couldn't catch the words. What was the accent, though—Scottish? Then she bent, offering an arm to the seated twin, and they moved away together across the garden to the break in the little hedge beyond, the twin who had stared at John leaning on her sister's arm. Here was the difference again. She was not quite so tall, and she stooped more—perhaps she was arthritic. They disappeared out of sight, and John, becoming impatient, got up and was about to walk back into the hotel when Laura emerged.

"Well, I must say, you took your time," he began, then stopped, because of the expression on her face.

"What's the matter, what's happened?" he asked.

He could tell at once there was something wrong. Almost as if she were in a state of shock. She blundered towards the table he had just vacated and sat down. He drew up a chair beside her, taking her hand.

"Darling, what is it? Tell me—are you ill?"

She shook her head, and then turned and looked at him. The dazed expression he had noticed at first had given way to one of dawning confidence, almost of exaltation.

"It's quite wonderful," she said slowly, "the most wonderful thing that could possibly be. You see, she isn't dead, she's still with us. That's why they kept staring at us, those two sisters. They could see Christine."

Oh God, he thought. It's what I've been dreading. She's going off her head. What do I do? How do I cope?

"Laura, sweet," he began, forcing a smile, "look, shall we go? I've paid the bill, we can go and look at the cathedral and stroll around, and then it will be time to take off in that launch again for Venice."

She wasn't listening, or at any rate the words didn't penetrate.

"John, love," she said, "I've got to tell you what happened. I followed her, as we planned, into the *toilette* place. She was combing her hair and I went into the loo, and then came out and washed my hands in the basin. She was washing hers in the next basin. Suddenly she turned and said to me, in a strong Scots accent, 'Don't be unhappy any more. My sister has seen your little girl. She was sitting between you and your husband, laughing.' Darling, I thought I was going to faint. I nearly did. Luckily, there was a chair, and I sat down, and the woman bent over me and patted my head. I'm not sure of her exact words, but she said something about the moment of truth and joy being as sharp as a sword, but not to be afraid, all was well, but the sister's vision had been so strong they knew I had to be told, and that Christine wanted it. Oh John, don't look like that. I swear I'm not making it up, this is what she told me, it's all true."

The desperate urgency in her voice made his heart sicken. He had to play along with her, agree, soothe, do anything to bring back some sense of calm.

"Laura, darling, of course I believe you," he said, "only it's a sort of shock, and I'm upset because you're upset . . ."

"But I'm not upset," she interrupted. "I'm happy, so happy that I can't put the feeling into words. You know what it's been like all these weeks, at home and everywhere we've been on holiday, though I tried to hide it from you. Now it's lifted, because I know, I just know, that the woman was right. Oh Lord, how awful of me, but I've forgotten their name—she did tell me. You see, the thing is that she's a retired doctor, they come from Edinburgh, and the one who saw Christine went blind a few years ago. Although she's studied the occult all her life and been very psychic, it's only since going blind that she has really seen things, like a medium. They've had the most wonderful experiences. But to describe Christine as the blind one did to her sister, even down to the little blue-and-white dress with the puff sleeves that she wore at her birthday party, and to say she was smiling happily . . . Oh darling, it's made me so happy I think I'm going to cry."

No hysteria. Nothing wild. She took a tissue from her bag and blew her nose, smiling at him. "I'm all right, you see, you don't have to worry. Neither of us need worry about anything any more. Give me a cigarette."

He took one from his packet and lighted it for her. She sounded normal, herself again. She wasn't trembling. And if this sudden belief was going to keep her happy he couldn't possibly begrudge it. But . . . but . . . he wished, all the same, it hadn't happened. There was something uncanny about thought-reading, about telepathy. Scientists couldn't account for it, nobody could, and this is what must have happened just now between Laura and the sisters. So the one who had been staring at him was blind. That accounted for the fixed gaze. Which somehow was unpleasant in itself, creepy. Oh hell, he thought, I wish we hadn't come here for lunch. Just chance, a flick of a coin between this, Torcello, and driving to Padua, and we had to choose Torcello.

"You didn't arrange to meet them again or anything, did you?" he asked, trying to sound casual.

"No, darling, why should I?" Laura answered. "I mean, there was nothing more they could tell me. The sister had had her wonderful vision, and that was that. Anyway, they're moving on. Funnily enough, it's rather like our original game. They are going round the world before returning to Scotland. Only I said Australia, didn't I? The old dears . . . anything less like murderers and jewel thieves!"

She had quite recovered. She stood up and looked about her. "Come on," she said. "Having come to Torcello we must see the cathedral."

They made their way from the restaurant across the open piazza, where the stalls had been set up with scarves and trinkets and postcards, and so along the path to the cathedral. One of the ferry-boats had just decanted a crowd of sight-seers, many of whom had already found their way into Santa Maria Assunta. Laura, undaunted, asked her husband for the guidebook, and, as had always been her custom in happier days, started to walk slowly through the cathedral, studying mosaics, columns, panels from left to right, while John, less interested, because of his concern at what had just happened, followed close behind, keeping a weather eye alert for the twin sisters. There was no sign of them. Perhaps they had gone into the Church of Santa Fosca close by. A sudden encounter would be embarrassing, quite apart from the effect it might have upon Laura. But the anonymous, shuffling tourists, intent upon culture, could not harm her, although from his own point of view they made artistic appreciation impossible. He could not concentrate, the cold clear beauty of what he saw left him untouched, and when Laura touched his sleeve, pointing to the mosaic of the Virgin and Child standing above the frieze of the Apostles, he nodded in sympathy yet saw nothing, the long, sad face of the Virgin infinitely remote, and turning on sudden impulse stared back over the heads of the tourists towards the door, where frescoes of the blessed and the damned gave themselves to judgment.

The twins were standing there, the blind one still holding on to her sister's arm, her sightless eyes fixed firmly upon him. He felt himself held, unable to move, and an impending sense of doom, of tragedy, came upon him. His whole being sagged, as it were, in apathy, and he thought, This is the end, there is no escape, no future. Then both sisters turned and went out of the cathedral and the sensation vanished, leaving indignation in its wake, and rising anger. How dare those two old fools practice their mediumistic tricks on him? It was fraudulent, unhealthy; this was probably the way they lived, touring the world making everyone they met uncomfortable. Give them half a chance and they would have got money out of Laura—anything.

He felt her tugging at his sleeve again. "Isn't she beautiful? So happy, so serene."

"Who? What?" he asked.

"The Madonna," she answered. "She has a magic quality. It goes right through to one. Don't you feel it too?"

"I suppose so. I don't know. There are too many people around."

She looked up at him, astonished. "What's that got to do with it? How funny you are. Well, all right, let's get away from them. I want to buy some postcards anyway." Disappointed, she sensed his lack of interest, and began to thread her way through the crowd of tourists to the door.

"Come on," he said abruptly, once they were outside, "there's plenty of time for postcards, let's explore a bit," and he struck off from the path, which would have taken them back to the center where the little houses were, and the stalls, and the drifting crowd of people, to a narrow way amongst uncultivated ground, beyond which he could see a sort of cutting, or canal. The sight of water, limpid, pale, was a soothing contrast to the fierce sun above their heads.

"I don't think this leads anywhere much," said Laura. "It's a bit muddy, too, one can't sit. Besides, there are more things the guidebook says we ought to see."

"Oh, forget the book," he said impatiently, and, pulling her down beside him on the bank above the cutting, put his arms round her.

"It's the wrong time of day for sight-seeing. Look, there's a rat swimming there the other side." He picked up a stone and threw it in the water, and the animal sank, or somehow disappeared, and nothing was left but bubbles.

"Don't," said Laura. "It's cruel, poor thing," and then suddenly, putting her hand on his knee, "Do you think Christine is sitting here beside us?"

He did not answer at once. What was there to say? Would it be like this forever?

"I expect so," he said slowly, "if you feel she is."

The point was, remembering Christine before the onset of the fatal meningitis, she would have been running along the bank excitedly, throwing off her shoes, wanting to paddle, giving Laura a fit of apprehension. "Sweetheart, take care, come back . . ."

"The woman said she was looking so happy, sitting beside us, smiling," said Laura. She got up, brushing her dress, her mood changed to restlessness. "Come on, let's go back," she said.

He followed her with a sinking heart. He knew she did not really want to buy postcards or see what remained to be seen; she wanted to go in search of the women again, not necessarily to talk, just to be near them. When they came to the open place by the stalls he noticed that the crowd of tourists had thinned, there were only a few stragglers left, and the sisters were not amongst them. They must have joined the main body who had come to Torcello by the ferry-service. A wave of relief seized him.

"Look, there's a mass of postcards at the second stall," he said quickly, "and some eye-catching head-scarves. Let me buy you a head-scarf."

"Darling, I've so many!" she protested. "Don't waste your lire."

"It isn't a waste. I'm in a buying mood. What about a basket? You know we never have enough baskets. Or some lace. How about lace?"

She allowed herself, laughing, to be dragged to the stall. While he rumpled through the goods spread out before them, and chatted up the smiling woman who was selling her wares, his ferociously bad Italian making her smile the more, he knew it would give the body of tourists more time to walk to the landing-stage and catch the ferry-service, and the twin sisters would be out of sight and out of their life.

"Never," said Laura, some twenty minutes later, "has so much junk been piled into so small a basket," her bubbling laugh reassuring him that all was well, he needn't worry any more, the evil hour had passed. The launch from the Cipriani that had brought them from Venice was waiting by the landing-stage. The passengers who had arrived with them, the Americans, the man with the monocle, were already assembled. Earlier, before setting out, he had thought the price for lunch and transport, there and back, decidedly steep. Now he grudged none of it, except that the outing to Torcello itself had been one of the major errors of this particular holiday in Venice. They stepped down into the launch, finding a place in the open, and the boat chugged away down the canal and into the lagoon. The ordinary ferry had gone before, steaming towards Murano, while their own craft headed past San Francesco del Deserto and so back direct to Venice.

He put his arm around her once more, holding her close, and this time she responded, smiling up at him, her head on his shoulder.

"It's been a lovely day," she said. "I shall never forget it, never. You know, darling, now at last I can begin to enjoy our holiday."

He wanted to shout with relief. It's going to be all right, he decided, let her believe what she likes, it doesn't matter, it makes her happy. The beauty of Venice rose before them, sharply outlined against the glowing sky, and there was still so much to see, wandering there together, that might now be perfect because of her change of mood, the shadow having lifted, and aloud he began to discuss the evening to come, where they would dine—not the restaurant they usually went to, near the Venice Theatre, but somewhere different, somewhere new.

"Yes, but it must be cheap," she said, falling in with his mood, "because we've already spent so much today."

Their hotel by the Grand Canal had a welcoming, comforting air. The clerk smiled as he handed over their key. The bedroom was familiar, like home, with Laura's things arranged neatly on the dressing-table, but with it the little festive atmosphere of strangeness, of excitement, that only a holiday bedroom brings. This is ours for the moment, but no more. While we are in it we bring it life. When we have gone it no longer exists, it fades into anonymity. He turned on both taps in the bathroom, the water gushing into the bath, the steam rising. Now, he thought afterwards, now at last is the moment to make love, and he went back into the bedroom, and she understood, and opened her arms and smiled. Such blessed relief after all those weeks of restraint.

"The thing is," she said later, fixing her earrings before the looking-glass, "I'm not really terribly hungry. Shall we just be dull and eat in the dining-room here?"

"God, no!" he exclaimed. "With all those rather dreary couples at the other tables? I'm ravenous. I'm also gay. I want to get rather sloshed."

"Not bright lights and music, surely?"

"No, no . . . some small, dark, intimate cave, rather sinister, full of lovers with other people's wives."

"H'm," sniffed Laura, "we all know what *that* means. You'll spot some Italian lovely of sixteen and smirk at her through dinner, while I'm stuck high and dry with a beastly man's broad back."

They went out laughing into the warm soft night, and the magic was about them everywhere. "Let's walk," he said, "let's walk and work up an appetite for our gigantic meal," and inevitably they found themselves by the Molo and the lapping gondolas dancing upon the water, the lights everywhere blending with the darkness. There were other couples strolling for the same sake of aimless enjoyment, backwards, forwards, purposeless, and the inevitable sailors in groups, noisy, gesticulating, and dark-eyed girls whispering, clicking on high heels.

"The trouble is," said Laura, "walking in Venice becomes compulsive once you start. Just over the next bridge, you say, and then the next one beckons. I'm sure there are no restaurants down here, we're almost at those public gardens where they hold the Biennale. Let's turn back. I know there's a restaurant somewhere near the Church of San Zaccaria, there's a little alley-way leading to it."

"Tell you what," said John, "if we go down here by the Arsenal, and cross that bridge at the end and head left, we'll come upon San Zaccaria from the other side. We did it the other morning."

"Yes, but it was daylight then. We may lose our way, it's not very well lit."

"Don't fuss. I have an instinct for these things."

They turned down the Fondamenta del l'Arsenale and crossed the little bridge short of the Arsenal itself, and so on past the Church of San Martino. There were two canals ahead, one bearing right, the other left, with narrow streets beside them. John hesitated. Which one was it they had walked beside the day before?

"You see," protested Laura, "we shall be lost, just as I said."

"Nonsense," replied John firmly. "It's the left-hand one, I remember the little bridge."

The canal was narrow, the houses on either side seemed to close in upon it, and in the daytime, with the sun's reflection on the water and the windows of the houses open, bedding upon the balconies, a canary singing in a cage, there had been an impression of warmth, of secluded shelter. Now, ill-lit, in darkness, the windows of the houses shuttered, the water dank, the scene appeared altogether different, neglected, poor, and the long narrow boats moored to the slippery steps of cellar entrances looked like coffins.

"I swear I don't remember this bridge," said Laura, pausing, and holding on to the rail, "and I don't like the look of that alley-way beyond."

"There's a lamp halfway up," John told her. "I know exactly where we are, not far from the Greek quarter."

They crossed the bridge, and were about to plunge into the alley-way, when they heard the cry. It came, surely, from one of the houses on the opposite side, but which one it was impossible to say. With the shutters closed, each of them seemed dead. They turned, and stared in the direction from which the sound had come.

"What was it?" whispered Laura.

"Some drunk or other," said John briefly, "come on."

Less like a drunk than someone being strangled, and the choking cry suppressed as the grip held firm.

"We ought to call the police," said Laura.

"Oh, for heaven's sake," said John. Where did she think she was—Piccadilly?

"Well, I'm off, it's sinister," she replied, and began to hurry away up the twisting alley-way. John hesitated, his eye caught by a small figure which suddenly crept from a cellar entrance below one of the opposite houses, and then jumped into a narrow boat below. It was a child, a little girl—she couldn't have been more than five or six—wearing a short coat over her minute skirt, a pixie hood covering her head. There were four boats moored, line upon line, and she proceeded to jump from one to the other with surprising agility, intent, it would seem, upon escape. Once her foot slipped and he caught his breath, for she was within a few feet of the water, losing balance; then she recovered, and hopped on to the furthest boat. Bending, she tugged at the rope, which

had the effect of swinging the boat's after-end across the canal, almost
touching the opposite side and another cellar entrance, about thirty feet
from the spot where John stood watching her. Then the child jumped
again, landing upon the cellar steps, and vanished into the house, the
boat swinging back into mid-canal behind her. The whole episode could
not have taken more than four minutes. Then he heard the quick patter
of feet. Laura had returned. She had seen none of it, for which he felt
unspeakably thankful. The sight of a child, a little girl, in what must
have been near danger, her fear that the scene he had just witnessed was
in some way a sequel to the alarming cry, might have had a disastrous
effect on her overwrought nerves.

"What are you doing?" she called. "I daren't go on without you. The
wretched alley branches in two directions."

"Sorry," he told her, "I'm coming."

He took her arm and they walked briskly along the alley, John with
an apparent confidence he did not possess.

"There were no more cries, were there?" she asked.

"No," he said, "no, nothing. I tell you, it was some drunk."

The alley led to a deserted campo behind a church, not a church he
knew, and he led the way across, along another street and over a further
bridge.

"Wait a minute," he said, "I think we take this right-hand turning.
It will lead us into the Greek quarter, the Church of San Georgio is
somewhere over there."

She did not answer. She was beginning to lose faith. The place was
like a maze. They might circle round and round forever, and then find
themselves back again, near the bridge where they had heard the cry.
Doggedly he led her on, and then, surprisingly, with relief, he saw
people walking in the lighted street ahead, there was a spire of a church,
the surroundings became familiar.

"There, I told you," he said, "that's San Zaccaria, we've found it all
right. Your restaurant can't be far away." And anyway, there would
be other restaurants, somewhere to eat, at least here was the cheering
glitter of lights, of movement, canals beside which people walked, the
atmosphere of tourism. The letters RISTORANTE in blue lights, shone
like a beacon down a left-hand alley.

"Is this your place?" he asked.

"God knows," she said. "Who cares? Let's feed there anyway."

And so into the sudden blast of heated air and hum of voices, the
smell of pasta, wine, waiters, jostling customers, laughter. "For two?
This way, please." Why, he thought, was one's British nationality

always so obvious? A cramped little table and an enormous menu scribbled in an indecipherable mauve ink, with the waiter hovering, expecting the order forthwith.

"Two very large Camparis, with soda," John said. "*Then* we'll study the menu."

He was not going to be rushed. He handed the bill of fare to Laura and looked about him. Mostly Italians—that meant the food would be good. Then he saw them. At the opposite side of the room. The twin sisters. They must have come into the restaurant hard upon Laura and his own arrival, for they were only now sitting down, shedding their coats, the waiter hovering beside the table. John was seized with the irrational thought that this was no coincidence. The sisters had noticed them both, in the street outside, and had followed them in. Why, in the name of hell, should they have picked on this particular spot, in the whole of Venice, unless . . . unless Laura herself, at Torcello, had suggested a further encounter, or the sister had suggested it to her? A small restaurant near the Church of San Zaccaria, we go there sometimes for dinner. It was Laura, before the walk, who had mentioned San Zaccaria . . .

She was still intent upon the menu, she had not seen the sisters, but any moment now she would have chosen what she wanted to eat, and then she would raise her head and look across the room. If only the drinks would come. If only the waiter would bring the drinks, it would give Laura something to do.

"You know, I was thinking," he said quickly, "we really ought to go to the garage tomorrow and get the car, and do that drive to Padua. We could lunch in Padua, see the cathedral and touch St. Anthony's tomb and look at the Giotto frescoes, and come back by way of those various villas along the Brenta that the guidebook recommends so highly."

It was no use, though. She was looking up, across the restaurant, and she gave a little gasp of surprise. It was genuine. He could swear it was genuine.

"Look," she said, "how extraordinary! How really amazing!"

"What?" he said sharply.

"Why, there they are. My wonderful old twins. They've seen us, what's more. They're staring this way." She waved her hand, radiant, delighted. The sister she had spoken to at Torcello bowed and smiled. False old bitch, he thought. I know they followed us.

"Oh, darling, I must go and speak to them," she said impulsively, "just to tell them how happy I've been all day, thanks to them."

"Oh, for heaven's sake," he said. "Look, here are the drinks. And we haven't ordered yet. Surely you can wait until later, until we've eaten?"

"I won't be a moment," she said, "and anyway I want scampi, nothing first. I told you I wasn't hungry."

She got up, and, brushing past the waiter with the drinks, crossed the room. She might have been greeting the loved friends of years. He watched her bend over the table, shake them both by the hand, and because there was a vacant chair at their table she drew it up and sat down, talking, smiling. Nor did the sisters seem surprised, at least not the one she knew, who nodded and talked back, while the blind sister remained impassive.

All right, thought John savagely, then I *will* get sloshed, and he proceeded to down his Campari and soda and order another, while he pointed out something quite unintelligible on the menu as his own choice, but remembered scampi for Laura. "And a bottle of soave," he added, "with ice."

The evening was ruined anyway. What was to have been an intimate and happy celebration would now be heavy-laden with spiritualistic visions, poor little dead Christine sharing the table with them, which was so damned stupid when in earthly life she would have been tucked up hours ago in bed. The bitter taste of his Campari suited his mood of sudden self-pity, and all the while he watched the group at the table in the opposite corner, Laura apparently listening while the more active sister held forth and the blind one sat silent, her formidable sightless eyes turned in his direction.

She's phoney, he thought, she's not blind at all. They're both of them frauds, and they could be males in drag after all, just as we pretended at Torcello, and they're after Laura.

He began on his second Campari and soda. The two drinks, taken on an empty stomach, had an instant effect. Vision became blurred. And still Laura went on sitting at the other table, putting in a question now and again, while the active sister talked. The waiter appeared with the scampi, and a companion beside him to serve John's own order, which was totally unrecognizable, heaped with a livid sauce.

"The signora does not come?" enquired the first waiter, and John shook his head grimly, pointing an unsteady finger across the room.

"Tell the signora," he said carefully, "her scampi will get cold."

He stared down at the offering placed before him, and prodded it delicately with a fork. The pallid sauce dissolved, revealing two enormous slices, rounds, of what appeared to be boiled pork, bedecked with garlic. He forked a portion to his mouth and chewed, and yes, it was pork, steamy, rich, the spicy sauce having turned it curiously sweet. He laid down his fork, pushing the plate away, and became aware of Laura, returning across the room and sitting beside him. She did not say anything, which was just as well, he thought, because he was too near nausea to answer. It wasn't just the drink, but reaction from the whole nightmare day. She began to eat her scampi, still not uttering. She did not seem to notice he was not eating. The waiter, hovering at his elbow, anxious, seemed aware that John's choice was somehow an error, and discreetly removed the plate. "Bring me a green salad," murmured John, and even then Laura did not register surprise, or, as she might have done in more normal circumstances, accuse him of having had too much to drink. Finally, when she had finished her scampi, and was sipping her wine, which John had waved away, to nibble at his salad in small mouthfuls like a sick rabbit, she began to speak.

"Darling," she said, "I know you won't believe it, and it's rather frightening in a way, but after they left the restaurant in Torcello the sisters went to the cathedral, as we did, although we didn't see them in that crowd, and the blind one had another vision. She said Christine was trying to tell her something about us, that we should be in danger if we stayed in Venice. Christine wanted us to go away as soon as possible."

So that's it, he thought. They think they can run our lives for us. This is to be our problem from henceforth. Do we eat? Do we get up? Do we go to bed? We must get in touch with the twin sisters. They will direct us.

"Well?" she said. "Why don't you say something?"

"Because," he answered, "you are perfectly right, I don't believe it. Quite frankly, I judge your old sisters as being a couple of freaks, if nothing else. They're obviously unbalanced, and I'm sorry if this hurts you, but the fact is they've found a sucker in you."

"You're being unfair," said Laura. "They are genuine, I know it. I just know it. They were completely sincere in what they said."

"All right. Granted. They're sincere. But that doesn't make them well-balanced. Honestly, darling, you meet that old girl for ten minutes in a loo, she tells you she sees Christine sitting beside us, well, anyone with a gift for telepathy could read your unconscious mind in an instant, and then, pleased with her success, as any old psychic expert would be, she flings a further mood of ecstasy and wants to boot us out of Venice. Well, I'm sorry, but to hell with it."

The room was no longer reeling. Anger had sobered him. If it would not put Laura to shame he would get up and cross to their table, and tell the old fools where they could get off.

"I knew you would take it like this," said Laura unhappily. "I told them you would. They said not to worry. As long as we left Venice tomorrow everything would come all right."

"Oh, for God's sake," said John. He changed his mind and poured himself a glass of wine.

"After all," Laura went on, "we have really seen the cream of Venice. I don't mind going on somewhere else. And if we stayed—I know it sounds silly, but I should have a nasty nagging sort of feeling inside me, and I should keep thinking of darling Christine being unhappy and trying to tell us to go."

"Right," said John with ominous calm, "that settles it. Go we will. I suggest we clear off to the hotel straight away and warn the reception we're leaving in the morning. Have you had enough to eat?"

"Oh, dear," sighed Laura, "don't take it like that. Look, why not come over and meet them, and then they can explain about the vision to you? Perhaps you would take it seriously then. Especially as you are the one it most concerns. Christine is more worried over you than me. And the extraordinary thing is that the blind sister says you're psychic and don't know it. You are somehow *en rapport* with the unknown, and I'm not."

"Well, that's final," said John. "I'm psychic, am I? Fine. My psychic intuition tells me to get out of this restaurant now, at once, and we can decide what we do about leaving Venice when we are back at the hotel."

He signalled to the waiter for the bill and they waited for it, not speaking to each other, Laura unhappy, fiddling with her bag, while John, glancing furtively at the twins' table, noticed that they were tucking into plates piled high with spaghetti, in very unpsychic fashion. The bill disposed of, John pushed back his chair.

"Right. Are you ready?" he asked.

"I'm going to say goodbye to them first," said Laura, her mouth set sulkily, reminding him instantly, with a pang, of their poor lost child.

"Just as you like," he replied, and walked ahead of her, out of the restaurant without a backward glance.

The soft humidity of the evening, so pleasant to walk about in earlier, had turned to rain. The strolling tourists had melted away. One or two people hurried by under umbrellas. This is what the inhabitants who live here see, he thought. This is the true life. Empty streets by night, and the dank stillness of a stagnant canal beneath shuttered houses. The rest is a bright façade put on for show, glittering by sunlight.

Laura joined him and they walked away together in silence, and emerging presently behind the ducal palace came out into the Piazza San Marco. The rain was heavy now, and they sought shelter, still walking, with the few remaining stragglers under the colonnades. The orchestras had packed up for the evening. The tables were bare. Chairs had been turned upside down.

The experts are right, he thought. Venice is sinking. The whole city is slowly dying. One day the tourists will travel here by boat to peer down into the waters, and they will see pillars and columns and marble far, far beneath them, slime and mud uncovering for brief moments a lost underworld of stone. Their heels made a ringing sound on the pavement and the rain splashed from the gutterings above. A fine ending to an evening that had started with brave hope, with innocence.

When they came to their hotel Laura made straight for the lift, and John turned to the desk to ask the night-porter for the key. The man handed him a telegram at the same time. John stared at it a moment. Laura was already in the lift. Then he opened the envelope and read the message. It was from the headmaster of Johnnie's preparatory school.

Johnnie under observation suspected appendicitis in city hospital here. No cause for alarm but surgeon thought wise advise you.
Charles Hill

He read the message twice, then walked slowly towards the lift, where Laura was waiting for him. He gave her the telegram. "This came when we were out," he said. "Not awfully good news." He pressed the lift button as she read the telegram. The lift stopped at the second floor, and they got out.

"Well, this decides it, doesn't it?" she said. "Here is the proof. We have to leave Venice because we're going home. It's Johnnie who's in danger, not us. This is what Christine was trying to tell the twins."

The first thing John did the following morning was to put a call through to the headmaster at the preparatory school. Then he gave notice of their departure to the reception manager, and they packed while they waited for the call. Neither of them referred to the events of the preceding day, it was not necessary. John knew the arrival of the telegram and the foreboding of danger from the sisters was coincidence, nothing more, but it was pointless to start an argument about it. Laura was convinced otherwise, but intuitively she knew it was best to keep her feelings to herself. During breakfast they discussed ways and means of getting home. It should be possible to get themselves, and the car, on to the special car train that ran from Milan through to Calais, since it was early in the season. In any event, the headmaster had said there was no urgency.

The call from England came while John was in the bathroom. Laura answered it. He came into the bedroom a few minutes later. She was still speaking, but he could tell from the expression in her eyes that she was anxious.

"It's Mrs. Hill," she said. "Mr. Hill is in class. She says they reported from the hospital that Johnnie had a restless night, and the surgeon may have to operate, but he doesn't want to unless it's absolutely necessary. They've taken X-rays and the appendix is in a tricky position, it's not awfully straightforward."

"Here, give it to me," he said.

The soothing but slightly guarded voice of the headmaster's wife came down the receiver. "I'm so sorry this may spoil your plans," she said, "but both Charles and I felt you ought to be told, and that you might feel rather easier if you were on the spot. Johnnie is very plucky, but of course he has some fever. That isn't unusual, the surgeon says, in the circumstances. Sometimes an appendix can get displaced, it appears, and this makes it more complicated. He's going to decide about operating this evening."

"Yes, of course, we quite understand," said John.

"Please do tell your wife not to worry too much," she went on. "The hospital is excellent, a very nice staff, and we have every confidence in the surgeon."

"Yes," said John, "yes," and then broke off because Laura was making gestures beside him.

"If we can't get the car on the train, I can fly," she said. "They're sure to be able to find me a seat on a plane. Then at least one of us would be there this evening."

He nodded agreement. "Thank you so much, Mrs. Hill," he said, "we'll manage to get back all right. Yes, I'm sure Johnnie is in good hands. Thank your husband for us. Goodbye."

He replaced the receiver and looked round him at the tumbled beds, suitcases on the floor, tissue-paper strewn. Baskets, maps, books, coats, everything they had brought with them in the car. "Oh God," he said, "what a bloody mess. All this junk." The telephone rang again. It was the hall porter to say he had succeeded in booking a sleeper for them both, and a place for the car, on the following night.

"Look," said Laura, who had seized the telephone, "could you book one seat on the midday plane from Venice to London today, for me? It's imperative one of us gets home this evening. My husband could follow with the car tomorrow."

"Here, hang on," interrupted John. "No need for panic stations. Surely twenty-four hours wouldn't make all that difference?"

Anxiety had drained the color from her face. She turned to him, distraught.

"It mightn't to you, but it does to me," she said. "I've lost one child, I'm not going to lose another."

"All right, darling, all right . . ." He put his hand out to her, but she brushed it off, impatiently, and continued giving directions to the porter. He turned back to his packing. No use saying anything. Better for it to be as she wished. They could, of course, both go by air, and then when all was well, and Johnnie better, he could come back and fetch the car, driving home through France as they had come. Rather a sweat, though, and a hell of an expense. Bad enough Laura going by air and himself with the car on the train from Milan.

"We could, if you like, both fly," he began tentatively, explaining the sudden idea, but she would have none of it. "That really *would* be absurd," she said impatiently. "As long as I'm there this evening, and you follow by train, it's all that matters. Besides, we shall need the car, going backwards and forwards to the hospital. And our luggage. We couldn't go off and just leave all this here."

No, he saw her point. A silly idea. It was only, well, he was as worried about Johnnie as she was, though he wasn't going to say so.

"I'm going downstairs to stand over the porter," said Laura. "They always make more effort if one is actually on the spot. Everything I want tonight is packed. I shall only need my overnight case. You can bring everything else in the car." She hadn't been out of the bedroom five minutes before the telephone rang. It was Laura. "Darling," she said, "it couldn't have worked out better. The porter has got me on a charter flight that leaves Venice in less than an hour. A special motor-launch takes the party direct from San Marco, in about ten minutes. Some passenger on the charter flight had canceled. I shall be at Gatwick in less than four hours."

"I'll be down right away," he told her.

He joined her by the reception desk. She no longer looked anxious and drawn, but full of purpose. She was on her way. He kept wishing they were going together. He couldn't bear to stay on in Venice after she had gone, but the thought of driving to Milan, spending a dreary night in a hotel there alone, the endless dragging day which would follow, and the long hours in the train the next night, filled him with intolerable depression, quite apart from the anxiety about Johnnie. They walked along to the San Marco landing-stage, the Molo bright and glittering after the rain, a little breeze blowing, the postcards and scarves and tourist souvenirs fluttering on the stalls, the tourists themselves out in force, strolling, contented, the happy day before them.

"I'll ring you tonight from Milan," he told her. "The Hills will give you a bed, I suppose. And if you're at the hospital they'll let me have the latest news. That must be your charter party. You're welcome to them!"

The passengers descending from the landing-stage down into the waiting launch were carrying hand-luggage with Union Jack tags upon them. They were mostly middle-aged, with what appeared to be two Methodist ministers in charge. One of them advanced towards Laura, holding out his hand, showing a gleaming row of dentures when he smiled. "You must be the lady joining us for the homeward flight," he said. "Welcome aboard, and to the Union of Fellowship. We are all delighted to make your acquaintance. Sorry we hadn't a seat for hubby too."

Laura turned swiftly and kissed John, a tremor at the corner of her mouth betraying inward laughter. "Do you think they'll break into hymns?" she whispered. "Take care of yourself, hubby. Call me tonight."

The pilot sounded a curious little toot upon his horn, and in a moment Laura had climbed down the steps into the launch and was standing amongst the crowd of passengers, waving her hand, her scarlet coat a gay patch of color amongst the more sober suiting of her companions. The launch tooted again and moved away from the landing-stage, and he stood there watching it, a sense of immense loss filling his heart. Then he turned and walked away, back to the hotel, the bright day all about him desolate, unseen.

There was nothing, he thought, as he looked about him presently in the hotel bedroom, so melancholy as a vacated room, especially when the recent signs of occupation were still visible about him. Laura's suitcases on the bed, a second coat she had left behind. Traces of powder on the dressing-table. A tissue, with a lipstick smear, thrown in the wastepaper basket. Even an old toothpaste tube squeezed dry, lying on the glass shelf above the wash basin. Sounds of the heedless traffic on the Grand Canal came as always from the open window, but

Laura wasn't there any more to listen to it, or to watch from the small balcony. The pleasure had gone. Feeling had gone.

John finished packing, and, leaving all the baggage ready to be collected, he went downstairs to pay the bill. The reception clerk was welcoming new arrivals. People were sitting on the terrace overlooking the Grand Canal reading newspapers, the pleasant day waiting to be planned.

John decided to have an early lunch, here on the hotel terrace, on familiar ground, and then have the porter carry the baggage to one of the ferries that steamed between San Marco and the Porta Roma, where the car was garaged. The fiasco meal of the night before had left him empty, and he was ready for the trolley of hors d'oeuvres when they brought it to him, around midday. Even here, though, there was change. The head-waiter, their especial friend, was off-duty, and the table where they usually sat was occupied by new arrivals, a honeymoon couple, he told himself sourly, observing the gaiety, the smiles, while he had been shown to a small single table behind a tub of flowers.

She's airborne now, John thought, she's on her way, and he tried to picture Laura seated between the Methodist ministers, telling them, no doubt, about Johnnie ill in hospital, and heaven knows what else besides. Well, the twin sisters anyway could rest in psychic peace. Their wishes would have been fulfilled.

Lunch over, there was no point in lingering with a cup of coffee on the terrace. His desire was to get away as soon as possible, fetch the car, and be en route for Milan. He made his farewells at the reception desk, and, escorted by a porter who had piled his baggage on to a wheeled trolley, he made his way once more to the landing-stage of San Marco. As he stepped on to the steam-ferry, his luggage heaped beside him, a crowd of jostling people all about him, he had one momentary pang to be leaving Venice. When, if ever, he wondered, would they come again? Next year . . . in three years . . . Glimpsed first on honeymoon, nearly ten years ago, and then a second visit, *en passant,* before a cruise, and now this last abortive ten days that had ended so abruptly.

The water glittered in the sunshine, buildings shone, tourists in dark glasses paraded up and down the rapidly receding Molo; already the terrace of their hotel was out of sight as the ferry churned its way up the Grand Canal. So many impressions to seize and hold, familiar loved façades, balconies, windows, water lapping the cellar steps of decaying palaces, the little red house where d'Annunzio lived, with its garden— our house, Laura called it, pretending it was theirs—and too soon the ferry would be turning left on the direct route to the Piazzale Roma, so missing the best of the Canal, the Rialto, the farther palaces.

Another ferry was heading downstream to pass them, filled with passengers, and for a brief foolish moment he wished he could change places, be amongst the happy tourists bound for Venice and all he had left behind him. Then he saw her. Laura, in her scarlet coat, the twin sisters by her side, the active sister with her hand on Laura's arm, talking earnestly, and Laura herself, her hair blowing in the wind, gesticulating, on her face a look of distress. He stared, astounded, too astonished to shout, to wave, and anyway they would never have heard or seen him, for his own ferry had already passed and was heading in the opposite direction.

What the hell had happened? There must have been a hold-up with the charter flight and it had never taken off, but in that case why had Laura not telephoned him at the hotel? And what were those damned sisters doing? Had she run into them at the airport? Was it coincidence? And why did she look so anxious? He could think of no explanation. Perhaps the flight had been canceled. Laura, of course, would go straight to the hotel, expecting to find him there, intending, doubtless, to drive with him after all to Milan and take the train the following night. What a blasted mix-up. The only thing to do was to telephone the hotel immediately his ferry reached the Piazzale Roma and tell her to wait, he would return and fetch her. As for the damned interfering sisters, they could get stuffed.

The usual stampede ensued when the ferry arrived at the landing-stage. He had to find a porter to collect his baggage, and then wait while he discovered a telephone. The fiddling with change, the hunt for the number, delayed him still more. He succeeded at last in getting through, and luckily the reception clerk he knew was still at the desk.

"Look, there's been some frightful muddle," he began, and explained how Laura was even now on her way back to the hotel—he had seen her with two friends on one of the ferry-services. Would the reception clerk explain and tell her to wait? He would be back by the next available service to collect her. "In any event, detain her," he said. "I'll be as quick as I can." The reception clerk understood perfectly and John rang off.

Thank heaven Laura hadn't turned up before he had put through his call, or they would have told her he was on his way to Milan. The porter was still waiting with the baggage, and it seemed simplest to walk with him to the garage, hand everything over to the chap in charge of the office there, and ask him to keep it for an hour, when he would be returning with his wife to pick up the car. Then he went back to the landing-station to await the next ferry to Venice. The minutes dragged, and he kept wondering all the time what had gone wrong at the airport and why in heaven's name Laura hadn't telephoned. No use conjecturing. She would tell him the whole story at the hotel. One thing was certain. He would not allow themselves to be saddled with the sisters and become involved with their affairs. He could imagine Laura saying that they also had missed a flight, and could they have a lift to Milan?

Finally the ferry chugged alongside the landing-stage and he stepped aboard. What an anticlimax, thrashing back past the familiar sights to which he had bidden a nostalgic farewell such a short while ago! He didn't even look about him this time, he was so intent on reaching his destination. In San Marco there were more people than ever, the afternoon crowds walking shoulder to shoulder, every one of them on pleasure bent.

He came to the hotel, and pushed his way through the swing-door, expecting to see Laura, and possibly the sisters, waiting in the lounge on the left-hand side of the entrance. She was not there. He went to the desk. The reception clerk he had spoken to on the telephone was standing there, talking to the manager.

"Has my wife arrived?" John asked.

"No, sir, not yet."

"What an extraordinary thing. Are you sure?"

"Absolutely certain, sir. I have been here ever since you telephoned me at a quarter to two. I have not left the desk."

"I just don't understand it. She was on one of the vaporettos passing by the Accademia. She would have landed at San Marco about five minutes later and come on here."

The clerk seemed nonplussed. "I don't know what to say. The signora was with friends, did you say?"

"Yes. Well, acquaintances. Two ladies we had met at Torcello yesterday. I was astonished to see her with them on the vaporetto, and of course I assumed that the flight had been cancelled, and she had somehow met up with them at the airport and decided to return here with them, to catch me before I left."

Oh hell, what was Laura doing? It was after three. A matter of moments from San Marco landing-stage to the hotel.

"Perhaps the signora went with her friends to their hotel instead. Do you know where they are staying?"

"No," said John, "I haven't the slightest idea. What's more I don't even know the names of the two ladies. They were sisters, twins, in fact—looked exactly alike. But, anyway, why go to their hotel and not here?"

The swing-door opened but it wasn't Laura. Two people staying in the hotel.

The manager broke into the conversation, "I tell you what I will do," he said. "I will telephone the airport and check about the flight. Then at least we will get somewhere." He smiled apologetically. It was not usual for arrangements to go wrong.

"Yes, do that," said John. "We may as well know what happened there."

He lit a cigarette and began to pace up and down the entrance hall. What a bloody mix-up. And how unlike Laura, who knew he would be setting off for Milan directly after lunch—indeed, for all she knew he might have gone before. But surely, in that case, she would have telephoned at once, on arrival at the airport, had take-off been canceled? The manager was ages telephoning, he had to be put through on some other line, and his Italian was too rapid for John to follow the conversation. Finally he replaced the receiver.

"It is more mysterious than ever, sir," he said. "The charter flight was not delayed, it took off on schedule with a full complement of passengers. As far as they could tell me, there was no hitch. The signora must simply have changed her mind." His smile was more apologetic than ever.

"Changed her mind," John repeated. "But why on earth should she do that? She was so anxious to be home tonight."

The manager shrugged. "You know how ladies can be, sir," he said. "Your wife may have thought that after all she would prefer to take the train to Milan with you. I do assure you, though, that the charter party was most respectable, and it was a Caravelle aircraft, perfectly safe."

"Yes, yes," said John impatiently, "I don't blame your arrangements in the slightest. I just can't understand what induced her to change her mind, unless it was meeting with these two ladies."

The manager was silent. He could not think of anything to say. The reception clerk was equally concerned. "It is possible," he ventured, "that you made a mistake, and it was not the signora that you saw on the vaporetto?"

"Oh no," replied John, "it was my wife, I assure you. She was wearing her red coat, she was hatless, just as she left here. I saw her as plainly as I can see you. I would swear to it in a court of law."

"It is unfortunate," said the manager, "that we do not know the name of the two ladies, or the hotel where they were staying. You say you met these ladies at Torcello yesterday?"

"Yes . . . but only briefly. They weren't staying there. At least, I am certain they were not. We saw them at dinner in Venice later, as it happens."

"Excuse me . . ." Guests were arriving with luggage to check in, the clerk was obliged to attend to them. John turned in desperation to the manager. "Do you think it would be any good telephoning the hotel in Torcello in case the people there knew the name of the ladies, or where they were staying in Venice?"

"We can try," replied the manager. "It is a small hope, but we can try."

John resumed his anxious pacing, all the while watching the swing-door, hoping, praying, that he would catch sight of the red coat and Laura would enter. Once again there followed what seemed an interminable telephone conversation between the manager and someone at the hotel in Torcello.

"Tell them two sisters," said John, "two elderly ladies dressed in grey, both exactly alike. One lady was blind," he added. The manager nodded. He was obviously giving a detailed description. Yet when he hung up he shook his head. "The manager at Torcello says he remembers the two ladies well," he told John, "but they were only there for lunch. He never learnt their names."

"Well, that's that. There's nothing to do now but wait."

John lit his third cigarette and went out on to the terrace, to resume his pacing there. He stared out across the canal, searching the heads of the people on passing steamers, motorboats, even drifting gondolas. The minutes ticked by on his watch, and there was no sign of Laura. A terrible foreboding nagged at him that somehow this was prearranged, that Laura had never intended to catch the aircraft, that last night in the restaurant she had made an assignation with the sisters. Oh God, he thought, that's impossible, I'm going paranoiac . . . Yet why, why? No, more likely the encounter at the airport was fortuitous, and for some incredible reason they had persuaded Laura not to board the aircraft, even prevented her from doing so, trotting out one of their psychic visions, that the aircraft would crash, that she must return with them to Venice. And Laura, in her sensitive state, felt they must be right, swallowed it all without question.

But granted all these possibilities, why had she not come to the hotel? What was she doing? Four o'clock, half-past four, the sun no longer dappling the water. He went back to the reception desk.

"I just can't hang around," he said. "Even if she does turn up, we shall never make Milan this evening. I might see her walking with these ladies, in the Piazza San Marco, anywhere. If she arrives while I'm out, will you explain?"

The clerk was full of concern. "Indeed, yes," he said. "It is very worrying for you, sir. Would it perhaps be prudent if we booked you in here tonight?"

John gestured, helplessly. "Perhaps, yes, I don't know. Maybe . . ."

He went out of the swing-door and began to walk towards the Piazza San Marco. He looked into every shop up and down the colonnades, crossed the piazza a dozen times, threaded his way between the tables in front of Florian's, in front of Quadri's, knowing that Laura's red coat and the distinct appearance of the twin sisters could easily be spotted, even amongst this milling crowd, but there was no sign of them. He joined the crowd of shoppers in the Merceria, shoulder to shoulder with idlers, thrusters, window-gazers, knowing instinctively that it was useless, they wouldn't be here. Why should Laura have deliberately missed her flight to return to Venice for such a purpose? And even if she had done so, for some reason beyond his imagining, she would surely have come first to the hotel to find him.

The only thing left to him was to try to track down the sisters. Their hotel could be anywhere amongst the hundreds of hotels and pensions scattered through Venice, or even across the other side at the Zattere, or farther again on the Giudecca. These last possibilities seemed remote. More likely they were staying in a small hotel or pension somewhere near San Zaccaria handy to the restaurant where they had dined last night. The blind one would surely not go far afield in the evening. He had been a fool not to have thought of this before, and he turned back and walked quickly away from the brightly lighted shopping district towards the narrower, more cramped quarter where they had dined last evening. He found the restaurant without difficulty, but they were not yet open for dinner, and the waiter preparing tables was not the one who had served them. John asked to see the *patrone,* and the waiter disappeared to the back regions, returning after a moment or two with the somewhat disheveled-looking proprietor in shirt-sleeves, caught in a slack moment, not in full *tenue.*

"I had dinner here last night," John explained. "There were two ladies sitting at that table there in the corner." He pointed to it.

"You wish to book that table for this evening?" asked the proprietor.

"No," said John. "No, there were two ladies there last night, two sisters, *due sorelle,* twins, *gemelle*"—what was the right word for twins? "Do you remember? Two ladies, *sorelle, vecchie . . .*"

"Ah," said the man, "si, si, signore, *la povera* signorina." He put his hands to his eyes to feign blindness. "Yes, I remember."

"Do you know their names?" asked John. "Where they were staying? I am very anxious to trace them."

The proprietor spread out his hands in a gesture of regret. "I am ver' sorry, signore, I do not know the names of the signorine, they have been here once, twice perhaps, for dinner, they do not say where they were staying. Perhaps if you come again tonight they might be here? Would you like to book a table?"

He pointed around him, suggesting a whole choice of tables that might appeal to a prospective diner, but John shook his head.

"Thank you, no. I may be dining elsewhere. I am sorry to have troubled you. If the signorine should come"—he paused—"possibly I may return later," he added. "I am not sure."

The proprietor bowed, and walked with him to the entrance. "In Venice the whole world meets," he said smiling. "It is possible the signore will find his friends tonight. *Arrivederci,* signore."

Friends? John walked out into the street. More likely kidnappers . . . Anxiety had turned to fear, to panic. Something had gone terribly wrong. Those women had got hold of Laura, played upon her suggestibility, induced her to go with them, either to their hotel or elsewhere. Should he find the Consulate? Where was it? What would he say when he got there? He began walking without purpose, finding himself, as they had done the night before, in streets he did not know, and suddenly came upon a tall building with the word QUESTURA above it. This is it, he thought. I don't care, something has happened, I'm going inside. There were a number of police in uniform coming and going, the place at any rate was active, and, addressing himself to one of them behind a glass-partition, he asked if there was anyone who spoke English. The man pointed to a flight of stairs and John went up, entering a door on the right where he saw that another couple were sitting, waiting, and with relief he recognized them as fellow-countrymen, tourists, obviously a man and his wife, in some sort of predicament.

"Come and sit down," said the man. "We've waited half-an-hour but they can't be much longer. What a country! They wouldn't leave us like this at home."

John took the proffered cigarette and found a chair beside them.

"What's your trouble?" he asked.

"My wife had her handbag pinched in one of those shops in the

Merceria," said the man. "She simply put it down one moment to look at something, and you'd hardly credit it, the next moment it had gone. I say it was a sneak thief, she insists it was the girl behind the counter. But who's to say? These Ities are all alike. Anyway, I'm certain we shan't get it back. What have you lost?"

"Suitcase stolen," John lied rapidly. "Had some important papers in it."

How could he say he had lost his wife? He couldn't even begin . . .

The man nodded in sympathy. "As I said, these Ities are all alike. Old Musso knew how to deal with them. Too many Communists around these days. The trouble is, they're not going to bother with our troubles much, not with this murderer at large. They're all out looking for him."

"Murderer? What murderer?" asked John.

"Don't tell me you've not heard about it?" The man stared at him in surprise. "Venice has talked of nothing else. It's been in all the papers, on the radio, and even in the English papers too. A grizzly business. One woman found with her throat slit last week—a tourist too—and some old chap discovered with the same sort of knife wound this morning. They seem to think it must be a maniac because there doesn't seem to be any motive. Nasty thing to happen in Venice in the tourist season."

"My wife and I never bother with the newspapers when we're on holiday," said John. "And we're neither of us much given to gossip in the hotel."

"Very wise of you," laughed the man. "It might have spoilt your holiday, especially if your wife is nervous. Oh well, we're off tomorrow anyway. Can't say we mind, do we, dear?" He turned to his wife. "Venice has gone downhill since we were here last. And now this loss of the handbag really is the limit."

The door of the inner room opened, and a senior police officer asked John's companion and his wife to pass through.

"I bet we don't get any satisfaction," murmured the tourist, winking at John, and he and his wife went into the inner room. The door closed behind them. John stubbed out his cigarette and lighted another. A strange feeling of unreality possessed him. He asked himself what he was doing here, what was the use of it? Laura was no longer in Venice but had disappeared, perhaps forever, with those diabolical sisters. She would never be traced. And just as the two of them had made up a fantastic story about the twins, when they first spotted them in Torcello, so, with nightmare logic, the fiction would have basis in fact: the women were in reality disguised crooks, men with criminal intent who lured unsuspecting persons to some appalling fate. They might even be the murderers for whom the police sought. Who would ever suspect two elderly women of respectable appearance, living quietly in some second-rate pension or hotel? He stubbed out his cigarette, unfinished.

This, he thought, is really the start of paranoia. This is the way people go off their heads. He glanced at his watch. It was half-past six. Better pack this in, this futile quest here in police headquarters, and keep to the single link of sanity remaining. Return to the hotel, put a call through to the prep school in England, and ask about the latest news of Johnnie. He had not thought about poor Johnnie since sighting Laura on the vaporetto.

Too late, though. The inner door opened, the couple were ushered out.

"Usual clap-trap," said the husband sotto voce to John. "They'll do what they can. Not much hope. So many foreigners in Venice, all of 'em thieves! The locals all above reproach. Wouldn't pay 'em to steal from customers. Well, I wish you better luck."

He nodded, his wife smiled and bowed, and they had gone. John followed the police officer into the inner room.

Formalities began. Name, address, passport. Length of stay in Venice, etc., etc. Then the questions, and John, the sweat beginning to appear on his forehead, launched into his interminable story. The first encounter with the sisters, the meeting at the restaurant, Laura's state of suggestibility because of the death of their child, the telegram about Johnnie, the decision to take the chartered flight, her departure, and her sudden inexplicable return. When he had finished he felt as exhausted as if he had driven three hundred miles nonstop after a severe bout of flu. His interrogator spoke excellent English with a strong Italian accent.

"You say," he began, "that your wife was suffering the aftereffects of shock. This had been noticeable during your stay here in Venice?"

"Well, yes," John replied, "she had really been quite ill. The holiday didn't seem to be doing her much good. It was only when she met these two women at Torcello yesterday that her mood changed. The strain seemed to have gone. She was ready, I suppose, to snatch at every straw, and this belief that our little girl was watching over her had somehow restored her to what appeared normality."

"It would be natural," said the police officer, "in the circumstances. But no doubt the telegram last night was a further shock to you both?"

"Indeed, yes. That was the reason we decided to return home."

"No argument between you? No difference of opinion?"

"None. We were in complete agreement. My one regret was that I could not go with my wife on this charter flight."

The police officer nodded. "It could well be that your wife had a sudden attack of amnesia and meeting the two ladies served as a link, she clung to them for support. You have described them with great accuracy, and I think they should not be too difficult to trace. Meanwhile, I suggest you should return to your hotel, and we will get in touch with you as soon as we have news."

At least, John thought, they believed his story. They did not consider him a crank who had made the whole thing up and was merely wasting their time.

"You appreciate," he said, "I am extremely anxious. These women may have some criminal design upon my wife. One has heard of such things . . ."

The police officer smiled for the first time. "Please don't concern yourself," he said. "I am sure there will be some satisfactory explanation."

All very well, thought John, but in heaven's name, what?

"I'm sorry," he said, "to have taken up so much of your time. Especially as I gather the police have their hands full hunting down a murderer who is still at large."

He spoke deliberately. No harm in letting the fellow know that for all any of them could tell there might be some connection between Laura's disappearance and this other hideous affair.

"Ah, that," said the police officer, rising to his feet. "We hope to have the murderer under lock and key very soon."

His tone of confidence was reassuring. Murderers, missing wives, lost handbags were all under control. They shook hands, and John was ushered out of the door and so downstairs. Perhaps, he thought, as he walked slowly back to the hotel, the fellow was right. Laura had suffered a sudden attack of amnesia, and the sisters happened to be at the airport and had brought her back to Venice, to their own hotel, because Laura couldn't remember where she and John had been staying. Perhaps they were even now trying to track down his hotel. Anyway, he could do nothing more. The police had everything in hand, and, please God, would come up with the solution. All he wanted to do right now was to collapse upon a bed with a stiff whisky, and then put through a call to Johnnie's school.

The page took him up in the lift to a modest room on the fourth floor at the rear of the hotel. Bare, impersonal, the shutters closed, with a smell of cooking wafting up from a courtyard down below.

"Ask them to send me up a double whisky, will you?" he said to the boy, "and a ginger-ale," and when he was alone he plunged his face under the cold tap in the wash-basin, relieved to find that the minute portion of visitor's soap afforded some measure of comfort. He flung off his shoes, hung his coat over the back of a chair, and threw himself down on the bed. Somebody's radio was blasting forth an old popular song, now several seasons out-of-date, that had been one of Laura's favorites a couple of years ago. "I love you, baby . . ." They had taped it and used to play it back in the car. He reached out for the telephone, and asked the exchange to put through the call to England. Then he closed his eyes, and all the while the insistent voice persisted, "I love you, baby . . . I can't get you out of my mind."

Presently there was a tap at the door. It was the waiter with his drink. Too little ice, such meager comfort, but what desperate need. He gulped it down without the ginger-ale, and in a few moments the ever-nagging pain was eased, numbed, bringing, if only momentarily, a sense of calm. The telephone rang, and now, he thought, bracing himself for ultimate disaster, the final shock, Johnnie probably dying, or already dead. In which case nothing remained. Let Venice be engulfed . . .

The exchange told him that connection had been made, and in a moment he heard the voice of Mrs. Hill at the other end of the line. They must have warned her that the call came from Venice, for she knew instantly who was speaking.

"Hullo?" she cried. "Oh, I am so glad you rang. All is well. Johnnie has had his operation, the surgeon decided to do it at midday rather than wait, and it was completely successful. Johnnie is going to be all right. So you don't have to worry any more, and will have a peaceful night."

"Thank God," he answered.

"I know," she said, "we are all so relieved. Now I'll get off the line and you can speak to your wife."

John sat up on the bed, stunned. What the hell did she mean? Then he heard Laura's voice, cool and clear.

"Darling? Darling, are you there?"

He could not answer. He felt the hand holding the receiver go clammy cold with sweat. "I'm here," he whispered.

"It's not a very good line," she said, "but never mind. As Mrs. Hill told you, all is well. Such a nice surgeon, and a very sweet Sister on Johnnie's floor, and I really am happy about the way it's turned out.

I came straight down here after landing at Gatwick—the flight O.K., by the way, but such a funny crowd, it'll make you hysterical when I tell you about them—and I went to the hospital, and Johnnie was coming round. Very dopey, of course, but so pleased to see me. And the Hills are being wonderful, I've got their spare-room, and it's only a short taxi-drive into the town and the hospital. I shall go to bed as soon as we've had dinner, because I'm a bit fagged, what with the flight and the anxiety. How was the drive to Milan? And where are you staying?"

John did not recognize the voice that answered as his own. It was the automatic response of some computer.

"I'm not in Milan," he said, "I'm still in Venice."

"Still in Venice? What on earth for? Wouldn't the car start?"

"I can't explain," he said. "There was a stupid sort of mix-up . . ."

He felt suddenly so exhausted that he nearly dropped the receiver, and, shame upon shame, he could feel tears pricking behind his eyes.

"What sort of mix-up?" Her voice was suspicious, almost hostile. "You weren't in a crash?"

"No . . . no . . . nothing like that."

A moment's silence, and then she said, "Your voice sounds very slurred. Don't tell me you went and got pissed."

Oh Christ . . . if she only knew! He was probably going to pass out any moment, but not from the whisky.

"I thought," he said slowly, "I thought I saw you, in a vaporetto, with those two sisters."

What was the point of going on? It was hopeless trying to explain.

"How could you have seen me with the sisters?" she said. "You knew I'd gone to the airport. Really, darling, you are an idiot. You seem to have got those two poor old dears on the brain. I hope you didn't say anything to Mrs. Hill just now."

"No."

"Well, what are you going to do? You'll catch the train at Milan tomorrow, won't you?"

"Yes, of course," he told her.

"I still don't understand what kept you in Venice," she said. "It all sounds a bit odd to me. However . . . thank God Johnnie is going to be all right and I'm here."

"Yes," he said, "yes."

He could hear the distant boom-boom sound of a gong from the headmaster's hall.

"You had better go," he said. "My regards to the Hills, and my love to Johnnie."

"Well, take care of yourself, darling, and for goodness sake don't miss the train tomorrow, and drive carefully."

The telephone clicked and she had gone. He poured the remaining drop of whisky into his empty glass, and, sousing it with ginger-ale, drank it down at a gulp. He got up, crossed the room, threw open the shutters, and leant out of the window. He felt light-headed. His sense of relief, enormous, overwhelming, was somehow tempered with a curious feeling of unreality, almost as though the voice speaking from England had not been Laura's after all but a fake, and she was still in Venice, hidden in some furtive pension with the two sisters.

The point was, he *had* seen all three of them on the vaporetto. It was not another woman in a red coat. The women *had* been there, with Laura. So what was the explanation? That he was going off his head? Or something more sinister? The sisters, possessing psychic powers of formidable strength, had seen him as their two ferries had passed, and in some inexplicable fashion had made him believe Laura was with them. But why, and to what end? No, it didn't make sense. The only explanation was that he had been mistaken, the whole episode an hallucination. In which case he needed psychoanalysis, just as Johnnie had needed a surgeon.

And what did he do now? Go downstairs and tell the management he had been at fault and had just spoken to his wife, who had arrived in England safe and sound from her charter flight? He put on his shoes and ran his fingers through his hair. He glanced at his watch. It was ten minutes to eight. If he nipped into the bar and had a quick drink it would be easier to face the manager and admit what had happened. Then, perhaps, they would get in touch with the police. Profuse apologies all round for putting everyone to enormous trouble.

He made his way to the ground floor and went straight to the bar, feeling self-conscious, a marked man, half-imagining everyone would look at him, thinking, *There's the fellow with the missing wife.* Luckily the bar was full and there wasn't a face he knew. Even the chap behind the bar was an underling who hadn't served him before. He downed his whisky and glanced over his shoulder to the reception hall. The desk was momentarily empty. He could see the manager's back framed in the doorway of an inner room, talking to someone within. On impulse, cowardlike, he crossed the hall and passed through the swing-door to the street outside.

I'll have some dinner, he decided, and then go back and face them. I'll feel more like it once I've some food inside me.

He went to the restaurant nearby where he and Laura had dined once or twice. Nothing mattered any more, because she was safe. The nightmare lay behind him. He could enjoy his dinner, despite her absence, and think of her sitting down with the Hills to a dull, quiet evening, early to bed, and on the following morning going to the hospital to sit with Johnnie. Johnnie was safe too. No more worries, only the awkward explanations and apologies to the manager at the hotel.

There was a pleasant anonymity sitting down at a corner table alone in the little restaurant, ordering *vitello allo Marsala* and half a bottle of Merlot. He took his time, enjoying his food but eating in a kind of haze, a sense of unreality still with him, while the conversation of his nearest neighbors had the same soothing effect as background music.

When they rose and left, he saw by the clock on the wall that it was nearly half-past nine. No use delaying matters any further. He drank his coffee, lighted a cigarette, and paid his bill. After all, he thought, as he walked back to the hotel, the manager would be greatly relieved to know that all was well.

When he pushed through the swing-door, the first thing he noticed was a man in police uniform, standing talking to the manager at the desk. The reception clerk was there too. They turned as John approached, and the manager's face lighted up with relief.

"Eccolo!" he exclaimed, "I was certain the signore would not be far away. Things are moving, signore. The two ladies have been traced, and they very kindly agreed to accompany the police to the Questura. If you will go there at once, this *agente di polizia* will escort you."

John flushed. "I have given everyone a lot of trouble," he said. "I meant to tell you before going out to dinner, but you were not at the desk. The fact is that I have contacted my wife. She did make the flight to London after all, and I spoke to her on the telephone. It was all a great mistake."

The manager looked bewildered. "The signora is in London?" he repeated. He broke off, and exchanged a rapid conversation in Italian with the policeman. "It seems that the ladies maintain they did not go out for the day, except for a little shopping in the morning," he said, turning back to John. "Then who was it the signore saw on the vaporetto?"

John shook his head. "A very extraordinary mistake on my part which I still don't understand," he said. "Obviously, I did not see either my wife or the two ladies. I really am extremely sorry."

More rapid conversation in Italian. John noticed the clerk watching him with a curious expression in his eyes. The manager was obviously apologizing on John's behalf to the policeman, who looked annoyed and gave tongue to this effect, his voice increasing in volume, to the manager's concern. The whole business had undoubtedly given enormous trouble to a great many people, not least the two unfortunate sisters.

"Look," said John, interrupting the flow, "will you tell the *agente* I will go with him to headquarters and apologize in person both to the police officer and to the ladies?"

The manager looked relieved. "If the signore would take the trouble," he said. "Naturally, the ladies were much distressed when a policeman interrogated them at their hotel, and they offered to accompany him to the Questura only because they were so distressed about the signora."

John felt more and more uncomfortable. Laura must never learn any of this. She would be outraged. He wondered if there were some penalty for giving the police misleading information involving a third party. His error began, in retrospect, to take on criminal proportions.

He crossed the Piazza San Marco, now thronged with after-dinner strollers and spectators at the cafes, all three orchestras going full blast in harmonious rivalry, while his companion kept a discreet two paces to his left and never uttered a word.

They arrived at the police station and mounted the stairs to the same inner room where he had been before. He saw immediately that it was not the officer he knew but another who sat behind the desk, a sallow-faced individual with a sour expression, while the two sisters, obviously upset—the active one in particular—were seated on chairs nearby, some underling in uniform standing behind them. John's escort went at once to the police officer, speaking in rapid Italian, while John himself, after a moment's hesitation, advanced towards the sisters.

"There has been a terrible mistake," he said. "I don't know how to apologize to you both. It's all my fault, mine entirely, the police are not to blame."

The active sister made as though to rise, her mouth twitching nervously, but he restrained her.

"We don't understand," she said, the Scots inflection strong. "We said goodnight to your wife last night at dinner, and we have not seen her since. The police came to our pension more than an hour ago and told us your wife was missing and you had filed a complaint against us. My sister is not very strong. She was considerably disturbed."

"A mistake. A frightful mistake," he repeated.

He turned towards the desk. The police officer was addressing him, his English very inferior to that of the previous interrogator. He had John's earlier statement on the desk in front of him, and tapped it with a pencil.

"So?" he queried. "This document all lies? You not speaka the truth?"

"I believed it to be true at the time," said John. "I could have sworn in a court of law that I saw my wife with these two ladies on a vaporetto in the Grand Canal this afternoon. Now I realize I was mistaken."

"We have not been near the Grand Canal all day," protested the sister, "not even on foot. We made a few purchases in the Merceria this morning, and remained indoors all afternoon. My sister was a little unwell. I have told the police officer this a dozen times, and the people at the pension would corroborate our story. He refused to listen."

"And the signora?" rapped the police officer angrily. "What happen to the signora?"

"The signora, my wife, is safe in England," explained John patiently. "I talked to her on the telephone just after seven. She did join the charter flight from the airport, and is now staying with friends."

"Then who you see on the vaporetto in the red coat?" asked the furious police officer. "And if not these signorine here, then what signorine?"

"My eyes deceived me," said John, aware that his English was likewise becoming strained. "I think I see my wife and these ladies but not, it was not so. My wife in aircraft, these ladies in pension all the time."

It was like talking stage Chinese. In a moment he would be bowing and putting his hands in his sleeves.

The police officer raised his eyes to heaven and thumped the table. "So all this work for nothing," he said. "Hotels and pensiones searched for the signorine and a missing signora *inglese,* when here we have plenty, plenty other things to do. You maka a mistake. You have perhaps too much vino at *mezzo giorno* and you see hundred signore in red coats in hundred vaporetti." He stood up, rumpling the papers on the desk. "And you, signorine," he said, "you wish to make complaint against this person?" He was addressing the active sister.

"Oh no," she said, "no, indeed. I quite see it was all a mistake. Our only wish is to return at once to our pension."

The police officer grunted. Then he pointed at John. "You very lucky man," he said. "These signorine could file complaint against you—very serious matter."

"I'm sure," began John, "I'll do anything in my power . . ."

"Please don't think of it," exclaimed the sister, horrified. "We would not hear of such a thing." It was her turn to apologize to the police officer. "I hope we need not take up any more of your valuable time," she said.

He waved a hand of dismissal and spoke in Italian to the underling. "This man walk with you to the pension," he said. "*Buona sera,* signorine*," and, ignoring John, he sat down again at his desk.

"I'll come with you," said John. "I want to explain exactly what happened."

They trooped down the stairs and out of the building, the blind sister leaning on her twin's arm, and once outside she turned her sightless eyes to John.

"You saw us," she said, "and your wife too. But not today. You saw us in the future."

Her voice was softer than her sister's, slower, she seemed to have some slight impediment in her speech.

"I don't follow," replied John, bewildered.

He turned to the active sister and she shook her head at him, frowning, and put her fingers on her lips.

"Come along, dear," she said to her twin. "You know you're very tired, and I want to get you home." Then, sotto voce to John, "She's psychic. Your wife told you, I believe, but I don't want her to go into trance here in the street."

God forbid, thought John, and the little procession began to move slowly along the street, away from police headquarters, a canal to the left of them. Progress was slow, because of the blind sister, and there were two bridges to cross over two canals. John was completely lost after the first turning, but it couldn't have mattered less. Their police escort was with them, and anyway, the sisters knew where they were going.

"I must explain," said John softly. "My wife would never forgive me if I didn't," and as they walked he went over the whole inexplicable story once again, beginning with the telegram received the night before and the conversation with Mrs. Hill, the decision to return to England the following day, Laura by air, and John himself by car and train. It no longer sounded as dramatic as it had done when he had made his statement to the police officer, when, possibly because of his conviction of something uncanny, the description of the two vaporettos passing one another in the middle of the Grand Canal had held a sinister quality, suggesting abduction on the part of the sisters, the pair of them holding a bewildered Laura captive. Now that neither of the women had any further menace for him he spoke more naturally, yet with great sincerity, feeling for the first time that they were somehow both in sympathy with him and would understand.

"You see," he explained, in a final endeavor to make amends for having gone to the police in the first place, "I truly believed I had seen you with Laura, and I thought . . ." he hesitated, because this had been the police officer's suggestion and not his, "I thought that perhaps Laura had some sudden loss of memory, had met you at the airport, and you had brought her back to Venice to wherever you were staying."

They had crossed a large campo and were approaching a house at one end of it, with a sign PENSIONE above the door. Their escort paused at the entrance.

"Is this it?" asked John.

"Yes," said the sister. "I know it is nothing much from the outside, but it is clean and comfortable, and was recommended by friends." She turned to the escort. "*Grazie,*" she said to him, "*grazie tanto.*"

The man nodded briefly, wished them "*Buona notte,*" and disappeared across the campo.

"Will you come in?" asked the sister. "I am sure we can find you some coffee, or perhaps you prefer tea?"

"No, really," John thanked her, "I must get back to the hotel. I'm making an early start in the morning. I just want to make quite sure you do understand what happened, and that you forgive me."

"There is nothing to forgive," she replied. "It is one of the many examples of second sight that my sister and I have experienced time and time again, and I should very much like to record it for our files, if you permit it."

"Well, as to that, of course," he told her, "but I myself find it hard to understand. It has never happened to me before."

"Not consciously, perhaps," she said, "but so many things happen to us of which we are not aware. My sister felt you had psychic understanding. She told your wife. She also told your wife, last night in the restaurant, that you were to experience trouble, that you should leave Venice. Well, don't you believe now that the telegram was proof of this? Your son was ill, possibly dangerously ill, and so it was necessary for you to return home immediately. Heaven be praised your wife flew home to be by his side."

"Yes, indeed," said John, "but why should I see her on the vaporetto with you and your sister when she was actually on her way to England?"

"Thought transference, perhaps," she answered. "Your wife may have been thinking about us. We gave her our address, should you wish to get in touch with us. We shall be here another ten days. And she knows that we would pass on any message that my sister might have from your little one in the spirit world."

"Yes," said John awkwardly, "yes, I see. It's very good of you." He had a sudden rather unkind picture of the two sisters putting on headphones in their bedroom, listening for a coded message from poor Christine. "Look, this is our address in London," he said. "I know Laura will be pleased to hear from you."

He scribbled their address on a sheet torn from his pocket-diary, even, as a bonus thrown in, the telephone number, and handed it to her. He could imagine the outcome. Laura springing it on him one evening that the "old dears" were passing through London on their way to Scotland, and the least they could do was to offer them hospitality, even the spare-room for the night. Then a séance in the living-room, tambourines appearing out of thin air.

"Well, I must be off," he said, "goodnight, and apologies, once again, for all that has happened this evening." He shook hands with the first sister, then turned to her blind twin. "I hope," he said, "that you are not too tired."

The sightless eyes were disconcerting. She held his hand fast and would not let it go. "The child," she said, speaking in an odd staccato voice, "the child . . . I can see the child . . ." and then, to his dismay, a bead of froth appeared at the corner of her mouth, her head jerked back, and she half-collapsed in her sister's arms.

"We must get her inside," said the sister hurriedly. "It's all right, she's not ill, it's the beginning of a trance state."

Between them they helped the twin, who had gone rigid, into the house, and sat her down on the nearest chair, the sister supporting her. A woman came running from some inner room. There was a strong smell of spaghetti from the back regions. "Don't worry," said the sister, "the signorina and I can manage. I think you had better go. Sometimes she is sick after these turns."

"I'm most frightfully sorry . . ." John began, but the sister had already turned her back, and with the signorina was bending over her twin, from whom peculiar choking sounds were proceeding. He was obviously in the way, and after a final gesture of courtesy, "Is there anything I can do?" which received no reply, he turned on his heel and began walking across the square. He looked back once, and saw they had closed the door.

What a finale to the evening! And all his fault. Poor old girls, first dragged to police headquarters and put through an interrogation, and then a psychic fit on top of it all. More likely epilepsy. Not much of a life for the active sister, but she seemed to take it in her stride. An additional hazard, though, if it happened in a restaurant or in the street. And not particularly welcome under his and Laura's roof should the sisters ever find themselves beneath it, which he prayed would never happen.

Meanwhile, where the devil was he? The campo, with the inevitable church at one end, was quite deserted. He could not remember which way they had come from police headquarters, there had seemed to be so many turnings. Wait a minute, the church itself had a familiar appearance. He drew nearer to it, looking for the name which was sometimes on notices at the entrance. San Giovanni in Bragora, that rang a bell. He and Laura had gone inside one morning to look at a painting by Cima da Conegliano. Surely it was only a stone's throw from the Riva degli Schiavoni and the open wide waters of the San Marco lagoon, with all the bright lights of civilization and the strolling tourists? He remembered taking a small turning from the Schiavoni and they had arrived at the church. Wasn't there the alley-way ahead? He plunged along it, but halfway down he hesitated. It didn't seem right, although it was familiar for some unknown reason.

Then he realized that it was not the alley they had taken the morning they visited the church, but the one they had walked along the previous evening, only he was approaching it from the opposite direction. Yes, that was it, in which case it would be quicker to go on and cross the little bridge over the narrow canal, and he would find the Arsenal on his left and the street leading down to the Riva degli Schiavoni to his right. Simpler than retracing his steps and getting lost once more in the maze of back streets.

He had almost reached the end of the alley, and the bridge was in sight, when he saw the child. It was the same little girl with the pixie hood who had leapt between the tethered boats the preceding night and vanished up the cellar steps of one of the houses. This time she was running from the direction of the church on the other side, making for the bridge. She was running as if her life depended on it, and in a moment he saw why. A man was in pursuit, who, when she glanced backwards for a moment, still running, flattened himself against a wall, believing himself unobserved. The child came on, scampering across the bridge, and John, fearful of alarming her further, backed into an open doorway that led into a small court.

He remembered the drunken yell of the night before which had come from one of the houses near where the man was hiding now. This is it, he thought, the fellow's after her again, and with a flash of intuition he connected the two events, the child's terror then and now, and the murders reported in the newspapers, supposedly the work of some madman. It could be coincidence, a child running from a drunken relative, and yet, and yet . . . His heart began thumping in his chest, instinct warning him to run himself, now, at once, back along the alley the way he had come, but what about the child? What was going to happen to the child?

Then he heard her running steps. She hurtled through the open doorway into the court in which he stood, not seeing him, making for the rear of the house that flanked it, where steps led presumably to a back entrance. She was sobbing as she ran, not the ordinary cry of a frightened child but a panic-stricken intake of breath of a helpless being in despair. Were there parents in the house who would protect her, whom he could warn? He hesitated a moment, then followed her down the steps and through the door at the bottom, which had burst open at the touch of her hands as she hurled herself against it.

"It's all right," he called. "I won't let him hurt you, it's all right," cursing his lack of Italian, but possibly an English voice might reassure her. But it was no use—she ran sobbing up another flight of stairs, which were spiral, twisting, leading to the floor above, and already it was too late for him to retreat. He could hear sounds of the pursuer in the courtyard behind, someone shouting in Italian, a dog barking. This is it, he thought, we're in it together, the child and I. Unless we can bolt some inner door above he'll get us both.

He ran up the stairs after the child, who had darted into a room leading off a small landing, and followed her inside and slammed the door, and, merciful heaven, there was a bolt which he rammed into its socket. The child was crouching by the open window. If he shouted for help, someone would surely hear, someone would surely come before the man in pursuit threw himself against the door and it gave, because there was no one but themselves, no parents, the room was bare except for a mattress on an old bed, and a heap of rags in one corner.

"It's all right," he panted, "it's all right," and held out his hand, trying to smile.

The child struggled to her feet and stood before him, the pixie hood falling from her head onto the floor. He stared at her, incredulity turning to horror, to fear. It was not a child at all but a little thickset woman dwarf, about three feet high, with a great square adult head too

big for her body, grey locks hanging shoulder-length, and she wasn't
sobbing any more, she was grinning at him, nodding her head up and
down.

Then he heard the footsteps on the landing outside and the hammering on the door, and a barking dog, and not one voice but several voices,
shouting, "Open up! Police!" The creature fumbled in her sleeve, drawing a knife, and as she threw it at him with hideous strength, piercing
his throat, he stumbled and fell, the sticky mess covering his protecting
hands. And he saw the vaporetto with Laura and the two sisters steaming down the Grand Canal, not today, not tomorrow, but the day after
that, and he knew why they were together and for what sad purpose
they had come. The creature was gibbering in its corner. The hammering and the voices and the barking dog grew fainter, and, Oh, God, he
thought, what a bloody silly way to die . . .

BILL PRONZINI
Booktaker

IT WAS a Thursday afternoon in late May, and it was gloomy and raining outside, and I was sitting in my brand-new offices on Drumm Street wishing I were somewhere else. Specifically, over at Kerry's apartment on Diamond Heights, snuggling up with her in front of her nice big fireplace. Thoughts like that seemed to come into my head all the time lately. I had known Kerry Wade only a couple of weeks, but it had already developed into a pretty intense relationship. For me, anyhow.

But I was not going to get to snuggle up with her tonight. Or tomorrow night either. She worked as a copywriter for Bates and Carpenter, a San Francisco advertising agency, and when I'd called her this morning she'd said she was in the middle of an important presentation; she was going to have to work late both nights in order to finish it to deadline. How about Saturday night? I said. Okay, she said. So I had a promise, which was better than nothing, but Saturday was two long days away. The prospect of spending the next forty-eight hours alone, cooped up here and in my Pacific Heights flat, made me feel as gloomy as the weather.

My flat wasn't so bad, but these shiny new offices left a great deal to be desired. They consisted of two rooms, one waiting area and one private office, with pastel walls, beige carpeting, some chrome chairs with beige corduroy cushions and venetian blinds on the windows. The bright yellow phone somebody in the telephone company had seen fit to give me looked out of place on my battered old desk. The desk looked out of place, too, in the sterile surroundings. And so did I: big hulking guy, overweight, shaggy-looking, with a face some people thought homely and other people—me included, when I was in a good mood—

515

thought of as possessing character. Sort of like the late actor Richard Boone.

I didn't belong in a place like this. It had *no* character, this place; it was just a two-room office in a newly renovated building down near the waterfront. It could have been anybody's office, in just about any profession. My old office, on the other hand, the one I had occupied for better than twenty years before moving here two weeks ago, had had too much character, which was the main reason I had made up my mind to leave it. It had been located in a frumpy old building on the fringe of the Tenderloin, one of the city's high-crime areas, and with the neighborhood worsening, I had finally accepted the fact that prospective clients wouldn't be too keen about hiring a private investigator with that sort of address.

This place had been the best I could find for what I could afford. And so here I was, all decked out with a new image, and the phone still didn't ring and clients still didn't line up outside my door. So much for transitioning upscale and all the rest of that crap. So much for detective work in general.

I was starting to depress myself. What I needed was to get out of here the rest of today and all day tomorrow; what I needed was work. So why doesn't somebody come in? I thought. I looked out across the anteroom to the access door. Well? I thought. Come on in, somebody.

And the door opened and somebody came in.

I blinked, startled. It was enough to make you wonder if maybe there was something after all to the theory of solipsism.

My visitor was a man, and I was on my feet when he limped through my private office and stopped in front of the desk. "I don't know if you remember me," he said. "I'm John Rothman."

"Yes, sir, sure I do. It's good to see you again, Mr. Rothman."

I had recognized him immediately even though I hadn't seen him in more than a year; I have a cop's memory for faces. He was the owner of San Francisco's largest secondhand bookshop—an entire building over on Golden Gate Avenue near the Federal Building, three floors and a basement full of every kind of used book, from reading copies of popular fiction and nonfiction to antiquarian books, prints and the like. I had first met him several years ago, when pulp magazines were still reasonably cheap and there were only a few serious collectors like myself around; he had acquired, through an estate sale, about a thousand near-mint issues of *Black Mask, Dime Detective, Dime Mystery, Thrilling Detective* and other pulps from the thirties and forties, and because I happened to be fairly solvent at the time, I'd been able to buy the entire lot at not much more than a dollar an issue. Those same thousand copies today would cost more than I made most years.

On four or five occasions since then, whenever a new batch of pulps came his way, Rothman had contacted me. I hadn't bought much from him, what with escalating prices, but I had purchased enough to keep my name in his files and in his memory.

But it wasn't his profession that had brought him here today; it was mine. "I've got a serious problem at the bookshop," he said, "and I'd like to hire you to get to the bottom of it."

"If I can help, I'll be glad to do what I can."

I waited until he was seated in one of the two clients' chairs and then sat down again myself. He was in his fifties, tall and aristocratic-looking, with silvering hair and cheekbones so pronounced they were like sharp little ridges. His limp was the result of some sort of childhood disease or accident—he had once made a vague reference to it—and he needed the use of a cane; the one he hooked over the arm of the chair was thick and gnarled and black, with a knobby handle. Its color matched the three-piece suit he wore.

"I'll get right to the point," he said. "I've been plagued by thefts the past few months, and I'm damned if I can find out who's responsible or how they're being done."

"What is it that's been stolen?"

"Valuable antiquarian items. Rare books at first; more recently, etchings, prints and old maps. The total value so far exceeds twenty thousand dollars."

I raised an eyebrow. "That's a lot of money."

"It is, and my insurance doesn't cover it all. I've been to the police, but there doesn't seem to be much they can do, under the circumstances. There seldom is in cases like this."

"You mean book thefts are a common occurrence?"

"Oh, yes," Rothman said. "Thieves are a thorn in the side of every bookseller. I lose hundreds, if not thousands, of dollars of stock to them each year. No matter how closely we watch our customers, the experienced thief can always find a way to slip a book into a concealed pocket or inside his clothing, or to wrap a print or an old map around himself under a coat. A few years ago an elderly gentleman, very distinguished, managed to steal a first edition of Twain's *Huckleberry Finn,* even though I can still swear I had my eyes on him the whole time."

"Do these people steal for profit—to resell the items?"

"Sometimes," he said. "Others are collectors who don't have the money or the inclination to pay for something they desperately want. A much smaller percentage are kleptomaniacs. But this is an unusual case because of the number and value of the thefts, and because of the circumstances surrounding them, and I'm fairly certain the motive is resale for profit. Not to other dealers, but to unscrupulous private collectors who don't care how the items were obtained and who don't ask questions when they're offered."

"Then you think the thief is a professional?"

"No. I think he's one of my employees."

"Oh? Why is that?"

"For several reasons. All of the items were taken from the Antiquarian Room on the third floor, a room that is kept locked at all times. I have a key and so do—or did—two of my employees; no customer has ever been allowed inside without one of us present. And after the first two thefts—a fine copy of T. S. Arthur's temperance novel, *Ten Nights in a Bar Room,* and an uncommon children's book, Mary Wollstonecraft's *Original Stories from Real Life*—I ordered the Antiquarian Room out of bounds to customers unless they were personally known to me. I also had a sensor alarm installed on the front entrance. You know what that is, of course?"

I nodded. It was an electronic gateway, similar to the metal detectors used in airports, through which customers had to pass on their way out. Any purchases they made were cleared by rubbing the items across a sensor strip. If someone tried to leave the premises with something that hadn't been paid for and cleared, an alarm would sound. A lot of bookstores used the device these days; so did most libraries.

"Three weeks later," Rothman said, "a sixteenth-century religious etching attributed to one of the pioneers of printmaking, Albrecht Dürer, disappeared. It was one of two I had recently purchased, and extremely valuable; if it had been authenticated, it would be priceless. Even so, I was in the process of realizing several thousand dollars from a collector in Hillsborough when it vanished." He paused. "The point is, I checked the Antiquarian Room that morning, before I went out to lunch, as I regularly do; the Dürer was still there at that time. But it had vanished when I checked the room again late that afternoon— and no customer had been permitted inside in the interim, nor had the door lock been tampered with."

"Did you take any further precautions after that theft?"

"Yes. I confiscated the other two keys to the Antiquarian Room. But that didn't stop him either. There have been four other thefts since then, at increasingly frequent intervals—all of them between eleven and two o'clock, evidently when I was away from the shop. The second Dürer etching, two seventeenth-century Japanese color prints and a rare map of the Orient; the map disappeared two days ago."

"The thief could have had a duplicate key made before you confiscated the originals," I suggested.

"I know; I thought of that, too. Any of my four employees could have had a duplicate made, in fact, not just the two who had keys previously. On occasion those two gave their keys to the other two, when they needed something from the Antiquarian Room and were too busy to get it themselves."

"Did you consider changing the lock?"

"I did, yes. But I decided against it."

"Why?"

"As clever as the thief is," Rothman said, "I suspect he'd have found a way to circumvent that obstacle, too. And I don't just want to stop the thefts; I want the person responsible caught and punished, and I want to know how he's getting the stolen items out of the shop so I can take steps to prevent it from ever happening again. The *how* of it bothers me almost as much as the thefts themselves."

"Couldn't the thief have simply cleared the items through the sensor when no one was looking and walked out with them later under his clothing?"

"No. The only sensor strip is located at the cashier's desk, and none of my people had access to it on the days of the thefts except Adam Turner. Adam is the only one of my people I trust implicitly; he's been with me twenty years, and he's loyal and honest to a fault. He'd taken to guarding the sensor since the thefts began, and on at least two of the days he swears he never left the desk for even a moment."

"Do you deactivate the alarm system when you close up for the day?"

"Yes."

"Well, couldn't the thief have stashed the items somewhere in the store and left with them after the alarm was shut off?"

Rothman shook his head. "I'm the last person to leave nearly every day. And when I'm not, Adam does the locking up. No one but the two of us has a key to the front door. Not only that, but each of the others has to pass through the alarm gateway on his way out, before it's shut off; that is a strict rule and there have been no exceptions."

I did some ruminating. "Is it possible the thief could have slipped out through another entrance during working hours? He wouldn't have to have been gone more than a couple of minutes; he could even have passed the stolen items to a confederate. . . ."

Rothman was shaking his head again. "All the other entrances to the shop—first-floor rear and fire-escape doors on the second and third floor—are kept locked and are protected by separate alarm systems."

"How many people have keys to those entrances?"

"Only myself. And even if one of the others managed to get hold of it and have a duplicate made, the alarm would still ring if any of the doors were opened."

"Where is the control box for those alarms located?"

"Behind the cashier's desk. But it's also kept locked, and Adam guards it as zealously as he does the sensor strip."

"What about a window?" I asked. "Are there alarms on those, too?"

"No, but they are all securely locked and also painted shut. None of them has been touched."

I ruminated again. "I can think of one other possibility," I said at length. "Suppose the thief *hasn't* gotten the stolen items out of the shop? Suppose he hid them somewhere with the idea of making off with them later, because he *hasn't* figured out a way to beat the alarms?"

"I'm afraid that's not the answer either," Rothman said. "For one thing, Adam and I have searched the shop on more than one occasion; it's quite large, granted, but I'm sure we would have found the missing pieces if they were there. And for another thing, at least one item—the first Dürer etching—appears to have surfaced in the collection of a man named Martell in Chicago."

"You've heard rumors, you mean?"

"More than just rumors. After each theft I notified other antiquarian booksellers throughout the country and in Europe, as well as *AB Bookman's Weekly* and other publications in the trade; that's standard procedure whenever anything of value is stolen. A dealer in Chicago called me not long after I publicized the theft of the first Dürer, to say that he'd heard Martell had intimated to another collector that he had acquired it. Admittedly, that's secondhand information. But I know of Martell; he's a passionate collector of fifteenth- and sixteenth-century religious etchings, and he has a reputation of being unscrupulous about it. My colleague in Chicago knows Martell personally and says that if he has bragged about having the Dürer etching, he really does have it."

"Did you try to contact Martell?"

"I did. He denies possession, of course."

"Isn't there anything you can do to prove otherwise?"

"No. Without proof that he bought it, there is no legal way I can have his premises searched or force him to admit to its current ownership."

"So the only way to get that proof," I said, "is to find out who stole it from you and sold it to Martell."

"That's correct."

"Do you suspect any one employee more than the others?"

"Not really. I've ruled out Adam Turner, as I told you; it could be any of the other three."

I had been taking notes as we talked; I flipped over to a clean page on my pad. "Tell me about those three."

"Tom Lennox has been with me the longest, next to Adam. Four years. He's quiet, intense, knowledgeable—a good bookman. He hopes to open his own antiquarian shop someday."

"So you'd say he's ambitious?"

"Yes, but not overly so."

"Is he one of the two who had keys to the Antiquarian Room?"

"Yes. Adam was the other. They both gave up their keys willingly."

"Uh-huh. Go ahead, Mr. Rothman."

"Harmon Boyette," he said, and spelled the last name. "He has worked for me a little more than two years, ever since he moved here from Seattle. He owned a bookstore there for several years, but he went bankrupt when his wife divorced him. He seems quite bitter about it."

"Do you consider him dependable?"

"Most of the time. But he does have an alcohol problem. Not that he drinks on the job—I wouldn't stand for that—but he comes in badly hungover on some mornings, and has missed days now and then."

"Does money seem to be important to him?"

"If so, he's never said anything about it. Nor has he ever said anything about wanting to go into business for himself again."

"And the third man?"

"Neal Vining. A Britisher, born in London. His father is a bookseller there. He married an American girl and came to San Francisco about eighteen months ago. I hired him because he has considerable expertise in English and European books, both antiquarian and modern. He learned the business from his father, and in a remarkably short time; he's only twenty-six."

"Is *he* ambitious, would you say?"

"Yes. He's eager, always asking questions, gathering more knowledge. His only apparent fault is that he tends to be a bit egotistical at times."

I took a moment to go back over my notes. "The thefts began how long ago?" I asked.

"Approximately five months."

"Were there many valuable items stolen in, say, the year prior to that?"

"Two books, as I recall." He frowned. "Are you thinking the same person might have stolen those, too?"

"It's possible," I said. "The man responsible could have started off in a small way at first and then decided to risk stealing items on a more regular basis. Particularly if he feels he has an undetectable method. Impatience, greed, a feeling of power—all those things could be driving him."

Rothman nodded speculatively. "Now that I think of it," he said, "an inscribed first edition of Henry Miller's *Black Spring* disappeared about three months after Neal Vining came to work for me."

"Lennox and Boyette are just as likely to be guilty, from what you've told me. Lennox could have been taking rare books off and on for four years, Boyette off and on for two."

"Yes, you're right." He ran spread fingers through his silvering hair. "How will you handle your investigation?"

"Well, first of all I'll run a background check on each of the three suspects. And it would be a good idea if I spent some time in the store, especially since the thief seems to be getting bolder; I might be able to spot something that'll tell us how he's doing it. You could introduce me as a new employee, give me some work to do and let me take it from there."

"Fine. Can you start right away?"

"This afternoon, if you like. But I think it would look better if I came in first thing in the morning. That way, I can spend the rest of today making those background checks."

Rothman agreed. He gave me addresses for Lennox, Boyette and Vining, after which we settled on my fee and I made out one of my standard contract forms and had him sign it. We also settled on what my job would be at the book shop—I would come in as a stock clerk, which entailed shelving books, filling customer orders and the like, and which would allow me to move freely around the shop—and on the name I would be using: Jim Marlowe, in honor of Raymond Chandler. Then we shook hands, and he limped out, and I got to work.

I called a guy I knew in Records and Identification at the Hall of Justice; he promised me he'd run the three names through his computer and the FBI hookup, to see if any of them had a criminal record, and get back to me before five o'clock. The next order of business was to get a credit report on each of the three, so I called another friend who worked for a leasing company and asked him to pull TRW's on the trio. He also said he'd have the information by five.

I got out my copy of the reverse directory of city addresses and looked up the street numbers I had for Lennox, Boyette and Vining. All three of them lived in apartment buildings, which made things a little easier for me. I made a list of the names and telephone numbers of all the other residents of those buildings; then I called them one by one, telling each person who answered that I was a claims representative for North Coast Insurance and that I was conducting a routine check in connection with a substantial insurance policy. Human nature being what it is, that was a ploy that almost always put people at their ease and got them to open up about their neighbors.

Two of Lennox's neighbors said that he kept pretty much to himself, had no apparent bad habits and seemed to be more or less happily married. A third person, who knew him a little better, had a somewhat different opinion of Lennox's marital status; this woman said that his wife, Fran, was a complainer who constantly nagged him about money matters. The woman also said that Lennox had a passion for books and that his apartment overflowed with them. She didn't know if any of the books were valuable; she didn't have time for such foolishness as reading, she said, and didn't know anything about books except that they were dust collectors.

Harmon Boyette's neighbors confirmed that he was a heavy drinker; most of his imbibing was done at home, they said, and he tended to be surly when he was tight. They didn't seem to like him much. Nobody knew if he had money to spend, or what he spent it on if he did. None of them had ever been inside his apartment.

Neal Vining, on the other hand, was friendly, gregarious, enjoyed having people in for small parties and was well liked. So was his wife, Sara, whose father owned a haberdashery shop in Ghirardelli Square that specialized in British imports; she and Vining had met during one of the father's buying trips to London. I also learned that Vining was the athletic type—jogged regularly, played racquetball—and that he liked to impress people with his knowledge of books and literary matters. As with Lennox and Boyette, he didn't seem to have a great deal of money and he didn't spend what he had indiscriminately.

There was nothing in any of this, at least so far as I could tell, that offered a clue as to which of the three men might be guilty. I considered running a check on Adam Turner, even though Rothman had seemed certain of Turner's innocence; I like to be thorough. But I decided to let Rothman's judgment stand, at least for the time being.

The guy at R and I called back at four-thirty, with a pretty much negative report: none of the three suspects had a criminal record, and with the exception of Boyette, none of them had ever been arrested. Boyette had been jailed twice, overnight both times, on drunk-and-disorderly charges.

Just before five, my friend at the leasing company came through with the credit reports. Not much there either. Vining had a good credit rating, Lennox a not very good one and Boyette none at all. The only potentially interesting fact was that Lennox had defaulted on an automobile loan nine months ago, with the result that the car—a new Mercedes—had been repossessed. Up until then, Lennox's credit rating had been pretty good. It made me wonder why he had decided to buy an expensive car like a Mercedes in the first place; he couldn't have been paid a very hefty salary. But then, it might have been his wife's doing, if what I'd been told about her was true.

By the time I looked over everything again, reread the notes I'd taken during my talk with Rothman and put it all away in a file folder, it was five-twenty and I was ready to pack it in for the day. I was feeling considerably better than I had been before Rothman's arrival; I had a job, and I would not have to spend tomorrow sitting around this damned office watching it rain and waiting for something to happen and pining away for Kerry.

The telephone was ringing when I let myself into my flat an hour later. I hustled into the bedroom, where I keep the thing, and hauled up the receiver and said hello.

"Hi," Kerry's voice said. "You sound out of breath."

"I just came in. *You* sound tired."

"I am. And the way it looks, I'm not going to get out of here until nine o'clock."

"How's the presentation going?"

"Pretty good. I'll probably have to work Saturday morning, but I should be finished by noon."

"We're still on for Saturday night, aren't we?"

"We are. What did you have in mind?"

"Well, I've been wondering—"

"Oh, damn," she said. "Can you hold on a minute? I'm being paged by the boss."

"Sure."

There was a clicking noise as she put me on hold. I shrugged out of my damp overcoat, tossed it on the floor and sat down on the rumpled bed. While I waited I occupied myself by visualizing Kerry in my mind. She was something to look at, all right. Not pretty in any classic sense, but strikingly attractive: coppery hair worn shoulder-length; animated face marked with humor lines; generous mouth; greenish eyes that seemed to change color, like a chameleon, according to her moods. And a fine willowy body, with the kind of legs men stared at and most women envied.

I wondered again, as I had on several occasions, what she saw in me. I was fifty-three to her thirty-eight and not much to look at, but she thought I was pretty hot stuff just the same. Sexy, she'd said once. Which was all a crock, as far as I was concerned, but I loved her for feeling that way.

I *did* love her, that was the thing, even though we'd only known each other a couple of weeks. I'd met her during a pulp-magazine convention, which she'd attended because both her parents—Ivan and Cybil Wade—were ex-pulp writers who had been well known in the forties, Ivan for his fantasy/horror stories in *Weird Tales* and *Dime Mystery*, Cybil for a hardboiled detective series under the male pseudonym of Samuel Leatherman. The pulp angle had been part of my attraction to her in the beginning, just as part of hers for me had been the fact that, as a result of her mother's writing, she'd always been intrigued by private detectives. So we'd struck up an immediate friendship, and had become lovers much sooner than I could have hoped for.

Meanwhile, things had been happening at the convention that culminated in murder, and I had found myself in an investigation that had almost got me killed. When it was finished I had asked her to marry me, surprising myself as well as her. She hadn't said no; in fact, she'd said that she loved me, too, after her fashion. But she'd been married once, a bad marriage, and she just wasn't sure if she wanted to try it again. She needed more time to think things over, she said. And that was where things stood now.

Not for long, though, I hoped. I had never been as sure of anything as I was that I wanted Ms. Kerry Wade, she of the fine legs and the wonderful chameleon eyes, to be my wife.

There was another noise as the line reopened, and she said, "You still there?"

"Would I hang up on a gorgeous lady like you?"

"Gorgeous," she said. "Hah. What were you saying about Saturday night?"

"I was just wondering," I said, "how you felt about snuggling up at your apartment in front of a nice hot fire?"

"Oh ho. So that's it."

"Yep. So how *do* you feel about it?"

"Well, I might be persuaded. Providing, of course, that you take me out first and ply me with good food."

"Done. How about Oaxaca's, over on Mission?"

"Mmm, yes. We could spend the afternoon together, too. Drinks in Sausalito, maybe?"

"Sounds terrific," I said. "Only I think I may be tied up during the afternoon. I picked up a job today." I told her about John Rothman and what he had hired me to do. "So unless I can wrap things up tomorrow, which doesn't seem likely, I'll be at the book shop all day Saturday. The place closes at six, though. I could pick you up around seven."

"Fine," she said. "Right now, I'd better get back to work. Call me tomorrow night? I'll be here late again."

"Okay. And Kerry . . . I love you."

"Me, too," she said, and she was gone.

Smiling, feeling chipper, I went out into the kitchen and opened myself a beer and made a couple of salami-and-cheese sandwiches. Kerry wouldn't have approved; she was of the opinion that my eating habits left something to be desired. Well, she could change them when she became my wife. I had been a bachelor too long to want to change them on my own.

After I finished eating I curled up on the couch in my cluttered living room—another thing Kerry disapproved of, and that she could change if she was of a mind to, was my sloppy housekeeping habits—with Volume One, Number One of *Strange Detective Mysteries,* dated October 1937. Norville Page's lead novel, "When the Death-Bat Flies," kept me amused for an hour, and stories by Norbert Davis, Wayne Rogers, Paul Ernst and Arthur Leo Zagat took care of the rest of the evening.

I got down to Rothman's book shop, dressed in a sports shirt and a pair of old slacks instead of my usual suit and tie, at five minutes to nine on Friday morning. The building, a big old structure with a Victorian facade, was sandwiched between an auction gallery and a Chinese restaurant. A pair of wide plate-glass windows flanked the entrance; behind them were display racks of books of various types. Both windows bore the same legends in dark red lettering:

J. ROTHMAN, BOOKSELLER
Fine Books—Used, Rare, Antiquarian

The front door was locked; I rapped on the glass panel. Pretty soon a stooped, elderly guy, coatless but wearing a white dress shirt and a bow tie, appeared inside. When he got to the door he peered out at me through rimless glasses and then threw the bolt lock and opened up.

"My name is Jim Marlowe," I told him. "I'm the new man Mr. Rothman hired yesterday."

"Oh, yes." He gave me his hand and I took it. "Turner, Adam Turner. Assistant manager."

"Pleased to meet you, Mr. Turner."

He nodded, stepped aside to let me come in. While he was relocking the door I glanced around the main floor. The cashier's desk was on the left, flanked by the wide gateway for the sensor alarm; you had to go through the gateway both entering and leaving, because there was a six-foot-high partition on the right-hand side. Beyond, several long display tables filled with sale books and recent arrivals were arranged for easy browsing. Floor-to-ceiling shelves covered the side walls, and stacks with narrow aisleways between them took up the rear half of the room. Off to one side toward the back, a flight of stairs led up to the second floor and another down to the basement.

I let Turner precede me through the gateway. He looked to be in his mid-sixties, nondescript and mild; but his rheumy blue eyes were alert and intelligent, and I thought that they would not miss much.

I asked him, "Is Mr. Rothman here?"

"Yes. He's in his office, upstairs on the second floor. He asked me to send you right up; he'll show you around personally."

"Thanks."

Most of the second floor was given over to stacks; according to a number of neatly painted signs, all of the books here were used hardcover fiction—general novels, mysteries, Westerns and science fiction. Another flight of stairs led to the third floor, but there was a chain drawn across the bottom and a sign that said, *No Admittance*. A wider corridor than the aisleways between the stacks extended the length of the far wall, and when I got over there I saw three doors, the middle one standing open. I stopped in front of the open one. Inside was a good-sized office—Rothman's, probably, judging from the size of the desk and the big old-fashioned safe in one corner—but nobody was in it.

I was standing there looking in when I heard a toilet flush. Then the third door opened and Rothman appeared. He saw me, caught up his cane from where it was leaning against the wall and limped over to me.

"One of the signs of advancing age is a weak bladder," he said, and gave me a rueful smile. "Have you been waiting long?"

"No, I just came up."

"You spoke to Adam, of course. I didn't tell him you were a detective; I thought it would be best if only you and I know your real purpose here."

I nodded. "Does he always come in this early?"

"Most days, yes. Sometimes he's here before I am, and I usually arrive by eight-thirty. His wife died a few years ago; he's lonely, and the shop is a second home to him."

"I see."

"Would you like to see the Antiquarian Room before I show you the rest of the shop?"

"Yes, please."

We went back to the stairs, and Rothman unhooked the chain and led me up to the third floor. There was a door at the top of the stairs; he unlocked it with his key, switched on the lights inside.

The Antiquarian Room was divided into two sections—the first and larger one containing several hundred books and pamphlets, the other one about a fifth as many prints, etchings, engravings, broadsides and maps. Half of the items were in glass display cases or inside glass-doored bookcases; the rest were openly shelved, most of those being sets of books: encyclopedias, histories, the collected works of nineteenth- and early twentieth-century authors. Refectory tables were set in the middle of each section, presumably so potential buyers could sit down and inspect whatever they were interested in. The good, musty smell of old books and old leather bindings was strong in the room.

I asked, "Are all the things in here valuable?"

"Comparatively, no," Rothman said. "Some are worth less than fifty dollars; they're kept here because of their age and because they're of interest only to serious collectors. I transferred a dozen or so of the most valuable items to my office safe several months ago, but there are still quite a few here worth a thousand dollars or more."

"Are most of those prints and the like?"

"No. Books."

"But the prints and engravings and maps that were stolen were worth more, weren't they?"

"Only in the case of the two Dürer etchings."

"Then why would the thief have taken prints and maps instead of the more expensive books?"

"I suppose because the people he's selling them to specialize in that sort of thing."

I moved around the room, examining the cases. Most of them were locked, but the locks were pretty flimsy; once the thief had got in here, it wouldn't have taken him long to break them open. The lock on one in the print section had scratches on it, as if it had been picked with a sharp instrument. That was the case, Rothman told me, which had contained the Orient map that had disappeared three days ago.

When I was done looking around, Rothman locked the door again and we descended to the second floor. He gave me a brief tour of the fiction section; took me down to the first floor, where most of the nonfiction was kept; and pointed out the location of the various categories. With the exception of a wall devoted to Western and regional Americana, and to travel books, the basement was full of trade and mass-market paperbacks of various types and back-issue magazines. There was also a stockroom down there, at the rear.

By the time we came back up to the main floor, it was a quarter to ten and the other employees were beginning to arrive. The first of the three to show up was Harmon Boyette. He was about forty, gaunt, with curly black hair, ascetic features and a bushy mustache. Judging from his bloodshot eyes and splotchy skin, the faint trembling of his hands, he'd had another rough night with the bottle.

Rothman introduced us. Boyette gave me a brief, appraising look, seemed to decide I was nobody he was much interested in and said he was glad to meet me without meaning it. He didn't offer to shake hands.

Neal Vining came in five minutes later. Rothman had excused himself and gone back upstairs to answer another call of nature, so it was Adam Turner who performed the introductions this time. Vining had brown eyes, lank brown hair, a bright smile with a lot of teeth in it and one of those lean, athletic bodies that make you think of long-distance runners. He was dressed in a sports jacket and slacks, very spiffy, and he looked older than the twenty-six Rothman had told me he was.

"Marlowe," he said, pumping my hand. "English name. But you don't look a bit English, I'm afraid."

"My mother was Italian," I said truthfully.

"Lovely people, the Italians. Have you ever been?"

"To Italy? No, I haven't."

"You should go someday, if you have the chance. Do you know books well, Jim?"

"Not as well as I'd like to."

"You'll learn them here, then. Won't he, Adam?"

"If he chooses," Turner said.

I did not get to meet Tom Lennox right away because he hadn't shown up yet when Turner hustled me down into the basement stockroom and put me to work. There were a couple of hundred newly acquired paperbacks on a table; my job was to sort them into categories and shelve them alphabetically in the proper sections. I figured I had better complete that task, to make the proper impression, before I did any roaming around. It took me more than an hour, and the place was full of customers when I finally went back upstairs.

Vining was over in the Occult section, trying to sell a fat woman a book on witchcraft; I could hear him regaling her with esoteric information on the subject when I passed. Turner was behind the cashier's desk, and so was a short, stocky guy with not much hair who was talking on the telephone. I didn't see any sign of Boyette.

The stocky guy finished his conversation and replaced the receiver as I came up. He was around thirty, freckled, with sad eyes and the sad, jowly face of a hound; what hair he had was a dark reddish color. I thought he must be Tom Lennox, and Turner confirmed it when he introduced us.

"Good to have you with us, Mr. Marlowe," Lennox said. He had a soft, cultured voice that belied his appearance.

"Thanks. I'm glad to be here."

"You've had previous bookstore experience, have you?"

"Some," I said. "I'm also a collector."

"Oh? What do you collect?"

"Pulp magazines."

He wasn't impressed. Maybe he was a literary snob, or maybe he just had no interest in pulps; in any case, he said, "You have plenty of company these days. The prices tend to be highly overinflated."

"I know," I said. "Supply and demand. That's why I collect the more inexpensive variety."

Lennox nodded and turned away. So much for me, and so much for pulp magazines.

Turner asked me if I'd finished shelving the paperbacks, and I told him I had. Then he said, "Harmon is upstairs working in hardcover fiction. I'd like you to go up and give him a hand."

When I got upstairs I found Boyette in the mystery section, weeding out the stock—evidently to make room for new acquisitions. Books were stacked on the floor to one side.

"Mr. Turner sent me up to give you some help," I said.

"I don't need any help."

"Well, those were my instructions."

He ran a hand over his splotchy face; he was sweating and he looked sick. "All right, then. Take that stack of books downstairs and put them out front in the bargain bins. But make sure you stop at the desk first."

"Why is that?"

"So Turner can clear them before you go out. They told you about the alarm, didn't they?"

"Oh, right. I guess that's a pretty good safeguard, the alarm system."

"Is it?"

"It prevents thefts, doesn't it?"

"Sometimes," he said. "Not always."

"You mean people can still manage to steal books? I don't see how."

"There are ways."

"What ways?"

"Didn't anybody tell you about the thefts we've been having?"

"No," I said. "What sort of thefts?"

"Valuable items from the Antiquarian Room upstairs. A half-dozen over the past few months. Nobody knows how it's been done." His mouth turned sardonic. "Rothman thinks one of us is responsible."

"One of the employees?"

"That's right."

"Is that what you think, too?"

"I don't get paid to think," Boyette said. "Personally, I don't give a damn who's responsible. Whoever it is can steal Rothman blind for all I care."

"You sound as though you don't like Mr. Rothman much."

"Maybe I've got reason not to like him."

"He seems like a decent sort to me. . . ."

"He is if you suck up to him. I've got five times as much bookselling experience as Lennox and Vining, but I'm the one who gets all the scut work around here. That's because I don't brownnose anybody."

"But Lennox and Vining do?"

"Lennox goes to garage sales, buys books and resells them to Rothman for a few cents apiece. Vining gives him fancy presents from his father-in-law's men's store. All I give him is a good eight hours of work."

"That ought to be enough."

"It isn't," he said bitterly. He narrowed his eyes at me. "What about you, Marlowe? Are *you* a brownnoser?"

"No."

"Then we're in the same boat. But I wouldn't care if you were. I wouldn't even care if you went to Rothman and told him everything I just said."

"I wouldn't do that—"

"He could fire me tomorrow and I wouldn't give a damn. I don't like him and I don't like this place and I don't like being under suspicion all the time."

"If you feel that way, why don't you quit?"

"That's just what I intend to do. As soon as I can find another job."

A customer came clumping up the stairs just then and over into the aisle where we were, and that put an end to the conversation. Boyette said, "Go ahead and take those books downstairs," and returned his attention to the shelves.

I carried the stack of books down to the cashier's desk, waited while Turner cleared them across the sensor strip and then took them outside to where two rolling bins of bargain items were set in front of the display windows. When I got back to the second floor I tried to talk to Boyette again, to see if I could get anything else out of him, but he had lapsed into a moody silence. He didn't have more than a dozen words to say to me over the next two hours.

Rothman went out for lunch at twelve-thirty, Vining around one and Boyette at one-thirty. Lennox and Turner ate brown-bag lunches on the premises, Turner right there at the desk. I also ate lunch in the shop— I'd made myself a couple of sandwiches before leaving my flat that morning—up on the second floor where I could watch the stairs to the Antiquarian Room. Rothman had told me that all of the thefts had occurred between eleven and two; I didn't want to leave, even for a half-hour, and risk missing something.

But there was nothing to miss. Nobody went near the Antiquarian Room and nobody did anything else of a suspicious nature, at last as far as I could tell.

Boyette came back at two-fifteen. He no longer looked quite so sick; his face was flushed and his eyes were a little glassy. I was downstairs when he came in, working in the section marked *Belles Lettres.* Lennox happened to be nearby, and I moved over to him as Boyette climbed the stairs to the second floor.

"Looks as though Harmon drank his lunch," I said.

Lennox made a disapproving noise. "He generally does."

"An alcoholic?"

"That's rather obvious, isn't it?"

"I guess it is. He seems to be a pretty bitter man, from some of the things he said to me this morning."

"Don't pay any attention to him," Lennox said. "The man has a chip on his shoulder. He thinks he deserves better than his present lot, and he can be damned unpleasant at times."

"Do you think he's honest?"

Lennox frowned. "What sort of question is that?"

"Well, he told me about the thefts from the Antiquarian Room," I said. "He says Mr. Rothman believes one of the employees is responsible."

"He had no business talking to you about that," Lennox said stiffly. "The thefts are none of your concern."

"Maybe not, but I do work here now—"

"Yes. And if you want to continue working here, you'll do well to tend to your work and mind your own affairs."

He stalked away toward the cashier's desk. As he did, Neal Vining appeared around the corner of the near stack and came up beside me; he had a fat book on archaeology in one hand. "Harmon isn't the only fellow who can be unpleasant," he said. "Tom's a bit tight-assed himself, you know."

"You overheard?"

"Accidentally, yes."

"What's Lennox's problem?"

"Oh, he takes himself and his work much too seriously. One would think *he* owned this shop, the way he acts."

"Those thefts do seem pretty serious," I said.

"They are, of course. Nasty business. I expect we're all on edge because of them."

"Do you agree with Mr. Rothman that someone who works here is responsible?"

He shrugged. "So it would seem, given the circumstances."

"Who do you think it might be?"

"I really don't have any idea," Vining said. "For all *I* know, Mr. Rothman himself could be slipping out with the spoils. Not that I believe that's the case, you understand," he added hastily. "He's quite above reproach. The point is, the thief could be anyone."

"Even Adam Turner?"

"Adam? I hardly think so. But then, two of the missing items were etchings attributed to Albrecht Dürer, and Adam does have considerable expertise in that area. He once wrote an article on Dürer's work.

He was also the person who arranged for Mr. Rothman to purchase the two etchings from the estate of a private collector."

"Oh? How was he able to do that?"

"The collector was an acquaintance of Adam's," Vining said. "They struck up a correspondence when the article was published."

Lennox returned and called Vining away to the telephone, so I didn't have a chance to press him for any more information. But what he'd told me was food for thought. If Turner was the guilty party, there was no real mystery in how he'd managed the thefts. He could have cleared the stolen pieces through the sensor at any time, working as he did on the cashier's desk, and walked out with them hidden in his clothes. Or he could have simply arrived early in the morning, as Rothman had told me he did periodically, and removed them from the store before Rothman showed up.

I decided that on Monday I would run a background check on Turner, after all.

The rest of the afternoon passed uneventfully. I spent most of it on the main floor, with occasional trips upstairs to check on Boyette. He was still uncommunicative, and by four o'clock, when the drinks he'd had for lunch had worn off, he had turned surly; he snapped at me and at a customer who asked him a question about a book. When closing time rolled around, he was the first one out the door.

I stayed until six-fifteen, making myself look busy; Vining and Lennox were gone by then. When Rothman came down he sent Turner and me on our way so he could shut off the sensor alarm and lock up as he usually did. I waited around for him outside. The rain had stopped and there were patches of clear sky among the clouds to the east; with any luck, the weather would be good for my weekend with Kerry.

Rothman came out a couple of minutes later. "Where's your car?" he asked when he finished locking the front doors.

"In the lot two blocks down."

"That's my direction. We can talk as we walk."

He set off at a brisk pace, in spite of his game leg. I asked him, "Everything okay in the Antiquarian Room?"

"Yes. I checked it this morning, and again tonight before I came down. Nothing's been touched. Have you found out anything so far?"

"Nothing specific, no," I said. I saw no purpose in telling him about Boyette's references to him, in making trouble for Boyette, unless it turned out to have some bearing on my investigation. And I didn't want to press him on Turner until I ran the background check. "I'm afraid this is the kind of job that may take some time, Mr. Rothman."

"I don't expect you to perform miracles," he said. "Time isn't important to me; finding out which of them is guilty, and how he's doing it, is what matters."

We had gone a block, and when we crossed the street Rothman stopped in front of a building that bore a sign reading: *Pacific Health Club.* "This is where I'm going," he said.

"You belong to a health club?"

He smiled. "I don't lift weights or play racquetball with Neal Vining, if that's what you're thinking. Mostly I use the Jacuzzi; it helps me relax and eases the pain in my leg."

"Oh, I see."

"You can join me if you like. Guests are permitted."

"No, thanks. I think I'll head home. I like to do my relaxing with a cold beer."

He glanced at my protruding belly. "So I see," he said, but gently, without censure.

We said good night, and he entered the building and I went and got my car and drove home. I drank two cans of Schlitz—the hell with health clubs and the hell with my belly—and then called Kerry at Bates and Carpenter. But she was busy and couldn't talk more than a couple of minutes. She did say that the presentation was going according to schedule and that she still expected to be done with it by noon tomorrow.

"Is it all right if I stop by the book shop when I'm finished?" she asked. "I like bookstores; and I'd love to see you shlepping books around."

"I don't see why not. As long as you don't tell anybody I'm really a private eye on a case."

"I'll try to restrain myself. See you tomorrow, then."

"Lovely lady, I'll count the minutes."

"Phooey," she said, and rang off.

I made myself something to eat, read for a while and turned in early. It had been a reasonably productive day and I was satisfied with it. I had learned a few things; maybe I would learn a few more tomorrow that would establish some kind of pattern. Maybe tomorrow would turn out, I thought, to be an even more productive day.

Saturday was a productive day, all right.

The thief hit the Antiquarian Room again, and he did it right under my damn nose.

It happened, as before, sometime between eleven-twenty, when Rothman checked the room before going out for an early lunch, and two o'clock, when he went up to check it again. I was on the main floor talking to Kerry at the time he made the discovery. She had been there about a half-hour, browsing, looking terrific in a black suit and a frilly white blouse; she was about to buy a book she'd found—a scarce old one of her father's, one of his early novels—and she was telling me how pleased he was going to be because he was down to only two file copies of that particular title.

I didn't like Ivan Wade—Ivan the Terrible, I called him—any more than he liked me; he was overprotective of Kerry, supercilious, humorless and something of a jerk. So I said, "I'm thrilled for him."

"Now don't be that way," she said. *"The Redmayne Horror* really is a scarce book. And they only want fifteen dollars."

"The Redmayne Horror is a dumb title," I said.

"It was a pulp serial, originally. That was the kind of title they put on weird fiction back in the forties, in the pulps and in book editions; you know that."

"It's still a dumb title."

"Oh, stick it in your ear," she said, and made a face at me. "Can't you see I'm excited about this? I almost knocked over a man with a cane upstairs when I found it."

"That would be Mr. Rothman. Nice going."

"Well, I'm sorry. But I—"

And that was when Rothman appeared on the stairs and beckoned to me urgently. I left Kerry and followed him up to his office, and as soon as he shut the door he told me about the latest theft.

"It was another rare map," he said. His face was flushed and his knuckles showed white where they gripped the head of his cane. "A sixteenth-century map by the Flemish cartographer and geographer Gerhardus Mercator."

"Valuable?"

"Very. Damn, I should have put it in my safe months ago."

"Where was it kept?"

"In one of the glass display cases. The lock was broken, just as in the other thefts."

"Whichever of them it is, he's bold and he's quick," I said. "I've been on this floor off and on ever since you left for lunch. He couldn't have spent much time up there; he had to know exactly what he was after."

"What do we do now?"

"What did you do after you discovered the other thefts?"

"Asked the customers to leave, closed up shop for the day, then gathered my people together and questioned them."

"All right. Do the same thing this time, only let me get rid of the customers. When you start the questioning, ask everybody if they mind being searched. If any of them refuses, press him on it. Then designate me to do the searching."

"Do I tell them you're a detective?"

"No. We won't get anywhere by blowing my cover. Just say you want me to do the searching because I'm new and you don't have any reason to suspect me."

"The thief won't have the map on his person," Rothman said grimly. "He's too clever for that."

"I know. But I want to see how they react and what they might be carrying in their pockets. I don't think he'll have the duplicate key on him either—he's probably got it stashed somewhere in the shop—but it's worth checking for."

"And if none of that does any good?"

"Then you'll have to let them go home. And you and I'll search this place from top to bottom. If none of them can leave with the map, then it's still got to be here somewhere."

We went downstairs together. Kerry was still waiting; when I joined her she said, "What's the matter? You look upset."

"Trouble. Another theft. You'd better go now; we're closing the shop."

"Oh boy. Will you still be able to make our date tonight?"

"I hope so. If I can't I'll call you."

It took twenty minutes to clear the store of customers and to get the front door locked. Turner and the others knew right away what was going on; none of them had much to say at first, and I could see them giving each other faintly mistrustful glances. Lennox looked aggrieved, as if he took the thefts personally and the money was coming straight out of his pocket. Boyette seemed more angry than anything else, but it was a put-upon kind of anger; he was suffering another hangover and his bloodshot eyes said the last thing he wanted to deal with was another crisis. Vining was subdued, the set of his face grave and concerned. Turner wore an expression of mingled agitation and worry—the look of a loyal company man whose boss is in trouble. None of the four seemed nervous. Or any more guilty, on the surface, than I was.

The six of us were gathered near the cashier's desk. Rothman started off by explaining what it was that had been stolen this time. Then he asked if anyone had seen anyone else go up to the Antiquarian Room;

nobody had. Had anyone seen anything of a suspicious nature between eleven-thirty and two o'clock? Nobody had. Who had left the store during that time period? Boyette had, and so had Lennox. But Turner had seen them both leave, through the alarm gateway as always, and nothing had happened.

Rothman said then, "I'm sorry, gentlemen, but these thefts have become intolerable; getting to the bottom of them calls for extreme measures. Do any of you object to being searched?"

The only one who did was Boyette. "Why the hell should I stand for that?" he said. "Even if I were guilty, I wouldn't be stupid enough to have the map on my person."

Lennox said, "Then you shouldn't object to being searched."

"I've had enough of this crap. Thefts, suspicion, body searches— pretty soon it'll be accusations. I won't stand for it; I'm leaving right now and I'm not coming back."

"If you do, Harmon," Vining said, "it will make you look guilty, you know."

"I don't care," Boyette said. He looked mean and belligerent; there was a pugnacious thrust to his jaw. "Is anyone going to try to stop me?"

Rothman glanced at me, but I gave him a faint headshake. I had no right to restrain Boyette, or to search him, without some proof of guilt; if any of us tried, it would leave us open to a lawsuit.

"All right, Harmon," Rothman said coldly. "Consider your employment terminated. I'll mail you what I owe you in salary. Adam, let him out."

Turner went through the gateway and unlocked the front door. The alarm was still operational, and when Boyette stomped through after him the bell didn't go off. It was still possible that he was guilty, but he wasn't walking out of here with the Mercator map.

When Turner relocked the door and came back to join the rest of us, Rothman said, "Does anyone else feel the same way? Or will you all submit to a search?"

There were no more objections. Rothman designated me to do the searching, as we'd agreed, and I frisked each man in turn. Turner first, because I knew he wasn't carrying the map; he'd gone through the gateway just as Boyette had. Then Vining, and then Lennox. No map. All three men had keys—no loose ones, though; they were all on rings or in cases—and Rothman examined each one stoically. His silence told me that none of the keys was the duplicate to the Antiquarian Room door.

There was nothing to do then but let the three of them leave, too.

Turner was the last to go, and he went reluctantly. "If you're planning to search the shop, Mr. Rothman," he said, "I can help. . . ."

"No, you go ahead. Marlowe will help me this time."

As soon as Turner was gone, Rothman and I began our search. We started with the Antiquarian Room; it wasn't likely that the thief would have hidden the Mercator map in there, but we gave it a good going-over just the same. No map. We went down to the second floor and searched the stacks, the storage room next to Rothman's office, the bathroom. No map. We combed the first-floor stacks and shelves, the display tables, the cashier's desk, even the window displays. No map. In the basement we searched the paperback sections, the Americana and travel shelves, the stockroom. No map.

We covered every inch of that building, from top to bottom. There was no way the map could have been gotten out, and yet there was no place an item of its size and fragility could have been hidden inside the shop that we had overlooked.

So what *had* happened to it?

Where the hell was the missing map?

It was ten of seven when Rothman and I finally called it quits, left the shop and went our separate ways. I was almost as frustrated as he was by then. On the drive home to my flat, I kept gnawing at the question, the seeming impossibility of the theft, like a dog gnaws at a bone. And the more I gnawed, the more I felt as if I were close to the marrow of the thing.

The answer was something clever and audacious, yes, but I also sensed that it was something simple. And that I had heard enough and seen enough the past three days to put it all together—a lot of little things that just needed to be shifted around into the right order. Damn it, I could almost taste the marrow. . . .

I gave Kerry a brief call, to tell her I would be late, and then showered the bookstore dust off me and put on my suit. Dusk was settling by the time I got up to Diamond Heights. The weather had cleared and the view from up there was spectacular; you could see both bridges, the wide sweep of the bay, the Oakland hills and the Pacific Ocean in the opposite direction. It was too nice an evening, I told myself, to let my frustration spoil things with Kerry, and as I parked the car in front of her building I decided I wouldn't let that happen.

I went into the vestibule and rang her bell, and she buzzed me in right away. When I got upstairs she was waiting for me in a shimmery green dress with plenty of cleavage—a dress designed to knock your optic out, as the pulp private eyes used to say.

"Sorry I'm so late," I said, admiring her. "It was some afternoon."

"That's okay. Did you catch the thief?"

"No. He swiped another rare map and managed to get it out of the store again, past the alarm system. I ought to be able to figure out which one of them it is and how he did it, but I can't seem to do it."

"Uh-oh. Does that mean you're going to be moody tonight?"

"No. I am not going to be moody tonight."

"You're *already* moody," she said.

"Bah. Let's go eat."

We went down and out to the car. Kerry said, "I'm starved. You must be, too."

"Yeah. They do a fine chorizo-and-peppers dish at the Oaxaca, very hot and spicy."

"So of course you have to drink a lot of beer with it."

"Sure. What's Mexican food without cold Mexican beer?"

"You put away more beer than any man I've ever known," she said. "I swear, sometimes I think you've got a hollow leg."

I leaned forward to switch on the ignition. Then I stopped with my hand on the key and stared over at her. "What did you say?"

"I said sometimes I think you've got a hollow leg. What's the matter?"

"That's it," I said.

"What's it?"

"The answer."

"I don't know what you're talking about. . . ."

I waved her quiet, started the car, switched on the headlights—it was full dark now—and pulled away from the curb; I tended to think more clearly while I was driving. By the time we approached Diamond Heights Boulevard, I had most of it put together. And when we were headed down the steep, curving boulevard, nearing Glen Canyon, I had the rest of it. All I needed was confirmation of one thing, and Kerry herself could give me that.

But before I could ask her about it, there was a roar of noise outside and the interior of the car was bathed in the bright glare of headlights. Another car had come boiling up behind us, so close that its lights were like huge staring eyes framed in the rear window. Damn tailgater, I thought, and took my foot off the accelerator and tapped the brake pedal gently, just enough to let the other driver see the flash of the brake lights.

Only he didn't slow down; he just kept coming. And his front bumper smacked into my rear bumper, hard enough to jolt the car and almost wrench the wheel loose from my hands.

Kerry twisted around on the seat. "My God! What's the matter with him? What's he *doing?*"

"Hang on!"

The other car jarred into us again, harder than before, shattering one or both of the taillights. Even though I was ready for it, I had to fight the wheel and feather the brakes to keep my car from fishtailing into a skid. The tires made screaming noises on the pavement; I could smell the burning rubber and the sudden sour odor of my own sweat.

The road had steepened and hooked over toward the long, narrow, tree-choked expanse of Glen Canyon; for a stretch of maybe five hundred yards, Diamond Heights Boulevard paralleled the canyon's eastern rim. In the reach of my headlights I could see that there was no guardrail, just a sidewalk and some knee-high brown grass on a strip of bank and then the drop-off, sheer, almost straight down. If we went off there, there wasn't much chance that we'd survive.

And that was just what the driver of the other car wanted, all right. It wasn't a drunk back there, or kids playing dangerous games; it was somebody bent on mayhem.

Downhill to the left, on the other side of the curve, a residential street cut away uphill. I yelled at Kerry again to hang on and got set to drop the transmission lever into low gear so I could make a fast, sharp left-hand turn into the other street. There was nothing else I could do with the trailing car hanging on my bumper the way it was.

But the driver saw the street, too, and before I got close enough to make the turn, his headlights flicked out to the left, into the uphill lane. In my side mirror I could see the bulky shape of the car outlined behind the glare; then he accelerated and pulled up abreast. I glanced over at him, but all I could make out was one person, his face a white smear in the darkness. Then I put my eyes back on the road and kept them there, muscles tensed, hands tightened on the wheel, because I sensed what he was going to try to do next.

It was only a couple of seconds before he did it, just as I started into the wide left-hand curve along the rim of the canyon: he pulled slightly ahead and then whipped over into me, hard along the front fender. There was a crunching sound, and Kerry cried out, and the car shimmied and the right front tire scraped against the curb on that side. But I was able to maintain control, even though we were still crowded together and he was trying to use his momentum to shove us up and over the bank.

I came down hard on the brake pedal, bracing myself, throwing my right arm out in front of Kerry to keep her from flying into the windshield. The tires shrieked again; we bucked and slid through the curve, losing speed. The other car glanced off, with another tearing-metal noise, yawing at a slight angle in front of me. Then the driver got it straightened out and braked as I had, swinging back full into the other lane so he could try ramming us again.

He would have done it, too, if it hadn't been for the third car that came sailing around another curve below, headed uphill.

I saw the oncoming headlights sweep through the scattered eucalyptus that grew inside the canyon further down, but the other driver was too intent on me to notice them because he didn't try to swing back into the downhill lane. Frantically I stood on the brake and got ready to yank on the emergency brake, if that was what it took to bring us to a stop; it seemed sure there would be a collision and all I could think was: Kerry might be hurt, I can't let her get hurt.

There was no collision. The driver of the third car saw what was happening, leaned hard on the horn, and managed to swerve up onto the sidewalk and across somebody's front lawn. But the guy who'd tried to kill Kerry and me had run out of luck. He saw the third car in time to swerve himself, back into the downhill lane, only he did it too sharply; he missed the third car, all right, by at least twenty feet—and he missed hitting mine by the same distance when he veered in front of me—but the rear end of his car broke loose and he wasn't able to fight through the skid and pull it out.

His car went out of control, spun all the way around, and then hit the curb and bounced up into the air like something made out of rubber. Its headlights sprayed the trees as it hurtled toward them, sideways. In the next second it was gone, and in the second after that the explosive sound of buckling metal and breaking glass and splintering wood erupted from inside the canyon.

I managed to bring my car to a stop. When I took my hands off the wheel they were as wet as if I'd dunked them in water.

"God," Kerry said, in a soft, trembly voice.

"Are you all right?"

"Yes. I . . . just give me a minute. . . ."

I touched her arm, and then opened the door and got out. People were spilling from houses in the vicinity, running toward the canyon; the driver of the third car, a heavyset woman, was slumped against her front fender, not moving, looking dazed. I ran up onto the sidewalk and ahead to where the other car had gone over. It was wrapped around one of the eucalyptus about a third of the way down the slope; the upper part of the tree had been sheared off and was canted at a drunken angle. From the mangled appearance of the wreckage, I didn't see how the guy inside could have survived.

But I was wrong about that. When I got there along with a couple of other people, and we dragged him out, he was alive. Unconscious and pretty badly cut up, but unless he had internal injuries, it looked as though he'd make it all right.

It did not surprise me when I saw who he was. Because he was the same person who had committed the thefts in John Rothman's book shop—the same clever, greedy, *stupid* young man.

Neal Vining.

Three hours later, I was sitting in a room at the Hall of Justice with Kerry, John Rothman and an inspector I knew named Jack Logan, who had been the investigating officer when Rothman first reported the thefts. Vining was in the hospital under police guard. He'd already been charged with attempted vehicular homicide, and had been coherent enough and frightened enough to confess to that, and when I got done with my explanations he would also be charged with several counts of grand larceny.

I was saying, "I knew even before Vining tried to run us off the road that he was the thief. And I know how he got the stolen items out of the store, too. It was a combination of things I'd seen and heard; and when Kerry made a comment about me having a hollow leg, because I like to drink beer, it triggered an association that put it all together."

"Hollow leg?" Rothman said. "I don't understand what—"

"You'll see what I mean in a minute. The whole thing is really pretty simple; it was Vining himself, in fact, who told me how he pulled off the thefts, either without realizing what he was saying or, more likely, because he was so sure of himself that it was his way of bragging. He said yesterday, 'For all I know, Mr. Rothman himself could be slipping out with the spoils.'"

They were all staring at me, Rothman with a look of incredulity. "Are you saying *I* took the items out of the shop for him? That's preposterous—"

"No, it isn't," I said. "You took them out, all right; that's the beauty of his scheme. He made you an unwitting accomplice."

"How could he possibly have done that?"

"By putting the stolen items inside your cane," I said.

"My *cane?*"

"Vining gave it to you, didn't he? Some months ago? Harmon Boyette told me Vining was in the habit of giving you presents from his father-in-law's haberdashery."

"Yes, but . . ." Rothman seemed a little nonplussed. He reached for the cane, propped against the side of his chair, and gawped at it as if he'd never seen it before.

Logan said, "You mean the cane's hollow?"

"Yes. That's the significance of Kerry's hollow-leg comment. And that's why Vining stole only etchings, prints and maps, instead of books that were more valuable, since you installed your alarm system: they could be rolled up and inserted inside the cane. They still make canes like that over in England; people keep money and other small valuable items inside them—as a safeguard against theft, ironically enough. It wouldn't have been difficult for Vining to have one imported through his father-in-law's store."

Rothman was running his fingers over the thick barrel of the cane, peering at it. "How does the damn thing work?"

"I don't know. But it shouldn't take us long to find out."

It took us about two minutes. The catch was well concealed, and so was the long hinged opening; you couldn't see either with the naked eye, you couldn't feel the grooves with your fingers and it wasn't likely that you could open it by accident. Fine British craftsmanship. Logan was the one who finally found the catch, and when the hinges released I saw what I expected to see: the hollow interior contained a rolled-up length of parchment.

Rothman took the parchment out and unrolled it gently. "My God," he said, "the Mercator map."

"Right where Vining put it this afternoon," I said, "after he stole it from the Antiquarian Room."

"But I keep the cane with me at all times; I need it to get around for any distance. I don't see how—"

"You don't take it into the bathroom with you, Mr. Rothman. When I got to the store yesterday morning, and went up to talk to you, you were in the bathroom; the cane was leaning against the wall outside. I remember you taking it from there when you came out."

Rothman nodded. "You're right, of course; I never took the cane into the bathroom because it was too cumbersome in that little cubicle. I always left it against the wall outside."

"And you used the bathroom fairly often during the day, didn't you? Because of your bladder problem?"

"Yes."

"So it was easy enough for Vining to put the stolen items inside the cane. He committed each of his thefts while you were out to lunch or otherwise away from the store in the early afternoons so he could be sure you wouldn't catch him red-handed. Then he either hid the pieces somewhere, or kept them inside his clothes, until you returned and he saw an opportunity to put them inside the cane while you were in the bathroom and there was nobody else in the vicinity. It only took him a few seconds each time.

"The whole idea was to beat the sensor alarm. Everyone who left the store after one of the thefts had to pass through the alarm gateway *except you;* you were always the last one to leave on those days, and you always switched the alarm off before you went through the gateway yourself to lock up. The *only* person who could have taken the items out of the shop was you."

"But how did Vining retrieve them from the cane after I'd left?" Rothman asked. Then I saw understanding come to him and he answered his own question. "Well, I'll be damned. The Pacific Health Club."

"Right. Vining is a member, too, isn't he?"

"Yes, he is. How did you know?"

"You told me so yourself, last night. You said you didn't go to the health club to lift weights or to play racquetball with Neal Vining; you wouldn't have phrased it that way unless he was also a member."

Logan asked, "How did Vining get the stuff out of the cane at the health club?"

"I go there every night to use the Jacuzzi," Rothman explained. "It's right off the locker room, so I've never taken the cane in there with me; there's no place to put it near the Jacuzzi."

"You left it inside your locker, is that it?"

"Yes. The locker has a combination lock, but I don't suppose it would have been difficult for Vining to get the combination. I remember him standing there talking to me on more than one occasion while I was opening it."

"So all he had to do," I said, "was to wait for you to go into the Jacuzzi and then open up your locker, transfer the stolen items from the cane to inside his clothing and walk out with them. Simple as that."

Rothman shook his head wonderingly. "The only other question I have," he said, "is why did Vining try to kill you and Miss Wade tonight?"

"He slipped up this afternoon at the store, while he was putting the Mercator map inside the cane. He'd been careful not to let anybody see him in the past; this time he wasn't so careful and somebody did see him."

"Me," Kerry said. "Well, I didn't exactly see him putting anything inside the cane; I just saw him with the cane in his hand."

"How did that happen?" Logan asked.

"I was browsing in the stacks at the rear of the fiction section. In the W's, along the rear wall directly behind the last stack, near what must be the bathroom. I guess he didn't see me when he looked down the aisles, so he didn't think anybody was around. I found an old scarce book of my father's—he's been a writer for forty years, you see—and I was excited about it; I grabbed it off the shelf and hurried out into the last aisle, and a man was standing there with that cane in his hand. I bumped right into him."

"She told me about that a few minutes later," I said. "At the time I naturally assumed the man she'd bumped into was Mr. Rothman. But later, I realized it could have been Vining. And it was."

"Then it was Miss Wade he was after tonight?" Rothman asked. "Because he was afraid she'd seen him put the Mercator map inside the cane?"

"Not exactly," I said. "Vining was trying to kill both of us. He was afraid Kerry had seen him with the map, yes, and he wanted to know who she was; from what he told the police at the hospital a little while ago, he hadn't formed any definite plans about her at that time. He'd followed her downstairs and overheard her talking to me, about the date we had tonight, so he knew we were friends. After he left the shop he waited around until I left at seven o'clock and then followed me until I led him to Kerry's apartment building. I was so preoccupied when I went inside to get her that I left my car unlocked. Vining looked inside and found out from the registration that I'm a detective. That really unnerved him. So when I drove away with Kerry a little while later, he followed us again—maybe with the intention of committing murder, maybe not. He said he didn't plan to try forcing us off the road; he just did it on impulse. Whether it was premeditated or not is up to a jury to decide."

And that was about it. Rothman still had the problem of recovering the other stolen items, but with a full confession from Vining—and it seemed probable the police would get one—he would know to whom they had been sold, and the chances were good that he would be able to force their return.

Saturday night may have been a bust as far as my date with Kerry had gone, but early Sunday morning at her apartment was something else again. Early Sunday morning was terrific.

"I love to watch you work," she said once. "You're a pretty good detective, you know that?"

"Well," I said modestly, "I do the best I can."

"Yes, you do. No matter what you're doing."

"The fire's getting low. Shall I get up and put another log on?"

"The heck with the fire," she said.

Neither of us noticed when it finally went out.

RAYMOND CHANDLER
The King in Yellow

1

GEORGE MILLAR, night auditor at the Carlton Hotel, was a dapper wiry little man, with a soft deep voice like a torch-singer's. He kept it low, but his eyes were sharp and angry, as he said into the PBX mouthpiece: "I'm very sorry. It won't happen again. I'll send up at once."

He tore off the head-piece, dropped it on the keys of the switchboard and marched swiftly from behind the pebbled screen and out into the entrance lobby. It was past one and the Carlton was two-thirds residential. In the main lobby, down three shallow steps, lamps were dimmed and the night porter had finished tidying up. The place was deserted—a wide space of dim furniture, rich carpet. Faintly in the distance a radio sounded. Millar went down the steps and walked quickly towards the sound, turned through an archway and looked at a man stretched out on a pale-green davenport and what looked like all the loose cushions in the hotel. He lay on his side, dreamy-eyed and listened to the radio two yards away from him.

Millar barked: "Hey, you! Are you the house dick here or the house cat?"

Steve Grayce turned his head slowly and looked at Millar. He was a long black-haired man, about twenty-eight, with deep-set silent eyes and a rather gentle mouth. He jerked a thumb at the radio and smiled. "King Leopardi, George. Hear that trumpet tone. Smooth as an angel's wing, boy."

"Swell! Go on back upstairs and get him out of the corridor!"

Steve Grayce looked shocked. "What—again? I thought I had those birds put to bed long ago." He swung his feet to the floor and stood up. He was at least a foot taller than Millar.

"Well, Eight-sixteen says no. Eight-sixteen says he's out in the hall with two of his stooges. He's dressed in yellow satin shorts and a trombone and he and his pals are putting on a jam session. And one of those hustlers Quillan registered in Eight-eleven is out there truckin' for them. Now get on to it, Steve—and this time make it stick."

Steve Grayce smiled wryly. He said: "Leopardi doesn't belong here anyway. Can I use chloroform or just my blackjack?"

He stepped long legs over the pale-green carpet, through the arch and across the main lobby to the single elevator that was open and lighted. He slid the doors shut and ran it up to Eight, stopped it roughly and stepped out into the corridor.

The noise hit him like a sudden wind. The walls echoed with it. Half a dozen doors were open and angry guests in night robes stood in them peering.

"It's O. K. folks," Steve Grayce said rapidly. "This is absolutely the last act. Just relax."

He rounded a corner and the hot music almost took him off his feet. Three men were lined up against the wall, near an open door from which light streamed. The middle one, the one with the trombone, was six feet tall, powerful and graceful, with a hairline mustache. His face was flushed and his eyes had an alcoholic glitter. He wore yellow satin shorts with large initials embroidered in black on the left leg—nothing more. His torso was tanned and naked.

The two with him were in pajamas, the usual halfway-good-looking band boys, both drunk, but not staggering drunk. One jittered madly on a clarinet and the other on a tenor saxophone.

Back and forth in front of them, strutting, trucking, preening herself like a magpie, arching her arms and her eyebrows, bending her fingers back until the carmine nails almost touched her arms, a metallic blonde swayed and went to town on the music. Her voice was a throaty screech, without melody, as false as her eyebrows and as sharp as her nails. She wore high-heeled slippers and black pajamas with a long purple sash.

Steve Grayce stopped dead and made a sharp downward motion with his hand. "Wrap it up!" he snapped. "Can it. Put it on ice. Take it away and bury it. The show's out. Scram, now—scram!"

King Leopardi took the trombone from his lips and bellowed: "Fanfare to a house dick!"

The three drunks blew a stuttering note that shook the walls. The girl laughed foolishly and kicked out. Her slipper caught Steve Grayce in the chest. He picked it out of the air, jumped towards the girl and took hold of her wrist.

"Tough, eh?" he grinned. "I'll take you first."

"Get him!" Leopardi yelled. "Sock him low! Dance the gum-heel on his neck!"

Steve swept the girl off her feet, tucked her under his arm and ran. He carried her as easily as a parcel. She tried to kick his legs. He laughed and shot a glance through a lighted doorway. A man's brown brogues lay under a bureau. He went on past that to a second lighted doorway, slammed through and kicked the door shut, turned far enough to twist the tabbed key in the lock. Almost at once a fist hit the door. He paid no attention to it.

He pushed the girl along the short passage past the bathroom, and let her go. She reeled away from him and put her back to the bureau, panting, her eyes furious. A lock of damp gold-dipped hair swung down over one eye. She shook her head violently and bared her teeth.

"How would you like to get vagged, sister?"

"Go to hell!" she spit out. "The King's a friend of mine, see? You better keep your paws off me, copper."

"You run the circuit with the boys?"

She spat at him again.

"How'd you know they'd be here?"

Another girl was sprawled across the bed, her head to the wall, tousled black hair over a white face. There was a tear in the leg of her pajamas. She lay limp and groaned.

Steve said harshly: "Oh, oh, the torn-pajama act. It flops here, sister, it flops hard. Now listen, you kids. You can go to bed and stay till morning or you can take the bounce. Make up your minds."

The black-haired girl groaned. The blonde said: "You get out of my room, you damned gum-heel!"

She reached behind her and threw a hand mirror. Steve ducked. The mirror slammed against the wall and fell without breaking. The black-haired girl rolled over on the bed and said wearily: "Oh lay off. I'm sick."

She lay with her eyes closed, the lids fluttering.

The blonde swiveled her hips across the room to a desk by the window, poured herself a full half-glass of Scotch in a water glass and gurgled it down before Steve could get to her. She choked violently, dropped the glass and went down on her hands and knees.

Steve said grimly: "That's the one that kicks you in the face, sister."

The girl crouched, shaking her head. She gagged once, lifted the carmine nails to paw at her mouth. She tried to get up, and her foot skidded out from under her and she fell down on her side and went fast asleep.

Steve sighed, went over and shut the window and fastened it. He rolled the black-haired girl over and straightened her on the bed and got the bedclothes from under her, tucked a pillow under her head. He picked the blonde bodily off the floor and dumped her on the bed and covered both girls to the chin. He opened the transom, switched off the ceiling-light and unlocked the door. He relocked it from the outside, with a master-key on a chain.

"Hotel business," he said under his breath. "Phooey."

The corridor was empty now. One lighted door still stood open. Its number was 815, two doors from the room the girls were in. Trombone music came from it softly—but not softly enough for 1:25 A.M.

Steve Grayce turned into the room, crowded the door shut with his shoulder and went along past the bathroom. King Leopardi was alone in the room.

The bandleader was sprawled out in an easy chair, with a tall misted glass at his elbow. He swung the trombone in a tight circle as he played it and the lights danced in the horn.

Steve lit a cigarette, blew a plume of smoke and stared through it at Leopardi with a queer, half-admiring, half-contemptuous expression.

He said softly: "Lights out, yellow-pants. You play a sweet trumpet and your trombone don't hurt either. But we can't use it here. I already told you that once. Lay off. Put that thing away."

Leopardi smiled nastily and blew a stuttering raspberry that sounded like a devil laughing.

"Says you," he sneered. "Leopardi does what he likes, where he likes, when he likes. Nobody's stopped him yet, gum-shoe. Take the air."

Steve hunched his shoulders and went close to the tall dark man. He said patiently: "Put that bazooka down, big-stuff. People are trying to sleep. They're funny that way. You're a great guy on a bandshell. Everywhere else you're just a guy with a lot of jack and a personal reputation that stinks from here to Miami and back. I've got a job to do and I'm doing it. Blow that thing again and I'll wrap it around your neck."

Leopardi lowered the trombone and took a long drink from the glass at his elbow. His eyes glinted nastily. He lifted the trombone to his lips again, filled his lungs with air and blew a blast that rocked the walls. Then he stood up very suddenly and smoothly and smashed the instrument down on Steve's head.

"I never did like house-peepers," he sneered. "They smell like public toilets."

Steve took a short step back and shook his head. He leered, slid forward on one foot and smacked Leopardi open-handed. The blow looked light, but Leopardi reeled all the way across the room and sprawled at the foot of the bed, sitting on the floor, his right arm draped in an open suitcase.

For a moment neither man moved. Then Steve kicked the trombone away from him and squashed his cigarette in a glass tray. His black eyes were empty but his mouth grinned whitely.

"If you want trouble," he said, "I come from where they make it."

Leopardi smiled, thinly, tautly, and his right hand came up out of the suitcase with a gun in it. His thumb snicked the safety catch. He held the gun steady, pointing.

"Make some with this," he said, and fired.

The bitter roar of the gun seemed a tremendous sound in the closed room. The bureau mirror splintered and glass flew. A sliver cut Steve's cheek like a razor blade. Blood oozed in a small narrow line on his skin.

He left his feet in a dive. His right shoulder crashed against Leopardi's bare chest and his left hand brushed the gun away from him, under the bed. He rolled swiftly to his right and came up on his knees spinning.

He said thickly, harshly: "You picked the wrong gee, brother."

He swarmed on Leopardi and dragged him to his feet by his hair, by main strength. Leopardi yelled and hit him twice on the jaw and Steve grinned and kept his left hand twisted in the bandleader's long sleek black hair. He turned his hand and the head twisted with it and Leopardi's third punch landed on Steve's shoulder. Steve took hold of the wrist behind the punch and twisted that and the bandleader went down on his knees yowling. Steve lifted him by the hair again, let go of his wrist and punched him three times in the stomach, short terrific jabs. He let go of the hair then as he sank the fourth punch almost to his wrist.

Leopardi sagged blindly to his knees and vomited.

Steve stepped away from him and went into the bathroom and got a towel off the rack. He threw it at Leopardi, jerked the open suitcase onto the bed and started throwing things into it.

Leopardi wiped his face and got to his feet still gagging. He swayed, braced himself on the end of the bureau. He was white as a sheet.

Steve Grayce said: "Get dressed, Leopardi. Or go out the way you are. It's all one to me."

Leopardi stumbled into the bathroom, pawing the wall like a blind man.

2

MILLAR STOOD very still behind the desk as the elevator opened. His face was white and scared and his cropped black mustache was a smudge across his upper lip. Leopardi came out of the elevator first, a muffler around his neck, a lightweight coat tossed over his arm, a hat tilted on his head. He walked stiffly, bent forward a little, his eyes vacant. His face had a greenish pallor.

Steve Grayce stepped out behind him carrying a suitcase, and Carl, the night porter came last with two more suitcases and two instrument cases in black leather. Steve marched over to the desk and said harshly: "Mr. Leopardi's bill—if any. He's checking out."

Millar goggled at him across the marble desk. "I—I don't think, Steve—"

"O. K. I thought not."

Leopardi smiled very thinly and unpleasantly and walked out through the brass-edged swing-doors the porter held open for him. There were two nighthawk cabs in the line. One of them came to life and pulled up to the canopy and the porter loaded Leopardi's stuff into it. Leopardi got into the cab and leaned forward to put his head to the open window. He said slowly and thickly: "I'm sorry for you, gum-heel. I mean sorry."

Steve Grayce stepped back and looked at him woodenly. The cab moved off down the street, rounded a corner and was gone. Steve turned on his heel, took a quarter from his pocket and tossed it up in the air. He slapped it into the night porter's hand.

"From the King," he said. "Keep it to show your grandchildren."

He went back into the hotel, got into the elevator without looking at Millar, shot it up to Eight again and went along the corridor, master-keyed his way into Leopardi's room. He relocked it from the inside, pulled the bed out from the wall and went in behind it. He got a .32 automatic off the carpet, put it in his pocket and prowled the floor with his eyes looking for the ejected shell. He found it against the wastebasket, reached to pick it up, and stayed bent over, staring into the wastebasket. His mouth tightened. He picked up the shell and dropped it absently into his pocket, then reached a questing finger into the basket and lifted out a torn scrap of paper on which a piece of newsprint had been pasted. Then he picked up the basket, pushed the bed back against the wall and dumped the contents of the basket out on it.

From the trash of torn papers and matches he separated a number of pieces with newsprint pasted to them. He went over to the desk with them and sat down. A few minutes later he had the torn scraps put together like a jigsaw puzzle and could read the message that had been made by cutting words and letters from magazines and pasting them on a sheet.

TEN GRAND BY THURSDAY NIGHT, LEOPARDI. DAY AFTER YOU OPEN AT THE CLUB SHALOTTE. OR ELSE—CURTAINS. FROM HER BROTHER.

Steve Grayce said: "Huh." He scooped the torn pieces into a hotel envelope, put that in his inside breast pocket and lit a cigarette. "The guy had guts," he said. "I'll grant him that—and his trumpet."

He locked the room, listened a moment in the now silent corridor, then went along to the room occupied by the two girls. He knocked softly and put his ear to the panel. A chair squeaked and feet came towards the door.

"What is it?" The girl's voice was cool, wide-awake. It was not the blonde's voice.

"The house man. Can I speak to you a minute?"

"You're speaking to me."

"Without the door between, lady."

"You've got the passkey. Help yourself." The steps went away. He unlocked the door with his master key, stepped quietly inside, and shut it. There was a dim light in a lamp with a shirred shade on the desk. On the bed the blonde snored heavily, one hand clutched in her brilliant metallic hair. The black-haired girl sat in the chair by the window, her legs crossed at right angles like a man's and stared at Steve emptily.

He went close to her and pointed to the long tear in her pajama leg. He said softly: "You're not sick. You were not drunk. That tear was done a long time ago. What's the racket? A shakedown on the King?"

The girl stared at him coolly, puffed at a cigarette and said nothing.

"He checked out," Steve said. "Nothing doing in that direction now, sister." He watched her like a hawk, his black eyes hard and steady on her face.

"Aw, you house dicks make me sick!" the girl said with sudden anger. She surged to her feet and went past him into the bathroom, shut and locked the door.

Steve shrugged and felt the pulse of the girl asleep in the bed—a thumpy, draggy pulse, a liquor pulse.

"Poor damn hustlers," he said under his breath.

He looked at a large purple bag that lay on the bureau, lifted it idly and let it fall. His face stiffened again. The bag made a heavy sound on the glass top, as if there were a lump of lead inside it. He snapped it open quickly and plunged a hand in. His fingers touched the cold metal of a gun. He opened the bag wide and stared down into it at a small .25 automatic. A scrap of white paper caught his eye. He fished it out and held it to the light—a rent receipt with a name and address. He stuffed it into his pocket, closed the bag and was standing by the window when the girl came out of the bathroom.

"Hell, are you still haunting me?" she snapped. "You know what happens to hotel dicks that master-key their way into ladies' bedrooms at night?"

Steve said loosely: "Yeah. They get in trouble. They might even get shot at."

The girl's face became set, but her eyes crawled sideways and looked at the purple bag. Steve looked at her. "Know Leopardi in Frisco?" he asked. "He hasn't played here in two years. Then he was just a trumpet player in Vane Utigore's band—a cheap outfit."

The girl curled her lip, went past him and sat down by the window again. Her face was white, stiff. She said dully: "Blossom did. That's Blossom on the bed."

"Know he was coming to this hotel tonight?"

"What makes it your business?"

"I can't figure him coming here at all," Steve said. "This is a quiet place. So I can't figure anybody coming here to put the bite on him."

"Go somewhere else and figure. I need sleep."

Steve said: "Good-night, sweetheart—and keep your door locked."

A thin man with thin blond hair and thin face was standing by the desk, tapping on the marble with thin fingers. Millar was still behind the desk and he still looked white and scared. The thin man wore a dark gray suit with a scarf inside the collar of the coat. He had a look of having just got up. He turned sea-green eyes slowly on Steve as he got out of the elevator, waited for him to come up to the desk and throw a tabbed key on it.

Steve said: "Leopardi's key, George. There's a busted mirror in his room and the carpet has his dinner on it—mostly Scotch." He turned to the thin man. "You want to see me, Mr. Peters?"

"What happened, Grayce?" The thin man had a tight voice that expected to be lied to.

"Leopardi and two of his boys were on Eight, the rest of the gang on Five. The bunch on Five went to bed. A couple of obvious hustlers managed to get themselves registered just two rooms from Leopardi. They managed to contact him and everybody was having a lot of nice noisy fun out in the hall. I could only stop it by getting a little tough."

"There's blood on your cheek," Peters said coldly. "Wipe it off."

Steve scratched at his cheek with a handkerchief. The thin thread of blood had dried. "I got the girls tucked away in their room," he said. "The two stooges took the hint and holed up, but Leopardi still thought the guests wanted to hear trombone music. I threatened to wrap it around his neck and he beaned me with it. I slapped him open-handed and he pulled a gun and took a shot at me. Here's the gun."

He took the .32 automatic out of his pocket and laid it on the desk. He put the used shell beside it. "So I beat some sense into him and threw him out," he added.

Peters tapped on the marble. "Your usual tact seems to have been well in evidence."

Steve stared at him. "He shot at me," he repeated quietly. "With a gun. This gun. I'm tender to bullets. He missed, but suppose he hadn't? I like my stomach the way it is, with just one way in and one way out."

Peters narrowed his tawny eyebrows. He said very politely: "We have you down on the payroll here as a night clerk, because we don't like the name house detective. But neither night clerks nor house detectives put guests out of the hotel without consulting me. Not ever, Mr. Grayce."

Steve said: "The guy shot at me, pal. With a gun. Catch on? I don't have to take that without a kickback, do I?" His face was a little white.

Peters said: "Another point for your consideration. The controlling interest in this hotel is owned by Mr. Halsey G. Walters. Mr. Walters also owns the Club Shalotte, where King Leopardi is opening on Wednesday night. And that, Mr. Grayce, is why Leopardi was good enough to give us his business. Can you think of anything else I should like to say to you?"

"Yeah. I'm canned," Steve said mirthlessly.

"Very correct, Mr. Grayce. Good-night, Mr. Grayce."

The thin blond man moved to the elevator and the night porter took him up.

Steve looked at Millar.

"Jumbo Walters, huh?" he said softly. "A tough, smart guy. Much too smart to think this dump and the Club Shalotte belong to the same sort of customers. Did Peters write Leopardi to come here?"

"I guess he did, Steve." Millar's voice was low and gloomy.

"Then why wasn't he put in a tower suite with a private balcony to dance on, at eighteen bucks a day? Why was he put on a medium-priced transient floor? And why did Quillan let those girls get so close to him?"

Millar pulled at his black mustache. "Tight with money—as well as with Scotch, I suppose. As to the girls, I don't know."

Steve slapped the counter open-handed. "Well, I'm canned, for not letting a drunken heel make a parlor-house and a shooting-gallery out of the eighth floor. Nuts! Well, I'll miss the joint at that."

"I'll miss you too, Steve," Millar said gently. "But not for a week. I take a week off starting tomorrow. My brother has a cabin at Crestline."

"Didn't know you had a brother," Steve said absently. He opened and closed his fist on the marble desk-top.

"He doesn't come into town much. A big guy. Used to be a fighter."

Steve nodded and straightened from the counter. "Well, I might as well finish out the night," he said. "On my back. Put this gun away somewhere, George."

He grinned coldly and walked away, down the steps into the dim main lobby and across to the room where the radio was. He punched the pillows into shape on the pale-green davenport, then suddenly reached into his pocket and took out the scrap of white paper he had lifted from the black-haired girl's purple handbag. It was a receipt for a week's rent, to a Miss Marilyn Delorme, Apt. 211, Ridgeland Apartments, 118 Court Street.

He tucked it into his wallet and stood staring at the silent radio. "Steve, I think you got another job," he said under his breath. "Something about this set-up smells."

He slipped into a closet-like phone-booth in the corner of the room, dropped a nickel and dialed an all-night radio station. He had to dial four times before he got a clear line to the Owl Program announcer.

"How's to play King Leopardi's record of *Solitude* again?" he asked him.

"Got a lot of requests piled up. Played it twice already. Who's calling?"

"Steve Grayce, night man at the Carlton Hotel."

"Oh, a sober guy on his job. For you, pal, anything."

Steve went back to the davenport, snapped the radio on and lay down on his back, with his hands clasped behind his head.

Ten minutes later the high, piercingly sweet trumpet notes of King Leopardi came softly from the radio, muted almost to a whisper, and sustaining E in Alt for an almost incredible period of time.

"Shucks," Steve grumbled, when the record ended. "A guy that can play like that—maybe I was too tough with him."

3

COURT STREET was old town, wop town, crook town, arty town. It lay across the top of Bunker Hill and you could find anything there from down-at-heels ex-Greenwich Villagers to crooks on the lam, from ladies of anybody's evening to County Relief clients brawling with haggard landladies in grand old houses with scrolled porches, parquetry floors, and immense sweeping banisters of white oak, mahogany and Circassian walnut.

It had been a nice place once, had Bunker Hill, and from the days of its niceness there still remained the funny little funicular railway, called the Angel's Flight, which crawled up and down a yellow clay bank from Hill Street. It was afternoon when Steve Grayce got off the car at the top, its only passenger. He walked along in the sun, a tall, wide-shouldered, rangy-looking man in a well-cut blue suit.

He turned west at Court and began to read the numbers. The one he wanted was two from the corner, across the street from a red brick funeral parlor with a sign in gold over it—*Paolo Perrugini Funeral Home*. A swarthy iron-gray Italian in a cutaway coat stood in front of the curtained door of the red brick building, smoking a cigar and waiting for somebody to die.

118 was a three-storied frame apartment house. It had a glass door, well masked by a dirty net curtain, a hall runner eighteen inches wide, dim doors with numbers painted on them with dim paint, a staircase halfway back. Brass stair rods glittered in the dimness of the hallway.

Steve Grayce went up the stairs and prowled back to the front. Apartment 211, Miss Marilyn Delorme, was on the right, a front apartment. He tapped lightly on the wood, waited, tapped again. Nothing moved beyond the silent door, or in the hallway. Behind another door across the hall somebody coughed and kept on coughing.

Standing there in the half-light Steve Grayce wondered why he had come. Miss Delorme had carried a gun. Leopardi had received some kind of a threat letter and torn it up and thrown it away. Miss Delorme had checked out of the Carlton about an hour after Steve told her Leopardi was gone. Even at that—

He took out a leather keyholder and studied the lock of the door. It looked as if it would listen to reason. He tried a pick on it, snicked the bolt back and stepped softly into the room. He shut the door, but the pick wouldn't lock it.

The room was dim with drawn shades across two front windows. The air smelled of face powder. There was light-painted furniture, a pull-down double bed which was pulled down but had been made up. There was a magazine on it, a glass tray full of cigarette butts, a pint bottle half full of whiskey, and a glass on a chair beside the bed. Two pillows had been used for a back rest and were still crushed in the middle.

On the dresser there was a composition toilet set, neither cheap nor expensive, a comb with black hair in it, a tray of manicuring stuff, plenty of spilled powder—in the bathroom nothing. In a closet behind the bed a lot of clothes and two suitcases. The shoes were all one size.

Steve stood beside the bed and pinched his chin. "Blossom, the spitting blonde, doesn't live here," he said under his breath. "Just Marilyn the torn-pants brunette."

He went back to the dresser and pulled drawers out. In the bottom drawer, under the piece of wall paper that lined it, he found a box of .25 copper-nickel automatic shells. He poked at the butts in the ash tray. All had lipstick on them. He pinched his chin again, then feathered the air with the palm of his hand, like an oarsman with a scull.

"Bunk," he said softly. "Wasting your time, Stevie."

He walked over to the door and reached for the knob, then turned back to the bed and lifted it by the footrail.

Miss Marilyn Delorme was in.

She lay on her side on the floor under the bed, long legs scissored out as if in running. One mule was on, one off. Garters and skin showed at the tops of her stockings, and a blue rose on something pink. She wore a square-necked, beige-sleeved dress that was not too clean. Her neck above the dress was blotched with purple bruises.

Her face was a dark plum color, her eyes had the faint stale glitter of death, and her mouth was open so far that it foreshortened her face. She was colder than ice, and still quite limp. She had been dead two or three hours at least, six hours at most.

The purple bag was beside her, gaping like her mouth. Steve didn't touch any of the stuff that had been emptied out on the floor. There was no gun and there were no papers.

He let the bed down over her again, then made the rounds of the apartment, wiping everything he had touched and a lot of things he couldn't remember whether he had touched or not.

He listened at the door and stepped out. The hall was still empty. The man behind the opposite door still coughed. Steve went down the stairs, looked at the mailboxes and went back along the lower hall to a door.

Behind this door a chair creaked monotonously. He knocked and a woman's sharp voice called out. Steve opened the door with his handkerchief and stepped in.

In the middle of the room a woman rocked in an old Boston rocker, her body in the slack boneless attitude of exhaustion. She had a mud-colored face, stringy hair, gray cotton stockings—everything a Bunker Hill landlady should have. She looked at Steve with the interested eye of a dead goldfish.

"Are you the manager?"

The woman stopped rocking, screamed, "Hi, Jake! Company!" at the top of her voice, and started rocking again.

An icebox door thudded shut behind a partly open inner door and a very big man came into the room carrying a can of beer. He had a doughy mooncalf face, a tuft of fuzz on top of an otherwise bald head, a thick brutal neck and chin, and brown pig eyes about as expressionless as the woman's. He needed a shave—had needed one the day before— and his collarless shirt gaped over a big hard hairy chest. He wore scarlet suspenders with large gilt buckles on them.

He held the can of beer out to the woman. She clawed it out of his hand and said bitterly: "I'm so tired I ain't got no sense."

The man said: "Yah. You ain't done the halls so good at that."

The woman snarled: "I done 'em as good as I aim to." She sucked the beer thirstily.

Steve looked at the man and said: "Manager?"

"Yah. 'S me. Jake Stoyanoff. Two hun'erd eighty-six stripped, and still plenty tough."

Steve said: "Who lives in Two-eleven?"

The big man leaned forward a little from the waist and snapped his suspenders. Nothing changed in his eyes. The skin along his big jaw may have tightened a little. "A dame," he said.

"Alone?"

"Go on—ask me," the big man said. He stuck his hand out and lifted a cigar off the edge of a stained-wood table. The cigar was burning unevenly and it smelled as if somebody had set fire to the doormat. He pushed it into his mouth with a hard, thrusting motion, as if he expected his mouth wouldn't want it to go in.

"I'm asking you," Steve said.

"Ask me out in the kitchen," the big man drawled.

He turned and held the door open. Steve went past him.

The big man kicked the door shut against the squeak of the rocking-chair, opened up the icebox and got out two cans of beer. He opened them and handed one to Steve.

"Dick?"

Steve drank some of the beer, put the can down on the sink, got a brand-new card out of his wallet—a business card printed that morning. He handed it to the man.

The man read it, put it down on the sink, picked it up and read it again. "One of them guys," he growled over his beer. "What's she pulled this time?"

Steve shrugged and said: "I guess it's the usual. The torn-pajama act. Only there's a kickback this time."

"How come? You handling it, huh? Must be a nice cozy one."

Steve nodded. The big man blew smoke from his mouth. "Go ahead and handle it," he said.

"You don't mind a pinch here?"

The big man laughed heartily. "Nuts to you, brother," he said pleasantly enough. "You're a private dick. So it's a hush. O.K. Go out and hush it. And if it *was* a pinch—that bothers me like a quart of milk. Go into your act. Take all the room you want. Cops don't bother Jake Stoyanoff."

Steve stared at the man. He didn't say anything. The big man talked it up some more, seemed to get more interested. "Besides," he went on, making motions with the cigar, "I'm soft-hearted. I never turn up a dame. I never put a frill in the middle." He finished his beer and threw the can in a basket under the sink, and pushed his hand out in front of him, revolving the large thumb slowly against the next two fingers. "Unless there's some of that," he added.

Steve said softly: "You've got big hands. You could have done it."

"Huh?" His small brown leathery eyes got silent and stared.

Steve said: "Yeah. You might be clean as an angel's wing. But with those hands the cops'd go round and round with you just the same."

The big man moved a little to his left, away from the sink. He let his right hand hang down at his side, loosely. His mouth got so tight that the cigar almost touched his nose.

"What's the beef, huh?" he barked. "What you shovin' at me, guy? What—"

"Cut it," Steve drawled. "She's been croaked. Strangled. Upstairs, on the floor under her bed. About midmorning, I'd say. Big hands did it—hands like yours."

The big man did a nice job of getting the gun off his hip. It arrived so suddenly that it seemed to have grown in his hand and been there all the time.

Steve frowned at the gun and didn't move. The big man looked him over. "You're tough," he said. "I been in the ring long enough to size up a guy's meat. You're plenty hard, boy. But you ain't as hard as lead. Talk it up fast."

"I knocked at her door. No answer. The lock was a pushover. I went in. I almost missed her because the bed was pulled down and she had been sitting on it, reading a magazine. There was no sign of struggle. I lifted the bed just before I left—and there she was. Very dead, Mr. Stoyanoff. Put the gat away. Cops don't bother you, you said a minute ago."

The big man whispered: "Yes and no. They don't make me happy neither. I get a bump once'n a while. Mostly a Dutch. You said something about my hands, mister."

Steve shook his head. "That was a gag," he said. "Her neck has nail marks. You bite your nails down close. You're clean."

The big man didn't look at his fingers. He was very pale. There was sweat on his lower lip, in the black stubble of his beard. He was still leaning forward, still motionless, when there was a knocking beyond the kitchen door, the door from the living-room to the hallway. The creaking chair stopped and the woman's sharp voice screamed: "Hi, Jake! Company!"

The big man cocked his head. "That old slut wouldn't climb off'n her fanny if the house caught fire," he said thickly.

He stepped to the door and slipped through it, locking it behind him.

Steve ranged the kitchen swiftly with his eyes. There was a small high window beyond the sink, a trap low down for a garbage pail and parcels, but no other door. He reached for his card Stoyanoff had left lying on the drainboard and slipped it back into his pocket. Then he took a short-barreled Detective Special out of his left breast pocket where he wore it nose down, as in a holster.

He had got that far when the shots roared beyond the wall—muffled a little, but still loud—four of them blended in a blast of sound.

Steve stepped back and hit the kitchen door with his leg out straight.

It held and jarred him to the top of his head and in his hip joint. He swore, took the whole width of the kitchen and slammed into it with his left shoulder. It gave this time. He pitched into the living-room. The mud-faced woman sat leaning forward in her rocker, her head to one side and a lock of mousy hair smeared down over her bony forehead.

"Backfire, huh?" she said stupidly. "Sounded kinda close. Musta been in the alley."

Steve jumped across the room, yanked the outer door open and plunged out into the hall.

The big man was still on his feet, a dozen feet down the hallway, in the direction of a screen door that opened flush on an alley. He was clawing at the wall. His gun lay at his feet. His left knee buckled and he went down on it.

A door was flung open and a hard-looking woman peered out, and instantly slammed her door shut again. A radio suddenly gained in volume beyond her door.

The big man got up off his left knee and the leg shook violently inside his trousers. He went down on both knees and got the gun into his hand and began to crawl towards the screen door. Then, suddenly he went down flat on his face and tried to crawl that way, grinding his face into the narrow hall runner.

Then he stopped crawling and stopped moving altogether. His body went limp and the hand holding the gun opened and the gun rolled out of it.

Steve hit the screen door and was out in the alley. A gray sedan was speeding towards the far end of it. He stopped, steadied himself and brought his gun up level, and the sedan whisked out of sight around the corner.

A man boiled out of another apartment house across the alley. Steve ran on, gesticulating back at him and pointing ahead. As he ran he slipped the gun back into his pocket. When he reached the end of the alley, the gray sedan was out of sight. Steve skidded around the wall onto the sidewalk, slowed to a walk and then stopped.

Half a block down a man finished parking a car, got out and went across the sidewalk to a lunchroom. Steve watched him go in, then straightened his hat and walked along the wall to the lunchroom.

He went in, sat at the counter and ordered coffee. In a little while there were sirens.

Steve drank his coffee, asked for another cup and drank that. He lit a cigarette and walked down the long hill to Fifth, across to Hill, back to the foot of the Angel's Flight, and got his convertible out of a parking lot.

He drove out west, beyond Vermont, to the small hotel where he had taken a room that morning.

4

BILL DOCKERY, floor manager of the Club Shalotte, teetered on his heels and yawned in the unlighted entrance to the dining-room. It was a dead hour for business, late cocktail time, too early for dinner, and much too early for the real business of the club, which was high-class gambling.

Dockery was a handsome mug in a midnight-blue dinner jacket and a maroon carnation. He had a two-inch forehead under black lacquer hair, good features a little on the heavy side, alert brown eyes and very long curly eyelashes which he liked to let down over his eyes, to fool troublesome drunks into taking a swing at him.

The entrance door of the foyer was opened by the uniformed door-man and Steve Grayce came in.

Dockery said, "Ho, hum," tapped his teeth and leaned his weight forward. He walked across the lobby slowly to meet the guest. Steve stood just inside the doors and ranged his eyes over the high foyer walled with milky glass, lighted softly from behind. Molded in the glass were etchings of sailing-ships, beasts of the jungle, Siamese pagodas, temples of Yucatan. The doors were square frames of chromium, like photo frames. The Club Shalotte had all the class there was, and the mutter of voices from the bar lounge on the left was not noisy. The faint Spanish music behind the voices was delicate as a carved fan.

Dockery came up and leaned his sleek head forward an inch. "May I help you?"

"King Leopardi around?"

Dockery leaned back again. He looked less interested. "The band-leader? He opens tomorrow night."

"I thought he might be around—rehearsing or something."

"Friend of his?"

"I know him. I'm not job-hunting, and I'm not a song-plugger if that's what you mean."

Dockery teetered on his heels. He was tone deaf and Leopardi meant no more to him than a bag of peanuts. He half smiled. "He was in the bar lounge a while ago." He pointed with his square rock-like chin. Steve Grayce went into the bar lounge.

It was about a third full, warm and comfortable and not too dark nor too light. The little Spanish orchestra was in an archway, playing with muted strings small seductive melodies that were more like memories than sounds. There was no dance floor. There was a long bar with comfortable seats, and there were small round composition-top tables, not too close together. A wall seat ran around three sides of the room. Waiters flitted among the tables like moths.

Steve Grayce saw Leopardi in the far corner, with a girl. There was an empty table on each side of him. The girl was a knockout.

She looked tall and her hair was the color of a brush-fire seen through a dust cloud. On it, at the ultimate rakish angle, she wore a black velvet double-pointed beret with two artificial butterflies made of polka-dotted feathers and fastened on with tall silver pins. Her dress was burgundy-red wool and the blue fox draped over one shoulder was at least a foot wide. Her eyes were large, smoke-blue, and looked bored. She slowly turned a small glass on the tabletop with a gloved left hand.

Leopardi faced her, leaning forward, talking. His shoulders looked very big in a shaggy, cream-colored sports coat. Above the neck of it his hair made a point on his brown neck. He laughed across the table as Steve came up, and his laugh had a confident, sneering sound.

Steve stopped, then moved behind the next table. The movement caught Leopardi's eye. His head turned, he looked annoyed, and then his eyes got very wide and brilliant and his whole body turned slowly, like a mechanical toy.

Leopardi put both his rather small well-shaped hands down on the table, on either side of a highball glass. He smiled. Then he pushed his chair back and stood up. He put one finger up and touched his hair-line mustache, with theatrical delicacy. Then he said drawlingly, but distinctly: "You ———— —— — ————!"

A man at a near-by table turned his head and scowled. A waiter who had started to come over stopped in his tracks, then faded back among the tables. The girl looked at Steve Grayce and then leaned back against the cushion of the wall seat and moistened the end of one bare finger on her right hand and smoothed a chestnut eyebrow.

Steve stood quite still. There was a sudden high flush on his cheekbones. He said softly: "You left something at the hotel last night. I think you ought to do something about it. Here."

He reached a folded paper out of his pocket and held it out. Leopardi took it, still smiling, opened it and read it. It was a sheet of yellow paper with torn pieces of white paper pasted on it. Leopardi crumpled the sheet and let it drop at his feet.

He took a smooth step towards Steve and repeated more loudly: "You ——— —— — ———!"

The man who had first looked around stood up sharply and turned. He said clearly: "I don't like that sort of language in front of my wife."

Without even looking at the man Leopardi said: "To hell with you and your wife."

The man's face got a dusky red. The woman with him stood up and grabbed a bag and a coat and walked away. After a moment's indecision the man followed her. Everybody in the place was staring now. The waiter who had faded back among the tables went through the doorway into the entrance foyer, walking very quickly.

Leopardi took another, longer step and slammed Steve Grayce on the jaw. Steve rolled with the punch and stepped back and put his hand down on another table and upset a glass. He turned to apologize to the couple at the table. Leopardi jumped forward very fast and hit him behind the ear.

Dockery came through the doorway, split two waiters like a banana skin and started down the room showing all his teeth.

Steve gagged a little and ducked away. He turned and said thickly: "Wait a minute, you fool—that isn't all of it—there's—"

Leopardi closed in fast and smashed him full on the mouth. Blood oozed from Steve's lip and crawled down the line at the corner of his mouth and glistened on his chin. The girl with the red hair reached for her bag, white-faced with anger, and started to get up from behind her table.

Leopardi turned abruptly on his heel and walked away. Dockery put out a hand to stop him. Leopardi brushed it aside and went on, went out of the lounge.

The tall red-haired girl put her bag down on the table again and dropped her handkerchief on the floor. She looked at Steve quietly, spoke quietly. "Wipe the blood off your chin before it drips on your shirt." She had a soft, husky voice with a trill in it.

Dockery came up harsh-faced, took Steve by the arm and put weight on the arm. "All right, you! Let's go!"

Steve stood quite still, his feet planted, staring at the girl. He dabbed at his mouth with a handkerchief. He half smiled. Dockery couldn't move him an inch. Dockery dropped his hand, signaled two waiters and they jumped behind Steve, but didn't touch him.

Steve felt his lip carefully and looked at the blood on his handkerchief. He turned to the people at the table behind him and said: "I'm terribly sorry. I lost my balance."

The girl whose drink he had spilled was mopping her dress with a small fringed napkin. She smiled up at him and said: "It wasn't your fault."

The two waiters suddenly grabbed Steve's arms from behind. Dockery shook his head and they let go again. Dockery said tightly: "You hit him?"

"No."

"You say anything to make him hit you?"

"No."

The girl at the corner table bent down to get her fallen handkerchief. It took her quite a time. She finally got it and slid into the corner behind the table again. She spoke coldly.

"Quite right, Bill. It was just some more of the King's sweet way with his public."

Dockery said "Huh?" and swiveled his head on his thick hard neck. Then he grinned and looked back at Steve.

Steve said grimly: "He gave me three good punches, one from behind, without a return. You look pretty hard. See can you do it."

Dockery measured him with his eyes. He said evenly: "You win. I couldn't . . . Beat it!" he added sharply to the waiters. They went away. Dockery sniffed his carnation, and said quietly: "We don't go for brawls in here." He smiled at the girl again and went away, saying a word here and there at the tables. He went out through the foyer doors.

Steve tapped his lip, put his handkerchief in his pocket and stood searching the floor with his eyes.

The red-haired girl said calmly: "I think I have what you want—in my handkerchief. Won't you sit down?"

Her voice had a remembered quality, as if he had heard it before.

He sat down opposite her, in the chair where Leopardi had been sitting.

The red-haired girl said: "The drink's on me. I was with him."

Steve said, "Coke with a dash of bitters," to the waiter.

The waiter said: "Madame?"

"Brandy and soda. Light on the brandy, please." The waiter bowed and drifted away. The girl said amusedly: "Coke with a dash of bitters. That's what I love about Hollywood. You meet so many neurotics."

Steve stared into her eyes and said softly: "I'm an occasional drinker, the kind of guy who goes out for a beer and wakes up in Singapore with a full beard."

"I don't believe a word of it. Have you known the King long?"

"I met him last night. I didn't get along with him."

"I sort of noticed that." She laughed. She had a rich low laugh, too.

"Give me that paper, lady."

"Oh, one of these impatient men. Plenty of time." The handkerchief with the crumpled yellow sheet inside it was clasped tightly in her gloved hand. Her middle right finger played with an eyebrow. "You're not in pictures, are you?"

"Hell, no."

"Same here. Me, I'm too tall. The beautiful men have to wear stilts in order to clasp me to their bosoms."

The waiter set the drinks down in front of them, made a few grace notes in the air with his napkin and went away.

Steve said quietly, stubbornly: "Give me that paper, lady."

"I don't like that 'lady' stuff. It sounds like cop to me."

"I don't know your name."

"I don't know yours. Where did you meet Leopardi?"

Steve sighed. The music from the little Spanish orchestra had a melancholy minor sound now and the muffled clicking of gourds dominated it.

Steve listened to it with his head on one side. He said: "The E string is a half-tone flat. Rather cute effect."

The girl stared at him with new interest. "I'd never have noticed that," she said. "And I'm supposed to be a pretty good singer. But you haven't answered my question."

He said slowly: "Last night I was house dick at the Carlton Hotel. They called me night clerk, but house dick was what I was. Leopardi stayed there and cut up too rough. I threw him out and got canned."

The girl said: "Ah. I begin to get the idea. He was being the King and you were being—if I might guess—a pretty tough order of house detective."

"Something like that. Now will you please—"

"You still haven't told me your name."

He reached for his wallet, took one of the brand-new cards out of it and passed it across the table. He sipped his drink while she read it.

"A nice name," she said slowly. "But not a very good address. And *Private Investigator* is bad. It should have been *Investigations,* very small, in the lower left-hand corner."

"They'll be small enough," Steve grinned. "Now will you please—"

She reached suddenly across the table and dropped the crumpled ball of paper in his hand.

"Of course I haven't read it—and of course I'd like to. You do give me that much credit, I hope"—she looked at the card again, and added—"Steve. Yes, and your office should be in a Georgian or very modernistic building in the Sunset Eighties. Suite Something-or-other. And your clothes should be very jazzy. Very jazzy indeed, Steve. To be inconspicuous in this town is to be a busted flush."

He grinned at her. His deep-set black eyes had lights in them. She put the card away in her bag, gave her fur piece a yank, and drank about half of her drink. "I have to go." She signaled the waiter and paid the check. The waiter went away and she stood up.

Steve said sharply: "Sit down."

She stared at him wonderingly. Then she sat down again and leaned against the wall, still staring at him. Steve leaned across the table, asked: "How well do *you* know Leopardi?"

"Off and on for years. If it's any of your business. Don't go masterful on me, for God's sake. I loathe masterful men. I once sang for him, but not for long. You can't just sing for Leopardi—if you get what I mean."

"You were having a drink with him."

She nodded slightly and shrugged. "He opens here tomorrow night. He was trying to talk me into singing for him again. I said no, but I may have to, for a week or two anyway. The man who owns the Club Shalotte also owns my contract—and the radio station where I work a good deal."

"Jumbo Walters," Steve said. "They say he's tough but square. I never met him, but I'd like to. After all I've got a living to get. Here."

He reached back across the table and dropped the crumpled paper. "The name was—"

"Dolores Chiozza."

Steve repeated it lingeringly. "I like it. I like your singing too. I've heard a lot of it. You don't oversell a song, like most of these high-money torchers." His eyes glistened.

The girl spread the paper on the table and read it slowly, without expression. Then she said quietly: "Who tore it up?"

"Leopardi, I guess. The pieces were in his wastebasket last night. I put them together, after he was gone. The guy has guts—or else he gets these things so often they don't register any more."

"Or else he thought it was a gag." She looked across the table levelly, then folded the paper and handed it back.

"Maybe. But if he's the kind of guy I hear he is—one of them is going to be on the level and the guy behind it is going to do more than just shake him down."

Dolores Chiozza said: "He's the kind of guy you hear he is."

"It wouldn't be hard for a woman to get to him then—would it—a woman with a gun?"

She went on staring at him. "No. And everybody would give her a big hand, if you ask me. If I were you, I'd just forget the whole thing. If he wants protection—Walters can throw more around him than the police. If he doesn't—who cares? I don't. I'm damn sure I don't."

"You're kind of tough yourself, Miss Chiozza—over some things."

She said nothing. Her face was a little white and more than a little hard.

Steve finished his drink, pushed his chair back and reached for his hat. He stood up. "Thank you very much for the drink, Miss Chiozza. Now that I've met you I'll look forward all the more to hearing you sing again."

"You're damn formal all of a sudden," she said.

He grinned. "So long, Dolores."

"So long, Steve. Good luck—in the sleuth racket. If I hear of anything—"

He turned and walked among the tables out of the bar lounge.

5

IN THE crisp fall evening the lights of Hollywood and Los Angeles winked at him. Searchlight beams probed the cloudless sky as if searching for bombing-planes.

Steve got his convertible out of the parking-lot and drove it east along Sunset. At Sunset and Fairfax he bought an evening paper and pulled over to the curb to look through it. There was nothing in the paper about 118 Court Street.

He drove on and ate dinner at the little coffee shop beside his hotel and went to a movie. When he came out he bought a Home Edition of the *Tribune,* a morning sheet. They were in that—both of them.

Police thought Jake Stoyanoff might have strangled the girl, but she had not been attacked. She was described as a stenographer, unemployed at the moment. There was no picture of her. There was a picture of Stoyanoff that looked like a touched-up police photo. Police were looking for a man who had been talking to Stoyanoff just before he was shot. Several people said he was a tall man in a dark suit. That was all the description the police got—or gave out.

Steve grinned sourly, stopped at the coffee shop for a good-night cup of coffee and then went up to his room. It was a few minutes to eleven o'clock. As he unlocked his door the telephone started to ring.

He shut the door and stood in the darkness remembering where the phone was. Then he walked straight to it, catlike in the dark room, sat in an easy chair and reached the phone up from the lower shelf of a small table. He held the one-piece to his ear and said: "Hello."

"Is this Steve?" It was a rich, husky voice, low, vibrant. It held a note of strain.

"Yeah, this is Steve. I can hear you. I know who you are."

There was a faint dry laugh. "You'll make a detective after all. And it seems I'm to give you your first case. Will you come over to my place at once? It's Twenty-four-twelve Renfrew—North, there isn't any South—just half a block below Fountain. It's a sort of bungalow court. My house is the last in line, at the back."

Steve said: "Yes. Sure. What's the matter?"

There was a pause. A horn blared in the street outside the hotel. A wave of white light went across the ceiling from some car rounding the corner uphill. The low voice said very slowly: "Leopardi. I can't get rid of him. He's—he's passed out in my bedroom." Then a tinny laugh that didn't go with the voice at all.

Steve held the phone so tight his hand ached. His teeth clicked in the darkness. He said flatly, in a dull, brittle voice: "Yeah. It'll cost you twenty bucks."

"Of course. Hurry, please."

He hung up, sat there in the dark room breathing hard. He pushed his hat back on his head, then yanked it forward again with a vicious jerk and laughed out loud. "Hell," he said. "*That* kind of a dame."

2412 Renfrew was not strictly a bungalow court. It was a staggered row of six bungalows, all facing the same way, but so arranged that no two of their front entrances overlooked each other. There was a brick wall at the back and beyond the brick wall a church. There was a long smooth lawn, moon-silvered.

The door was up two steps, with lanterns on each side and an ironwork grill over the peep hole. This opened to his knock and a girl's face looked out, a small oval face with a Cupid's-bow mouth, arched and plucked eyebrows, wavy brown hair. The eyes were like two fresh and shiny chestnuts.

Steve dropped a cigarette and put his foot on it. "Miss Chiozza. She's expecting me. Steve Grayce."

"Miss Chiozza has retired, sir," the girl said with a half-insolent twist to her lips.

"Break it up, kid. You heard me, I'm expected."

The wicket slammed shut. He waited, scowling back along the narrow moonlit lawn towards the street. O. K. So it was like that—well, twenty bucks was worth a ride in the moonlight anyway.

The lock clicked and the door opened wide. Steve went past the maid into a warm cheerful room, old-fashioned with chintz. The lamps were neither old nor new and there were enough of them—in the right places. There was a hearth behind a paneled copper screen, a davenport close to it, a bar-top radio in the corner.

The maid said stiffly: "I'm sorry, sir. Miss Chiozza forgot to tell me. Please to have a chair." The voice was soft, and it might be cagey. The girl went off down the room—short skirts, sheer silk stockings, and four-inch spike heels.

Steve sat down and held his hat on his knee and scowled at the wall. A swing-door creaked shut. He got a cigarette out and rolled it between his fingers and then deliberately squeezed it to a shapeless flatness of white paper and ragged tobacco. He threw it away from him, at the fire screen.

Dolores Chiozza came towards him. She wore green velvet lounging pajamas with a long gold-fringed sash. She spun the end of the sash as if she might be going to throw a loop with it. She smiled a slight artificial smile. Her face had a clean scrubbed look and her eyelids were bluish and they twitched.

Steve stood up and watched the green morocco slippers peep out under the pajamas as she walked. When she was close to him he lifted his eyes to her face and said dully: "Hello."

She looked at him very steadily, then spoke in a high, carrying voice. "I know it's late, but I knew you were used to being up all night. So I thought what we had to talk over— Won't you sit down?"

She turned her head very slightly, seemed to be listening for something.

Steve said: "I never go to bed before two. Quite all right."

She went over and pushed a bell beside the hearth. After a moment the maid came through the arch.

"Bring some ice cubes, Agatha. Then go along home. It's getting pretty late."

"Yes'm." The girl disappeared.

There was a silence then that almost howled till the tall girl took a cigarette absently out of a box, put it between her lips and Steve struck a match clumsily on his shoe. She pushed the end of the cigarette into the flame and her smoke-blue eyes were very steady on his black ones. She shook her head very slightly.

The maid came back with a copper ice-bucket. She pulled a low Indian-brass tray-table between them before the davenport, put the ice-bucket on it, then a siphon, glasses and spoons, and a triangular bottle that looked like good Scotch had come in it except that it was covered with silver filigree work and fitted with a stopper.

Dolores Chiozza said, "Will you mix a drink?" in a formal voice.

He mixed two drinks, stirred them, handed her one. She sipped it, shook her head. "Too light," she said. He put more whiskey in it and handed it back. She said, "Better," and leaned back against the corner of the davenport.

The maid came into the room again. She had a small rakish red hat on her wavy brown hair and was wearing a gray coat trimmed with nice fur. She carried a black brocade bag that could have cleaned out a fair-sized ice-box. She said: "Good night, Miss Dolores."

"Good-night, Agatha."

The girl went out the front door, closed it softly. Her heels clicked down the walk. A car door opened and shut distantly and a motor started. Its sound soon dwindled away. It was a very quiet neighborhood.

Steve put his drink down on the brass tray and looked levelly at the tall girl, said harshly: "That means she's out of the way?"

"Yes. She goes home in her own car. She drives me home from the studio in mine—when I go to the studio, which I did tonight. I don't like to drive a car myself."

"Well, what are we waiting for?"

The red-haired girl looked steadily at the paneled fire-screen and the unlit log fire behind it. A muscle twitched in her cheek.

After a moment she said: "Funny that I called you instead of Walters. He'd have protected me better than you can. Only he wouldn't have believed me. I thought perhaps you would. I didn't invite Leopardi here. So far as I know—we two are the only people in the world who know he's here."

Something in her voice jerked Steve upright.

She took a small crisp handkerchief from the breast pocket of the green velvet pajama-suit, dropped it on the floor, picked it up swiftly and pressed it against her mouth. Suddenly, without making a sound, she began to shake like a leaf.

Steve said swiftly: "What the hell—I can handle that heel in my hip pocket. I did last night—and last night he had a gun and took a shot at me."

Her head turned. Her eyes were very wide and staring. "But it couldn't have been my gun," she said in a dead voice.

"Huh? Of course not—what—?"

"It's my gun tonight," she said and stared at him. "You said a woman could get to him with a gun very easily."

He just stared at her. His face was white now and he made a vague sound in his throat.

"He's not drunk, Steve," she said gently. "He's dead. In yellow pajamas—in my bed. With my gun in his hand. You didn't think he was just drunk—did you, Steve?"

He stood up in a swift lunge, then became absolutely motionless, staring down at her. He moved his tongue on his lips and after a long time he formed words with it. "Let's go look at him," he said in a hushed voice.

6

THE ROOM was at the back of the house to the left. The girl took a key out of her pocket and unlocked the door. There was a low light on a table, and the Venetian blinds were drawn. Steve went in past her silently, on cat feet.

Leopardi lay squarely in the middle of the bed, a large smooth silent man, waxy and artificial in death. Even his mustache looked phony. His half-open eyes, sightless as marbles, looked as if they had never seen. He lay on his back, on the sheet, and the bedclothes were thrown over the foot of the bed.

The King wore yellow silk pajamas, the slip-on kind, with a turned collar. They were loose and thin. Over his breast they were dark with blood that had seeped into the silk as if into blotting-paper. There was a little blood on his bare brown neck.

Steve stared at him and said tonelessly: "The King in Yellow. I read a book with that title once. He liked yellow, I guess. I packed some of his stuff last night. And he wasn't yellow either. Guys like him usually are—or are they?"

The girl went over to the corner and sat down in a slipper chair and looked at the floor. It was a nice room, as modernistic as the living-room was casual. It had a chenille rug, café-au-lait color, severely angled furniture in inlaid wood, and a trick dresser with a mirror for a top, a kneehole and drawers like a desk. It had a box mirror above and a semi-cylindrical frosted wall-light set above the mirror. In the corner there was a glass table with a crystal greyhound on top of it, and a lamp with the deepest drum shade Steve had ever seen.

He stopped looking at all this and looked at Leopardi again. He pulled the King's pajamas down gently and examined the wound. It was directly over the heart and the skin was scorched and mottled there. There was not so very much blood. He had died in a fraction of a second.

A small Mauser automatic lay cuddled in his right hand, on top of the bed's second pillow.

"That's artistic," Steve said and pointed. "Yeah, that's a nice touch. Typical contact wound, I guess. He even pulled his pajama shirt down. I've heard they do that. A Mauser Seven Sixty-three about. Sure it's your gun?"

"Yes." She kept on looking at the floor. "It was in a desk in the living-room—not loaded. But there were shells. I don't know why. Somebody gave it to me once. I didn't even know how to load it."

Steve smiled. Her eyes lifted suddenly and she saw the smile and shuddered. "I don't expect anybody to believe that," she said. "We may as well call the police, I suppose."

Steve nodded absently, put a cigarette in his mouth and flipped it up and down with his lips that were still puffy from Leopardi's punch. He lit a match on his thumbnail, puffed a small plume of smoke and said quietly: "No cops. Not yet. Just tell it."

The red-haired girl said: "I sing at KFQC, you know. Three nights a week—on a quarter-hour automobile program. This was one of the nights. Agatha and I got home—oh, close to half past ten. At the door I remembered there was no fizzwater in the house, so I sent her back to the liquor store three blocks away, and came in alone. There was a queer smell in the house. I don't know what it was. As if several men had been in here, somehow. When I came in the bedroom—he was exactly as he is now. I saw the gun and I went and looked and then I knew I was sunk. I didn't know what to do. Even if the police cleared me, everywhere I went from now on—"

Steve said sharply: "He got in here—how?"

"I don't know."

"Go on," he said.

"I locked the door. Then I undressed—with that on my bed. I went into the bathroom to shower and collect my brains, if any. I locked the door when I left the room and took the key. Agatha was back then, but I don't think she saw me. Well, I took the shower and it braced me up a bit. Then I had a drink and then I came in here and called you."

She stopped and moistened the end of a finger and smoothed the end of her left eyebrow with it. "That's all, Steve—absolutely all."

"Domestic help can be pretty nosy. This Agatha's nosier than most— or I miss my guess." He walked over to the door and looked at the lock. "I bet there are three or four keys in the house that knock this over." He went to the windows and felt the catches, looked down at the screens through the glass. He said over his shoulder, casually: "Was the King in love with you?"

Her voice was sharp, almost angry. "He never was in love with any woman. A couple of years back in San Francisco, when I was with his band for a while, there was some slapsilly publicity about us. Nothing to it. It's been revived here in the hand-outs to the press, to build up his opening. I was telling him this afternoon I wouldn't stand for it, that I wouldn't be linked with him in anybody's mind. His private life was filthy. It reeked. Everybody in the business knows that. And it's not a business where daisies grow very often."

Steve said: "Yours was the only bedroom he couldn't make?"

The girl flushed to the roots of her dusky red hair.

"That sounds lousy," he said. "But I have to figure the angles. That's about true, isn't it?"

"Yes—I suppose so. I wouldn't say the only one."

"Go on out in the other room and buy yourself a drink."

She stood up and looked at him squarely across the bed. "I didn't kill him, Steve. I didn't let him into this house tonight. I didn't know he was coming here, or had any reason to come here. Believe that or not. But something about this is wrong. Leopardi was the last man in the world to take his lovely life himself."

Steve said: "He didn't, angel. Go buy that drink. He was murdered. The whole thing is a frame—to get a cover-up from Jumbo Walters. Go on out."

He stood silent, motionless, until sounds he heard from the living-room told him she was out there. Then he took out his handkerchief and loosened the gun from Leopardi's right hand and wiped it over carefully on the outside, broke out the magazine and wiped that off, spilled out all the shells and wiped every one, ejected the one in the breech and wiped that. He reloaded the gun and put it back in Leopardi's dead hand and closed his fingers around it and pushed his index finger against the trigger. Then he let the hand fall naturally back on the bed.

He pawed through the bedclothes and found an ejected shell and wiped that off, put it back where he had found it. He put the handkerchief to his nose, sniffed it wryly, went around the bed to a clothes closet and opened the door.

"Careless of your clothes, boy," he said softly.

The rough cream-colored coat hung in there, on a hook, over dark gray slacks with a lizard-skin belt. A yellow satin shirt and a wine-colored tie, dangled alongside. A handkerchief to match the tie flowed loosely four inches from the breast pocket of the coat. On the floor lay a pair of gazelle-leather nutmeg-brown sports shoes, and socks without garters. And there were yellow satin shorts with heavy black initials on them lying close by.

Steve felt carefully in the gray slacks and got out a leather keyholder. He left the room, went along the cross-hall and into the kitchen. It had a solid door, a good spring lock with a key stuck in it. He took it out and tried keys from the bunch in the keyholder, found none that fitted, put the other key back and went into the living-room. He opened the front door, went outside and shut it again without looking at the girl huddled in a corner of the davenport. He tried keys in the lock, finally found the right one. He let himself back into the house, returned to the bedroom and put the keyholder in the pocket of the gray slacks again. Then he went back to the living-room.

The girl was still huddled motionless, staring at him.

He put his back to the mantel and puffed at a cigarette. "Agatha with you all the time at the studio?"

She nodded. "I suppose so. So he had a key. That was what you were doing, wasn't it?"

"Yes. Had Agatha long?"

"About a year."

"She steal from you? Small stuff, I mean?"

Dolores Chiozza shrugged wearily. "What does it matter? Most of them do. A little face cream or powder, a handkerchief, a pair of stockings once in a while. Yes, I think she stole from me. They look on that sort of thing as more or less legitimate."

"Not the nice ones, angel."

"Well—the hours were a little trying. I work at night, often get home very late. She's a dresser as well as a maid."

"Anything else about her? She use cocaine or weed. Hit the bottle? Ever have laughing fits?"

"I don't think so. What has she got to do with it, Steve?"

"Lady, she sold somebody a key to your apartment. That's obvious. You didn't give him one, the landlord wouldn't give him one, but Agatha had one. Check?"

Her eyes had a stricken look. Her mouth trembled a little, not much. A drink was untasted at her elbow. Steve bent over and drank some of it.

She said slowly: "We're wasting time, Steve. We have to call the police. There's nothing anybody can do. I'm done for as a nice person, even if not as a lady at large. They'll think it was a lovers' quarrel and I shot him and that's that. If I could convince them I didn't, then he shot himself in my bed, and I'm still ruined. So I might as well make up my mind to face the music."

Steve said softly: "Watch this. My mother used to do it."

He put a finger to his mouth, bent down and touched her lips at the same spot with the same finger. He smiled, said: "We'll go to Walters— or you will. He'll pick his cops and the ones he picks won't go screaming through the night with reporters sitting in their laps. They'll sneak in quiet, like process-servers. Walters can handle this. That was what was counted on. Me, I'm going to collect Agatha. Because I want a description of the guy she sold that key to—and I want it fast. And by the way, you owe me twenty bucks for coming over here. Don't let that slip your memory."

The tall girl stood up, smiling. "You're a kick, you are," she said. "What makes you so sure he was murdered?"

"He's not wearing his own pajamas. His have his initials on them. I packed his stuff last night—before I threw him out of the Carlton. Get dressed, angel—and get me Agatha's address."

He went into the bedroom and pulled a sheet over Leopardi's body, held it a moment above the still waxen face before letting it fall.

"So long, guy," he said gently. "You were a louse—but you sure had music in you."

It was a small frame house on Brighton Avenue near Jefferson, in a block of small frame houses, all old-fashioned, with front porches. This one had a narrow concrete walk which the moon made whiter than it was.

Steve mounted the steps and looked at the light-edged shade of the wide front window. He knocked. There were shuffling steps and a woman opened the door and looked at him through the hooked screen —a dumpy elderly woman with frizzled gray hair. Her body was shapeless in a wrapper and her feet slithered in loose slippers. A man with a polished bald head and milky eyes sat in a wicker chair beside a table. He held his hands in his lap and twisted the knuckles aimlessly. He didn't look towards the door.

Steve said: "I'm from Miss Chiozza. Are you Agatha's mother?"

The woman said dully: "I reckon. But she ain't home, mister." The man in the chair got a handkerchief from somewhere and blew his nose. He snickered darkly.

Steve said: "Miss Chiozza's not feeling so well tonight. She was hoping Agatha would come back and stay the night with her."

The milky-eyed man snickered again, sharply. The woman said: "We dunno where she is. She don't come home. Pa 'n me waits up for her to come home. She stays out till we're sick."

The old man snapped in a reedy voice: "She'll stay out till the cops get her one of these times."

"Pa's half blind," the woman said. "Makes him kinda mean. Won't you step in?"

Steve shook his head and turned his hat around in his hands like a bashful cowpuncher in a horse opera. "I've got to find her," he said. "Where would she go?"

"Out drinkin' liquor with cheap spenders," Pa cackled. "Pantywaists with silk handkerchiefs 'stead of neckties. If I had eyes, I'd strap her till she dropped." He grabbed the arms of his chair and the muscles knotted on the backs of his hands. Then he began to cry. Tears welled from his milky eyes and started through the white stubble on his cheeks. The woman went across and took the handkerchief out of his fist and wiped his face with it. Then she blew her nose on it and came back to the door.

"Might be anywhere," she said to Steve. "This is a big town, mister. I dunno where at to say."

Steve said dully: "I'll call back. If she comes in, will you hang onto her. What's your phone number?"

"What's the phone number, Pa?" the woman called back over her shoulder.

"I ain't sayin'," Pa snorted.

The woman said: "I remember now. South Two-four-five-four. Call any time. Pa 'n me ain't got nothing to do."

Steve thanked her and went back down the white walk to the street and along the walk half a block to where he had left his car. He glanced idly across the way and started to get into his car, then stopped moving suddenly with his hand gripping the car door. He let go of that, took three steps sideways and stood looking across the street tight-mouthed.

All the houses in the block were much the same, but the one opposite had a *FOR RENT* placard stuck in the front window and a real-estate sign spiked into the small patch of front lawn. The house itself looked neglected, utterly empty, but in its little driveway stood a small neat black coupé.

Steve said under his breath: "Hunch. Play it up, Stevie."

He walked almost delicately across the wide dusty street, his hand touching the hard metal of the gun in his pocket, and came up behind the little car, stood and listened. He moved silently along its left side, glanced back across the street, then looked in the car's open left-front window.

The girl sat almost as if driving, except that her head was tipped a little too much into the corner. The little red hat was still on her head, the gray coat, trimmed with fur, still around her body. In the reflected moonlight her mouth was strained open. Her tongue stuck out. And her chestnut eyes stared at the roof of the car.

Steve didn't touch her. He didn't have to touch her or look any closer to know there would be heavy bruises on her neck.

"Tough on women, these guys," he muttered.

The girl's big black brocade bag lay on the seat beside her, gaping open like her mouth—like Miss Marilyn Delorme's mouth, and Miss Marilyn Delorme's purple bag.

"Yeah—tough on women."

He backed away till he stood under a small palm tree by the entrance to the driveway. The street was as empty and deserted as a closed theater. He crossed silently to his car, got into it and drove away.

Nothing to it. A girl coming home alone late at night, stuck up and strangled a few doors from her own home by some tough guy. Very simple. The first prowl car that cruised that block—if the boys were half awake—would take a look the minute they spotted the *FOR RENT* sign. Steve tramped hard on the throttle and went away from there.

At Washington and Figueroa he went into an all-night drug store and pulled shut the door of the phone booth at the back. He dropped his nickel and dialed the number of police headquarters.

He asked for the desk and said: "Write this down, will you, sergeant? Brighton Avenue, thirty-two-hundred block, west side, in driveway of empty house. Got that much?"

"Yeah. So what?"

"Car with dead woman in it," Steve said, and hung up.

7

QUILLAN, HEAD day clerk and assistant manager of the Carlton Hotel, was on night duty, because Millar, the night auditor, was off for a week. It was half past one and things were dead and Quillan was bored. He had done everything there was to do long ago, because he had been a hotel man for twenty years and there was nothing to it.

The night porter had finished cleaning up and was in his room beside the elevator bank. One elevator was lighted and open, as usual. The main lobby had been tidied up and the lights had been properly dimmed. Everything was exactly as usual.

Quillan was a rather short, rather thickset man with clear bright toadlike eyes that seemed to hold a friendly expression without really having any expression at all. He had pale sandy hair and not much of it. His pale hands were clasped in front of him on the marble top of the desk. He was just the right height to put his weight on the desk without looking as if he were sprawling. He was looking at the wall across the entrance lobby, but he wasn't seeing it. He was half asleep, even though his eyes were wide open, and if the night porter struck a match behind his door, Quillan would know it and bang on his bell.

The brass-trimmed swing-doors at the street entrance pushed open and Steve Grayce came in, a summer-weight coat turned up around his neck, his hat yanked low and a cigarette wisping smoke at the corner of his mouth. He looked very casual, very alert, and very much at ease. He strolled over to the desk and rapped on it.

"Wake up!" he snorted.

Quillan moved his eyes an inch and said: "All outside rooms with bath. But positively no parties on the eighth floor. Hiyah, Steve. So you finally got the axe. And for the wrong thing. That's life."

Steve said: "O.K. Have you got a new night man here?"

"Don't need one, Steve. Never did, in my opinion."

"You'll need one as long as old hotel men like you register floozies on the same corridor with people like Leopardi."

Quillan half closed his eyes and then opened them to where they had been before. He said indifferently: "Not me, pal. But anybody can make a mistake. Millar's really an accountant—not a desk man."

Steve leaned back and his face became very still. The smoke almost hung at the tip of his cigarette. His eyes were like black glass now. He smiled a little dishonestly.

"And why was Leopardi put in a four-dollar room on Eight instead of in a tower suite at eighteen per?"

Quillan smiled back at him. "I didn't register Leopardi, old sock. There were reservations in. I supposed they were what he wanted. Some guys don't spend. Any other questions, Mr. Grayce?"

"Yeah. Was Eight-fourteen empty last night?"

"It was on change, so it was empty. Something about the plumbing. Proceed."

"Who marked it on change?"

Quillan's bright fathomless eyes turned and became curiously fixed. He didn't answer.

Steve said: "Here's why. Leopardi was in Eight-fifteen and the two girls in Eight-eleven. Just Eight-thirteen between. A lad with a passkey could have gone into Eight-thirteen and turned both the bolt locks on the communicating doors. Then, if the folks in the two other rooms had done the same thing on their side, they'd have a suite set up."

"So what?" Quillan asked. "We got chiseled out of four bucks, eh? Well, it happens, in better hotels than this." His eyes looked sleepy now.

Steve said: "Millar could have done that. But hell, it doesn't make sense. Millar's not that kind of a guy. Risk a job for a buck tip—phooey. Millar's no dollar pimp."

Quillan said: "All right, policeman. Tell me what's really on your mind."

"One of the girls in Eight-eleven had a gun. Leopardi got a threat letter yesterday—I don't know where or how. It didn't faze him, though. He tore it up. That's how I know. I collected the pieces from his basket. I suppose Leopardi's boys all checked out of here."

"Of course. They went to the Normandy."

"Call the Normandy and ask to speak to Leopardi. If he's there, he'll still be at the bottle. Probably with a gang."

"Why?" Quillan asked gently.

"Because you're a nice guy. If Leopardi answers—just hang up." Steve paused and pinched his chin hard. "If he went out, try to find out where."

Quillan straightened, gave Steve another long quiet look and went behind the pebbled glass screen. Steve stood very still, listening, one hand clenched at his side, the other tapping noiselessly on the marble desk.

In about three minutes Quillan came back and leaned on the desk again and said: "Not there. Party going on in his suite—they sold him a big one—and sounds loud. I talked to a guy who was fairly sober. He said Leopardi got a call around ten—some girl. He went out preening himself, as the fellow says. Hinting about a very juicy date. The guy was just lit enough to hand me all this."

Steve said: "You're a real pal. I hate not to tell you the rest. Well, I liked working here. Not much work at that."

He started towards the entrance doors again. Quillan let him get his hand on the brass handle before he called out. Steve turned and came back slowly.

Quillan said: "I heard Leopardi took a shot at you. I don't think it was noticed. It wasn't reported down here. And I don't think Peters fully realized that until he saw the mirror in Eight-fifteen. If you want to come back, Steve—"

Steve shook his head. "Thanks for the thought."

"And hearing about that shot," Quillan added, "made me remember something. Two years ago a girl shot herself in Eight-fifteen."

Steve straightened his back so sharply that he almost jumped. "What girl?" he almost yelled.

Quillan looked surprised. "I don't know. I don't remember her real name. Some girl who had been kicked around all she could stand and wanted to die in a clean bed—alone."

Steve reached across and took hold of Quillan's arm. "The hotel files," he rasped. "The clippings, whatever there was in the papers will be in them. I want to see those clippings."

Quillan stared at him for a long moment. Then he said: "Whatever game you're playing, kid—you're playing it damn close to your vest. I will say that for you. And me bored stiff with a night to kill."

He reached along the desk and thumped the call bell. The door of the night porter's room opened and the porter came across the entrance lobby. He nodded and smiled at Steve.

Quillan said: "Take the board, Carl. I'll be in Mr. Peters' office for a little while."

He went to the safe and got keys out of it.

8

THE CABIN was high up on the side of the mountain, against a thick growth of digger pine, oak and incense cedar. It was solidly built, with a stone chimney, shingled all over and heavily braced against the slope of the hill. By daylight the roof was green and the sides dark reddish brown and the window frames and draw-curtains red. In the uncanny brightness of an all-night mid-October moon in the mountains, it stood out sharply in every detail, except color.

It was at the end of a road, a quarter of a mile from any other cabin. Steve rounded the bend towards it without lights, at five in the morning. He stopped his car at once, when he was sure it was the right cabin, got out and walked soundlessly along the side of the gravel road, on a carpet of wild iris.

On the road level there was a rough pine board garage, and from this a path went up to the cabin porch. The garage was unlocked. Steve swung the door open carefully, groped in past the dark bulk of a car and felt the top of the radiator. It was still warmish. He got a small flash out of his pocket and played it over the car. A gray sedan, dusty, the gas gauge low. He snapped the flash off, shut the garage door carefully and slipped into place the piece of wood that served for a hasp. Then he climbed the path to the house.

There was light behind the drawn red curtains. The porch was high and juniper logs were piled on it, with the bark still on them. The front door had a thumb latch and a rustic door-handle above.

He went up, neither too softly nor too noisily, lifted his hand, sighed deep in his throat, and knocked. His hand touched the butt of the gun in the inside pocket of his coat, once, then came away empty.

A chair creaked and steps padded across the floor and a voice called out softly: "What is it?" Millar's voice.

Steve put his lips close to the wood and said: "This is Steve, George. You up already?"

The key turned, and the door opened. George Millar, the dapper night auditor of the Carlton Hotel, didn't look dapper now. He was dressed in old trousers and a thick blue sweater with a roll collar. His feet were in ribbed wool socks and fleece-lined slippers. His clipped black mustache was a curved smudge across his pale face. Two electric bulbs burned in their sockets in a low beam across the room, below the slope of the high roof. A table lamp was lit and its shade was tilted to throw light on a big Morris chair with a leather seat and back-cushion. A fire burned lazily in a heap of soft ash on the big open hearth.

Millar said in his low, husky voice: "Hell's sake, Steve. Glad to see you. How'd you find us anyway? Come on in, guy."

Steve stepped through the door and Millar locked it. "City habit," he said grinning. "Nobody locks anything in the mountains. Have a chair. Warm your toes. Cold out at this time of night."

Steve said: "Yeah. Plenty cold."

He sat down in the Morris chair and put his hat and coat on the end of the solid wood table behind it. He leaned forward and held his hands out to the fire.

Millar said: "How the hell did you find us, Steve? I didn't know—"

Steve didn't look at him. He said quietly: "Not so easy at that. You told me last night your brother had a cabin up here—remember? So I had nothing to do, so I thought I'd drive up and bum some breakfast. The guy in the inn at Crestline didn't know who had cabins where. His trade is with people passing through. I rang up a garage man and he didn't know any Millar cabin. Then I saw a light come on down the street in a coal-and-wood yard and a little guy who is forest ranger and deputy sheriff and wood-and-gas dealer and half a dozen other things was getting his car out to go down to San Bernardino for some tank gas. A very smart little guy. The minute I said your brother had been a fighter he wised up. So here I am."

Millar pawed at his mustache. Bedsprings creaked at the back of the cabin somewhere. "Sure, he still goes under his fighting name—Gaff Talley. I'll get him up and we'll have some coffee. I guess you and me are both in the same boat. Used to working at night and can't sleep. I haven't been to bed at all."

Steve looked at him slowly and looked away. A burly voice behind them said: "Gaff is up. Who's your pal, George?"

Steve stood up casually and turned. He looked at the man's hands first. He couldn't help himself. They were large hands, well kept as to cleanliness, but coarse and ugly. One knuckle had been broken badly. He was a big man with reddish hair. He wore a sloppy bathrobe over outing-flannel pajamas. He had a leathery expressionless face, scarred over the cheekbones. There were fine white scars over his eyebrows and at the corners of his mouth. His nose was spread and thick. His whole face looked as if it had caught a lot of gloves. His eyes alone looked vaguely like Millar's eyes.

Millar said: "Steve Grayce. Night man at the hotel—until last night." His grin was a little vague.

Gaff Talley came over and shook hands. "Glad to meet you," he said. "I'll get some duds on and we'll scrape a breakfast off the shelves. I slept enough. George ain't slept any, the poor sap."

He went back across the room towards the door through which he'd come. He stopped there and leaned on an old phonograph, put his big hand down behind a pile of records in paper envelopes. He stayed just like that, without moving.

Millar said: "Any luck on a job, Steve? Or did you try yet?"

"Yeah. In a way. I guess I'm a sap, but I'm going to have a shot at the private agency racket. Not much in it unless I can land some publicity." He shrugged. Then he said very quietly: "King Leopardi's been bumped off."

Millar's mouth snapped wide open. He stayed like that for almost a minute—perfectly still, with his mouth open. Gaff Talley leaned against the wall and stared without showing anything in his face. Millar finally said: "Bumped off? Where? Don't tell me—"

"Not in the hotel, George. Too bad, wasn't it? In a girl's apartment. Nice girl too. She didn't entice him there. The old suicide gag—only it won't work. And the girl is my client."

Millar didn't move. Neither did the big man. Steve leaned his shoulders against the stone mantel. He said softly: "I went out to the Club Shalotte this afternoon to apologize to Leopardi. Silly idea, because I didn't owe him an apology. There was a girl there in the bar lounge with him. He took three socks at me and left. The girl didn't like that. We got rather clubby. Had a drink together. Then late tonight—last night —she called me up and said Leopardi was over at her place and he was drunk and she couldn't get rid of him. I went there. Only he wasn't drunk. He was dead, in her bed, in yellow pajamas."

The big man lifted his left hand and roughed back his hair. Millar leaned slowly against the edge of the table, as if he were afraid the edge might be sharp enough to cut him. His mouth twitched under the clipped black mustache.

He said huskily: "That's lousy."

The big man said: "Well, for cryin' into a milk bottle."

Steve said: "Only they weren't Leopardi's pajamas. He had initials on them—big black initials. And his were satin, not silk. And although he had a gun in his hand—this girl's gun by the way—*he* didn't shoot himself in the heart. The cops will determine that. Maybe you birds never heard of the Lund test, with paraffin wax, to find out who did or didn't fire a gun recently. The kill ought to have been pulled in the hotel last night, in Room Eight-fifteen. I spoiled that by heaving him out on his neck before that black-haired girl in Eight-eleven could get to him. Didn't I, George?"

Millar said: "I guess you did—if I know what you're talking about."

Steve said slowly: "I think you know what I'm talking about, George. It would have been a kind of poetic justice if King Leopardi had been knocked off in Room Eight-fifteen. Because that was the room where a girl shot herself two years ago. A girl who registered as Mary Smith— but whose usual name was Eve Talley. And whose real name was Eve Millar."

The big man leaned heavily on the victrola and said thickly: "Maybe I ain't woke up yet. That sounds like it might grow up to be a dirty crack. We had a sister named Eve that shot herself in the Carlton. So what?"

Steve smiled a little crookedly. He said: "Listen, George. You told me Quillan registered those girls in Eight-eleven. *You* did. You told me Leopardi registered on Eight, instead of in a good suite, because he was tight. He wasn't tight. He just didn't care where he was put, as long as female company was handy. And you saw to that. You planned the whole thing, George. You even got Peters to write Leopardi at the Raleigh in Frisco and ask him to use the Carlton when he came down— because the same man owned it who owned the Club Shalotte. As if a guy like Jumbo Walters would care where a bandleader registered."

Millar's face was dead white, expressionless. His voice cracked. "Steve—for God's sake, Steve, what are you talking about? How the hell could I—"

"Sorry, kid. I liked working with you. I liked you a lot. I guess I still like you. But I don't like people who strangle women—or people who smear women in order to cover up a revenge murder."

His hand shot up—and stopped. The big man said: "Take it easy— and look at this one."

Gaff's hand had come up from behind the pile of records. A Colt .45 was in it. He said between his teeth: "I always thought house dicks were just a bunch of cheap grafters. I guess I missed out on you. You got a few brains. Hell, I bet you even run out to One-eighteen Court Street. Right?"

Steve let his hand fall empty and looked straight at the big Colt. "Right. I saw the girl—dead—with your fingers marked into her neck. They can measure those, fella. Killing Dolores Chiozza's maid the same way was a mistake. They'll match up the two sets of marks, find out that your black-haired gun girl was at the Carlton last night, and piece the whole story together. With the information they get at the hotel they can't miss. I give you two weeks, if you beat it quick. And I mean quick."

Millar licked his dry lips and said softly: "There's no hurry, Steve. No hurry at all. Our job is done. Maybe not the best way, maybe not the nicest way, but it wasn't a nice job. And Leopardi was the worst kind of a louse. We loved our sister, and he made a tramp out of her. She was a wide-eyed kid that fell for a flashy greaseball, and the greaseball went up in the world and threw her out on her ear for a red-headed torcher who was more his kind. He threw her out and broke her heart and she killed herself."

Steve said harshly: "Yeah—and what were you doing all that time—manicuring your nails?"

"We weren't around when it happened. It took us a little time to find out the why of it."

Steve said: "So that was worth killing four people for, was it? And as for Dolores Chiozza, she wouldn't have wiped her feet on Leopardi —then, or any time since. But you had to put her in the middle too, with your rotten little revenge murder. You make me sick, George. Tell your big tough brother to get on with his murder party."

The big man grinned and said: "Nuff talk, George. See has he a gat—and don't get behind him or in front of him. This bean-shooter goes on through."

Steve stared at the big man's .45. His face was hard as white bone. There was a thin cold sneer on his lips and his eyes were cold and dark.

Millar moved softly in his fleece-lined slippers. He came around the end of the table and went close to Steve's side and reached out a hand to tap his pockets. He stepped back and pointed: "In there."

Steve said softly: "I must be nuts. I could have taken you then, George."

Gaff Talley barked: "Stand away from him."

He walked solidly across the room and put the big Colt against Steve's stomach hard. He reached up with his left hand and worked the Detective Special from the inside breast pocket. His eyes were sharp on Steve's eyes. He held Steve's gun out behind him. "Take this, George."

Millar took the gun and went over beyond the big table again and stood at the far corner of it. Gaff Talley backed away from Steve.

"You're through, wise guy," he said. "You got to know that. There's only two ways outa these mountains and we gotta have time. And maybe you didn't tell nobody. See?"

Steve stood like a rock, his face white, a twisted half-smile working at the corners of his lips. He stared hard at the big man's gun and his stare was faintly puzzled.

Millar said: "Does it have to be that way, Gaff?" His voice was a croak now, without tone, without its usual pleasant huskiness.

Steve turned his head a little and looked at Millar. "Sure it has, George. You're just a couple of cheap hoodlums after all. A couple of nasty-minded sadists playing at being revengers of wronged girlhood. Hillbilly stuff. And right this minute you're practically cold meat— cold, rotten meat."

Gaff Talley laughed and cocked the big revolver with his thumb. "Say your prayers, guy," he jeered.

Steve said grimly: "What makes you think you're going to bump me off with that thing? No shells in it, strangler. Better try to take me the way you handle women—with your hands."

The big man's eyes flicked down, clouded. Then he roared with laughter. "Geez, the dust on that one must be a foot thick," he chuckled. "Watch."

He pointed the big gun at the floor and squeezed the trigger. The firing-pin clicked dryly—on an empty chamber. The big man's face convulsed.

For a short moment nobody moved. Then Gaff turned slowly on the balls of his feet and looked at his brother. He said almost gently: "You, George?"

Millar licked his lips and gulped. He had to move his mouth in and out before he could speak.

"Me, Gaff. I was standing by the window when Steve got out of his car down the road, I saw him go into the garage. I knew the car would still be warm. There's been enough killing, Gaff. Too much. So I took the shells out of your gun."

Millar's thumb moved back the hammer on the Detective Special. Gaff's eyes bulged. He stared fascinated at the snubnosed gun. Then he lunged violently towards it, flailing with the empty Colt. Millar braced himself and stood very still and said dimly, like an old man: "Good-bye, Gaff."

The gun jumped three times in his small neat hand. Smoke curled lazily from its muzzle. A piece of burned log fell over in the fireplace.

Gaff Talley smiled queerly and stopped and stood perfectly still. The gun dropped at his feet. He put his big heavy hands against his stomach, said slowly, thickly: "'S all right, kid. 'S all right, I guess . . . I guess I . . ."

His voice trailed off and his legs began to twist under him. Steve took three long quick silent steps, and slammed Millar hard on the angle of the jaw. The big man was still falling—as slowly as a tree falls.

Millar spun across the room and crashed against the end wall and a blue-and-white plate fell off the plate-moulding and broke. The gun sailed from his fingers. Steve dived for it and came up with it. Millar crouched and watched his brother.

Gaff Talley bent his head to the floor and braced his hands and then lay down quietly, on his stomach, like a man who was very tired. He made no sound of any kind.

Daylight showed at the windows, around the red glass-curtains. The piece of broken log smoked against the side of the hearth and the rest of the fire was a heap of soft gray ash with a glow at its heart.

Steve said dully: "You saved my life, George—or at least you saved a lot of shooting. I took the chance because what I wanted was evidence. Step over there to the desk and write it all out and sign it."

Millar said: "Is he dead?"

"He's dead, George. You killed him. Write that too."

Millar said quietly: "It's funny. I wanted to finish Leopardi myself, with my own hands, when he was at the top, when he had the farthest to fall. Just finish him and then take what came. But Gaff was the guy who wanted it done cute. Gaff, the tough mug who never had any education and never dodged a punch in his life, wanted to do it smart and figure angles. Well, maybe that's why he owned property, like that apartment house on Court Street that Jake Stoyanoff managed for him. I don't know how he got to Dolores Chiozza's maid. It doesn't matter much, does it?"

Steve said: "Go and write it. You were the one called Leopardi up and pretended to be the girl, huh?"

Millar said: "Yes. I'll write it all down, Steve. I'll sign it and then you'll let me go—just for an hour. Won't you, Steve? Just an hour's start. That's not much to ask of an old friend, is it, Steve?"

Millar smiled. It was a small, frail, ghostly smile. Steve bent beside the big sprawled man and felt his neck artery. He looked up, said: "Quite dead. . . . Yes, you get an hour's start, George—if you write it all out."

Millar walked softly over to a tall oak highboy desk, studded with tarnished brass nails. He opened the flap and sat down and reached for a pen. He unscrewed the top from a bottle of ink and began to write in his neat, clear accountant's handwriting.

Steve Grayce sat down in front of the fire and lit a cigarette and stared at the ashes. He held the gun with his left hand on his knee.

Outside the cabin, birds began to sing. Inside there was no sound but the scratching pen.

9

THE SUN was well up when Steve left the cabin, locked it up, walked down the steep path and along the narrow gravel road to his car. The garage was empty now. The gray sedan was gone. Smoke from another cabin floated lazily above the pines and oaks half a mile away. He started his car, drove it around a bend, past two old box-cars that had been converted into cabins, then on to a main road with a stripe down the middle and so up the hill to Crestline.

He parked on the main street before the Rim-of-the-World Inn, had a cup of coffee at the counter, then shut himself in a phone booth at the back of the empty lounge. He had the long distance operator get Jumbo Walters' number in Los Angeles, then called the owner of the Club Shalotte.

A voice said silkily: "This is Mr. Walters' residence."

"Steve Grayce. Put him on, if you please."

"One moment, please." A click, another voice, not so smooth and much harder. "Yeah?"

"Steve Grayce. I want to speak to Mr. Walters."

"Sorry. I don't seem to know you. It's a little early, amigo. What's your business?"

"Did he go to Miss Chiozza's place?"

"Oh." A pause. "The shamus. I get it. Hold the line, pal."

Another voice now—lazy, with the faintest color of Irish in it. "You can talk, son. This is Walters."

"I'm Steve Grayce. I'm the man—"

"I know all about that, son. The lady is O. K., by the way. I think she's asleep upstairs. Go on."

"I'm at Crestline—top of the Arrowhead grade. Two men murdered Leopardi. One was George Millar, night auditor at the Carlton Hotel. The other his brother, an ex-fighter named Gaff Talley. Talley's dead— shot by his brother. Millar got away—but he left me a full confession signed, detailed, complete."

Walters said slowly: "You're a fast worker, son—unless you're just plain crazy. Better come in here fast. Why did they do it?"

"They had a sister."

Walters repeated quietly: "They had a sister. . . . What about this fellow that got away? We don't want some hick sheriff or publicity-hungry county attorney to get ideas—"

Steve broke in quietly: "I don't think you'll have to worry about that, Mr. Walters. I think I know where he's gone."

He ate breakfast at the inn, not because he was hungry, but because he was weak. He got into his car again and started down the long smooth grade from Crestline to San Bernardino, a broad paved boulevard skirting the edge of a sheer drop into the deep valley. There were places where the road went close to the edge, white guard-fences alongside.

Two miles below Crestline was the place. The road made a sharp turn around a shoulder of the mountain. Cars were parked on the gravel off the pavement—several private cars, an official car, and a wrecking-car. The white fence was broken through and men stood around the broken place looking down.

Eight hundred feet below, what was left of a gray sedan lay silent and crumpled in the morning sunshine.